P9-ECZ-445

YAMATO

A RAGE IN HEAVEN

A RAGE IN HEAVEN

THE EPIC BEGINS...

KEN KATO

A Time Warner Company

Warner Books, Inc., 666 Fifth Avenue, New York, NY 10103
A Time Warner Company

Printed in the United States of America
First printing: October 1990

10 9 8 7 6 5 4 3 2 1

Library of Congress Cataloging-in-Publication Data

Kato, Ken.
Yamato : a rage in heaven / Ken Kato.
p. cm.
ISBN 0-446-51570-1
I. Title.
PR6061.A79Y36 1990
823'.914—dc20

Book design: *H. Roberts*

For James Clavell
who certainly asked for it

My thanks are due to my parents, and to all who have read, corrected, translated, revised or criticised this work prior to publication, or who have contributed suggestions to it, scientific, literary or inspirational. I should like to mention by name: Ishihara Shintaro for the spirit of *pachinko*, Kawasaki Kiichiro for digging up and bringing home, Ninagawa Yukio and Akimoto Matsuyo for the spirit of *Genroku*; Chris Clarke of UCL observatory, Stephen Boyle and his stellar database; Takahashi Masae for herself; Lillian Chia for her "uranographie Chinoise," C.J.R. Lord of Braybrooke; Steve Turnbull and Yamamoto Tsunetomo for the spirit of *bushido*; Martyn Brain for IBM contact, Gerry Santoro and Steveley-san for cosmic views, Dr. F. Richard Stephenson of JPL for novae and the heavenly mansions; Nakadai Tatsuya, Tsutomu Yamazaki, Kurasawa Akira and Tanaka Tomoyuki all for the fox spirit of Nagashino; Ohno Yuji for the music of the spheres, Iwasaki Kazuaki for his visualisations; in England, Blackwell's for hospitality, Tom Robinson in memory of fine days in Tokyo and Hiroshima and better ones to come in the Big Apple—and finally to Mary Judah.

Particular thanks are due to two men in New York, agent Richard Curtis and editor Brian Thomsen, for the spirit of *nazukeru*, and to my dear friend in London, David Wingrove, magnanimous in victory and brave in defeat, for the spirit of *go*, our intellectual martial art.

Atari!

CAST

Four Traders

Ellis Straker	Trader captain, grade-one psi-talent and astrogator. Born A.D. 2396. Appointed commander of the nexus ship *Dwight D.*, A.D. 2421. Cruising in quest of profit in the disputed region of Known Space between Yamato and Amerika called the Neutral Zone.
Duval Straker	Chaos theorist and weapons engineer. Ellis Straker's brother, younger by two years, graduate of RISC. Sent into the Zone aboard the *Thomas J.* on an illegal trading expedition, his mission to ship-test a new species of weapon.
Jos Hawken	Commodore. Ex-Navy, now private trader. Leader of the expedition. With his brother Billy Hawken, outstanding agitator of the Expansionist faction to promote Amerikan trade in the Neutral Zone.
John Oujuku	One of Hawken's captains.

Thirteen Power Brokers of Amerika

Alia Kane	Expansionist President. Past opposition to the policies of the Henry clan meant that she spent many years under house arrest. Her election to power in the turbulent year A.D. 2411 caused the overthrow of Lucia Henry's power and the ending of the pro-Yamato policy.
Lucia Henry	President, A.D. 2407–11. A pro-Yamato President, now confined in internal exile to suppress a return to power of that faction.

Stratford Henry	President, A.D. 2362–2400. Original dynast of the powerful Henry clan who have run Amerika during most of the century. Father of Lucia.
Halton Henry	Vice-president, brother of Lucia Henry, and schemer for power. His betrayal of his sister opened the way for Alia Kane to gain the presidency.
Conroy Lubbock	Chief ally of the President and leading influence on Expansionist thinking.
Reba Lubbock	Daughter of Conroy Lubbock.
Jiro Ito	Ex-ninja, confidential messenger for Conroy Lubbock.
Pharis Cassabian	Adroit spymaster and manipulator. A more extreme Expansionist than Conroy Lubbock.
Timo Farren	Pharis Cassabian's intellectual companion.
Ganesh Ramakrishnan	Psi-savant and psientific theorist. Founder of the Liberty ashram.
Kurt Reiner	Heir to the powerful Halide Corporation, the servant-manufacturing mega-corp. Intended husband of Reba Lubbock.
Otis le Grande	Financier and politician. His ambition is to marry Alia Kane.
Kim Gwon Chung	A Free Korean privateer.

Ten Samurai of Yamato

(Where two names are quoted, the Japanese convention of giving the family name first and the personal name second has been followed.)

Mutsuhito	God-Emperor of Yamato. Ascended in year one of the reign era Kanei, A.D. 2402.
Baron Harumi	Supreme military commander of Yamato's military forces.
Okubo Shigenori	Yamato ambassador to Amerika, resident on Liberty, the capital world of Amerika.
Nishima Jun	Daimyo lord appointed to take command of the strategically important world of Sado in the Neutral Zone.
Fumiko	Nishima Jun's wife.

Kurita Imari	Admiral of an Imperial convoy in the Neutral Zone, commander of the *kin kaigun,* officer of the Yamato Guard.
Kondo	An officer subordinate to Admiral Kurita.
Hasegawa Kenji	Principal fief-holder on Sado.
Katsumi	Hasegawa Kenji's son.
Michie	Hasegawa Kenji's daughter.

Eight Others

Cao	A *sangokujin* escapee from Yamato oppression.
Choi Ki Won	A Korean of high principle.
Fukuda Ikku	A zealous *metsuke*, inspector general of the *kempei*.
Helene di Barrio	A captain of Hawken's fleet.
Horse Smith	A nexus rat and isotopist.
Ingram	A nexus rat aboard the *Richard M*.
Wataru Hoshino	An old soldier, friend of Duval Straker's.
Yao Wen-yuan	The *sangokujin* head of Hasegawa's technical facilities.

PROLOG

The old pond,
A frog jumps in,
Resonance and ripples.

"In the beginning there was the Earth, the cradle, where all life began, and the Earth was as a rock and its bounty scant, but the waters that surrounded the Earth were deep and warm and they gave succor to the creatures and the fishes that began to dwell there.

"Then, after a long age, a beautiful forest clothed the land, then the waters stirred and there arose from the deeps insects and other beasts that breathed the air and great monsters that went upon the land, and it was from these beasts and these forests that the frogs and the snakes and the birds and all the fur-clothed animals came.

"And beast fought beast, and beast begat beast for another, long age, until at last, Man appeared in all his races, and Man was different from the lesser animals that had come before, because Man has a tongue and two hands and a brain, and so Man conquered, and Man prospered, and in time Man made the Earth his own.

"Then, like the tides of the Ocean, the Kingdoms of Men rose and fell for ten thousand years. And one kingdom warred upon another with weapons that filled the Earth with terror, and great slaughter was brought upon the sons of Men so that blood flowed as if in an ever-increasing fountain.

"Then, as day followed night, it came to pass that a weapon was created so terrible in its power that none dared use it for fear it would destroy all the Earth and every living thing that walked or grew upon it. So Man's numbers multiplied and he became ever more numerous and his living was made slender and he looked to the Heavens for succor as once he had looked to the continents across the Ocean; but the Heavens were silent and cold and distant and the many cultures of Mankind were forced to live in chaos one upon the other until all was madness and until the means were found whereby Man could go abroad in the deeps of space and find other planets to make his own and there to change them.

"And in those final days the Edict was spoken that each breed of Man shall leave the Earth, and each shall have his place in the Hours of Heaven. And the first two Hours were given back to the gods. And the Men of the Middle Kingdom and the Men of Hindostan were given six Hours of the Heavens to share between them. And the Men of Europe two Hours likewise, so too the worshipers of Islam, and for the Slavs two more Hours were given, and the Latins also had two Hours. For Brasilia another two Hours, then two Hours for the Men of Afrika, and two more Hours for the Men of Yamato. In this same way also, two Hours were given to the Men of Amerika. . . ."

The Book of Earth

YAMATO

A RAGE IN HEAVEN

BOOK 1

20TH YEAR OF KANEI/A.D. 2421

The Domain of Yamato
Is equal with the Heavens,
It is I who rule it all,
It is I who reign over all.

Yoriyaku
Japanese Emperor
reigned A.D. 457–79

Material excerpted from "A Manuscript Found in Space," by A. Hacker:

Ozma Vault Transmission Package KVFG #0131,
Copyright Synthetic Educator Corp, Orenburg, VIR.,
By Permission of the Central Authority,
Old Earth. A.D. 2420

[Ref. Module MCXXIV-024.240354 /Engl.]

[Cross-references to other SEC modules in CAPS.]

YAMATO

First, see [Ref. Module MMVII-124.288762] KNOWN SPACE.

Begins: YAMATO, one of the twelve Sectors of KNOWN SPACE. After the EDICT was proclaimed, under which principal EARTH cultures were apportioned specific Sectors of Known Space, there followed the GREAT DIASPORA beginning approximately A.D. 2100#

. . . HACK INTERRUPTED . . .

#one of the original twelve equal Sectors, in form like a segment of orange, bounded by the pole line of Known Space referred to galactic coordinates, the envelope of exploration and the Three-Thirty Degree and Three-Sixty (or Zero) Degree Boundary planes of galactic longitude. (The Earth system itself is omitted since it is surrounded by a three-light-year-diameter Exclusion Zo#

. . . HACK INTERRUPTED . . .

#ne Empire of Yamato is the name adopted for the Sector occupied by the cultural and linguistic traditions of Japan, bordered by the Sector of XANADU (G. Long 300–330), also known as China, the Central Realm, etc., and by the NEUTRAL ZONE (G. Long 0–30). Yamato contains many thousands of star systems, hundreds of which are now inhabited. They are organised into four QUADRANTS. More than sixty systems contain very well developed planets of a billion or more inhabitants. The earliest settled systems, closest to Earth, are approximately three hundred years old at the time of writing. The Sector capital world is KYOTO; the form of government is a monarchy, headed by the EMPEROR, who is conventionally held to be divine. Although much actual power now resides in the office of SHOGUN, or generalis#

. . . HACK INTERRUPTED . . .

#Ato has been effectively closed to the citizens of other Sectors for many years, first by the creation of high-price conditions, by the imposition of anti-immigration laws, and by bans on the sale of planetary land to foreign citizens or legal entities, then later by physical closure of the Sector so that now no Yamato citizen is permitted to leave, and no outsider can gain entry, through the boundary NEXI. De facto annexation of the Neutral Zone has been an unstated but primary policy of the government of Yamato since the start of the KANEI reign era. Insofar a#

. . . LINE ABORTED.

1

SOMEWHERE IN THE NEUTRAL ZONE

Captain Ayrton Rodrigo died at the midnight of the blue sun.

Before first light, they had made planetfall, his body had been loaded into a freezee, the freezee sealed into a plex coffin, and the still-living remains consigned to eternity in an unmarked grave on the rawest most godforsaken continent of this remote world.

The near-corpse would remain suspended inside the freezee forever. No natural force could burst the plex armor shell. Neither volcanic heat nor oceanic pressure; neither deep burial by geologic forces nor the jaws of whatever monsters might ultimately evolve here. The body would stay put in its refrigerant, wailing its beacon like a banshee, locked into molecular stasis until a time when it might conceivably be found by a technology that had the ability to open a sealed plex unit. That might just be a technology advanced enough to make Ayrton Rodrigo live again. It was a vanishingly small chance, but even so a consolation, an eternal destiny that befitted a master psi-astrogator. But it didn't soften by one degree the hearts of the tough people who had come to pay their last repects. For them, there was only hate.

As soon as the captains of the battered Amerikan flotilla congregated, the weather began to worsen, and the last of them to arrive, Ellis Straker, stared down at the bloodied ensign with its stars and bars and fringe of gold as it whipped in the thin-oxygen wind. Enclosed within was the body of the man who had taught him everything.

By the Lord Christ Jeezus, I'll get vengeance for your soul, amigo! I swear it! he told himself, stiffening with anger. One day the Empire of Yamato would pay, but first an urgent decision must be made for the sake of the four hundred Amerikan souls in their care. He thought again of his wife, Janka, and their young son back in Lincoln, the capital, and damned the psi-tempest for the fiftieth time. Had it not come upon them, they would have been safe home, in sight of Liberty, by now.

But this was a region where fierce psi-storms, the tsunami as the Japanese-speakers called them, buffeted the fabric of space-time unpredictably, when not even chaos theory could pin down exactly the nexus through which a ship must transit to get home. At times, passage towards the Amerikan Sector was almost impossible to predict, which was why this region had first been designated the Neutral Zone, not part of any Sector, and perhaps also why Yamato had been allowed to annex it.

As if mirroring the rage in heaven, the barely breathable atmosphere of this poorly terraformed world filed at their suits with sharp sand spicules. The sky foamed angrily from the cloudtops, and the camouflage patterning of the seven-thousand-ton flagship, *Thomas Jefferson,* adjusted crazily to the swells of light under an overcast of salmon-pink marble. The four other ships were parked close by like huge, resting catfish. The warm wind harped in the aerials of one of them, making the heads of the men and women who lined the graveside turn and look for what was making the eerie sound.

Beside the coffin their commodore, Jos Hawken, stood stern-faced, his cropped black hair quivering in the wind as he greeted his captains: di Barrio and Hampton, Geneva, Oujuku, and Straker. Behind them, soldiers in plex battle suits and helmets formed an honor guard with their weapons quartered, and at the head of the grave Angela Rodrigo stood ready, her bare feet moving on the sand heaped beside the roughly cut slot as she bent to pick up a handful of alien dust.

The captains made a tight group around the body, keeping a minute's peace out of respect, but it was not Ayrton Rodrigo's death that turned the silence bitter in their mouths, it was the way it had happened: he had been burned in the belly at close range by a Yamato sniper during their landing on Palawan. The weapon had carried away his testicles and most of his intestines, and he had lain in a twilight world of neuro-drugs and emergency life support for seven weeks before giving up his will to live.

Ellis Straker regarded the proceedings grimly. Tall, blond-bearded, and bareheaded under the raging skies, like the other astrogators he was wondering if he had figured correctly where the psi-storm had pushed them, for on that calculation they would, all of them, live or die.

Fifty days ago they had left Palawan under heavy fire from a beam weapon sited in orbit around the planet. As traders seeking profit from the settlers of the Neutral Zone they had not wanted their voyage to end like this, but they had met with heavy opposition. Every place they went their wares were shunned, even though the traders could see it in their customers' eyes that they wanted desperately to buy. The goods on offer were desired, but still the answer was "*Iye.*" No.

When they had asked why, there had been shrugging shoulders and nervous smiling, then fear, and eventually some had whispered that Yamato would not like it. That the *kempei* would come soon.

"Filthy secret police," Jos Hawken had spat. "They got no goddamned jurisdiction out here. This ain't Yamato."

But the *rikugun* rolled in the next day. The military. Black boots. Black uniforms. And guns. They came into the trade emporium, a huge space-frame filled with sale items and contract booths, ghostly since the rumors. They turned the place over, and then they started getting nasty.

Hawken gave his orders, and everyone in the fleet was superb. Discipline, self-control, and impeccable manners under provocation from crew and salesmen alike—when all anyone wanted to do was take the baggy pants off those arrogant little slimes and tan their hides.

Then one of them shot Ayrton with a flame blaster for no psi-damned reason at all, except maybe they thought he hadn't shown them enough respect.

They withdrew then. Leaving everything. Dropping everything. Just into the landers and a white-lipped "Look, goddamn you, we're leaving!"

They tried scrupulously to avoid conflict and to make an eventless passage to the nexus that lay close to one of the Trojan points of Palawan's gas giant neighbor, but they were fired on again by a *rikugun* orbiter, and when they arrived at the gravitational anomaly that would allow them to take passage home, all they found was one gigantic junkyard of rock debris scoured from the sloppy and overhasty terraforming that had been done in the system.

A raging psi-storm caught them in the approach phase to the choked nexus. It was at the moment when their velocity and direction had to be precisely correct if they were to hit the nexus and effect a subspace transit, but the storm ruined everything. For three days their ships clung desperately together, as Ellis Straker and the other astrogators went terrifyingly insane. The intensity of the storm induced blasts of alpha waves in the brains of all the psi-talents. There followed eerie pauses in electrical activity in those who persisted in trying to "feel out" the nexus, and finally severe epileptic seizures gripped them.

The bridge lights started to flash.

"We've got to hang it and peel off," Hampton said. "This is killing my psi-people!"

"Ayrton's gonna die if we don't get him back to Liberty!" Oujuku blasted him from the *John F*.

Ellis shouted in his rage, haggard, blood streaming from his nose, "I'll feel out that sonofabitch, if I have to bleed my guts all over the ship!"

And he stuck at it until the blood pumped in his brain and the agony drenched him. But it was no good. Dal Givens, the most sensitive astrogator, stationed aboard the *Richard M*., threshed in a frenzy and then bit off the tip of her tongue in a fit whilst sending the lead ship into a blind approach. Without steering advice the tidal lobes of the nexus almost tore the plex skin off their rotting twenty-five-year-old scout ship, then, as they overshot, the *Millard Fillmore* disappeared into the mass of Trojan debris and the shields on all the ships sheared to maximum to deflect the hail of rock debris that spewed out. One after another they fell out of communication so that each astrogator thought the others dead, and when, a week later, the ships regrouped, there was no option but to run a manual make on the subspace topography charts and cruise in real-time for the swamping gravitational safety of the star at the center of the system.

But where precisely in the G-field of that great sapphire-blue giant were they now? How many astronomical units out had they drifted? And when might the Index rise enough to make the nexus safe? It was to answer these questions that Hawken had signaled for them to come aboard. For that and to witness the burial of a brother astrogator.

Those close to Rodrigo could still smell the stink of death gusting from the sealed freezee. Ellis remembered carrying Rodrigo to the ship. He had heeded the man's cries not to be left to die on Palawan, and when Rodrigo saw the purple mass of his own intestines, saw what the blaster fire had done to his testicles, he had begged Ellis to finish him there and then, but Ellis had not had the strength to do it and those cries still rang in his ears, haunting him like the growling pronouncement of Lieutenant-Surgeon Grosse, who said that a wound like that took away a man's will to live and that he'd be dead inside thirty days, whatever they did for him.

So Ellis had been given command of Rodrigo's ship, the *Dwight D. Eisenhower,* and Rodrigo had been taken aboard the *Thomas Jefferson* to suffer seeing his lower half turned to a shit-stinking mire before his eyes. He had died in torment. Torment born of Yamato temperament and Yamato treachery. And it wounded Ellis doubly because he alone knew that this was to have been Ayrton Rodrigo's last trip before retiring to keep a welcome house on Liberty and watch his dozen grandchildren grow up around him.

He looked to the two Shinto priests and the Yamato citizen, Mr. Iwakura, whom they had taken on board two weeks ago from a lost and fleeing shuttle that had turned up on their scanners. They stood together mutely now in the gusting wind, their silk kimonos fluttering like bunting, but Ellis hated them and wanted suddenly to bundle them into a dust crater, get them downwind where they could no longer pollute the air of a Christian burial service. Lord God, he vowed as he tore his eyes off them and watched instead the far horizon, if ever we get home to Liberty, I'll pay Yamato back ten thousand times over for your suffering, Ayrton! I'll come back to Palawan with a good ship and a dozen beam weapons and I'll square things with the *kempei,* so help me Jeezus!

"Man that is born of woman hath but a short time to live and is full of misery. . . ."

John Oujuku, stocky and black and barrel-chested, fire-eyed and with a beard sparse as desert scrub, read solemn verses from his prayer book over the corpse. His family had escaped off Nigeria during the Afrikan coups forty years ago, and like the sons and daughters of most refugees to whom Amerika had given asylum, he had grown up to be 101 percent Amerikan.

". . . looking for the resurrection of the body when the firmament shall give up her dead. Amen."

Then, at Hawken's nod, Brown and Chiminski pulled shut the lid of the freezee and Ayrton Rodrigo's remains were slid into the shallow groove in the sand.

As they held silence, Ellis looked across the red-dust sea to where his own weather-beaten command, the *Dwight D.,* slumbered, her hull scintillating softly. Beyond her stood the *Richard M.* and the *John F.,* and alone, ahead of them all, Oujuku's little five-hundred-tonner *Judith L.* Together, they had penetrated deeper into the disputed Sector than any Amerikan trading fleet for many years, shattering the Emperor's decree that had created a Yamato monopoly of half of explored space. In three pioneering voyages, Hawken's ships had driven a wedge into the golden heart of the Neutral Zone, establishing a lucrative trade that suited all parties—except the jealous *rikugun* military that represented the Imperial Court.

Ellis had been with Hawken on his first two yoyages. Both trips had made a very handsome return, and the third had started off just as profitably. At first, settlers at Buru and Ceram had been anxious to trade. They had been most willing to ignore the prohibitions imposed by the Emperor against these unlicensed and therefore illegal merchants because the colonists needed machinery, manufactures, and genetic stock from the established worlds, and they had bought from them readily. Trading with the Amerikan fleet avoided the crippling *shizo,* or sales tax, that all Yamato supply ships were ordered to exact. But on Halmahera things had begun to change. There the Imperial authorities had forced Hawken to land his cargoes under armed guard. There had been interference and double-dealing and so they had cruised on to Sula, where they had discovered only the *rikugun* and unsheathed aggression. Hawken had pulled the fleet out of orbit after the first skirmish to think again, taking with him half a dozen wounded men and leaving behind two dead.

Yes, Ellis thought with regret, the days of peaceful trading are over. If we are to move at all in the Neutral Zone, we must come in force. Our beam weapons must show the Empire of Yamato that they can't exclude us from the Zone. We must never surrender to any unilateral declaration of ownership, or one day we'll see them carve up our own Sector, like they've carved it up here.

Up on the bridge of the *Thomas J.*, Duval, Ellis Straker's younger brother, the one they called "the Gunner," set the sky ablaze with a light show. The beam weapon jerked and a hundred shimmering colored streamers crackled into the air in salute. The long black snout glowed crimson, and ozone scented the air acridly. The first power discharge boomed out over the site, followed by another and another, a fourth and a fifth, in an irregularly spaced roll, like echoes of thunder. Then it was done and the assembly was dismissed, and Hawken led the astrogators alone to conference on his high, narrow observation gallery at the very aftmost part of the bridge. Ellis, last of the five to climb the gangway past the ensign whom di Barrio had posted for privacy, stooped down to see the chart that Hawken was manipulating in the visualiser.

Laid out before them was the familiar five-foot globe of Known Space across which ley lines fanned out, and on which were drawn the limits of human exploration. The diffuse shadows of nebulae and the color-coded symbols showing stars and planetary systems and nexus points cast from the central projector. An opal sheen shifted back and forth over it as Hawken circled a finger above the area of uncertainty. His voice, as ever when he was worried, was soft and thoughtful.

"My best estimate puts us here—a planet they've called Tanimbar. Thirty light-years from here is the Yamato Boundary, thirty or more the other way is Liberty, and home. Our closest planetfall in the Amerikan Sector is probably no more than ten parsecs in the same direction."

"And the other way?" Geneva asked.

"That way is certain death." Hampton's phlegmatic eye measured their faces. "Against the flow of the nexus chain the *Richard M.* would founder before reaching the second jump, and I judge that the *Thomas J.* is in no condition to face a crossing. We should make for Biak, here, and head back. Then follow the chain that crosses into the Tuamotu."

"I say we head out," Oujuku said, shaking his head. "We need to find a place to link into the Marquesas Main and there's a crossover there. The psi-storm's gotta blow out before long. We can make planetfall at Midway, or one of them other dustballs. That way we might get a chance of meeting our *rikugun* friends again. This time with beam weapons—and no need to pussyfoot!"

"Sure, and cause an inter-Sector incident," Hampton growled.

"We've as good as done that already, in their eyes! Or worse."

"Worse?"

"Sure, Hampton," Oujuku said. "We've started a war!"

Hawken moved between the two men. "John, we're not at war with Yamato. We want nothing other than cordial relations with His Imperial Majesty, the Son of Heaven, and his subjects. Remember that at all times."

Oujuku's fuse burned brighter and he showed his teeth whitely. "How does it help us to be at peace with Yamato *when they are at war with us?*"

Hawken's face froze. "I've said it twenty times. The success of this and future missions depends on Yamato remaining at peace with Amerika, and upon our exemplary conduct. Even in the face of provocation."

"Sheeeeee-it!"

Hawken turned to his most experienced captain. At forty-six years, Helene di Barrio was older than any other present except Geneva. She was also the most cautious among them.

"Helene, what do you say?"

Di Barrio scratched at her cleft chin. She was normally a woman of few words and did not enjoy being called upon to speak. "I don't know. There's not a whole lot to choose. The Yamato system's death to any that venture across the Zero Degree Plane. I don't doubt that's true after what happened to Ayrton. Those guys with the swords terrify me." She looked about her, sour-faced. "Anyway, these damned ships're in no fit state to make heavy transits after what they've been through. We just don't have the power to get home by the most direct route. Try that and we'll get stuck for sure."

"Faye, what do you think?"

Ellis considered as Geneva crouched low and studied the visualiser. He knew that like many outworld astrogators both di Barrio and Geneva had a superstitious dislike for structured time. They hated planning ahead, preferring instead to rely on instinct alone, that unerring feeling when an entry was right.

Ellis had spent time in each of Hawken's three voyages into the Neutral Zone, talking with all the Yamato astrogators he came across and assiduously recording what they told him. Di Barrio's beliefs appeared to tally with that, but something still disturbed Ellis. Although he had waited his turn to voice his opinion, it was his belief that Hawken had miscalculated their position badly.

Geneva looked up challengingly. "I say go direct."

"Direct?" Oujuku hissed.

"Yep. Make for Midway via Sado."

"That's suicide! Sado's right next to the Yamato Boundary!"

Hawken quieted Oujuku and invited Geneva to continue.

"If we try to fight the nexus by going against the flow, we'll have to cross two hundred light-years and make twenty transits before we see Guam. It's not just the *Thomas J.* and *Richard M.* that are in poor condition. We're all short of repair materials. Go via Sado and we could be home in two easy jumps."

"*Easy?* We'd lose everything," Oujuku said flatly.

"It's likely." Geneva glanced at Oujuku. "And if we tried to do a ten-, maybe twenty-jump chain with the hulls we have, we'll be blown out of at least one of those nexus points as a fine mist."

"Better to chance that than be crucified as interlopers because we strayed into the Yamato Sector. They nail foreigners up on wooden crosses for the hell of it there. Think about that, Faye." Di Barrio turned to appeal to Hawken directly. "Don't forget, sir, you were loaned the *Thomas J.* and the *Richard M.* by the Navy—by the President herself—they're listed officially as Amerikan warships. To go around violating Yamato's sovereignty in Navy ships will be seen as an act of war!"

Ellis looked at their worried faces in the hiatus: Oujuku was sunk in an angry silence. Hawken was nodding; Don Hampton seemed to be in agreement. Each knew that the President's policy towards the Empire of Yamato stopped well short of open warfare. For the flotilla to enter the Sado nexus without permission would count directly as an act of aggression against Yamato, leaving the way open for the Emperor to retaliate massively.

To Ellis, the situation seemed fraught with dangers that extended far beyond the perils of their own position. Of all the cultural Sectors set up by the Edict, only Amerika had resisted the slide into totalitarianism. Only in Amerika was the ideal of democracy still revered and given succor. Only in Amerika was free speech unsuppressed and held to be a virtue. And only in Amerika was the free mixing of men of all races, creeds, and colors encouraged.

According to the Emperor, such freedom was a dangerous disease. It had been his personal dream, his life's dedicated mission, to stamp out the Amerikan aberration—to reunify mankind beneath the Standard of the Rising Sun and under the authority of the Son of Heaven. He would be seeking any excuse to turn his savage legions loose on Amerika.

Hawken bent over the visualiser once more. "Why Sado, for Chrissakes?"

Faye Geneva's leathery face creased. She had spent her childhood on Arizona, a world with insufficient ozone in the atmosphere, and orbiting an A-type primary; the high UV dose had left its mark on her. A slim finger darted over the shimmering surface of the charts. "Why Sado, Commodore? Because there's a small, poorly defended nexus nearby, because it's flowing our way, and because we're already heading for it. We'll get there with around a week's dilation. If we show ourselves in force before anyone can get there, play a close hand about what a pitiful state we're in, then they might offer us all we require without any need to threaten them."

"Sado is a mantrap," Oujuku said scornfully. "And the *rikugun* have had all voyage to bait it."

Hawken seemed undecided. "Ellis?"

Ellis's thoughts solidified suddenly and he stirred. "I don't like Sado. It's too dangerous. But we must lay up somewhere with a well-equipped apron to effect repairs. That's unavoidable. And wherever we go we'll lack for a welcome. It's my belief that running out at Sado will involve less dilation than you think. We could be there in one jump."

"One jump?" Hawken asked. "Sado is a dozen parsecs away."

Each parsec was about three and a quarter light-years. If the Index kept up, their ships might make the transit first time. According to Ellis Straker, by midnight, Universal Time, just sixteen hours from now, they could hope to emerge with a three-day dilation.

Ellis shook his head. "See, Commodore, I believe our true position is here." He stabbed a finger at the visualiser. "I reckon that psi-storm carried us much further than we thought. I don't think this planet is Tanimbar. I think it's Talaud. If I'm right, we've no alternative but to jump via Sado."

There was a commotion at the forward scanner, then the ensign's voice canceled the alarm. When Red Bowen shouted down again, his message stunned them.

"I'm sorry to interrupt you, sir, but the scanners are picking up a second satellite rising."

"Confirmed?"

"Yes, sir."

"Okeh, thank you, Mr. Bowen."

Hawken stood up, his gray eyes searching the screens gravely. According to the 'labe, Tanimbar had only one large moon, Talaud had two.

"Well, now, people, it seems that my decision has been made for me. We must make a passage close to Yamato territorial space. Sado it is. I suggest we get about our business."

2

SADO

Gunner Straker had come onto the gallery that surrounded the bridge of the *Thomas Jefferson* as soon as they came within visual range of Sado.

"Land ho!" he said, and punched his palm. Many of the crew had already crowded onto the observation deck, and he had to slap a few backs to get to the rail. All eyes were searching the pale limb of the planet, trying to make out the irregularities that the scanner showed. As the ship powered on towards its destination and entered a high elliptical orbit, the scanners revealed more and more of the day side of Sado, flat coastlines of murky reddish browns and greens backed by ranges of purple mountains, riven like molars. The scanner blackout lasted ten minutes as they reentered through the zone of high meson flux, then everyone gasped at the brilliance of the colors that flooded the screens. As the ship burned white in Sado's atmosphere, the perspective grew ever more real. An archipelago here, the massive sea of a sand desert and huge stretches of dark blue ocean. Three tiny islands speckled the shore as the landing bell sounded over the talkback: two low atolls, little more than reefs that flared white under the power of the breakers, and a third, larger, with buildings and outworks, then the coastline and the white apron with a dozen Yamato ships parked on a strip. This was Niigata, the port of entry Mr. Iwakura had spoken of when they had questioned him yesterday, its position on the continental coast marked by a little dogleg island that was nowhere more than six feet above the sea along a seaboard battered by deep-sea rollers that had fetched across six thousand miles and crashed now continually into its rock-rubble.

Beyond the apron the forests had been cleared and the Yamato authorities had mounted a series of docking modules along the terminal where ships were attached to umbilicals.

He went up to the weapons bay to check that his equipment was stowed for landing.

"Hey, Red."

"Hey, you dumb sucker."

Jeff "Red" Bowen, the *Thomas Jefferson*'s third officer, stood with the Japanese-speaking trio beside him. He was a stocky, muscular man, shag-bearded with thick brows and high cheeks that made slits of his eyes. He was as redheaded as it was possible to be.

"Move yourself, Ingram, you lazy sonofabitch," he told the big engineer who barred his way.

Ingram looked down at him with a puckered face, hiding his sullen disrespect poorly, and loped off.

"He's a lazy bastard, and he stinks too."

Duval shook his head and the movement tossed blue-black needle-straight hair about his ears. Half a head taller than Bowen and leaner, he smoothed his wispy moustache out between finger and thumb and leaned on the firing pins, long chrome steel rods that had to be locked home to allow the prototype gun to fire. He looked away from the crowded gallery and through the transparent plex blister a couple of hundred yards distant off the *Thomas Jefferson*'s starboard beam, where his brother was striding restlessly round the bridge of his ship, the *Dwight D*. Like a tiger dressed in a blue jacket, shouting orders under a big see-through plex dome. That's my brother, he thought proudly. Although nobody believes it.

He looked about some more. Their five ships made an impressive squadron, bearing down on the port of Niigata, but the Gunner remained uneasy. What if the governor had received the same instructions as the authorities at Palawan and gave them the same fiery welcome? He looked over the dark and dormant weapons that were his special care and compared them with the big, clumsy beam weapons of the terminal batteries. If they give us any grief, my beauties, he said silently, slapping the universal mounting of the nearest experimental gun, then we'll have a sharp answer ready for them, eh?

"Is that Niigata?" Bowen asked scornfully. " 'Tain't hardly much."

"The commodore says this planet's got the only spaceport with a repair station in the entire godforsaken quadrant."

Iwakura and the Shinto priests listened suspiciously as Duval spoke. Iwakura's eyes were downcast, a weaselly half-smile on his face.

"It's good enough for space-going ships, and not far away is the city of Niigata, which lies beyond the forests," Duval went on. "This is where the aurium from all over the planet ends up—truck ships laden with semirefined ore dug out of this lump of Population One supernova wreck. Mountains of the stuff, element 114, isotope 298, as heavy as hell, but stable! Aurium like you've never seen, and just as a by-product argentium, element 112, isotope 296, nuggets the size of grapes. Isn't that so, Iwakura-san?"

Iwakura inclined his head, giving nothing away. "Sir, I have never been to Niigata."

"Don't the Yamato people say there are argentium nuggets as big as grapes . . . as *budo*, Iwakura-san? Think of that, Jeff!"

"You speak Japanese?" Iwakura said guardedly.

"Not too good as yet, Iwakura-san. All I've learned of your language I learned from holos, but they say I've got a talent that way. And next voyage I mean to sharpen it up."

"Gunner Straker has Yamato looks, don't you think?" the third officer asked, planting his feet and knitting his muscular arms together. "Some of the crew give him hell, calling him 'Yambo.' He don't like that—do you, Gunner? You seen his brother? Blond as a Finn and fair-skinned. But this Joe—yep—eyes like that and he's got to be a bastard to some Yambo."

"Better a bastard than a ginger sonofabitch from Arkansas!" Duval grinned. Bowen's fooling had never bothered him at all, but Iwakura looked away in disgust. To Duval he seemed watchful and tightly drawn under his surface calm, as if he was hiding something. Iwakura had come aboard with the two Shinto priests when the *Thomas Jefferson* had caught their distress signals yesterday. A samurai by his dress and hairstyle, and treated with due courtesy by Hawken, but for all that, his reasons for taking a ship offplanet were only half-reasons, and Duval had been wary of him. Overnight, Duval had listened openly to his whispered conversations with the taller priest, picking up small details here and there until he had learned enough.

Hawken came up behind them and Iwakura turned to him. "It is as I told you, a most suitable facility."

The commodore eyed the spaceport glassily. He was a wiry man in his prime, dark-haired, thin-faced, and with hood-lidded eyes that gave him a look of remoteness that went with his commanding rank. Intersystem trading had been his life for as long as he could remember. He had worked the nexi since the age of sixteen, as had his father before him, and the love of the Void ran pure in his veins. He had put on his pressure suit for the landing, the one with the big silver badge.

"Easy as she goes at the head, pilot."

Bowen stared with his customary bluff expression at the fuselages of four or five hulks that stood like half-picked chicken crates on one end of the apron, now almost completely stripped of their plex skins. Robot salvagers crawled all over them, the violet points of their meson arc torches flickering in the heat haze. Bowen said, "Looks like down this neck of the woods any ship that can't make the nexus gets to be made into goddamned samurai swords, huh? Make sure you post sentries, Commodore, or those robot jiggers'll be all over us with their arcs, cutting slices off of our tail."

Hawken grunted. "What are those hulks, Mr. Iwakura?"

The Japanese shrugged. "You must know, Commodore, that the aurium fleet of Yamato comes here every year to carry aurium to Honshu. Maybe some old ships have been left here to be broken up. But nothing for you to worry about. Believe me, Sado is very safe. The nexus is very safe."

"I hope you're right, Mr. Iwakura. Keep the shields up, Bowen."

"Yes, sir!"

As they closed with the port, the flotilla swung southeast, turning parallel with the main runway, and passing along an approach lane just two hundred yards wide between the parked ships and the low, white terminal building of Niigata passenger port. The other way, a headland jutted into the surf and intermittently threw up great fans of white spray. The roof of the terminal was painted with the striking symbol of Yamato: the sunburst with rays, in red and white.

The approach had been kept deliberately narrow to discourage any maneuver or demonstration of war-like intent. Duval Straker knew that, but the fleet was unmarked and unlooked for, and the ground station that had interrogated their communications computers had been met with silence. Their arrival had probably caught Niigata, and the whole of Sado, by surprise.

As they put down and began to taxi, a beam was discharged from the shore battery, then a moment later, a second. They watched the white vapor billow quickly up from the red shafts of super-heated air and disperse. Two blasts of three. It was a challenge.

Hawken's order was sharp. "Signal our intentions, Gunner. Let them know we mean them no harm."

"Stand clear of the weapons bay!"

The twin-muzzled gun, a matt-black mechanism thirteen feet long, swiveled as he climbed into the harness. Duval put the switches to power the gun into arm mode and the assembly jerked back powerfully, roaring like static in a sharp triple burst. The weapon was totally secret, unlike anything yet invented, and terrifying. It projected space-time anomalies—minute antimatter quasi-singularities—space-time sinks capable of sucking in a few thousand pounds of matter as they seared along their short-lived trajectories. They were not as energetic nor as violent as beam weapons, but they were utterly unstoppable. No kind of shield—even a plex hull—could impede them, and their wailing when they fired was like a thousand banshees.

The helmsman shouted up at Hawken. "Mean them no harm? Jeezus, Commodore!"

"All right, pipe down, you people."

"My God! Get an eyeful of that!"

It was Bowen. He began to point and roar with laughter. "Look at it, will ya?"

Duval saw the palanquin, a platform carried by eight men, each shouldering a pole, with a tasseled, gilded booth swaying on the top and the whole thing absurdly canopied with silk, blasted by the wind of their engines. It was heading across the runway towards the *Thomas Jefferson,* a totally incongruous sight.

Hawken watched the bizarre vehicle approach for several seconds, then he went down to the cargo deck to welcome the disarrayed Japanese official aboard, taking Iwakura with him.

"Come down too, Gunner. I need your Japanese."

The palanquin was set down and the curtains parted. The visitor was a fleshy man weighed down with rich turquoise ceremonial silk. A long spire of stiffened silk whipped up from his hat, and his silver and sharkskin chain of office chinked as he stepped out. He wore block-soled *geta* sandals held with a toe stud and white *tabi* socks. A kimono of turquoise silk, bound at the waist with an obi, fell from winged shoulders to just above the ground, and a pair of samurai blades jutted from his hip.

He approached the side of the ship flanked by two of his seminaked bearers, then he saw Hawken and stopped dead.

At Hawken's order, the visitors were addressed by Iwakura as soon as they halted. Duval saw how they were seized by a sudden loss of dignity when they realised that the ship they had admitted onto the Niigata apron was not manned by racial Japanese.

Hawken pulled off his glove and offered his hand in a gesture of friendship, but the robed figure stared and made no move to reciprocate the gesture.

"I am Commodore Josiah Hawken, and this is my fleet. We are traders sailing under the merchant flag of the United Worlds of Amerika. I request berths for my five ships and facilities to repair them. Be assured it is our wish to return home to our own Sector as soon as possible and that we intend fair payment for all facilities we use and any materials we take aboard. Translate that, if you please, Mr. Iwakura."

As Iwakura conveyed the greeting, the official blanched, his eyes flickering from the translator to Hawken and back. He shook his head strenuously and produced a rapid stream of words that Duval struggled to comprehend.

"His name is Ugaki Nobutaka, governor of Niigata. He says you cannot come here, Commodore."

Duval added, "He also calls it piracy to arrive without proper identification, to deliberately deceive honest men."

Hawken's face hardened. "Tell him we're not pirates. The consoles we carry cannot be successfully interrogated by Niigata's ground station, or any on Sado. Tell him our ships are in need of repair. We do not have enough power to return to Amerika except via the Sado nexus. We *must* hook up here. Tell him!"

There followed a lengthy exchange during which the official looked imploringly to Hawken. At last, Iwakura spoke. "Governor Ugaki is sorry, but that is out of the question. You must go. *Now.* There can be no berth for your ships here."

Hawken asked Duval, "Does he report the man truthfully?"

"He does, Commodore."

Hawken turned to the governor once more, his hands resting on the blaster butt that jutted from his suit holster. "Ask the governor why he refuses us. There are no more than twelve ships on his apron, and sixty empty berths."

The governor spoke through Iwakura again. "He says that soon there will be many Yamato ships here. Great ships. The Emperor's war fleet, with many thousands of settlers for the Greater Yamato Co-prosperity Sphere, and many heavy beam weapons, commanded by the respected veteran Admiral Kurita. His biggest vessels are twice the size of this fine ship in whose shadow we now stand, Commodore."

Duval frowned at the governor's blustering words. He said in a low voice to Hawken, "The aurium fleet is due, Commodore. I heard the Shinto priests say that last night."

Iwakura flashed him an ugly expression that was quickly gone.

"Is this true?" Hawken pierced the governor with a penetrating stare. "Is this fleet of which you speak the *kin kaigun?*"

The governor swallowed fearfully at the Japanese phrase. He was sweating. That's why he's dressed in his Imperial finery, Duval realized suddenly with mounting wonderment. They've mistaken us for the lead ships of the aurium fleet. He's come hurrying down the apron with his speech of welcome scrolled in his hand! Look! He's terrified. Doubly so now we know the fleet's due. Christ alive! Niigata must be packed to the rafters with aurium and argentium awaiting transshipment to Honshu!

"Answer me."

"*Hai*. Yes. He says he looks for the warships of the Yamato Guard daily. He adds that they will certainly be most disappointed to find an Amerikan—trader—here in their place."

Hawken slid out his blaster and touched its muzzle to the governor's sharp chin. "Then your fleet will be disappointed, sir, and maybe a little surprised, eh?"

Ugaki nodded carefully.

"He regrets that he cannot vouch for your safety, Commodore."

"My safety is my own concern."

"He says you are either a very brave man, or you are *baka*—insane."

"Tell him that my requirement is for five berths. I don't see any reason why we can't get along just fine for the five days it'll take us to get our vessels shipshape. I'll hold him personally responsible for the actions of his security men both in the terminal and out on the apron."

At Hawken's order, an explanatory communiqué was drafted to the Yamato presidents and Council in Kanazawa, explaining the flotilla's presence in innocuous diplomatic terms, then Ugaki and his officers were dismissed and sent to the terminal, comforted by an armed "honor guard." They remained under escort until Duval Straker oversaw the disarming of the beam weapons installations by his own contingents. Then the ships were taxied in close, side by side, so that the service umbilicals could be attached, and all of them were made secure.

In the terminal Duval found a small Shinto shrine artfully made from the bodies of wrecked ships, and at each extremity of the long building there was a Zen temple with a low wall enclosing an austere garden of tortured bushes and raked gravel. They made a good open site for their sensors away from spurious waveband noise. He stationed two sensor crews of five men each to cover both approaches and set about the long job of installing the machines that would warn them of the approach of any vessel using the Sado nexus.

The distractions as Duval Straker worked were increasingly hard to ignore. Because Hawken had omitted to make a general confinement order, men and women without duties began to wander about in the terminal, ignoring the openmouthed stares of the Japanese who staffed the concourse. They began going in and out of the little boutiques and tea houses and eating houses and bars where there was beer and stingo and a rough rice liquor they called *sake*.

Private trading and bartering got under way for all kinds of souvenirs and rarities. Then some of the men and women discovered the terminal's pleasure house and they began to compete for the attentions of the boys and the strange little painted dolls—geisha—who regularly entertained and serviced the passengers coming through the Sado terminal. There was plenty of choice. Geisha and prostitutes had collected here from Niigata and Kanazawa and all over Sado, anxious for the arrival of the aurium fleet. The cries of the mama-sans could be heard all night. Cries and moans and laughter and table-banging songs, escaping through the paper-screen walls, making Duval Straker sweat and curse and desire the freedom his fellow Amerikans were enjoying. But there was work to do.

Tom Fleming, a big sandy-haired New New Yorker from the *Richard M.*, came past with a tiny, delicate woman on his arm as Duval secured the last of his sensor batteries.

"They've got gels who can do things you wouldn't believe, Gunner," he shouted up with a greasy smile. "It's damned near heaven's gate. I'm coming up for number four myself. You ought to get yourself down there before the best of them are trugged out."

The geisha giggled and waved up at him, then hid her painted lips behind a fluttering fan.

"Not for a few hours yet, Tom."

"Please yourself!"

"I wish I could."

He worked on, wilting under the summer heat. As the officer responsible for nondestructively disarming the port's beam weapons he was to report to Hawken at regular intervals and attend the meeting with the other captains tonight. Since Ayrton Rodrigo's shooting, and Ellis's promotion to the *Dwight D.,* the brothers had seen little of each other. He missed that, enjoying those calm nights in the mess, making music or drinking and playing *go,* the intriguing Yamato board game that had become such an obsession with him recently, under a brilliant dome of stars; watching teams of crew members tumbling and colliding in the space between the ships in their games of win ball and robopolo. At one time they had fallen in with a school of vast, genetically engineered space whales, living creatures a mile or more long that cruised the asteroid belts of some systems blindly gorging on debris with their huge maws. Their hides carried mysterious luminescent patches, pulsing and patterning under strange wave-like impulses, as if they were talking between themselves, indulging in huge philosophic discourses for which they had all the time in the universe. There had been a whole catalog of new things to see, new experiences never dreamed of at home. But also perils that he could not have imagined either.

When the flotilla had been scattered by the psi-storm off Palawan, he had wondered if he would see Ellis again, but he had never doubted his brother's psi-talent or his ability to take the *Dwight D.* home. This was Ellis's third voyage for Hawken, and he knew how to handle the trim of a nexus ship better than almost any Amerikan alive. He had been in love with space since being apprenticed at the age of twelve. Duval had laid a bet of ten credits to five of Bowen's that when the ships established communication again, it would be the *Dwight D.* that raised the flagship first. Bowen was still mourning the loss of a week's credit in real-time.

Duval remembered it was Thanksgiving. On Thursday nights, by custom, the officers ate and drank at the commodore's table aboard the *Thomas Jefferson*. Tonight would be special. Ugaki had stiffly declined the invitation and was conveyed to his office in the terminal to pray for his own deliverance and beg the spirits of his ancestors to arrange the speedy arrival of Admiral Kurita's fleet.

The mango-scented breeze gave the warm, close air of the terminal an artificial smell as the Gunner made his way to the berths. He sweated into his thin cotton coveralls, staining them at back and armpits. Clouds continued to race across the sky, and the high-tide breakers slapped implacably at the seawall beyond the apron wire. Occasional flashes of dry sheet lightning lit the eastern sky soundlessly. Without realising what it was and where it had come from, the terraformers had made a good job of this planet. It was comfortable, if a little primeval, but now it was showing ill temper. Inside Hawken's cabin the light flickered from a dozen festive wax candles, and the drafts that filtered from the aircon were icy against the sickly humidity outside. The air was charged with rain and tasted as thick as glycerine.

For a reason Duval could not at first identify the atmosphere at table was equally tense. They sat in full dress uniform, complete with high collars and silver buttons and dirks at their belts. John Oujuku said grace movingly, thanking God for giving them a safe haven, but after they broke bread Duval found the conversation became strained and subdued. Sam, the commodore's youngest cadet, played steward. He refilled their glasses twice, but still no one relaxed. We've been away eleven months now, Duval reminded himself, the worst time for morale, and there are other reasons to feel down too. After the storm the *Millard Fillmore* had never reappeared. She's either lost, or safe at home in Liberty now, he reflected. Either way it's a sore subject for a man to think about. But that alone can't account for the hostility I can feel simmering around the supper table.

For Duval Straker it had been an exhilarating first voyage. His "rank" of gunner was a nominal one; he had won his place aboard the *Thomas Jefferson* at Ellis's recommendation and out of necessity: his skills had been learned in the physics laboratories of the Amerikan Institute of Technology and, later, the RISC Foundation on Liberty, with whose resources he had helped to develop the first mountable prototypes of the singularity gun. "My investment in your voyage shall be in kind," the head of grav-phys at RISC had told Hawken at their first meeting. "You agree to take Straker and his prototypes out on your trading mission and I'll fix it for you to get a ship big enough for you to put them aboard. How would the Navy's *Thomas Jefferson* suit you?" Hawken had always had a gut reaction against weapons, but still he had readily agreed. His defensive guns were mostly beam weapons; but after the demonstration RISC had put on, anyone could see that the singularity gun was going to make beam weapons obsolete aboard nexus ships very soon. There would come a day when Yamato would have singularity guns too, and that disturbed him even more. It would do no harm to scratch the government's back. Hell, there were even a couple of free ships in it, a big one and the smaller Navy sloop *Richard M*.

"Good old Amerikan know-how," Duval Straker had said when the installation was done. "That's what we have here."

"Oh, yeah?"

"Sure. And if we don't develop this technology, somebody else will."

"Like Yamato, you mean?"

"Shit, Commodore! What the hell did they ever invent? They steal other people's ideas. They always have."

"And then improve them."

"That's a matter of opinion."

"Well, I still don't see how your weapons're going to help us trade in the Neutral Zone. Or how our trading helps you to improve your guns."

Duval had explained: only by going with the weapons and handling them in real-action situations could the practical difficulties of protecting a trading fleet so far from home be understood and solved. Wasn't it a bitch that every new invention had to have some kind of military application first, before it was beaten into a useful plowshare? Sure, but it was the way of the world. The universe even.

Duval drained his second glass of lite beer and looked from his brother to the commodore. Hawken had treated him well, and in return he had worked hard to train the beam weapons engineers and gun crews of the *Richard M*. and the *Thomas Jefferson*. At the same time he had experimented with novel solutions to the equations that his own abstruse branch of math occasionally threw up. Spin and strangeness, love and devotion and anger were the names of the parameters he dealt with. All in the search for the manifold solutions to the fractal limit plane they called "aleph prime."

But there were practical developments too. By now he had brought the ships' gunnery to the point where they could trade beam for beam with any vessel in orbit or at long range, should it be necessary. Now his equations had showed pretty conclusively that no shield could be possible against a singularity gun.

As he carved into the breast of their Thanksgiving turkey, Duval saw from his brother's demeanor that the weighty matter that lay upon him was about to be cast off.

"So what's it to be, Commodore?"

Di Barrio's question brought the matter to a head.

"What's it to be?" Hawken smiled and sat back in his chair, studying their faces. In each he saw dangerous thoughts; at their last meeting there had been a preoccupation with survival, with the cost of restoring the flotilla to seaworthiness and computations of their chances of making a straight run home with their shares intact. This time it was different: a brooding sense of expectation, something no one was willing to voice first. Hawken had seen it before, and he recognised it now. It was the most destructive form of greed that could be placed in a person's heart: the chance to get stinking rich without working for it.

All their eyes were upon him. Shafts that stung. Dare I lay the alternatives before them openly? Hawken asked himself. Or do I keep quiet so they know nothing of my thoughts? Take care, Jos Hawken! You chose as your astrogators people who can damn near read other people's minds. Perhaps they can read yours. A year in the Neutral Zone is long enough for that. Can you—should you—deceive them? *Or can you trust them?* Already the rumors have started. The Yamato officials in Niigata are skulking about like frightened rabbits. The ships hooked up alongside the *Dwight D.* have two hundred billion credits in aurium in their bellies. Divided among four hundred Amerikans, that's half a billion each—*two million years'* pay for a third officer! Crews have murdered their captains for a whole lot less. And captains their commodore.

Hawken said very deliberately, "There's a store of treasure in Niigata to rival that of King Midas's."

He saw Oujuku's eyes flare up like novae, and Hawken looked away from him. Three hundred and eighty-six senators and a hundred and ten congressmen of the United Worlds—the most powerful group of men in Amerika—had personally invested in the venture. William Conroy Lubbock, the President's most intimate confidant, had staked a sizable fortune, and much more. For ten years Lubbock had recognised the need for Amerika to challenge the seventy-five-year-old Central Authority decree that was allowing Yamato to loot the entire Neutral Zone, but it needed more than fine words carried between Liberty and Kyoto, the Imperial capital, to end the monopoly; it required men prepared to die or else win their fortunes by testing Yamato's mettle, and such men were hard to dissuade from a course once they were determined upon it.

At length Geneva's cold blood stirred in her veins, prompting her to speak. "We've gambled in the past and won. Why not now? Are we gonna stand shaking in our boots when there's a prize worth two hundred megs next door? All that aurium they ship out of the Neutral Zone year after year, half of that's ours by rights! If Yamato can claim it, so can we! Half of it belongs to Amerika. God gave us free will, and the strength to choose. Why do we always gotta play by the marquis of Queensberry's rules when the other guy's holding a blaster?"

Oujuku jumped in hotly. "I say we take Niigata apart!"

Hawken's shoulders braced and he sat back. "If a single credit of the Emperor's wealth is touched, we'll stand accused before our own courts as pirates and common thieves. And rightly. I remind you all that the *Thomas Jefferson* and the *Richard M.* are both still listed as Amerikan Navy vessels. Are you ready to steal them too? Because you'll have to take them off me if you mean to lay your hands on a single credit's worth of that consignment."

"Yamato owes us more than a single credit, Commodore," Don Hampton said darkly.

"Ayrton was a fine astrogator and a lifelong lover of mine," di Barrio muttered. "A thousand-carat nugget or two would ease the hurt to his widow and seven youngsters."

"Right! And we should take compensation for injuries to our trade," Geneva added.

Hawken's drinking glass froze in midair. His free palm moved minutely towards the jeweled pommel of his dress-dagger. "By God, Geneva, then you'd better tell me who you are! A loyal Amerikan? *Or a thief?*"

"Can't a person be both?" Oujuku whispered, touching the hilt of his own knife.

"No, he cannot!"

"*I say he can!*" Oujuku spat.

"Thou shalt not steal! Ever hear of that?"

"Thou shalt not kill! But they killed Ayrton!"

The silence pounded in the veins of Hawken's head, brittle and loaded with pain. Beneath the table the feet of both men moved back on each side of their chairs. If either man snapped, the other would be forced to draw.

"*It means war, John.*"

Ellis Straker's voice was clear, reasonable, vastly calming in the silence.

Oujuku flashed a glance at him; he bared his teeth and hammered a big black fist into the table. "God's death! We're damned near at war now!"

"But we're *not* at war." Hawken put his glass down with conspicuous care. "When is the aurium fleet due herc, Gunner?"

Duval Straker answered smartly. "Mr. Iwakura spoke of it as being two days late already, Commodore."

Oujuku, his shoulders broad as the table, grasped a handful of air. "Whenever they arrive, we should wait and take them!"

"Come on! The opportunity is heaven sent, Commodore," Geneva said persuasively.

Hawken judged it right to reason. One false step and Amerika could be plunged into war, he told himself, controlling his anger with Faye Geneva. "With the psi-storms we've had lately their fleet might not appear at all."

Oujuku appealed to them, imploring. "In that case we have time to repair, to reprovision—and take honest damages away with us from the treasury of Niigata!"

"Honest damages? I think not, Mr. Oujuku! The law—"

"Amerikan law does not apply here, Commodore. And even if it did, the Supreme Court sits in Liberty, seventy light-years away!"

"Still close enough to glue your ass to a prison cell bench."

"All our asses."

Hampton said, "The commodore gave his promise to the governor that we would pay in full and leave peaceably. Do you want him to break his word?"

"Fuck the promise!"

"That's enough!"

Their eyes turned to Hawken. I've drawn them, he thought. Now I must impose my will. Hc leaned towards Oujuku threateningly. "Understand me plainly, sir. I will not have this treasonous talk on my ship. From you or from anyone!"

His eyes locked on Oujuku's and they struggled. The older man finally faced the younger down. In a more composed voice Hawken said, "The Emperor has closed the Yamato Sector against us, but it will not always be so. The Neutral Zone colonists have shown they're anxious to trade with us. Profits are good, so we must be patient until relations between the governments of Amerika and Yamato grow friendlier again, which I believe they will eventually do. Then will come the likelihood of our securing a regular concession to trade in the Neutral Zone and in Yamato as well. Never forget, we're traders, and it's our aim to win for ourselves a constant and acknowledged portion of the market of the Zone."

"I agree with the commodore," Hampton said. "If Yamato has wronged us, then Yamato must be made to pay. But it will pay dearest in the long term. We've turned a good profit on this trip. Let's go home and leave the goose laying golden eggs for tomorrow."

Hawken watched Oujuku sit back sourly, but he nodded his assent. Perhaps now, he thought, they'll remember who's in charge.

Before the dinner ended, Hawken spoke to them grave-faced. "People, I hope we're agreed on this. I want it posted on all your screens. And make sure your crews are left in no doubt." He addressed the ship's command bank. "This is Commodore Hawken of the *Thomas Jefferson*. I'm implementing executive officer's extraordinary powers under section ten, subsection two, of the Amerikan Merchant Venturers' Code. From midnight UT tonight no crew member or trader shall approach within a hundred yards of any Yamato ship docked on Sado, whatever his or her reason. No crew member or trader shall attempt to enter the terminal building except at the specific order of Gunner Straker here. An armed guard will be posted. And thirdly all those without a disembarkation permit allowing them to leave their own ship are confined thereto. The penalty for breaking any of these three rules is summary freezeeing. This is my order, signed by me this Thursday, being the twenty-fourth day of November, year of Our Lord twenty-four hundred and twenty-one."

As the Straker brothers left the ship, Duval heard noises, a series of high-pitched squeaks coming from the darkness of the ship's shadow. He turned and saw movement as small patches of darkness broke from the shadows and scurried across the crete, making for the storm drains.

"Shipneys," Ellis said. "Looks like Voss is gassing the runs."

"I guess."

Then the last of the rats from the *Thomas J.*'s belly disappeared into the drain and all was quiet again.

3

Ellis Straker returned to the *Dwight D.* and stood his men to, ordering three sergeants at arms to scour the terminal and have those insensibly drunk put in the flow showers. Then he acquainted his complement of thirty-three with the order. It made sense. Though it was unenforceable, it made Hawken's wishes quite clear, but it also pulled the pin on a great big self-destructor charge, and the longer they remained on Sado, the tenser everyone would get, until some poor schmuck got freezeed. It would take at least seven days for the *Thomas Jefferson* to get spaceworthy again, and in that time Ellis knew he must keep the people under his command too busy to think. During the fifteen daylight hours of this world that would be hard enough; after nightfall, when the air grew sultry and still, it would be impossible.

In the early evening, under the light of two rising moons, one of them the huge red Chi no Tsuki that raised the high tides, he mounted the steps to his customary and now familiar place of command. He felt an ache in his stomach, probably the fault of the fruit he had eaten at supper. He broke wind noisily. His crew were mostly aboard and sleeping, just one man of the watch walking the bridge slowly, back and forth, aware of his captain's presence.

God, I don't like this place, he thought. I wish we were under full power and speeding from it. Now. Tonight. Another month gone and we're further from home than ever. I wonder what time it is in Liberty. Is Janka asleep? Is she feeding Harry at her breast? Is he still suckling? Christ! He's almost two years old now. And this trip's spanned almost half his life. She's twenty now, long fair hair, and slim as a willow sapling. How easy it is to forget. What a pity there's no magic to transport a man home on Sundays, just one day in seven to check on things and see that everything's all right. That's a provision the engineers overlooked when they figured out the way to use the nexi. How much easier it would be for my peace of mind, how much it would comfort Janka. She's delicate but she's strong-minded and she knows what being an astrogator's wife means, and a long homecoming has a special sweetness all its own.

In the southeast the big moon's red bloated disc struggled up through rags of cloud that threatened storm. He shrugged the tiredness from his muscles, took a final stroll around the bridge, and then hit the sack.

In his cabin he passed a restless night in his strap hammock. A pair of striped bush monkeys caged in his first officer's quarters screamed each time anyone passed in the corridor, and rumbles of thunder rolled in on the comm. All night demonic visions plagued him. Out of the swaying, creaking darkness of his strap hammock that he usually found so comforting, he conjured only vile images: the living skeletons of the Tien Shan famine seen in his mind's eye.

Time and again he thought he saw the fires of Texas burning in the night sky, and the rotting head of John Oujuku, with raucous black crows picking the eye sockets hollow on the railings of the White House.

When at last dawn came bloody red through his cabin blister, he got up and pulled on his boots. The gauge showed that the wind had slackened, the pressure in this oxygen-rich atmosphere had fallen. Rain fell in huge, heavy drops, refreshing him as he walked down onto the apron, inspecting the tompions that plugged the ship's fans. The decaying smell of big tropical trees was on the wind, and the apron was spotted with gorgeous green moths that had been drawn by the arclights and downed by the cloudburst. He saw the damp copy of the commodore's order he had had posted hardcopy on the gangway that led to the forward bulkhead. It was untouched by the crew graffiti artists. Though none of them would agree with it, it served as a powerful reminder. They respected printed laws, and it helped him as master to gauge their attitude.

"Captain! Captain!"

He whirled round, then looked up, shielding his eyes against the brightness. Cadet Morton was leaning down from the bridge gallery, gesticulating like a mad thing. He had been playing with the sensors.

"What is it, lad?"

"Ships, Captain! Ships! Dozens of 'em, bearing down from the north, eighty miles distant!"

Straker was instantly alert. "How many?"

"I can't tell, sir. But there's dozens."

And I can't see from here, he thought, cursing. But the boy can't count. There can't be dozens. Is he seeing things? Or panicking over a glitch on the screens?

When he swung onto the elevator plate and kicked it into action, the machinery felt slower than usual. The first sign of anxiety, he thought. Calm down. It's bound to be a mistake.

When he reached the gallery halfway up the *Dwight D.*'s bridge, he jumped out and saw a sight that sent his mouth dry.

There on the fore scanner screen, streaming down onto Sado under full power, was a big four-engined armed bulk carrier, another a couple of miles behind, then another and another. There were smaller vessels also, but he counted thirteen great ships in all, too distant to discern their origin, but there could be no doubt who they were.

It's the aurium fleet! The Yamato Guard. And here at the worst possible moment with repairs hardly started and our vessels in total disarray. They might be on us within minutes!

He punched the alarm that screamed the entire ship to alert condition. Crewmen appeared, half dressed, scrambling from their cabins. "You there, Ingram! Weiser! And you, Fleming! Get the word to the other ships that the Yamato fleet's coming!"

Alarms sounded on the other Amerikan ships, the orders shrilled from the command banks, sending personnel onto the gangways and swarming up to the bridge. The gun crews raced to their stations on the ships and in the terminal, and began to reinforce their defenses with the six beam weapons still functioning on the ships.

Hawken took Ellis Straker aside and tossed his head towards the *Thomas J.*'s shuttle. He dispatched him under a truce signal to go parley with the Yamato admiral.

"Tell him I control the Sado batteries and that I must have an accord agreed before I can admit him. I trust you'll dress up my meaning in whatever polite terms they require."

"However that's said, Kurita won't like it."

"He'll like it less if we keep him up in the air for lack of a treaty."

"Can we do that?"

"With your brother's guns we can."

"But if we deny him entry to his own ground port, his ships'll have nowhere to go. They can't stay in orbit very long, and they've got to put down on this apron. There isn't anywhere else with landing facilities, and those big babies aren't built for putting down on rough terrain. Force them to do that and they'll have casualties, and you'll be so deep in the shit no kind of paddle will get you out."

"Then Kurita'll have to treat with us on our terms."

"Samurai pride will never—"

Hawken's temper broke. "Samurai pride don't enter into it, Ellis! Their admiral's responsible for two hundred billion credits' worth of cargo. He won't risk losing that. Now get under way!"

Ellis left with that fabulous sum running unstoppably through his mind. Two hundred billion credits was more than the entire Liberty economy raised in tax revenues in a whole real-time year . . .

His shuttle returned within the hour, bringing down to a parley on the apron a straight-backed messenger in fine Yamato attire of blue and gold, a captain with two swords and a shaved head and topknot who spoke English fluently.

"I am Vice-admiral Kondo, representing Admiral Kurita and His Excellency Nishima Jun, daimyo-designate of Sado. I bring His Excellency's greetings. He asks what business you imagine you have here and invites you to vacate his port immediately."

Hawken's stomach had clenched convulsively at mention of the daimyo. If he was aboard, then the Emperor's own instrument of government was here. *In person.* He looked at the haughty bearing of Kondo and knew that by a cruel twist of fortune he had been brought suddenly to the very edge of disaster.

"Then you agree to our terms?"

Kondo stepped forward stiff and formal, his mouth betraying disdain. "I regret to say, Commodore, that your demands are utterly refused. Your ships will leave our port within the hour."

The next step was unavoidable. Hawken shook his head.

"That I cannot do, sir. Please inform His Excellency that his ships are at this moment in no position to dictate to me. I must have my terms met."

Kondo hid his outrage manfully. "That is your final answer, Commodore?"

"It is."

"Then I will convey it faithfully to His Excellency."

Kondo turned arrogantly on his heel and took his leave. Ellis watched him weighing the strength of the port's defenses as he went. Despite himself he had been impressed by the vice-admiral's easy assumption of superiority.

Oujuku kept his voice low, hating the aristocrat on sight. "They're a pack of treacherous dogs. We'll have to shoot the shit out of them to save ourselves now. Let's take them, Jos. Come on! We'll never get a better chance."

Hawken's stare was like a dagger. "They'll be back. This time on our terms."

Oujuku hissed. "You're going to let them in? They'll disable our shields and have us wrecked as soon as piss!"

"If they agree to bind over a dozen of their first-rank samurai as hostages and suffer our keeping control of the port's guns, I'll admit them."

"You can't trust them, Commodore. Samurai're disgusting bastards. No respect for human life. Why, they cut their own guts out as soon as piss. The concept of a hostage don't mean a thing to them."

"I hope you're wrong."

Ellis went again to Kondo later that day and carried back with him the daimyo's answer. This time the message was honeyed with fine words and agreed to all of Hawken's conditions. Twelve hostages were exchanged and, as Friday night fell, the aurium fleet began to drop out of the sky and land.

From the bridge of the admiral's flagship, *Chiyoda*, Choshu no Nishima Jun looked at the preparations with satisfaction. He was a tall, darkly handsome figure with steel-gray beard and the characteristic oiled and bound topknot of the samurai class curved up across the shaven top of his skull. He wore a blue kimono underneath a matching pair of *hakama* trousers and a *haori* jacket decorated on the sleeves, breast, and back with the triple-leaf crest of his family. His Imperial Majesty, the Son of Heaven, had commanded him to take over as daimyo of Sado, and this was his first visit to the planet.

But it was an inauspicious first visit. The wind had begun to blow again, and the sky which an hour before had been scoured of cloud was darkening once more.

In the sky, the wind,
Is a sword blade, cutting out,
Patterns of white cloud.

The haiku poem came to him, crystalising the moment perfectly. Below him the last of the passengers were climbing down into air-cars. They included Confucian monks and Shinto priests, the secretaries and staff of the new Imperial administration and, of course, the women.

Dressed in a stiff, peach-colored silk kimono tied about the middle with a white obi, and climbing delicately into the air-car now, was the delightful Urawa no Hasegawa Michie.

Michie-san had been Nishima's wife's traveling companion aboard the *Chiyoda,* and what a sublime torture she had proved for every man aboard. Even Kurita's all-male crew—rough-handed veterans, most of them—had risked humiliating punishment willingly, loitering at their tasks whenever she had appeared on the observation promenade that straddled the flagship's aft superstructure. Now, along with the other ladies and noncombatants who had voyaged to the godless planet of Sado in the Yamato Guard, she was being taken to Niigata, where she would be safe. She needs to be taken in hand, he thought, relishing the prospect. But first, there is an important duty to perform. I have chosen noon as the time to restore our honor and serve the Emperor, as I know I must.

It had taken two days to assemble all the truckships in the vastly overcrowded apron, but by the morning of *mokuyo*—Jupiter's day, or Thursday as the Amerikans called it—all was prepared and the Amerikan vessels were sectioned off together like carp in a pond.

Everything he had heard about the barbarous Amerikans was true. They were utterly mannerless, worse than *hinin*—the lowest of the *burakumin* outcastes, the nonhumans. And they were incredibly stupid. By stalling and applying constant interference, Nishima thought, we have made the filth lose almost three days repair time, and they are now trying to make it up as rapidly as possible. Understandably they are distracted by their anxiety to leave. But they are soon to be disappointed.

"Why do these Amerikans behave the way they do?" he had demanded of Kurita as they approached Sado. "It's hard to believe that they have absolutely no understanding of civilised ways. I think they insult us deliberately."

"They are mongrels, Excellency," the admiral had replied, disgust rippling his falcon-like face. Kurita had looked squarely back, using his five years' advantage and the fact of his position as absolute master of the aurium fleet to try to speak on terms of equality with an Imperially appointed daimyo. "They are well known in the Neutral Zone and appear there every year."

"Have they been granted a *ryoken* to trade in the Greater Yamato Coprosperity Sphere?" he had asked doubtfully, stressing his use of the new term for the territory that had just been annexed. "Are they licensed like some of the Chinese traders?"

Kurita had laughed. "No, Nishima-san. This Hawken has tried many times to wheedle his way into the Sphere with official blessing. He has given bribes, devised all kinds of clever schemes. He has even offered to use his influence at the White House—to help Yamato gain official recognition by the Amerikan government for half our claim!"

"May the gods piss on their impudence!"

"They appear in the Neutr—that is, the Co-prosperity Sphere, every year with an assortment of shoddy merchandise to peddle."

"Which our colonists flock to buy illicitly wherever they can."

"Ah, only under duress, Excellency."

"And to avoid the sales tax, eh, Kurita?"

Kurita had smiled. "The Sphere is a frontier, Excellency, full of dangers and offering few pleasures to a civilised person. No settler comes to the planets of the Sphere without thoughts of enriching himself—unless he has to. The Amerikans are soft people, silly people. They are very good at dreaming up ephemeral playthings—luxuries and entertainments and things to help childish fantasies. It's natural in a way. Our settlers have to work hard, and they like to play hard also. A small amount of illicit trade is to be expected."

Nishima had flamed inside at that remark. During the voyage he had pledged a hundred times to knock some of the arrogance out of Kurita once the aurium fleet put down on Niigata apron and officially passed into his jurisdiction.

It was entering *juji,* the tenth hour, when Nishima watched the last of the ladies lift the hem of her kimono and step up into the air-car. He thought irritably of the inconvenience that the Amerikans had caused him. I could be entrained for Kanazawa now, enjoying the *cha-no-yu,* the tea ceremony, in the company of my ladies, were it not for these detestable pirates. They're *hinin* with no respect for the law. But here *I* am the law! With the help of my ancestors, I will see the Amerikans dangling from crosses before sundown. They give me just the excuse I've been waiting for to make Kurita jump to my command. And it will be the admiral's own ships that will have won me my victory!

Preparations were almost complete. The previous evening he had received the murderer, Iwakura, and promised him clemency for his crimes in return for a favor. Iwakura's escape from the convict settlement on the Blood Moon had been clever, and the idea of using him had sounded worthwhile. Three messengers had carried secret letters to Governor Ugaki, who was at this moment quietly mustering a thousand soldiers of the Sado garrison and smuggling them aboard the nexus ship hulk lying beside the Niigata apron. Beam weapons were being inched into place aboard a great ship of nine thousand tons, open ports cut in her plex so that at Kondo's signal they could be trained on the enemy. Even now she was secretly being packed with samurai next to the Amerikan *Richard M. Nixon* so that on the signal three hundred armed men would come rushing out and throw themselves onto the Amerikans.

Kondo appeared, bowing, at his side with one of the pirates.

"The Amerikan commodore has sent this man to crave your indulgence once more, Excellency," he announced formally.

"Indeed?"

The man was strikingly oriental in appearance for an Amerikan. The daimyo had noticed him several times, working on the shore batteries that the Amerikan guarded so jealously. He had even asked Kondo to discover if the man was a deserter and therefore of some use—as Iwakura had been.

"What is it?"

The Amerikan cleared his throat. "If it please you, Excellency, my commodore counts too many men passing back and forth on the apron, more than your agreement stipulates. He asks if you would be good enough to order them back aboard your ships."

Nishima felt a flush of indignation at so insubordinate a question delivered in such appallingly poor Japanese. Certainly an insult, since this man was clearly not of equivalent rank.

"These laborers—they are merely my admiral's work parties. They are necessary to the proper order of his fleet."

"Then may I tell my commodore you will order them back, sir?"

The daimyo's eyes blazed with anger. "This is a Yamato port. I have authority here."

The Amerikan had already accepted Nishima's assurances that the activity they saw was no threat to them, and he had salved their suspicions twice with carefully worded explanations. Their insistence was becoming tedious, but he knew he must control his anger a little longer.

"But the agreement specifies—"

"Yes, yes! Tell your commodore what he asks will be done."

The Amerikan remained at Kondo's side.

"Well?"

"I beg your pardon, sir?"

"What is it? There's more you wish to say?"

"I apologise for my poor Japanese, sir, but my commodore also questions the purpose of the ship now being brought alongside our second vessel."

Kondo started forward, his eyes flashing anxiously, but the daimyo motioned him to be still. Nevertheless, his hand tightened on his sword hilt as Nishima said with an artificial lightness in his voice, "As you see, the apron is crowded. The ship to which you refer is simply coming alongside to take on cargo. There is nowhere else to do it."

As soon as the Amerikan bowed and withdrew, Kondo said, "They are suspicious. You should have let me cut him down, Excellency."

"Patience, Kondo-san."

"But, Excellency—"

"At this moment the Amerikan pirate chief is preparing to lunch with Iwakura. I hope the secrecy of our purpose will endure two hours more."

Kondo was trembling with anger. He had read the signs and judged the daimyo's plan too complex to work once the Amerikans were alerted.

When Nishima moved away, he balled his hand and struck the side of the bulkhead in frustration, then he made for thc samurai-packed hulk before Nishima's plan fell completely into chaos.

5

The table in the *Thomas Jefferson*'s main dining room was set with a white cloth and silver and, in deference to the guests, the sharply pointed Yamato chopsticks that were so difficult to manipulate and so easy to lose face with. The table was spread with the finest delicacies that could be synthesised in the ship's Dover machines. Di Barrio and Hampton were present beside Ellis Straker. So too Iwakura and his priestly companions. He had asked to be allowed to say his farewells to Hawken with due ceremony, and Hawken had agreed. It had seemed to Ellis an unlikely, if appropriate, gesture. Today they had finally begun manifesting the trade goods that had been off-loaded and stockpiled on the apron whilst the overhaul was completed. With any luck by tomorrow night they would be able to light out for the nexus.

As Hawken sat down at the head of a table of six guests, Chambers, his steward, poured a tiny ceramic thimble of *sake* provided by Iwakura. Silently Ellis congratulated his commodore, feeling that he had somehow traversed a difficulty by diplomacy and firm dealing. His ships were in good transit condition, he had secured, albeit at a high price, the stores he required, and above all he had convinced a Yamato nobleman of ancient lineage, the daimyo of Sado, that an orderly withdrawal was the best course for them both. Nishima's chop was impressed in red and white on the treaty, and all without a single beam being fired. Then why, Ellis wondered, were the muscles of his chest and neck as tight as the bracing arms on the main engine?

Iwakura's thimble was raised in salute.

"To our Amerikan hosts and their gracious President!"

"To our friends in the Neutral Zone and the people of Yamato!"

Ellis muttered the words and sipped. As pretty a party as you could hope for, the mocking part of him said. What's wrong? Can't samurai and Amerikan compliment one another in friendship? Do you hate them that much? Wasn't it Yamato settler trade that bought you your mansion in Lincoln? Isn't it Yamato aurium that'll buy you your own ship when you get back? Go along with it. Smile. Treat the commodore's guests civilly.

"To Jos Hawken of Liberty: a great commodore!"

"And to you, Mr. Iwakura—or should I say Iwakura-san: an honest samurai."

Ellis raised his thimble, but this time he could not touch it to his lips. It was a samurai that gave you your first command too, the other, suspicious part screamed back, samurai temper that burned Ayrton's guts out, and Yamato treachery that will smash the whole fleet! Look at it! Stop ignoring it! Stop fooling yourself! They've already broken the treaty. They're shifting vessels all over the apron. They're swarming all over the place. Shaven-headed men who don't ever look you in the eye, all doing the work of slaves. It doesn't add up.

"To your fine captains: may they never lose their ships in a psi-storm."

"To the Shinto priests: that one day they'll learn to speak and understand Amerikan."

They're soldiers! Soldiers! They're waiting to fall on us!

At the moment the thimbles were raised, Ellis's eye caught a flash of steel. Iwakura's capacious right sleeve was hidden under the table, and with a deft flick of his forearm he slid from under it a glittering *tanto* blade a foot and a half long.

Hawken leaned forward, unaware of the dagger poised in the man's hand. Desperately Ellis realised that Iwakura was about to strike. Iwakura was too far across the table for Ellis to stop him, too distant to reach directly, and if he gave warning, the man would snap like a steel spring. There was no time to think, no time to consider. No time to save the life of the man who had been like a father to him . . .

Ellis's instincts shut out his helpless brain. He acted blindly, instantly. Without warning, he sent his fist crashing into Hawken's jaw and threw him sprawling backward over his chair. The commodore's *sake* swilled across the tablecloth as the *tanto* darted from view, then Ellis leapt at Iwakura's throat, scattering the amazed guests in confusion.

"He's got a knife!" Hawken's young steward shouted. Hampton lunged for Ellis's arm.

"He's gone mad!" di Barrio cried as the priests jumped to their feet.

When Iwakura's hand came up, it was in a deadly arc. The killing blade sliced through the air and deeply into Ellis's tunic, but he twisted away from the strike with incredible agility, shrugging Hampton off him as he did so. Then Iwakura's arm jerked wide, caught now in Ellis's iron grip. Hawken had recovered his feet and flung himself across the table, pinning the man's wrist back so that the *tanto* fell to the table. Immediately the steward grabbed it up and held it to the assassin's throat, stopping the priests in their tracks.

The door burst open and Bowen spilled into the cabin with two burly crewmen who instinctively seized the Shinto priests. Hawken forced Iwakura to face the murderous redness in his eye. He pounded the man's head against the dining room wall.

"You lying Yamato filth!"

Iwakura breathed hard, sweating, enraged at his failure. "*Oshii desu ne!*"

he replied through gritted teeth, then spat. "*Sonno! Joi!*" Revere the Emperor! Expel the barbarians!

Hawken stepped back and swung. Iwakura's head catapulted. His eyes rolled up in pain and he fell limp.

"Bowen! Lock him up before I kill him! Lock them all up!" He threw off his *sake*-sodden velvet jacket and pushed his way out of the room, tearing his loaded blaster off the rack as he went.

Ellis searched the chest of his jerkin inside the tear where the knife point had opened his shirt. It had barely scratched him. He shouted for the armorer.

"Break out the guns and beat to arms! Bowen—get on the talkback and rally the crew! Get everyone suited up!"

He followed Hawken out and sprang after him down into the gaping cargo bay of the *Thomas Jefferson*. On the far side the big Yamato bulk carrier had sent a thick flexiplex hawser looped from her beakhead over the *Richard M.* and down to one of the ring bolts set into the apron. Five men heaved on it, desperate to physically anchor the *Richard M.* down and prevent her taxiing. The man orchestrating the task was Kondo.

"What the—?" Hawken shouted in amazement, and loosed a bolt of air-searing energy at him. Kondo staggered back as one of *Richard M.*'s sharpshooters blew open the chest of the man beside him, spattering the vice-admiral with gore.

"*Banzai!*" Kondo shouted back defiantly, ripping out his sword. The Yamato war cry echoed across the apron and hundreds of the daimyo's samurai swarmed to the call. Alarm sirens blared and Amerikan crews appeared everywhere, some in plex armor, others half into their pressure suits or closing helmets over their heads, many with weapons to hand.

The hulk had burst open beside them. Yamato troops rushed out eager to blood their ancestral weapons in personal combat. They began hacking the defenders down with swords as they closed. Blasters fired and raked the cargo bays, slaughtering the *Richard M.*'s crew. They retreated before the onslaught, Hawken falling back with a dozen men to call up support from the *Thomas J.*

Ellis was isolated. Trapped against the bulkhead, he fought back desperately with wild swings of a fire ax until in the counterattack the samurai were driven away under a blaze of fire from the *Thomas J.*'s high stern. Amerikans were now pouring into the melee but their own attack had caught them in a trap. The first group found themselves pinned in the *Thomas J.*'s cargo bays, under a withering cross fire from decks above. But already the samurai were mounting a second wave, attacking from all quarters.

My own command? Ellis thought desperately. No time to think of the *Dwight D.* Trust your crew to keep their heads. You must get the *Richard M.* away. Stop them getting aboard. Stop them coming across her open bays again.

A bolt flashed past his head and struck off the plex in a sizzling refraction fan. He flung a heavy plex cutter to the nearest man, a racial Chinese they had "liberated" from Palawan named Cao.

"Get that hawser!"

Cao bounded forward, lithe and muscular. The plex cutter stuttered twice and then struck. A violet jet of mu-mesons played over the thick woven line that secured the ship, and with agonising slowness it began to part. There was no time to think about flight checking, and no chance of maneuvering her onto a taxiway, but he had to get her moving. He sent men to the bridge to enable the ground effect motors on the *Richard M.*'s stern to try to ease the three-thousand-tonner out.

The beam weapons on the terminal thundered. Looking that way, he saw Kurita's men bringing round the big guns to bear on the unshielded Amerikan ships.

Duval! Where's Duval! he thought as he saw Ally de Soto, the *Thomas J.*'s chief armorer, and able hand Dexy Jordan both cut down by energy beams. All across the apron samurai soldiers had fallen on the Amerikans; the parking pads were littered with bodies. A hundred or more had been cut down near the storm gullies so that they ran red with blood. It was disgusting bestial bloodlust at its crudest. Sickening animal butchery. There would soon be no chance for Duval to get aboard. Already the *Richard M.* was pulling away from the *Thomas J.*, whose own open cargo bays were swarming with Yamato troops.

A heavy bombardment began. Deadly beams whipped from the terminal batteries searing down the *Thomas J.*'s fin and ripping her beetle-wing cargo doors off at the hinges, but both the *Richard M.* and the *Thomas J.* were free, taxiing slowly as the motors caught hold of them.

Shaking with a terrible fury, Ellis climbed into the flagship. He swept up a lost samurai sword and charged screaming into three plex-armored men who turned on him with their own swords. His steel rang against one sword and on the upswing struck sparks from the second's plex helmet, but a blow from the third's foot knocked him sideways and he was forced hard up against the hull by their leader.

He saw the *katana* raised to strike at his skull, saw the white teeth of the man in jointed lamellar breastplate and crested warbonnet, and as he dodged felt his shoulder absorb the blade. It bit with the force of an ax and stuck deep in the flesh.

I'm a dead man now, he thought, *dead.*

Instinctively he gripped the sword hilt with outstretched hands and kicked the man away from it. His adversary cast about for another weapon. He picked up a second discarded sword, but as the battery fire raked them again he was carried off balance. Shattered metal rained down in the bay around him, but he recovered, towering now over Cadet Preston. The boy tried valiantly to fight back but was hacked down almost at once. Jeezus! Ellis mouthed as he watched the slaughter. He's almost cut him in two. But I'm not dead yet. I must work the steel loose and endure the pain.

The seconds seemed like agonising minutes as the blade ground sickeningly inside his shoulder just above the scratch Iwakura had given him. Though he hung his full weight on it, the blade would not come free. Ellis's blue jerkin was now sodden with blood, and the tattered shirt beneath soaked deep red. The samurai turned again.

Ellis gathered himself for one last furious heave and forced his body against the bulkhead stanchion. A surge of pain and horror flooded him as he levered the hilt and the blade came free. He could not stop the blood or the pain, but at least he could defend himself now.

The samurai hacked at him. He dodged the slash badly and the man's sword point caught the *katana*'s handguard, spinning him round. With an immense effort he drove his assailant back and thrust his own sword left-handed into the samurai's bull neck directly above the center line of his breastplate.

The man staggered. Then he hugged Ellis to him and crashed to the deck plates on top of him. Ellis felt the blade spring under his back and the sudden crack as it snapped off against the *Thomas J.*'s grip flooring.

I must get help, he told himself. Must stop the bleeding, find some way to plug the gash. He felt his strength and rage ebbing as the shocking wound fuddled his brain. I must get out, he told himself. I must not faint away, or I'll never wake up. I must get back to my ship, get hold of my brother . . .

Then the weight of the dead samurai crushed the wind from his lungs and darkness closed over him.

6

"Don't shoot! It's Duval down there!"

"Jeezus! It's the Gunner!"

Duval Straker touched the hull of the *Richard M.* and allowed himself to be heaved up over the loading ramp. As he lay gasping for breath on the bloodied decks, he saw bodies being thrown out. Of his weapons crew he was the only one alive; at the terminal out of a hundred and fifty only three had gotten away alive when the sensors had started screaming. He watched Hawken, now suited up in his fighting gear and giving orders.

You stubborn bastard, he thought savagely. If you'd listened to my report, we would have been prepared. But you wouldn't. You thought you'd got away with it, that these guys were impressed by your firm and open dealing. Ellis told you that you should have been more vigilant. He tried to warn you that the daimyo was planning treachery. Now two hundred of us have paid for your stubbornness with their lives.

"Where's my brother?"

Hawken whirled. An ugly bruise purpled his cheek. "Gunner!"

"Where's Ellis?"

"His ship's taken. Maybe him too."

"Dead?" Duval felt the force of the word in the pit of his stomach.

"Like us all if you don't get those shooters working."

Bowen shouted. "I saw your brother board the *Thomas J.* in a blood-spitting temper just before we lost sight of him. He was aiming to drive the attackers off her."

The flagship was taxiing in crazy circles, her aerials and gantries in ruin, her bay doors dragging on the apron. There was no sign of Ellis, nor anyone moving on the bridge.

Despite intense battery fire, the *Richard M.* was coming to battle order. She had been taken out two ship's lengths, her anchoring lugs cut and her engines firing up. Both ex-Navy ships were now beyond boarding range, but they were being cut to pieces each time the terminal's guns fired. To protect the *Richard M.*, Hawken worked her close to the *Thomas J.*, and seeing this the Yamato admiral ordered his ships to cut loose and come across to bring their guns to bear.

Duval Straker got his gunners to work quickly, sending cadets to the magazines below to arm the argentium tubes. In the fury of the battle he looked inward for the knot of calm determination that would sustain him but found only furious questions. He knew that Ellis would not have waited to throw himself into the assault. He had always said that in a fight the man who acted on psi-instinct, abandoning himself to action and to his fate, was safer than the man who thought and cowered. It was especially true when the instinct had been ingrained by long psi-training.

This is the moment Ellis must have foreseen, Duval thought. This is why I was brought along. He knew I would somehow have the chance to prove my singularity weapons, and the unspoken prophesy has come true.

Duval realised suddenly that Ellis was almost certainly dead. The idea was shocking, but the pain was numbed as if he couldn't believe in it and he found refuge from it in his own skills. He narrowed his mind to the task in hand and gathered his crew, pressing others to stand in for those who had died on the apron. Methodically they readied the barrels of his five experimental guns, charging them with argentium, arming them with the big arming keys, fusing them, energising azimuth and elevation on the complex recoil mounts.

He shouted down the talkback to the bridge where the astrogator signaled his readiness to accept the gunner's aiming directions. He code-signaled back: "Forget the terminal! Get me clear! I want the bogey ships!"

Hacking orders and the sharp whistles of the *Richard M.*'s takeoff engines had driven the crew to their stations. Already they had got themselves into fighting order, then the turbos flared and, as they came up to power, the ship's nose came around, swinging a line of blockading Yamato ships past his waiting muzzles.

"Fire at will!"

"Firing!"

An infinitesimal gap of time as simultaneously five triggers slotted home, then *Richard M.*'s structure was hammered by a tightly synchronised concussion that filled the interior of the ship with the acrid smell of ozone.

The first strake was wide, the unstoppable lances of ionised air glowing unnaturally as baseball-sized singularities appeared from the guns and propagated through free space at their characteristic rate, quasi-micro-black holes dragging the air into them in long, moaning shafts. Immediately the crews set about reloading and the second attempt was brilliantly on target.

The Yamato admiral's ship, *Chiyoda*, was hit just above the lateral line: an inspired shot that penetrated the magazine, and the prow of the vessel was ripped apart by a concussion that shook the whole apron. Men were blasted high by a searing orange explosion that littered the entire spaceport with burning wreckage.

Duval tore his eyes from the devastation. The *Richard M.*'s crew were cheering wildly and they cheered again seconds later when her guns set the Yamato vice-admiral, *Shinano,* on fire. One after another the singularities shafted into the fabric of the great ships, a bulk carrier, then the *Chiyoda* again, which lost her undercarriage and settled on her belly, smoke and flames issuing from her.

"That's the ship Nishima's aboard!" someone shouted. The stink of ozone filled Duval's nostrils and the roaring of the weapons deafened him. He saw the engines flash over on Oujuku's *Judith L.* as it stood off to give covering fire. At least John's safely off the ground.

You've got your wish, he blamed Hawken silently, filled with the spirit of vengeance. These bastards have paid a heavy price, but our fleet's doomed: The *John F.* is burning, the *Dwight D.* has been taken, and the shuttles are all overrun. The *Thomas Jefferson* is abandoned and useless. Only the *Richard M.* and *Judith L.* remain. God damn you for Ellis's death.

7

Across the apron, close by the terminal, Kurita Imari listened to his samurai with alarm. The resistance had taken him completely by surprise, and the unknown weapons that were punching holes in the plex hulls of his ships had struck fear into him. Now there was this new problem. The sergeant had disobeyed orders to leave the burning flagship in a six-wheel apron caddy to tell him that the daimyo was refusing to come off his burning ship.

The man's expression was imploring through the streaked dirt of his face.

"What?"

"His Excellency's anger is beyond all reason! He will not listen. The danger to his person is extreme but he will not leave the *Chiyoda*."

Cursing, Kurita told the sergeant to find where the fire appliances were quartered and order the cowardly crews to assist the daimyo's ship whatever the state of the battle—under pain of death—then he went after Kondo, his vice-admiral. If anything will blast Nishima Jun out of his fury, he thought sanguinely, the sight of Kondo will. Together they boarded the caddy and raced across the battle chaos of the apron, and he found the daimyo white-faced, stiff-limbed with rage, still brandishing his sword and a blaster pistol at the Amerikans, utterly powerless to do anything about the wrecking of his ships.

Kurita sent the firemen away to fight the blazes as best they could.

"Excellency!"

Immediately the daimyo saw Kondo, his face began to suffuse with blood.

"You dare come aboard my ship? Report, you traitorous *shirami!*"

Kondo paled under the attack, but knelt and humbly gave his version.

"I had no choice, Excellency. We were discovered. I myself was almost killed by a blaster bolt at the hands of the Amerikan commodore himself. My first officer was shot down at my side. I had to give the signal."

Kurita watched Kondo kneeling in supplication. That's right, he told Kondo silently, humble yourself. You know you gave thc signal to attack an hour too soon. We were not fully prepared. If we had been ready, the Amerikans and their ships would have been obliterated just as surely as those who were slaughtered in the terminal. Instead we have lost three capital ships, and still the Amerikans live. What a disaster! And it's worse because Nishima's obviously never been in battle before. He doesn't realise what's happened, and there's no way I can bring it up now without his losing face completely. *What, by all the gods, is that weapon they're using?*

Nishima's eyes opened wide in disbelief at Kondo. "The Amerikan pirate lives? You lie! Did Iwakura not have my orders to kill him? You raised the signal to save your own miserable skin!"

"Not so, Excellency. The plan was known to them. We were betrayed. I swear it!"

Nishima recoiled from the insolence, and in that moment Kurita stepped forward.

"My men have taken the batteries. Look, Excellency! They are crushing the Amerikan flagship, and the one with those terrifying new guns has ceased firing."

The daimyo turned to stare at the pirates. "What are they doing? They have their shields up and they're just hovering there. Why don't they retreat?"

"Excellency, they are crippled. Everything they have is aboard their flagship down on the apron. Without that they have nowhere to go."

"Prepare a kamikaze ship!"

"But Excellency, the circumst—"

Nishima's eyes burned like the coals of the deepest fire-hell. "You *dare* to question my orders?"

"Certainly not, Excellency." Kurita took hold of Kondo angrily. The man was still on his knees. "Did you not hear the daimyo-designate's orders? Prepare a ship for a kamikaze attack immediately."

Kondo looked helplessly back, but got to his feet, bowed, and left to do his admiral's bidding.

Across the apron the beam weapons were hitting the Amerikans' shields. Kurita's men in the *Chiyoda*'s belly were bringing the fire under control so that the need to formally request the daimyo to alight from his ship had subsided. Despite the freshening breeze, the air tasted sickeningly of ozone, but through the ragged smoke Kurita could see that both Amerikan ships had managed, through a feat of extraordinary pilotage, to get off from the apron. Undoubtedly the pirate's flagship was stricken, her cargo bay doors shot off, and, even as he watched, a cheer went up from the samurai on shore when her hull began to spasm with death-throe colors as her organic-computer nervous system died.

She is old and obsolete; her hull patterning is going crazy, Kurita thought with satisfaction. Soon her nervous system will be dead and she will be a transparent hulk, her chrome response motes unable to switch on and reflect, unable to keep the beams from burning her interior. Soon we will have these remaining Amerikans in irons. Then Nishima will have his revenge. By all the gods, what is that weapon they have? The daimyo has no understanding of warfare, or he'd know it isn't a beam weapon, he'd know it was revolutionary! I hope he takes the captives and crucifies them all for the *gaijin* pirates they are, but first, I hope he finds out about those weapons. He stifled his disgust. But a kamikaze ship is madness!

The daimyo's hands remained tight on his *katana* hilt, but as the truth of the enemy's plight grew clearer, he began to calm. I am Choshu no Nishima Jun, honorary commander of the Imperial Army, daimyo of Sado, admiral of the Home Systems, and trusted vassal of His Imperial Majesty, the Emperor Mutsuhito, he told himself proudly. I know how to deal with godless *gaijin,* and soon they will be mine.

"When will the kamikaze ship be ready?"

"Excellency, may I prevail upon you to reconsider? If—"

"When will it be ready?"

Kurita stifled his insubordination. "As soon as Kondo-san can execute your order."

"Good. None of them must escape."

For the next few minutes Nishima paced the deck restlessly, his burnished plex armor hot and heavy on his sweat-drenched body. He was bleeding inside at the loss of his admiral's finest ships.

How had they done it? How had these obsolete Amerikan vessels inflicted such disproportionate damage? How was he to know that the insects had the stings of scorpions? How would he explain the situation to the Emperor's chamberlains?

It would be useless to count on the admiral. He had detected overt reproof in Kurita's manner, and hadn't he heard him say "daimyo-designate" to Kondo—it was the truth, but it was also a slight. An unconscious slip? Unlikely. In which case Kurita Imari would have to be taught a lesson.

Calmer now, Nishima watched as the helpless Amerikan flagship was lacerated by fresh bolts of energy from the beam weapons batteries. The chroming was definitely close to failure. A grim smile curved his long face, making his black moustaches lift like raven's wings.

He turned to Kurita. "Have the Amerikan corpses heaped like logs on the apron below the batteries as a taunt."

Kurita passed on the order emotionlessly.

"It will be a long time before the *gaijin* come to Niigata again, eh, Kurita-san?"

The admiral seemed about to betray himself, then said only, "Perhaps."

"Are they not utterly destroyed?"

"The Amerikans are an obstinate people, Nishima. They did not stop coming to the Co-prosperity Sphere when the Central Authority ordained it, they did not desist at the Emperor's command, and I doubt if they will heed you."

"Then you would have treated them differently?"

"It is not my place to criticise your actions, Excellency."

"Who can say I acted incorrectly? If the Amerikans were too stupid or too cowardly to believe I would try to destroy them, is that not their failing?"

The admiral fixed his eyes stiffly on the Amerikan flagship and made no reply, infuriating Nishima.

"What binds the word of a samurai when given to a *gaijin* and a blackmailer? Nothing!"

"Who can say what binds the word of a samurai?"

Nishima stared at his admiral.

"Damn you to each of the eight ice-hells in turn, Kurita! Have not the planets of the Co-prosperity Sphere been made the possession of Yamato by the Central Authority itself? That edict has made everything within one nexus jump of the Yamato borders a dependency and a protectorate of the Empire. Is it not the will of the gods that the Empire be protected against these marauders?"

Again Kurita made no reply, but his stare hardened, forcing the daimyo to a greater pitch of anger.

"Now I am daimyo there will be a new regime. I carry the Emperor's personal brief to make Sado secure, and by all the blood in hell I shall do so!"

Kurita Imari's family was not of great rank. His lineage was ancient, but his flatish face betrayed more than a hint of low blood. The daimyo had seen too many like him not to be wary of them. Such men must be watched carefully, their ambitions stifled before they grew too dangerous. More than once on the crossing from Honshu the admiral had showed himself to be overly self-important. He would not be content until he had risen high up the golden stair of power, and he was foolish enough to believe that he could do it through tireless service and loyalty in ferrying the Emperor's aurium across space. But this is where your loyalty has been tested, Admiral of the Nexus! You are flawed by disobedience, and I will see you brought down for it, ferryman!

He began to sketch the opening of his first dispatch to his Emperor's chamberlains. He would begin by revealing how the fool Kondo had been responsible for confounding his excellent plan by giving the battle signal too soon. He would make sure Kondo was put to death ignominiously and then he would deal with Kurita's disobedience.

The smile on the daimyo's lips faded. He saw that the smaller Amerikan vessel had managed to work back towards the flagship. It was then that the impossible began to happen.

8

On the *Richard M.*'s bridge, Duval Straker listened intently to the commodore. Jos Hawken's face was alight as he exhorted his crew to greater efforts. John Oujuku had made off under full power and was heading for orbit, but Hawken had seen that his own ship could not follow. There were two reasons: The *Richard M.* had not even begun loading by the time the battle had started, and there was no Dover catalyst aboard. Without that they'd starve. The other reason was brought up by Duval: the *Thomas Jefferson*'s armament. They couldn't leave singularity gun prototypes behind intact.

One chance remained. If only the *Richard M.* could be brought under cover of the *Thomas Jefferson*'s bulk, she would be protected from the deadly fire of the Sado batteries, even though in landing she would have to close down her shields. Then they could try to take on board the precious cargo that was stowed in the flagship's cargo hold and give themselves a slim chance of survival.

The battery fire faltered as the *Richard M.* turned. It was as if the Yamato gunners could not believe the ship was coming towards them instead of running for orbit as the other had already done. They had covered the runways, anticipating retreat, and it took them some seconds to re-aim their weapons on the apparently crippled Amerikan. They cruised low over the terminal in a gut-wrenching arc, and the interval was long enough for Duval Straker's gunners to disable the three main batteries that were pouring beams into the *Thomas J.*

Then the ship put down again, and as the hulls of the two Amerikan vessels touched, Hawken's orders to his officers were explicit:

"Take twenty crew each aboard the *Thomas J.* Put them to work in gangs of four, transferring provisions manually. Water and any Dover catalyst you can find—whatever you get we can use. Now go to it!" Hawken turned to Hampton. "Come with me. And you, Sanders—get your tight ass shifting or lose it to those shit-shoveling snipers! Help get our wounded below. We'll get the *Richard M.* home if we have to push her all the way!"

Sanders saluted, her own face streaked with blood. Then the crew scattered as a tangled mass of metal and plex sheets was ripped from the *Thomas J.*'s bridge and flung down among them. A man who moved too slowly was axed down by the debris. Two of his crewmates moved to help him. They turned him and saw the face of Purser Rosencrantz. He was dead.

"You heard the commodore!" Duval heard himself shout. His heart hammered at his ribs, but his head was clear and cool as he considered Hawken's orders. Inside the *Thomas J.*'s strongroom were the profits of their entire expedition. But the combination was lost, locked beyond recall now in the dead purser's head, and this was no time to worry about credit: nobody could eat inter-Sector exchange cards. Still, the injustice of it gnawed at him.

As young Schenk, Appa Browne, and Dale Hooper lowered the *Richard M.*'s hatch manually alongside the flagship, Horse Smith, the isotopist and number two on the starboard gun crew, pulled on the side hatch release. The container-shifting waldos were kicked into life and they began the hazardous operation of transferring stores.

The *Thomas J.*'s hull was breaking up in random blips of color: her computer nervous system was failing. Despite the remote aid the *Richard M.*'s sister organism was administering via hookup, it would not be long before the spurious patterning started up again, making her half-chromed hide easy prey for energy beams. She was already a shambles inside. Many crew had been killed aboard her; Yamato and Amerikan bodies were strewn across her decks, some whole, some torn into slaughterhouse meat by the blasters. Duval Straker fought down his revulsion and the urge to turn them over in case one had the face of his brother. All around him, his shipmates were like monkeys, fast, alert for the searing, stabbing beams that still crashed into the *Thomas J.*, showering them with fractured metal from external apparatus. The main fluid tanks had been ruptured and were gushing thousands of gallons of water and lube and bilge and refrigerant into the holds. Hawken himself had gone aboard and appeared with Don Hampton at intervals carrying data modules and navigation instruments, the ship's log, and her remote self-destruct key.

For almost half an hour, they labored under withering beam fire. Duval's men brought out twenty dideuterium-oxide containers, each one of a hundred and twenty-six gallons' capacity, hoisted from the hold and loaded across by power arms and waldos rigged to *Richard M.*'s main power loom. If all else failed, they could drink it neat. They brought out fifty full cargo units containing everything from genetic bank stocks and translation cards to atmospheric monitors and super-hardy wheat seeds. Duval helped carry phials of food catalyst across, followed by fifteen freezees of suspended fish which di Barrio had brought at Palawan, and all the while they worked knee-deep in bilge, breathing choking smoke, amid terrifying danger in the holds.

Sado's gunners had holed the flagship and reduced the bridge to a wasteland of splintered steel struts and ruined upholstery. Her starboard side was smashed in and all her beam weapons thrown back from their plex blisters in disarray, making Duval's stomach churn with anger. Coldly he began to rig the melt-outs so that they could not fall into enemy hands. Angrily his mind searched for other ways to make the enemy pay for what they had done, and he hit upon a plan.

"Sir, she's cleaned out for'ard," Cornelius reported, his eyes straying towards the comparative safety of the *Richard M*.

Hawken and Sanders had already left with their detail. Duval watched Diaz, who leapt down into the arms of her crewmates from the *Dwight D*. They were now the last aboard and orders were being shouted in the *Richard M*. to raise the hatches and lift off.

Duval seized the handles of the remaining singularity gun and pushed it on its swivel. It was almost as big as one of the beam weapons they had mounted in the bow, and the swivel was made with end stops that prevented the gun being aimed at the interior of the ship. He kicked it and faced the Irishman. "Do you want to go home a pauper or a rich man, Cornelius?"

"Well, now ye mention it, I'd rather take our wages home, that's for certain."

"Then you six get aft to the strongroom! Get on talkback and guide me in. While we're alive we'll not leave a brass button for those sonsabitches."

Pollak protested. "The commodore said to take only necessaries. I ain't breaking no orders."

"You gonna eat dirt back home? You're under no compulsion. Do I see half a dozen volunteers? Okeh, so stick with me!"

Five hands, the last aboard, swarmed into the guts of the ship after Cornelius. As Duval Straker smashed off the end stops from the gun mount, he saw piercing bright turquoise through the shattered flooring of the blister. Bilge water gushing from smashed pipework swilled underfoot, illuminated by a piercing blue alarm light, and a body lolled grotesquely in the latrine filth, its head mashed into a bloody mush, surrounded by a halo of red. He stepped over it and jammed the dangerously overloaded gun against the deck support. Then he fired.

There was a bright flash, a tremendous scream which carried away the side of the bay, wrecking the mounting, then he heard Cornelius swearing over the talkback.

"By Jeezus! You'll kill us all! Aim to yer left, can't ye?"

Two parallel shafts the diameter of dinner plates had sliced through the ship, leaving precisely cut edges to anything and everything that the propagating singularities had encountered.

He adjusted his aim and fired again. Another flash and scream. Then again and again. Then there was a whoop over the talkback.

"Ye've busted it wide open, Gunner! Damn near blew me to hellfire too, ye crazy bastard. Don't fire that thing again, for Godsakes!"

Duval pulled the melt-out pins out of the gun, held them in his palm for an agonising second as he bit the skin off his bottom lip, then threw the pins down and torched them with his blaster.

He went after Cornelius and the others. He ducked into the strongroom, and as his eyes grew accustomed to the blackness within, he saw the glint of plex sheets cut cleanly by the scalpel action of the singularity gun. Refined aurium in heavy five-inch cast spheres had been scattered across the deck. In addition, there were three huge locked flasks of radioactive aurium 297 tri-nitride, and ten million credits' worth of exchange data.

"Get the flasks—damn you, Ingram!"

"They've stopped firing." Ingram, insubordinate and broody, wild hair like a horse's mane, flashed anger.

Rively and Cadet Morton pushed towards the jagged hole in the *Thomas J.*'s flooring. Cadet Morton's round eyes were on the floating corpse; Rively's were on the observation blister and the huge bulk carrier taxiing across the apron.

"Jeezus H. Christ!"

"What is it, man?"

Rively, an effeminate doe-faced man, shook his head in disbelief. "We've got to get out of here! Look! They're coming right at us! It's a kamikaze ship!"

"What the hell's that?" Jaye Moon, the *John F.*'s Dover chef, shouted. Her knee was in an immobiliser sleeve and her voice was urgent. "Come on, Rively! Give!"

"A suicide ship! I heard they do that stuff. All their ships got self-destruct circuits. That's why they're taxiing, to keep the shields from turning on automatically and suppressing the explosion. We've gotta get out of here!"

His cries panicked them. Duval fought to gain control, then put his own head up to the blister. The Yamato admiral had lined up one of his two-thousand-tonners, and the sight of its hull flashing with the Yamato sunburst, alight from stem to stern with red and white rays, was enough to drive fear into the minds of any Amerikan. For Duval it was the purest liquor of dread. His earliest memory, one that had wiped out all that had gone before, was of the red and white sunburst standards raised on Oregon, when as a four-year-old boy he had seen the crucifixes of Mad Kajiwara's executioners. Then twenty Amerikan tourists had been nailed up for no obvious reason by a fanatical Yamato sect in a park-planet beach resort. He forced his terrors deep down inside him. If this was a kamikaze ship, they would all be dead very soon.

But there might yet be enough time. Or if they were very lucky, the computer in the heart of the approaching ship would go insane and it would refuse to respond.

"Bring the tri-nitride flasks out, I said."

Rively was first to snap. "She'll blow us to hell, Gunner! *Richard M.*'ll make a run for it and we'll be left to roast alive!"

"Or run!"

"I can't run!" Moon shouted helplessly, her knee strapped up.

"And I won't run," the Irishman replied.

"You're wasting time." Duval stood foursquare in the exit. When Ingram tried to pass, he slapped him down into the sluicing, bloodied water that was welling up from the bilges below, but Ingram leapt up and braced himself as if to spring, and only Duval's strength of will stopped him.

"Ignore my orders, you sonofabitch? Take that flask, Ingram, or we'll all burn together!" Duval held his stare. Five pairs of eyes nailed him, darted past him to judge a rush to freedom. But no one dared enough to try. When you give an order, make it stick. Never, never go back on it, he remembered—that was the second rule of command, a lesson his brother had drummed into him. The first rule was never to make orders you needed to countermand.

In the sudden silence the bilge water rushing in the hull grew loud. Then the roaring sound of flame came to them from down the corridor. Cadet Morton was shaking. His pathetic whimpering almost unnerved Duval. He grabbed the eighteen-year-old and heaved him towards the hatch. "Go on! Get aboard *Richard M*. This is man's work."

The moment passed. Cornelius the Irishman began heaving on the flask. It was heavy and big enough to contain two men; it weighed three or four hundred pounds and was worth a fortune. Duval prayed that the ensign had picked the most valuable of the three. Then there were five pairs of hands dragging the first flask out of the strongroom.

In the time it took to hoist the flask on deck, the kamikaze ship had come on halfway across the apron—a half mile. Her hull was blazing with the Yamato ensign, her engines screaming. She had held her intent and was closing with all speed, jinking through the debris that obstructed her.

Hand over hand they hauled on the jury-rigged waldos, swinging the flask clear of the cargo bay and into *Richard M.*'s belly, where it crashed down into the loading deck.

Duval froze as he stood in the *Thomas Jefferson*'s loading bay, the last man aboard, surrounded by bodies, his terror now too much to conceal. Pilot Linex had started the *Richard M.*'s apron engines. The gap between the hulls widened. He could feel the presence of the kamikaze as its roaring lanced the air, and then he was knocked down by the impact of a big internal explosion. Choking black smoke gusted over him, filling his head with the acrid smell of ozone and charring flesh. He sprawled across the decking, and then he saw a flash of red beside him. An arm clad in an astrogator's dress jacket. A hand with a gold ring on the last finger, a ring bearing a jet-black stone.

"Jump, Gunner! *Jump!*"

"Ellis!"

The face was waxen, the color of ashes.

In horror he rolled the body off his brother's chest, and as he did so, dark blood welled from an appalling gash in Ellis's shoulder. The sight horrified him.

God in heaven, he's alive!

Power looms crackled overhead in the intense heat.

Beams refracted in multicolored fans off the crazily patterning hull.

"Jump! For Christ's sake!"

"Save yourself!"

He slipped his fingers under his brother's outstretched arm ready to drag him out. With a maniac's strength he heaved Ellis's body over his shoulder. Ten feet, twelve, fifteen feet now lay between the two ships. Too much to jump now—even to save himself.

Fire blazed all around him, incinerating everything it touched.

Staring round in desperation through the rippling air, he saw a shattered waldo attached to a grapnel snaking slowly over the side—one of the hoists they had been using to move the stores. It was secured to the *Richard M.*'s cargo bay, and as she pulled away, the loading arm followed, dragging its hook across the deck. He dived for the steel hook and rammed it under Ellis's belt. The arm tautened so that his brother's body jerked up like a dead thing come suddenly to life. Blood ran down his arm and dripped from his fingers as he was lifted clear and hung grotesquely over the gap between the ships.

Hawken's men pulled the stricken captain inboard and watched helplessly in horror as the kamikaze wheeled into its final, unobstructed approach.

Suddenly the *Richard M.*'s engines thrust, powering her steeply away. Those watching from the *Richard M.*'s cargo bay stared down at Duval running across the apron after her, helplessly, hopelessly, until the tiny figure was enveloped in black smoke. Then the kamikaze smashed into the *Thomas J.* and there was a vast, head-shattering explosion and the Gunner was gone from sight.

CHI NO TSUKI

Overnight the *Richard M.* hugged the darkside of the big red moon of Sado, the one ominously called in Japanese "Chi no Tsuki"—Blood Moon. Oujuku's ship, the *Judith L.*, had vanished; the *Dwight D.* was captured and the *John F.* destroyed. Hawken was forced to use up most of his remaining lander fuel finding a suitable hiding place, but the surface was peppered with dry dust quags and very unstable, and as the winds got up, the *Richard M.*'s undercarriage began to sink, threatening to stick them fast on this dirty and inhospitable satellite.

Hawken took little comfort from knowing they were now out of range of the Niigata batteries. Pursuit was not too hazardous to attempt, the new daimyo's rage would be boundless, and Kurita's cruisers would hunt them down mercilessly, unless, like Oujuku, they had escaped over the nexus event horizon by 0600 or 0700 UT.

But the crew were in a pitiful state. Every inch of space was taken by a human form. Though the surgeons worked continuously, the facilities were unable to meet the disaster. They had no more freezees. With the aircon inoperative, the darkness below breathed stale with a hundred men and women, while on the upper decks, the pitiful whimpering of the wounded was mixed with the prayers of those who looked fearfully towards death.

"All we made is lost! All of it!"

"God have mercy on us!"

And there were those who spoke in low voices, words of despair that by morning had become words of mutiny.

Hawken sent Bowen among them, to encourage them with the special civility of a master sergeant.

"Come on, ya slobs! Shift ya butts! Move it, boys and girls! Are ya Amerikans, or aincha? Then fall to it!"

"Shut your hole, Bowen! You sonofabitch! Can't ya see there's people here trying to sleep?"

"Come on, shift your ass, Ingram!"

"Ah, blitz out!"

"Come on, Commodore's orders!"

As Bowen mustered the able-bodied in the main congress, Hawken saw they were almost completely exhausted. At his back were Don Hampton, the *Richard M.*'s captain, Bowen and Jeen Ben, an assortment of ensigns, and Tix Pollak, Ben's cadet, all serious-faced and attentive. The officers Hawken most wanted by his side, Helene di Barrio, Ellis Straker, and the fiery John Oujuku, were absent. Faye Geneva was dead.

As Hawken stepped forward, a hush of respect automatically fell.

"I'll tell you this," he began in his stilted public style. "A heavy piece of treachery has been dropped on us, but we've shown the Yamato authorities that they cannot treat Amerikans as slaves and receive no reply."

The crew hung back like shocked zombies, shuffling and swaying with the pain of their injuries. Some muttered assent, few dared meet his eye.

"This is no time to be afraid. We're not yet taken and we never will be so long as we keep faith."

Below him some faces peered up, sullen and resentful.

"Keep faith with what?"

Hawken stared hard at the man who spoke. It was Ingram, a stubborn, shifty man, a dealer in grubby rumors whom he had fined at Palawan for sleeping on guard duty.

"With each other and with God, Mr. Ingram! Only then can we bring our ship home again."

"Your ship!"

A swell of muttering rose up, and Ingram called out again. "Some of us thought it was a dumb thing to land on Sado in the first place."

"Yeah!"

"That's right!"

"Some of you? And which of you wise captains is that? If any one of you knows better than your commodore, I suggest you step forward."

No one moved, then the man beside Ingram spoke up. "None of us wants to die, Commodore!"

"Then tell me what you do want. I'd rather have you tell me now than start with the wisecracks after the fact. What's your plan? What would you have me do?"

The conflict rose up again and Hawken cut it short. "Yeah, well, it's like I thought, you don't have a plan. You don't know what to do."

"We want to see Liberty!"

"And so you shall. But under my command. Or not at all! There's two hundred people here and without discipline we'll get nowhere. Understand this: if anybody breaks ship's rules he'll be confined in the brig, or else hung on the outside of the hull in a pressure suit if the brig gets full. I will not have dissent, so don't try me out."

He went down the gangway and passed among them, then dismissed them to specific duties in groups of two and three.

"Ration the water to half a cup per day and guard the tanks," he told Bowen. They had brought aboard precious little water and not much more Dover catalyst to make food. Of the four hundred that had landed on Sado, only half remained. But still there were too many. Too many to take home. Hawken knew that the chances of a quarter of them seeing Liberty again were very small indeed.

The nexus probability Index lifted over the next three hours, answering their prayers, and had raised itself just enough to let them risk heading for the nexus.

"What will you do, Jos?" Hampton asked when they were alone at the commodore's command seat.

Hawken looked at his sweating, dirt-streaked face. Hampton was a quiet man, lean and secretive about his feelings. As a captain he was cold and distant from his men. He commanded his ship efficiently, but he could be ruthless. Hawken had first employed him ten years ago, and in all that time had found him utterly loyal.

"First, we have to find water."

Hampton's creased cheeks moved mournfully. "With the recyling plant shot to bits, even full tanks'll see us to the Guam side chain, no further. Then we'll need to make a landing and pick up water. But by then I reckon water'll be the least of our problems."

"Huh?"

Hampton kept his voice low. "The Dover machines are shafted without catalyst, Jos. With two hundred mouths aboard we've enough food for just five days. On quarter rations, twenty."

Hawken knew that even with a good Index the crossing to Amerika must take at least seventy-five days, probably nearer a hundred. Many of the wounded would die, after a month on a starvation diet many more would fall sick, and those left would be vitamin-deficient skeletons too weak to climb out of their strap hammocks. The idea of trusting a hunger-delerious astrogator to judge a tough transit on which all their lives depended appalled him. I have no choice, he thought. If two hundred of us set out for Amerika, nobody'll reach home—except maybe a few cannibals.

"Put everyone on a strict quarter ration of whatever the Dovers can be made to turn up. Save the emergency dried stuff in the shuttle for the psi-talents. Give narcos to the wounded, but none to the able hands. And make sure the dead are dispatched smartly."

"Then?"

"Then I've got a hard decision to make."

Hampton nodded, understanding.

Hawken went aft and closed the cabin door on his troubled ship. Alone, he took from the drawer his commodore's badge and held it tight in his fist, meditating. He sank onto his strap hammock, kissed the badge, and prayed silently, fervently, seeking an answer, a sign from somewhere that would strengthen him in his difficult task and help him decide what to do. Then he got up and stepped through into the tiny space where the thrust converters rose up through the deck. It was the astrogator's booth, and was hung about with psi-devices and the black chair in which the talents suffered; an antique brass quadrant and dividers hung on the wall, as well as the cord-bound hilt of a samurai sword, its blade melted off six inches from the *tsuba* handguard.

Pete Grosse stood with his red face brooding down and his black surgeon's skullcap pulled tight on his head. Sweat beaded his forehead where Ellis Straker lay, his body close to death and his spirit drawn deep inside him as if doing battle with great evil.

"He's got uncommon strength of will, Jos, but I think the fight might be too much—even for him." Grosse spoke gruffly, kneading his hands clean on a lump of jellosept. His surgeon's flexiplex apron was still stained with blood from his night's labors; his weird side-whiskers and piggy eyes and bizarre manner made the crew shun him, but he swore that his deep interest in ancient medicine had saved lives when the medomats were overwhelmed by numbers. Few could forget the way he had carved the limbs from some of the sick just like a carpenter cutting off a chair leg.

"They used to call it amputation," he had explained. "An ancient remedy. It looks pretty nasty but the idea is that it keeps a body alive long enough to get back to civilisation and grow another limb." The crew had been disgusted at him and stopped him from experimenting.

"Maybe I ought to operate again," Grosse said, staring at Ellis Straker.

"Leave him be."

"At least I ought to acupuncture him again. Bad *chi*. Bad *chi* kills a man. There's no remedy but to let it out."

"Let him be, I told you!"

Grosse straightened. "The wound will get infected and he'll die."

"He don't need any more of that needle stuff. Who sent you down here anyway?"

"Captain Hampton."

"Well, get on about your business below. Or catch some sleep if you can."

As the surgeon left, Hawken looked at the compress that had been strapped across Straker's chest. He had been swabbed with jellosept and the air had been sweetened with something to ease his labored breathing. I might have been lying here, Hawken thought, with him standing over me instead. He fingered his own cheekbone tenderly where he had been punched, and probed the place where his tooth was now loosened.

When he had been struck, Hawken had reeled back in amazement. For a split second he had been unable to understand, and the suspicion that it was treachery had flashed through his mind. He regretted that unworthy thought now, leaning closer. Your blood is mixed with that of my own wife's family, Ellis. Mohawk blood. That's why I took you and trained you up from a boy. And now you've saved my life. Hell, you're a brave man and a clever one. Janka's lucky to have a husband, and little Hal a father, like you. She deserves better than that you die here.

He got up as Bowen appeared at the iris with his report. He seemed unsure of Hawken's state of mind, and was unusually subdued.

"Commodore, if I can report, sir, I sent out drones. They say the hull's sound, and the engines are okeh. The water in the bilges might be got out by tonight if the aft recycling plant can be repaired. Our power supplies are good enough for a lift-off in this low gee. Though we lost capacity in the action, we can have them both restored by tomorrow. Index is rising, and the astrogator wants a decision."

"I'll speak to him, Bowen. Keep the men busy and rig strap hammocks in the fore congress so that the wounded can be brought up until night."

"Yes, sir."

"And, Bowen?"

"Sir?"

Hawken eyed his officer carefully. "Do you think I've been too severe to the crew tonight?"

Bowen shuffled with embarrassment. "I . . . I can't say I think about that, Commodore."

"See they're kept busy and the work apportioned fairly."

"Yes, sir."

Hawken's eyes followed him from the cabin. A pity there aren't more like you, he thought. Never a complaint in five years' service. I'm only sorry I probably won't live to promote you further. And by God, your own tasks will grow tricky enough before long.

Hawken set a course, following the terminator. In sight of vegetation the crew would be more hopeful and more easily persuaded when the time came to deal toughly with them. Alone, Hawken turned his mind to the ruin of his enterprise. We've lost everything we ever hoped to gain, he thought as he slumped into his chair. Nothing is left to show for our year of labor except two flasks of tri-nitride and a casket of convertible credit. Ten million, maybe fifteen million credits in all. We're ruined! Ruined!

The loss of the *Thomas J.* was Hawken's heaviest single burden. The naval loan had been made on the understanding that any damage sustained by her on the voyage would be made good at the Hawken brothers' expense, but if she was destroyed completely, then the government would bear the loss. Had the *Thomas J.* been lost in a nexus accident or wrecked on a godforsaken moon like this, he could have fairly claimed an excuse. He felt his heart falter as he imagined the interview at which he explained to his President's face that he had lost her ship to a Yamato attack.

At worst, he thought, my brother Billy might suffer the same ultimate penalty. None of us can expect to get away with this one.

Alia Kane was a supremely capable President. She had ruled Amerika with a semblance of her father's iron authority, but with her own special political genius, for the last decade. Loved and feared within her own administration, adored by the people of Amerika, hated across the Empire, she was everywhere respected. Her single purpose had been to maintain Amerika as an independent Sector, but to do so and to remain President she had had to rewrite the rules of diplomacy. If the universe worked to a system that disadvantaged Alia Kane, then Alia Kane must change the universe. Which, in part, was why she had become Hawken's sponsor. Other key investors were Conroy Lubbock, the President's closest and most trusted advisor; Nissa Ottoman, the leader of the House; Otis le Grande, the President's ally in Congress. And there were other powerful individuals, all members of the Security Council. Hawken imagined their pique when he told them that the millions he had promised to multiply for them were lost—and yet *he* had returned alive to tell them so.

Shares in his expedition had been sold on a strictly speculative basis, all loss and all gain to be borne according to the size of the original stake. But these men were not common traders, and his venture no simple trading mission. Not one of them, he was certain, would stand their loss like traders. Each would reassure him, then try to squeeze a return by taxing their influence higher, by extortion over trade permits and licenses, or simply by pricing high their next favor. Because they stood between Hawken and the President, there were a thousand small ways they could arrange the settling of their losses against his future.

He had undertaken a volatile mix of commerce and politics that magnified the rewards—*but also the risks.*

If this was simple misfortune, he mused bitterly, I could sell my ships and my Liberty house, and liquidate all assets. The Hawken brothers can muster perhaps twenty million in credit. That would easily be sufficient to cover the debt to the President and to appease her allies, but this is not a simple misfortune, and I can see no escape from the coils of this particular serpent.

He got up and began to pace about, thinking feverishly of the political ramifications of what had happened, and as he thought, the prospect grew bleaker and bleaker. Now that the guns were silent and he was alone, he could meditate on it. The President's Security Council was split into two main groups: the party of peace, who thought Yamato looked to Amerika as a valuable potential ally against their main rival, the Chinese, and the party of war, who saw Yamato as an inevitable enemy, implacable and determined to crush the stronghold of freedom and democracy and free trade. The latter group wanted the President to arm massively against the Yamato threat; it was also the group that had invested in his expedition. But there was one major exception: Otis le Grande, the immensely rich financier, whose investment had been made in secret.

The situation was perilous. The le Grandes, as many knew, were a tribe of traitors. Otis's grandfather had been a groveling sycophant in the administration of Alia Kane's pro-Yamato predecessor, Lucia Henry—he had been exiled for treason by Alia Kane. Le Grande's father had styled himself spokesman of the people when acting treasurer to the same pro-Yamato administration; he had died at the hands of an assassin. Gifford le Grande, Otis's brother, had been married to the pretender Queenie Duquesne; both had been exiled.

So how can I use him? Is there a way to make Otis le Grande support me? He's the only man except Lubbock close enough to the President to dampen her passion. How can he be made to speak for me? Perhaps there is a way! He'd be unwilling for the rest of the Security Council to learn that he's invested in me while at the same time publicly supporting the reconciliation with Yamato. Oh, yes, Otis le Grande, that would reveal you as the three-faced liar you really are. Against that, what would be the loss of a few million in credit?

Hawken quailed at the thought of blackmailing le Grande. His blood is bad, he thought sourly. There's the taint of treason in everything he does. He is ambitious and he has no loyalty except to himself. Yet the President tolerates him. He remains her favored man in Congress. How can she be so blind to his true character? How can a woman so wise in other matters be so easily taken in by a man like him?

He had been a childhood companion of the President, sharing the same upbringing and many adolescent confidences. And she would hear no wrong of him.

He's wormed his way nicely into her affections, Hawken thought. Can't she see that he won't satisfy his ambition until he's married her and then become President himself? They say that eight years ago he murdered his wife to whitewash a scandal, and I believe it.

Hawken put thoughts of le Grande aside. He sat down again. There was a vastly bigger picture to consider. One more dangerous still, where the stakes were the very existence of Amerika.

Undoubtedly, one of the daimyo of Sado's fast dispatch ships was even now preparing to transit for Honshu with the Yamato account of the incident. If the Emperor was goaded to anger, war might easily be the outcome. And it was not a war Amerika could possibly win against the mighty Empire of Yamato. We are an economically poor Sector, he reminded himself, a Sector of three and a half billion people, approximately an orange segment of space between galactic longitude planes thirty degrees and sixty degrees, coexisting with totalitarian regimes: China, barbarous Afrika, Izlam, and the mighty Yamato. We mind our own business and tend to business, manufacturing and trading, and we survive. But Yamato—mighty Yamato! Fifteen billion Japanese-speakers under an Emperor who thinks of himself as the Son of Heaven with a divine right to command Known Space, whose tough samurai troops are raised in every planetary system in the Empire. They've never lost a battle in a hundred years. Those invincible battalions even now scourge the Europans, driven by a maniac whose veins run with Neutral Zone aurium and whose conquering convictions go utterly unquestioned by the Central Authority. A single transport of their aurium fleet carries more wealth in her guts than the entire planet of Liberty! The exchequer of the Honshu quadrant alone exceeds that of the whole of Amerika! Once the Emperor decides to crush our Sector, he will do so with no more difficulty than stepping on a roach. And with as little compunction.

This Sado fiasco has been mega-bad. For me, and for Amerika.

How fiercely would the President fight to avoid war? How artfully would she try to knit the wound and heal the scar with the Emperor? In order to steer a course away from a war with Yamato, she would fight like a wildcat. Nothing was beyond her. She would offer marriages, make gifts of restitution, appease the Emperor's haughty ambassadors, and order executions. To save her realm she'll shovel me and mine into the furnace of the Emperor's wrath until we're all gobbled up.

The prospect weighed heavily on Hawken. He called for Sam and ordered him to bring him a cold beer. The creaking of the *Richard M.*'s damaged internals and the sound of his repair drones hammering on the deck above reminded him with each blow that she was a Navy ship. He took the lite beer and dismissed the steward curtly before drinking it down in one. It would be better if the *Richard M.* were to crack up now and put an end to it all, he thought sourly. The suffering ahead will be terrible! The one vision capable of sustaining such hardship is the desire to see that pretty ball of blue-green: Liberty lighting up the forward scanners again. But not now. Not when that sight means impeachment, execution, a traitor's freezee inside the wire at Camp Worth. It's hopeless. Should I take a walk to the aft magazine now? Should I blow the *Richard M.* to hell and save a whole lot of suffering? But there was Kate. And his eight-year-old son, Ritchie. He pursed his thin lips, wiping them on his sleeve, and knew that he could do no other than try to bring the ship home, whatever the cost, whatever the consequences. Loyalty to the President, loyalty to his family, and loyalty to his crew all demanded it. It was the only decision an Amerikan could make.

10

All that night the ship groaned in complaint as the engines worked from time to time to keep her on the surface of the dry quags that tried to suck her down. It was as if every piece of metal had been loosened against every other. They sighted no pursuit craft, and if pursuit had been attempted, it had failed. By noon UT the next day fourteen of the most severely wounded had died and been put outside with as much ceremony as could be mustered. Thirst turned the officer's voices to dry croaks as they shouted their orders over the talkback, and hunger began to gnaw at their stomachs, but they had continued to lie low just darkside of the terminator, under a blanket of stealth and radio black.

In the astrogator's chamber where Straker lay, Hawken studied the visualisers. He had been hoping for the bore holes to reveal subsurface water to fill their tanks, but none was found. They must try to lift off and look for fresh water at the Blood Moon's equator, he had decided. There had to be water somewhere. This was the place Sado sent its criminals, and they had a colony and a penitentiary complex in the warmer zone to the south. That was eight thousand miles away, and to get there they would have to spend days crawling along under minimal power to avoid detection. He laid down his log pad and was about to go back to the bridge when a groan made him turn.

Ellis Straker's mouth was open, his eyes dully half lidded, and his limbs were stirring like a man emerging from nightmare.

"Easy," Hawken said, and shouted for Chambers to bring a medikit and a cup of precious water spiced with painkillers.

The man was still deathly pale and his lips puckered with dry skin, but he was conscious. Hawken eased him up, cradling his head.

"We're in flight?" Straker said weakly.

"Sure, we're safe and going home, Ellis. You're coming with us."

"We're aboard the *Thomas J.?*"

Ellis tried to sit up but the effort creased his face and he collapsed back, breathing heavily.

"We're aboard the *Richard M*. Heading for water, and all our people with her."

"The *Dwight D.*—who's at the console? Is she damaged?"

"Hey, now, calm yourself. We're making good time. Soon we'll be standing on Harrisburg apron and wishing ourselves offplanet again."

"How long have I been—" Ellis tried to raise himself again but a jag of pain exploded across his chest.

What's the matter with me? he wondered groggily. Why can't I sit up? I feel sicker than a shit-eating bilge worm. He felt the burning skin of his chest. There was soreness round his neck and he ached all down his left side.

"You're too slow, Ellis. You were hog-spiked by a samurai and damned near done in."

Ellis groaned again. He looked hazily at his shoulder and the jello pad. As he pulled it aside he saw a ragged purple cleft, and raw meat, four inches deep. All around it he was bruised black.

It's nothing, he thought. Nothing at all. I've seen a man fight on with half his arm missing.

"This is all?" he croaked. "Why ain't I stitched up?"

"Later. They say the men of the Yamato Guard often poison their swords with nerve venom. Pete Grosse reckons the wound ought to breathe a while."

"So—a samurai bit me, huh?"

"You're lucky he missed your vitals."

"Who's commanding the *Dwight D.*? Is Duval aboard her?"

His head was spinning, but his memory of the battle was beginning to come back. The small port above his head was phased clear, and the light of the stars moved in dancing patterns beyond. A cooling breeze from the aircon washed over his body.

He could remember the samurai that had chopped him. A bull of a man, with flying silk robes and burnished plex armor. I killed him. Sent him to hell for his treachery, like I promised Ayrton Rodrigo I would. And what treachery! They set on us like rats from a stinking bilge hole, after their daimyo's word of honor was given.

"We gave as good as we got. The *Dwight D.*'s captured, Ellis."

His mouth puckered with pain at the news. "How many were killed?"

"Two hundred."

"Half our men—and my brother?"

Hawken's face was grave, his eyes hooded. "Left behind."

Hawken told him of the kamikaze, of the way the *Richard M.* had been forced to cut loose, and how he had been waldoed aboard at the last possible moment.

"Then he may be alive!"

"He died on the apron."

"You sure?"

"Yes. If he was taken by the samurai—well, they showed little mercy to our people in the terminal."

"But nobody saw him die?"

"That I can't say."

Ellis felt the anguish surge up within him. I'm to blame, he told himself. It's my fault. I've broken the solemn promise to my mother that I would look after him. It was me who fixed him a place on this trip, me who got cut up in the first bit of trouble, me who caused him to wait too long on the *Thomas Jefferson!*

He closed his eyes and panted for breath. Hawken was called urgently to the bridge, and Chambers came in with a cup and the medikit to take his place. The steward gave him a drink to clear his throat and fed him a little soup with a spoon, then laid him back gently. But he would not lie still. A hundred questions boiled in his brain. Was the *Richard M.* alone? Who else had got away? Two hundred people aboard the *Richard M.* was impossible. What about John Oujuku and Don Hampton and Helene di Barrio? Had anyone actually seen Duval die?

When Chambers turned his back, Ellis struggled to get up. He swung his naked legs out of the strap hammock and stood swaying, grasping the chair, but collapsed into the steward's arms.

"You're still very weak, Captain. Try to rest."

Ellis's eyes clouded, but he was fighting to keep them open. Chambers spoke softly to him, mesmerically, soothingly.

"We're going home. Going back to Liberty and our loved ones, Captain. You'll be seeing your wife and son, and I'll be seeing my sweetheart again soon. With my share of the voyage I'm going to marry. I'll buy land on Iowa and settle down. She's a sweet one, my girl. Becky's her name, sweet and gentle with cheeks like apples in high summer and hair the color of a chestnut mare. I'm a lucky man to have her, Captain. We'll have six sons, and six daughters too, and they'll help me fetch and carry, just like I did for my father when I was a youngster. And all because of this voyage and Commodore Hawken and your brother's neat work. I saw the *Thomas J.*'s flasks come aboard, Captain. There's a heap of credit in our hold. Aurium and argentium by the kilo. Some for the President and some for the commodore, and some for us who he lets ride his ships . . .

"Sleep now, Captain. That's it. Sleep's the best remedy. And when you dream, dream of home."

As Ellis's eyes closed, Chambers swabbed his face gently.

Ah, but you're a lucky one, Chambers thought. Psi shines out of you, Ellis Straker, and it lights you up like a beacon, so it does. By rights you should be burned to a cinder, just like your brother was. I saw the *Thomas J.* blasted to smithereens. It was a sight to see. And a tale to tell my grandchildren. Her hull melted out in a blaze of purple mesons, her innards flaming like the Fourth of July. She's gone now, just like the Gunner, who I saw burn with her. Saw it with my own eyes.

11

Ellis stared hollow-eyed through the phased open hull along one side of the blue assembly. His empty belly ached. His wound was healing slowly. The malaise had not left him and he was still weak. I need water to flush it out of me, to let the air at it, he told himself. Better than stewing in a strap hammock. Stand up, walk around, do anything instead of lying here in a daze.

Five days had passed and the crew had taken to snaring shipneys and the other vermin that slinked about in the cable runs. Yesterday the monkeys had disappeared. He had had the *John F.*'s supercargo, Leon Swarbrick, confined for killing and secretly gorging himself on half of one of them, but the rumor of the punishment had sobered the crew to their true condition.

With new engine converter bypasses rigged, *Richard M.* had come on, but there had been no bore-hole strikes and their water was down to the last tank. He forced his mind away from the tragedy, and in the long empty hours had begun calmly, quietly hatching a plan. Then he heard the shout.

Hawken's steward was waving madly.

"What's he say?"

"Houses," Cao said.

"He's spotted habitation!"

Orders rang out. Hands hurried to the bridge.

"He's right!"

Ellis followed. "There's a danger they have guns, or at least a communications link with Sado."

Hampton acknowledged the information with a nod and began to bring the *Richard M.* down. They worked in an arc for a few minutes, then slackened their headway. An instrument pod was rigged forward with a broad frequency comms monitor attached. Each time the ship passed over the signs of habitation, Hampton listened out for the monitors and any sign of a message being beamed into orbit. Silence. So the undercarriage was dropped.

As the *Richard M.* touched down, Ellis joined Hawken at the command chair. "I'd like to put this to you, Commodore," he said slowly, formally. "We're in a pretty tight bind, but I think I know a way we can get out of it."

Hawken turned to face him, his thin lips unsmiling. "Go on."

"According to Iwakura, this place is used by Sado as a penal settlement. We picked him up in a D Class lunar-shuttle transport, so maybe he was an escapee. Whatever he was I guess they send other ships here—I saw plenty on the Niigata apron. They may not be too frequent, but if we create a secret supply base here, then lie in wait, we can run one of them down, take their arms—"

Hawken cut him short. "You're advocating aggressive action, Captain. Piracy."

Ellis hesitated. "You can call it that, but the way I see it—"

"I do call it that!" Anger flashed suddenly across Hawken's face. "I won't have you speak of this here. The *Richard M.* is a ship of the Amerikan Navy fleet. My duty is to bring her home."

"Commodore, after what happened we have a right to—"

Hawken's eyes pinned him. "Don't provoke me, Captain. You forget yourself. I raised you up, and I can just as soon bust you down. I'm taking the *Richard M.* home, or I'll die trying."

Ellis watched Hawken's face trembling. That's right, he thought, his belly tightening, you will die trying, and you'll kill us all. When it's the jokers who jumped us that should die!

"Please hear me out, Commodore," he said levelly. "The *Millard Fillmore* may not have been lost. John Oujuku, too, might somehow struggle home again. We're out of touch. A year away from the politics of the capital, can you be sure of anything? John was right: in that time war might have been declared, legitimising everything. Alia Kane may have been assassinated, or Lucia Henry taken her place!"

Hawken's hand came up and struck him across the face. It was a slap that anywhere else would have brought on a fistfight, but it was so unexpected it took Ellis aback and so sudden it went unnoticed by anyone else.

"You're talking piracy and treason, Straker!"

Ellis's frozen stare melted. Inside he seethed with anger, and he controlled it only by the memory of the blow he had dealt Hawken before the battle. He breathed tremulously and forced his eyes away from Hawken's own.

"I apologise," he said, finding discipline at last. "And I thank you, Commodore."

"Do you, by God?"

"I shouldn't have said what I did."

Hawken waited for him to continue but he stayed silent.

"In that case, I accept your apology. And we'll consider it unsaid."

As he watched Hawken go across the bridge, Ellis's whole body shook with anger. You damned fool, he told himself. You know how to persuade Jos Hawken. You should have known he would react that way. What were you thinking of? What the hell made you say it? You spent days working that plan out, couldn't you have chosen a better time than this? Spewing it out on the moment like an asshole? Now it's dead. Dead. And my revenge riding on it.

He wiped the sweat from his numb face and looked out at the settlement. Its white compounds were no more than a couple of hundred yards away, and he could hear the desolate wind breaking thinly against it. The monitors showed it was deserted.

You're getting old, Jos Hawken, Ellis thought. Time was you'd have taken me up on that. We could survive on this moon indefinitely with a singularity-gun-equipped ship to prey on the Sado convoys. Think of it! There's plenty of fresh water and time to get ourselves shipshape again. If convicts eat here, we can eat here too. With half our men in a hidden stronghold and the rest raiding on the *Richard M.*, we could menace anything and everything that came into the system. We could paralyse the entire Yamato aurium trade, and when we'd had our fill we could force down one of their big transports and take her home in triumph with a ton of refined aurium in the coffers! Then if we get branded pirates, so be it!

The sirens blew the crew to standby and the order went out to assemble in the empty cargo bay, a space much bigger than the fore congress. Hawken stood at the center of the rail and planted his feet on the deck. His voice was raised, strong and firm. He read out a prepared list, commanding the thirty-six named crew members to stand together on the starboard side of the ship.

"I have walked among you every day and I've listened to a mess of rumors and tales," he said portentously. "It's clear to any fool that you already know we can't all go home. So some of you want to surrender. Others want to stay here on this moon. Hear my decision then. I intend to split the ship's company into two equal halves. The people I have named and who stand to starboard of the hatch will brave starvation and psi-storms and whatever else there is to face and try for Amerika. Any of you who so desire may join them. The rest will stand to port of the hatch. That group will make planetfall here and take their chance as they will, to look out for themselves with the Sado convicts, or with the Yamato authorities, as they choose. If you find no agreement, you'll draw lots."

The crew shuffled uncertainly now, staring up at the raised ramp and into the light, then they began to look to one another anxiously. All those essential for the ship's working and maintenance had been named. Sixty more were to go.

Ellis spoke up. "Commodore, I want to stay."

A hush descended. Then a chorus of voices began to ask for Ellis's place.

Hawken silenced them. "Ellis Straker was named. He must remain aboard."

Ellis's voice came back at him. "The people to be landed are leaderless. There must be a recognised captain among them or there'll be chaos."

Again, dissent blazed from the crew.

Hawken motioned down to where a container stood on the ramp. Hampton threw open the lid and dug his hands into the convertible currency. It glittered there with the blue surface sheen meant to look like aurium metal as Hawken let the credits spill through his fingers so that everyone saw them.

"I have not forgotten your pledges of loyalty. No one has broken his oath to me—in fact, many of you have far exceeded my expectation—and no one shall see me break my word either. All who choose to stay are due their share. Each crew member will therefore have money—pay, bonus, and voyage share is ready for you to take, or if you prefer it will be given to your family should the *Richard M.* escape disaster and reach Amerika. I further pledge to you now that I will return here next year, or when the government allows it, to bring you home, awarding double pay for the interval."

The lid of the container stayed open, and the light played over the thick credit plates as Hawken told them to choose.

Fuller stepped forward. "I have a wife and three children at home, sir. You can take them my share."

A second crew member made her decision. "And mine."

"So be it."

Three more came forward and were handed their share. Then another and another.

Ellis looked on. Across the deck some began to argue, others to cross themselves and pray for guidance.

It can't be far to a Yamato settlement from here, he thought. Light gravity, a thin atmosphere, low oxygen, fever swamp and proto-forest thick with dangers, and no guarantee that the Yamato authorities won't nail you to a cross the moment they see you. But I have a reason to stay. I must know if my brother is still alive. Maybe that was what prompted me to say what I did to Hawken earlier. Maybe.

Thirty crew members had come forward and no more. Hawken recorded their names in the log, and when the rest requested a proper space of time to consider, he adjourned the proceedings. The big shuttle was lowered, and those that had chosen to depart were motored to a disembarkation point some miles from the ship and on the other side of the swamp without delay.

Back on the ship a scratch water testing and filtration plant was set up. It was a slim chance but they might even be able to process enough deuterium and tritium to engage one of the Dovers. The task of filling the water tanks began and was carried on throughout the afternoon. During it, Ellis busied himself with transferring data and notes compiled in the ship's computer rutter module into his own astrogator's log. He said nothing more to Hawken until 1800 UT. Hampton told him that those appointed to return home had been ordered to remain on board, but he went to Hawken to ask permission to accompany the shuttle to the swamp from which they were taking water.

"If I can find anything edible, it will help on the voyage."

Hawken looked at him closely, then said, "Take Chambers and two others from the watering party."

"Thank you, Commodore."

As they skimmed a mile or two northward, fringing the swamp, the low primary star was sinking with painful sloth in a retrograde path towards the flat eastern horizon. It was to be the last trip to the swamp, and the driver took them slowly, the quality of the moon's thin, unfamiliar atmosphere, clumsy light gee, and the long day's work making them drowsy. Ellis took his place in the rear seat and eyed the darkening western sky with caution. Above them, the disc of Sado hovered immovable in the sky. The Blood Moon's orbital period was around twelve days. To call it a moon was stretching a point; technically Sado and Chi no Tsuki made up a double planet: they were comparable in mass and orbited about one another so that the center of rotation was well outside the surface of Sado, but Sado was much the larger and the Blood Moon's large subsurface iron bathylith had been gravitationally captured so that it presented the same face to Sado apart from a large libration. The planetary architect had done a good job. The system was interesting from an orbital mechanics point of view, but the two worlds were not much to Ellis's taste in terms of climate and comfort, and the inhabitants' ideas of hospitality were somewhat lacking.

The long local day-month was fading as the terminator crept across the equator. The scrubby land sped under them. All around the shuttle the air was chopping up, and a fresh breeze was blowing up stronger by the minute.

A night storm coming, he decided as he watched pregnant rain clouds rolling down from the north. It's a bad omen. The season of electrical storms mentioned in the computer's rutter module has probably started. It might give us problems. Our ships just aren't built to work in overly hostile weather. We need an apron or something pretty flat and firm to land on. We find it tough getting off worlds with greater than two gees by way of local gravity without equatorial assist. We usually need to taxi to get off the deck. Without a well-equipped terminal to put in at every now and again we lose our capacity to stay in flight. It was a great idea to have a ship that could shoot nexus *and* reenter atmospheres, but I sometimes wonder if the old ideas of orbiter-plus-planetary-lander wasn't better. We're streamlined for atmospheric flight and planar-bottomed for surfing in on the stratosphere, power-configured for acceleration mode when we need to approach a nexus at 0.9 cee, attack-configured for beating up on hostile ships in orbit. Maybe we're building ships that are just too adaptable, too convenient. To work the Neutral Zone we must have ships with a deeper hull, fins that sit lower along the lateral line, allowing as near a perfectly spherical shield as possible: as small a target as possible for beam weapons. And now the new singularity guns . . . He groaned inwardly at the memory the thought had stirred up.

They landed on a mud bank that flanked a sluggish estuary, and while the tanks were being filled he led his detail along the fringe of the swamp. They found guavas and obanions and took a few hundred in a flexiplex bag. Chambers returned laden with what looked like small cucumbers. "They call the fruit *kyuri*. I brought all I could carry and there's *momo* and *suika*."

"Are there more?"

"Sure, Captain."

Ellis adjusted the strapping on his arm sling and looked at the twilight sky. It gets dark slow here, he thought, but the primary star's gone and this atmosphere doesn't diffuse much light. An overcast was blotting out Sado and the budding stars now. In the distance the *Richard M*. was showing landing lights. He checked how long the water tanks would take to fill and picked up the last fruit sack.

"There's time. Show me where."

They reached the clearing quickly and began to pick the fruit. Overhead, large bats whirled in spectacular loops, and all around in the forest night insects and frogs began their chirruping calls.

"I've been thinking, Captain. Maybe I should volunteer to stay."

Ellis looked at the steward with surprise. He liked the man's gentle nature, one he kept well, and with dignity, among the coarseness of shipboard life.

"I thought you planned to marry, Chambers."

"I do, Captain, but I have debts. Becky and me would benefit from double pay over a year's marooning. It'd be like making another two voyages. I know she'll wait for me."

"If you want my advice, Chambers, you'll take your chances in the lottery with the others and put thoughts of volunteering right out of your head. Leave decisions like that to psi."

"But you volunteered to stay, Captain."

Ellis cleared his throat. "Yeah—but that's different."

Chambers fell silent and Ellis moved away, regretting his words. It had set him thinking about home again and had opened for inspection the raw complications of his position. He had a wife and son at home, and he owed a debt of duty to them. But there was more than one kind of duty. How could a man ponder the debts of his life when that life was owed to his brother? A brother who was probably dead, but who might even now be chained in some stinking Yamato torture hole, looking vainly for rescue? How could he begin to set a value on such a thing, when it was in terms of his own family? Then there was the duty he owed Jos Hawken, a debt sharpened by the loss of the *Dwight D.* and by his unpardonable insubordination. Finally there was the duty he had to the crew—all of them. Many he had known for all the years of his life, all now facing either marooning or starvation. It was too much for an honest man to properly comprehend.

He reached up for another wild fruit and felt something whistle past his head. He heard it thud into the trunk of a tree and realised instantly what it was.

"Jeezus God, Chambers! Run for the shuttle!" he shouted, dropping his bag of fruit and pulling a primed blaster with his good hand. Another arrow speared the ground by his foot. In the semidarkness he could not see how many there were, but he knew that technology-deprived convicts who had been forced to live on their wits would be pretty adept at ambushes.

They ran back towards the shuttle, Ellis trailing, trying desperately to set the mechanism of his blaster. It was slick with condensation. When it clicked home, he steadied it and attempted to discharge it into the foliage at his back. An agonising quarter second passed as the trigger snapped home and the muzzle fizzed, then there was a bright streamer of light and a loud *phshzzzang!*

He heard a yell and caught a movement in the brush but did not wait to see what emerged. He and Chambers gained the clearing together, scrambling breathlessly towards the shuttle. More arrow shafts whistled through air and stuck in the mud ahead of them. The blaster had alerted the men who were waiting in the shuttle and they had acted, one heaving himself into the pilot seat, another coming forward to cover their retreat with blaster fire.

Only when all five were inboard and the hatch closed did a dozen long-haired figures break from the tree line and run into the clearing, yelling and waving their arms.

The shuttle carried the Amerikans away from the clearing quickly and into the treetops.

Ellis counted heads. Two of the work party were missing. It's too late, he thought. Nothing for it but to put back to the ship. The wind buffeted them as they came alongside and put down. Hampton questioned him about the missing men.

Ellis explained.

"Bastards!" he grunted. "Better say nothing to frighten those who've gotta stay here. Their lots have been cast already."

As soon as they discharged the water tanks, Hampton ordered the big shuttle filled with the luckless. In their absence, Chambers and four of the watering party had been appointed to stay.

"Looks like my decision has been made for me," he said to Ellis. His eyes were full of fear now. The attack had badly shaken him.

"Godspeed to you, Jon."

"And you, Captain."

They clasped hands.

"Tell your shipmates I got a strong psi-feeling they ought to try for the penitentiary complex. It's fifty miles away. You might find some kind of safety there."

Ellis twisted off his ring. It was gold and bore a large black stone on which was carved the Aquila eagle. It was the first time he had taken it off in seven years.

"Take this."

"Oh, no, Captain—" Chambers tried to protest, but was quieted.

"I'll see your Becky receives her due. If ever you find my brother Duval alive, give him this ring as a pledge that I intend to come back for him—and for you all."

The steward slipped the ring inside his shirt pocket and climbed into the shuttle. As it pulled away from the nexus ship's shelter, a dousing, chemical rain began to whip the landing site. The crew lined the *Richard M.*'s open bays, waving and shouting words of hopeful parting.

Chambers watched the ship grow small. After landing he stood on the wet ground a little way apart from the hundred others who huddled together for comfort. The *Richard M.* wasted no time in lifting off, and they watched her go. Chambers drew the ring from his pocket and slipped it on, but it was too big for any of his fingers. Although the rain drove into his eyes, he continued to watch, staring blindly at the points of light that were all that could be seen of the old, familiar world, until they at last were extinguished in the cloud base and he knew with finality that he would never see Amerika or his Becky again.

12

SADO

The sight of the newly captured Amerikan filled her with wonder and excitement. She was Urawa no Hasegawa Michie, daughter of Urawa no Hasegawa Kenji, one of the greatest fief-holders on Sado and owner of the richest *han* near Kanazawa. At the request of her father she had left Kyoto to join her family, to attend at her mother's sickbed. That was the official reason Hasegawa Kenji had put in his letter to the Emperor's court; he had, of course, said nothing about the rape, nor the delicate matter of Prince Kono.

Opposite Michie sat the regal Choshu no Nishima Fumiko, meticulously considering a *go* board with its complex patterns of black and white stones. In her early forties, devout in her Confucian philosophy, upright, and of the generation that had flowered in the glorious days of the last Emperor, she had been brought to Sado by her husband, the new daimyo. But she had suffered constant sickness on the voyage after transiting the first nexus. She hated the ship, she hated Sado, she even appeared to hate her husband. And she hated with such vehemence that, by the end of the passage, Michie thought she must hate life itself.

The two women sat playing the intricate board game together, alone at the rear of Governor Ugaki's house, in the cool shade of an open veranda amid a riot of heavy-scented blooms. But their peace had been shattered by the new prisoner. A little way along the street, the Amerikan captives began a chorus of shouts. They yelled raucous oaths at the guards, and their dirty, bearded faces crowded the barred window of the prison, no longer listless and brooding but alight with rejoicing.

The new prisoner, Michie saw, wore nothing but ragged underwear and caked filth. He was shackled at wrist and ankle. Each of the three soldiers who led him held a long rope attached to his heavy wooden disc collar like those used to subdue badly behaved criminals. The two-inch-thick solid wheel extended a foot or so from the neck, just far enough to prevent the wearer putting his hand to his mouth. It was designed to be incredibly humiliating. The loss of face a man suffered when unable to feed himself was quite literal. But the last thing the prisoner seemed interested in was eating. Mud matted his hair and beard, and he was bleeding from several superficial wounds, but even so he looked around him with unbounded interest, and there was something else about him, a certain pride of bearing that gave him a peculiar dignity.

It's two weeks since the great battle, she thought. During that time he must have been hiding in the swamps or in some secret lair in the giant plantations that lay beyond the fringes of the town. Had the security forces captured him?

Had he given himself up? Or was he perhaps trapped by his need to come out in search of food?

The noise from the prison increased. At the sound of his shipmates, she saw him try and fail to put his fingers to his lips, but he still managed to blow a distinctive piercing whistle that brought a clamor of approval from the captives. When he passed the veranda, he was fifteen paces from them. What happened next brought a rush of blood to her cheeks because he looked directly at her, stopped, and before the guards could react he bowed from the waist. He was swiftly kicked down for his insolence, but he fought back even though he was weak and the punishment wheel that he wore was heavy.

With deft jerks on the ropes the soldiers strangled him into the dust and began dragging him along like a dog. But he was not a dog, he was a man. And he showed them that he had great spirit.

"They should all be crucified," the older woman snapped. She slapped a white *go* stone onto the board and slid it into position on the strategic three-four point. "They are not men, they are not even *hinin!*"

"Oh! How can you say that, Fumiko-san? They have souls, for all their evilness."

"Atari!" Check!

"Oh! That's *shi-cho*—a running capture to the edge of the board, no?"

"So sorry, Michie-san."

Michie saw that she had lost a five-stone group. Recklessness. But it was hard to concentrate on the game. Despite herself Michie's eyes continually strayed towards the jail. She found herself fanning the blood from her cheeks under Fumiko's questioning eye.

"They are even worse than savages. They stink! Can't you smell them, Michie-san? It's like rotten milk."

"No man smells sweet in a prison cell."

"But Michie-san, theirs is a reek no water can wash away. These Amerikans smell of piracy. Remember your history. The Tokugawa shoguns were absolutely right to close the country of Japan to foreigners. Absolutely right. Contamination was all that could result. And the eternal wheel of history has come round again, thank the gods. The only remedy for a stink like that is crucifixion."

Fumiko regarded the younger woman silently. She had seen the way the officers of the guard looked at her with the kind of half-concealed longing men reserve for the beautiful and the impossibly out of reach. Michie's skin was blemishless, honeyed gold, and her eyes dark and moist under fine black brows that sometimes arched with annoyance.

I can see you secretly glancing at the prison, Hasegawa Michie, she thought. How delighted you were in your foolish pride when that *gaijin*—foreigner—bowed just then. Are you still a virgin? Or did you let some Kyoto courtier spoil your prospects? We've been together nearly three months now but you've told me almost nothing about yourself. Have you been disgraced at Court like your sister was? Are you secretly with child? Is that really why you've come to this dirty industrial planet beyond the Boundary of Yamato? Well, pregnant or not, your good looks won't last long here, my dear. Sado is the uttermost end of the universe. I hate it. And I rue the day my husband's honor forced him to involve himself with the Emperor's personal intrigues. He should have taken his life—committed *seppuku* and finished himself honorably.

She scratched through the stiff material of her sleeve at the bites that itched and itched. Why did they insist on letting insects loose on terraformed worlds? What possible use were midges to any planet? You gave no thought to my comfort, Jun-san. You should have listened to me. Why couldn't you see that it would all end in misery? Can it be that you still imagine that the Emperor has honored you by sending you here? Perhaps you were infected by Prince Kono's devils. This is exile! You should have known better than to have anything to do with the heir.

She shifted to ease the pain in her back and made another corner play on the *go* board.

Michie said, "Governor Ugaki tells me that Niigata is the oldest city on Sado, that the first ships came here two hundred and fifty years ago to found it."

Fumiko sighed. "Did he also tell you that the captain of that first ship had to disable his own vessel to prevent his crew deserting him?"

"He says that the shoji screens in the tea house are from that ship."

The drone of voices filtered from inside the house. The daimyo's anger punctuated the proceedings at intervals as the inquiry into the battle continued. Michie strained her hearing, following the testimony, knowing already what the outcome must be.

"Are you listening to me, Michie-san?"

"Yes, Fumiko-san. Of course. You know I am."

Michie touched the minutely finished *ginkyo* wood of the veranda's rail. Close by, a trail of tiny red ants followed a sinuous path up the whitewashed wall, carrying tiny offerings of tribute to their ant-shogun. Yes, she thought, I listen to you far more than you imagine. I'm listening to you now; I listened to you on the ship and I listened to your sleeping secrets. I understand what is going on in your husband's inquiry, and I know that it's little to do with the truth.

Nishima-sama was trying to insulate himself against blame for the loss of the Emperor's ships, but the admiral was too experienced, too wily to be entrapped by words. His vice-admiral, however, was much younger, full of courage and enterprise, the sort of man who considers only the problem in hand and pays little regard to consequences. Ex-Vice-admiral Kondo would be easy prey, the perfect choice for a scapegoat. How I despise you for what you are doing to him, Lord Nishima. I know what kind of man you are. You have no honor—in battle or out of it.

She remembered standing at her high balcony that terrible morning two weeks ago. At first she had thought it a ceremonial salute, but as the weapons had begun to fill the wind with huge noises, the verandas had become crowded with excited watchers and she had run to her own. There were shouts of encouragement and the sight of running men in the street below. Out on the apron ships had begun to move, then she had watched in disbelief as the biggest of them, a great transporter of ten thousand tons, had blossomed into an enormous ball of fire. Seconds later she had felt the shock as the sound of the explosion carried to her; she had felt it across her chest and stomach like a physical blow.

"No doubt my husband will deal with them very soon," Fumiko said. "I can't imagine why he hasn't hung them up on crosses already. That way they could have been burned with the dead bodies. Ugh! How they make my flesh creep to watch them. They are base and filthy and they gabble away in their impossible tongue, saying I don't know what terrible things."

Michie fluttered her fan and watched Fumiko's fingers turn the white *go* stone over and over. "The Amerikans have caused your husband so much trouble, but aren't these the honorable hostages that were exchanged before we were permitted to land?"

"You cannot call them honorable, Michie-san. You cannot call any Amerikan that. Because they have no tradition, they are aimless. They trust only their feelings in everything. They drift on the winds of existence, living chaotic lives without meaning or honor. They disgust me, and they should disgust you too."

"I suppose your husband is right to call them pirates."

"Did you see the gesture that one just made to me? Such indecency! Such lewdness."

"He only bowed to us, Fumiko-san."

Fumiko placed another white stone down on the board. Mildly she reproached her companion. "How dare you defend him, you good-for-nothing? Let me tell you, Michie-san, I know their Amerikan manners very well indeed. Fourteen years ago, when I was little older than you are now, I was taken to their despicable Sector in the retinue of our good Emperor. He was a prince then, twenty-six years old, and the woman he was to meet was thirty-seven. She was President Lucia Henry. Of course, she was purest Amerikan filth, spawned by that fat, godless swine Stratford Henry. Although Lucia was supposed to be pro-Yamato, there is no doubt that the curse of her father's seed passed to all his offspring."

Fumiko fanned herself.

"It was the height of summer, *Shichigatsu*—July, they call it. I remember we landed at a port called Harrisburg, on Liberty, and went from there to Lincoln, the capital city, where the ceremonies were to take place. *Summer?* By the ice-hells of Jigoku's suffering demons! It was so cold and wet, you can't imagine. It rained all the while. I tell you! All our ceremonial horses were skidding and sliding. All my wigs and fine dresses were ruined by rain before we got halfway there."

"You make it sound a very sad place."

"Sad? It's no more than they deserve. They are not civilised people. They live in hovels with plex floors and solid plex walls. And they smell! I can't tell you how bad! Oh, yes, it's true that there is no life outside Yamato. They're cultural mongrels, these Amerikans. They have no concept of duty. Amerika today is like the Old World almost became under their insane twenty-first-century ideas." She shivered with deeply felt revulsion. "You must have seen pictures of Sacred Japan and what they did to it after they overran it. Steel and glass office towers like boxes. Little iron ground-cars everywhere. Gah! They almost made the whole of mankind into a disgusting mass of uniform, coffee-colored consumers, identical the world over. Classless. Tasteless. Raving about their rights, but with never a thought about duty. A filthy conglomerate mass with no distinctions, no pride of place, and no dignity. They are totally weak and self-indulgent. That's what Amerika stands for."

"Even here, in the Neutral Zone, Fumiko-san?"

"Especially here in the Co-prosperity Sphere, Michie-san."

Michie snapped her fan shut. You talk as if Yamato was paradise, she thought. But it's not. And for years the Court on Kyoto has been a terrifying hell. The Emperor had married in his teens and his wife had borne him a lunatic son, Prince Kono. The thought of that cackling, misshapen monster haunted her still. Insanity had run in his mother's family for generations, heightened by dynastic inbreeding. The Prince had been born mad, and as the years passed and his father secluded himself more and more absolutely in his palace complex, Prince Kono's vindictive rages had steeped the Imperial Court in fear and loathing.

Michie's stomach tightened as she recalled her sister and the Imperial maniac who had terrorised her with sexual toys and made her time in Kyoto a living nightmare. Oh, yes, I remember you, Prince Kono. The Shinto priests had to cut a hole in your head to let out the evil *kami* that tortured your soul. The same hell-demons drove you to torment anyone that came near you. You who in high summer slept naked on a bed of ice. You who roasted dogs and kittens alive in your apartments. You who flayed horses to death to glory in their agony. And you who whipped my sister half to death before you raped her. And nothing could be done because you were the Son of Heaven's son. You're dead now but your immortal soul will never rest in the deepest ice pits of Jigoku.

Michie forced the evil thoughts away. Very soon now she would meet her mother and father again. It was almost ten years since they had been together as a family. Ten years! When as a young girl she had been sent into Honshu with her sister to live with her aunt, a lady-in-waiting at the Imperial Court, and learn refined manners. Very soon, she thought, and breathed the air of a new planet that meant freedom to her.

Fumiko played with the white glass *go* stone, turning it over between finger and thumb. Her nasal voice grew far away, and her eyes became glazed with reminiscence.

" . . . on his state visit to Amerika the Emperor was all in blue, accompanied by my father, who as the Emperor's representative was to give the Amerikans a gift as a token to recognise the opening of our embassy. Naturally the Emperor wanted his son to come with him, but for reasons of protocol he could not. He preferred to stay at home with his second stepmother. We saw the Amerikan President receive the Emperor on the White House lawn. Lucia Henry was not a beauty, my dear. She reminded me of an old horse wrapped up in a washing cloth. Her eyes were like a Siamese cat's and she was cursed with hair the color of roasting chestnuts—they say her father's hair was bright orange!—and her skin was pale and wrinkled like an octopus. They met face-to-face on Peace Day, but all protocol was ignored. Do you know she had the affrontery to keep the Emperor waiting at the Capitol? And she had her flags of state marched in procession before her so that the ceremony was delayed again until the Emperor's banners could be brought."

Michie shook her head, thinking it a great honor to have gone with Emperor Mutsuhito's retinue to attend at his state visit. She had been too young and her family too far from Imperial favor when the Emperor had visited Amerika. Still she remembered the stories of the lust Prince Kono had had for his second stepmother in the Emperor's absence.

Fumiko's voice became resentful. "After the state visit such a quantity of money was spent, gifts spread ahead of the retinue for the pleasure of the people as we progressed to the Capitol. But still the Amerikans hated us. We could see it in their eyes as we passed by. Hostile, mannerless, brooding like hogs. Nobody knelt. Even the common people gawped and no one compelled them to take their hats off to us, and when we came to their Capitol they gave our divine Emperor only the same deference they would afford to an ordinary human being. The Emperor forbade any reaction. We were to bear all insults, whatever the humiliation. We were jostled and subjected to contemptuous indignities at every turn until every last shred of honor was stripped from us. As long as I live I will never, never forget it. Nor will I forgive."

"It must have been very difficult for you, Fumiko-san."

Michie clasped her hands together on her lap and looked down at her manicured fingernails, still listening. She was glad she had worn her lightest, plainest kimono. Fumiko's obi stood out stiff and white. Her gray-streaked hair was pinned up in the Kyoto style with long silver skewers, and her charcoal-gray kimono ruffled about her feet. She was a woman of dowdy tastes that belied the dark passion of her moods.

"Yes, they were cruel to us, but they paid for their sins. On the Emperor's return Yamato was closed to all *gaijin*. All foreigners were given seventy-two hours to leave. And just as their infamous Jesus Christ god was crucified, so were those who attempted to defy the Emperor's ruling. Yes, they paid for their bad manners when Lucia Henry was President. We cut them off—just like that! *Atari!*"

A white stone clicked onto the board and Michie saw another of her black groups surrounded by white with no possible way out. Fumiko was an accomplished five-dan player, giving away a full complement of nine handicap stones at the start of the game: Amerikans were not the only ones to be crucified! Her concentration slipped as she recalled the stories she had heard about Amerika and its appeasing ways.

In her consuming desire to bring the Amerikans to accommodate the wishes of the Emperor, and perhaps in some vain hope of bringing prosperity back to Amerika once more, Lucia Henry had rounded up the chiefest and loudest among the Expansionists and had had them assassinated. Hundreds were killed, all denied the luxury of *seppuku*. But wasn't that another example of Amerikan barbarity? They did not allow *seppuku,* the honorable slitting of the belly, that permitted a person to leave this mortal world with his or her honor intact.

Only after three years, when unfortunate fighting broke out on the Amerikan-held planet of Honolulu, did Lucia Henry stop hunting down the Expansionists, and then for just four months. Again the calls for Amerika to officially allow Amerikan settlers into the Neutral Zone were heard, again the Emperor refused. Honolulu fell and the President was sucked down into a deepening crisis. Amerika was a democracy—a bizarre state where a majority periodically had its say in who would govern. Lucia Henry's own people, whose salvation she had so strenuously sought, hated her and blamed her for losing the last Amerikan foothold in the Neutral Zone. Her policy must have seemed so futile, Michie thought. Her people estranged from her, alone and denied respect, her all-important majority gone. With nothing more to live for she had retired to Nevada, a strange monastic world, so it was said, utterly despised, leaving the White House and the mantle of power to Alia Kane.

". . . so that hellcat, the bastard Alia Kane, usurped power."

"I'm sorry, Fumiko-san, what did you say?"

"That mistress of *hinin* who sits on the throne of Amerika—she stole the presidency, no?"

"Oh, yes."

A *sangokujin* servant—a Korean or Chinese—brought them green tea in a fine porcelain pot from the kitchens under the house. It tasted bitter and delightful on her lips. Michie looked again at the prison. Was it true that in Amerika there were no servants? That they sometimes constructed flesh robots, synthetic life, to do the menial labor? A horrifying thought! But there were many strange and impossible stories about Amerika. Like the curious system of democracy. How could it possibly work? After a while, she made another play and saw immediately how foolish it was. She said, "What do you think your honored husband, the daimyo, will do with the hostages?"

Fumiko laid down another stone, sealing the game. She frowned, glancing up at the prison once more. "Let us go indoors, Michie-san. I can see the heat is affecting you."

As they reached the open wooden staircase and began to climb, Michie heard the sound of challenges. The daimyo's guard drew arms on a visitor. It was Admiral Kurita, come with impeccable timing, to plead, no doubt, for the honor of his second-in-command.

13

"Was it not Japanese enterprise that discovered the secret of faster-than-light travel? And the size and efficiency of Japanese corporations that made terraforming possible? Then, by my ancestors, it will be to Yamato that the tribute of the galaxy will run!"

Kurita heard the daimyo's words blustering from the chamber. A gaunt chief retainer knelt impassively at his side, and around the huge, formal room were numbers of Shinto priests and lieutenants, officers and *hatamoto-yakko*—the daimyo's personal retainers.

The walls of the council chamber were shoji, paper screens, some of which slid back to form doors. The floor was covered in high-quality rice tatami imported from Honshu. Behind the daimyo a carved wooden wall containing the clan symbol of Ugaki had been hung over with a large Nishima standard of three fan-shaped *ginkyo* leaves arranged with their stalks curling like the *yin* and *yang*, yellow on red.

In the corridor outside, the admiral stopped, pulled off his gorgeously worked helmet, and dabbed at his forehead where the headband had impressed a red mark. Above it his hair was cropped short, an even mix of gray and black. His shoulders were plated in lacquered bands like a lobster's tail, and his hands, forearms, and elbows were encased in ceremonial armor in the *Yukinoshita-do* style, woven with tassels and crimson cordage. He wore baggy lime-green *hakama* pantaloons and a cobalt-blue jacket under his segmented breastplate, a white obi into which his swords were thrust.

Real lacquered armor cooks the body like an oven out here, he thought as he felt the sweat trickle down his back. He rubbed absently at his forehead. Beyond the open windows the wild waters of the bay rippled invitingly. How I wish I could throw off my gear and run down to the shore. Just five minutes! Two! I would give a thousand *koku* for the pleasure of a swim. Instead I must attend the Council and endure Lord Nishima's rhetoric. How a samurai suffers for his position in this world. Oh, to be serving in Guam now, under General Yoshida. Oh, to be a man of action once more!

He passed his helmet to a servant who received it reverently. He had spent a difficult morning on the apron at Niigata, watching Shinto priests reconsecrating the shrines there after the unpleasantness. For two weeks the stench of death had blown into Niigata from the bloated corpses of the Amerikans that the daimyo had ordered left there as a reminder.

"A reminder to whom?" he had asked, astounded. "To my crews? To the townspeople? To their slaves? To Captain Kondo? We are not here to punish the people of Niigata. Let me fire the bodies, Nishima-sama, before they corrupt the air and the whole of Niigata suffers unnecessary shame."

Three days later, the daimyo had permitted it.

The shoji slid aside and he entered.

Nishima acknowledged his bow curtly and motioned him to vacant space on the floor. The governor and two of his councilors were present. As were various officers of the daimyo's staff and of the *kin kaigun*. All sat stiff-backed, watching the proceedings gravely.

Nishima faced Governor Ugaki with a list of charges. "You permitted Amerikan vessels to enter the Greater Yamato Co-prosperity Sphere. You know that is now forbidden. You permitted them to land on Sado. That also is forbidden. You did not try to attack them and drive them away. You were derelict in your duty. What have you to say?"

Ugaki stared sightlessly forward, his face blank parchment but streaming with sweat. He said nothing.

"However," the daimyo went on, "it is recognised that you could not have defeated the invading barbarians without the probable loss of the terminal facility. Therefore"—he paused, looking round the assembled faces grimly—"it is my decision that you will be permitted to commit *seppuku*."

Visible relief flooded through Ugaki. The reprieve had been so totally unexpected he had not even brought a second to deliver the killing blow.

"My retainer will act as your second," Nishima said, seeing the man's embarrassment. He doesn't deserve it, he thought, but heads must roll and in as tidy a way as possible.

Ugaki knelt, opened his stiff-shouldered *kataginu* robe, and readied himself. In the silence his deep, steady breathing was audible, then he lifted the razor-sharp blade and plunged it into his abdomen, managing to draw it across him and up as tradition demanded before the *katana* sang down onto his bare neck.

The head lolled forward, still connected at the Adam's apple by a piece of flesh, then Ugaki's body pitched forward in a fountain of blood.

After a few moments' silence the body ceased to twitch and Nishima turned next to Kondo. "You deliberately acted against my explicit orders, and your precipitate action cost the Emperor ten thousand *koku* of aurium, including four hundred *koku* of semirefined ore without which the Advance Colonisation Program will come to a complete halt. Seven ships are destroyed or irreparably damaged. Four hundred of my men are killed. I have written to the Emperor informing him of this. I'm bound to say that you should prepare to have your belly opened and your entrails stretched around Niigata by *hinin*." He glanced briefly at Kurita. "However, your admiral reminds me that because you are an officer of the Yamato Guard I am technically obliged to hold you until I receive instructions from Kyoto. What have you to say?"

Kondo's stare was flinty. "I acted wholly in good faith, Excellency."

"You acted without honor, Captain Kondo. You failed me. You are a traitor."

"No! I cannot stand the shame!" Kondo lowered his head and stared fixedly at the floor before him. Kurita could smell fear on his breath.

"So. You have nothing more to say for yourself?"

"Nothing, Excellency."

"Then hear my pleasure. I will not take a traitor to Kanazawa with me. You will await the Emperor's reply here in Niigata. In the jail. Take this worthless *hinin* out of my sight."

The captain of the guard hesitated, and Nishima's face darkened.

"I beg your clarification, Excellency. Am I to confine Captain Kondo *with the Amerikans?*"

"That was my instruction."

The man still hesitated, appalled at the gigantic dishonor that had been heaped on Kondo.

Nishima brought his hand crashing down onto his knee. "Do as I say! Immediately! Or you will go with him!"

Kurita held his silence as Kondo was marched, white-faced, from the room. As he passed, his eyes darted to his admiral and away again. Only when the tribunal had been cleared and the lowly *burakumin* had removed Ugaki's corpse and replaced the ruined tatami did Kurita draw the daimyo to the veranda and speak softly to him alone.

"The fleet leaves for Honshu the day after tomorrow, Nishima-sama. I must have Captain Kondo with me."

Nishima turned to face him. "That's impossible."

"I cannot forget that it is I who am responsible for delivering the Emperor's aurium safely to the Home Worlds. Captain Kondo has assuredly shamed himself by his impetuous act, but he is a most able officer—and, unfortunately, quite essential to the security of the Emperor's aurium."

"He stays here."

"Surely in the interests of expediency—"

The daimyo's eyebrows jerked up. "Expediency, Admiral?"

"In the interests of *justice* may I suggest a compromise?"

"There are no compromises where justice or samurai honor is at issue."

"It is to protect your honor and mine, Excellency, that I beg this favor of you."

Nishima bit each word off angrily. "You—do—*what?*"

"I give you my word that the captain will be delivered to the jail in Kyoto to await His Imperial Majesty's decision."

"It's absolutely out of the question. The matter is closed."

Kurita took a pace back. Don't crowd him, he thought. Give him every chance to comply with good grace. It was always difficult knowing precisely how to deal with Choshu no Nishima Jun. He took surprisingly little account of the realities of his position, and he was as unpredictable as a left-handed swordsman.

"Then . . . I cannot guarantee the contents of my own report to His Imperial Majesty concerning the losses."

Nishima stiffened. "Am I to understand that you intend sending *separate* dispatches to the Imperial Court?"

"That depends, Excellency."

"On what?"

"On whether you and I can agree on Captain Kondo's future."

The daimyo bristled, then nodded shortly. "Very well. I shall order him loaded with a punishment wheel and confined aboard the *Hiei*, where he will pass into your jurisdiction." He added tiredly, "Then you may do with him as you like."

"Thank you. A very wise decision, Excellency."

Ugaki's successor hovered by the shoji, then he came in and groveled.

"Speak."

"Lord, please may I ask what you intend to do with the *gaijin* hostages?"

"I shall have them marched to Kanazawa, where they will be examined and then executed. You have no room for *gaijin* interlopers here."

"Of course they are contraband traders and smugglers, but perhaps they are not interlopers, Lord," the new governor suggested hopefully. "If their arrival was not premeditated before the Imperial edict which closed this region."

Nishima grinned faintly at Kurita. "Perhaps this man looks for the return of Amerikan ships carrying a ransom?"

The man's voice quavered, and his knees cracked audibly. "Oh, no, Lord! I seek only justice!"

"Well, if they are not interlopers they are certainly *gaijin*, and don't you crucify barbarians here in Niigata as Imperial decree demands?"

The new governor's chin quivered, and the admiral took up his cause.

"Doubtless the *bonze* would condemn them to be nailed up without hesitation. Shinto priests are responsible for the purity of Yamato, Nishima-sama, but perhaps they are narrower in their understanding of practicalities than we are. It strikes me that no matter how unlikely the chance of an Amerikan vessel coming this way again, perhaps the governor may be successful in trading the lives of a few worthless *gaijin* for a ransom. I'm sure Niigata has a good use for any extraordinary sums of revenue that may turn up."

Still kneeling, the new governor began to nod, then stopped abruptly.

"You seem remarkably ready to make light of the Emperor's law. I say these men are interlopers!" Nishima insisted, adding acidly to Kurita, "Was not your own ship, the *Chiyoda*, blown to hell by them? Did you not see with your own eyes the *Zuiho* burned to a hulk? Yes, they are interlopers, and they must be stamped out!"

The governor said distantly, "Perhaps they will be back."

Kurita saw the disquiet in the new governor's eyes. Long gone were the days when an Amerikan freighter might appear quietly through a nexus and land at a Neutral Zone port with a hold full of cheap merchandise. Gone too were the commissions amicably arranged in a spirit of mutual gain.

Nishima inspected the governor, dropping his voice to a growl. "That is why the Emperor in his wisdom sent me here. A new sword cuts clean and His

Imperial Majesty's orders are quite explicit. He foresees further incursions unless the Amerikans and Chinese can be shown that we have the will to protect our Empire. All ports are to be fortified and garrisoned in strength. No foreign shipping is to be permitted leave to trade or suffered to use our aprons or facility houses. If the previous daimyo of Sado had been more scrupulous about His Imperial Majesty's laws, we would not be in this position now."

"Fortification is very expensive, Lord," the governor said, aghast at the daimyo's words. "How will His Imperial Majesty be able to pay for the work?"

"You will find a way. I'm sure of that. You seem to have a most—energetic town."

"Only when the aurium fleet comes is Niigata as you see it, Lord. Ordinarily our city is a humble and wretched place."

The frenzied *ya* that sprang into being upon the arrival of the ore fleet transformed Niigata and every settlement within fifty miles of the port into a boisterous market packed with traders, *ronin* (freebooting warriors), geisha, and *bakuto* (gamblers). As far away as Ogi the *ya* blistered with samurai and various traffickers dicing and drinking for weeks on end, buying and selling *sake,* religious charms, weapons, silks, highly illegal comic books and "art pictures," anything and everything disgorged by the ships.

"As I see it, the sole reason for these *ya* is that on Sado no one is willing to work for a living. You're all too busy digging aurium and argentium to manufacture artifacts for yourselves. Everything has to be brought in from Yamato. Isn't that so, Kurita-san?"

Kurita made an ambiguous gesture. As he watched the daimyo pick fastidiously at a speck on his otherwise spotless silk sleeve, questions came unbidden to his mind. Why were you sent here? Is it, as you claim, to enforce the Emperor's orders and to protect the Co-prosperity Sphere from Amerikan traders? True, these smugglers undercut Yamato goods, but they are hardly threatening the stability of the Empire. Did the Emperor send you here to deal with them? Or was it for another reason altogether? To remove you from the Court? Perhaps it's easy to understand why the Emperor would want to banish you to faraway Sado, Nishima-sama. You're a zealot, a rash champion of lost causes, and because of that you're a danger to him despite your devotion to the Imperial Court.

Ugaki's successor, who was still on his knees, wafted at a fly. "Please, Lord. This talk is too complicated for my humble status. Have I permission to ransom the Amerikans?"

"Perhaps I need to make my position quite clear to you. I will tolerate no infraction of His Imperial Majesty's law while I am daimyo."

"Of course, Lord. May I ask what you plan to do with the Amerikans in the immediate future?"

"I have not yet made a decision. Since I intend to remain here for some weeks yet, there is no need."

The governor raised a cheerless grimace of delight. "It's just that with so many extra people in town, so many malefactors and rogues, we have need of prison space."

"Don't trouble me with the details of your petty arrangements. You can't expect me to deal with every minor problem."

"Of course not, Lord. But if we could just make a little bit more room—"

"Enough. I will inform you when I have made my decision."

Kurita's thoughts turned once more to the Emperor. Whatever else he may be, Mutsuhito is meticulous. He makes no move unless it is thrice considered, laid aside, and considered once again. His method is all to him. Nishima-san's impetuousness must therefore affront him. So what better place for the man than slumbering Sado? Here he can busy himself with trifles while the Emperor's favored vassals like Baron Harumi, who is now virtual shogun, direct his Empire through the *bakufu* in Kyoto, the *real* center of power. So long as aurium continues to flow across the nexus chains as it has done uninterruptedly these past fifty years, then you can do as you please. You do not fool me with your sanctimonious pride, Nishima-san. You forget that you have paced my bridge for two months and that I have taken your measure. My bet is that the Emperor sent you here to oversee his slaves, to keep account of his subjects' plantations, to play at fort building—and to rot in obscurity. I'd give a year's pay to know what you did to upset the Emperor! What precisely was it that brought you here?

The admiral's reverie was disturbed by a commotion at the door; it was the lieutenant whom Nishima had put in charge of the hostages, exquisitely uniformed, immaculate, pleased with his own efforts. He came into the daimyo's presence.

"We have captured another piece of Amerikan filth, Excellency."

Nishima regarded the man coldly. "Another Amerikan?"

"Yes, Excellency. I personally caught him on the south side, trying to creep into the city."

"What have you done with him?"

"I threw him in with the others, Excellency."

"Quite correct. Good work."

"Thank you, Excellency."

Kurita's eyes followed as the man scurried away loaded with the daimyo's approval. Why incarcerate this one with the others? he thought. If I were you I'd interrogate him before he infects the rest with lies. Aloud he said, "I wonder how many more of them escaped. I shouldn't be surprised if they retired up to Chi no Tsuki and landed an armed party on the darkside. That's what I would have done. There could be hundreds of them crouching in the swamps up there. Personally I'd double the guard."

The governor paled, but Nishima leaned back and folded his arms. "Let them come. We're a match for any vermin-ridden Amerikan. How many does that make in your jail?"

"Thirteen, Lord."

"Ah, an appropriate number to eat a Last Supper together, no?" And he laughed.

They roared with delight when he told them.

"We hit her just right. Drilled a hole right into her magazine and she went to pieces with a couple of hundred samurai aboard."

"You're shit-hot, Gunner!" Torven Jones said, grinning broadly so that his big gravestone teeth and red gums showed.

"It's a good eye you got, Duval Straker. Yessir!"

"More luck than judgement, Helene."

"It was a bang that shook the foundations of this place, I can tell you. We thought it was the *Thomas Jefferson* done got blowed up by their trickery."

"So the bastards said nothing to you?"

"They taunted us with promises beforehand, the sonsabitches. But nothin' since! They daren't admit what really happened."

"None of us speaks enough of their shit-gobbling language, Gunner."

"Maybe that accounts for their bad manners in putting you in this no-star hotel."

Di Barrio cleared a space on the bare floor. "When we were first brought here, the governor had us locked up. These asshole jailors took our Wessons and communicators and our credit and anything else they could filch and locked us up in here."

"They even confiscated my comb," Horner said sourly.

The cell where they were confined was cramped, five paces square, with a central plex pillar and a high slit window in each of the two end walls, one looking into a bare yard, the other onto the street. The yard was sinister, with a punishment stake so that the prisoners preferred to take the air by the higher front window. Despite the primitive conditions, the door was sheeted with plex and secured with an ion lock, while into all four walls, on which had been scrawled a thousand *kanji* characters, plex rings were bolted. Half of the captives were chained up, the rest were chained to one another and had been taking turns to ride shoulders at the windows. Now most were standing, some sitting with their backs to the wall.

Juli Dexter, an experienced woman who had lost an eye on the first Hawken trading venture, spat in disgust. Immediately flies settled on her face again.

"The big feller with the keys at his belt come in here boasting of what they planned. He threatened to nail us up."

"If this was on Ohio, a girl like you'd've eaten him for breakfast, Dexter."

"That's for sure."

Di Barrio rubbed her cheeks. "If only one of us had gotten to the ships. Just one!"

"Well, it wasn't to be."

Davey Marks, an able hand, said, "Yep, locked up here with three basins of shitty rice between us a day, nothing to drink, and not knowing what's happening. 'Tain't right."

"Think yourself lucky you aren't aboard the *Richard M*. She's a starvation ship right now," Duval said, thinking about his brother. Had he survived so far? Or had Pete Grosse killed him with his doctoring? Could the *Richard M*. possibly get back to Amerika?

"At least she's going somewheres," Marks said.

"The commodore'll get her home."

"Oh, yeah?"

"I saw a crew starve two years ago," Dexter said darkly. "Chinese they was, out of Tien Shan, and got the worst end of an argument with some pirates off of the Taiwan nexus. There was one guy aboard could feel his backbone through his belly. Weren't above sixty pounds, poor guy."

Di Barrio lowered her voice. "What's become of the others, Gunner?"

He told them of his escape. He had been suffocated by thick clouds of smoke that came from the *Richard M*.'s engines, and he had run blindly across the apron to escape the blast he knew was coming. When the kamikaze ship blew, he had been thrown twenty yards by a searing shock wave. Incredibly, with his shirt and hair all in flames he had fallen into one of the deep storm drains whose cover grille had been blown off and landed up in six inches of water where he thrashed the fire out. The lasting image of an arm thrust through a sewer hole in the drain's sump, and Iwakura's terror-white face imploring him to come back and release him from the drowning hole, had stayed with him for a long time.

"I just couldn't get him out," he said, shaking his head.

"Ah, let 'em all roast in hell." Matt Kaiser, a scrawny sea cook with thinning hair and quick, darting eyes, let himself down from the window, his chains rattling. "Seeing as the daimyo's thrown his treaty over his left shoulder and gone off upcountry, what's likely to become of us?"

Dexter stretched herself. "You can speak their weird chat, Gunner. Are they going to kill us?"

Duval made no answer.

"Yeah!" Marks's voice was thick with scorn. "I was on the *Alabama* in 'twenty-five when we went privateering against the Koreans, an' all. We never had much mercy for Yambo crews. If'n we caught 'em, we used to roll 'em up in their own silk pajammies and shoot 'em out the garbage ports."

"We don't know what they intend," Duval said, hating the way hopelessness turned quickly into easy acquiescence in some of them.

"That's the worst part, Gunner—not knowing!"

"Jeezus, I feel as rough as a Turkish astrogator's asshole."

Jeb Womak was despairing. He came out of the corner and stood close to Duval and breathed on him. His body was sour and his teeth busted; the stink made Duval recoil. Even aboard ship he was soap-shy. He was a maintenance man and had spent most of his time festering in the ship's guts fixing leaks. He had lost a lot of weight. "They're starving us. We've been stuck here to die. I haven't had a mouthful in two days. Did you bring any water with you, Gunner?"

Duval looked at the man, then turned quickly away.

"Ignore him, he's raving. He's bleeding at the arse, Gunner. It's some kind of disease he's picked up."

"They got nasty ticks here."

Forrest, an able hand whose feet were anchored in plex chains, laughed bitterly. "Just shut it, Womak! He drinks all the water and then bleats for more, and he stinks the place out."

Duval continued to recount how he had got off the apron after abandoning Iwakura to his fate. The *Richard M.* had been no more than fifty yards away before the blast came, but then she had powered away. He had known enough about the Yamato mind-set to realise that to try to give himself up at that moment would have meant certain death, so he had struck out for the coast, wading through the tide-line shallows with the last of his strength. He had lived for two weeks in an abandoned sensor shack, sleeping in short bursts, ranging the spaceport at night, rooting up shellfish to eat at low tide, trying to get hold of a weapon with which to rescue his compatriots.

Duval eyed the rough stone gutter that led from the corner of the cell. It was black with midden flies and stank worse than Womak.

"I guessed I'd find you in some such hellhole, but before I could devise a scheme to get you out I was taken."

"Hellhole is right. Sorry, boys, but I gotta go." Toni Jacob, one of the *Thomas J.*'s two biologists, got up. She unpopped the seam of her coveralls and squatted over the open sewer, sending the flies up in a cloud. The men looked away automatically. "We're greatly annoyed by night bugs," she said to fill the embarrassed silence as she urinated. "The locals call them *hae*. They're some kind of genetically engineered mosquito. They've got a wonderful appetite for blood. If you kill them while they're sucking, the bite swells up in an itching weal, but if you let them drink their fill, they do no damage other than a fleabite."

Womak screamed and brushed at his lap in a frenzy. There was a chorus of mouth-filling oaths, then raucous laughter.

"Get it off me! Get it off!"

Dexter elbowed him viciously. "Keep still, you little shit-head!"

A great ginger-colored spider the size of a man's hand had dropped onto Womak from above. At the street window there was the sound of childish laughter and running feet.

"What's the matter? Scared of a goddamned spider?"

Dexter picked up the spider by its bulbous abdomen and turned it over so that its jointed legs grasped at the air. "That's the best yet! Little brats!" She offered it to Womak, who cowered back in horror, his face twisted and flushed pink. "No! Please! Take it away, Jools. I can't take spiders. I hate 'em, I tell you!"

"Woooo!" Dexter held the spider closer and squeezed it so that its legs struggled. "It's only a little ol' spider, Jeb boy. Listen at him pleading for mercy."

Jacob came over and examined the creature. "What say we drop it on the next Yambo lady to pass this way?"

The two went across to the window, leaving Womak panting in his corner.

"Listen!" Duval said, turning to di Barrio. "Don't you hear that?"

All eyes turned to stare at him, listening.

"Jeezus!"

Those who could, crowded to the rear of the cell to watch what was happening in the courtyard. The screams grew louder and then a troop of samurai came in sight with two Chinese slaves struggling fearfully in chains. Duval pressed up against the bars and watched.

"What they saying, Gunner?"

"I can't tell."

"It's a whipping!"

"No."

An officer read sentence—something about running away, as far as Duval could tell. Then he barked orders at the soldiers, who stripped the slaves and hoisted them to hang side by side, spread-eagled and upside down from the timber whipping frame. Their ankles were tied to the crossbar, and their heads dangled a foot off the ground. A Shinto priest stood beside them mouthing incantations and splashing them with water.

Jesus Christ, they can't be! Duval thought as he realised what he was about to witness. No crime, not even treason, warrants that. They're going to use the meat cleaver on them.

He turned his face away, unable to watch. Only Dexter remained, gripped by the grotesque horror of it. Her face contorted as the screams intensified and they heard the sounds of a butcher's ax biting into flesh.

Then one of the voices stopped.

There was a deafening silence. Straker felt the sweat pouring from him as the methodical chopping began again. When the screams died altogether, Dexter shook her head and slid down to the floor.

"They've cut them in two," she said. "From ass to Adam's apple. They're dripping there like four sides of beef."

Not one of them spoke for many minutes. The truth of their position was suddenly very real to them. Despite the futility of trying, escape was on all their minds, and when they spoke again, they began to ask Duval sober questions.

"The city's packed with people. Yesterday I lay up in one of the flood-lamp gantries that line the road, quietly, to check out the town and look out for an opportunity. I saw a procession. It passed right under me—the daimyo on horseback with five of his guard around him in some kind of weird ceremony—and I could have dropped on him if I'd had my shark knife and slit his throat."

"It's a pity you didn't, Gunner. He's gonna slice us up for sure."

"How were you captured?"

"I made a mistake. A slave child saw me when I hid in a ditch. She went running from the field to her mother. The mother raised a hell of a yell."

"Then what?"

"Next I know there's most of the garrison pointing swords at my head."

"Bad luck, Gunner. This place has bad *feng shui*." It was Tim Soo. He had been badly shaken by the executions.

"The dice are agin us."

"No doubt about that."

"My balls are aching. Damn these fucking chains!"

Marks shrugged. "There weren't no chance of getting us out of here anyways, Gunner. When we saw you coming, clamped up at the neck like that, we hoped you'd been caught in a skirmish. We had hopes of a rescue landing."

Dexter snorted. "It ain't like the commodore to just hightail it away without seeing what can be done for his folk."

"Sure, a decent ship with singularity guns blazing would get us out."

"The *Richard M.* was packed tight with crew when she lit out," Duval told them, quick to squash false hope. "It was all she could do to get off the apron. There are still plenty of samurai in Niigata, and they'd like nothing better than a second chance to get hold of a singularity gun."

Dale Seebeck held up a hand swaddled tight in a rag torn from his bloodied shirt. "Cruel bastards as my hand here testifies, Gunner. They'd've cut a landing party to bits like these here fingers."

Yamato's samurai regiments were the fear of Christendom, well drilled, well equipped, and arrogantly certain of their prowess. All had heard the horrible stories that had come out of the Neutral Zone shortly after Baron Harumi had descended on a rebellious system with his units.

"Well, now. We're not dead yet."

"Did you find out anything that might save us, Gunner?"

There were machine noises outside. An ion key cycling in the lock.

A blast of shouted Japanese, and the door of the cell swung open, pushing Jones aside. Then the sergeant-jailor, as fat as a sumo wrestler, entered. He stood just inside the doorway, a steel-tipped cane in his hand. His black moustache was shaved in the middle but his hair was not in the samurai style. He wore grubby clothes, and his baggy *ko-bakama* trousers were tucked into gaiters below the knee. He grunted as he looked about him, then spoke again rapidly. It was an order. *"So-re!"*

"What does he say, Gunner?"

"He wants one of us."

"Which one?"

A second jailor, the one with the ion key jangling at his belt, pointed to di Barrio and motioned her back.

"Go to hell, you son of a whore!"

Another took hold of Duval's wrist chain, but he pulled the man down, over him, looking for his knife. Dexter threw herself at the third, tearing at the man's face with her bare hands. Then other soldiers began pouring into the cell, dragging out those who were not chained to the wall, beating down the others with truncheons.

They separated Duval and took him out into the yard, slamming the cell door shut once again on the others who crowded to the window shouting and reaching out to him helplessly.

One of the guards cracked a thonged whip at the window, laying open Dexter's face where it pressed against the bars.

"By God! I'll have your eye for that, you bastard!"

"Give me strength!"

"They're going to kill us all!"

Womak's voice quailed from the corner. "We'll never get out of here alive!"

Dexter turned on him. "Shut your mouth, I told you!"

"You too, Dexter!" di Barrio shouted.

"Jeezus, what are they doing to him?"

More faces pushed the bars to witness the Gunner's fate. The Yamato sergeant had a thick bullwhip coiled in his hand. He ordered Duval stripped and shackled to the whipping post.

A Shinto priest in a huge black robe and holding up a spade-like *gohei,* a symbol of divinity, came to stand before him. The complicated robes were secured at the neck and waist with knotted cords and had voluminous sleeves. The equally massive hood was thrown back, revealing a man in his seventies, a long gray beard, a broken nose, face pinched and directed downward in silent inner contemplation. A peculiar hat that looked like a lunch pail was tied onto the top of his head. Under his block-soled *geta* the flagged yard was sticky with blood, and flies buzzed up around them.

A strange mumbling began.

He's chanting, Duval thought, his sweat frozen to his flesh. Devil knows what he's saying, what kind of weird, unknowable thoughts he's thinking. Wasn't it the Black Brotherhood who ran the *kempei* in Yamato? Who tortured their captives into degradation until they abandoned their sanity? His heart thumped faster and he felt his testicles shrivel. This is it, he thought. This is where I die. An example to the rest. They'll flay me and leave me to dangle. At least I'm first. At least I don't have to watch the others. I hope I can bear the pain without shouting out. What if I shit myself? Jeezus, I hope I can die well. Oh, God, help me . . . He began to stare about him, the repetitive lines of the priest's reverberant chanting marching unceasingly through his mind, blotting out the world.

They unlocked his huge collar and removed it. A Chinese laborer wearing a shoulder yoke brought two pails of water, and the sergeant poured one out over Duval's head. Then the Chinese began to scrub at his body. The rubbing hands worked over his head and face, down across his collar-raw neck and shoulders, then his chest and belly. His limbs were sponged right down to his fingers and toes. When he was quite clean, the second bucket was dashed over him and the Chinese began to towel him down with a rough cloth.

After a minute he was unshackled. He was still too shocked to speak, but when a loose jacket and a pair of baggy trousers were handed to him, he put them on. Then plex leg clamps and manacles were snapped back again on his ankles and wrists, and the disc collar refitted.

The priest motioned to the chief jailor.

"Koko e dozo!"

"Where are you taking me?" he asked shakily.

The priest replied in heavily inflected English, "We go to daimyo."

Duval felt the mix of relief and soaring hope in his belly turn to water. "The daimyo?"

"His wish is to question you."

"Me?" Duval's mind raced. The shock still gripped him and he felt light-headed and shivery. "But why me? What about the rest?"

The priest gazed at him with an unsettlingly earnest expression. *"Kamai masen. Dozo, okamai naku. Ikimasho ka?"* It doesn't matter. Please don't trouble yourself. Can we go?

Duval's flesh crawled at the insincere politeness of the priest's formal language. His accent was ancient high Court Kyoto, and it recalled terrors from his youth. Oh, yes, he thought, you're probably pretty adept at the devil's tongue—all that politeness and obsessive rank stuff for putting other people in their place. There's a hundred ways of saying "me" in that language! And it's a hell of a form of communication that leaves the verb to the end of a long sentence so nobody can follow your intentions until you've finished speaking. And words that negate are at the end too, so you can easily reverse what you meant to say if you judge it's not going down well with the listener. But plain speaking would show everyone what a bunch of dangerous two-faced liars you Black Brotherhood priests are. In my childhood I remember seeing men dressed like you blessing the terrorists as they tightened wire nooses on the necks of Amerikan women and children. Using fear as your weapon, you fanatics tried to discourage our settlers setting up home on the systems of the Neutral Zone. My parents died because of pain-loving filth like you!

"But, why am I—"

"Perhaps His Excellency has ordered that you be separated from the others."

"But why me?"

"So sorry. I cannot tell you that."

They marched him down the street the Amerikans had nicknamed the Ginza, past the long, raised veranda where he had seen the young woman, and turned left into a flagged square. On one side, fruit vendors crouched in the shade, wrapped in black padded coats and wearing conical straw hats, succulent fare spread out in front of them on rush mats; on the other a squad of thirty soldiers drilled in unison with wooden swords to the insulting commands of a sergeant while an officer astride a white horse looked on.

He blinked at the bright sun, which was about the same size and color as the sun of his home planet, and also about the same as the original Sun. The parameters came back to him from the *Thomas J.*'s pilot console: a G0-type star, luminosity class V, with apparent visual magnitude −27.2 and absolute visual magnitude 4.4. The color indices were B−V = 0.62, U−B = 0.1, effective temperature 5,800 K.

The star of the Sado system felt very similar to Liberty's primary. Paradoxically the very sameness of it riding high over these strange curved roofs made him feel all the more distant from home. Ahead was the administrative building, brilliantly white under the sun, with massive rampart-like base, a pair of great bronze doors, and above, the complex graphite-gray tilework of a traditional pagoda-style roof. Duval was led up the steps of the other big building that fronted the square. There was a featureless column on each side of the main entrance, and within, deep pools of darkness that hid from the sun. It was surprisingly cool inside; a breeze channeled from windows on the seaward side played on his damp skin. He ran his hand through his hair, making it squeak as it flowed back over his head.

They made him kneel on a mat placed in the middle of the room. Through the open shoji he could see a wooden-railed balcony and the apron of Niigata terminal. His eyes went immediately to the *Dwight D.*, his brother's old command, and he thought again of Ellis and knew that whatever happened he had already cheated death twice, the first time swapping a better man for himself in the burning cargo bay of the *Thomas J.* A death for a life, that's more than fair. Let them kill me now. I've already won and I'll go to the stake laughing. And I'll laugh in their faces now.

Then he thought of his shipmates stewing in filth and degradation and he knew that fate had appointed him their spokesperson whether he liked it or not. He had a duty to try his best to secure their lives.

The daimyo was seated at the center of a small, slightly raised stage, set squarely across the back of the room; he was a silhouette ten yards away, his shoulders winged and star-like. There were others beside him, samurai in similar *kataginu* robes, also priests with the brick-shaped hats tied on the tops of their bald heads, town functionaries in less decorative robes, and a woman.

A pack of proud cats! Look at their vanity and disdain. What does he want with me? Duval asked himself, trying to impose discipline on his chaotic thoughts. Concentrate! It's hard to imagine, but what would I do in his position? What would I want to know? Our ships? Our trade? An account of Commodore Hawken's mind? What? Sure, there are the singularity guns. But I have to put them out of my mind! I can't afford even to think about them. They don't exist. Perhaps there's been a landing, like Dexter thought. God help me to think! How do I keep Helene di Barrio and the others alive?

"Anata no onamae wa? Wakari masu ka, Amerikanu?" What is your name? Do you understand me, Amerikan?

Duval stared stupidly at the daimyo. There was a short, muttered exchange between him and the woman, then she asked in Amerikan, "What is your name, please?"

"I am Duval Straker, and I protest my confinement."

"What did he say, Fumiko-san?"

She translated accurately.

"Perhaps you should warn him to be less proud. Tell him I am the lord of this planet and to mind his manners or I may choose to cut out his tongue."

There was a pause, then Fumiko spoke again. "He says—he says he could tell you nothing if you did that."

Angrily, "Make him understand that it is the daimyo of Sado he addresses."

He listened without reaction.

"He understands that you are the daimyo, Nishima, and calls you 'the one responsible.' "

"Good. Ask him where he thinks the two escaped Amerikan ships have gone."

Fumiko's voice was at once staccato and breathy, the prisoner's reply calm and deliberate.

"He knows nothing of the intentions of the rest of the Amerikan nexus fleet and adds that he would not tell you if he did."

"Fleet?"

Beside him, the scribe dipped his brush, recorded, and dipped again. Nishima's eyes roamed over the prisoner. An insolent puppy, he thought. I will drown you in the sea for your hubris. There is not enough time to let you learn deference by rotting in jail like your fellows. In any case, Fumiko says that all Amerikans have the manners of animals; perhaps a spell hanging like a bat from the walls would make you more respectful. To hell with them all, he decided suddenly. The governor of Niigata is crying for the return of his prison, so I'll simply let the priest crucify them as he wants. But first there is an important duty to perform.

"He says that a fleet of Amerikan ships is waiting in the cold outer orbits of this system to ambush the aurium fleet. He knows that our ships orbit round Sado for several days before they leave the system, then they take advantage of the Blood Moon's gravity to assist them towards the nexus."

The daimyo narrowed his eyes. You answer like an astrogator, he thought. You are clearly very intelligent, no ordinary crewman, and by your bearing I judge that you are used to academic thought. Perhaps it's you who can unravel the mystery.

"Who are you, Duval Straker? What's your rank and what do you know about the strange guns your compatriots were using?"

Duval's reply was rudely concise.

The answer was translated and the daimyo fumed in rage. His chief retainer stepped forward and half drew his sword, shaking with anger. "I warn you!"

he shouted. "Answer the lord respectfully and honestly! Or I will order the eyelids and lips cut off all the captives!"

Duval was sickened as a bolt of fear speared him. The daimyo's got me totally in his power, he thought. I can't stall and I daren't lie.

"I am—or was—gun captain of the nexus ship *Thomas Jefferson*," he admitted slowly. "The same one that you blew up with your suicide ship. So I know quite a lot about the guns."

Nishima's pulse hammered. A gun captain! he thought exultantly. Now we'll find out what caused so much havoc among Kurita's ships.

He returned to the stage and looked once more to his wife, his face deadpan. "Tell me about them."

"We have developed a weapon from which there is not—and can never be—any shielding. Its range is short, but within that range there is no defense against it. It shoots straight as a beam but cannot be reflected, refracted, or dispersed. It will penetrate any shield and open any thickness of plex, yet it fires nothing at all."

When Fumiko translated his words, the room erupted with gasps. A glance from the daimyo quieted them. This was truly a gift from the gods! Such a prize!

Fumiko was still translating. ". . . he says he went to the shore after the battle. Several days ago."

"Ask what mischief he has been causing in the interval."

Duval gave a brief account.

"He claims that he has lived in a disused hut for two weeks since then."

"Stealing food, no doubt?"

The man replied, but Fumiko shook her head and laughed shortly.

"What does he say?"

"He's lying! A laughable transparency! He knows that you have trapped him. His answer was that he ate by raiding garbage cans."

"Tell him not to be afraid. I pardon him for the food he has stolen."

"But Nishima-sama!"

"No, no. Tell him that exactly."

The daimyo's eyes watched Duval Straker carefully. He saw that his clemency had been understood the moment he had said it, not as the words were interpreted. So you understand Japanese too, eh? Of course! Yes, I know you. You were the man Hawken sent aboard my ship to ask about the ship movements across the apron. Then you must be a trusted man, in your commodore's confidence, perhaps party to his strategies. I can certainly use you, Duval Straker.

He spoke directly to the prisoner: "And the fleet of which you speak?"

Duval hesitated, but saw he had been found out. In Japanese he said defiantly, "I can say nothing of that except that it's in the Guam system, lying in wait for your aurium fleet."

"Is that where your commodore was heading? To a rendezvous at Guam? A rendezvous with Amerikan warships?"

"I can tell you nothing more."

Nishima sat back in his chair and stroked the tab of hair under his lip. He was disinclined to play cat and mouse with this arrogant young liar any longer. Apart from anything else, protocol required that such a game must be played out before the local dignitaries; necessity had meant that Fumiko was present. It was demeaning for a daimyo to be resisted in front of his wife and his functionaries. That morning he had read dispatches from the governor of Kanazawa, and others from Iwo Jima. None of them had made mention of a fleet of Amerikan ships. I understand your reasons but you are a poor liar, Amerikan. However, you have your uses. As for the rest, they can tell me nothing that I don't already know. I will let the priests crucify them on the beach at low tide as an entertainment for the townspeople. How poetic to watch the sea rise around them and snuff them out.

Like a harvest gift,
Pale offerings to the sea,
All drowned by the Moon.

"If you are obedient I may spare your life."

"Obedient?"

"If you do as you are told. If you do not, I will order you crucified along with the others."

"You'll slaughter helpless prisoners of war?"

"War? Amerika and Yamato are not at war. We are neighbors, no? Good neighbors who respect one another's privacy, no? You, on the other hand, are dogs who have got into our garden. Piratical smugglers who need to be taught a lesson."

"You fired without warning on two Amerikan Navy vessels."

"No insult to your government was intended. I merely wished to rid my system of a gang of smugglers."

"We are not smugglers."

"You are undeniably barbarians. In Yamato we always—"

He stopped. Ah, but this is not Yamato, Nishima reminded himself, thinking again of the reason he was here. I was sent out of Yamato by His Imperial Majesty. Apart from Fumiko, my wife, only the Emperor and I know the real reason I was sent here. Mutsuhito was at his wits' end. It was I who acted. It was I who saved his throne. It was I who prevented his insane son, Prince Kono, fleeing to become a focus of intrigue against the Empire. Yes, and it was I, with my own hands, who murdered him.

And how the Emperor has repaid my loyalty! By assigning to me the task of fortifying the new territories of the Co-prosperity Sphere he has swept me into obscurity temporarily. But I will return to Yamato one day in triumph and the Emperor will see that I am indispensable to him. For that, guns are required. Not old, obsolete beam weapons, but guns like the Amerikans now make, that combine power and accuracy and are unaffected by any known shielding.

He knew that hitherto the best *gaijin* weapon-makers were English. Their foundries, which clustered around the rich systems of London, Manchester, and Bristol, had manufactured most of the big beam weapons on Yamato vessels. But the arms companies were Europan and could not be tempted to give away technological secrets to Yamato at any price for fear of confiscation of funds by the Europa government. And since the closure of Yamato there had been little trade. If I can bring much better secrets into Yamato, our ships will become as invincible as our armies, he thought with growing excitement. We will be able to conquer the Chinese and obliterate the so-called Neutral Zone. Then, finally, we will destroy the Amerikans in their homeland and unify the territories of Yamato into a single domain. Any honor will be mine for the asking.

He folded his arms and regarded Duval Straker thoughtfully, his decision made. Then he turned to the Shinto priest and said, "You will crucify this barbarian in thirteen days' time. Tomorrow you will begin crucifying the rest of them on the beach. One each tide. In the manner of their Jeezus god."

BOOK 2

21ST YEAR OF KANEI/A.D. 2422

Beautiful, my domain,
My Yamato,
Land of the dragonfly.

Jomei
Japanese Emperor
reigned A.D. 629–41

Autoscript captured from hacks on NEWSWIRE AK.22034,
and
Central Obituary Datachord, record P.555435
Copyright A.D. 2425 Hearstcorp, Lincoln, LIB.

Obit. Pending: ALIA KANE (b. A.D. 2386)

President of Amerikan Sector of Known Space. Only child of Ottoman Kane and Anne O'Boston. Born at Lincoln, LIB., and succeeded to office A.D. 2411. With aid of Ames, K.R., and Lubbock, W.C., attempted to reconcile Expansionists and Amerikan pro-Yamato factions. In A.D. 2412 refused dynastic marriage to Mutsuhito, Emperor o#

. . . *HACK INTERRUPTED* . . .

#ments being made around the President also to marry her diplomatically to the nineteen-year-old Kan (Chinese) prince. She cannot now reject the idea out of hand without provoking a major political rift with Xanadu#

. . . *HACK INTERRUPTED* . . .

#Yeh-chun, the intended consort of Mutsuhito. If she becomes his latest quasi-wife, this daughter of the Korean puppet, Ho Kum-sun, will represent a useful acquisition. She is presently on Seoul, at the port with the biggest nexus terminal and apron in Known Space, and may embark soon for the long transnexus voyage to Kyoto. Intelligence reports say the vast escort that would be required, for purposes of protocol as well as necessary discouragement to Korean pirates, is already beginning to assemble in that system. Mutsuhito may choose to interpret the Earth Central decree as an excuse to mount his long-expected invasion of#

. . . SECURITY INTERLOCK. HACK ABORTED.

15

WYOMING

A dark shape melted from the blackness and moved swiftly out from the cover of a rain-drenched pine grove before dissolving into sodden ground ten yards from the crossroads. There it waited in lethal silence for the lights to come closer.

They were ten yards away when they slewed to the side of the road, just as the watcher knew they would. It was where the big storm drain had collapsed and the metaled surface of the road had turned to filth. Three—no, four of them in a ground-car pickup that skidded, then wallowed in the mire. The three men got out, put their backs to freeing it from the sticky mud while the girl cursed impatiently at the wheel. Without grip the engine whined. Mud flew up from the big tires and splattered in the red glare behind. Ahead, four headlights blasted the dark, picking out the downpour.

The lights had made Jiro Ito get off the road, park his own beat-up ground-car where it could not be seen, and ready himself for murder. Heedless of the rain, he squeezed himself against the ground and drew a concealed dagger smoothly from his boot as he watched the wavering light. With this serrated knife he had many times severed the strings of a man's throat. He held his breath, feeling the hairs on his neck begin to rise like needles.

Reports said that this road had seen very strange movements these past six months: unexplained landings, visitors going up to the Cassabian mansion, foreigners and jacknasties of all kinds, but by their actions he could see that these people were locals.

There were parts of Wyoming where the rain was incessant, and Sweetwater was one. Sweetwater, some joker had called it—some shit-for-brains at the Terraforming Authority. When all it did was rain, the locals must have found that one hell of a joke. Normal air-cars were banned across the whole of this continent because of the "survival tourism." Corporate fatsoes who liked to play at soldiers.

But these people were not two-weekers. They knew the road well, had traveled it many times at night, but still the washout had caught them as he had known it would. By their accent and the resignation in their rough voices and the way they swore, he knew they were locals, from Green River or Black Buttes maybe. They were working. In the middle of the night. Very strange.

There could be only one explanation, Ito thought, not allowing himself to relax. There had been snow all week, turning in the thaw to hail and freezing rain. This was the first night in five when tire tracks would not be left in the morning. The townspeople of Green River were probably bringing contraband off the same freighter that had brought him here yesterday, landing it by night and moving it inland along the river. Damn their hides! How they'd shout if they knew they were being watched by Conroy Lubbock's man, he thought. It's a powerful temptation to send them down the mountain and freewheel their pickup into the river. Summary justice, as scum who bleed the Revenue deserve, but justice must wait. Secrecy drove me off the road and secrecy must drive me on to the Cassabian mansion.

He watched the pickup lumbering on until the engine note deepened. Doors slammed and the old-fashioned red taillights disappeared around the next bend. Ito stood up. He wore black boots and a black cloak. He had chosen a black sedan from the rental, smeared the white tourist flash with greasepaint before departure. Half a lifetime in the Shinto-Buddhist monastery of Shugendo and the other half in Conroy Lubbock's pay had taught him cunning in the art of carrying a message. From Liberty via twelve nexus jumps, riding twelve different two-credit freighters, he could cross Amerika. Kalifornia in two days, or two days to Texas, Amerika's second system, or four to Hawaii, on the fringes of the Neutral Zone, arriving sick in the stomach from too many half-assed jumps and next to dead from the food they served shipboard. The ordinary mail took twice that time, by scheduled flights, but a courier for the President's most trusted ally must carry letters in person, and secretly. The security of the Sector might even now depend on it.

He walked back down the road along the exposed sweep where rain and darkness cowled him. The stream gushed and roared in the precipice, swollen with the melt. Wyoming was a hard country, and Sweetwater deliberately made the hardest, packed the length and breadth with unforeseen dangers. It had been designed as a national park-world, but had fallen into chaos and for a hundred years had attracted the wrong type of settler—moonshiners and backwoods types. Lately there had been efforts made to start tourism up again. Survival holidays and the frontiersman fad had helped investment, then the federal government had declared Wyoming a Technology Free Zone—nothing beyond gas engines and wire electricity allowed—but most of Wyoming was too hard for that. And too wet. Here, beyond the Shirley Mountains, there were vast forests and a maze of blind canyons on the badlands, wolves, bears, and stupidly introduced Siberia tigers. And worse, certain of the human inhabitants preyed on the lone traveler, hillsmen with mantraps and others who stretched cords neck-high on fast straights looking to bring down bikers for what they could steal from their panniers. Each season brought its peculiar difficulties. Now it was the back end of Wyoming's long year: a time of freezing fogs and mud-clogged roads and pitch-blackness when a man needed the gift of psi to be a courier. Jiro Ito had that gift. For half a dozen years he had been the best courier in all Amerika, good enough to become what he was now: not simply a deliverer of the government's most secret messages, but an agent for his master, and for his President.

Only ten parsecs as the beam flies from all the comforts and sophistications of the District of Columbia on Liberty, but night and dirty weather had turned the land here as dark and hostile as any wilderness world. And beyond the clouds, Liberty would be just an invisible speck circling a fifth-magnitude star, itself on the very fringe of visibility, the very light of which was nearly thirty-three years out of date. He climbed back into his rental and cleared the rain-spangled windshield, hating the prohibition on air-cars. A stand of gaunt birches glowed ghostly where the car's exhaust touched them. Once back on the track, he sped on, following the stream up from Kemmerer where the Green River road had taken him. A mile and a half further on he saw the sullen glare of house lights on the hill. The Cassabian mansion: an old three-story Gothic-style house, tall and solemn, a wooden beam and red brick facade, a steeply pitched roof with dormer windows, and a garden of shrub hedges surrounded by a high wall with studded steel gates locked against the night. It was quaint and out of style.

He pulled into a narrow track two hundred yards away. There was no sign of activity but he knew that the master of the Cassabian mansion always posted a synth servant to watch the road. Tonight, foul weather or no, would be no exception.

Grimly he knew that he could afford to take no chances. Ito had never married. A wife and children were baggage he could not afford to carry, they were hostages to fortune. In the world of politics, friendships shifted, alliances were melted down to be poured into new molds, powerful structures were intrigued against and undermined. And there were times when an ethnic Japanese had to be particularly careful. Half a century ago, the Henry dynasty had taken their hold on the presidency only by ruthlessly dismantling democracy. Stratford Henry's son, Halton Henry, had broken with the even greater power of the Central Authority in his days as ambassador there, and then consolidated his success by stripping Authority-owned assets of their wealth to pay off those he recognised as allies. Under the violent political turnabouts the Sector had endured, first under Halton's shenanigans, then Lucia's misrule, the last of the Henrys, and now the diamond-hard Alia Kane; constant purgings of its ruling caste had occurred until all Liberty seethed with the dispossessed. And in such circumstances there had always been the need for scapegoats . . .

The new men who had risen up were insecure, watchful, and given to swift realignments in order to protect their positions. The man I seek may be Conroy's most confidential associate, Ito thought, a member of the House and a zealous Expansionist, but a year ago his name was unknown and a year from now he might be plotting rebellion against President Kane. Didn't he angle for my services when we met at the White House? Didn't he want to put me in his pay? He asked some pretty subtle questions that don't amount to much on paper, but the intention was real enough. He'll catch the unwary. But I'm not weak and I'm not greedy. I know my duty is to my own master, and I'll give that loyalty to one man alone. And to one woman.

He swore silently as the ground-car lurched in a pothole, his nearside scraping branches. He searched the darkness but there was nothing. He had swerved at shadows. Careful! It's on nights like this, after a long journey, twelve hundred miles by ground, that a man gets sloppy. He begins to think of his comfort and cuts corners, but I'm different because I was ninja-trained to despise comfort. And I make it my unbending rule to take elementary precautions. Which is why I'm alive and others are not.

Again he took the rental off the road and camouflaged it with foliage. He found a fence post and took out his skeleton keys and security sensor, taking readings from the network of invisible rays that scanned the area within the wall to calibrate and retune his neural implants. He made his way to where the wall backed onto the mansion's garages. He stared up at the circular tower, then pulled his black neck scarf up over his mouth and nose to soak up his steaming breath. The wall was ten feet high. At its foot he leapt and caught the top. Silently, with great strength, he pulled himself up the brickwork and dropped over into the yard. Rain drummed on the tile roofs of the outbuildings and dripped from the garage eaves. Inside he saw a pickup, two black sedans, and, on its own in a separate locked garage, a big gray air-car.

As he peered through the small window a glow of satisfaction surged through him and he smiled. Discipline, he thought. That's all it takes. Nine times out of ten no result, but every now and then . . .

The air-car they had tried to hide was a Bristol. An English luxury model. Very costly, and very rare in Amerika. Ito knew it could not belong at the Cassabian mansion. Then its sensors began to pan, sniffing him out, but were unsure, perhaps confused by the rain. A servant chauffeur woke up, rose in his seat, alerted by the car's behavior, and began to look about warily.

Ito ducked out of sight, his ninja implants screaming warnings into his nervous system. He lowered himself down, paused, listening, then left and crept back to his own car, blowing softly on his hands to dispel the cold. Then he swung back onto the road and drove on until he reached the gate.

A small, rectangular aperture opened in it, framing a thin, white servant face. Ito hated conversing with synthetic life.

"Who are you?" the face asked in an unnaturally flat voice.

"Jiro Ito, messenger to Secretary Lubbock, on official business."

"Where's your ID?"

A smart card was drawn from Ito's glove compartment and passed through. The small shutter closed. After a time the heavy gate began to swing open.

He was admitted by a man in a cape raincoat and hood. The chauffeur appeared and took his rental away, remarking on what a comfortable car the beat-up was. His overpowering pleasantness was typical of a servant. The Staff and Servant Division of the Halide Corporation had great technique but little imagination. Synthetic genes could be turned out any way a customer liked. The majority liked "submissive, honest, and hard to insult." The chauffeur was all three—plus security-conscious.

By the plastic whores of Disney World, Ito thought, they make my real, live, genuine flesh crawl with shivers. Have a nice, disposable life, you monstrous pink block of neutered gristle.

Then the house servant, Thomas, met him at the door: huge, slow-moving, powerful, drawling, and as stupid as a Chinese dumpling.

"Hello, sir. My name's Thomas. Can I be of assistance to you?"

"Announce me, Thomas."

"I can't do that, Mr. Ito . . ."

"Just do as I say."

Thomas looked dully past the windows of the vestibule and into the carpeted hallway. The dark plastic walls were cast in relief by electric light that spilled from what looked like original glass globes. The hall contained photo portraits and incredibly old items of furniture from Earth; Ito was taken by the superb veneer-and-chipboard table and bench seat, set conspicuously under the lamp holders. Five hundred years old if it was a day, and priceless. Shame about the Earth, Ito thought. All those legendary places and ancient treasures. And now . . . ?

A tragedy.

The servant banged the heavy door shut behind them but seemed to remain unconvinced that he should place Ito's instruction above his master's. Rainwater darkened the carpet, where it dripped from the corner of Ito's cape.

"He said no one was to disturb him. On no account."

"Yes," Ito said, barely controlling his irritation with the servant. "But he doesn't know that *I* am here."

Thomas turned his moon face away and began to slouch down the hall. Ito followed him. Wooden doors stood to his left, all furnished with stout panels and ornate iron mechanisms that bore the obsolete arms of the sheriff of Sweetwater, and, to his right, small diamond-leaded windows bowed and shivered in their frames as the rain lashed them. Thomas's light knock on the furthest door was rewarded by silence: the hum of conversation beyond had paused. Impatiently Ito tried the door handle. It was locked and would not move.

"Is that you, Ito?"

The voice was not entirely composed, a little irritated at the intrusion. Ito spoke up. "Forgive me, sir. I have an urgent message for you."

"Just a moment."

Seconds later, the door swung open revealing a brightly lit interior, warmed by a roaring wood fire. It was opened by a man of about forty years. He wore a black felt skullcap, an unpretentious jerkin with squared linen collar, and he sported a graying beard, clipped short. He was of medium height and light build, but he had piercing, dark brown eyes and a rich, soothing voice that revealed something of the qualities of mind that had carried him in a single year to a position of almost unparalleled influence in Amerika. Officially, until last year, Pharis Cassabian had been representative for Wyoming. Now, although he held no official post, he had good cause to lock his doors securely and point his sensors at the road with care. He had lately assumed control of Amerika's new Sector Intelligence Bureau and was now coordinator of a network of spies scattered throughout thc Ncutral Zone and even in Yamato itself.

"Thank you, Thomas, it's all right." Cassabian closed the door and turned to Ito. "Please sit down. It's an evil night and you're soaked."

"Thank you, sir."

Ito went over to one of two armchairs that had been pulled up close to the fire. As he sat down, a second door into the room opened, and a grotesque figure entered.

"Good news, I hope?" Timo Farren asked. The cipher expert remained in the draughty doorway, hesitant. He was an old man: bent, rheumy, and myopic. Ito shivered inwardly. Farren was malodorously diseased. Where the fleshy parts of his nose had eroded, the septum was exposed, but over the deformity he now wore a hollow platinium nose that made his voice ring incisively when he spoke. The bandaged, ravaged flesh of his hands was his greatest handicap, and by the way he held objects Ito judged there was no feeling at all in the stumps of his fingers where the infection had first attacked. The filthy perverted bastard.

"Good news, Mr. Farren. That depends on your point of view."

"Ah, well, bad news travels quickest. Isn't that so?"

"And always on the dirtiest of nights."

Farren watched the messenger sit down. Ito was in the flush of his manhood, virile, sturdy, and full of arrogance. Gloved and booted, he was clearly in command of his occupation, but Farren did not like him. He seemed always to be sneering. And he was disgusted by the leprosy, though he tried not to show it. You crude, untutored lout, Farren thought genially, you're out of the same military mold as Yamato's samurai. Paranoid maniacs, thrashing around madly, destroying, cutting civilisation to ribbons with your razor blades. Why does a man like Lubbock surround himself with men like you?

Cassabian offered the courier an expensive glass of beer, and Farren watched distastefully as Ito accepted it, then set it down unsipped.

Thank you, Mr. Cassabian, he could almost hear Ito thinking. *But I don't drink alcohol. Not even imported brew. I know that alcohol gives a man loose lips and I'm too goddamned clever to fall for that.*

Farren nodded at Cassabian as if to say, I told you so. The owner of the Cassabian mansion had sophisticated tastes. He was always mindful of small courtesies, he had a fine intellect, though unskilled in mathematics, was a fervent Expansionist and a powerful accumulator of allies. They had first met on London, in the years when Lucia Henry occupied the White House, fifteen years ago. As prudent men, they had both left Amerika at the start of her administration; Cassabian then a student, fresh from his studies at Yale College, Cambridge, and RISC, Timo Farren an angry fifty-year-old academic, late of Cambridge and RISC. They had planned to keep out of Amerika until such time as a more liberal President could be found for the Sector, and they had done so, traveling and traveling in every foreign Sector they could enter, Farren indulging a newly discovered masochistic sexual desire with any sadistic woman who would go to bed with him, Cassabian all the while spinning a delicate web of contacts and acquaintances. Finally they had come home for President Kane's inauguration ten years ago, and Farren had stayed close by his friend since then. The designer disease had never seemed to bother Cassabian.

Their recent associations with Conroy Lubbock had filled Farren with hope. Lubbock had long been chancellor of the Ivy League, and how dearly Farren would have loved to be installed in one of the prestige colleges to research the new mathematics that was presently unfolding. But there had been no professorial chair granted him. He had so far hoped in vain, his mathematical genius unrecognised within the gnarled carcass of a man who had inexplicably inflicted a ghastly disease on himself.

I shall wait, he thought. Wait and rot a little more. Soon I'll no longer be able to hold a pencil stub. But still the work these hands can do you'll think is worth a university sinecure soon enough, Conroy Lubbock. You'll see!

In five years together abroad in Known Space, he and Cassabian had visited Korea and Manchuria, Europa and Xanadu, the Chinese Empire, scores of planets, making hundreds of contacts. When, last year, Lubbock had been approached, they had been able to divulge to him the names, whereabouts, and current doings of all parties across the whole of Known Space who wished Amerika ill.

"So what bad news brings you here so urgently, Mr. Ito?"

"Some pretty bad news." The leather of Ito's boots steamed as he unbuttoned his jerkin. Strapped next to his heart was a wallet; inside that, one of Conroy Lubbock's distinctive smart envelopes.

"Real leather, eh, Mr. Ito? I shouldn't think they'd be as hard-wearing as flexiplex."

"I understood that certain modern technologies are banned on Wyoming."

"As you can see, we live very simply here."

"You have installed no modern equipment?"

"As you say, it's against the law."

"Your synthetic servants don't count?"

Cassabian shrugged. "Who's to say they're synthetic."

Ito's granite face hardened. He turned to Cassabian. "How did you know it was me at the door?"

"I beg your pardon?"

"I asked you how you knew it was me. Just now. Through a closed door?"

Cassabian took the smart envelope, examined the seals, and lowered himself into the second fireside chair, answering without looking up. "A man writes his signature in many ways, Mr. Ito. You have a certain brusque way with door handles."

The Cassabian mansion had been in the Cassabian family for forty years, and its owner was reluctant to leave it, despite its mounting upkeep and the inconvenience of its remoteness from Liberty. Cassabian had been born here, and knew every corner, every sound of each loose board, each crack in every worn stair. He had remarried a year ago, again to a widow. Ursula was a good wife and like his first had brought from her previous marriage two grown sons and a juicy check account, which was fortunate since Cassabian was not himself the owner of a large credit balance, and the maintenance of a private network of foreign contacts was an expensive undertaking.

He turned over the envelope again, opened it, and saw immediately that the information it contained was of the first order of importance. As he read, he decided that the situation it described was potentially ruinous for Amerika.

His mind flipped immediately into analytical mode. Can it be true? Has there really been a disaster? If not, who would want to make me think there has been? What vested interests would profit from a tale about a massacre? Which of the President's satellites would strengthen his or her position most as a result? Or could the letter be a forgery?

The fire spat a burning spark onto Jiro Ito's lap and he dashed it to the hearth with a quick movement.

"A *real* fire. I didn't realise!"

"Like I said: we try to keep it simple here, and lawful. What you see is what you get."

A significant detail about Ito's appearance caught Cassabian's attention momentarily and was quickly put to the back of his mind. He had met Ito twice and knew him to be dogged and determined, and above all physically tough. He possessed the best qualities of a sergeant, with just enough of an inquiring nature to make him useful in carrying back answers. If the message was important, Secretary of State Lubbock could know that short of death, whatever the circumstance, whatever the bribe, to give it into the care of Jiro Ito was like handing it personally to its intended reader.

But Ito was also vainglorious, and thought of himself as unsurpassed at hitching rides on tramp freighters and skulking round the various worlds of the Sector. Which was lately no longer true. Nevertheless, Ito was unswervingly Lubbock's man, a loyal servant. And the letter was certainly from Lubbock.

Then what about Lubbock? Does the secretary of state stand to gain in any way by lying? On the surface of it, he surely has most to lose. Lubbock has invested three hundred thousand credits in Hawken's expedition and, much more important, three years of painstaking foreign policy making—all of which could be plunged into doubt by this letter. True, Lubbock has begun to use my network, but it's possible he feels himself becoming overdependent on me. Perhaps he sees my Expansionist principles as an obstacle: too firm, too righteous—too extreme? So, do I trust Conroy Lubbock? Do I judge he trusts me? Do I still hold him to be Amerika's sole hope of deliverance? Yes, yes, and a third time yes! I can do nothing else. The dispatch has to be taken at face value.

"So? What is it?" Farren inquired gently.

"You should read it."

Farren took it and put on his eyeglasses. After a space he spoke again. "Josiah Hawken is dead?"

"If Sumitomo is to be believed."

"Lubbock clearly believes it. And Eli 'Billy' Hawken, on Liberty—he will believe it too, when he hears tomorrow that his brother is dead, all his nexus ships burned, and four hundred personnel atomised by beam weapons. No jollies for him—or us—this Christmas."

"Premature, Timo."

"Ah! You mean you don't believe it?"

"I didn't say that."

Farren cackled. "How much did you have in the venture?"

"A small sum."

"Then beware wishful thinking. Do you think Sumitomo would make up such a tale?"

Cassabian did not answer. Sumitomo, the Yamato bank, were represented on Liberty by Sumitomo Nomura himself, but the source of this intelligence was their executive Yi To Man, a Korean who had come from the Neutral Zone to the Amerikan fringe planet of Puerto Rico some days ago.

"Mr. Ito? What do you think of Yi To Man?"

"A Korean. And probably as damnable a liar as any of them."

"But capable of the truth—for a consideration?"

"I paid him well, and I think he spoke the truth to me, and to Secretary Lubbock."

"The truth as he knows it?"

"He said that Yamato was on fire with the news of the daimyo of Sado's handiwork. Yamato isn't calling it treachery. They say that the Neutral Zone aurium fleet has safely sailed for the Yamato Home Worlds after Hawken tried to destroy it in a surprise attack. The rumor is they want a trade embargo imposed on Amerika."

"Hah!" Farren scratched at his armpit. His face was like a pudding, a kneaded, moldering mass on which silver whiskers had sprouted. He was grinning. "All Yamato rumors get bigger by the hour! And let's not forget that if Sumitomo can exaggerate the matter to their advantage, they will certainly do so. Why shouldn't they? Their main interest lies in undermining Amerikan trade. They make big profits on every freighter Amerikan Lines operates. That's where the biggest profits are. It might look like an independent banking corporation, but Sumitomo's directly under the control of the Yamato government. Now, if Yamato is accusing Hawken of piracy—"

Ito twisted round. "If Hawken is dead and his fleet destroyed, no one will be able to refute that allegation. It's a perfect pretext and the door to the Neutral Zone can be slammed in Amerika's face completely. The Empire of Yamato has been looking for a means to strangle us for years. If they close the Neutral Zone to all traffic, there will be chaos and panic on Liberty. Amerikan corporations will be ruined, Amerikan goods will cease production, and Yamato will have lost nothing except a trade competitor."

Cassabian closed his eyes and leaned back, lacing his fingers tightly. "I don't know. I believe Sumitomo are deliberately passing on false information to panic the Amerikan credit markets."

Farren answered: "They might have achieved just that. If you ask me there's a crash ahead like we've never seen."

Cassabian shook his head. He cursed Farren's masochistic delight, and also the slow suspicion that was growing in his own mind. He tried to suppress his rising excitement.

"By God, Timo! Don't you realise, we could be talking about war?"

"A war in the Neutral Zone? You reckon that'll happen?" Farren's voice rose with derision. "Sure! Baron Harumi's murdering hordes are just waiting to flood into the nexi."

"Come on! Our Mr. Ito here may be right. This could be the excuse they've been waiting for. Military annexation of the entire Neutral Zone. Forcible exclusion of all non-Yamato shipping—exactly as they've done with Yamato itself these past fifty years. Why not? Yamato could do it."

Farren laughed shortly. "Hawken's okeh. I don't believe a word of that bullshit."

"Why don't you take the message at face value?" Ito said darkly. "Maybe there *has* been a disaster. Yi's words seemed to be spoken honestly. He gave details—the itineraries of Hawken's ships, the names of captives imprisoned at Niigata—just as if they had been set down by the daimyo's own hand. The timing's right. Two months and one week is a good crossing from Sado, but Yamato dispatch ships can be very fast."

"No." Cassabian fell silent again, then he stood up and began to pace. What game are they playing? he asked himself. What is Yamato about? And Sumitomo? They're just as samurai as the Emperor's government, and a hundred times more dangerous at the moment. Using leverage gained from loans made all over Known Space, Sumitomo has infiltrated all the Sector governments there are. They maintain agents in every port, spies on every ship, and servants in every significant household, and since the time of the Edict, merchant bankers like Sumitomo and Yasuda have grown fabulously rich by financing the Central Authority's terraforming program.

The legendary Bank of Sumitomo could defeat any army, they could make invincible any fleet of ships, prop up any sham government. Their wealth could hire the most proficient mercenary soldiers and their bribes could unlock the doors of any fortress. It was Sumitomo who had secured the election of two complete Central Authority councils and smoothed the way for the accession of Emperor Mutsuhito, and it was Sumitomo that continued to mortgage the wealth of the Empire.

Cassabian sat down again, and the courier stirred, warmed now by the decaying fire.

"If you're hungry, I'll ask Thomas to bring you a piece of pumpkin pie. You've got a long trip ahead."

Ito sighed, but roused himself and sat up, scrubbing at his head. "No. No thank you. Is there a message of reply to the secretary?"

"Yes."

Cassabian asked Thomas to have Ito's ground-car brought out, then he told Farren to find his pen and began to dictate slowly. Farren's nib scratched rapidly across the paper a sequence of numbers recalled with faultless precision directly from memory. It was checked, sealed with Cassabian's security code, and handed over in a matter of seconds.

"Give Conroy this, and tell him he ought to use module sixteen of the red protocol to crack it."

Ito got up and put the letter into his pouch, and the pouch back in his pocket. Then he left. As the door closed on him, Farren looked to Cassabian.

"So you intend to counsel patience?"

Cassabian nodded. "Without doubt. There is little to be gained from an incautious move now."

"But the news will be all over Liberty tomorrow!"

"That's why it's imperative we get to the markets first. I want our people to put about an alternative story: that Hawken landed secretly in—better make it Delaware—a week ago with an aurium cargo so rich that he's looking for a way of disposing of it before paying duty and coming into Amerikan Revenue jurisdiction. The story must be passed along with an embroidered Japanese tale that his ships have been blown up, so the Sumitomo rumor may be dismissed as a jealous lie. That will keep the markets in flux for a week or two."

"Next, we'll make it quietly known in Harrisburg and Norfolk and the other Liberty aprons that all shipping should watch for Yamato vessels attempting to use the Neutral Zone in convoy. Any found by Amerikan Navy vessels must be intercepted immediately. Any found by armed freighters ought to be —let's say 'politely investigated.' "

Farren's face puckered. "You expect to see a convoy?"

"I think so, five or six ships, fast, small, probably out of a Yamato port and making for Guam. That's what we should look for. Under no circumstances must such a convoy be allowed to reach its destination."

"I don't follow—"

Cassabian silenced him impatiently and began ticking off the points on his fingers. "Firstly, Baron Harumi has one million samurai troops in the Neutral Zone. They cost money to maintain. Sure, I know they'd volunteer to go without pay tomorrow if Harumi asked them to, but they still have to eat. A million samurai consume a vast amount, Timo. How can Baron Harumi keep his iron fist closed on the Neutral Zone if he can't feed his troops?"

Farren made to interrupt, but Cassabian stayed him with a sharp gesture and continued. "Secondly, by the greatest good fortune early attempts to terraform in the Neutral Zone weren't always so accomplished. Three of the four main strategic systems where Harumi's men are billeted, Lombok, Guam, and Marshall II, are desert worlds. They don't grow rice and they don't farm seafood.

Very few species have been introduced and they hardly support the few settlers who carve a living there. On the other hand, the fourth world, Marshall I, is almost all ocean. Just a few specks of land and the sea cut with heavy metal salts. So no natural food whatsoever."

"So," Farren said, "there are just two ways in which food can reach them: either by bulk convoy from offworld—which is a fabulously expensive alternative—or by using the system they've always used."

Cassabian nodded, knowing that Farren meant food synthesis through the many variants of the Dover process. Instant fresh ham salad on rye from a pint of water and a few handfuls of whatever rock might be available, he thought. We're so used to it, it seems the most natural thing in the world. But there weren't always Dover synth units. A horn of plenty at the touch of a button—but only *if* you have the dimethyl aurium to make the Dover process catalyse the proteins and fats you need. Once aurium fails to arrive, Yamato's plans sink.

Cassabian's mind snapped back to his line of reasoning. "Thirdly, we know that the Emperor raises funds with Chinese banks on surety of aurium arriving at Sado. Those same bankers are now well aware of the progress of the aurium en route from Sado. There is no guarantee that the shipment will reach Yamato's Home Worlds, but the aurium fleet has left Sado, so the most hazardous part of its journey is already complete. The risk is therefore good. Good enough for the banks to extend their best customer any sum of credit he cares to name. Mutsuhito has the soul of an accountant. I believe I know his mind well enough to predict that he's already dispatched the exact amount of refined dimethyl aurium required to feed Harumi's troops for the next six months."

Farren gasped. "At two thousand cals per man, per day, and a million troops, that's plenty of chicken soup, Pharis. Maybe a thousand gallons of catalyst. Four or five ships to share the mass, and the burden of risk in jumping the nexi. A convoy will be faster than one ponderous heavy freighter. They could arrive in Guam anytime during the next few weeks!"

"It's vital they are found and taken—as a retaliation."

"So you *do* think Hawken has been destroyed."

We may yet cause the Emperor the agony he deserves, Cassabian thought. If the ships under the President's orders can arrest Harumi's aurium, and if I can persuade Conroy to take a strong diplomatic line by demanding the release of the hostages held in Niigata, we might seize and retain the initiative for months!

He moved to the window and touched the polariser. Through the crystal panes he could see the forecourt and Ito's cowled figure swinging into his groundcar.

"Yes, maybe," he said. "We've got cause to plan hard, Timo. If Baron Harumi's troops are supplied, there will be a potential invasion force already assembled in the Neutral Zone. His samurai are crack assault troops. I've no doubt at all that if they were this side of the Boundary, on Oregon or any of the planets of the Kalifornian system, they'd be walking up the steps of the White House come Sunday afternoon with their ancestral swords drawn."

A tremor passed over Farren's face. His hand twitched so that he dropped his pen. He scowled. "Yeah, but they're not across the Boundary yet; they're five light-years away from Kalifornia. That means at least one nexus jump."

"And in that alone may lie our deliverance."

Cassabian went from window to door, the one from which Farren had appeared. He opened it and passed through into the next room. From there he went to the next again, to where his wife practiced classical ballet at a wall rail.

"He's gone."

Ursula was a tall woman, magnificent, approaching forty. She had dismissed both of her visiting dancing instructors two hours ago, but still went over the graceful movements time and again, anxious to make them perfect.

She shivered theatrically, sweat spangling her face and exposed chest. "That man is the very devil incarnate."

"Perhaps, my dear, but Amerika depends on men like Ito."

"Well, then. I'd call that regrettable."

The room was mirrored to above head height with mirrors edged in carved scrollwork and decorative beading that hid an invisible force field in the second panel from the door. The mirror rippled, like a pool of mercury now under Cassabian's knowledgeable hands. It was one of the snoop-proof hiding places that had been built into the house during Lucia Henry's murderous crusade, a bolt hole for the various covert Expansionists whom his mother, Zelka, had encouraged during the witch-hunts. As the surface dissolved, an interior, a dark space not quite two feet wide, appeared between the double walls. Ursula had shown the guest where to hide and had pushed her reproduction antique piano in front of it. It was impossible for the occupant to have overheard anything of the conversation with Ito.

"It's OK, the danger's passed. You can come out now, Otis."

The figure who appeared from the darkness was Otis le Grande. In his mid-thirties, tall, dark-haired with long moustaches which slanted down to his jaw each side of a Zappa tab. His clothing was exceptionally plain, the plainest clothes Cassabian had ever seen him wear, but still of conspicuously fine quality. To have come here with his Bristol air-car, ignoring the prohibition, had been a piece of Carolina vanity, the kind of thing a man as rich as le Grande might do out of pure ego.

Despite his wait, le Grande had maintained his dignity. He bowed and smiled charmingly at Ursula. "For the trouble you've taken to safeguard my anonymity, I thank you kindly, madam."

Cassabian found himself regretting again that le Grande had not been more security-conscious. How could a man reputedly so skilled at political deceptions, and able to disarm the President almost at will, have been so careless?

Ursula smiled, taken by le Grande's stately manners. "You honored our home, sir, by coming here. It's the very least we can do."

"You realise that before the end of the week Conroy Lubbock will know you've been here?" Cassabian said, frowning.

"Oh? How?"

"The air-car was a mistake."

"You let him see my car?" le Grande asked, astounded, as he was conducted back to the room where Farren waited.

"I don't doubt that he saw it. Conroy's courier is a careful man. He's ninja-trained. I understand he carries poison implants in case he needs to silence himself, and he has another to drive him on day and night until his heart bursts if need be. It's like a second system of endocrine glands that dumps synthetic hormones into his bloodstream. If he finds himself in trouble, he can summon up fantastic physical strength and endurance just by meditating."

"You don't say."

"I do say. That black getup he wears isn't just for show, you know."

"I understand that on Liberty they call Jiro Ito 'the Crow,' " Ursula said, toweling herself.

Cassabian sighed. "I saw faint green stains on his jerkin. At first, I didn't notice them. Then, when I did, they puzzled me. I finally realised what they were—the wall. It's mossy because of the rain we get here. Ito's been sneaking around. He saw your air-car. You can bet on that, Otis."

Color rose visibly in le Grande's face. "Maybe you should have hidden it better. If Lubbock finds out I came here, we're both in big trouble!"

Yes, Cassabian thought. Conroy loathes your innocent manner and resents your wealth and the way the President confides in you. He thinks you're an unreliable opportunist, and he's tried on at least two occasions to revive the story that you murdered your wife. He'll continue to hound and isolate you until you've followed the rest of your clan into the political boneyard. You can rely on that, le Grande.

"I'd say I have more to fear than you do from Lubbock's knowledge of our meeting, Otis."

"Oh?"

"Well—you're probably Amerika's wealthiest private individual. You can protect yourself from Lubbock. But I'm just an unofficial advisor. Which of us do you think has most to fear?"

"Conversely, I've got more than you all to lose. If Lubbock hears that we've been talking, we're both in the nexus cusp."

Cassabian noted the way le Grande's tone had hardened. Had he begun to suspect duplicity?

"You know that Conroy despises you? He thinks you're in league with the VP."

"Whereas you seem to have become his bosom buddy." Le Grande's eyes narrowed. "Lubbock is a danger to us all. President Kane isn't safe so long as he's prowling around the White House."

"I guess your plans are well advanced in that regard?"

Le Grande adopted a puzzled look. "What do you mean?"

"You and Halton Henry have settled a pact against Lubbock."

"A pact?" The question was echoed with disarming innocence.

Cassabian smiled. "The astrogator who feels a psi-storm building in a nexus is a fool if he makes no corrections for the safety of his ship."

Again that incredible blankness. "You're talking in riddles, Mr. Cassabian."

That's for the safety of my own ship, Cassabian thought. We both know why you're here. Lucia Henry's arrival in Liberty threatens you just as it does the President. If the President should die, Halton Henry will succeed her, and you'll be out. You'll have lost all your power and influence. Unless . . .

"Otis, if you want my help, you're going to have to level with me."

Le Grande looked aside at Farren, who had retired to a corner and seemed oblivious to them, engrossed in a spreadsheet hologram. His disgust was more intense than Ito's had been.

"I can't speak with that here."

Farren sat up prissily. "What Pharis Cassabian knows, I know. Automatically. We confide everything."

Ursula smiled at le Grande. "You came here to discuss Lucia Henry, didn't you?"

Le Grande hesitated. "Yes, I did."

"Then go ahead, and don't worry that my husband lets his wife and associate listen in. Timo's right. When he says we're Pharis's confidants, that's exactly what we are."

Lucia Henry had virtually inherited the presidency from her strong father, Stratford Henry, but her ruinous mismanagement of the economy and her abandonment of her father's Expansionist ideals had cost her her popularity. She had been forced to relinquish the presidency ten years ago by Alia Kane, whose pro-Expansionist views were well known.

Lucia Henry had lost a confidence vote and had been forced to resign. But Kane could not have done it without the help of Lucia's brother, Halton Henry, and in gratitude, Alia Kane had appointed him vice-president. Everyone had seen it as Halton's own bid for power, his obsessive need to outplay his older sister overcoming family loyalty. It was shabby, but it worked. He had bought the number two position in Amerika by selling out his own sister's presidency to Alia Kane.

Lucia had left Liberty, retiring to her vast estates on Nevada, but now she was back, and it had begun to look like a deal had been struck between Halton and his sister.

I wonder what precisely is going on, Cassabian thought. Whatever it is, Alia Kane has got to be protected. That's unavoidable. If she falls, it's a domino endgame: Expansionism falls. The Isolationists take back power. The Neutral Zone gets surrendered in its entirety to Yamato. If that happens, the Amerikan Sector will have lost. It would be dismembered and absorbed into the Greater Yamato Co-prosperity Sphere within ten years.

"I hear the President's getting pretty uncomfortable," he said.

Le Grande braced himself and spoke. "I want to help secure her position. I believe Lucia Henry can be run off Liberty. I want to impeach Halton Henry for treason. But I want to know what support I can expect before I start out on that."

I bet you do, Cassabian thought. He knew that any influence over the President's authority was minimal. Only through the judicious manipulation of funds could anyone hope to direct Alia Kanc's hand, and it had been her policy to enrich the presidency with private capital so that funds voted through Congress were unnecessary for the prosecution of her favorite policies. He said, "Alia doesn't want to take Lucia on directly. Why should she when she has the presidency to lose?"

"Because Lucia is a threat to the President's security. No doubt about that. In the Kalifornia system there are plenty of Isolationists who regard Alia as Satan, and Lucia as the true upholder of the Amerikan way. Half the Isolationists want to see Alia Kane appease Yamato; the rest want nothing less than Lucia Henry back in the White House. Alia has to act."

"I'm sorry, Otis. I don't think she'll play that game."

"If she wants evidence of Lucia's attitude, she doesn't have to look far. All Lucia Henry's speeches indicate that she hasn't given up hope of moving back into the White House one day. Most of Alia's people regard her as dangerous. What more does she need?"

"Halton Henry is Amerika's vice-president. As such he stands to step straight into power if anything happens to Alia Kane. Why should Lucia help put Halton in the White House after what he did to her?"

"The reason Alia won't move against Lucia no matter what she does is that Yamato sees Lucia as their woman. While she's a credible prospect Yamato can play the waiting game. They know that once she becomes President they've won. If Lucia is broken, Yamato will give up its plans to take Amerika by puppetry. They'll have to do it by force."

As le Grande absorbed that, Cassabian considered the alarm he felt as dispassionately as he could. Why was le Grande allowing him, and therefore almost certainly Lubbock, to hear his thinking? The pretext that he had come merely to canvass opinions on his plan to impeach the VP was utterly transparent. Perhaps he thinks I'll carry the plan to Lubbock and in so doing expose the secretary to attack. It is no secret that le Grande hates Conroy, but does he have the nerve to go against the President? He's her lapdog. He draws his power and prestige from her alone. The moment she's gone, he'll be cut to pieces.

Cassabian felt his palms dampen as he made the connection. The heightening threat of war with Yamato. An invasion force massed in the Neutral Zone. The arrival of the despicable Lucia Henry. And now le Grande's unscrupulous twisting. In Cassabian's powerful mind it had all suddenly begun to make coherent and terrifying sense.

16

THE NEUTRAL ZONE, BETWEEN NAURU AND PALMYRA

"They say that space whales are sensitive to the nexi, Captain."

Ellis Straker stirred from his doom-laden thoughts at the helmsman's words. He had not slept for twenty-four hours, wanting to see the *Richard M.* through this new crisis despite his tiredness and hunger. The hours on the bridge had finally brought him to a decision, but they had done little to improve his foreboding humor about Palmyra's Aleph-Three-Oh nexus.

"What's the matter, Brophy? Lost your nerve?"

"Only trying to help, sir."

"Your best hope is to attend to your own duties and leave the astrogating to me."

"Sir."

The entire crew was in a terrible state: shuffling, gray-faced skeltons. Most who had come through the Sado nexus were dead already; the rest were starving or stricken with the same fever that had attacked the commodore. The very strangeness of infectious disease had terrified them all; epidemics had not happened for three hundred years in Amerika, but without medical support they were powerless to resist the one that had broken out now. It had come from the ship's rats.

Ellis steadied himself and watched the forward scanners of the *Richard M.*'s bridge showing up the relativistic blue image of the star they were rushing towards. The last nexus had irised wide for them, its probability Index very low. It had let them transit smoothly down a soft gradient, but the price they had paid was an extremely low exit velocity. Nauru aleph null had spat them out at only 0.01 cee, ensuring that they would have to overuse the big primary engines to accelerate to the necessary speed to hit Palymra Aleph-Three-Oh with transit momentum. A constant acceleration of one hundred gee would see them up at 0.9 cee in three days six hours. The fields used to stabilise the interior of the ship used up a lot of power at one hundred gee. Without that, everything contained within the plex hull would be mashed into tinfoil and strawberry jam. Both stabilisers were virused and heavily bypassed already.

He stifled a sigh and felt himself drifting.

The forward scanners had been showing the herd of space whales for most of those three days—great tubes of living tissue a mile long that cruised some systems sweeping up debris with the vast lobes of their maw magnetic fields. They fed sparsely but continuously, converting ingested material into flesh, getting ever bigger, living like comets in vastly elongated orbits, diving in towards the primary star from time to time to experience summer warmth and perhaps to breed. They were masterpieces of bioengineering, with a vast but bovine intelligence so some said, freed from the aging process so others said, immortal and eerie and infinitely gentle. They were certainly able to communicate between themselves and to intelligently correct their courses by expelling jets of gas, and certainly provided a service to nexus ship operators by vacuuming huge quantities of dangerous material from systems. Some had been discovered thousands of astronomical units from their primaries, on hyperbolic orbits that seemed destined to eventually carry them across interstellar space the hard way in a great dreaming migration.

"I heard they were the work of the Adventer scientist Colkin," Brophy said to Bowen painfully, seeing Ellis watching the herd with a trance-like gaze. "They say he spent his life cruising Known Space in a one-man ship, seeding them in every system he visited. Incredible, ain't it? That such a thing could grow from something the size of a hot dog."

"Brophy, will ya shut up about food?" Bowen said briskly, his tough good humor sustaining him and raising the spirits of all those on the bridge.

By the monitor stack, two of the duty watch were in desperation over the herd which cruised blissfully ahead. Their dogged levity tinged with the lassitude of death.

"But don't you see? If we could capture one, we could eat it!"

"I never heard of that, Lunk."

"Don't mean it can't be done. Just think of it. Juicy space whale steaks! Huge platter-fillers with gravy and sauce and all the trimmings!"

"I'll wring your goddamned neck, Lunk. So help me!"

"Jeezus! Look at that sucker blow off!"

Simultaneous blasts of gas jetted from each of the herd, fine-tuning their orbit with beautiful precision.

"See, ya crazy lummock. They're getting the hell out of here now you said that. Probably read your mind."

"What a life, eh? Farting your way round space!" Infinite regret filled Lunk's voice. "I guess we were too close to the nexus anyways."

There was a pause, then Brophy said, "I don't like their course correction. Do you think it's maybe sign of a psi-storm in Palmyra Aleph-Three-Oh, sir?"

Bowen muttered. "The best sign of a psi-storm is the look on the astrogator's face."

Ellis's voice cut at them from above. "Keep your thoughts to yourself in my hearing, Bowen."

"Aye, Captain." Privately his eyebrows rose, saying, See what I mean?

"General order to the ship: clear for transit. Alert condition one. And stand by for coordinates, Brophy."

"Aye." Brophy's reply was toothless and indistinct. His mouth was festering with black sores—none of them had eaten at all for many days—nevertheless he got about his business. Ellis knew that if they were hit by one more psi-storm they would break up, and if the Index dropped they would starve. It had become his habit never to lie to himself, whatever the circumstances, and he had known for three days that they could not possibly reach the Amerika Sector on a straight run. That was why he had ordered the change of course.

The webbings and braces were made secure, and he saw to it that the mass distribution was corrected. An hour to go to transit. He remoted the helm control and went down to the ship's center of gravity and locked himself into the astrogator's chamber to prepare himself meditatively for the coming ordeal.

He allowed his mind to run through its most obtrusive concerns prior to clearing it for the transit. After Sado they had rapidly run out of things to eat. One by one, all living things had been caught and stewed, then the pangs in their bellies had driven some into the bilges to hunt down shipneys. The name was a corruption of the Japanese word *ne;* a specialty in times of famine aboard a stranded nexus ship. When skinned, topped, and tailed and cooked in pepperwater, they tasted like chicken, but on a starvation ship they were scrawny and stringy and lacking in meat, and a rat was a rat all the same.

"Amerikan crews have stomachs strong enough to eat horseshoes," Hawken had told Ellis once in better times. Hunger made anything sweet. And when on this passage Ellis had watched an older hand showing a younger how to render down paper with the last dregs of dimethyl aurium in the Dovers and extract agar-like sustenance from organic fabrics such as silk and wool and cotton, he had remembered Hawken's words. Ensign Vander had sung of his fantasy. "When I gets my credits away, I'm gonna have myself one helluva day: a congressman's breakfast, a sumo wrestler's lunch, a purser's dinner, and a bowl of punch. Chug-a-lug-a-lug to wash it all down. I'm gonna get so drunk in Lincoln town!"

But he had died a week later and he had left a pitiful note weaved in the strings of his violina saying that they could have his credit and take his big day out instead.

Ellis thanked God for his constitution. He had been overmuscled while they had traded. Too much good living and too much respect for his past not to lend a hand on all physical tasks had given him plenty to spare.

He had always been keen to do everything himself, no matter how arduous. If that was his failing as an officer, Hawken had put him right. "Keep yourself a bit more aloof from your men, Ellis. Give them a chance to show you what they can do by themselves. Jump in like that when you're commanding a ship and your crew won't thank you for it." It had been like that on the *Dwight D.* Days of vigilance and giving orders. He had become the mind of his ship, tightening a schedule here, slackening off a rota there, finely tuning her organisation like the strings of the ensign's violina so that the ship ran tight and happy.

That was being captain: a comfortable suit to wear, a suit of responsibility patched with old errors, and it had been experience with the Amerikan Merchant Adventurers, cruising short runs across the Sector to Virginia, that had given him those early trials, and later, on his first Neutral Zone voyage, when he had first supervised a trans-Sector nexus ship and lost his first crewman to a stupid airlock accident, he had learned again. He could remember it clearly, seared onto his mind like a criminal's brand. There was nothing he could have done, but it had not stopped him blaming himself. The old lessons had come the full circle of experience. He had remembered then the day that he had been caught drowsing on watch, years before. It was rare and unlooked for and memorable because of it. Ayrton Rodrigo had cuffed him and treated him to a tongue-lashing, then he had said something he had never forgotten. Never let boredom get at you, Ellis. A good ship's officer is never bored. And if he is, then his mind's where a shipowner can't afford it. At the time, he had felt the threat cut into him, then wondered what else Ayrton had meant. Then the days had never been long enough, when he was seventeen.

The *Thomas Jefferson* had been a big ship with plenty to occupy a person who was prepared to seek work out. There had been deck upon deck of her, four in the huge fore section alone, and he had made it his business to acquaint himself with every inch. Before his day she had been one of the ships in Amerika's Navy that had repulsed the Chinese in the Alaska system, when the *Theodore Roosevelt* had turned turtle and split. It had been the *Thomas J.* and her sister ship the *Loomis McKecknie* that had tried to salvage her, but that had been a task beyond her, and the Navy ship had been abandoned forever.

He had learned and learned, assiduously, every day, until he thought he knew everything that made a captain, but it was only when he had put on Ayrton Rodrigo's helmet aboard *Dwight D.* that he had discovered command was something beyond learning. He had had cause to remember the hundreds of small lessons an excellent astrogator had taught him about that, and he had understood that the rest was down to him.

A half hour to go to injection. He shifted his weight in the command chair, watching the patterns in the visualiser swirl fitfully and thinking of Hawken.

The commodore had fallen into a decline and the disease lingered in him. He was still unable to stand. Even though the vermin fever had broken, it had left him weak and covered in sores. In the next few days, Ellis knew, he would either gain strength or the malady would kill him. Perhaps that was what Hawken wanted. He had reached his limit and lost hope, and that ultimately was what invited Death to call on some and not on others.

"By God," he said quietly. "We are going home."

Since the Sado nexus and the passing of the *Richard M.* beyond the last dangerous psi-effects of that system and into deep space, he had tried to put hunger out of his mind by keeping himself engrossed in the minutiae of the ship. Concentration was a powerful weapon against pain, and only those who could master themselves could hope to master a nexus ship. Though he had eaten no more than any of *Richard M.*'s crew, he had stayed strong because he had been economical with his exertion, had slept in a deep state that conserved energy, had rationed his consumption strictly, had refused the pitiful offal that passed among the crew, and because he had needed to prove himself worthy to be their captain.

"Six-oh-six-decimal-nine-five-seven, green. Five minutes to transit."

Brophy's voice grated on the talkback. "Six-oh-six-decimal-nine-five-seven, green, sir."

"Lock in."

"Locked in, sir."

As the helmsman complied weakly, the coordinates appeared and the ship's angle of attack veered minutely. He felt the psi coursing through his spine. A complex pattern, churning like a maelstrom. Though he used all his concentration he could not accomplish the solution. Hunger was obtrusive in him and Ellis had to adjust the oxygen level in the chamber. He put his weight on the foot bar, enriching the mix.

"Helm's off!"

He felt the *Richard M.*'s course drifting once more into the eye of the nexus. Brophy's gritty voice shouted over the singing in his ears. "Four-two, four-two. Velocity kick coming. Ready to let go!"

The power of the engines forward of the ship's center of gravity slackened. As soon as the indicators began to touch, they felt the buffeting, then she came right, and the second-order correction was made.

A hollow sound filled Ellis's head. The helmet sang flat in his ears. The chamber felt cold as death.

Not quite good enough.

She's come to within a point, the rational part of Ellis's mind told him, looking into the indicator display that burst with a gorgeous visualisation. Feedback from his own mind amplified his talent. He could see he wasn't performing well at all, and that doubt too fed on itself, threatening to blow the transit until he savagely disciplined his thoughts. Damn it! She's within three points now, and dragging her belly as if she's full of lead. He watched the Index vibrating on the big indicator—eddies making the fabric of the ship shake and shudder noisily.

"Off forward main!"

Brophy repeated the order to the ragged remnants of the bridge crew and the shaking stopped, but still he was unsatisfied. At the best of times the *Richard M.* was liable to sternway, and he eased the attack into feathering so that tidal forces acting on the starboard side of the hull pushed her stern back to optimum. The bastard Index was falling off.

Great bursts of hologram white dashed up out of the visualiser and across the chamber like ectoplasm, alarming him at the last minute. He sweated coldly. His body strained, his teeth gritting into the safety gumshields. Sinews stood out on his neck as he felt the way. The ship's velocity was falling off rapidly, and when the after engines began to bite he heard the distant word given by Brophy, "Ten seconds! And good luck."

From his position, deep in the ship's belly, his talent surged loose. That necessary state descended over his mind and coalesced like something concrete. He became one with the ship.

He felt the computer surveying the ship rationally, trying to recalculate a final escape course should he command an abort. It was academic. No abort was possible now. The *Richard M.*'s fate was locked, her probability already set. The nexus was a bastard, but he was equal to it.

Blood dripped from his nostrils. He screamed. And then they were all in dream time.

When they came through, he was slicked with sweat. The decelerators were performing like darlings—one hundred gee and not a complaint from the stabilisers. Tinfoil and strawberry jam, he thought again. He watched the helm drifting and ordered Bowen up to give the helmsman a hand. He cleaned up as best he could with tight water. Then he went aft to Hawken's cabin.

The commodore's eyes were yellowed, his pallor grim.

"Where are we, Ellis?"

"Korea."

"What system? How far in?"

Ellis breathed deeply and bent over the terminal, exhaustion crushing him. "Six or seven AU, good enough to make orbit."

Hawken struggled to sit up. "No. You'll not take my ship to Seoul! The Koreans won't—"

"Not Seoul, Cheju Do."

"Cheju Do?" Hawken's voice was breathy, as if his mind was half in trance.

"The Index is against us as it has been all the way from Sado. We can't run directly home."

Cheju Do was a system in the Korean quadrant, that part of the quadrant that Yamato had claimed some years ago. It contained two inhabited planets, Cheju itself and Mokp'o, the totally isolated Sun Myung Moon religious colony. But there were sometimes Amerikan traders on the apron at Cheju, ships like the *Richard M.* that plied the short chains. There they might just find help.

"Do you know what day it is, Commodore?"

Hawken slumped back. "No."

"Christmas Day."

"Christmas?"

"Yeah," he replied bleakly. "Season's greetings to you, Commodore."

He went below into the ship's guts and sent Ingram and Bonetti, the men who had been taken off the gee stabiliser work, back to their drudgery, but Ingram turned on him with five other crew and reported that during the day the stabilisers had shown fresh signs of failing.

His anger was on a knife edge. "We're fighting and losing. The whole bag of shit's fucked."

Ellis listened to the fear in Ingram's voice, saw the unspoken question on every man's face. *What are you going to do, Captain?* It was a question that had no ready answer. He had gone below and seen the mass of bypass equipment that surrounded the essential modules, and had felt each discontinuity in acceleration grow more sluggish and difficult to compensate. Like Hawken himself, many of the crew had fallen to the fever. Each day another marble-gray corpse had been rolled stiff from its strap hammock and carried to the chutes. Some days there were none, others three or four; last week, with the oxygen low, they had begun dying so fast it was hard to keep count. With barely thirty crew left to handle the ship—crew weak from starvation, or whose guts were bleeding over faster than water could be brought to them—Ellis knew that their chances of survival were now thin. Half the crew had already been driven close to madness. They did no work, they did not sleep, but starved and wasted and stared. There was only one way to fight it, and that was by discipline.

A voice came into his head.

"Put your crew first. Be good to them," Ayrton Rodrigo told him. His first psi-tutor whispered back across the years as he watched his people hollowed-eyed and staring, demanding his explanation. "Give them your respect, always treat them like you wanted to be treated when you were a rating. Even the lousiest of them. Save their lives, because they alone stand between you and your grave."

"It's bad seepage caused by engine overburn on the last nexus," Ellis said. "But I've looked at it and it'll hold until we get to Cheju."

He sounded confident, but the deputation remained. Ingram's question was direct. "Where are we now, Captain? We're losing that stabiliser."

Bonetti was in utter despair. "She won't last another day. Cheju's too far away!"

"She'll hold. I promise you," he lied.

"How's that? Because you tell us so? Because you've got a *feeling* about it?"

"Listen, Ingram—"

"No! *You* listen, Captain!"

Ellis controlled his temper. "Get about your work. We'll keep *Richard M*. cruising. A week is all we need."

"A week?"

"Cheju Do. A few AU from the next nexus."

"We can make planetfall on Mokp'o! With the Index against us we can get there tomorrow!"

Ellis's voice dropped to a growl. "You're not astrogating the *Richard M*., Ingram."

"She's fucked, I tell you! She was rotten with virus before we put down on Sado!"

"Let's make for Mokp'o, eh, Captain? That's best, eh?" Bonetti pleaded, his eyes bulging from his head.

"He's right, Captain!

"Yeah! It's that or die!"

"Well, Captain?" Ingram said.

Ellis flared with anger. For days he had known that the bypasses of the *Richard M*.'s starboard stabiliser were in a critical condition. It was jury-rigged and nothing more could be done about it. He also knew that it was essential to make Ingram and the rest of them believe the stabilisers would hold and that they could still get home. I'll make them believe, he swore inwardly. I'll make them take this shit bucket home despite themselves. And no filthy nexus rat is going to tell me how or where to take any ship that I command!

"You want to go to Mokp'o, eh?"

"Sure, we do. We all do!"

"You want to spend the rest of your lives toiling in a state of brainwash?"

Mention of the religious slavery where prisoners minds were broken by repetitive labor and detained forever filled them with confusion. The woman behind Ingram shrank back visibly.

"Remember that Korean ship we rendezvoused with at Bunguran?"

Ingram shifted his weight. "Jeezus, Captain, even that's better than starvation! I'm tired of trying."

"Like I thought, it's not the stabiliser that's bothering you. You're quitting! What waits for you on Mokp'o, Ingram, is ten thousand times worse than anything on this ship. Do you want to go to that? They're maniacs. They'll burn your mind out and take your soul before they kill you, and they'll be watching for us. Now get back to the stabilisers."

"Don't order me around, you sonofabi—" Ingram started forward but Ellis took his shirt front in two fists and sent him crashing into the console. He wheeled on the others.

"We're all in the same ship. That's the only certainty. But I promise you that those stabilisers are strong enough. We're going home. If anyone else wants to dispute that with me, I'm ready for him."

Bonetti fell to his knees, his hands laced together and his face raised pitifully. He prayed hoarsely. "Please, Captain, I beg you! Take us to a planetfall—"

Ellis dragged him to his feet with difficulty, strength draining from him, but he made Bonetti face him, on his feet and with the semblance of a man's dignity.

"Now get back to the stabilisers!"

Bonetti staggered, raving now. He rose up in a fury of possession. For a split second, Ellis saw a satanic light in his eyes, heard him laugh frighteningly. He grinned with a bright, unnatural strength and went for his captain's throat. Ellis was rooted by the terror of Bonetti's madness as it took him. His mind slipped from his control and into panic. Then Bonetti froze. His arms fell limp; he turned and walked sniggering in triumph to the egress hatch. Before anyone could stop him he had opened it and dived inside and opened the gas cock.

The men broke away and saw their shipmate's unsuited body take raw vacuum. His eyes boiling in their sockets and mouth bursting wide open across his face.

One of them faced him, her features full of revulsion.

"You got what you wanted, Straker," she said.

"Get to your stations! Now!"

They turned, and in silence Ingram took the rest of them away, his surly anger utterly shattered. Ellis knew that neither he nor any of them could be trusted now. And they would have to put down on Cheju.

17

SADO

"What're they going to do with us, Gunner?"

"We're dying in here!"

"A hundred and thirty days in this stinking hole!"

Four pale faces crowded the bars of the prison window rattling their chains on the sill as he passed beneath. It was two months since they had taken the Gunner from them. Still they were in Niigata, still the daimyo had not departed for Kanazawa, the inland capital of Sado, and the threat of death had hung over them until at last they had begun to wish for the mercy of an execution, any relief from their crushing misery.

The chorus of cries was daily more plaintive. Their laughing jailor rattled the bars with his cane and bowed low to the officer as the guard passed, making Duval do the same. He had brought the captives news of an Amerikan landing in the north of the continent, and day after day he had told them of how a force was raiding ever closer to Niigata before cruelly dashing their hopes by revealing that it had all been a pack of lies. After that, Duval Straker had seen all hope desert them, their spirits crushed.

"Hey, Gunner, what do they want with you?"

He was prodded forward by the jailor's cane. "I don't know."

"*Sugu!*" The voice commanding him came from the horseman following. It was the same man who had arrived shortly after Duval's capture. He had appeared twice since. And twice Duval had noticed and disliked his frosty manner. Clearly he was the soldiers' commander, because whenever he approached they became tense and cruel.

Duval raised his eyes to the prison window defiantly. "They say the daimyo's leaving tomorr—"

"*Sugu!*"

A blaster butt crashed down on his neck and he staggered. It was dangerous to ignore this proud young officer of the daimyo's staff. He wore a smart gray uniform kimono and everything about him was neatly ordered, down to the soles of his polished boots. Arrogant bastard, Duval thought. You treat us like dogs just to win the daimyo's praise, but every bruise you raise hardens me. We have strength because right is with us and against you. What's your name, you bastard? I promise you, one day I'll find out. And then I'll kill you.

He fell into a cold sulk in which his survival instincts closed his mouth and opened his eyes. The town was quiet now. It had been slowly emptying for a month, but today it seemed especially deserted. Duval knew that the battle losses had thrown the fierce markets of the Niigata *ya* into an unprecedented convulsion that sent prices up to the cirrus clouds. In his daily escorted trips through the town he had seen the commerce boiling up to a climax: despite intense bargaining, key merchants had sat on the rarest cargoes, forcing their buyers to send far along the chain, to the systems of Palawan and Iwo Jima and to Korea, to hunt down news of cheaper alternatives. Slaves were brought ashore, owners and traders haggled in the Ginza. Monks came for their consignments of paper and wood and paid in thick, square coins of gold wrapped in silk. Soldiers bought swords and the newest marque beam firearms that were coming here now by the shipload. Fine silks from the Home Worlds, or brought out of the Philippines from Manila Mitsukoshi, or laboriously brought across all Yamato on small craft from inside Xanadu, Fukien, and the best mulberry farms in Known Space. Weakly radioactive isotopes of argentium and platinium were traded in return, along with rare nuggets of native aurium that would be carried eventually up the Home World chain to the customs houses of Honshu, where the Emperor's revenue men would put them under bond and assess them for punitive import taxation.

Each morning for twelve weeks Gunner Duval had been taken in a guarded air-car to the remote defense facility of Hasegawa Industries near Niigata; each afternoon he had been put in a small room with carefully selected manuals. He had read them assiduously, slipping quickly into the way of the technical *kanji* and the twin *kana* syllabaries of the Japanese language. After a while it had become quite simple. During his breaks he had been allowed to sit with other technicians. He had watched and listened and recently he had begun to engage in conversation. At first, he had been kept apart from the men who built the beam weapons for the newly annexed Co-prosperity Sphere. Hasegawa's headquarters were at Chiba, near Kanazawa, but the small installation facility in Niigata, which served the port and the ships that passed through it, was adequate to confirm Duval's claims to be a weapons specialist.

At Hasegawa they resented the new daimyo's interference in their work and had little desire to admit a *gaijin* to their workshops—that went against every principle of the war commerce that had been waged against Amerika and its Earth predecessor since Showa times. But Nishima was daimyo, and his word was law.

Duval had encountered typical Japanese obstructionism at first. Lately, though, he had begun to win their respect, and that of Wataru Hoshino, the old man who secured his chains in the animal byre and brought him raw fish and rice each night. Hoshino had taught him much about Sado: the *ya*, the system of *han*, or lordly domains, that parceled out the land and industry and apportioned the people, and he had begun to understand a little of what a massive achievement had been made in industrialising so huge a portion of Sado's single continent and bringing its climatic excesses under control.

It was something he tried to fight, but Duval knew that he harbored a genuine respect for his captors, and many times as he watched the brilliant equatorial stars shooting up out of the eastern seas and tumbling across the sky to the mountains of the west he had thought how distant Amerika was and how immediate and real this strange place. "No matter where you go in Known Space, Orion is much the same." That was a Yamato saying he had learned. It comforted him strangely as he watched the Belt stars rising.

As they always did, the soldiers chained him to a ring in the doorway of the horse stable and left him alone, their duty discharged. He usually filled the time before Hoshino arrived with his food thinking of home, but tonight he relaxed, watched the Blood Moon rising above the horizon, and allowed his mind to range where it would.

When they had first taken him from the others, he had been chained in this same place. He had awoken from nightmare to find great sucking ticks, their abdomens filled and distended like black grapes, clustering on his neck and chest. He had pulled them off and burst them bloodily in disgust, and for the rest of the night he had been unable to find rest. But in the calm warmth of a new dawn he had awoken to find the future stretching out before him like a golden carpet, and he had known that a part of his life had been left behind forever. The toothless man who had brought him a pail of water and a bowl of seafood noodles had sat by him at the door, nodding amiably as the *gaijin* washed.

"Excuse me, but it is hard to wash in chains, sir. May I not be unlocked, please?" he had asked in his imperfect Japanese.

The old man's eyes had narrowed and his hand had strayed suspiciously to the pocket in which he kept the ion key. "You are a *gaijin*."

"I am a man, and not an animal."

"*So desu ka?* All men are animals, no? Charu-resu Daru-in, no? And a man must know his place."

"Charles Darwin or not, I have always thought my place was alongside other men."

"Ha! An interesting answer! And will you give your word that you will not try to run away?"

"Where can I run?"

"Your word, *gaijin?* On your life?"

"You have it. On my life."

"Then you may wash as a man."

The old man's hair had been wispy iron-gray but it had seemed to Duval that his spirit was still young. As he had washed, Duval had talked, wanting to know more about his captors and about the daimyo. Anything Hoshino could tell him might be useful. As he had begun to eat, he found that the old man slipped easily into conversation.

"My name is Wataru Hoshino. When I was your age, I too was an adventurer. A soldier. Then, one fortunate year, I joined with my lord, the famous Yoshida Shingen, on a great enterprise. Ah, what a man he was! I too—young and strong and full of ideas about glory as a young man should be—and for the glory of the Emperor we followed the nexus chain all the way down to this planet to break it for habitation. We raised our banners high that first day. Two thousand men, to build a planet where soft settlers could follow! Sado was savage in those days. The terraformer who made this place had a fine sense of humor. Five million introduced species crafted into a very stable ecological pyramid, but most of them obnoxious to man in one way or another. There are poisonous plants and biting insects of every kind, carnivorous animals, serpents that can swallow a horse whole! The terraformers didn't know about Sado, or how special it was. They had no idea it was a piece of ejecta from the Gum Nebula that had been captured by a star. They didn't know it had been born in a supernova, and they didn't know what it contained. It was twenty-five years ago, when we pioneers came here, *gaijin-san,* but I remember it as if it was yesterday. Some things a man may never forget. Many of us came here but few survived. Is that not always the way of the pioneer? Every man must have his time, eh? He must face death, or how may he know life?"

"All for the glory of the Emperor?" Duval had asked in Japanese between noisy, ravenous spoonfuls of noodle. "And of your lord, eh?"

The old man grunted.

"You live here in Niigata?"

"Here, yes, but mostly in Kanazawa. It is my good fortune to go forever between these two great cities with the ore rail-cars. I am a transport under-supervisor. But I have been sent here by Hasegawa Industries because I know some of your language and because Hasegawa Kenji is my lord. He hopes you will trust me."

"Your lord?"

"He is *oyabun,* I am *kobun*—parent and child, you see?"

"Not just your employer, then, I guess."

Hoshino chuckled. "*Ii-ye!* No! Much more than that Amerikan idea. Hasegawa-sama provides protection and advice and my living, and in return I render him total loyalty for all my life."

"Do you have anything to do with the shipment of aurium from Kanazawa?"

Hoshino's chest swelled with pride. "Yes, but only in a very small way of course. I am of lowly status, but my lord has allowed me to supervise the schedules from Bizen. It is a place in the heart of Sado, and in its center is a mountain veined with aurium ore. Hasegawa Industries has the contract for moving that ore by automatic rail trucks."

"That must be a great honor."

Hoshino tossed his head modestly; inside he was bursting with pride. "The tracks go from a great plateau ten thousand *shaku* above the sea, across the place we call the Plain of Stones, down past the lakes of salt and sweet water and the fuming volcanoes that guard the inland highlands—the land where the sunsets are the best. Below them the broad-leaf jungles begin. They grow densely like a peasant's own garden, all the way here to the sea, dark and dangerous because of the *gurentai,* the slaves that have escaped from the plantations and criminals who make their homes there."

"Why move the ore by rail?"

"It is too voluminous to move economically by any other means."

"That's only because ninety-nine-point-nine-nine-nine percent is impurity. Why isn't it refined at the mine heads? If the metal was extracted, it would be much easier to transport."

"Perhaps when the rail was built, there was no way to refine the ore. Refining plants are still hugely expensive, and . . . strategically important."

Hoshino fell silent and the peace of the moment descended on them, but after a while, Duval asked, "Are you samurai, Wataru-san?"

"*Iiye.* Few families in Yamato are samurai, fewer still here on Sado. Most people are *ikki* class—peasants and workers. I was born *doso*, merchant."

"Doesn't it bother you that you can't change classes?"

"I am what I am."

The big bronze bells hanging in the open wooden framework of the shrine across the way had begun to sound deeply. Three men in *fundoshi* loincloths, sandals, and white *hachimaki* headbands were swinging a great suspended log against it like a medieval battering ram; the sound brought Duval back to the present. He watched the robed priest peg back a hanging awning and release the water in its folds. Hoshino bowed low to the altar within.

"I must go."

"You will go with the daimyo's ceremonial procession when it leaves for the interior?"

"*Hai.* Tuesday. And if the daimyo desires it, he will take you to Kanazawa also."

Duval looked up suddenly. "Do you believe he will?"

Hoshino shrugged, picking up the shackles. "It is possible."

Duval watched as people appeared from side streets, heading for the shrine across the parade square of red compacted earth. Yesterday the morning's rain had dappled it with pools of water that had steamed gently in the rising heat of the day. He had watched the fierce sun of noon bake the horseshoe marks into hard semicircular ridges that would eventually be worn away by the bare feet of *ikki* and *hinin* and slaves, the *geta* of the priests and the rice straw sandals of samurai and what traders remained in Niigata. By night the Ginza had been peaceful once more and it had been then that he'd seen her. She'd come from the governor's house alone, her mane of black hair unpinned, dressed in a loose silk gown as if she had stolen from the house unobserved, and he had watched her hurry across the square towards him, oblivious of his presence. He had felt a pang of shame at his wretchedness and had hidden himself among the shadows, but he had continued to watch as she came inside the stable door and stood by the horses, patting their necks, speaking softly to them and blowing onto their nostrils.

"My lady, you are so kind to visit us here," he had whispered in throaty Japanese, and she had jumped back in surprise, unable to see anyone in the darkness.

"Who's there?"

"Only we horses."

"Horses?"

"Did you not know, my lady? On Sado we horses all talk."

She had seen the white of his smile then and tossed her head.

"And donkeys too!"

She left, not hurriedly, not scared by him, not embarrassed, but boldly and with a natural dignity. All day he had been unable to put that impression of her out of his mind. Now he looked at the governor's residence until the glare from its splendid tile roof hurt his eyes. The ornate house stood over the square in great authority. At its door the immaculately groomed officer on the white horse sat erect, exchanging words with that same graceful woman who had come unannounced into his reverie. She was dressed in a blue kimono and white obi, her hair pinned up now, and he saw that she was without doubt the young woman he had bravely bowed to when he had been captured.

He flicked his head towards the horseman. "Tell me, Wataru-san, who is that man?"

"He is the officer of the guard. My lord's son and heir and an important man in Kanazawa. His name is Hasegawa Katsumi."

"And the lady he talks to?"

"His sister, Michie. She is beautiful, is she not?" Hoshino grinned, showing the stump of one canine tooth. "If only I was a young man again!"

Duval smiled wistfully. He felt something—what? He couldn't say. Passion and apprehension coiling and uncoiling in his belly as Hoshino bolted home the chains on his wrists and ankles again.

Across the square the horse shimmied and was still. Katsumi reined it in tightly. Michie saw the spur marks on the horse's ribs and frowned.

"What do you call him?"

"The horse? His name is Moku." Jupiter.

She snapped her fan shut, nettled by her brother's unyielding poise. Can't he understand it is I, Michie-san, his sister? she asked herself. Can't he show just a little emotion in his face for me? It is as though he doesn't really want me here. That I am nothing to him.

"Something troubles you, Michie-san?"

"It's nothing. I was thinking of the journey ahead. Is it very arduous?"

"You will be well looked after. Don't forget that I'm here to protect you."

"They say there are dangerous criminals in the jungles between here and Kanazawa. Is that true?"

"They will not dare trouble us. We are many and they are curs that will not dare to fight. Their stolen weapons are no match even for those of our local escort, much less the arms of my own men."

She looked away, thinking of the sadness that had been in his eyes at their parting. "Please may I ask a favor of you?"

He smiled. "You know that you may ask anything of me, Michie-san."

"May I ride Moku when we leave for the interior?"

"My horse?" His smile disappeared.

"It would make the journey more bearable if I am free to ride alone—

within the bounds of the column, of course." Her eyebrows knitted and she bit lightly on her lip, lowering her voice. "I've been in the company of Fumiko-san for weeks."

"I'm sorry, but you must realise you are no longer in the Home Worlds. Here in Sado, horses can cost a thousand in credit."

"You have a horse, Katsumi-san."

"And you will have the most comfortable seat in the best palanquin that I can contrive. I will personally select your bearers and warn them to carry you carefully—under pain of death."

She sighed. "I'm sure your order would make them very careful, Katsumi-san, but even so I don't think I can stand bumping all the way to Kanazawa in a *kago* and listening continually to the daimyo's wife's grumbles. I would be certain to lose my politeness."

Katsumi seemed suddenly shocked but he demurred diplomatically. He rippled his heels over the horse's flanks and reined in, giving contradictory signals. "Think of your complexion, Michie. This miserable star we call our sun puts out too many ultraviolet rays. And, look, this horse is so skittish. Sado is too hot for them, they get sore under the saddle. If he were to throw you and you were to hurt yourself, our father would never forgive me. And of course I could never forgive myself."

"Forgive yourself, Hasegawa?" The daimyo's elegant figure appeared at the door. His eye moved over Michie's powder-pale face, searching her, before meeting his lieutenant's. "What is there for you to forgive?"

Katsumi dismounted immediately and bowed low. "Excellency."

Nishima's voice was superficially genial. "I ask myself why you sound so guilty, Hasegawa. It was a simple question."

Katsumi's back straightened and his chin jutted. "I was merely explaining to my sister, Excellency, that for her to ride to Kanazawa would be out of the question."

"Oh? How so?"

"It . . . it would not be fitting, Excellency."

Michie put her hand to her mouth and made a self-deprecating laugh. "It was only a silly girlish fancy, Nishima-sama. Oh, please do not trouble—"

"It's no trouble. I'm sure your brother will be delighted to loan you his horse. In any case, I have other duties in mind for him."

Katsumi fought to keep his face blank. "Other duties, Excellency?"

"You've shown commendable interest in the Amerikan captive. Your notion that the Hasegawa weapons facility might be interested in the new weapon also was worthy. Your father is head of Hasegawa Industries, is he not? The Amerikan has proved that he's knowledgeable, and so I've decided to bring him with us. He has much to tell us, but he must be persuaded to unburden himself of his own free will. You'll be responsible for his safety. See if you can imagine a way to unlock his secrets."

As the daimyo moved out of earshot, Michie turned her eyes to Katsumi in apology. He put the reins into her hand and said, "Here, take the horse. But you'll do well in future to curb your tongue in front of my superiors. And to remember that I have big responsibilities now."

18

By ten o'clock the next day their journey had begun.

The road that snaked out of Niigata was modern, paralleling the ore rail-track, and as they reached higher ground it became dusty and dry. They passed many small old-style settlements, houses made of wood and thatched with traditional reeds. *Ikki* downed tools and came rushing from the fields to press their foreheads to the ground at the curb, and small children did likewise, held still and silent by terrified parents. At each halt there was refreshment, and at night fires were lit and tents rigged for the soldiers who lay down on colorful bedrolls of quilted cotton. A guard was diligently posted on the fringes of settlements which had been hacked from the screaming forest. In daytime, at high points of the road, the vistas were of unbroken foliage, an ocean of steamy, tropical jungle stretching unendingly to the four horizons, clothing hills and valleys alike.

Nishima Jun rode in the center of the train. Three other high-ranking horsemen rode with him, one a Shinto priest and two others, the *karo,* or marshal of the military region around Niigata, and the *taisho,* his second-in-command. Ahead, there were three platoons of samurai, marching in formation with long *sashimono* flags attached to their backs; behind, the *doso* merchants with their guild symbols and formal presents for the outgoing daimyo, who was still at Kanazawa. Then came the *kago* of the ladies, each palanquin of traditional design carried by bearers whose heavily tattooed torsos gleamed in the sun. In the rear there were more soldiers, a thousand in all, and lines of ceremonial slaves chained three abreast, and the ground-cars in which the baggage was carried.

Michie had been given special permission to ride outside the column on the white horse. Sometimes she rode ahead of them all, sometimes at the tail. She liked to let the horse range as he would up and down the line, but she rarely fell in beside the *kago* of the ladies. She had taken her maid's advice and wore a long, loose-fitting robe and a wide-brimmed straw hat tied under her chin with broad white ribbon.

Katsumi walked a few yards behind the main body, keeping the Amerikan in sight. At the halts he would watch with disapproval as old Hoshino came to the Amerikan's side and shared a little food with him or shaved his beard. The chains had been taken from the Amerikan's legs, but still his hands were looped together.

"I see you did find yourself a horse, after all, my lady," he had called to her in his best Japanese. "How about getting me a ride, too?"

Naturally she had ignored him, but she had blushed unstoppably and told herself that it was not his fault that he could not understand the solemnity of the daimyo's inaugural procession into his domain.

That night, at her lodging in the Inn of the Three Waterfalls, Katsumi had warned her not to approach the captive again.

"Oh! Katsumi-san, I did not—"

"You know he is a dangerous *gaijin,*" he had said fiercely. "And polluted with filthy Amerikan ideas. I shall not be able to restrain myself from drawing my sword on him if he insults you again."

She had stared in disbelief at the intensity of the warning.

Of course, Katsumi-san was right to warn her. But then he had also warned her to ride obediently in one place in the procession, not to stray and not to go within ten *shaku* of any of his soldiers.

"This is a dangerous place, Michie-san. I have warned you time and again, and still you defy me."

"Please excuse me, but why shouldn't I exercise the horse? He likes to walk the verges and so do I, and the daimyo gave me special perm—"

"Willful girl! Have respect! I have already told you once: there are *gurentai* in the jungle who are armed! There are escaped slaves who will carry you away!"

"*So desu ka?* But I am not afraid. The road is good and you said the criminals were cowards who wouldn't dare to attack so large a body of soldiers."

"Do as you are told, Michie-san! For your own good! And keep away from the Amerikan!"

She had slid the shoji door closed after him then, and wished her brother on a different planet. And then she had cried, realising that the old Katsumi-san was dead and the new one a complete stranger.

Now she looked at the Amerikan again. He was tall, more than six *shaku*, which was big even for well-fed samurai, and now that he was allowed to wash and comb his hair he seemed almost handsome. His features seemed almost Japanese, but he was not Japanese, he was Amerikan, and that made him *gaijin*. Michie felt a seeping dread deep within her. He had no understanding of civilisation or of proper behavior and so he must not be treated as a normal man. That was what Fumiko said. That was what the priests said. It must be true.

Then why did she disbelieve it? And why should disbelieving scare her? Was not the Amerikan's behavior his own concern? If he had no sense of the uncouth state in which he was existing, was that not a problem for him alone? And why shouldn't these barbarous foreigners go to the nine hells in their own way if they so chose?

She nudged her horse into a canter and rode forward to the head of the train. The thought of her mother and father unsettled her now. What if they had been hardened by Sado too? What if they attempted to imprison her spirit as Katsumi had already tried to do?

Oh, I'll never be a good daughter with good manners, no matter how hard I try. I have such different thoughts to everyone else. Or perhaps it is just that they are better at disguising them.

Michie prayed silently, thinking of the hopes and fears that attended the meeting with her father. Hasegawa Kenji had traveled to Sado ten years ago. A graduate of the University of Honshu, a samurai of high rank but impoverished, he had decided to take his wife and son to the place where opportunities were blossoming. He had approached several important people on Kyoto about starting a technical corporation, but his enemies at the Court on Kyoto had gained the upper hand, and, unable to brook the rigid system of rank and status in Yamato, he had chosen a new settlement in the Neutral Zone—Sado—as the place to rebuild his ancestral wealth. His two young daughters, Michie and Kinuyo, he had left with his sister on Kyoto, partly as a sign to his enemies that he intended one day to return, partly that the girls might be educated and schooled in the ways of the Court. Such a thing would have been impossible on Sado. Later, as holder of a large *han* and with growing influence in the Sado administration, Hasegawa Kenji had begun to dream of a return to Yamato, but the news of his first daughter's violent death at the hands of the Emperor's son had thrown his hopes into ruin and he had sent to Kyoto for Michie and to sever his last links with the Home Worlds.

Katsumi, she knew, still harbored a desire to go to Yamato. To repair his father's reverses and avenge the death of his sister. He cannot show me love, and yet he thirsts to avenge Kinuyo, she thought, not understanding him or the *bushido* code he had absorbed so totally. He would do better to think of me than to throw himself at the Imperial Chamberlain who had been Prince Kono's principal guardian. That would only bring shame down on our name. Yes, far better that he think of keeping what family he has.

Ahead, the mountains were rising majestically. The road across the plains was ending, leaving the dense, forested region and heading up into the high, treeless savannah. There was a shining, rippling sparkle on the road ahead. It looked like a river. Perhaps there was a ford. She urged Moku forward, past the lead body of soldiers who looked up at her passing and began to call out to her to come back.

The horse was thirsty. She would let him drink. Katsumi's men had no right to shout at her. Already they were left behind, as the horse's hooves beat out a gallop.

The road narrowed. She saw something red-brown and thick as a tree trunk slung across its metaled surface and the horse shied, pulling up, stamping nervously. The red-brown thing was moving loathsomely from one side of the road to the other, rippling, tumbling like a snake, but it was no snake. It was a mass of huge insects, like ants but half a finger in length and with long, sharp jaws.

They *were* ants. Jungle ants. Thousands of them. They moved like a military column, carrying leaves and insects and other booty tirelessly in their flow from the left-hand verge to the right.

She watched them, at once horrified and amazed, thinking what clever haiku might capture such a phenomenon tonight, and perhaps draw the comic parallel with the daimyo's own procession so that everyone would laugh.

And then she saw the bodies. Two human forms, clothed thickly with a prickling mass of red-brown. They had been deliberately staked out in the insects' path and then, with a second spasm of horror, she realised that the *gurentai* perpetrators were not long gone—both their victims were still alive.

They came by midday to a town of two hundred inhabitants surrounded by groves of longan and persimmon and pomegranate and built by the great river beside which broad salines had been cut and in which slaves labored.

Hoshino brought a bowl of rice and divided it, grinning. They talked, seated comfortably in the shade, Duval listening to the old man's reminiscences, all the while keeping an eye on Hasegawa Katsumi, who was inclined to watch him secretly.

"It was the work of the *gurentai* bandits," Hoshino told him. "Two in every five of the Kan slaves on Sado have deserted their masters. They live in the forests and worship pagan gods and eat pig flesh, as they do in Xanadu. Sometimes they attack isolated settlements and steal away slave women to increase their numbers. They hate us because many of the *han* owners are cruel men who think only of profit."

"And the men they killed?" Duval had seen the shocking sight as they cut the victims out. The rescuers had had to prise each soldier ant head from the flesh individually, but much of their skin was gone and their eyes had been devoured down to the nerves.

"Also *sangokujin*. People of the Three Domains—Chinese, Taiwanese, Koreans. Or maybe local *ikki*. The *gurentai* are no friends of the peasantry. The *ikki* buy salt here and carry it into the interior. They are often robbed." He sniffed comically. "Yes—you can smell *sangokujin* slaves on the air all around this district. Dirty people. Pig eaters. At one time I myself used to bring salt down to Niigata where it is taken by nexus ship to Guam . . ."

Duval began to drowse. The noon stops were often of two hours or more and afforded welcome respite from the heat and the chafing of his plex leg irons. The sound of his own breathing filled his ears, and as he lay back he caught the faint waft of pigpens on the air and he slit open an eye, looking for the source of the smell. Then he stirred and sat up.

Hoshino roused himself suddenly. "What is it?"

Duval shook his head. "I thought . . . it's nothing. For a moment I thought I heard Amerikan spoken."

"You are dreaming of home."

"Perhaps."

Duval forced himself to relax and Hoshino settled once more, pushing his broad-brimmed straw hat forward over his eyes, and was soon breathing regularly.

It came again. This time Duval got to his feet, slowly, so that the chains made the minimum of noise. He walked in the direction of the hog sties.

"I must relieve myself," he said to a nearby soldier, who watched him disinterestedly. When he turned the corner of the nearest building, he saw the face at the gate. It was pressed against a narrow gap and he recognised the man. It was Hawken's steward.

"Jon Chambers, can that be you?"

The face stared back at him. "Gunner!"

"Quietly!"

Through the gaps he could see that there were perhaps twenty of them confined in the sty. They were naked and the smell of ordure rose powerfully from them in a stifling wave.

He went as close as he could.

"The commodore, is he with you?"

"No."

"How the hell did you get here?"

"We were marooned on the Blood Moon."

Chambers explained how the party had divided into three, twenty-five going north, another thirty south, and the remainder striking east towards the penal settlement. His group had been attacked by the Blood Moon's own *gurentai*, who had stripped them of everything useful but had left their credit smarts. They had gone six days without water and had finally come to the prison, where they had been taken by the authorities and sent down to Niigata. They had been set walking on the road to Kanazawa and then imprisoned here for no apparent reason.

"They need to ask their big boss what to do with you, I guess."

Chambers was in a miserable state. His eyes bugging out at the horror and injustice, his voice breaking up with hysteria. "They shut us all up in this hole and threatened to crucify us, Gunner! They gave us pig swill to eat! Many of us have been hurt, and we told them we needed medical treatment but they don't take any notice! Nobody can get through to them! We've been in this shit for days!"

"What happened to the *Richard M.?*"

"Gone home, I guess. I hope."

"Was my brother alive?"

"Yeah—or he was when I last saw him."

Duval raised his eyes skyward. "Thank God for that!"

"He gave me something. A ring—Jeezus, those psi-talents are sure plugged into the future. He musta just *known* we'd meet up somehow, Gunner."

Duval heard movement behind him and saw the white horse. He stood up and pointed angrily to his shipmates' misery. "They are my compatriots, locked up here in worse squalor than I would permit pigs to suffer in. Is this the way the famous samurai treat their prisoners?"

Michie stared down at him and at the sty, then she nodded, turned her horse, and left, returning with her brother almost immediately.

A great moaning rose from the captives when they saw the soldiers. They feared death and implored Duval to help them because Hasegawa Katsumi's men carried nooses.

Duval's heart pounded as he listened to their cries helplessly.

"They're going to hang us!"

"Jeezus, Gunner! Help us!"

His heart raced. He looked from Chambers to the officer and stepped forward, asking Hasegawa to reconsider. The samurai brushed him aside.

"No. Please! They don't deserve to die! You can't hang them."

"Get out of my way immediately!"

"What is their crime?"

"Stand aside, *gaijin!*"

Duval's eyes flashed around for a weapon, but there was none. Next, he heard himself scream and felt his bare hands tearing at Hasegawa's throat, then he was down on top of him, his grip on that vile neck unbreakable. He wanted no more than to strangle the life from this little man. It felt like freedom and like justice, but it was madness. Six soldiers lifted him bodily and prised his fingers from the flesh and Hasegawa came alive again, gasping and choking.

He had changed nothing.

A dozen drawn swords pinned Duval's chest to the ground, the points digging through his shirt to draw blood. He saw the woman dismount and run to her brother. She held his head and helped him to breathe, and her eyes flashed at Duval, full of anger and hatred.

"Foreign devil!"

"Lady, he was going to hang them!"

"He should hang all of you!"

Hasegawa's sergeant staked the point of his long *daito* sword over the Amerikan's heart, looking to his superior for a nod of command. When none came from the coughing, gasping officer, he asked with relish, "Shall I kill him now, sir?"

"No!"

The sergeant hesitated, expecting another answer. Then he put up his weapon reluctantly.

"Bring him!"

Duval was hauled savagely to his feet and brought before the daimyo.

Hasegawa, recovered now, his *haori* torn open, dragged his lapel aside and showed the marks where the Amerikan's fingernails had clawed into him. He explained angrily that he had tried to kill him and demanded the satisfaction of seeing him nailed up immediately.

Nishima looked up from his papers icily.

"He tried to kill you?"

Hasegawa showed again the weals on his neck.

The daimyo turned to the accused man. "Is this true?"

"Your pardon, Excellency," Duval said breathlessly. "He was going to hang my friends."

"I ordered these filthy pirates taken from their hole and bound up."

"His men had nooses—"

"Did you expect them to be marched to Kanazawa unbound?"

"I thought—"

"You thought?" Nishima motioned to his guards. "Take him out of here."

As Duval was led away, Nishima turned to Hasegawa, a half-smile on his mouth.

"So the Amerikan saw fit to assault you, after all, Hasegawa?" he said with mild reproach. "I thought you said you had tamed him."

"These Amerikans are never tamed. They respect nothing but force."

Nishima regarded Hasegawa thoughtfully. "You're a hasty young man, but you've proved something about the Amerikan's temper that you yourself did not suspect."

When Hasegawa had suggested Hasegawa Industries as a test of the Amerikan's knowledge of beam weapons, he had agreed to postpone the crucifixions. And when the head scientist at the remote facility had made an excellent report of his abilities, he had canceled the order. The Amerikan had obviously worked for many years as a theoretician and knew well the practices of the weapons industry. In that, he had not lied, but neither had he offered any important information. He was wary still, and unwilling. If he is to truly render his secrets to us, we who have made him captive and whom he hates, he must be persuaded by means other than bare compulsion. But there is time enough, and I am not impatient.

Hasegawa began to speak, but Nishima overrode him.

"I have already told you that the Amerikan was to be brought to Kanazawa alive. That he is valuable."

"Yes, Excellency."

"And you can think of no way to loosen his tongue, other than by force? That's very sad."

"I think I understand you, Excellency. If a man will not be obedient for the sake of his own skin, often he will be so for his friends. He was willing to die to save his comrades."

"Quite so."

Hasegawa brightened. "Shall I order them all brought to Kanazawa?"

"Do that. And send word to the governor in Niigata to deliver the Amerikans in his jail to me also. Next, send these instructions ahead to Kanazawa. Then you will see how the strength of an enemy may be used against him."

Two days later they arrived at Kameyama.

There they rested. The Amerikan prisoners were treated well by the Confucian monks at the temple there, given clothing and food and ointments to heal their wounds. From there, they came to Otani, forty *ri* from Kanazawa, a town of three hundred, where they were lodged in the house of the Black Brotherhood. Their stay at Kofu, where the argentium mines lay, was of two days and nights, and five days later, stopping off at various *han* estates along the main Nakasendo road, they came to within five *ri* of Kanazawa, accompanied by a great many townspeople.

Nishima watched the Amerikan carefully throughout all that time and saw that he was as a brother to his countrymen. He also saw the way that Hasegawa's sister attracted his eye time and again. And he began to see another way to wrest the Amerikan's secrets from him.

At Gifu they halted at the seminary of more Shinto priests, and from there they were taken to the shrine of Mount Isu, where the healing springs eased their bodily hurts. Before they departed, each samurai of the train, of whatever rank, mounted or on foot, would not pass by the shrine until he had first entered it, knelt before the image, and made an offering to the *kami* of Isu to deliver him from misfortune.

At *yoji*—four o'clock—on the next day they entered Kanazawa by the street called the Most Fortunate Boulevard of the Cherry Trees where the residence of the daimyo stood. In Nishima's mind, a plan concerning the Amerikan and young Hasegawa's sister had begun to form.

LIBERTY

"Are we at war, Sparky?"

"Not as far as I know, Jos."

The man's reply came as he appeared from the *Richard M.*'s boarding umbilicus port. He was Sparky Hoover, owner of a Liberty nexus salvage ship, on his way from Liberty to the moons of the sub-Jovian gas giant, Arcadia, where some heavy plants needed busting down. He had happened upon them as they appeared from the nexus and came over to check them out. Hawken questioned him anxiously for news, knowing that all their futures hung on what he had to tell them.

Hoover was stocky as a barrel, whiskery, with a round face and cleft chin; his cheek was packed with a baccy quid and he was still amazed at having come across Hawken's ship. He took off his skewed cowboy hat and kneaded its brim in hands that were as big and red as Connecticut crabs.

"Well, hell, Jos, I sure didn't think I'd be seeing you out here this trip. I didn't think I'd be seeing you ever. War or no war."

The Index was low and the nexus wreathed in Boeing debris from last month's disaster, but still it was home and the Liberty system star shone with indescribable beauty to everyone aboard the *Richard M*.

"Do you know why the Yamato authorities are seizing Amerikan merchantmen in Neutral Zone ports?" Ellis asked.

Hoover spat juicily into the water cooler set into the bulkhead. "That's the blockade. It's common to all trade this past month. They say Yamato's furious over some seizure of aurium made at Marshall I—stuff set to feed them sammy-rays garrisoned in the Zone. They have us embargoed out of all the nexi they control. Nothing's going in or out of the Zone."

"Sonofabitch! That's bad. Very bad!" Hawken's eyes were deep-set in a gaunt and disease-ravaged face. He looked to his fortunes with a bleary eye. "The President can be as sulky as a child after a tantrum. She'll ruin us all and in as high-handed a way as the Emperor himself!"

"Not if what they say in the bars around Liberty's all true," the salvageman told him, relishing the chance to pass on his thoughts. "In the business of seizures we've had the best of it so far. Those Yamato boys forget they can't communicate with Korea except by the nexus chain that runs right by Kalifornia, and there's plenty Korean pirates waiting to get on their backs. They won't let a single Yamato ship through the chain if they can help it. Up in Lincoln they say Okubo, the Yamato ambassador, is fuming mad, that he's got just the one thought in his brain—an embargo of Amerika."

Ellis asked incredulously, "Korea is closed?"

"Yep. Tight as a duck's asshole."

"But that's suicide!"

"For the Koreans maybe."

"For Amerika!"

"You been away too long, old buddy."

"We're well enough informed. Since New Year's Day we've been a week in Cheju Do. They told us there had been some seizures and a slackening of trade. But this!"

Hawken explained how on the point of death they had found the Korean system and got men and provisions from the impounded ships of Amerikan small traders, effecting hasty repairs and putting out before the Yamato authorities came to understand what was happening. He and Ellis had picked up the confused rumors that abounded about an embargo and the incident at Sado, and they had kept their identity secret just long enough to escape to the nexus again.

"It's a psi-storm that's gotta blow itself out soon," Hoover said. "Any play Yamato makes, short of force, loses them the game."

"Yeah! Short of force," Hawken replied. "But that's always their ace."

The salvageman sniffed a dewy drop from his nose and told them how trade was flowing the other way now, through Europa, where the Germans and United Baltic States traders were taking all the manufacturers that Amerikan ships could land. As Hoover spoke, it seemed to Ellis that the situation was not as bleak as Hawken had supposed. He was fervently loyal to the President, but his fevered brain had imagined a traitor's welcome and no way out of it. But things had changed. Yamato supply ships had been driven into the Kalifornian system by Korean pirates. There they had fallen legally under Amerikan jurisdiction. So long as the President released the Yamato vessels she contravened no laws. She could even claim to have acted in good faith by giving them safe haven against hostile pirates. However, there had been no reason to release the ships' *cargoes*. The owners of the dimethyl aurium on board, and those responsible for its safety until it reached Guam and the Marshall systems, were Chinese financiers. Ellis saw that their position must have been a sorry one. Faced with Amerika's request to land the dimethyl aurium in Kalifornia, they had taken the only course possible and agreed. And now the whole consignment of that fantastically precious material was impounded on Liberty—for safekeeping.

Ellis considered the position carefully. "The Emperor of Yamato will certainly interpret this action as a piece of diplomacy designed to damage and humiliate him," he told Hawken exultantly. "You know what I think? I think the President may have chosen it as a method of squaring the outrage inflicted on our ships on Sado!"

"In which case our return may only heat up the situation."

"Will Alia back us or will she bury us? Hard to say, but I'd guess the former."

Hawken sacrificed his caution regretfully, but hope was beginning to stir him. "That's her character from what I know of her: always ready to play the injured party in order to gain an advantage, always willing to clench her fist against Yamato—*if* there's something to be gained by it."

"If the embargo's hurting Korea, that will suit her too. If what we heard in Cheju Do's right, Yamato's big corporations will soon be crying for a settlement. Perhaps Baron Harumi's beginning to regret listening to Ambassador Okubo. And perhaps our return is well timed, after all!"

Ellis's thoughts soared as they prepared to separate from the salvage vessel.

"We must get down to Liberty as fast as we can," was all Hawken would say of his plans. He seemed to Ellis to have drawn other, darker threads into the pattern of his thoughts, threads he would not hint at. Still his assessment of their prospects and the reception they might yet meet with seemed unduly guarded.

News of their arrival had gone before them from Philadelphia to Boston, carried in all the Liberty airwaves like an Oregon forest fire. The word was relayed via the main communications links, then across the system so that by the time the *Richard M.* touched down on the Harrisburg apron she had drawn a crowd of air-cars all shooting their searchlight beams at her. In reply, her hull markings cycled through a victorious light show for the people who had crowded the terminal to see them home. All Harrisburg had come to a halt.

A familiar black face grinned up at him from the ground-car that came alongside as they dropped the bay ramps.

"Well, damn me to hell! Can it be?"

"You got me up from my bed, you lousy sonofabitch!"

"That's a goddamned miracle!"

"Jeezus, it's good to see you, Ellis. You're a lucky bastard."

"You too, John. But if that was luck we had aboard, it was all cross-grained."

"You're looking fine!"

"Healthy enough—for a dead man."

Oujuku scrambled aboard and the two men clasped each other's forearms in the way of men made brothers by the nexi. The cold, almost windless calm had turned the apron into an ice rink, and despite the earliness of the hour the frosty terminal was swelling: half the people in Harrisburg had come down to the apron to see who had lived and who had died in the Zone.

Oujuku looked around him. "A difficult passage, by the looks of your ship's innards. And you too."

"Not so bad since Cheju Do. We took on twelve good guys, and the rest of us have fattened up like buffaloes since then. Those of us left." Ellis's breath steamed as he looked away from the ship's empty cargo bay in disgust. He was in no mood for bantering and could think only of his Janka and their son now.

"Where you been?"

"We sighted the system two days ago. You?"

"I beat your ragged ass home by five days. While you were wishing yourself here, I've been making a nest out of a bed with Mary Newman the last two days up Kingston way. No callers on pain of death! Call yourself an astrogator, you big, no-hope nexus-trasher?"

Ellis scowled down at his friend. "I may be out of trim, but I've enough left to sink your ass, so watch your mouth, lubber!"

Oujuku roared and slapped his thigh. "Come on down, it's past time I stood you a round with some of them credits you owe me. There's a lot of news you'll be wanting to hear. Me too, I can tell you."

"Eh—don't spoil a man's privacy. I've some haymaking of my own to do first."

"Aye, there's a few priorities, if I knows Ellis Straker!" As Oujuku looked around him, he saw that those lining the *Richard M.*'s walkways were not people of her original crew. He became suddenly serious. "How many did you bring back with you?"

"Fifteen."

"Christ in heaven!" Oujuku's voice was low.

"You?"

"Sixty-three."

Ellis was warmed at the news, but it did not show on his face. He said, "We had a marooning."

Oujuku's pride guttered. "Marooning? Jeez, that's bad."

"A hundred put down on Chi no Tsuke. Make of that what you will."

By the terminal, Billy Hawken waited where hundreds of husbands and wives congregated, anxious for their own. The tearful meetings of the lucky few leavened the sickly disappointment of the many as they disembarked. He saw Jon Chambers's girl, Becky, her face showing how her heart had been struck hollow. She heard Hawken read the list of those who had been left behind on the Blood Moon.

He was hardly aware of it. The charge of emotions around him penetrated his chest, filling him with expectation. Suddenly his control burst and he gave in to the feeling he had kept bound up these many months. He strained his eyes searching the concourse for Janka and young Hal. The press of familiar people dazzled him. Damn it! Where was she? It would be like her to hang back in a doorway with their son and watch him search her out, then come to her privately, away from the rest, to hug wife and son tight in his arms.

His eyes roamed the concourse and then he felt Becky tugging at him, her tear-stained cheeks pale with shock.

"Captain Straker?"

He heard her distantly, not wanting to be caught up in her grief for her man at this thousand-times-looked-for moment. Where was Janka? *Where was she?*

"Captain Straker? Listen to me. Please listen!"

Again she clutched at his sleeve.

"Not now, please, I—"

"For God's sake!"

Then he saw the faces of the people around him and their looks reflected his sudden agony.

"Your Janka's not here."

The girl's words cut his heart from him.

"*Not here?*"

"She and the baby, Captain Straker. An air-car accident two months ago."

He threw off her grasping fingers and closed his mind. But the words continued to wound him like hot knives. *Air-car accident? Could it be true? Could it?*

"They're dead, Captain."

"No!"

He bellowed out his anger. Strode off. Threw his fists at the elevator doors. Then he sank down to his knees, wrapped up in himself so tight that no one approached him, nor dared speak to him. Even Oujuku left him, wishing his tongue could be cut out for what had passed between them minutes before. He had not known about Janka's death. He went back to the apron where Billy

Hawken, in a gray suit and standing by the big limo, embraced his emaciated brother. He led his employees through the concourse and to the assembly point where press conference tables had already been set up for the tri-vee broadcasts. As they walked, their gladness turned to business. Oujuku saw that Billy Hawken kept his words private, and tried to overhear.

"Some reports had you down as destroyed, others said you'd gone to Delaware."

Jos spat. "Delaware? That's a crazy notion!"

"There were plenty of investors in Lincoln who believed it, and many who believe it still. The word is that you landed a quarter ton of argentium and two hundred million credit units of aurium there. It'll take a lot of denying to shake the press off that one."

Jos Hawken grunted. "Let them think what they like."

"Yeah, but it'd be a powerful disappointment to people if we were to shake such a belief too early," Billy said.

"And a mess of trouble for us both if we don't. We were down on Cheju Do two weeks ago. All Korea was swarming with lies about us."

"Were you recognised?" Oujuku asked.

"They found us out, eventually. And a great meal they thought they'd make of us, too. The Yamato line is that we attacked Nishima out of greed. That we had a go at knocking off his aurium shipment. It's vital I get up to Lincoln at once."

"The President and her staff must be told the truth. And we ought to keep it secret."

"And quickly if we're going to avoid big trouble. We've a flask of trinitride and some bits and pieces, but precious little else. Thirteen, maybe fourteen million in credit, depending on the state of the market. That's all told. *Richard M.*'s fit only for selling to Sparky Hoover's boys. We're damn near busted."

The elder Hawken nodded gravely. "So it seems our Zone adventures are over. I wish I knew what Alia intended."

"Will she see me personally?"

"That's what Otis le Grande is paid for. He's fixing things."

"You never know—we might avoid the slammer at Camp Worth yet."

Billy glanced around and said quietly, "The President too is looking over her shoulder since Lucia Henry came down. The whisper is that Alia's cornered in Congress, adversaries to left and right. They even say a ninja assassination squad's in town. Some think it's time Lucia Henry was encouraged."

Jos showed his disbelief. "Assassins? To kill the President? How the hell can anyone say there's ninja here? They don't exactly advertise themselves."

"Tread with care, Jos. Alia may want your balls in payment for your getting her in deeper than she wants with Yamato. But she has need of friends right now, so be discreet in how you present your case to her."

"If any trade is to go forward in the Zone from now on, we've got to have her clearance. Her tacit approval, at least."

"We've got to have the President's clearance, it's true. But who knows who'll be sitting in the Oval Office a month or two from now? And who knows if a pro-Yamato administration would give you right of passage across the treaty line? When the Emperor and Lucia Henry were playing footsie, at least some commerce was allowed—"

"What about your promise to go back to Chi no Tsuki?" Oujuku broke in.

Jos Hawken eyed him irritably. "What?"

"Come on, Commodore! The rescue! We got a hundred people marooned up there."

"That'll have to wait."

"Waddaya mean, wait?"

Hawken turned on him. "I mean wait!"

As the press conference began, Oujuku moved away. His stomach had been knotted by Hawken's reply. He collected Cao, the Chinese who had come back stronger than anyone aboard the *Richard M.*, and went pushing through the crowds in search of Ellis. War was coming, and in war it was not enough to think like a merchant thinks. A man had to have the balls to do what others could not face. In war, a certain kind of person was needed. And he knew a way that would bring Ellis to his cause. Since pulling the *Judith L.* out of Sado, he had spent many hours constructing an elaborate plan of revenge. For the first time, he had the money and could raise powerful backing, and at last giant affairs of state were swinging the right way. Now was the time to cancel his contract with Hawken and put his ideas to the test.

At dusk Oujuku found Ellis alone in his empty home. He knew what must be done and led him to the bar called the Black Hole on the corner of Potomac Boulevard and Mockingbird. The big blond man went like a zombie, stiffly, with Oujuku's hand clamped under one arm and Cao's under the other. The footing was icy. Tri-vee comedy shows shone dimly in windows of homes. Since he was last at the Black Hole, James Cagney's smiling portrait had been taken down from the walls; now a rough cartoon of the Emperor arm-wrestling with Alia Kane filled the space above the pool cube.

The night was frosty, but inside it was warm and full of familiar smells. A one-armed bandit filled a space in the corner with cheery light. Oujuku gave him a coin and threw him out. Nexus-rat faces gaped at them until Oujuku raised his fist to them.

"Come on! Wassamatter? Never seen an astrogator before?"

He ordered a beefie, some new-crisped zots, and a jug of sour mash and cleared a corner table for them. The broken slave ring in Cao's ear scintillated, its mechanism disrupted but its dependency circuit still lethal enough to stop its surgical removal, as he watched the man who had astrogated him to this cold world and kept him from starvation and madness.

"Coming down here's the only way," Oujuku said, chewing on the beefie, but he got no answer.

He knew Ellis wanted only to be alone, but he would not let him be. He was a captain and he had his duty. A debt to pay after the stranding. Oujuku told him to eat, and then to drink the pain out of him amongst his people, as was only right. That way no one's sorrow could fester. Within half an hour, as Oujuku knew it would, the bar became a smothering hell for Ellis. The place had filled to bursting for the catharsis. Down its entire length, dead men's relatives were shouting and throwing up their hands, the uncommonly piercing voices of women who were still looking vainly for their husbands, and children wanting fathers that would never return. Often the names turned to shrieks, and rucks of violence flared up among the husbands.

A catharsis was a family's right after a disaster. They wanted accounts by those that had seen it happen. Stories that paid in full for the agony in their souls. It was a survivor's obligation and a captain's solemn duty. The agony of the marooning on Chi no Tsuke had to be faced squarely, but all the while Ellis sat mute, frozen inside his own heartbreak. Another jostle broke out at the door. Oujuku made him drink another swallow. And he compiled, gulping the burning Kentucky down mechanically as though he could not taste it. Then a shower of credit slottees ricocheted off the table where he sat.

"You bastards! You fucking liars! A curse on all your children and your children's children, you scum!" In a frenzy of words the woman flew at them. She was a marooned man's wife, held back by Angela, Ayrton Rodrigo's widow. "There's your blood money, you godless bastards! I hope you burn in hellfire!"

The woman was grappled and pulled outside. Cao calmly gathered up what credit he could see into the empty mash jug and handed it to the woman's brother.

"I'm right sorry, Captain. She's crazy with grief. She's got a family of three youngsters to explain it all to and she don't know how to start."

The man left them, seeing suddenly the bloodless gray of Ellis's face. It was different when a ship was lost with all hands. Then the grief was shared equally. With a marooning it was as if they had all died but then some had been resurrected, as if the families thought the survivors had cheated the victims out of their homecoming.

"Where's Hawken?" Ellis said in a lost whisper.

"It's his place to be here."

"And mine. This place stinks. I gotta get out." Ellis looked suddenly like he was about to vomit.

Oujuku steadied him. "If you go now, they'll never forgive you, Ellis. You know that. You've got to show them plain that you've got no guilt over what happened. Face-to-face!"

"I'm burning in hell, John!"

"Drink!"

He lifted the jug to Ellis's lips again and made him swallow until the amber liquor coursed through his beard.

"I want to die."

"You will. When your time comes."

Ellis's rigid paralysis gave way to a mighty shaking. He heaved himself to his feet and staggered to the door. Oujuku stood over him outside as he brought up a belly full of pungent bile.

"That's the way. Get it all out!"

The cold night air seeped into him. The circumpolar stars above pitiless and white, like needles. And Cao's hand on his back slapping him until his eyes watered. When he straightened he was sucking in breath and panting.

"I want to go home."

"There's things I want to say before we part."

"It can wait."

"No! It can't!"

"Get off my arm, John!"

Oujuku let go, and Ellis shrugged his sleeve and began to walk.

"You want to go back for your brother, don't you?"

He stopped, but did not turn.

"My brother's dead. My blood is dead. All I ever loved."

"You're brother's *alive*, Ellis."

Air-cars roared overhead, their lights slashing the night. The life drained from his body and he sank down against the wall. For a moment the din from the bar seemed to fade away, and the knitted wound in his shoulder seeped pain all across his breast.

"Alive?"

"It's my practice to ask questions of my crew. Duval was seen. By two of his people who'd been left for dead on the terminal. They crawled out from the corpses and got off in a shuttle. We tractored them alongside when we hit Sado orbit."

Ellis's mouth hung open, his eyes shot with glistening light. "Is it true?"

"One of them says he saw your brother running from the *Thomas J.* before the explosion, and the other swears he watched him climb out of a storm drain and make for the beach."

"He knew it was Duval?"

"Only one man I know wore a red neckerchief."

"They're lying! Hoping to pick up a reward from me!"

"I know when a crewman of mine is telling the truth."

Ellis's voice was a breath. "Christ Jeezus!"

Oujuku leaned forward, his eyes wrinkled and his mouth split, showing a set of pearl-like teeth in a devil's grin. "How would you like to come in with me on another trip? A return journey to Niigata? This time with a belly full of weapons to trade? Eh, Ellis? How 'bout that?"

21

The air-car ride east from Harrisburg apron to Lincoln was above a continent made white by winter. Their salvaged cargo had been packed into four twelve-seater Fords and watched overnight by guards from the Hawken organisation; the journey began at first light.

Jouncing over the thermals thrown up by the Harrisburg Mountains had made Ellis sick in the belly, and each time he stood up, the dizzying movement of the floor under his feet made him stagger. Almost everything outside was hidden under a blanket of snow. The heated ground-car roads were ribbons of black, the towns jewel boxes of orange sodium lights, and the forests bright fleeces that hurt the eyes. Everywhere he looked was laid out in familiar patterns with rivers and mountains and habitations and painful memories. Even later, when a watery sun warmed his aching shoulder through the plex blister, the cold night of winter and everything on Liberty were dead to him.

Beyond St. Paul the ride improved. They traveled over parklands where frozen lakes showed through the snow, and the plains where the big corporations had built their factories, and soon enough they came into the valley of the Potomac, thick with skeletal trees and a promise of arrival, because from here they would descend. As he saw the metropolis of Lincoln rising ahead, some of the pain in Ellis's heart melted and he felt his soul begin to thaw.

When Hawken had asked him to accompany their salvaged cargo to Liberty, Ellis had been silently obedient. He had taken the order mutely and done as he was told, nothing more nor less, walking, speaking, and doing now, all without spirit or commitment. When Hawken told him he was to accompany him to the White House, Ellis refused. In this he was adamant, clinging to the words John Oujuku had spoken. Only when Hawken explained that he needed him as a trusted witness of events did he agree.

"I intend to lodge a complaint with the Security Council about the treatment we've received at the hands of the Yamato authorities. And to demand reprisals. Will you come with me?"

"Do you want me to?"

"Yes."

"Then I will—if you'll undertake to get the President's permission for the rescue that you promised. Our people on Chi no Tsuki."

"I can't ask for that."

"Then I can't back you up."

Hawken spoke sternly to him then, of a scheme that must secure all their futures against a turmoil that would soon sweep across Amerika. Ellis acquiesced, and the bitterness and pain that had attended his homecoming were diluted by the prospect that was now opening up. The promise that Hawken made kept the fire that Oujuku had ignited within him alight. Without it, he might have let his spirit burn out.

They cruised in over the western suburbs and passed the splendid civic buildings of Wilmott and Piedmont and Richmond. The university was built of real red brick, with soaring towers, verdigris-green domes, and castellated turrets. Ellis was glad to see the Sector Library at Richmond, which stood along the river's edge, flanked by herringbones of outbuildings and the RISC research center. It rose up six stories, full of big, square glass windows in soaring twentieth-century style, and the transparent plex of its roof contained a heated pool full of dolphins and decked with metal gantries. There were many river craft here, pleasure cruisers and fishing loafers and a busy towpath on which he saw a family getting out of a ground-car: five little children dressed in colored tats. A bit further on there was a girl riding a palomino, and for some reason unknown to him Ellis smiled painfully at the thought that the family he and Janka had planned would now never be.

The riverside drive grew more congested with ground-cars and truckettes as they overflew Lakeview, and Ellis began to smell salt in the tidal river mud. This was where the President's psi-advisor, Ganesh Ramakrishnan, lived. Many times, he knew, Hawken had gone to his big rambling ashram and there consulted him for the latest in classified astrogation research, or to discuss the possibility of using marginal nexus chains in seldom-traveled parts of the Zone.

"He's a psi-talent of great power. A man of tremendous intellect. He has the biggest psi-library in Amerika," Hawken told him, pointing at the Ramakrishnan place. "He has collected a complete set of Records."

"Ramakrishnan's ashram—I've heard some pretty odd stories about that. Yeah, they say he's a maniac."

Hawken nodded. "He's a strange man, all right. A weird Hindu. Drinks a pint of his own urine every day, that kind of stuff. But he's an authentic genius. That's a word that gets bandied about far too much these days, I grant you, but what else can you call a person of his achievements? He's close to a unification theory of matter, energy, and psi, in which he'll truly be able to describe the universe, the Six Interactions, the Acausal Principle, and all."

"Do you believe that?"

"The President believes it, and that's good enough. Politically he's sound too. Under all the mystic bullshit he sees Yamato as a parasitic entity with a ravening appetite to prove itself superior to its host—that's us and the other Sectors, in case you're in any doubt. It's what stops his enemies prising him away from Alia Kane and ruining him. He's been smeared plenty of times, but now she's made it clear that persecution of Ramakrishnan—academic or otherwise—is tantamount to treason."

"Hands off the guru, eh?"

"That's what Alia Kane's protection means. What the hell, he might succeed in his theoretical work."

"And when she leaves office?"

"There will be a new President. Depending on who it is, Ramakrishnan is at liberty to leave Amerika, and his talents will be lost to us."

"You rate the guy?"

"I rate him."

Ellis folded his arms, unsure of his own belief. His head told him it was impossible and against the fundamentals of science, but at the same time he gloried in the notion of there being such a thing as a unified theory of matter, energy, and psi.

Hawken detected his withdrawal, handed him a stiff black coffee. Below, the ground-car lights on Bleeker turned to red. He saw a bowl of oranges in a restaurant window, a gingham tablecloth. This was Lincoln. Instantly he felt the vital force that only this fabulous capital city could create. As they touched down and dropped onto the cold lot, he felt like a ghost, an invisible eye, watching but ignored, and in his detachment he saw the truth of the place. It was astonishing! An exciting, aggressive, intense stew of human endeavor. A city growing fast, drawing all things and all men to it like a magnet, so that it doubled in size every ten years. It was sure to become soon the most populous city outside of the Kan Empire, and the most diverse anywhere. He saw men and women and children in the streets, workers and walkers; there were the great mansions of the rich and powerful, cathedrals and civic amenities, shopfronts and low shiels and malls crammed in side streets. Everywhere from Hythe Square up to Poland Drag there was a bedlam of noise. Street athletes attacked their personal bests, aggressive commerce happened with loud cries, popular art busking too, cleaning carts rattled down attractive arcade streets, whipjacks cried for credit, watched by Squad catchpoles who would take a share or maybe arrest them. Every minute, it seemed, each man, woman, and child fought psi and his or her fellow human being for profit in the middle of this most scoffing, most respectless and unthankful city there ever was.

They spent the night at Hawken's mansion on fashionable Pennsylvania Avenue, where his staff of synth servants fussed after them and attended their stay with sugar-sweet artificiality, and in the morning they ate a magnificent extended breakfast and got up from the table at noon, taking a black ground-limo to the other end of the avenue, its synth chauffeur chatting like a philosopher until Hawken commanded him to be quiet.

"No air-cars because of security," Hawken said, shrugging. "The place is surrounded by a trigger shield that would stop a suicide attack."

"Great."

"Remember what I told you if you get called to the stand."

"Don't worry about it."

On the other side of the railings they saw the rose gardens, and beyond, the quasi-replica of the imposing state buildings that had once stood in Washington, D.C., in the United States of Old Earth.

Marine guards in chrome helmets and blue neckerchiefs challenged them and took away their ID. But they saluted when it was given back, and they were waved through the tunnel. They got out and were conducted within the precinct of this old and venerable wing to the hall and chamber where the Security Council met.

It was a maze of doors and covered ways that smelled like floor polish and institutions. Within, ministers and civil servants and senators and congressmen occupied themselves with work and gossip and dancing round the issues. There were stately pieces of period furniture everywhere and huge paintings in gilt frames, carved busts of the great survivors, and below them a separate estate of office expeditors, aides, sergeants-at-arms, and beneath them a bustling underworld of servants, secretaries, spies, caterers, security men, cleaners, and administrators.

Hawken's petitions to the Council had preceded them, and they were met courteously by congressional officers who brought Hawken to the inquiry. When Ellis tried to follow, guards clashed their weapons together across his path, their stony lack of response leaving him in no doubt that he had been excluded unnegotiably.

Uninvited, he lingered outside the chamber of the Security Council for an hour, pacing the deep-carpeted corridor, wondering what was happening with Hawken, when or if he would be called as witness to events on Sado, and, if so, what he should say. Anxiously he imagined the councilors in their heavy robes, grave-faced, pompous, outwardly deploring Hawken's actions of piracy, and inwardly soured that he had failed to bring them the profit he had promised. This was the moment Hawken had dreaded in his fevers. The moment of account when credit tripped into deficit. When erstwhile political allies kissed the cheek and then turned their backs to call in the soldiery.

Ellis looked up as a troop of twelve white-and-blue-uniformed Marine guards, each carrying a folding-stock blaster, turned into the corridor. They clashed to attention ten yards away from him and remained at attention, staring glassily ahead.

Their arrival unsettled Ellis, who saw no reason for their presence. When he was approached by a man who might have been a lawyer, he felt alarm course through him. Dressed in a fawn half-cloak and skullcap, he seemed to be of some consequence. His face showed him to be a man of intellect and he had a sonorous voice to match the brown liquidity of his eyes.

"Captain Straker?"

Ellis returned the stare. "Yes."

"Would you be kind enough to follow me?"

Ellis remained rooted where he stood and the man turned back after three steps.

"I'm waiting for Commodore Hawken. He's in the council chamb—"

"Yes, I know. Please come with me."

Still Ellis did not move.

"What's the problem?"

Ellis's guarded words came slowly. "I don't know who you are. And I don't know how you know me. Am I under arrest?"

The man glanced at the Marine guard and shook his head. "These fine fellows have nothing to do with me, Captain. My name's Pharis Cassabian."

Cassabian put out a hand, but Ellis ignored it. "What do you want?"

Cassabian's eyes sparkled. "You've become quite famous around here just lately. I want to talk with you. That's all."

Ellis recoiled from the intensity of the man, the presumption of his manner, but something in Cassabian's face held him, and when he asked him to follow a third time, he followed.

22

It was another cold February night, eight o'clock by the chimes of the Sears clock tower, and Ambassador Satsuma no Okubo Shigenori sat cross-legged and alone on the tatami, sweating over a piece of diplomacy that he had been postponing for days. It was hard to know how best to proceed—in a begging letter to the Emperor of Yamato.

"*Sacred and Imperial Majesty,*" he wrote, obedient to the formula. "*My obligation to serve your Imperial Majesty, and the natural faith and love to your Imperial Majesty, induce me, with the greatest submission, to propose that which appears to me most fitting. . . .*"

Okubo was a heavy man, thickset, with a bullet head. His kimono had a military cut, the same black as his eyes, and his gray moustaches reached out across his cheeks like the moustaches found embossed on a *hoate*—the grotesque samurai warrior mask. He ran a hand uncertainly through the stubble of his pate, straight back from his forehead, as he searched for words, but his concentration was unfocused and his eyebrows rode querulously as he listened to the sound of a ground-car rattling through the streets below. Could this be the visitor he was expecting?

The man—a merchant captain, or so he said—had written a letter of proposal and that too lay on the tatami beside his writing stand. It was cautious but at the same time extravagant, and the promise it held out was tantalising, and Okubo had already decided that it was no longer a question of whether, but *when* he must act on it.

The ambassador applied himself anxiously to the other, vastly more important letter again. All Yamato's stars are in the ascendant. We must seize the moment now, he thought. If we hestitate we'll let fall the finest opportunity there'll ever be to destroy the Amerikans.

Okubo labored under no illusions about his position. He knew that he had replaced his well-liked and well-respected predecessor, Kuroda Kansuke, as a reprisal in kind. At the same time, in the ninth month of last year, the Emperor had expelled the uncouth Amerikan ambassador-resident and ex-academic, Dr. Ali Akhbar Smith.

He remembered Smith with indignation; his vitriolic temper and vile manners had outraged the whole of Kyoto. He had picked his teeth like a Kan Chinese, got disgustingly drunk, and, before hosts of the royal blood, had referred to the Emperor as "a canting little Yambo." Eventually the Court had been driven to petition the Emperor, who was spending time at Lake Biwa in Zen contemplation, and within six months he had complied, but Smith had refused to surrender the apology Mutsuhito had demanded of him, and so he had been thrown out. Surely it must have been a deliberate insult delivered on Alia Kane's behalf, the Baron Harumi, a man vastly experienced in the iniquities of the Amerikans, had told the Emperor. The fact that she had sent such a low-born, ill-bred creature, a fellow unskilled in all but the most vulgar social graces, can only have been a calculated slight—especially when the Emperor's ambassador to Amerika had been so elegant, so punctilious, and so refined.

Four months ago I thought the same, Okubo decided sadly, but four months on this planet has convinced me that such delicacy of understanding is utterly beyond the Amerikans. They think themselves a civilised people, but in reality they are as barbarous as the Kan. However, ignorance is no defense against infractions of diplomacy. It's time to show Alia Kane that she can't affront the Emperor of Yamato with impunity. It's time to remind Known Space that Yamato is the heir to greatness, and that at any time we can do to Amerika what we have already done to Korea and are presently doing to the Chinese.

"If harmonious relations are to be preserved between Amerika and the Court of Heaven," the Emperor's chamberlain had instructed him coldly just before he had embarked on the outward-bound nexus ship, "those relations must be based on tributary respect. Failing that, there must be an embassy of antagonism."

The shame of that parting burned in Okubo still. The Emperor's words had transmuted a golden, crowning moment into a leaden shame. Insult and innuendo had followed. Okubo thought hotly of the story he had picked up on board the transnexus ship to Liberty that the Emperor's half brother, Prince Sekigahara, had suggested sending a pig, wearing ambassadorial velvet over an Amerikan-style suit, to the White House. Of course, the story had gone, Mutsuhito's unsmiling sobriety had overruled that idea, and instead, he had sent Okubo Shigenori to teach the Amerikans manners!

And teach them he would.

Four months! Four months on this terrible planet. Four months spent huddled inside, four months of blackness when the cool primary star rises at nine in the morning and sinks at three in the afternoon. But it had been an immensely important four months in a place where history was at its rawest. Huge upheavals were afflicting the Sector, and each successive tremor nudged Alia Kane's downfall an inch closer. Yes, he told himself, heartened by the thought, the shame of my appointment is subsiding only slowly, but it's subsiding nevertheless. It has been my burden as well as my honor to carry out my duties to the Emperor, and I've been better served by the gods than by my master's courtiers, but I understand well that the ambitious diplomat can only forge himself a successful career in the furnace of conflict, and even if it sinks me in debt, I will buy my Emperor the victory he craves. *Hai!* And at the same time I will buy a victory of my own, for I long to see the streets of Lincoln lit up as bright as day by the funeral pyres of Alia Kane's Expansionists, and in this, the merchant captain may help me.

Okubo knew intimately his master's fervent passion. Since the death of his son, Prince Kono, the Emperor had been increasingly insular and increasingly concerned to extend the seamless cloak of Confucian stasis over the whole of Known Space. He knew that it was a mission appointed him by the gods. A task that would redeem the spiritual sins of Prince Kono and his own complicity in the murder of his son by Nishima Jun. If only Okubo could bend those pious hopes to his own ends. He had written a letter to Baron Harumi, trumpeting and martial, begging him to see the opportunities that the situation presented. An audacious move against Amerika was vital, and Harumi-sama's interest had been whetted. Now it was essential to convince Kyoto.

The letter he must now write to the Emperor would be superficially a request for funds. The embassy which was his residency was the legacy of a former age, when the old Anglo-Amerikan alliance had flourished. It had been provided by the grace of the English Crown; his own Emperor had budgeted a mere sixty thousand credits per annum to finance a staff of twenty-four. It was a figure that had not changed since the cutbacks of Alia Kane's first days, but prices were rising all over Amerika, and on his imperial funding he was expected to keep up appearances and to pay the multitude of informants and spies who fed into the Yamato network. So ran the text of the letter. But artfully concealed, interspersed among the old Kyoto flourishes, and readily decoded only by Prince Sekigahara's private secretaries were key *kanji* that spelled out the real difficulty: Okubo could ill afford the extra expenses that invasion plans would incur.

Though a man of some status, with a comfortable income from his industrial *han,* Okubo had found his lordly budget strained after just two months in this freezing hellhole. The extravagant demands of the gathering crisis had bankrupted him. Emperor Mutsuhito had to be made to understand. His Amerikan embassy must have funds. Now. Immediately!

Should this letter fail to sway the Emperor, Okubo knew, all these careful efforts would fall into dust. Starved of funds, the choice would then be to languish impotently, or turn to the detestable Chinese, whose financial tentacles were everywhere. Anything but that, he thought, running his eye reverently over his ancestral *katana* that rested on its customary stand by the door. The curved *saya,* or scabbard, was wooden, lacquered black and plain. The *tsuba,* handguard, was of silver, pierced so as to suggest the petals of a chrysanthemum—or the twelve Sectors of Known Space. The *tsuka,* hilt, was artfully wrapped in ray-fish skin and overwound with cords and finished with two decorative black and silver pommel pieces. No, if the Chinese were brought in to underwrite a Yamato Emperor's policies, there would be interference and constraint and all secrets would be compromised.

Truly the moment is coming, he told himself, weighing the *katana*. If the Amerikan Sector were not so unfortunately situated in Known Space, Baron Harumi's men would have annihilated this filthy hole and cut the throats of every last one of its obstinate inhabitants months ago. But soon enough the Amerikans would learn that their insularity was no protection against the might of Yamato.

The very air of Liberty is heavy with flammable vapors, and the Court of the President is tinder dry, he thought with anticipation. A spark! A single, sword-struck spark at the right instant would set Amerika ablaze. The entire Sector would rage with war, and not just war, but an era of destruction that would consume, once and for all, the vile barbarians.

He went to the sword, half drew it, and looked along the blade lovingly. At a single stroke all difficulties would be eliminated forever! And I, Satsuma no Okubo Shigenori, knight of *bushido*, member of the Council of His Imperial Majesty, will have touched off their destruction!

He closed his eyes and willed the images that cascaded through his mind to be still. This was no time for flights of fancy; there was still much to be done, he thought, growing suddenly severe with himself. The merchant captain talks big, but are not all Amerikan nexus rats loose-tongued braggarts? Surely he cannot possibly deliver what he says. Better to write the letter to the Emperor and leave dreaming to idle men.

He dipped his brush and wrote, couching the letter to his Emperor in flowery, subservient terms, struggling to strike the correct tenor and appending the standard "first priority" close:

"May the gods preserve, for many years, the sacred and celestial person of your Imperial Majesty. From the embassy of Yamato to Amerika, this twenty-eighth day of the second month, in the twentieth year of Kanei, your Imperial Majesty's unworthy ambassador and most humble servant."

Before the ornate Sears clock struck its third quarter, Okubo heard the knock at his door. He hurriedly put his papers and the sword in their proper places, then stood up and gave permission to the attendant for his visitor to be afforded entry.

The shoji slid aside.

Revealed was a tall, blond, barefoot man dressed in a rib-fronted jacket the color of an ocean wave and fashionable trousers. His teeth were white, he smelled of Amerikan bathwater, and he carried a gold stud, enameled with an outspread Aquila eagle, in his earlobe. But the most exquisite and the most provocative item of his apparel was a spiral-linked platinium chain looped three times around his neck and hanging inside his jacket. It was clearly of Japanese origin and too expensive to have been got honestly.

Okubo was caught momentarily speechless.

"*Konnichi wa,* Your Excellency!"

"*You?* You are—Captain Straker?"

"Got it in one."

A broad smile. Okubo looked the man up and down in amazement, then he recovered and quickly stifled his incredulity. This man was a full head taller than him, and built in proportion, though he had little fat about him. His hair and neatly-trimmed beard were coarse and wiry and his skin was bronzed; he had the assured presence of a psi-talent. And his finery no doubt came of profit he had made in the Neutral Zone. The man's hand came forward to clasp his own in a crushing squeeze.

"You—you will of course take tea?"

"Sure. Thanks."

He had expected someone very different: one of the shiftless apron scum that clustered about the local orbiter port of Norfolk, or a cloaked sneak thief from the seedy district. But this man was no spy. By his accent he was of this planet, bluff and uncultivated, and there was a fierceness in his eyes, but it was not a fierceness that threatened. Perhaps I can tame this lion, Okubo thought, pouring from a porcelain pot that had appeared at his elbow. In his letter he spoke of a great advantage to me and my cause. He's worth a cup of green tea at least.

"Do you have any preference, Captain? This is tea made with a leaf grown on Kyoto, from the *han* which my family owns."

The captain hesitated. "My taste is for Wu-i from Fukien, if you have it."

Okubo smiled delicately. "Ah, the black teas of China. Regrettably I do not keep a stock of Chinese leaf. You have been there?"

"Indeed I have. And I'm sure I can arrange for a pack or two of whatever leaf you like to be delivered to Your Excellency, if you wish it. I can even supply it to you at cost."

Okubo's hand hovered. "Thank you, but perhaps not, Captain. My position requires that I, more than any other, am seen to remain loyal to the produce of my own Sector. And loyalty is important, is it not?"

"Loyalty?" Straker laughed scornfully. "You'll pay through the ass if it's loyalty you want to drink."

Okubo replaced the pot and smiled again. "I know well the cost of service. Do you know that an ambassador must pay his own expenses?"

"Yeah? But his Emperor will underwrite him, if necessary, eh?"

Okubo paused. Then he nodded slowly, understanding. Dealing with barbarians and liars was an education in itself; they invariably called proceedings down to business with unseemly haste.

"So," he said genially. "You have your audience. What is this 'great advantage' of which you speak?"

Straker leaned forward gloatingly. "Something that can give you what you want and at the same time make me a few credits. If you're prepared to hear me out, you might think so too."

Straker began to talk business. Okubo learned first who he was, and then with shock that he had been at Sado on Hawken's ship. As he listened he took comfort in the guard that waited at his shoji and in the sword of Tsunetoshi steel standing beside it, but he swiftly discovered that he would need neither.

"A hundred men were left on Chi no Tsuki, Your Excellency. My brother among them. And I want to recover them all. My proposal is this: in exchange for their safe release and delivery here, a sum of aurium, and certain guarantees—I will give you the key to Amerika."

Okubo stared at Straker, inwardly unsure whether to throw him out or to hear him further, but the look in his visitor's eye held him and at last he said, "Go on."

"Your Emperor has an army of invasion in the Zone. He knows that that is a blaster pointed at the head of Amerika. Conversely, Korean pirate vessels, vessels under the President's covert orders, are swarming in the nexus chains of Korea and paralysing your communications at will, and you are powerless to prevent them."

"That is a common belief here," Okubo said, attempting nonchalance.

"And with good reason. As you know perfectly well, unless Baron Harumi's samurai are fed, they will have to retreat from Guam and the Marshall systems and bring unbearable shame down on the Emperor. The Koreans will renew their attempts to get free from Yamato rule, and they'll succeed. How long do you think it will be before the Chinese recover their wits and wrest that quadrant from you?"

Acid bubbled in Okubo's stomach. This rude nexus captain had described the situation accurately. His analysis was perfect, his insights uncommonly well informed, and uncannily, Straker's views were identical to his own worst fears. Okubo decided, then, to hear the man out.

China, "the Middle Kingdom," as they called themselves, was Confucian and hugely populous. Her ruling imperial house of Shan was wrestling with other internal factions for control of the Sector. Astrographically she occupied the choicest slice of Known Space, and her trading position connecting the Asian, Europan, and Amerikan quadrants posed a massive potential threat to Yamato. Kyoto's greatest nightmare was that once China's countless billions were united again under a strong leader, she would rival Yamato for mastery of Known Space, and a China that had annexed the rich heartlands and controlled satellite quadrants like Korea and Manchu would be a China of unthinkable dominance.

"You need to keep Korea under your economic yoke," Straker insisted, seizing the initiative. "But Korea is slipping away from you. And there's nothing you can do to stop it. While Alia Kane remains President of Amerika the Korean chain will never be Yamato's artery and Korea will never be secure!"

Okubo's palms were damp with anxiety. "The new tariffs into and out of Korea will soon raise enough credit to feed Baron Harumi's garrisons."

"Wrong! Harumi's a fool if he believes that." Straker laughed scornfully. "Yamato's new import tariffs are resented. They will be resisted. And in imposing them Yamato will make enemies of the men who create and control the Korean Quadrant's wealth. If every hundredth credit of property, and every twentieth credit of land sales, and every tenth credit of all other sales is to be clawed from them and spent on oppression, what must the Koreans begin to think? You take no account of their liberties, Mr. Okubo. Even the factions friendly to Yamato perceive that the baron means to make slaves of them!"

Okubo recoiled from the vision Straker had thrown up before his eyes. The words of that arch-rebel, Keun Whan Pai, burned in his mind: "We have come to drive out the intruding, foreign, and shameful tyranny of these cruel ravishers and persecutors of Korean blood, to bring back your old privileges . . ." He felt his hands turning cold now and fought to steady them. "I don't accept what you say," he began slowly, "and if I did, I could not expect a man like you to provide a remedy."

Ellis leaned back, a humorless grin on his face. "Now, that's not the attitude at all, Mr. Okubo. As well you know, conditions here are ripe for change. It's a mistake to think that everyone in Amerika wants this situation to continue."

"Are you not loyal to your President?"

"Merchants are loyal to themselves! Men like me are always hurt by embargoes. I've had commerce in the Neutral Zone with many Yamato traders who think just the same."

"And do they propose rebellion as an answer?"

The fierceness in the Amerikan flared up. "Listen! Presidents come and Presidents go. I mean to prosper whoever sits in the White House. I've been up there with the men who stand between Baron Harumi and Liberty. And I know their minds. Just you think about this: a handful of trusted agents, spending credits in the right places, can keep the Korean chains clear of hostile ships long enough for your baron's men to make the crossing into Amerika. I can put five armed nexus ships of two thousand tons mass at your disposal at any time. Five ships that will guarantee a successful landing."

Okubo made an effort to marshal his thoughts. "Why would you do that, Captain? You enjoy low rates of interest in Amerika. There are no tenth or twentieth credit taxes here. Why should an Amerikan merchant wish to be put in the same ship as his Korean competitors? You know that could happen if Amerika falls under Yamato dominion."

"If that happens, then doubtless some merchants will be more highly favored than others, eh? Come the day, those that've shown themselves most friendly can expect the best cuts in return, isn't that right?"

"Ah! Now we return to questions of loyalty, do we not, Captain?" Okubo said. Inwardly he was thinking: Careful! Amerikans have twisted minds. They have no clear concept of honor or of loyalty. They all think like the rabid filth of the merchant class. How many times have I heard their phrase "to make a quick buck"? It seems unthinkable madness to us who revere our Emperor totally and are prepared to think in terms of very long-term strategies, but it is entirely possible that this Amerikan is prepared to sell out his Sector and betray his President for a quick handful of credits.

The Amerikan sucked in his cheeks and placed his hands flat on the table before him. "Look, it's a simple business transaction. I'm offering you the aid you require. The cost is two million credits in freely convertible inter-Sector bonds. Take it or leave it."

"Two million credits represents a lot of buying power."

"That depends on what you're buying."

"I will think about it."

"Well, Mr. Okubo, don't think about it too long. My offer is limited. And like your tea, it doesn't stay on the boil forever."

Okubo watched the man rise massively from the tatami and leave him to his thoughts. It was true that the Amerikan President had never been in a more bellicose mood. It was also true that without safe passage across the Korean chains, intervention in Amerika would be impossible. According to his spies, there were millions put out of work by the trade embargo in Amerika, many of whom were reaching the limit of their patience with Alia Kane. Sooner or later, someone would stand up and do something. Perhaps this man really had brought him the key that would open the door to Amerika. And if so, he, Okubo, must surely grasp it.

As the echo of Ellis's boots died away on the cedar planking outside, Okubo opened the drawer of an exquisite maroon lacquer chest and brought out his Imperial letter, feeling a stab of annoyance. If the sum of payment the Amerikan had demanded was to be included, the whole letter would have to be redrafted.

23

Ellis left the residency on foot and made his way back across Lincoln via the groundways and precincts of Lower East that any sane man avoided at night. Marginals and lowlifes bayed at him and were ignored as he strode down the middle of trash-strewn sidewalks under overhanging upper stories where porno holos filled the windows and hookers shouted down. Kicking aside heaps of filth and swinging his arms for warmth, he was almost willing some slime to jump from the shadows and attempt to take him. There was a reason to come this way. No one would dare follow him here, and if they did he would detect them more easily. Woe betide anyone who got in his way!

Two weeks of inactivity in Lincoln coming on the top of the paralysing tragedy of his homecoming had made him ready for anything this city might bring to him. Suddenly he felt a powerful need to discharge the dirty burden that dealing with Okubo had put on him. Talk of his brother had opened a sewer seething with maggots, and the feeling was too much to bear.

"I've stuck a meat hook right through your jaw, Okubo," he said aloud, flexing his fists. "I've got you dangling right where I want you, you sonofabitch."

Hawken had disclosed little of what had passed at the meeting with the Security Council. To Ellis's dismay all he would say was that he had delivered a statement of facts concerning the events at Sado and that the meeting had been adjourned to a later date. He had expressed neither hopes nor fears about the outcome, but he had ordered Ellis to remain on call and to await further instructions.

Ellis longed to be released from that arrangement now. He wanted only to go back to Harrisburg, to find John Oujuku and further their plans. What was needed was action! A definite course, plotted with intent and powered with strength and courage! This two-bit politicking was a waste of time, and its hourly passage served only to cool the temper and blunt the steel.

In a barely suppressed rage he moved across a city that mirrored his mood. Lincoln fumed with crisis. The atmosphere was thunderous with revolt and charged with rumors of every kind. He emerged into a main thoroughfare, into streets lit by blue floods and thronged with night people, beggars, hookers—synthetic and real—and drunken packs of people, all blowing here and there in a wind of purposelessness. He lost himself in the jostling night that no curfew had ever been called to quieten, and then, recognising the dark stump of the RISC building, he made for the appointed meeting place. By the brash, lit-up colossus of the Vegas Strike and next to it the Slottee Palace, and down the Spanish Steps with its chow houses, out by Amalgamated Continental and into Highboro. A gang of half a dozen nexus rednecks came shouldering by him with tri-shirts bearing the pulsing Japanese characters for "Yamato" and the belligerent words "Send me!" At the bridge over the river an evil stink rose up, poisoning the air. Upstream was Con-Park, he knew, discharging warm water, and this place was the foulest running sore that ever ran tributary into a Liberty river; if it went on like this, the famous East Side crayfish would stop living in it. He closed his mouth and tried not to breathe in the fetid mists as he waited.

In minutes he was met by "Butler," Hawken's chief synth servant, and another synthetic he had never seen before. Both constructs were thin and pallid in the city light. They reminded Ellis of ship's rats as they invited him into the plush limo interior.

"If you'd like to get in, sir."

"Park it. I want to walk."

"Yes, sir. If that's your wish."

Butler told him that the master had left a message to join him at a place downtown when he could do so conveniently.

"Where?"

"You're to come with us."

"How far?"

"Just along, Captain, sir."

The scrubbed pink subservience of the synths made him ashamed. He just couldn't bring himself to be ordinarily polite to artificial life. What kind of status thing is this? he asked himself. Yet all the very rich seem to surround themselves with them. Only the rich can afford them. They're real hard to make and take a long time to program and mature and so expensive that everyone wants one. Sick. Sick! Sick!!

"That your only name? Butler?"

"I am Butler, sir. He is Driver."

"Not Joe Butler? Or Frank Butler? Or *Charlie* Butler?"

"Just Butler, sir. It's my . . . function."

"Jeezus . . ."

They walked for a half hour, the two synthetic men flanking him, warding off the bums that crept from holes and doorways as they passed. They seemed strangely hard and programmed to be streetwise. In his expensively cut clothes Ellis drew envious stares. He flipped small credit slottees as he went, feeling touched by the plight of the poor schizo bastards that had nowhere to rest their bones on such a freezing cold night, not slackening his pace until one ragged heap of filth moved into his path and looked up at him with an ageing human face. It was vilely tattooed and silvery threads were swinging from a wound in the bald head. Direct stimulation of the fantasy centers of the brain for anyone who could afford to wire up to a code outlet.

"C'mon, c'mon, c'mon," it shrieked in a hideous singsong. "Rats and mice and ev'thing nice. Got the price of shot for a veteran of the Ho Chi Minh massacre?"

Ellis handed a silver slottee to the freak and walked on. Slottees were being hailed as a relatively new idea: discs of ID-free read-only credit for gamblers and lowlifes to spend anonymously. He felt more disgusted now than ever he had aboard the starvation ship. He knew it was because the old man's voyage of degradation was a result of human weakness. He had no destination but the autopsy slab.

"Please don't do that, Captain, sir. Please don't. Not a whole credit slottee. Others'll see and there'll be a riot!"

Ellis ignored Butler's wheedling complaint, and a little later as they passed into a broad, less congested street, the complaint came again. "Please, Captain, sir. Never again. There are the Squads for them. They'll jump us like a pack of ditch dogs if you flash your cash. You've been away a long time, Captain. Perhaps you've forgotten the value of credit down here."

"What the hell do you know about human suffering? You never hear of charity?"

"Yessir." Butler put his hand to his breast hastily. "I beg your pardon, Captain."

The other chimed in explanation. "Most of them are fakers, sir. Just syndicated fakers."

Ellis replied with irritation. "Who'd want to fake that kind of distress?"

"That's syndicate work, Captain. They aren't *real*. No more than Driver or myself. Though some are just assembled from real spare parts. They have an 'E' or an 'R' printed on their arms, or crosses of blue in their armpits. There's a trade in synthetics that go wrong. Big corruption in the corporation. Rejects operated by hoodlums. That's where the hookers come from."

Driver spoke. "A difficult moral question, you'll agree, Captain. If they seem real, it's because they practice the art of deception habitually. Hoodlums."

"Driver's right." Butler nodded vigorously. "The Squads will arrest them and melt out their—"

"Shut it! You think I can't tell a synthetic at twenty paces?"

They had come to the gate of an impressively large mansion of plex shingle and new French brick. The vogue for big staffed houses where politics was done was growing. There was, it seemed to Ellis, more window than wall to it. Partying sounds emanated from inside. As he passed the guard, he was obliged to leave his Wesson with the trog. Without it on his hip he felt naked, but as he was admitted he began to stare around comfortably. The mansion's main congress was spacious and tastefully furnished with a giant holo fire blazing to give atmosphere. Liveried synthetics went about the tables with serving dishes; there were some top-slot Dover creations. Maybe even a few realfood delicacies.

There were high-status people here, many young preppie types dancing to vambo, intellectuals, party post-holders—the owner was definitely a powerful man in political circles. Above them, a high plex frieze was lit up by a hundred holo candles and, above that, an ornate white ceiling, filled with exquisite vambo music, played on wire and pipes.

He picked out Hawken almost at once.

"What happened?" the shipowner asked, keeping his voice low. He could not disguise his anxiety.

"Plenty. Why are we here?" Ellis looked around again at the lavish decor. "Who's the owner?"

"Tell me, damn it! Did Okubo bite?"

"You could say that his interest was aroused. What the hell is this place?"

Hawken pursed his lips. "Ellis, there's somebody who wants to speak with you. All hell's breaking loose tonight. You could say that the ulcer's burst at last."

"Is Mr. Cassabian here?" Ellis asked, surprised at Hawken's tense restlessness. Immediately he thought of the Security Council adjournment. Was Hawken priming him because he had wind of some immediate danger? He had never forgotten that all their futures hung by a thread, but then caution and responsibility had supplanted raw faith in Hawken's soul long ago. Hawken could never fully abandon himself to his fate as an astrogator must. As a man grows older and richer, Ellis warned himself, he loses his will to fight and his taste for trying Destiny's hand. But I will! See if I don't. I'll take Destiny outside and kick the shit out of him until he submits to my demands. And I'll never surrender.

"Ellis, a quiet word!"

"Sure, but will you please tell me whose place this is?"

Before Hawken could reply they were approached by a tall, bony woman of middle age and serene expression. She held the hand of a small boy with an elfin face, five or six years of age. Beside her stood a young woman of delicate looks and shy manner, her features showing a close resemblance to her mother. Ellis was first struck by her willowy beauty, but was then shocked to see in her the ghost of another. He realised who her father was, and whose place this must therefore be.

Hawken presented him deferentially.

"Vara Lubbock, Captain Ellis."

"I'm very pleased to meet you, Captain."

"Likewise, Mrs. Lubbock." His smile was crisply formal.

"This is my son, Bobby—say 'Welcome to my father's house,' Bobby."

The boy did as he was told and smiled. Ellis reached down and took the boy's small hand briefly.

"May I present my elder daughter, Reba?"

"Charmed."

The young woman took his hand in silence. She was elegance itself, and Ellis felt the warmth in her smile. He was aware of a finely attired youth watching them intently from a couch some distance away. He seemed mean-tempered and to have indulged a mite too liberally in the hospitality. Ellis saw how Reba looked to him modestly. Her smile disappeared and she stepped back.

Her mother detected the urgency in Hawken. "We won't detain you, Captain. I believe you have some business with my husband."

As he led the way, Hawken whispered fierce words that sent a shock through Ellis's guts. "This is where the Security Council's adjournment has brought us. Choose your words carefully and understand that tonight we're pleading for our lives. I heard from Otis le Grande that we're to be indicted for piracy. Take care now. The man we're going to meet could be our executioner."

They drew close to the holo fire. Nearby, on an upholstered couch, an austerely garbed man dandled a child on his knee and told another three or four standing about him a fantastic tale that captivated their attention. He was in his mid-fifties, his face was long, his eyes deep-set but alight with a warm humor, and he gently disengaged a tiny hand from his long beard as Hawken came to him, acknowledging him with a nod. He was William Conroy Lubbock, principal secretary of state of Amerika. Though not from a long-standing political family, he had risen to become the most powerful man in the administration. At length, he stood up tall and straight and ushered Hawken and Ellis to a door and along a shining plex corridor to a large room stocked with hundreds of paper books and displaying seven or eight small pieces of archeological sculpture. A Freemason crest and historical prints adorned the walls.

Ellis scanned the bookshelves with awe. The room was an old-style library, twenty yards by ten, dominated by a ceiling star from which hung a candelabrum of fifty pure wax candles which a silent servant patiently lit for them. Chairs were brought and the fire was blazed up. This was no holo, but a real fire of burning wood. There was more paper here than Ellis had imagined could ever be left outside the tragic original planet of Earth. The smell of the paper that filled the room reeked wealth and delighted him.

The oak desk at which Conroy Lubbock sat was huge and neatly arranged and genuine. He listened intently, all trace of levity erased from his face and replaced by a solemnity that was graven deep, as Hawken explained that Ellis was the witness of whom he had spoken to the Security Council.

A charge of power emanated from Lubbock, Ellis saw, but it was not a dead authority born of cold responsibility. It was said that Lubbock had the capacity to interlace fifty separate thoughts in his mind simultaneously, that it was impossible to outguess him. When he spoke, his voice was distinctively nasal and soft; his words were admirably to the point.

"You have been at the residence of Ambassador Okubo. What did you say to him?"

Ellis cleared the burr from his throat. "Well, sir, I told him that I would give him help in his enterprise."

"You told him exactly what Commodore Hawken told you to say?"

"I did, yes, sir. And more. The proposal I put to him went like this: for a million credits in convertible bonds he will have the service of five nexus ships, if and only if he will free our people on Sado."

"Your brother is among them, isn't he?"

"Yes."

"And Okubo accepted?"

"Not straight out. But I believe he will."

"Good! Now tell me word for word what was said."

Conroy Lubbock sat back as the captain made his report, listening and judging. As Hawken had said, Straker was a psi-talent with an impressive presence and a quick, clear mind. The detail in which he laid out the interview with Okubo confirmed that amply. Hawken had vouched that Ellis was reliable, describing his loyalty in the highest terms and praising his political understanding. Above all Hawken had said that Ellis's personal loss fitted him for his task exactly. As Lubbock watched and listened he saw that Ellis's feelings for his stranded brother shone through like a heat ray. He had faith, and that faith, though surely misplaced, gave his manner an earnestness that was impossible to fake. It would be hard to order the killing of a man like this.

Lubbock decided with regret that such an order would probably be necessary. The great test is coming, he reminded himself. It doesn't take a statesman to see that the pulse of the city is quickening by the hour. The leviathan of war is stirring from sleep, and it inflames and terrifies the people. Ito has brought me intelligence of unease from all the worlds of Amerika. It's fortunate that Otis le Grande plans to move against me tomorrow. If he carries the President, I will fall. *Therefore, I must decide on Hawken tonight.*

Lubbock's knuckles cracked as he squeezed his left hand with his right. If Mutsuhito has decided on invasion, as Hawken insists, then it's imperative that he be countered and confounded. In that case, Ellis's desire for his brother's release may serve to convince and mislead Okubo to great effect. That much is plain. *But is Mutsuhito's mind made up to invade?* If it's not, then to back Hawken will enrage the Emperor and push him into war. That's futile. Appeasement would make much better sense.

Lubbock considered the latter course carefully. Perhaps I should cease to oppose le Grande and make my peace with those who're trying to heal the rift with Yamato. Then I would cease to be their target. Wouldn't it be better to stop this double-dealing now? To square things with Okubo and arrest Hawken and Straker in a grand gesture of friendship with Yamato? Cassabian's meddling had already made that more difficult—but not yet impossible.

Lubbock silently cursed the timing of events for the thousandth time that day. Crushingly, just as the million seeds he had planted during his incumbency as secretary were coming to fruit, there had sprung up an overwhelming combination of circumstances from which escape seemed impossible. They dragged at him with the force of a black hole.

The toil had been immense, he thought proudly. My program to cut expenditure and restore the value of the currency has provided a sturdy base for the economy. Years of peace have prospered the Sector. For a decade I've sought to build up Amerika's weak defenses, the Army, the Navy, and industry. I've striven to attract foreign investors and manufacturers to Amerika. Last year I ordered the formation of the R&D Agency. That's now bringing in Europan aurium prospectors to attempt to locate captured Gum ejecta, sources of the super-heavy metals essential for modern life. What a tragedy of waste if it's allowed to collapse now!

Lubbock toyed with his heavy chain of office as Ellis finished his report, still unconvinced about Hawken's game. Of course, the man was looking out for his own interest, but there was a good deal of truth in what he said. However, the growing enmity with Yamato was throwing the gains of ten years to the winds. That could not be ignored lightly, even if it meant sending patriotic men to face Yamato justice.

"We must have a united Sector, secure and strong," Lubbock told them openly. "That is paramount. We cannot afford to contemplate a war with Yamato. My foreign policy is on a knife point. It seems that Harumi's samurai legions must eventually win in Korea and that the puppet government will soon crush the Independents in Manchu."

"Then what?" Hawken asked tightly.

"A Chinese-Yamato alliance against Amerika. It's the only sensible course for our enemies, an opportunity they can't afford to overlook to destroy us. Already Pharis Cassabian has intercepted correspondence between the Chinese hegemony and Mutsuhito. A meeting in two months' time, so he says, to plot our downfall. What can I do? Tell me. How do I save Amerika from two titans?"

Hawken's words were brave and unswerving. "You must have a defensive alliance with Europa. You must suckle the newborn rebel movements in Manchu, shutting the back door against the Chinese Dowager, who for years has used Manchu against us. You must stamp out the plots in Latina, where Yamato seeks to establish bases that will encircle us, and you must step up aid to the Taiwanese and the Koreans, who, while they remain free, continue to exhaust and distract Yamato."

"We don't have much time."

"Then you should decide to start now."

"All that is still not enough. Europa is too far away, the Manchu rebels are weak, and the Koreans divided. Our only hope against Yamato is to cement an alliance with the Chinese, and the only way to do that is for the President to agree to the Dowager's demands that the Ten Degree tract of the Neutral Zone will become their sole property. My attempts to secure such an agreement have so far failed."

Lubbock's mind ranged free over the bleak political landscape as he tried to think of a way to save Hawken, Straker, and one or two other scapegoats from being extradited, tried in Yamato for piracy, and ceremonially executed. If Cassabian was right, the Chinese civil wars would soon cease. The Dowager Empress, head of the Shan, was ambitious to enthrone each of her three male offspring. Though attempts to marry Alia Kane to Prince Fa Hsien had foundered, and his brother, Fu Chih, was married, there was another. It was still minutely possible that an alliance with China could be made through the nineteen-year-old Prince Pi Wu. If Cassabian was right . . .

Lubbock brought his thoughts back to the matter in hand severely and decided to lay the central aspect of the maze before Hawken.

"You can't hope to know the answers to this riddle, because the greatest threat comes from within," he said throatily, his words coming like a confession. "I am at the center of a power struggle. A vicious conspiracy to unseat me. Otis le Grande has opposed me consistently, searching out support in Halton Henry and other branches of the Henry clan. The representatives of Dakota particularly, Waters and Westmoreland and their allies, detest the President's reliance on me. They complain of my influence. Jealousy and resentment are my chief enemies. And if the President is prised away from me now, we've lost everything."

"So we're all in the same position, Mr. Secretary," Ellis said suddenly. "For Chrissakes let's stand together! Those who want to make peace with Yamato are the same people who want to usher in direct rule from Kyoto. They want to destroy us. Are we going to let them take us down that road without a fight?"

Lubbock's attention fastened on his words like a talon. "Brave sentiments, Captain. *But I must have a plan.*"

"I have a plan."

Hawken's disquiet rose visibly. His eyes flashed a warning, but Ellis ignored it, seizing his chance. "The Korean leader, Keun Whan Pai, is no fool. He has an official policy whereby he condemns the pirates that riddle his Quadrant, but the truth is he maintains most of the armed nexus ships in the Korean chain. He's got at least fifty so-called pirates cruising under his orders. Inside a year, he could have eighty big nexus ships under arms. Korea's by no means lost yet. Let's give them all the aid we can. If we support their privateers on all Amerikan aprons, they can patrol the Neutral Zone chains too, and stand between Amerika and Yamato as a protection."

"Another cause for Yamato to resent us?"

"Give me command of six ships, Mr. Secretary, and if, through Okubo, I can draw Baron Harumi into a premature invasion, I'll fall on his transports and blow them to hell. Imagine it! His samurai division defenseless as they accelerate towards the Kalifornian nexi, when his mercenary escort turns on him with singularity guns! Think of the loss of face! It would deal Yamato such a blow of shame that they wouldn't get up off their asses inside ten years!"

"If only it were that simple, Captain."

"Which of us ain't a pirate at heart?" Ellis said quietly. He braced himself, clearly aware that his life and the future of Amerika depended on what he was about to say. "Mr. Lubbock, I'm an Amerikan, and I know that if Amerikans are to succeed, we must dare to do what no one else dares. We are not as rich as Yamato, and our Sector is comparatively underpopulated and without resources. But our people have courage. Put your trust in them and they won't fail you."

A knock at the door prevented Lubbock from replying. The man who entered was of middle height, corpulent, and with the white curly hair of a sixty-year-old. Nikolai Belkov was Lubbock's immensely rich ally in Council. He and Lubbock had first met during their student days on Massachusetts, and since then Belkov had benefited hugely from Stratford Henry's defiance of Central Authority constraints on trade in the Neutral Zone and had weathered the storms of Lucia Henry's days despite his firm Expansionism. He owned land in six systems and now occupied the position of treasury secretary. It was Belkov who had championed Hawken at the giving of his depositions before the Security Council and it was he who had protected him by calling for the adjournment.

He greeted Hawken warmly, nodded amiably at Ellis, and sank into an armchair, red-faced, sweating, and breathless.

"Bad news. I've sounded Morgan and Caesare. They're with the vice-president and his buddies on the Neutral Zone recognition question. They favor an immediate restoration of relations with Mutsuhito." He turned bulging eyes on Hawken. "And you guys extradited to Kyoto to face trial!"

Hawken's pale face was unmoving. Belkov went on, this time to Lubbock. "But there's better. The President this afternoon slapped down Otis le Grande in a savage argument for opposing you. It was wonderful to behold, Conroy! All riled up in a terrible fury. She stabbed him with her finger and sent him away like a little boy! A remarkable performance! You should have been there."

Lubbock experienced a tremendous wave of relief. He had been fearing what would happen when le Grande poured his poison in the President's ear. He had worried that Alia would be swayed sufficiently by her favorite billionaire to let events ride their course. Without her explicit protection, Lubbock knew, he was as good as dead. But she had confirmed him in her esteem by preempting le Grande's attack.

Lubbock turned to Ellis, knowing that he needed time to consider these new developments. "We'll have to talk further. Please, Captain, enjoy the hospitality of my house, but excuse us. There's a few things I need to discuss."

Ellis rose stiffly and left with a show of unwillingness.

When the captain was gone, Lubbock told Belkov about Hawken's plan and what had happened that evening with Okubo.

"We must move fast!"

"What will you do?" Hawken asked.

"Follow my instincts—as always. I may yet have a use for your Captain Straker."

Both men watched Lubbock go over to the fireplace. Nikolai Belkov had been his closest friend for many years now. They had stood godfather to each other's children, they had been through many political crises together, planned together, seen their fortunes rise together. In this time of troubles they would have to stick together.

Lubbock stooped over the real hearth and picked up a bundle of twigs. He turned and held up the bundle, flexing it in his hands.

"See that, gentlemen!" he said with all the dignity of the ancient movie hero John Huston. "Together I can't break them. It's beyond my strength. But singly—" He pulled out one twig and snapped it, then another and another. "One at a time, Nikolai, they are at my command. One at a time."

When Ellis returned to the main congress, he saw that the younger children had been put to bed and the party had fizzled out. The evening's gathering was settling to more leisurely matters, turning to cards and tables of backgammon and conversation. He was urged to make accounts of his thrilling voyages and to be polite to all the couch lizards that asked.

Vara Lubbock found him drowning in a tide of young people eager to learn the truth about the Sado incident. She extricated him and brought him along with her, talking inconsequentially all the while, but examining him so subtly that Ellis had no doubt that her appraisal of him would reach her husband that night.

They walked the long gallery, Ellis enduring a string of elaborate introductions, until they came to a knot of spectators; the sight arrested Ellis's attention. An adjoining room had been cleared of furniture and strung with a net. Two young men in shirt sleeves were playing a game. They appeared to be swiping a feathered gewgaw back and forth with bats shaped like snowshoes. After the weighty proceedings in which Ellis had been engaged it seemed frivolous and trivial behavior.

"Kurt Reiner. And his opponent, Art Logan."

Ellis recognised Reiner as the arrogant chancer who had caught his attention in the main congress when he had first arrived. So that's Kurt Reiner, he thought. He remembered the rumor he had picked up from one of Hawken's servants that Reiner had attacked a synthetic of the Lubbock household a couple of years before and killed him. Watching his vicious slashings with the bat, Ellis felt certain his first impressions had been correct.

"Kurt has lived with us here as one of my husband's protégés. My husband hopes that one day soon he will become a member of the House and also our family by marrying our elder daughter. He's a keen player."

"What is the aim of it, Mrs. Lubbock?"

"We often amuse ourselves with classical games here, Captain. This one you may not know. It's called 'badminton.' "

"I've never seen it. I doubt whether it has ever been played aboard a nexus ship."

Vara looked askance at him. "We play other games, some of a more intellectual kind. Little riddles with which we entertain ourselves. I understand you're an astrogator, so try you this: Suppose you were a Yamato admiral. What would be your chief concerns?"

"A Yamato admiral?" Ellis balked at the idea. "That's a hell of a mind-set to get into."

"Give it a try. How would you advise your Emperor?"

"I'd have to tell him to ground all his ships and be less of a nuisance to law-abiding traders in neutral territories."

Conroy Lubbock's wife tutted. "Give me a proper answer."

The gewgaw flew toward Ellis and he caught it from the air deftly. Reiner demanded its return and threw down his bat in pique as it was tossed to his opponent. He was obviously beer drunk. Ellis's gesture of apology was respectless, and he noticed that Vara Lubbock took note of it as he pondered her question.

Strange how all the important politics in the Sector gets done in these mansion soirees, he thought. The power being brokered in this house tonight is astonishing. If this is some kind of test, he thought, then okeh. He would answer as honestly as he could. When at Cheju Do, he had heard news of the Chinese in the newly ceded system of Hainan. Mutsuhito had demanded explanations why their numbers had been allowed to exceed those of racial Japanese. He had outlawed their language, destroyed their ghettoes, prohibited their Chinese dress, and ordered the doors of each Chinese household to swing open on each and every day to expose the depth of their iniquities. Pushed beyond endurance, they had risen against the *kempei* and had called upon the Dowager for aid. It gave Ellis an idea to answer politics with politics.

"I think I would advise His Imperial Majesty to watch his back."

"His back?"

"Hainan."

"Ah! The Chinese. You think the suppression in Hainan was Yamato's big mistake?"

"Sure. Ever since the system fell to Yamato the Chinese have brooded on its recapture. When the Dowager's father defeated the Yamato fleet ten years ago in the Zhanjiang system, the Chinese gained control from there to the Boundary chain. It's only a matter of time before the Dowager sends an army to attempt the return of Hainan."

"So, Admiral, you would beg the Emperor to build ships? Ships that might easily invade Amerika?"

"To build ships, yes. But not ships fit for the Neutral Zone. In chains like those spurred from Zhanjiang, the Emperor needs vast freezee transports, globe vessels like those he already has, to keep the Chinese out of the Home Worlds."

"You think like a Japanese, Captain."

"You asked me to, ma'am."

"Let's hope the Emperor has few advisors as wise as you. Or none of us will be able to sleep safe in our beds."

"So long as Amerikan ships remain loyal, you can sleep secure. There's not a fleet yet built that could overcome us. Nor will there be, if I have any say in the matter."

"I like your spirit, Captain. But perhaps you're a little too outspoken. If you don't mind me offering you advice, I suggest you employ rigorous logic where my husband is concerned. He has a high regard for facts, and he mistrusts those who attempt to appeal to his emotions." Vara Lubbock's eyes strayed to her daughter and back. "Do you play *go?*"

Ellis sighed. "I've played once or twice."

"What rank are you?"

"Sho-dan."

"Is that right? Well, why not have a game against equal opposition? If you will."

"I'd be delighted," he said, feeling otherwise, but was pleasantly surprised when Reba Lubbock came to him and set up a *go* board on a small carved table between them. They sat quietly in a corner on little stools, well apart from the noise and hubbub at the center of the room, but as they played, Ellis's thoughts were interrupted time and again by stratagems wholly unconnected with the board. Had he wrestled well enough with Okubo for Hawken's plan to be taken up by the ambassador? Had his outspokenness jeopardised the plan with Conroy Lubbock? What was the meaning of the news that Belkov had brought?

He tried to shut from his mind the possibility that Conroy Lubbock would decide to extradite them, and explored instead the damning consequences of success. Suppose that Yamato agreed to surrender Duval and the other survivors—what then? Wouldn't they murder them all in rage if he betrayed Okubo at the crucial time? What tortures would they not inflict on a man whose brother had destroyed an entire Yamato invasion force? They'd probably Probe Duval to death in as lingering a way as possible.

Reba's voice came to him again. "It's your move, Captain Straker."

Absently he picked up his white stone and began to place it at a cut point, then he saw her frown and he corrected his mistake. She played well. Too well. He watched her slender hands as she fingered one of his captured stones. He had thought she was shy at first, but there was an undeniable boldness about her. Strands of brown hair had escaped from her clip and trailed beside her ear and she twisted them as she concentrated. With a pang he realised that it was a gesture that reminded him of Janka. Poor dead Janka.

"*Atari.*"

"I missed that."

"Your mind is somewhere else, Captain."

"I guess so."

"Would you rather we didn't play?"

"No, no." He sat back, looking at her. "Tell me. Who taught you to play *go?*"

"My father." She looked up at him guilelessly, pleased to have opened conversation with him. "He's always been very interested in the education of his children. And he's a very clever man."

"I noticed that."

She smiled at him and the smile touched him. "You did, huh? My father likes to fill his house with friends. He says that makes him feel at home."

"Few men have a more prestigious circle of friends to invite home."

Her smile withered. "His position has its drawbacks. My father's work load has been crushing him lately. The President is a hard taskmistress. She refuses to marry and that's worrying him. Alia Kane is a difficult woman to get along with. She leans on him heavily. His health suffers, I think."

Ellis knew that for years Lubbock had urged upon the President a politically astute marriage to one of the princes of the Chinese Empire. It was an unpleasant, not to say ludicrous, idea to most Amerikans, but the Chinese would have found it the most sincere expression of a top-level diplomatic alliance. Horrified by the prospect, Alia Kane had brought all negotiations to a halt over trivialities.

He asked, "Did you think Prince Fa Hsien was a good choice?"

"It's hardly my place to say, Captain Straker. Diplomacy is a complex matter, only for those of high understanding."

Ellis noted her modesty. They were both aware of the risks surrounding the fact of a woman ruler—when two thirds of humanity considered women to be chattels and political marriages a normal aspect of interfamily and inter-Sector diplomacy. Since the arrival on Liberty of Lucia Henry, the Chinese marriage had grown even more important as an issue.

She asked him, "Do you think the President should marry?"

Ellis guarded his thoughts with care, wanting to trust her but not sure if he could. "I can't say. What's your opinion?"

A frown passed over her face briefly. "Her marriageability is quite a useful political tool. If she took an Amerikan husband, she would raise one of her allies to preeminence and thereby create in him a focus of jealousy. If she marries into a foreign dynasty like the Chinese Shan, she'll bring Amerika under the influence of an alien power. If she chooses not to marry at all, there's always potential, and she can keep a lot of factions jockeying for the prize."

Ellis nodded, impressed with her grasp of the political realities, but he forced himself to remember where he was and with whom he was speaking. Reba's father had obviously educated her in the elements of statecraft, and it passed through Ellis's mind that he could learn much from her that might be useful. He said, "What about those who think the President is neglecting her duty? That she ought to marry."

"Do you think that?" She appeared shocked.

"No, but there's always Lucia Henry."

At that, Reba's face betrayed her inner disquiet, and it became clear to him where one of Conroy Lubbock's great fears lay. If enough support could be marshaled behind Lucia Henry, Alia Kane might be unseated and Amerika returned to a pro-Yamato stance that would give Mutsuhito's government all it desired without any need for an invasion.

What wouldn't I give, Ellis thought ruefully, to have a true picture of the inner workings of the White House? It seems a place where treason walks hand in hand with self-preservation and where treachery lurks in every corner. And at the center of everything is the President. Like a queen bee, radiant with royal splendor, with the power of life and death over ordinary mortals. Yes, he thought, suddenly awed, she is the key to all riches and status in Amerika: the higher the closer, and the closer the higher! And there was no one—as yet—closer to her or higher up the pecking order than Conroy Lubbock.

He thanked his fate that circumstances had brought him here to the Lubbock mansion. There could be no better place from which to launch his own schemes of retribution and reprisal against Yamato once Duval's rescue was brought off. Two million credits he had demanded of Okuba, but one million he had agreed with Hawken and reported to Lubbock. Much could be achieved with the difference. But that was thinking too far into the future. He was forgetting that in ten days he might easily be heading for a meeting with the judges of Yamato's kangaroo court. Nothing was decided yet. He must ready himself for any eventuality. He remembered what Vara Lubbock had said and knew that from now on he must be very careful.

They returned to the game, Ellis capturing two groups to his opponent's one. As she took his one-eyed army of ten stones from the board, she asked him innocently, "Are you married, Captain?"

"I was. My wife died recently."

"Oh! I didn't mean to—"

She fell silent and looked away, but he spoke up. He had remembered how painfully exhausting his grief had been, but realised that for the first time he wanted to speak of it.

"It happened while I was in the Zone. A psi-storm and then Yamato treachery delayed our return. When I stepped down onto the Harrisburg apron, I found that my wife and son had been killed in an air-car malfunction. It takes time to understand what something like that means. Why fate would take them from me so cruelly. What was their crime? I asked myself that a lot. Could her psi have been so bad? Surely my son was too young to have—" He felt a sudden intolerable constriction in his throat and swallowed to dissolve it. "Then I stopped asking. To save myself from pain, and perhaps to wash away the guilt."

"Guilt?"

"I couldn't be with her on her last day—" He choked up again. "Some people believe in the law of conservation of psi. I'm one of them. I'd got away from Sado by a miracle; and now it's paid for."

She put a comforting hand on his sleeve and he looked to her and managed a smile, but a braying laugh distracted him.

He looked up to see Kurt Reiner, drenched in sweat and drinking from a foaming jug. He wiped his full lips, his head of dark, curly hair plastered and wet, then his gaze fell on Reba Lubbock's hand.

"I see you've found suitable entertainment," he told her drunkenly, ignoring Ellis.

Immediately she withdrew inside herself, acutely embarrassed, fearful even, but Reiner seized her wrist and squeezed until she looked him in the eye. "You told me you were too tired to watch me thrash Art. Why don't you introduce me to this—*go* player?"

"Kurt, this is Captain Ellis Straker," she said tightly. "He's here at my father's request."

"Ah! The spaceman! Tell him who *I* am."

Reba looked helplessly around for assistance but found none. Moving to contain Reiner's anger, she complied quickly. "Captain, this is Kurt Reiner, of the Halide Corporation."

Ellis perceived the warning in her voice. "How are you?" he asked.

"The *heir* to the Halide Corporation," Reiner slurred, turning glazed eyes on the still-seated Ellis. "We're a very rich family. I'm the greatest poet in Amerika, the greatest polo player, and the greatest lover. So I like people to stand when they're presented to me. In fact, I insist."

Ellis acknowledged him with a single nod, detesting the rudeness of the intrusion and the swaggering conceit of the man. Talk of Janka had drained him of all belligerency.

"Stand up, I said!"

Ellis remained seated on the low stool. He watched with ill-concealed disgust as Reiner lifted the corner of the *go* board, scattering the pieces across the floor and sending a shock through the appalled watchers.

Ellis steadied himself, knowing that to rise would inflame Reiner's histrionic display to blows. Reiner caught up Reba's wrist again and ordered her cruelly, "Tell him to stand up!"

She turned her head from him defiantly and Reiner increased his grip until a jag of pain twisted her mouth and she cried out.

Instantly Ellis was on his feet. He covered the distance to his adversary in two steps and broke Reiner's fingers away from Reba Lubbock's wrist with ease.

"C'mon! You're hurting her."

Reiner's enraged voice rose up. "You *dare* to touch me?" he demanded. With sudden ferocity his fist lashed out, catching Ellis on the side of the head, then Ellis felt hands grappling him. Effortlessly he thrust his assailant back and pulled himself free.

"Ellis!"

It was Hawken's voice, stern and strained. The tall, black-robed figure of Conroy Lubbock was beside him. Ellis took a pace back, his ear ringing from the blow. Every nerve in him wanted to snap Reiner in two, but he knew that for Hawken's sake, and his own, he must exercise supreme restraint.

He forced himself to say slowly, "Hey, relax."

The music had ceased so that the entire main congress was in silence. A hundred eyes were staring at them. Reiner's face had passed from ruddy to a pallor of rage. His lips were tight and he was shaking with the will to fight. "Apologise!"

Reba stepped forward, pleading. "Kurt, please—"

Reiner's eyes jumped from Ellis to her and back. "Get out!"

He swept her aside, and as Ellis instinctively made a move towards him, Reiner darted back and made a grab for the handle of a long carving knife that skewered a hock of beef on the table beside him.

"You'll apologise, I said!"

Reiner's words rang in the rafters, demonic, insane. Something inside Ellis triggered. He shrugged off the restraint he had been imposing and lunged at Reiner as he would a mutineer.

The knife was thrust forward but Ellis sidestepped and allowed Reiner's outstretched arm to pass under his own. With a steel grip he seized the knife hand, trapping the forearm under his armpit, and turned with perfect balance so that all his weight bore down on Reiner's elbow. The arm snapped straight, from wrist to shoulder, and the fingers splayed convulsively so that the blade rang to the floor.

What happened next was unnecessary, but Ellis thought Reiner deserved it. Few saw the knee raised sharply in Reiner's groin; they heard only a gasp of pain as Amerika's greatest lover crumpled.

Suddenly a dozen hands were on Ellis and he was lifted bodily from the hall.

Hawken took him from the guards, incensed. He marched him to the exit, spitting oaths.

"Sweet Jeezus in heaven! What the hell do you think you're about? Can't I trust you to hold your temper for just five minutes?"

"*My* temper? What the hell are you talking about? The sonofabitch started it! Wasn't my fault!"

Hawken squared up to him. "Fault is it? *Fault?* It *was* your fault, by God!"

"If that bastard was aboard my ship, I'd—"

Hawken's shout rent the night. "Shut it! And damn your brawling ignorance! He's a piece of the apparatus that runs this town and Lubbock's pet. He's Kurt Reiner of the Halide Corp. They make every goddamned synthetic in Amerika. And that's enough to make the fault yours whatever he did. I expected you to understand that! You should have kissed his ass if he asked you to!"

The night air washed over Ellis, cooling him. He bent to get inside the limo that had been brought out, then turned to Hawken unapologetically as the heavy doors clicked shut. "Well, fuck it, Jos! I've had about enough bullshit tonight! This is Amerika, Jos! *Amerika!* That means something to me. And I don't see why I should take shit from anybody. And that goes for you too! I may as well be hanged for a wolf as for a goddamned sheep!"

Hawken shook his head. "You're not to be hanged at all. Neither of us is—and no thanks to you."

"What do you mean?"

"Conroy Lubbock has swallowed the bait. Belkov has brought news from Cassabian that the youngest Chinese prince, Pi Wu, will entertain Alia's suit. And you're to have your damned squadron of nexus ships."

SADO

When Michie heard the sound of air-cars and the chatter of Chinese, she ran to the window.

It was Katsumi, come from Kanazawa. Then her stomach turned over as she saw the Amerikan standing with them and remembered the day several months ago when he had tried to kill her brother with his bare hands.

Nishima-sama had had two of the captives horribly executed in the Place of Public Chastisement because of that. A shudder passed through her as she watched him. Demon man! Katsumi was right about you. Your pride is too great. You killed those poor men just as certainly as if you'd executed them yourself. And now you've come here to defile the harmony of my father's house, following me like an evil *kami*.

The lands of her father's *han* were spread out as far as she could see, flooded rice terraces and tilled fields where land slaves labored ceaselessly to cultivate the hard earth of the high plateau. To the west and south lay the great mineral lakes of Fukuoka and Chiba and the factories and domiciles of Hasegawa Industries; to the southeast the serrated horizon where Matsuyama and Fuji-san, the great volcanoes revered by all the peoples of Sado, smoldered threateningly.

Hasegawa Kenji had brought order and civilisation to this place. He had dispelled barbarism and ruled here as a great *han* lord and industrialist, paying strict attention to discipline, going the rounds from dawn to dusk, seeing that his people did their duty. Though he had now been made a *hatamoto* of the daimyo, Nishima Jun, he placed little value on silk finery, but dressed plainly, attended by only a few pages and retainers to illustrate his rank; he kept faith with his religion and treated all whom he ruled with fairness and justice.

Michie's reception had been splendid. The whole household had been assembled to receive her, and the low side table had been filled with a great variety of choice foods, enough for a wedding, and she had sat like an Emperor's consort, as honored guest, and all those of the household that had known her before wondered at her being a grown woman. All except her mother, who saw her unchanged and still fussed over her as if she was a child.

Michie had bowed to her father, tears welling. He was a little stouter now, his temples wholly gray and his face brown-grained. He seemed the most magnificent man. Her mother, Masae, had been by his side and Michie had bowed to her also, her feelings dammed up behind the formal facade of family ritual. Only now was she completely sure that the report of her mother's wasting illness had been a pretext to get her off Kyoto. And the maids had hugged and chattered and pressed cheeks as the glow of the reunion had spread through the household like warm *sake*.

The great house was a heavenly mansion in the sun, spaces sculpted by shadow, the timbers beginning to darken with age, the wooden shutters lifted like skirts from the ground floor; shoji at the front gleamed white, and graphite-gray tiles were pitched shallowly all down the magnificent roof. There was a broad walkway, knee-high round the house, covered by the eaves, clean gravel beyond set with stepping-stones and a big threshold stone on which shoes could be left.

At the back of the house was a formal bamboo garden with a stream and a small waterfall that played into a pool of pea-green water. And woven windbreaks with the Hasegawa *mon* of a red octagon on a black background were stretched between poles.

Yao Wen-yuan, her father's Chinese comprador, was talking with Katsumi. Her brother was now once more astride his Moku and among his *tsukai-ban* samurai: all hardy, athletic men who ran errands for the daimyo, spanning Sado to expedite orders of state. They were climbing out from a military Datsun air-car, looking about them and getting their gear down. They had brought with them a troop of Chinese in a second vehicle, yellow-skinned, with sinister flat faces who squatted and gabbled in their singsong language.

"When I came here, there was only a newly terraformed wilderness," her father had told her proudly. "Then we brought labor and machinery and built everything. Over there are the factories. The lands of the *han* stretch as far as you can see, near the *ikki* domiciles. The houses of the other classes, except the samurai of course, are near the factories. Our own house is fashioned after the one that I was born in, on Satsuma in the Kyushu quarter. Traditional materials take a long time to mature, my daughter. And appropriate trees need time to grow. But look, now! It's almost like a civilised place. We grow rice and every kind of fruit and vegetable here. There is cleanliness and order and the *kami* have come to settle here with us!"

Below, Moku's tail twitched at flies. Beside the horse, a little apart from the samurai, barefoot and dressed in tatters, was the Amerikan.

"Why has Katsumi brought him here?" she asked her mother, pointing to him.

"Yao says that the barbarians are being given to main landowners to oversee the Chinese slaves."

Hasegawa Masae was a woman of regal bearing, always patient with her daughter's questions. She had passed her fine looks to her daughter, and though in her middle forties, she had kept her lustrous black hair and her trim figure; she bathed daily, rode often, and enjoyed the ruling of her husband's domain as much as he did.

"But *this* one. He—" She picked up her favorite fan, the one of plain white paper and bamboo, and splayed it. Though she did not know why, Michie stopped herself from speaking of the Amerikan's attempt to strangle Katsumi.

"What of him?"

"I remember he came with the daimyo's procession from Niigata. He was one of the Amerikans who caused so much trouble there. I think he was their leader."

"Katsumi takes his orders direct from Nishima-sama. We are close to the capital and must expect at least one. It's proper and fitting that the leader should be given to your father. Does it matter now? Here he will be your father's subject, and he will behave."

They went down to greet Katsumi and found him shouting terse commands to his samurai to marshal the Chinese. When he saw his mother, he broke away and came to speak. He seemed distracted by his duties, but bowed to his mother and smiled pleasantly at Michie.

"Mother, I cannot stay. This is an official visit, you understand."

The older woman nodded. "Of course, but you'll take tea with us, won't you, Katsumi-chan? Your men can eat in the kitchens and your Chinese may stay here in the yard with Yao." She used the very familiar form "chan" to make her son feel at home, and perhaps to allow him to relax a little.

"I must speak with my father. Urgently."

She put her hands together and nodded with finality. "That's settled, then, because your father's driven to Osaka, on the far side of Lake Chiba. He won't be back before dusk."

The Amerikan sat some distance away, on the stone lip of the water trough, with one ankle resting on his knee, surrounded by moss. He seemed fascinated by the Chinese who had congregated in the far corner of the open court under the shade of a heavily wired pine tree. Several of the coolies were drinking water from flasks, or pinching their nostrils closed and swallowing fumes from a tortoiseshell pipe.

"What about the captive? Shouldn't he be chained up?"

Michie looked askance at her mother. She was amazed when Katsumi said, "He is not a captive, Mother. He has behaved well for the past four months. He put himself in charge of his countrymen and has convinced them to act lawfully in return for some small liberties. Nishima-sama has made his welfare my personal responsibility. I will ask Father to put him to some useful task where he may learn to forget his piratical ways." Katsumi's eyes avoided Michie's studiously. "I know that he'll flourish here, in my father's enlightened *han*."

His mother's eyebrows had lifted at the word "piratical." They began to walk back towards the house together. "A pirate, you say? Michie-chan tells me he's dangerous."

"Only when provoked."

"Provoked? How can I know what will provoke a barbarian?"

"Let him take tea with us, and you may ask him."

"Tea? So sorry! I'll not have a *gaijin* in your father's house! The *wa* will disappear and we shall have no harmony for seven years."

"He did not surrender himself. It was I who captured him. He has honor. He's our guest."

"So sorry! On behalf of your father, I cannot permit it."

She hurried away, scattering a group of clucking, bobbing Chinese, and as she left, Michie faced Katsumi. He was grinning.

She said, "Oh, Katsumi-san. You shouldn't upset our mother deliberately. Please tell me why you really brought him here."

He glanced at her with irritation. "Michie-san, it has been a long ride."

"Please! You must tell me."

"I have told you. I am his keeper. Where else should I bring him?"

She snapped her fan shut. "Katsumi-san, he tried to murder you!"

He shrugged. "It was nothing. These Amerikans think differently to us. It is not as bad as our mother imagines. He is a person from a family of some status—sort of samurai in Amerika, I think."

"Excuse me, but there is no such thing."

His eyes moved evasively. The levity in his voice was paper thin. "Michie-san, I will not be interrogated by you."

"So sorry, but I don't feel safe now. Why did you bring him, honorable brother? It was you who warned me about him in the first place. And you were right. He tried to kill you. Now you've brought him here. He of all of them. Why have you changed your mind?"

"It's the natural solution. He must be kept under scrutiny. What better place than this? And I saw the way you looked at him."

He said it lightly, but she fanned herself to keep the color from blooding her cheeks and took a pace back. Still, she forced herself to say, "How? How did I look at him?"

"Like a woman who has spent too many months on board a nexus ship full of men."

She couldn't believe her ears. That Katsumi-san, her own brother, could think, could speak to her like that. Shame rose in her and she made for the steps.

"Where are you going?"

"I cannot stay!"

He followed, catching her halfway up the flight. He was smiling, but his voice was urgent, almost pleading. "I'm sorry. It was an insensitive joke. If you must know, the daimyo himself ordered me to bring the *gaijin* here because he knows about a special type of gun, Michie-san. He can make superb instruments of war! Even the sister of an insensitive joker can understand the importance of that. You know we all have *giri,* our duty to our lord, and *chu,* our sacred duty to the Emperor, and that even the most complete rendering of our efforts is only partial fulfillment of the debt we owe to the Son of Heaven."

Don't lecture me like a fool, she wanted to shout back at him, but of course she checked herself, and more calmly said, "Katsumi-san, why don't you say what is upsetting you?"

He shook his head slowly, then straightened. "It is Nishima-sama's earnest wish that . . . that is, he hopes that you might be prepared to . . . to try to gain the Amerikan's confidence for us. For the honor of the family. For Yamato."

He lay in the straw staring up at the light that seeped in through crevices in the barn roof. Flies buzzed round his head, settling on the dried blood of his face and arms, maddening him. Every bone of his body seemed to ache and it was agony to brush the insects away. He put on the ring that Chambers had given him. His brother's ring that bore the outstretched eagle of Aquila. It fitted snugly on his middle finger, and the sense of wearing it in defiance of his captors gave him a sort of secret pleasure.

The afternoon and evening of the first day on the Hasegawa *han* had passed tensely for Duval. He had awaited the moment when he would be confronted with his sins—his attack on Katsumi was surely unforgivable—but instead had been brought to the kitchens and served a bowl of noodles and thinly sliced spring onions swimming in hot stock water. It was brought by a fear-stricken maid who had been told of the demonic *gaijin* that now inhabited the kitchen.

The soup had tasted salty but refreshing, and contained slices of what might have been raw potato; it was, the watching samurai had told him, *takenoko.* He had licked his fingers and eaten it anyway, breaking off pieces of the white discs and nibbling them.

A shallow cup of water was put before him, but he had not drunk enough to counteract the saltiness of the soup, and he had said politely, "*Gochisosama,*" and dabbed his lips to signal he had finished.

Hardly anything in Amerika was a ritual; everything here was that. He had feared the ritual of confrontation that must come soon. He knew he would be expected to atone for his bad manners and insubordination towards Katsumi. He had let drops of water fall to the table, drops like blood. A plague on your house, Hasegawa Kenji, whoever you are, he thought darkly. Something irrational made him remember the Jewish Passover ritual: blood and frogs and flies and hail. May your cattle die and the locusts strip your fields. But most of all may the Lord God seize your firstborn and send him to hellfire . . .

The guilt he felt over the executions of Ron Howell and Jerry Walsh had shaped all his actions in Kanazawa. He had negotiated terms, promising and praying: favors in exchange for good behavior, a bloodless solution to the problem of what to do with thirty desperate, costly survivors who just didn't fit into this society and probably never could. He had seen how the samurai in Sado would not stoop to giving orders directly to coolie labor, that they had need of go-betweens and compradors and men to serve them as they went about, and weren't Amerikan servants a novelty? Weren't they better than Chinese? An expression of status to have an Amerikan servant, and they'd soon learn the basics of the language and respectful manners. It was to Katsumi that he had been forced to swear his own oath of bail. Miraculously the samurai had backed down from his demands for further retribution, but he had asked the daimyo if he could personally take charge of Duval, receiving him into his father's *han* at Chiba.

What does the bastard really want with me? he had wondered. Now that my shipmates are sold out into servitude all over the planet, what more chance is there they'll be used to squeeze me? Now I'm alone and I have only myself to answer for. Katsumi ought to know that I'll see us all in hell before giving him any real secrets.

He had dreaded that which awaited him on the *han*. Two hours before midnight he had been brought, hands bound, before the lord and his son, and rank upon rank of *han* retainers who flanked the main congress of the house. He had expected to feel only hatred, but he had seen in Hasegawa Kenji a man of honor, straight and principled. Still, he had had the uneasy conviction that Katsumi was using his father.

"You will work for your living here," Kenji had told him plainly as he was made to kneel before the lord. "If you work well, you will have sufficient rest and food and shelter, and after a time money to buy possessions. If you do not, these things will be denied you. If you trouble me—cause hurt to any of my people or damage anything on my estate—I will have you whipped as I would any other man. Do you understand that?"

"Yes."

"Tell me, Amerikan, what was your work title?"

"I'm a technical academic. Although my last job was a little different—specifically the destroying of Yamato nexus ships. Since then I've been on vacation."

A great gasp had passed round the hall at that, fifty samurai retainers drawing breath as one. Katsumi had gone rigid with anger; his pretense of control over Duval was shattered now. "You invaded an apron belonging to the Yamato government!" he shouted.

Kenji had grunted impassively from the raised platform on which he sat cross-legged. He quieted his son. "Amerikan, I warn you not to be flippant.

Sarcasm is not a form of humor that suits the Japanese language. It is disrespectful and not appropriate on Yamato worlds. It will be severely punished in future."

Duval had moved his head in an ambiguous gesture, but it seemed to satisfy the lord of the *han*.

"Now, I have work for you. First you will write specifications for the building of a facility. You'll choose the site and have an advisory role in all aspects of its design and construction. It is to be a place where singularity guns can be made, equipped as closely as possible to your facility in Amerika. There are five technically proficient men at your disposal, an encycloputer, and a quiet place to meditate. Anything more you require you will report daily to my comprador, Yao, who reports directly to me. I will personally inspect your progress every third day. Is that clear?"

Duval had stared straight ahead and absorbed the orders thoughtfully. Is this so bad? a voice inside him had asked. They could have killed you instead of Howell and Walsh. They could still do so, and as painfully as the cruelties of their culture allow. What's there to object to in this? To build a facility? And for a man you could easily respect.

But you have no respect for his son, the harder side of him had answered. I don't trust Katsumi. And these're his orders, or, more exactly, the orders of Nishima Jun. And he's asking me to dig my own grave, and the grave of my comrades. And it's not just a research facility he wants, it's a gun factory! Look at the way they've still got you tied up like a criminal. Jeezus, have you no pride?

The persuasive voice came back. What's the harm in it? Build them a factory. They can't make singularity guns without the secret of argentium tube vortex linkage. They don't understand quasi-gravitics at all. So—waste their time! Spend their money! Deceive them! Then you will have played them for fools.

He had looked at Kenji's open, expectant features and shook his head tightly in refusal.

Katsumi's face hardened. "What's the matter? Don't you understand my father's command?"

"I understand. But I refuse it utterly. You're an unscrupulous bastard and your father's a dupe and the daimyo is a wicked tool of an even more wicked sonofabitch on Kyoto, and I piss on the entire lot of you!"

The entire assembly had been on their feet instantly. At the intolerable insult, the lord himself had drawn one of the brace of swords that lay within reach on the platform beside him and pointed it at Duval's heart, his fist shaking in rage. "You dare speak to me like that? In my own house?"

Duval had stared fixedly at the *katana*, filled with the satisfaction of his defiance, glad that he had sealed his course but suffering the agonising seconds before the pain started.

"Go on, kill me! And if you're too much of a coward, tell your slaves to do it."

Kenji had brought down his weapon in a slashing arc, severing the rope that held Duval's wrists. The rest had dragged him into the yard and savagely beat him with wooden *keyaki* swords—practice swords—raining blows on all the places of his body where bone was near skin.

"That is for my lord's honor! And that is for his son's! And that is for His Excellency the daimyo! You were warned, Amerikan! You were warned, but you chose not to listen!"

The blood and the bruises had been spectacular, but the beating had been controlled and careful, and Kenji had known when to stop it.

"That is for your defiance! That is for your refusal! And that is for your insults!" he said in the throaty growl of the samurai class. "I have broken this land and made it tame, and I will break you and make you tame also!"

Katsumi raised his hand again.

"Leave him!"

"But, Father—"

"Leave him."

Duval had fallen limp, feigning unconsciousness, and he had heard Kenji say, "Don't kill him. Don't forget that Nishima-sama requires him alive."

"No man who speaks like that should be allowed to live!"

Father and son had faced one another then. "Do as you are told! Kill him and you'll forfeit your own life. He's not worth that."

He had looked up at them from one eye, blood streaming from his nose.

Kenji's truncheon fell to the earth. "What do you mean?"

"Remember Nishima-sama's orders. We must use every means to persuade him. *Every* means. If he does not comply, I will be dishonored and lose everything."

And they had gone back to the house, and the Chinese had come and dragged him by the ankles, groaning and hideously hurt, across the gravel, to the stable barn.

The sunrise was two hours old when Duval awoke. He raised himself and felt about his body for broken bones, then he turned onto his side painfully, remembering the night. The straw nestled him as if he were a fragile pot and he felt the unimaginable joy of relief from torment.

I've got you, Hasegawa-Godalmighty-Kenji, he thought with elation. You're as much in my power now as I am in yours. And now the respect is mutual.

A shadow fell across him, eclipsing the brightness of the morning sun. The blurred silhouette of a woman, carrying a pail of water. She looked at him for a long moment before approaching further.

"You?"

It was Michie. Her hair was down and her face without makeup. She wore an old kimono loosely fastened.

"You are injured," she said haltingly, using the form of address reserved for inferiors, and set down her pail. "Let me see your face."

He turned his chin up and she knelt and sponged his neck and shoulders, removing the rope bracelets that still hung on his wrists. The cool water thrilled him, taking the burn away from his wounds, and he flinched.

"Try to keep still."

"Why are you here?" he asked, amazed that she, the lord's daughter, had come to tend him.

"If you do not keep still, I cannot tend your wounds." Her voice was as gentle as gossamer but also as hard as obsidian. "My father asked me to come. I did not refuse his request. In Yamato it is very bad manners for a daughter to refuse her father. Nor did I question him. He is a good man and deserves immediate obedience. Perhaps this will convince you that he has now put the regrettable incident of last night behind him."

"Then I am forgiven?"

She searched his face for an explanation and found none. In this light, and with his features marred by the bruising, he could have been a racial Japanese. But his sentiments were alien. "Forgiveness is not a meaningful idea in Yamato. You would do better to think in terms of duty. You wronged my father last night by insulting him. Therefore you owed him a debt of *giri*. He simply took back his injured reputation when he had you beaten. Now it is finished, just as much as if you had insulted yourself and then beat yourself for doing so, all inside your mind."

"You're all as mad as hatters!"

"I don't understand. Are you trying to insult me now? Perhaps lack of manners is to be expected of a barbarian?"

"Please excuse me, lady, but I am neither ill mannered nor a barbarian."

The reproach rose in her voice. "Don't you know that you're lucky to be alive? My father is a good man, a kind man. Within hours you have infected him with your savagery. What you said to him was insufferable."

"Did he send you here? Or was it your brother?"

She ignored his question and continued to scrub the dried blood from his hairless chest and arms. Twice when she leaned forward her kimono grew slack across her and he was amazed to catch the delicious sight of a small, golden breast, brown-tipped and firm. The glimpse sent a thrill through him. When she finished, she dried her hands, then she looked directly at him and said with sudden deliberateness, "Please, Duval Straker, for your own sake, forget your old life and do as Katsumi-san wishes."

Her delicately lidded eyes flashed dark fire at him, and he saw how lovely she was. He steeled himself, hardening his feelings as he knew he must. "You're asking me to betray Amerika."

"You don't have to do that. Please, for my father's sake as well as yours, go along with what is asked of you. You must."

He propped himself up, knowing that he must oppose the temptation she was laying before him. It's just another trick, he told himself, delighting in her appealing words nevertheless. She doesn't mean it. She was ordered here to coax me with her attentions. Yet she seems genuinely worried for me. How can I oppose her without hurting her?

"Please couldn't you do that?" she asked again.

"I could. But it would be for the daimyo and not for you."

"Please. I saw the executions in Kanazawa. I don't want to see them take you too."

He summoned up all his strength and spoke scathingly, wanting, and yet not wanting, to drive her away. "I'd heard that samurai have a talent for persuasion. But I thought it extended only to swords and to fear. I had no idea you were so advanced."

"What do you mean by that?"

"You know very well, lady."

She stood up, he rising with her, then she bunched her fingers as if to beat on him. Open your eyes and see what you're doing, she thought. I wish you'd never come here. I wish I'd never set eyes on you, demon *gaijin!* I hate you!

"You are a very strange man," she said distantly.

"That's no way to persuade me," he told her, the mocking gone from him now. He knew there was one sure course that would send her away.

There was a long pause before she asked, "Then how?"

"Like this." He seized her in his arms, taking her off balance, and kissed her full on the lips.

For a moment she seemed paralysed. He pulled back from her and looked into her eyes, unsure what he would see there. Then she hit him in the face with all the force she could muster.

"Bitch!"

His cheek stung, and he kissed her again, this time forcefully, so that she struggled against his strength in vain. Her pail was kicked over. Then he opened his arms and she fell to the floor. He scissored his hands as if clapping dust from them. The place she had hit him hurt like hell, his vision popped; she had put skill and a good deal of feeling into the blow, but he was not going to let her see how it troubled him.

She stared up at him, burning with emotion. "You're a demon! A foolish, proud man! Like all men, you must always be right. You're too proud to see anything. You are blinded by your own stupidity!"

He sat down on the ground slowly and put his hand to his mouth, like a man disgorging a cherry pip. When his hand came away, there was blood in his saliva and an ivory-white lump in his hand. He thoughtfully probed with the tip of his tongue the place where his tooth had been.

Her anger suddenly collapsed. A tooth! She had done that? Oh, *ko!* But an Amerikan tooth was probably irreplaceable in Sado. It was a damage that could not be reversed. Feelings of horror flushed through her, washing away her astonishment at his unaccountably barbarous actions, making her forget everything.

It was a molar. A big one.

"Let me see," she said with concern.

He braced his elbows behind him and meekly leaned his head back. Then she knelt beside him, put one hand softly on his forehead and delicately hooked the left side of his open mouth with her little finger, and peered inside.

Blood welled in the hole where the tooth had been. It was dark and pulpy, but the tooth had come out cleanly and no splinters were left. She kept her face straight, rocking back on her heels. "I think it's all right."

"Good," he said, nodding, and handed her the tooth. Then he turned and spat with as much delicacy as he could. She looked at the tooth guiltily. It was a fine, white tooth. And a pity to lose it.

"I'm sorry," she said. "Truly, I never meant to hurt you."

"I'm not hurt."

"Really? No pain?"

"No."

"I'll bring you something from the medikit. If you plug the gap with it, the wound will heal quickly."

He nodded his head slowly. It was not one of his Amerikan mannerisms, but subtle and very Japanese. You're learning quickly, she thought. Your Japanese is nine times better than it was when you startled me that night in the horse stable in Niigata. How long will it be before you're like one of us?

A voice in the back of her head nagged at her. It was her mother's voice, or perhaps just one of the aunts with whom she had lived on Kyoto when she had sought refuge from Prince Kono's cruelty. The voice told her to beware. Though this man was physically handsome under his bruises and more clever than she had thought and obviously attracted to her, he was still an Amerikan and therefore barbarian through and through.

It was hard to believe he had the soul of a demon as she watched him sitting there like a child in sorrow over a broken possession. He seemed like other men, only more wild and somehow more—

She broke off the unruly thought suddenly, remaining outwardly calm, and renewed her plea. "Please won't you do a little of what Nishima-sama wants?"

"How can I?"

"Hasn't he been good to you? He should have crucified you all at Niigata in order to comply strictly with the Emperor's law. Instead, he's brought you to the capital, given your men shelter and food and now the chance to earn for themselves a living and a place to fit in."

"Overseeing slaves?"

"It is dignified work in Kanazawa."

"Huh!" He grew stiff again. "My duty is to my compatriots in Amerika."

She sighed in exasperation. "Duty! The men settled on the *han* are your compatriots too. Do you not owe them something?"

"I owe them less than I owe anyone. I've already paid them their due. Tomorrow it will be six months to the day that we were fired upon by Nishima-sama's ships. That half year has been my gift of life to them. They cannot expect more."

"Just a small compromise. That's all my father asks. Surely that's possible?"

He saw her face and the pleading it held, and he looked past her and saw the sun shining on the distant lake and the orderly fields of red earth and the distant blasted slopes of the volcanoes, and suddenly he felt that Amerika was a hundred thousand parsecs away.

"Never," he whispered in his own language, but he knew as he said it that there would be no escape from Sado for himself or for his shipmates, now or at any time, and that she was right—the day for compromise had dawned.

26

LIBERTY

Night had begun to fall when Ellis Straker left the heavily armed nexus ship that put down on the apron at Norfolk. It was a warm, northern hemisphere spring evening over the salt marshes of the Potomac estuary, a westerly breeze rippling the water and the reed beds of Fish Creek. He was reminded of the broad skies of Sado and that it was now almost nine months since his life had been saved by his brother's heroism.

Very soon, he thought. Very soon now. If all went well, he would get the two million credits from Okubo tomorrow. Added to the million he had been apportioned from the profits carried home aboard the *Richard M.*, and the half million Oujuku had got, there would be enough to mount the revenge expedition he had conceived.

As he rode the elevator plate to ground, he decided that the Korean he had just spoken with, and whose pledge-print was on the smart card he now carried, could be trusted.

The *Seoul*, owned and captained by Kim Gwon Chung, would lift off during the next launch window and make for the Neutral Zone in search of Yamato traders that might be stacked in orbit or plying the nexus approach lanes. Kim called them "schmoo," and went after them with the fiery enthusiasm of a schmoo-catcher. But this time he would find none. Would pursue none. Would board none. Precisely as planned.

Kim was a fanatical Korean, a native of the Koje Do system, as were all his crew. Koje Do had been overrun by Yamato at the turn of the century, and each of his men and women had an implacable hatred of Yamato born in the massacres of '06. With others like him he had fled to the outer ports of Amerika to menace shipping and to supply the ragged bands of rebels that hid in the soft nexus territory on the fringes of the Neutral Zone where they could elude the big armored battlewagons of the oppressor and prey upon his transports. For Kim, arguments that depended on credit stood a poor second to those whetted by blood. It had taken much to persuade him that a punishing strike against Yamato could be delivered in exchange for a piece of good faith and a little patience. But at last the crazy Korean had agreed.

Ellis walked through the tumbled shacks of Norfolk's Fun Mall, thinking of the three secret trysts he had had with Reba Lubbock. In the first, she had told him of her father's increasing doubts over the wisdom of antagonising Yamato; in the second she had spoken of Otis le Grande's increasingly contrary view; and in the third she had revealed with breathless fear precisely what her father knew of the vice-president's scheme to aid Lucia Henry to usurp the presidency.

The information had been priceless. It had sparked a plan in Ellis Straker's mind to throw Conroy Lubbock's doubts into confusion and to carry Ambassador Okubo beyond all suspicion—by setting up an act of outrageous intended piracy.

He had shed his dress uniform in exchange for a shabby duraplex anorak, a Texas hat, and the sharp blue snakeskin boots he had last worn aboard the *Richard M*. Normally, as night closed in, Norfolk's hundred rowdy bars competed noisily for custom, and when, as now, hulls on the apron were as thick as catfish on a creek bed, the maze of narrow conduits would be packed with men and women, spending their pay or profits shares on quick and sublime pleasures. Trader money was hard-earned and easily spent, and the credit would run through their fingers like quicksilver, descending always until it reached the gutter, where pimps and thieves and gamblers made it their own. But tonight, though there were a hundred merchant captains in port, the malls were deserted and credit, honest or not, was hard to come by.

Ellis smiled. He had hoped for just this state of affairs.

The blockade of Pusan had once more pinched off trade to a trickle, and until the big fleets sailed again to open the Korean ports, the only nexus rats to be found spending in the dives were those who had lifted their profits direct from dangerous work in the Neutral Zone. Idle nexus trash must wait, unpaid, until the Merchant Traders' convoy gathered. Then the great stores of merchandise would find dispatch and Amerika's trade would once more be set moving and her prosperity assured. But now there was no trade, and idle crews grew restless. It was just such men and women that Ellis had come to find.

He made his first port of call a bar called the Star-mangled Spanner. He grinned. The name was one of those grim in-jokes appreciated only by Old Nexus Hands who had seen a nexus accident and what the tidal forces could do to metal and flesh alike when a nexus entry was badly goofed up.

Inside the bar, low beams made him stoop. It was hot and airless and greasy, built and hung like an old Aleph-class starship's interior. The Spanner, he knew, was frequented by men hankering after a trip. Immediately he saw several of his old crew: van Keef's burly frame, and young Morton, a cadet no more, sprouting a thin beard now, with his face in a bar girl's cleavage and his jock straining at the laces. And in a corner, face sallow and jaw unshaven, Ingram staring around him suspiciously.

"Captain!"

The voice was Bowen's. Despite the season's warmth he was bundled up in a quilted stevie jacket and his neon jerkin was filthy as if he had eaten and slept in it for six months. He was in the brown stuff.

"Hey, what's what? Take a beer?"

"Gimme that hand, you sonofabitch! Long time, eh? Sure I'll crack a Bud." Bowen's expression turned from glad surprise to hope. He lowered his voice. "You're in Norfolk, Ellis? That mean you got work?"

Ellis made no offer.

"Hey, hey. C'mon, Ellis, I'm more than willing. If you need a whole man and a fair stevie who knows his way around a cargo hold."

"Don't put yourself down, Red. I know you've a ticket or two to your name, and there's a third officer's berth for you in any ship I command."

"Command? Jeez!" Bowen's hope flamed up and he asked, "You got a ship, then? And a cargo?"

"Neither."

The light went out of Bowen's eyes, but they slitted as Ellis told him about Hawken and Lincoln and how he and John Oujuku had a plan to return to the Zone. He said nothing about Kim or any of his dealings with the ambassador.

"Hey, take me with you, Captain!" Bowen whispered. "I'd sooner lay both hands on the Zone than piss in the wind here."

"I like to hear that kinda talk. The berth's yours, but first you gotta do something for me."

"Hey, anything!"

"It'll not be to your liking, eh."

Bowen's face creased as a stack of silver credits was pressed into his palm. "What's this?"

"I want you to put it about quietly that Kim Gwon Chung and myself are readying to fall-on against the Merchant Traders' fleet. That we've secretly turned privateer, totally jacked off with the delaying in Lincoln, we've gone over. Say we have a pact with Baron Harumi and that Halton Henry's money is behind it."

Bowen was aghast. He could say nothing.

"Well? Will you do it, Red?"

"But surely it ain't right, Ellis—to make dirt out of your good name? You'll be right in the brown stuff."

"Hey, can I have your word?"

"But the boys 'n' girls hereabouts are waiting to take ship on that fleet. They'll not take kindly to being told of them that wants to jeopardise it."

"I want you to do that. Exactly like I said. Well?"

"If you want to get smeared—to death."

"I want to get smeared. Blacken me as a man willing to throw in with Yamato." Without looking up, Ellis felt Ingram's dull eyes locked on them. "And you can start by buying booze for a cable rat by the name of Ingram. He'll lighten your task by half."

27

"Otis le Grande, I want to speak with you on a matter of importance!"

"Can't it wait, Mr. Secretary?"

"No, by God. It can't!"

Lubbock's cadaverous figure, swathed in somberness and leaning heavily on the balustrade, distracted le Grande. The sun flashed on his opponent's plexer as it stabbed forward and he did not see its point at all. He felt only the swipe and heard ripping air, so that he stumbled back and was brought down.

A ripple of comment passed through those who watched and jeers from a knot of Reiner's friends.

"For Chrissakes, Kurt!"

"You're too slow. I could have shaved your chin twice." The young man's voice was hard and laced with sardonic humor, very different to the sweet side of himself he showed to the President.

The holidays had brought the President here to Lexington, to the spa retreat of Looie's Shattoe. Around them, the manorial lawns stretched out in mowed green. Despite the dryness of Liberty's August, these gardens were verdant where they had been nourished by symbiotics. Tables and chairs had been brought outside and a blue-and-white-striped windbreak pitched close by. High summer, and finally the day had dawned, a day le Grande had been anticipating for three years!

For Otis le Grande, the plexer match with Reiner had been ill considered and dangerously vain, and the thrashing he was getting was ignominious. Though merely a spar-practice, there had been no quarter offered by Reiner. The bastard was half his age and touched with ruthlessness. It took all le Grande's strength with the blunt plex samurai swords to maintain his dignity in the face of it. He got to his feet, recovering himself.

"You're sparring well. As for myself, I guess I'm a little stiff from yesterday's hunting."

Reiner looked to Lubbock with a half-smile. "And how's your own back, Daddy? Bent with too much thinking, as usual? Well, I suppose old age must have some compensations, eh?"

Le Grande bristled at the implied insult to his vigor. He said acidly, "Your elbow is fully healed, then?" Adding under his breath, "And your balls?"

When Reiner had appeared at the White House with his arm strapped up in February, he had claimed he had wrenched it in the auto-gym, but the story of his drunken brawl with a shipper had preceded him—to the delight of many, not least le Grande, who hated him cordially.

According to the story, a big astrogator had taken exception to Reiner's wit, had thrust him halfway up a wall and swore to cut off his prick and feed it to the pigs on Kentucky II if he didn't apologise.

He placed his opponent once more *en garde*. The youth had often jibed him over his age, thinking that any man older than forty-five could be wounded like that, but especially le Grande, knowing the delicacy of his position and the President's taste for surrounding herself with young toy-type men.

Le Grande hid his feelings now, reminding himself of the intricacy of the links that tied them all together. Kurt Reiner was a prickly problem: not yet twenty, he had been an academic guest at Lubbock's house in his minority and had succeeded his father as head of Reiner Inc., the umbrella corporation that included Halide, seven years ago. It was only that vital politico-industrial connection that had made his future—and saved him from his enemies—so far.

They touched plexers savagely. Around them, the Shattoe's neatly clipped hedges surrounded a grassy bank. The patchwork garden beyond was green with fabulous biogen cross-plants and the air was tinctured with herbal smells and exotic blooms. In the silence sweat ran down le Grande's back and he was suddenly keenly aware of the warbling note of a distant Squad car.

Reiner circled ominously, and le Grande concentrated on him once more. You're rich, but you're an immoral bastard; you're pretty schwartzy and you try your damnedest to be fashionable, but you're also spoiled and possessed of one hell of an evil temper; you're athletic and you get all the girls slavering over you, but you're also a selfish prick-head that all Amerika is learning to hate. And I'll see you eat shit one day soon, boy!

Le Grande resumed his sparring stance. I know that Lubbock has long planned to use you as a lever against me, but what a mistake he's made! He imagines that if you can be brought to Alia's private parties with your pretty-boy looks and your pathetic flattery, you'll capture the President's attention. But you're young, inexperienced, and transparent. You're not content to play that game, and too hot-headed to succeed. And there's still the small matter of a charge of synth slaughter against you.

Lubbock and the Halide labs would doubtless get him off the consequences of that offense. It was an interesting point of law. After all, the dead synthetic was only a grade-four servant, stabbed by the head of the Halide empire that had created him in the first place. But whatever the legal arguments, the fact was that Reiner had been in one of his famous temper tantrums, and it would take time and money to convince a Liberty jury that the victim had flipped out and run onto Reiner's knife. And there was the very vocal Campaign for Synthetic Rights getting into the broadcasts just lately. For a space of time at least, Lubbock would have to run Reiner on a very short leash.

Le Grande eyed the murderer's blade. But I'm no synthetic, he told his opponent silently. I'm as smart as you are, and then some! He circled his plexer and lunged. Reiner was forced to step back once, then again. Le Grande skipped to his left and brought the plexer round in a neat parabola. The strike was swift. Surgical. It drew no blood, but was done with intent to wound Reiner's pride. As they withdrew to the mark, he permitted himself a smile.

Lubbock stood ten yards away. In his heavy jacket and dark colors, he was at home in the gray cloisters of power. Here, in Lexington's high summer, amid the entertainments and trivialities of the President's Vacation Week, he sweltered uncomfortably, a fish out of water. Le Grande kept him waiting.

Standing in the shade, as yet unseen by Reiner, were Lubbock's handsome daughter and a big man in a high-cut blue jacket. Surely this must be the man who had put Reiner into a sling that time, and whom the maniac had sworn to kill. Or could it be that the dalliance between Reba Lubbock and Kurt Reiner was in decline? The man seemed more than a match for Reiner.

What about the way Reiner had called Conroy "Daddy"? There was, of course, no blood relationship between them, but Reiner had at one time been as good as Lubbock's son-in-law. That was Lubbock's weakness. The secretary had spent plenty of time and effort searching the registers for the hint of psi-talent. He had paid Ramakrishnan's ashram a fortune, only to have Reiner proved totally psi-talent-free. Beneath his affectations, Conroy Lubbock was nothing but a preppie fashion slave. It was chic to have your kids marry psi, but not just any old psi. Too bad, astrogator. You've got no chance!

Conroy had been able to find no psi-connections whatsoever, nothing with which to legitimise Reiner among the mansion party set who were all marrying into psi like crazy. The jibes that he was trying to get a stake in Halide through the young heir had punctured his pride, so he had done the next best thing: he had taken Reiner under his wing as a RISC student. In Lubbock's mansion, Reiner's private tutors had doubtless tried to educate him in more than cosmic analysis, but the project had failed, and Reiner had turned out to be an ungrateful monster.

However, one aspect of Kurt Reiner's genealogy was becoming daily more pertinent to le Grande's own plan: Reiner was first cousin to le Grande's great enemy, Halton Henry, the VP. The exquisite prospect of entrapping and then obliterating the pair of them *and* sending Lubbock to his reward at the same time sent a sensation of such delight through him that he decided to call off the sparring.

"What, Otis, tired already?" Reiner inquired, seeing Lubbock's daughter for the first time.

Le Grande ignored the jibe and turned to Lubbock. "C'mon, tell me, Mr. Secretary, what's so urgent?"

Lubbock's voice was grave. "The entire Sector is in crisis, sir."

"Crisis? Well, now. Why don't you tell me about it? Like what there is to fear."

"Baron Harumi's army is perched like a vulture on the Boundary."

"But he has no means of getting through the Kalifornia nexus with them. And nothing to feed them on en route."

"That may be true—at the moment."

Le Grande put up his plexer and handed it, sheathed, to his sparring tutor, then he picked up a small towel and began to soak the sweat from his face and neck. A political animal's got to keep in trim, he thought, but look at how we do it. Plexing's only Amerikan-style *kendo.* I guess it's the way of the universe that the lesser Sectors become cultural slaves of the giants. Yamato's a cultural imperialist, and because we run an open society they're pouring their influences into Amerika and we don't stop them. One-way trade. Still, plexing's good exercise no matter where the plexer blade was manufactured. And you know what they say about knowing your enemy, boy! As he sat down he took a long swig of orange juice, letting Lubbock wait until he had drunk his fill.

Reiner, sulking now at the sight of his protector's daughter and her impressive companion, and unable because of Lubbock's watchful presence to start trouble, stalked away towards the house with his gaggle of friends.

He turned to Lubbock. "C'mon, tell me—what is there to fear?"

Lubbock leaned on the balustrade, severe in black beside le Grande's own embroidered white shirt. "Take a look at this."

Le Grande took the sheet and read it, dropping it carelessly on the table when he was done with it. Inside him, acid bubbled up fiercely.

Lubbock picked the intelligence report up again and asked flatly, "Cat got your tongue, le Grande?"

Le Grande laughed tauntingly. "I find it—fascinating."

"Here's *proof* that Halton Henry and his cronies plotted with the Yamato ambassador three months ago against Amerikan interests."

"Hold on a minute. What it seems to say to me is that a bunch of merchants organised a fleet to cruise to Europa, since they sure as hell could not go to Korea, and that Henry and his friends and Okubo tried to stop it."

"They asked Yamato—Baron Harumi—to halt the Amerikan Merchant Traders' convoy!"

Le Grande shrugged at Lubbock's anger. "Okeh, and they enlisted the help of Korean pirates. So? Was the convoy stopped?"

Lubbock drew himself up. "You know perfectly that it wasn't."

"So what's the big deal?"

"The fleet got through only because it lighted out two days early. Prewarned by an unknown source."

"Again—so what? The private interests of Henry and his cronies are his own affair."

"By God, deliberately plotting to panic the financial markets is a criminal offense! He's plainly trying to make conditions rife for rebellion inside Amerika!"

Le Grande could not contain his delight. "You infer a good deal from a goddamned two-bit intelligence report, Mr. Secretary!"

"And I'll imply more. To the President! If you were a part of this scam and didn't divulge it to me—"

"Yeah?"

Lubbock contained himself, stopping short of an overt threat. He turned and marched away, gathering his daughter and her companion as he went. Le Grande poured another jug of juice. He felt a twist of anger at Lubbock's unique high-handedness and at the damage that any revelation against Halton Henry could do to his intricate plans at this stage. Incredible that Henry could have been so foolish!

Lubbock really believes I'm cooking something up with the VP, he thought, touched by the irony of the situation. He's seen me kiss Henry's ass and he believes it's genuine! Well and good, then! Let him believe I'm a friend to Henry. I can prove to the President which of her advisors has had secret dealings with Ambassador Okubo and which has not.

Le Grande picked up the jug once more and drank deeply, down to the squeezings. Whatever happens, he thought guardedly, Lubbock must not be allowed to upset my plans for Halton Henry. Henry must die.

If all went well, the vice-president would arrive at the Shattoe that afternoon, and at the meeting le Grande would tell him of his fate.

Le Grande took himself off, needing solitary thought. Already the warmth had driven Alia to seek the shade of the inner sanctum to protect her complexion from Liberty's star and its UV. The scented air was light; children and dogs ran freely and the President sat among her family friends observing the niceties of light conversation. He glimpsed Carola Ford at her side, and he withdrew. There was no point in stirring up Alia's jealousy, he reasoned, trying to bury the knowledge that the President did not believe his assurances. It was fortunate that Carola was with her now. At least Alia's suspicions would not be aroused today. He had been accused of being Carola's secret lover and had made it known that he was wounded deeply by the charge, but it was true, and the wound to Alia had been deeper. Women! he thought, half exasperatedly, half reverently. They'll never understand a man's urge is beyond his command, beyond sense, even beyond threat of death.

Of course, some men needed more than the usual outlets for their sexual energies, he thought with a smile. What I really need is two women in my bed at the same time to satisfy me; pity that only synths would play that game without explosions of jealousy. But synths are tiresome. Real women, powerful women are my passion. To stalk them and to stick them. The taking of Carola had been such a hunt, and just lately there had been another, the widow of Clayton Sheffield. Both had served to satisfy and comfort him in the defeats he had suffered in his quest for Alia Kane's body, but never both at once. And it was dangerous for any man, especially one so dependent on the President's favor, to shoot his seed so indiscriminately. Ever since the days of the Pink Death that whole area of human expression had gone suddenly taboo, but since the cure was found, sexual freedom still hadn't made a full recovery. Social hysteresis, he thought, but you can't keep a good sex drive down.

He had thought he would bring Alia an expensive present and declare humbly, "I am only a man!" and all would be healed. But she had been as cold as ice. And she had worked him hard for months, giving thin reward, showing her favor instead to Lubbock and complimenting Reiner to his face. She had engaged them both in conversation to his exclusion, but he had used it to advantage, stalling Halton Henry again and again, until today. Today was the day le Grande had chosen to bring Halton Henry to his knees. That Conroy Lubbock had uncovered some of the VP's clumsy dealings only added weight to the hammer blow that would crush Henry. But the man that Lubbock had brought with him, this astrogator, stank of counterplots. It was imperative that the matter be carried out swiftly.

A motion at the Shattoe's guardhouse window caught his eye. A beam interrogating an approaching air-vehicle. Then his aide signaling: Halton Henry's air-car had arrived.

Le Grande hurriedly rounded the outer court and passed the guard before coming to a place where he could see the VP. He watched Henry climb out of his air-car alone, hating him with a rare, unsatisfied intensity. The VP had been his special quarry since their rivalry had spilled embarrassingly into violence before Amerika's press some three years ago. Henry, furious at being bested in a big corporate deal and inexpressibly jealous of the familiarity le Grande had shown to the President in public, had threatened him. He had come with his father-in-law, General Waters, to intimidate him and call him names.

It had taken every moment since that time to coax Halton Henry into compliance with a scheme that would destroy him. The first real victory had been during a secret meeting in the formal garden of le Grande's own magnificent estate at Concord. That had come after meeting with Cassabian at his retreat on Wyoming—a ruse to ensure Lubbock was made aware of at least part of the plan. It was the culmination of years of delicate web spinning. Le Grande had visited Halton Henry several times now, and each time had droppered a little more venom into his ear about his sister, Lucia, a woman who as ex-President could make the perfect comeback in these difficult times. Without that, Henry would remain a VP, a lesser partner, the controller of very little, and forever displaced in the President's favor by le Grande himself.

At the same time, there was another reason to try to use him, which was why le Grande trod his ground with care, testing the way secretly and alone. Those presidential death threats were causing concern; were Alia to die at the hands of a ninja, all protection would evaporate like the morning dew and he would reap the whirlwind of a thousand bitter jealousies. That was the reason he had chosen to adopt an intricately roundabout approach: First, he had offered Halton Henry flattery, then a morsel of hope. Hope of putting behind him the three disastrous gambits the VP had already made. Each of his plans to bring back Lucia from exile had failed. Every time public opinion had swung against the idea. Next, le Grande had played on Henry's dormant pro-Yamato leanings, reminding him of the position he had held as a young man in his sister's administration.

At last the flattery had begun to work its magic. It was no coincidence that when Lucia Henry took ship to Liberty, it was to Philadelphia that she came, and into the bosom of Henry's business partner, Silas Quirk. There, Halton had visited her, held out his promises of restoring her to power.

According to the Constitution's one hundred ninety-third amendment, the President could call a snap election at any time on sixty days' notice. That meant that any issue could be tested by a direct electronic plebiscite, and the President could choose to gain the backing of a popular vote of confidence. Conversely elections could be called against her, given the approval of a sufficient percentage of Congress.

Delicately le Grande had pointed out that *the man who controlled Lucia* might control the destiny of Amerika. Such a man, if he went about it correctly, could become first VP to Lucia—nominally, of course—and then when Lucia was forced to resign, he would inherit the presidency! Surely there could be no better way for Halton to cement all his interests and ambitions than to listen to the scheme le Grande had drawn up. Surely there could be no greater prize! As soon as the VP's mouth had begun to slaver with greed, he had retired, leaving his potent suggestions to ferment in Halton's uncomplicated mind. There had been much to do elsewhere.

Immediately le Grande had sent a secret message via private courier to Philadelphia, where Lucia was now living, suggesting that he would use his best efforts to secure a snap election on the Neutral Zone issue if she wanted it. He then decided to cover himself so far as Alia was concerned. He had gone to the President to propose openly but gently that a solution to the embarrassment of Lucia Henry might be found in a snap election. If the small matter of Lucia's secret offer of marriage to the Chinese prince could be exposed, what better chance would Alia ever have to neutralizing the threat Lucia posed than by exposing her promise of marriage to a two-bit foreign despot? He had waited patiently for Alia to show her displeasure, or at least give some sign as to her thoughts, but she had remained utterly silent over the matter. And so, taking the biggest gamble of all, he had visited Cassabian to convince him and therefore his master, Conroy Lubbock, that a plot was simmering.

Le Grande had considered his next move carefully, then after a week of incredible patience he had offered to talk with Halton Henry at Concord. The Chinese marriage, he had decided, would be no problem at all to arrange.

The Japanese cipher reply le Grande received from Lucia had come in the dead of night, handed to him from the sleeve of her personal messenger. He had read it with quiet satisfaction, noticing the way that Lucia's meandering *kanji* hand grew more and more excited as she dwelled on the glittering prospect he had opened up for her. So the way had been made clear.

Le Grande smiled, recalling the way Henry had come running to Concord, exhibiting the anticipation that he had been unable to hide. Henry, gullible, trusting now, and completely disarmed by the glaring vision le Grande had worked so hard to fix in his imagination, had arrived alone and unattended. He had hated the man so completely then—hated his smug face, hated the asthmatic sound of his breathing, hated the smell of cheap after-shave that accompanied him, and above all he had hated his weakness.

"My dear Halton."

"Otis."

"It's all looking good. We've played poker and plotted together enough, now it's time to get right down to it."

"Sure," Henry had said eagerly.

He had pinched his finger and thumb together. "You're *that* far away from winning everything, but to make certain, you've got to have allies. First, Lubbock must be disarmed and then the proposal put to Alia in a way she'll find hard to refuse. I'm willing to undertake that, but first I want your solemn promise that you'll go through with it."

"O—keh."

He had smiled then and laid his hand on Henry's shoulder. "You know, I've always thought we could pull this off. If only we stood together. My God, you're a clever man, Halton, and I agree with your analysis of the way Lubbock is pushing Alia into war with Yamato. You know as well as I do that it's a war Amerika can't hope to win. And when Alia falls, you'll fall with her. But with your connections in the pro-Yamato camp, you could destroy that threat at a stroke. A lot can happen in sixty days, and by raising public opinion against Alia you stand a chance of supplanting her as President yourself."

Never before had the full consequence of the scheme been so brazenly stated, and it hit Halton Henry with the force of a beam weapon. He had hesitated. They were talking the highest form of sophistication.

"I could. But not without your initial help, le Grande."

"If you depend on me, think how much more I depend on you. My part would be simple, and once done, I guess I'd be in your power."

"Oh, don't worry about that. One good turn deserves another."

"It's a favor that as President you could well afford to give. You would have all of Amerika at your disposal."

"What sort of favor did you have in mind?"

"Oh, I don't know. If you could think of a way to get a hold of the Halide Corporation maybe. I know Kurt's not exactly your favorite person. And I know you could persuade Silas Quirk to part with a little of his stock . . ."

"And in the meantime? You're putting me in the President's firing line. And you're saying I have to trust you."

Le Grande had spread his hands in an open gesture. "In this line of work, Halton, nobody can cover his ass all of the time. You got to speculate to accumulate. Ever hear of that? I can't do everything for you. There's just some things you have to do yourself."

"Why should Alia agree to an election? What persuasion can you possibly offer her against Lubbock's advice? She's not a fool. And with Lubbock by her side she's hard to persuade. What if you're trying to trap me?"

"Aw, c'mon, Halton," he had insisted. "I'm forty-seven; the President is forty-six. I've known her since she was five years old, and I've always been able to get closer to her than anyone. I know her mind better than anyone alive and my arguments always carry weight with her."

"Yeah, but in all that time she hasn't agreed to marry you, has she?"

"Do you think I'm still ambitious for that? She'll never marry anyone. I know that. I accept it. So there can never be any hope for my ambitions while Alia lives. And I'm tired of waiting for scraps at her table. I know what the broadcasts say, but I'm not just another hag-fag hanging around the President's neck. What I most want is to see Conroy Lubbock brought down. For that I'd take just about any risk and pay just about any price."

Henry laughed conspiratorially. "Yeah."

"So you agree?"

Halton Henry's eyes narrowed. He asked, "When would you put it to her?"

"As soon as we've drawn up the Halide contract. Naturally it'll remain secret until you're in a position to act on it."

Henry hesitated once more. "Like I said, you want me to lay myself open."

"Uh-huh. I can't see how else it can be done."

"What if Alia refuses your request? What if she explicitly forbids an election?"

"She won't."

"But what if she does?"

Le Grande's impatience had bubbled up, but he had covered it with persuasive pleas. "There's no chance of that, Halton, but if she does, so what? You've nothing to fear. You're VP. A statesman. A protector of the best interests of Amerika. It's your duty to look out for the best interests of the Sector. You'd only be seeking the public good, doing what almost everyone else in a position of power and influence in the Sector has been doing—trying to make an honorable and lasting peace with Yamato for the future good. Go on the broadcasts. Ask the people: Is it a crime for a man to want to see peace in Amerika? No! Is it a crime to ask my President's permission to put that before the Amerikan people? No! Can't you just see it? No, Halton, there's no danger to you that a mouthful of bullshit won't soothe down."

"There's shit in somebody's mouth, all right."

He had shrugged. "Hey, you're a politician, Halton. That's the way it goes down in the District."

"You must think I'm a retard to lecture me like this."

The distant way Henry had said it had for a moment frozen le Grande's stomach solid, and for a moment he had thought he was about to hear a revelation that the conversation was on tape and that he himself was caught in a trap—but nothing came. Hurriedly, smoothly, he had moved on.

"Listen, I'm sorry, Halton. But you know how it is. I apologise for any rudeness. I didn't intend it like that."

"I'm glad of that, Otis. You should know it's dangerous to cross me. We're very different in that respect, you and me, but then we've always been very different types, haven't we?"

He had swallowed his pride, thinking of the greater victory. "Yeah, I guess we have. No offense."

"I tell you, the price you're asking is too high. Consider: Lucia's possibility of reclaiming the presidency is good—her standing in the popularity polls is now almost as high as Alia's. Then there's what can be done with the hundreds of millions of credit that I can bring to a campaign. There's a simpler way: a coup. Waters and Westmoreland can win the Army over. And there's always

Baron Harumi. As you yourself pointed out: his presence in Guam raises the ante significantly."

Le Grande had hissed at him. "An armed coup? But that's crazy! A rebellion would pitch Amerika into civil war—pro versus con in a piece of bloody butchery that'll lay the Sector open to invasion by Yamato! Threat of invasion can be a weapon in your armory, sure! But the Amerikan people would never trust a man who brought Baron Harumi's murderers down on them. Not for five minutes."

Halton Henry's wheezing laugh had been contemptuous. "I'm impressed by your concern for the people of Amerika, Otis. I would be more impressed by it if you'd offered to intercede with Alia freely, without talk of Halide stock and secret binding contracts."

"There you have it," he had told Henry, unmoved. "As you so eloquently argue, you can go it alone and try to take the presidency by force, or you can do it my way. You can take Lincoln by storm, or you can walk in smelling of roses and loved by the people. Which is it to be?"

The time had come for a decision, and Henry had been unhesitating. "Give me the contract."

They had sat down then and argued over the details, a corporation here, a controlling vote there, and he had seethed inside, watching Henry's convoluted signature being scratched to more than he had ever hoped for or dared to dream about.

Le Grande remembered that meeting with glee. All the while he had sweated, desperately thinking through the alternative Henry had divulged. What if he really did opt for that route? A rebellion in the outermost worlds of Amerika! A ransacking army sweeping out of the Boundary, gathering support as it went. Jeezus God! What a terrifying prospect! There came a vision of Waters's Army command hammering on his door, making him a public scapegoat, a show trial for treason—and then the rare use of capital punishment—

There had been a cold, black void in his mind, a trickle of sweat on his temple, and then he had forced his mind back to the present, thought the matter through, and seen that his own fear was the last enemy of this contract. Henry was an asthmatic fool, and no warlord. He could never inspire a *coup d'état!*

When he had added his own signature to the documents, he had made a bargain that had sealed Henry's future, and the rest had been mere puppet play.

Now, as le Grande spied on him from the doorway, he saw that Henry had come alone. This time there was no General Waters to lean on, nor Kurt Reiner to lend him smirking support. His face was ruddy with expectation as he got down from the air-car driving seat. He snapped the gull-wing door shut and paced across the pad, glancing up at the ornamental clock in the guardhouse tower. Le Grande watched him a full minute, until the ornate Swiss chimes of Looie's Shattoe struck the hour. Henry wrung his kid gloves nervously, his hacking cough punctuating the silence, then he moved out of the sun. The VP's scent brought in a hunting dog in a velvet collar of unsettling bright red. It was patted until its tail began to wag, then spurned.

Unable to contain his own anticipation any longer, Le Grande composed himself and made his appearance.

The VP took two steps towards him, an agony boiling in his belly. "Well?"

"Halton."

"You've come from the President? She's going to call a snap?"

"The President is listening to her godchildren play. I've just come from her."

Henry searched for a clue, but le Grande's face was a maddening blank, put on deliberately.

"But you put it to her? Like you said you would?"

"I . . . did."

Henry's agitation increased. "Come on, Otis! Is the election going to be called, or isn't it?"

Le Grande's sigh was tremulous. "I'm sorry, Halton. She wouldn't wear it."

"*Wouldn't wear it?*"

Henry's mouth fell open, his eyes flicked to left and right and then settled immovably on le Grande's smile. He took an involuntary pace forward, his hand on the butt of his blaster, but before the rage of his betrayal could come over him, le Grande's hand was raised. At the signal three boar-faced synths in sky-blue coveralls stepped out from the arches and came to their master's heel. They carried guns in their hands and looked built for butchery.

Halton Henry felt a tide of utter disbelief wash over him. Bands of steel tightened around his chest. He turned without a word and walked back to his limo, knowing that if he could persuade Waters and Westmoreland within the week, and if the Korean chain could be secured and Harumi's troops brought in before the end of the month, he could still carry off the default plan.

If! If! If! The word hammered inside his head, filling it with pain like a rotten tooth as he walked away. He fought to steady himself and to keep his thoughts on vengeance. Le Grande would pay for this with his life. He would grind the faces of the entire le Grande faction into the dust. Their disciples and hangers-on, all of their adherents, no matter how insignificant! None would escape. He would make them pay just as he had once made his sister pay.

As he came to his air-car he was racked with a bout of uncontrollable coughing. Another inner voice spoke to him, this one cool and distant and utterly terrifying. He suffocated as he tried to shut it out, gasped for air as he refused to listen, but it kept on speaking to him all the same. Laughingly, in le Grande's voice, it told him that the reason he could not breathe was that he was already shut inside a freezee.

28

Ellis Straker lay back on the soft grass, sated, drowsing in an ecstasy of peace, Reba's naked body in his arms. Overhead the leaf-laden boughs of this private part of the big Shattoe estate shivered, dappling them with Arcadian sunlight. This is what heaven must be like, he thought hazily. A virgin and a man who's not slept with a woman for damned near two years. Such a release dissolved all problems, all thoughts, in a wonderful golden halo.

He rolled his lover onto her back beside him and caressed her gently. Then he looked deep into her eyes and saw that she wanted to hold the moment forever, but when he laid her down, the spell was broken, and her words, as she covered herself, brought him back to reality, and he remembered that they were both minor players in a desperate game and that this was not paradise but a secluded place in a wood somewhere near Lexington.

"You'd be in great danger if Kurt found out what had happened between us."

"He's a harmless fool."

"His mind is seldom motivated by reason, Ellis, but he is no fool. He would act first and think later. He already detests you for the way you stood up to him."

He saw the sudden regret in her face and sought her hand. "Don't talk about him."

"He's far from harmless. He's rich and he has powerful associates. He could have you followed and set up at any time."

"Not while I'm lodging at the Lubbock mansion. I'll snap the weasel in half if he so much as—"

She silenced him with a shake of her head, getting suddenly up on her elbow. "You don't understand! My father would have you horse-whipped and sent into exile on Yukon if he imagined that you and I—"

"Do you regret that we came here?"

"No. How could I? But there are greater powers than love in our world. To some people's minds, we've just committed a heinous crime."

He clenched his teeth and felt a ripple of muscle move over his jaw. "I'm a man. You're a woman. Where's the crime in that?"

"I've told you that my father wants me to marry Kurt. That is sufficient to send you to Yukon."

"While I'm entangled with the Yamato ambassador? Not a chance."

"How long can that save you? What if—"

She stopped, seeing that he looked at her elfin face, and let him put a finger to the faint freckles that spangled the bridge of her nose. There was real fear for him in her doe-like eyes, and it made him feel worthy.

"Crazy talk," he said, admonishing her kindly. "You can't hedge everything in life with 'what ifs.' An astrogator learns that there's a lot of psi in life, a current that carries events. There is a power within us all, which, if we take notice of it, carries us around difficulties and enables us to reach our goals."

She looked into his eyes. "Do you believe that? Truly?"

"It's axiomatic."

She seemed suddenly perplexed. "So men and women don't meet by chance?"

He smiled at her earnestness and ran his hand lightly over the firm smoothness of her body, wondering at the way his touch raised the down on her arms in gooseflesh. "This was meant to be. I can feel it. It's all up there, in those broad spaces between the stars. The same stars I astrogate by."

"The same that will take you from me soon?"

"That's meant to be too." He fell silent, his mind turning to his brother and the oath he had sworn. The psi-current was straining to carry him back to the Zone. He could detect its pull, could feel the rightness of it, and knew that if he faced any danger it would be through opposing this force. *Don't resist it,* his inner self cried to him at nights, sternly and sometimes in his mother's voice. *You've divided your loyalties in a way I told you that you must never do!*

He hated the impatient feeling that came over him in those quiet times. After months of waiting, it was past time to leave. To catch up on his destiny. To recharge the power pack of his soul.

He told Reba of Duval's capture and of his desire to search for him, and she took it well, understanding the power and the passion that motivated him, and loving him because he tried to be true to it.

"What's he like, your brother?" she asked softly, laying her head on his chest so that her hair fanned out across it like the down of a dandelion clock.

He sighed. "Younger and a foot shorter than me, and dark. He took after my mother, whereas I was more my father's son."

"Is he a gentle man, with a woman's softness?"

Ellis smiled. "He's a man. No doubt about that. And if it were questioned in his earshot, he'd prove as much. But you're right. He has a calmer nature than me, more patience with fools, more skill in intricate things."

"I can see that you love him a lot."

"I do. He's my only living relative. My mother's dead. My son and my son's mother. My father was killed for his Expansionist beliefs in the Philadelphia riot; before that he was an adventurer, then a merchant." Ellis's voice was reinforced by pride. "He was the stiffest-necked bastard in all of Amerika. Under Lucia he would not be silent. He knew little of humility, he never preached to Duval or me, but he had strong beliefs and he was protesting at Harrisburg because he could not endure the impositions of Yamato when the Squadsmen opened fire."

"He was a patriot. And a martyr to the cause?"

"I guess you could say that."

"And you'll be a martyr too, if you don't take very great care with Ambassador Okubo."

He sat up, feeling the sudden chill of perspiration on his limbs. "Think so?"

"My father is using you. He must consider bigger things than justice to one man. When set against the affairs of the Sector, you're insignificant, Ellis. I know that he'll toss you aside the moment you no longer supply him with the means to further his policies. His aim is to astrogate Amerika as you would astrogate your nexus ship." She reached out a hand to his body, gently touching him. "You know that Amerikan high politics is conducted through allegory and metaphor, don't you? It's because of the influence of our neighbors—Byzantium infecting Greece. When I was a child, my father taught me that in Yamato they consider the anatomy of Amerika like a human form: the President is its head; ministers of state are its eyes, which never wink or sleep; the press are ears, to hear complaint; the armed forces are the shoulders and arms that bear the burden of war and of peace, and defend the head with strength; the corporations are the trunk, the chest, and the belly with the vital organs of commerce and manufacture. But the people—the people are down at the bottom: the legs to run errands and do all the work and support everything else."

"Now you're using allegory. Why don't you say what's on your mind?"

She sighed at his impatience. "You've played *go* against me. My father taught me that too. You've seen his attitudes in the plays I make: to him, all stones are expendable—and all men."

He smiled at a stray thought that flitted through his mind as he listened, but Reba insisted, "When my father has finished with you, he'll cast you aside like a tissue. Be warned— What are you laughing at?"

"Oh, not at you—just your rundown of Yamato political thought. I was wondering who, in all this great allegorical acupuncturist's catalog, is the asshole. I think, maybe, that must be Kurt Reiner."

She dissolved in a laughter born of tension rather than humor. It decayed quickly. "What's going to become of us all, Ellis?"

"With faith we'll be victorious. With faith there's always hope. Untune that string, and note what discord follows."

She looked at him calculatingly then. And, as if she had made up her mind, told him deliberately, "Shakespeare, huh? Well, the discord of change is sounding in Amerika right now. The President has issued a holding order on the VP. He can't leave Liberty. If he complies he'll be arrested, tried, and then executed for treason. If he does not, but manages to get offworld, then there will be war by Christmas."

As they walked together back up to the Shattoe, high-piled lightning clouds sent rollers of sound over the fields, and big spots of rain pelted the seven-fingered leaves of the horse chestnut trees. Ellis found himself wishing that this golden summer could go on and on endlessly, an endless train of golden days, an idyll without worries or cares, but he knew it could not. The word at the house was that Halton Henry had fled. That he would not obey the President.

Before night fell, Ellis learned that Secretary Lubbock had ordered him to return to Harrisburg immediately. There was a squadron of nexus ships to be readied.

29

Jiro Ito made straight for the White House, arriving at noon. He carried the report directly to Secretary Lubbock, brooking no nonsense from the security staff who tried to delay him. The grade one security pass he flourished at them was enough to open any door in Amerika beyond the Oval Office. The committee was in plenary session—the President alone was absent.

The chamber was echoic, high-vaulted, and paneled in oak and Oregon marble that resounded in the uproar. Among the committee, Nikolai Belkov, Raich Sadler, and General Earls flanked Lubbock. Opposite them, seated along a vast and ornate plex table, were Daven Zaentz, in charge of Finance, and le Grande and his supporters.

Lubbock hushed the noise as he saw the stony look on Ito's face. This news was urgent, he judged. Urgent and of bad tenor.

Ito's bow was curt. "Mr. Secretary, the news from Dakota is very bad. General Waters's men are burning their Oath of Allegiance cards at Fort Naseby."

"When?"

"November fourteenth. Three days ago. At their head is General Kulross and a hundred of her senior staff officers."

"It's another civil war," Lubbock said, stunned.

Lubbock knew that resentment burned in the younger generation of Army officers over the way they had been subordinated by Alia Kane. She had removed all political power from them. How eager would they be to avenge their deflated prestige now? How many would rally to the rebellious banner as it moved Liberty-ward?

"Elements are even now preparing to take control on New New York with five hundred thousand troops. All across the Boundary the calls are going out, calling men to arms. The port of Frisco on Kalifornia III is taken."

"Lucia must be arrested," Zaentz said urgently.

"Instruct the Guard to see to that at once."

"And the President?" le Grande asked.

"We're working on it!" Lubbock's fingers danced over the keyboard and he began to write swiftly. He said, "The District of Columbia is the President's best protection. In the capital at least we can be sure the population is ninety-nine percent loyal."

"You think the rebellion will reach Liberty?" Sadler asked, aghast.

General Earls rubbed her hands together and advised caution. "I can't be sure of my men. Sixty thousand troops are billeted here, but I can't guarantee they'll follow orders. I guess they have as little taste for a civil war as I do. Let's try to arrange a parley, to cool the rebels' heels a while. Then perhaps the fire will burn itself out."

Le Grande sneered at her. "Sure! Like it did for you in the Carolinas?"

"I'm a soldier. And a realist!"

Lubbock turned on them both. "People! We're facing collapse. In ten days, Lincoln may be facing a Yamato army. We cannot afford to be caught unprepared."

"Reports say that Harumi's troops are gathering in Guam," Ito said.

Lubbock spoke to Earls. "Where's the Yamato ambassador?"

"Still at his Lincoln embassy."

"The President must summon him."

Le Grande grinned. "Let her summon General Waters and that sonofabitch Westmoreland too. She summoned Halton Henry and look what happened."

It was normal practice at times of state alert for the President to command any factions suspected of disloyalty to be called to Liberty. There they could be watched closely and removed from dangerous associates. "The Army rebels won't come, but Okubo has to." Lubbock bent over his keyboard, writing hasty directives. He looked up with eyes that impaled le Grande. "There was time for Halton Henry to repent of the evil into which you led him. I hold you responsible for making a traitor of Amerika's vice-president. Yes, and for your own deceitful ends!"

Le Grande leapt to his feet. "Conroy, you're a filthy liar! It's no fault of mine that Henry planned an uprising. Your head is so stuffed with the shit of your own intrigues that you just can't see straight anymore!"

Lubbock was pleased with le Grande's crude outburst. It was now on the committee record. The man's resentment at being manipulated had flooded out, showing that he was a worried man. If the President chose mercy and Halton Henry did not fall, how vast would le Grande's chagrin grow? How huge his fear of Halton Henry's eventual reprisals? Le Grande had staked everything on Halton Henry's downfall. And though he had yet to lose, he had not won either.

One at a time! Lubbock thought mercilessly, looking to Belkov and then to le Grande. Otis's twig humbled, then bent double! Lucia's branch pegged to earth! Halton almost sawn off! Almost. Next would come the Army rebels of Waters and Westmoreland. Those I'm going to snap in two!

When Lubbock spoke, it was calmly to his ally, Raich Sadler, warden of the Boundary Worlds. "The President is hoping to see Halton Henry curbed but not broken. What do you think about that?"

Sadler, sixty years old losing some of his flesh, stared out from under shaggy brows. "Congress will see it very differently. He's a traitor."

Lubbock dropped his voice. "It might yet be a good idea to allow the President her own way in this matter. Back me and I'll see you're appointed to supervise Zaentz at Finance."

Sadler smiled briefly. "You seem pretty confident of victory."

"I am. Ito!" When the messenger came to him, Lubbock spoke rapidly. "Take this message to my Lincoln house immediately: Captain Straker is to put Hawken's plan into effect. He'll understand what you mean. Harrisburg and Norfolk are on alert. This is to order the Navy to its alert station with all strength, and using stealth. Make sure they understand that Hawken's ships are not to be interfered with, whatever they appear to do. Got that?"

Ito bowed and hurried from the chamber with the orders, still hot from the terminal and security-sealed, in his gloved fist.

Good, Lubbock thought with satisfaction. Perhaps it's time to humble le Grande a little more. He's spent too much time this year strutting around the District like a turkey cock, reingratiating himself. Last week he went to the White House in that ostentatious Bristol air-car of his and told her he had sure knowledge of my plans to kiss the feet of the Emperor. Now he's called me a liar, openly and in front of the committee. He's getting well above himself and he deserves to suffer a reminder that'll demonstrate to him his true status. What better way than to show him the contract?

He thought back with pleasure to the day of Halton Henry's surrender. Henry must have taken the presidential summons from his messenger as if it was a viper. On that fateful summer day at Looie's Shattoe, when le Grande had snapped the jaws of his trap closed, Henry had fled back to Lincoln and then to his fortified estate in the obscure system of Ossining.

In a frenzy, he had begun stitching together the tatters of his contingency plans. At first it must have looked impossible, but as the leaves of his maple forests turned first to gold and then to bloodred, there had grown in him renewed hope. Cassabian had intercepted communiqués written by Waters and by Westmoreland, showing they were both solid to the Henrys' cause. Lucia herself, filled with righteous indignation against her house arrest, had encouraged him also. Baron Harumi, though his temper had been put under considerable pressure, had extended his undertaking to send troops. Against the odds, Okubo's repeated intercessions had persuaded him that the hazardous crossing of the Korean chain was possible before winter set in—with Amerikan help. As a result of Yamato pressure the puppets of the Central Authority had agreed to withdraw Alia Kane's name from the register of recognised governmental heads and try to turn her subjects against her. That would be a gigantic blow to her prestige.

Just as it must have seemed to Halton Henry that he would succeed, Lubbock had spoken to Alia. Then he had reworded her document of presidential summons to Henry, drafting it in conciliatory terms, to make her seem eager for rapprochement. Henry had wavered. In a few more days, everything would have been ready. So he had held out on Ossining, pleading a transport problem.

"*Play for time!*" Lucia's voice had screamed at him from Liberty. "*Delay them. Alia must be made to wait.*"

Henry had spoken hoarsely to his secretly disloyal secretary. "Tell the courier that I'm unable to get offplanet today. That I'll come in three days—no, four. Say that I've made every effort to comply."

Then he had asked Waters, "I'll be safe on Ossining, won't I? I can raise twenty thousand troops here and we have a few ships. If I can hold out for a week, I'll be safe. A week! God grant me that!"

Lubbock's spy had told him how, three days later, the color had drained from Halton Henry's distraught face, how he had coughed flecks of blood as he broke the seal on the President's second, this time unaltered, summons.

"*This manner of reply I have not been accustomed to receive from any person,*" she had written in a high passion, demanding that he come. Instantly. In the Navy ship she had sent.

He had read the terrifying demand twice, seeing the naval personnel booting impatiently about in his courtyard and the vast belly of their warship hovering above his house, blotting out the sky. The two lieutenants who faced him wore studded jerkins of blue leather and looked like they meant business. Desperation had crawled over his skin, then he had fired off a message to Waters on Dakota to stay the rebellion.

"I'll go to Liberty and throw myself on the President's mercy!" he had told Westmoreland, who was on the vidilink. He was in orbit.

"You can still go through with it!"

"No!"

"Coward! Betrayer! You'll murder us all!"

When the screen went dead, a group of his own guards had tried to stop him. They had stood in his way, but he had pushed them aside in his anxiety to go aboard the *Portland* and thereafter fling himself in abject repentance at Alia Kane's feet.

And when he had arrived at the White House, how she had screamed at him, sending his blood cold, launching threats without mercy, one after another, down upon his head. He had been dragged from her, begging forgiveness, pouring out the pathetic sentiments le Grande had fed him about neutralizing Lucia and guarding the succession, all the while choking for air asthmatically as the grip of restraint on his arms had reminded him of the penalty he must now pay.

It had been extraordinary to watch. And after, it had been so simple to extract from the quivering Halton Henry the damning contract he had made with le Grande for control of Halide. Shall I snap le Grande now? Lubbock asked himself, feeling utterly in control of all he surveyed. Shall I show him a facsimile of the contract? It would be like showing him his own death warrant, and sure proof against any pompous spite on his part. Perhaps not. Perhaps I'll save it until I need it. A wise man would.

He thought once more of the bundle of firewood twigs he had shown to Nikolai Belkov. One twig remained: Ellis Straker. The next letter he would draft would be to Baron Harumi. A diplomatic message to be passed on in total secrecy by the Korean executive Yi To Man, via Sumitomo Bank, warning that the escort Baron Harumi had arranged for his troops would turn on him and attempt to destroy his invasion force.

30

THE KALIFORNIA I SYSTEM

When Jos Hawken saw her, the *Constitution* was riding in orbit about the closest planet to the nexus of Kalifornia I; along with four other neat two-thousand-tonners, she drew a watchful curtain across the terminus of the Korean chain. Each of the vessels belonged to Hawken; all were merchantmen bought after the Merchant Traders' successful summer convoy to Europa, and all were mass light as if waiting to pick up cargo. But Hawken knew that there was no cargo: each ship was heavily armed with beam weapons and singularity guns; the reduced mass was to make the ships more maneuverable and to allow them to make a looser approach to the nexus when the time came to get the hell out.

He had come to talk business and stood in the egress port of a supply grab, a small craft out of Los Angeles. It was creepy up near this huge, oblate gas giant. Its fractal-patterned surface was cold and dark, a long way from the primary. The Index was as low as he'd ever seen it.

Hawken saluted and clasped Ellis's hand tightly, as usual, but there was something in his grip that put Ellis on his guard as he came out of the umbilicus.

"Welcome aboard, Commodore," he said with shipboard formality.

"Thank you, Ellis."

"Any news from Liberty?"

Hawken faced him, his glance warning off eavesdroppers. "News that'll not please you. First, I want your report."

They climbed up to the bridge together, Ellis made uneasy now by Hawken's reticence. I've nothing at all to report and you know it, he thought. Twelve days going round this rotten mandarin of a planet without result. You've come to tell me the reason, and it'd better be good. I wish I knew what twisted ideas Cassabian's been planting in your head and what his position is now. Jeezus! And what about the rebellion? It's a fact that knowledge is power—without knowledge I'm hobbled out here. And you know that too.

He said, "The Yamato transports know we're here. Either they'll come to rendezvous when they're ready, or they won't. I'm damned if I'm cruising through the nexus to fetch them."

Hawken grunted and hooked his thumbs into his belt knowingly. "You think they suspect what you have in store for them? Eh? Wouldn't that explain their reluctance?"

Ellis cast him a sudden, savage glance. Since receiving Conroy Lubbock's order two weeks ago, he had been relishing the prospect of paying off Okubo in very final terms. The ambassador had given him payment and sealed communiqués to pass on to Harumi's emissary. Half the credit had gone to Hawken, and the remainder, in Red Bowen's possession, had been sent down to Harrisburg at John Oujuku's request. The letter to Harumi was still under lock and key in his suite.

Ellis's spirits had been high then. It had been exhilarating to get back aboard a nexus ship after so long kicking about up in Lincoln. To move and to see events move, it was good. He had discussed the operation to the penultimate detail with Okubo, then he had cruised to his appointed station on the Boundary exactly as the ambassador had desired. As soon as the troop-laden globe ships appeared, he would fall in beside them, his squadron formed up tight, and he would take them to within sight of Los Angeles and the four Navy cruisers which were orbiting there. Then the real payment would be made, the part he had not told Okubo about: a nice opening up with singularity guns!

If only Duval were here now, he thought. With expert handling, these thirteen-foot-long Stanton weapons, each weighing four thousand pounds, could puncture any hull—extraplex or balsa wood, it made no difference, shield or no shield. Such a gun locally altered the value of the gravitational constant. It propagated a two-ton antimatter quasi-singularity with an initial event horizon a foot in diameter across three to five miles of free space. It would drill a neat hole through all solid matter, suck in any gas or liquid it encountered, and fill itself up, the matter it absorbed destroying the antimatter it contained, until it petered out. In vacuum it would collapse naturally and blink out unfilled at the end of its life, birthing a "plumstone" of matter, a polished sphere of pure iron 56 a little over two and a half feet across that would continue to propagate with the same velocity as the original singularity. If the *Constitution* and her sister vessels could get close enough, Baron Harumi's globe ships would be lanced into lumps of inoperative junk, and the other ships that would act as escort would be put out of action in the same way, their systems disrupted, their atmospheres leaking away, and their crews not knowing what the hell had hit them.

But nothing had happened. No ship from the nexus. Nothing so much as a salvager had made a transit. And those ships that had been cruising for the other side of the nexus had used hyper-cautious and expensive go-ahead drones to blip through and back with a surveillance snapshot of the far side. They had cut away as soon as they detected his ships in the destination system, increasing the confusion in the Marshall II interface where Kim Gwon Chung and his pirates were hanging around in predatory fashion.

"I hear that Oujuku's bought himself a fast ship and two shuttles," Hawken said.

Ellis waited for Hawken to say more.

"I hear that he's sailed from Harrisburg without clearance or passport. Do you know anything about that?"

"We're a long way from Harrisburg here, Commodore."

Hawken grunted. "Yeah. But that's no answer to a direct question."

"I have a few preoccupations of my own. Too many to think too much about what John Oujuku may be doing."

The secret plans Ellis had made with Oujuku just before the man's wedding in July had been far-ranging. They had sat together in Hawken's Lincoln house and without Hawken's knowledge had drunk to the voyage-hungry nexus trash of Norfolk and Harrisburg and advanced their ideas to send a privateeing ship into the Neutral Zone. Since then, Oujuku had settled matters admirably. With credit of his own and later with the credit Ellis had taken from Okubo, Oujuku had bought a fast, light ship, and Stanton guns, and had immediately started equipping her for a return voyage to Sado. If Oujuku could reach there before news of Baron Harumi's smashed army did, he might be able to rescue or ransom Duval and the other Amerikans and escape without penalty.

"Nothing spectacular," Oujuku had said, grinning at the prospect. "Just a little piece of midnight horse-trading with Governor Ugaki. Open and honest and friendly like. Then, when the boys and girls are all aboard, we'll overfly Niigata and leave our answer branded across Nishima's double-crossing ass."

The thick-accented words of Kim Gwon Chung had come to him then: "Yamato generosity is very big and glowing! Me, I ask only for their credit, but many times they try to give me their lives also!"

Since that time, Ellis had dwelled on the succulent notion that it was Okubo's credit that would finance everything. And if John was true to himself, the ransom money would just be used as a lure and would return with him multiplied a dozen times over. But something had miscarried. Ten days had passed and no contact had been made with Baron Harumi's emissary. Was it possible that the rebellion was swelling with troops and arms? What if Halton Henry had succeeded? If Lincoln itself had risen against the President? A sudden fear reared in Ellis's mind and his thoughts turned to Reba Lubbock's safety.

"You're to set the coordinates for home, Ellis."

Ellis felt the words break in on him like hammers. "*What?*"

"Now. Immediately. I've got other work for you."

This was what he had feared the moment he had seen Hawken marching down the umbilicus with that no-nonsense walk of his. He had known that backhanded politicking in Lincoln had robbed him of his chance of action.

"What's been happening?" he demanded.

Hawken slapped his hands flat on the rail before him. "The Boundary ports are closed, and I'm defying Conroy's order to come here. You know that Waters and Westmoreland have mustered in Dakota and Iowa? They've taken control of Ohio and chosen the Akron chain as the nexus for Harumi's troops to make first planetfall."

"They'll never reach Akron, by God! They have to come through here first."

Hawken shook his head. "Perhaps. But it's not your efforts that'll stop them. Halton Henry's in the penitentiary at Camp Worth, just outside Lincoln. The President is in her War Room at Mount Rainier, and her cousin, General Hunsdon, is commanding the military push that will oppose the rebels. In Lincoln rumors are circulating that Baron Harumi's sworn to pay his samurai with credit from the vaults of Bank Amerika and make the President bow to him publicly on the steps of the Washington Memorial, on live broadcast. Waters is stirring it up at the head of his army. Even now they're preparing to transit into Illinois with seven hundred thousand troops."

Ellis's stomach tightened. "Then I can't leave this station! Harumi must be contained!"

Hawken looked up then. All he had come to say was in his mouth. "You'll do as I tell you. The rumors are false. Harumi will not attempt to come through here. And without his help the rebellion will crumble."

"Not attempt to come through? But it's the only way he can get into Amerika. Have we been betrayed to Okubo?" Ellis's mind reeled.

"No. Harumi's written a letter to Okubo saying that help will now only be dispatched following the release of Lucia Henry. He considers that to be the best test of Amerikan feeling against Alia Kane, and proof that the rebellion is not a lost cause. But the rebel army can never release Lucia because they can no longer get to her. They don't know where she is. Tansi Dousenne and Raich Sadler have moved her to someplace up the Alaska chain, and that's too far for Waters's army to penetrate without Harumi's help."

Ellis saw at once that the rebels' dilemma was total: no support without Lucia, and no Lucia without support. Unless the circle was broken, the rising was doomed. Such a vicious catch had the stamp of Conroy Lubbock's fertile mind about it.

"How was Harumi persuaded to impose that condition? By the secretary, I'll bet!" Ellis said angrily. The twin-tongued bastard! he thought. Lubbock tipped Harumi off. And I've been here all the while for nothing!

Hawken shrugged, saying less than he knew. "Conroy is not wholly in accord with our ideas, Ellis."

It was enough for Ellis. "Come on, Commodore, give it to me straight!"

Hawken shot a glance at his subordinate's display of ill temper, but he held his course. "Consider: Conroy's object is to stop the rising. The rising may be stopped by the preventing of Yamato support. Therefore, Yamato support must be prevented. There was never a desire to destroy a Yamato army. Simply a need to prevent it reaching an Amerikan system."

Ellis's sarcasm was heavy: "Oh, sure! Harumi's army is no big deal. It'll just sit there minding its own business on Guam forever. Guam obviously needs a million troops to keep it subdued. Who's trying to kid who, Jos?" Ellis slammed his fist down on the breech of a singularity gun. "What the hell did we mount these sonsabitches for, heh?"

"You may just as well have a cargo hold full of scrap iron."

"It'd be easier to digest than what's burning in my belly now!"

"That may be"—Hawken became suddenly conciliatory—"but don't you see? Our way was irreversible. Conroy had a more subtle and flexible balancing act to perform. He's saved Harumi from destruction and signaled to Yamato that he's not looking for war. He's made a gesture to Yamato without accepting their line on the Zone. And he's made a fool out of Okubo in Harumi's eyes."

"Yeah! And a fool out of me!"

"He's buying us time to organise."

"He's lost us the chance of a decisive blow!" Ellis slammed his fist into the breech once more so that his knuckles bled. The thought flashed into his mind that Kim Gwon Chung's anger would know no bounds. That he had worked up his crews and his associates with false promises of glory and he'd have to stand there and tell them it was all off. Now nothing—nothing at all—would restore confidence in his name among those from whom he most wanted respect. "Devil take Mr. Secretary Lubbock as the snake that he is!"

Hawken's eyes narrowed. "Steady, Ellis. Conroy's a powerful man. Dangerous as a snake, true, but it's better that he's not set against us. When the looked-for pro-Yamato rising in the heartworlds fails to appear, and when the rebels are cut off and crushed to dust by Earls and Hunsdon, Conroy will have carried the day. It'll not be long before Lucia and Halton Henry are both tried for treason and sent to their reward, and Conroy appointed VP, and all that accomplished without provoking Yamato to invade. Total victory in his eyes. He will see it as a rout. And why not? It's you, with your hair-trigger temper and your private war and your independent action, who's the real danger. Well, as of now, I've seen to it that you're not dangerous any longer."

Ellis looked across the ship's bridge where his men stood at their posts, wrapped up in private thoughts, listening but trying to seem not to be. He saw Moss and Rively, Brown, and Gruber, all of whom had come back survivors of the Sado fiasco. It had been more than a year now. He knew how they itched to settle their old shipmates' scores. Good crew, reliable crew, crew that'd run to hell and kick the devil's ass for you. Not people to leave dangling as puppets, as Hawken is dangling you. Don't fail them now.

"What's our position with the government?" he asked Hawken bitterly.

"Officially we're nothing more than pirates. However, Yamato is most likely to resort to diplomacy once the rising is put down and she may be disposed to let matters be. In effect, Conroy will have bought a stalemate."

"And Okubo? I guess our credibility's blown as far as he's concerned."

Hawken drew a deep breath and expelled it slowly, considering the question carefully. "I doubt that. I think Conroy's hand was played as subtly as ever. Harumi was warned against mutiny within your crews. The most Okuba will suspect will be the loyalty of your men."

Ellis nodded tightly and Hawken folded his arms. "I think we'd better talk with Cassabian from here on in. He has a new task for you."

"What sort of task?"

"One you should perform well—smuggling."

"*Smuggling?*" Ellis's reply was explosive. "You think I'll let myself be used again?"

"Goddamn you, Ellis! Won't you accept a single order without talking back? This is important work. For a trusted man. It's not small-time stuff I've got in mind."

Ellis looked at Hawken with a murderous glance. "Then what?"

"You're to convey a Korean banker into Amerika. And with him comes the best hope of all our futures."

The argument had cleared the anger from Ellis's brain. He was thinking clearly and with perspective now. There was no point in exposing useful duplicity needlessly, and Lubbock would surely wring every last drop of advantage from Okubo's credulity. But this new task was an extension of duties both unagreed and unwelcome.

"I won't do any more of your dirty work," he told Hawken. "I've got a task of my own. My brother—"

"You'll go nowhere without a ship or a passport."

Ellis flared. "And who'll stop me?"

"I will. And all the forces at the President's command. You'll be a dead man inside a weak if you defy me, Ellis. But bring me this banker and I'll see you obtain a passport to go to the relief of those left marooned on Chi no Tsuki."

Ellis thought it over, then he said, "Who is he?"

"His name is Yi To Man. His mission is of great importance."

"How's that?"

"He's vital to presidential security. More I can't say. On my life."

"On your *what?*"

"Yes. My life. And on Alia Kane's. Good enough?"

He slacked off a point or two. "All right, then, in that case what's in it for me if I agree? It ought to be more than some pissy paper of permission."

"If you're successful, your payment will be a ship of your own."

"This one—or you can whistle through your ass."

Hawken spat rancorously. "Damn you, Ellis Straker! Didn't I take you on as a boy? I've grown you from a seed! And for what? To have you demand—*demand*—of me my best ship!"

Ellis's hand gripped the hilt of his blaster. "Well, I'm a grown oak tree now. I already have your best ship and four more. If I learned anything from you, Jos Hawken, it's that a captain is master of all when his ship's offworld. More than secretaries of state. More than Emperors. Yeah, and more than an owner. You're on *my* ship now, and she's in orbit and we can go anywhere I decide. I'll have the *Constitution* for my trouble, or the squadron lights-out for Korea and the aid the Korean Confederation will gratefully give me to harass Yamato. And make no mistake—every Jack and Jill on board will follow me."

Hawken eyed him silently, then nodded assent.

Ellis felt a surge of elation that conquered every doubt. What a prize! In ancient times, the Constitution was an idea. A document that defined the Universal Rights of Man, very powerful it was and hard to defy, an idea that had destroyed many despots. The *Constitution* was the perfect ship to carry forward his plans: newly built, lean, fast, well designed, and capable, as he had seen, of mounting great firepower.

His mind roamed over the debris cast up on the accretion disc of fortune by the latest turns of this political psi-storm. So far, the pluses had been Okubo's credit and Reba Lubbock. If the next piece of space flotsam turned out to be the *Constitution,* he would have that too. He would wait for Oujuku to return with Duval and then they would go out cruising the Zone chains together and Yamato would see there was more to Amerikan pride and Amerikan vengeance than old men who dissembled and wanted stalemates and political balance, men who shrank back from justice.

Hawken's eyes pierced him, reading his thoughts. His warning was delivered softly. "You make me very angry, Ellis. But be careful. Conroy's ruthless and clever. Yes, even more than you think. And he's a thousand times more connected to events than you or I will ever be, psi or no psi. He has hundreds of spies all over Known Space feeding him secrets. He's fanatically loyal to Alia Kane. You saw the way he worked things round to put himself in line for the vice-presidency. He'll do anything to maintain power and to elevate himself. You called him a snake. So he is. He turns this way and that just as it suits him. Just now, he's turning towards Yamato and towards Kurt Reiner. If you want to keep your leaves, oak tree, you'll remember that. And you'll keep away from his daughter."

Ellis stiffened, thinking suddenly of the clashing antlers of the stags in the deer parks at Looie's Shattoe. It was a universal male urge to lock horns with anything that stands between an individual and his desire. The temptation to tangle with Lubbock was overpoweringly strong, but Hawken was right. It was an urge that was lethal, and, for the moment, it would have to be be resisted.

But no one would keep him away from Reba forever. No one.

31

LIBERTY

On the morning of May Day, Jiro Ito brought his master the item he had been dreading. It shattered Lubbock's inner serenity more completely than if his President had ordered him out of government.

When Ito came to him, Lubbock was hard-pressed with work, drawing up a list of trials and executions that would best illustrate and punish the crimes of the rebels. Until today, events had proceeded to Lubbock's satisfaction.

Hadn't Kurt Reiner finally agreed to marry his daughter? Hadn't the Sector been pulled back from the very brink of war with Yamato? Hadn't the systems of the Boundary been harshly disciplined and all his enemies reduced and diminished?

Apart from a brief flurry of violence by the diehards, a flurry soon quieted by General Hunsdon's forces, the revolt had been gutted even before Thanksgiving. By the end of February, it had been utterly smashed. Waters's ragged army had been slammed, Lucia Henry's few remaining sympathisers in Dakota had surrendered, and their leaders had been humiliatingly captured. Only the weasel Westmoreland had succeeded in evading capture, bolting to the Honshu haven for high-ranking renegade Amerikans in Yamato. The two outstanding questions now were how to deal with Lucia and what to do with Halton Henry.

Lubbock had given the matter great thought. It should be simple, he had told himself two days ago. An orchestrated Congress was howling for Lucia's head, and efforts were daily being made to whip up opinion against her. It was a simple matter of convincing Alia that Lucia's execution was inescapable.

But when he had gone to her, Alia had become intractably, resolutely, intransigently set against the idea.

Lubbock recalled how he had gone too far with her—the way Alia's eyes had darted at him from that humorless face, the single pendant pearl earring under her red hair quivering, and her lips pursed in disapproval. Under the President's thin eyebrows, her pupils, large as saucers, rimmed with irises that were near black, had been turned on him with the full force of her considerable personality. Thin lips, painted pale, clashing garishly with a head of bright spun copper. Her head had seemed disembodied, then, raised on her neck, a fearsome mask, because he had brought her to within a hair's breadth of overt anger. Yes, and deliberately. She had been President a dozen years and she had learned how to demand and how to get. But he had been a statesman longer and knew how to make his President want what he wanted. A glance had commanded silence. Her two-fisted gestures, though from the body of a woman, had been recognisably her father's. The pure, insistent power of Ottoman Kane himself.

Of course, it was all staged and calculated to terrify those who surrounded her instantly, and so it did. He had backed off obediently as he had left the Oval Office, feeling he had maneuvered her precisely as he wanted.

But beneath the mask, in private, he had seen her face racked by a warring conscience. There had been no further discussion that week about the delicate matter of Lucia's death sentence—which was a pity, but could wait—nor of Halton Henry's, which was a consolation. The foolish ex-VP was better alive, for there was a clear use for him. And with the President riled in a passion over both, Halton might survive. He would present that, eventually, as the will of the Amerikan people. The offer would be clemency for Halton and death for Lucia. And Alia would accept that, because it was just and it was wise and because she trusted him absolutely.

Ito's unfussy bow was followed by no preliminary explanation. Instead, he laid a large plex poster sheet on the table. Its formal paragraphs made Lubbock gasp.

This nightmare was why he had closed the Boundary nexi before Christmas and kept them closed throughout the rising and after. This was the high retribution come down on them from above, the thunderbolt he had tried to stave off, and it shot him full of fear to find that it had appeared before him without warning.

"They were found distributed on printed plex throughout the District of Columbia, Mr. Lubbock."

"Thank you," he said, shocked utterly, though he had expected it in some small way at the back of his mind. "Thank you, Ito. I don't imagine this is an isolated copy?"

"Everyone knows about it. The Squad have found copies in Philadelphia and Harrisburg and—all over. The newscasters have got hold of it and are saying that there's no longer any point in suppressing it because the story's broken. They'll take a lot of hushing. And soon it'll be common knowledge offworld, I think. They're probably ahead of any embargo we can get out."

"You brought it straightaway?"

"Of course."

"Then you did well. Wait for me here, I'll be back shortly."

He folded the sheet, got up, and marched directly to the Oval Office. Le Grande was with the President, and a dozen aides, and Lubbock saw at once that the interruption was enormously inopportune. It made her waspish, and she chose not to look at him, addressing le Grande instead.

"You're ill at ease, Otis."

It was not a question.

Le Grande rubbed languidly at his forehead. Lubbock saw that he had arrived just as le Grande was hatching some scheme to amuse her and enrich himself. To scheme in the presence of Alia Kane was an electrifying experience at any time. Now, with Lubbock's arrival, it was too much for le Grande. There were few who could withhold the truth from her for long, fewer still who could lie openly to her face, and none who could do it successfully when Conroy Lubbock was at her side.

Lubbock waited patiently for le Grande to scuttle away.

"I'm getting the sweat," le Grande said, getting up from his seat. "It feels like that new Europan influenza virus might have got to me."

Alia's voice was feline. "I'll call Dr. Caius to you."

"Thank you, Alia, but please, don't trouble him."

"He's eminent and knows about viral strains. He'll tell you if you've got the sweat and give you a shot of mucolin."

"No trouble. It's nothing."

She looked penetratingly at Carola Ford, her attractive chief aide and le Grande's mistress, and then back at him. "So why mention it, Otis?"

"Tell you the truth, Alia . . ."

"Yes."

"Tell you the truth, I think I'm just tired. I . . . didn't get much sleep last night."

Alia's pout of annoyance was fleeting. He tried to touch her hand uninvited but she drew it back, remembering that Lubbock was watching.

"Go on, get the hell out of here, Otis. There's no more for you here today."

As he passed Lubbock, le Grande strutted like a peacock. He whispered pleasantly, "Up your ass, Mr. Secretary."

"And yours, Otis, with a glass samurai sword." Lubbock smiled and inclined his head with exaggerated politeness, calling after him, louder, "Sideways."

Le Grande turned, then turned again and stalked out, his fists flexing. A ripple of sniggering passed through the President's aides. Those that were in earshot looked suddenly stunned. The whispering began, eyed coldly by Carola Ford, but the exchange with le Grande had done nothing to unfreeze the secretary's baleful expression.

Alia gestured peremptorily. Lubbock approached, sheet in hand, adopted a suitably deferential stoop, and whispered to her. Immediately she got up and cleared the room with a clap of her hands.

"Okeh, time out. Let's go."

Her face had lost all softness; all around her, terminals and datacorders and hard copy were gathered up swiftly.

When Alia took the sheet to her desk, she pushed a finger through the holes where the Central Authority's decree had been fixed to, and later roughly torn from, one of the White House side doors. She studied it carefully and made no comment until she finished its archaic legalese lines.

REGARDING ONE Alia Kane: By the power vested in the Judges of this Committee, and with the authority of Earth Central, to whom is given all final and binding arbitration in Known Space and in the worlds thereof, and in which has been committed full exercise of Heavenly and Supreme Law, over and above the laws of constituent Sectors, to be governed with plenary authority . . .

We, seeing that improper and unlawful actions are multiplied one upon another, also that the prosecution of the Supreme Law grows every day weaker and weaker, through instigation and by means of the said Alia Kane, and since We understand her heart to be so hardened and obdurate that she has not only ignored the wholesome requests and admonitions of this Central Authority concerning her restitution and recompense but also has not so much as suffered the lawful Agents of this Authority to cross into the Sector of Amerika for this purpose, are constrained to betake ourselves to the weapons of justice against her.

We do out of the fullness of our Authority declare the aforesaid Alia Kane to be a usurper and a favorer of usurpers, and her adherents in the matters aforesaid, to have incurred the sentence of death, and to be cut off from the unity of the body of Humankind. And moreover We do declare her to be deprived of her pretended title to the Sector aforesaid, and of all dominion, dignity, and privilege whatsoever; and also the government, subjects, and people of the said Sector, and all others who have in any sort sworn unto her, to be forever absolved from any such oath, and all manner of duty of dominion, allegiance, and obedience; and We also do by authority of these presents absolve them, and do deprive the said Alia Kane of her pretended title to the Sector, and all other things before named. And We do command and charge all and every officer, subjects, people, and others aforesaid that they presume not to obey her or her orders, mandates, and laws; and those which shall do the contrary We do also and by this decree include them in the like sentence of anathema.

When the President looked up, her face was composed but her eyes flickered wildly. She stared penetratingly at her secretary and let the paper fall in her lap. Her breathing was shallow and fast.

"I am, by this decree, murdered. All my subjects are made either traitors or damned to death with me."

"Alia . . ."

Lubbock could say nothing more. Hell of hells, he thought. This proves, if any proof were needed, the extent to which Yamato controls the Authority of Earth Central. This is a statute last used three hundred years ago! In the days when the Sectors were being set up and there was a need for the Central Authority to come down hard on factions splintering away and setting up their own Sectors without permission. The punishment for any self-made ruler was death. The reward for any assassin carrying out the Authority's sentence was a secret known only to the cloistermen of Earth Central, the forbidden secret of everlasting life.

Now the menace of Lucia Henry is raised to a new and insistent pitch, he thought. Now the President *must* agree to sign her death warrant! Will she? She must!

"Hold me." Her cold hand tried to squeeze his fingers. "Hold me until I say let go."

She trembled, quaked, like a woman in labor. Sweat spangled her high forehead.

"Will they desert me? Will they, Conroy? Tell me!"

"The love of your people is a firm rock, Alia."

"And my enemies? Will they rise up against me now?"

"All your subjects love you dearly. More than they love life itself."

She snapped to her feet and began pacing. All around her, blue-and-white-clad elite Marine guards stood waxen, immobile in their niches, not daring to flinch. Lubbock watched her, terrified, knowing that the massive tension that pressured the President's heart would kill a buffalo.

Her voice daggered him. "There's a more formidable and immediate threat to consider. From this day on, a fantastic price is put on my head. There will now be assassins by the thousand willing to buy immortality for themselves in exchange for the life of this canceled President. Not least, perhaps, the arch-bastard himself, the self-appointed commander of the Known Universe, Mutsuhito!"

"Alia, please!" Lubbock pleaded. She whirled and clapped her hands, and like a discharge of lightning it poleaxed him. He took a step back from her, then saw her face split and her teeth, yellow against the bone white of her face. She was laughing.

32

It was two days later, around sundown, when Lubbock received another urgent visit from Ito.

"You've been successful in your errand?"

"Mr. Secretary. Elton Bowery, a software grower from Harrisburg, has admitted his guilt."

"He distributed the sheets?"

"That is his confession. Bowery is under arrest."

"You've examined him with the Probe?"

"So I guessed you would have ordered me, sir."

"Yes. Well . . . give him a restful night to think it over, but sing him this lullaby: if he doesn't reveal his accomplices, then he'll face the Probe again tomorrow. I want the name of the person who brought the master copy into Amerika."

Ito's eyes glittered in the lamplight. "I have already persuaded him to reveal that, sir."

"Who was it?"

"One Yi To Man. A Korean. A financier and agent of the Sumitomo Bank. He brought the master in from a Boundary nexus."

Lubbock's hand gripped Ito's sleeve. "What nexus? How did he get it into Amerika?"

"That's something we have yet to learn, sir."

Lubbock watched Ito gather up his satchel and prepare to go. Though the man was his most stalwart lieutenant, Ito had been born and raised in Yamato. Fleetingly he wondered if the man could still be trusted, then dismissed the thought as a loose-headed fear. There is no one more fanatic than the convert—especially one who has been ninja-trained. A samurai who has allowed himself to surrender is dead in his own eyes. Ito's psychology underwent a flip and he renders every assistance to his captors, as fanatically antagonistic to Yamato as he had previously been loyal to it. But only the future could reveal the power Earth Central's venomous order had to poison other men against a Sector's lawfully elected ruler, and by that time, it might be too late.

Who? he asked the empty room. I must know who is behind this. Who?

Cassabian? No. He's an Expansionist through and through. Then who? Le Grande? Yes! Oh, cowardly, ambitious Otis le Grande. Treacherous butterfly flitting about the President. Obstacle. Hated enemy. I'll bring you down. I'll show the President that ploy which you hatched with Halton Henry—yes, and have Henry come before you in the flesh to confirm every line of it to your face. Escape from that, perjurer! Shrug that away, you filthy liar!

What if I've misjudged, he thought, suddenly doubting his own cleverness. For the sake of Amerika, Lucia must die and Halton must live. But what if Lucia lives and Halton dies? Too bad. Too bad! For Amerika, and for me. I can't impeach le Grande without first impeaching Halton Henry. Then I'll have to wait again. Halton must be released. That's the promise I made to Kurt Reiner, and without his cousin's release there will be no marriage for Reba.

He looked at the vase of withered daffodils that stood on his windowsill. Beyond the open panes, the lawn was shot with long shadows, and in the sunset the west was cut out by the Lincoln skyline. The sky was a rich velvet blue, raked by streamers of high cloud, waves of salmon pink and molten gold dotted with air-car traffic, and below there were smaller, dimmer lights in the windows of the presidential apartments.

Alia stood silently at her balcony, alone, choosing to take the calm warmth of the night as an omen. She had been thinking of the despicable arrangements being made around her to marry her diplomatically to the nineteen-year-old Chinese prince, and regretting that she could not squash the idea immediately and out of hand without provoking a major row with China. The thought led her to consider the Emperor's latest dynastic move: Yeh-chun, the new consort of Mutsuhito. This latest quasi-wife was the daughter of the Korean puppet Ho Kum-sun, and a useful acquisition. She was presently on Seoul, at the port with the biggest nexus terminal and apron in Known Space, and would embark soon for the long transnexus voyage to Kyoto. Intelligence reports said the vast escort that would be required, for purposes of protocol as well as necessary discouragement to Korean pirates, was already beginning to assemble there. How simple it would be for Mutsuhito to interpret the Earth Central decree as an excuse to mount his longed-for invasion.

It was a delicate situation. For the first time in over a year the opportunity for an invasion was coming together. In terms of available hardware and suitable pretext it was very dangerous and the Navy would have to be extremely vigilant. According to Cassabian's spies, Westmoreland had found a home in the renegade corral of the Honshu quadrant, among a pack of exiles that daily petitioned Yamato with requests for war. An example made of his fellow conspirator, Waters, might douse passions in Yamato, but it could equally inflame them.

She had received Lubbock's report on Waters and had signed the document of execution which even now lay facedown on her desk. Why was it never easy to snuff out a man's life? she asked herself. No matter what he did, no matter what he had planned for me, I can't hate him enough to enjoy this duty. Why does there seem to be less steel in my veins than in my father's? If he suffered an unquiet conscience, he never showed it. Perhaps that was his secret. But, then . . . he was Ottoman Kane.

She examined her feelings more closely. It was never easy to order the death of citizens who held immovable convictions, and it was invariably unwise to try. Even so, it was not the suffering *but the cause* that made martyrs who endured.

For her comfort she decided to commute Bowery's sentence to exile, then she passed on to the next case: Lucia.

Conroy urges me to judicially murder her, she thought, but for what advantage? It's a dangerous precedent to set! And one only contemplated by such men as the filthy cloister dogs at Earth Central. Lucia plotted against me—she did exactly what I would have done in her place. Now she's my captive and she leaves me no alternative. I've taken her freedom, but I will not take her life.

And Halton, sweet, arrogant, foolish Halton! The bumbler, always the tool of others. But he did confess everything. And for that I should commute his sentence to exile.

Amerika will endure, and I will remain its President. But what if the maintenance of that power is achieved by dishonesty? What President can enjoy power when it's tainted by corruption? When she is surrounded by ruthless and ambitious people who barely acknowledge the concept of right and wrong?

She thought fondly of the darkest of her days. The sallow morning, sixteen years ago in the time of Lucia's presidency, when a congressional committee had ordered her brought from Philadelphia to Lincoln. It had taken all the steel in her then to hold her head erect as she had climbed the intimidating steps of the Capitol. Accused of plotting with Eli Wyatt against the state, of conspiracy against the friendly power of Yamato, and of orchestrating demonstrations against the disarmament treaty to be signed by Lucia and Mutsuhito, she had been put on trial for her life. And for a year under arrest in Lincoln as the trial continued, and the following four years of terror spent on Maine and Rhode Island as the sentence was considered, she had been held close captive, the shadow of the samurai blade—the same that had almost severed Amerika's head—maintained above her.

But Lucia Henry, repeatedly advised to move and often tempted to move, had always drawn back her hand, Alia remembered. Though daughter of Stratford Henry, and responsible for many, many executions, she had not ordered the ultimate penalty for her arch-rival.

And so, on that fateful November day after Lucia's political power sank disastrously into armed insurrection, it was I who came finally out of exile and back to Liberty to be proclaimed President in her place, the people welcoming me with a parade of flowers as their protector as if there was some magic in the name of Kane, and in the same breath damning Lucia to hell for her mishandling of the Sector and the détente she had encouraged with Yamato.

I have known the terror of a death sentence, Alia told herself, seeing the sunset shadows lengthen across her lawn now. I have known it too intimately to welcome it back or to lay it on another that easily. Just as Lucia Henry did with me, so shall I do with her. Neither she nor her foolish brother deserves the death sentence; neither shall have it. No matter what the threat to my life, Lubbock's persuasion or no.

She straightened, sighed, eased fingers over the bridge of her nose. From below she became aware of the sound of a ukeclave amateurishly plucked by a youth of eighteen or nineteen—Travis Hilton, one of Zaentz's nephews and now a Marine guard. He was off duty and seemed unaware of his presidential eavesdropper.

"Oh, say can you see,
By the dawn's early light,
What so proudly we hailed,
At the twilight's last gleaming?"

Alia stepped back inside, smiling at the concentration in the youth's voice and the way he had managed to elude the tune. As she reached her writing desk, she felt an unexpected giddiness and grasped the arm of her chair, willing the feeling to pass, but it would not pass and she sat down, feeling the weight of the whole planet suddenly press on her back. As she breathed deeply, the pain left her, and in that moment she saw the universe and her place in it with lucid clarity. Her lips broadened in a smile and she whispered to the night:

"Oh, say does that star-spangled banner yet wave,
O'er the lands of the free, and the homes of the brave?"

Ah, foolish Halton. Foolish ambitious meddler. How quickly would Otis and Conroy see you in your grave. But you did confess, and even God asks no more than that. She picked up her stylo and wrote ordering Halton Henry to be released from custody.

"Halt!"

Whoever they were, the looming man in orange robes and the man with the nose of tarnished silver had no business here, the young Marine guard was certain.

Both the guru and the foul, lion-faced Timo Farren were known to him. Farren was often to be seen in the company of Pharis Cassabian, and throughout the administration had showed up wherever the President's entourage appeared.

He was a mathematician and psientist; Ramakrishnan was a spook connected with all kinds of weird research, but even so he would not get into the presidential apartments without a Grade One security pass. Not when Travis Hilton stood on guard.

His uncle's orders were definite. Since the scandal of the Earth Central declaration, the White House guard had been doubled, then trebled. The secretary's fears had led to checking and double-checking in the guardhouses, until every man was alert to the sneaking dangers of ninja assassins.

All items—documents, equipment, records, synthetics—anything that might come near Alia Kane's person was to be screened. The kitchens were to be inspected continuously. All water, liquors, wines, and other drinks to be randomly tested. All prepared foods tasted by the cooks, table servants, and housemen. Only Grade One passes were allowed in. It didn't matter if he was a maniac with a butcher's knife, a sweet little five-year-old girl, or a ninja murderer posing as a staff member, the pass was the important thing, and all entries had to be monitored and cleared after that, pass or not.

"Wassamatter, don't you know me?"

"I—yes, sir."

"Then admit me!"

"I can't do that, sir."

Hilton's fellow guards ranked behind him, barring entry. Their eyes were on the figure in orange robes, barefoot and wearing a long gray beard, forked like two huge tusks, who dominated the space behind Farren. He smelled powerfully of patchouli oil and seemed to swell with sinister power as he stepped forward.

The loathsome Farren shuffled closer, the pass gripped in his ruined hand. "See that! Secretary Lubbock's own clearance couldn't be higher!"

The guard examined the card reluctantly and put it on the pad until it was snatched back.

"Well?"

"It *looks* like a Grade One," he said grudgingly.

"Then let us pass!"

"My orders are that no one can pass today, or any other, without specific clearance from—"

Farren drew himself up so that the morning sun caught in his spectacle panes, blotting out his eyes. "What's your name, boy?"

The young guard was perplexed. He seemed to Farren no more than a boy, no doubt appointed to his position here through a family connection. Lads like him were frequently dull-witted, always looking out for a means to distinguish themselves. But this one seemed gutless too. In front of his colleagues he wavered, unsure whether to bluster or order them away from the checkpoint. Lamely the youth said, "The President's not here."

"I know that. D'you think she'd have a young lad with half a mind and no balls at all to guard anything except an empty room? Let us past, I told you."

The youth screwed up his courage. "And I told you: I can't do that, sir!"

"What's your name!"

"I don't see that that's relevant, sir."

"You will do as my associate says, boy!" The new voice was deep and resonant and commanding. The rest of the guards eyed him uncertainly.

"I'm sorry, sir."

"Sorry?" Farren's nasal shout made the young man swallow. "I'll report you to your superior for interfering with the President's business. Didn't you confirm the pass? Or aren't you following orders now?"

Despite his confusion, the guard's chin jutted. "I'm following them to the letter, sir. That's just the point. I'm—"

Farren's words cut him off. "You know who this is?"

"I know he doesn't have a Grade One pass."

Suddenly the dark face smiled. Ramakrishnan spoke again. He asked the guards somberly, "You would deny me entry on this most significant of days?"

"Why significant? What's your business here?" the boy replied shakily.

Farren's grin glittered. "Psi, boy. Psi. We've come to examine the President's bedroom. You know that Professor Ramakrishnan is the President's only protection against ninja infiltrators. He can look inside men's heads and know all their secrets."

Ramakrishnan's voice boomed. "He is speaking the truth, Travis Hilton!"

The guard paled. "You know me?"

"That's his name, all right," the Marine behind whispered.

"Then let me pass and you can keep it."

"Keep it?"

"You cannot do anything else. I see you are an honest man who would die to save his President. You cannot do anything else. *You cannot do anything else.*"

Hilton stepped aside involuntarily, and the rest of the guard seemed suddenly preoccupied with a difficult mental problem. They made no move as Ramakrishnan strode through the checkpoint and down the long corridor, Farren hobbling after him.

"That's a helluva trick, Ganesh."

Ramakrishnan snorted scornfully. "Soldiers are fools. Young ones the more so. And that one especially. As I have told you, it is easiest when they are a little bit disquieted. That is why it helps for you to pick an argument with them each time."

"Yeah, but it never fails to amaze me when they switch off like that."

They came to the President's bedchamber, and to the great canopied dragon bed that had been a gift from the Dowager Empress Wen-lan of Shan China. Alia Kane had risen from it half an hour ago. Its mattress was huge under a gorgeous Chinese brocade cover. It was still mussed and bore the imprint of the President's body.

Farren watched the door anxiously as Ramakrishnan flung the sheets back and took from his jacket a long pair of tweezers and a razor scalpel. He levered open a concealed recess in the dragon's eye with great dexterity. Inside a hole in the polished wood was a large, tawny chrysalis an inch long. He removed it with the tweezers, then he replaced it with a similar chrysalis. He crushed the first one into the palm of his hand and smeared the brown juice from it round and round until it was completely destroyed.

They had come on this same mission of deceit, always the same time, once a week, for seven consecutive months.

"That it?"

"It is done."

"Why do you always grind them up?" Farren asked.

"To make sure they are dead. In case those to whom they belong know something that I do not."

Farren snickered and looked about. "Don't you ever wonder what kind of butterfly they'd turn into?"

"The White Emperor, if that concerns you."

"Your pardon, Professor." Farren put his hands together and bowed low, grinning. "I forget myself, master. You're Ganesh Ramakrishnan, a guru of unmatched reputation: arch-psientist of Amerika, confidant of the President, advisor of astrogators, friend of the great Zen masters of Kamakura, translator of the . . ."

Ramakrishnan raised a finger. "Psssht!"

In the listening silence, Farren strained his ears. A creaking board, scuffling noises—synthetics here to fix the room.

"We should be gone."

As they passed back through the checkpoint, Ramakrishnan faced the young guard, shoving him aside, despite his size. He tottered, staring into space.

"Come back and speak to me, Travis Hilton. All of you, come back."

The men blinked and shuffled as if they had suddenly forgotten something important, just as they always did. Then they were fully alert again.

"I asked if we could go in?"

"Not without a Grade One pass, sir."

"I . . . see."

"I'm sorry, sir. I have my orders."

"That's quite all right, Marine, I understand you're only doing your job," Farren said pleasantly.

The guard saluted and his men watched as the strange Hindu and the even stranger Farren went back the way they had come.

As they passed from the west wing into the courtyard, Ramakrishnan grinned and led Farren to his ground-car. It was time they were heading for the ashram.

34

The ground-car which carried the astrogator and the spymaster negotiated the northward bend in the freeway, past weeping willows and a patchwork of green fields the few miles towards the river and Ramakrishnan's monstrous home. Cassabian pointed out to Ellis the meadows of Morningford and the mansion he was building there to reflect the increase in his fortunes.

"I need a house in Lincoln these days. This is the place I've chosen."

"You've really arrived," Ellis said drily.

"That's right. I have. I like it here. It's close enough to the river and RISC, as well as the White House."

"As Ramakrishnan has found out."

Cassabian nodded appreciatively. "You'll find out that our mad guru is really no fool. You'll see he has some pretty good ideas."

Ellis watched as a flight of wild ducks took off from the water, trusting Cassabian better than anyone else he had met in Lincoln except Reba. When the news of Yi To Man's actual mission had been explained to him, Ellis had wanted to cut the man's throat, but Cassabian's candid logic had persuaded him.

"What does it matter that Earth Central has sentenced Alia Kane to death?" he had said. "All Known Space realises that the Cloisters are full of Yamato's puppets. If security is tightened around the President as a result, so much the better. And listen: Expansionist feeling is running warmer, making Conroy's position less cozy. The declaration is too late to stir up an Army mutiny, which has already been defeated. So the pro-Yamato faction are caught in a bind: to suffer in silence or stand up and be counted. The glove of challenge has been thrown down, but they are in no position to take it up now. Our first requirement is for a treaty with China. If arrangements for a marriage between the President and the Dowager's son are set in motion, the chances of Yamato and the Chinese agreeing to leave one another alone so they can both concentrate on carving us up are very much lessened. You've done only good by bringing Yi and the master copy of the declaration here. And even better: if Yi does what he says he intends and gets in touch with Halton Henry, it won't be long before both of them are hog-tied, I can promise you that."

Cassabian had deliberately steered Ellis's thoughts towards Reba then. "Listen, you know that if Halton Henry is executed, Reiner will lose all reason to marry Lubbock's daughter?"

"At least that's some consolation for me, Pharis. I can't marry her, though I love her, and I know she loves me."

"Shame you're not a few million credits richer."

"Hmmm. Give me time."

Ellis watched Cassabian's deep brown eyes surveying the land on which he was planning to build. "So," he said, "you have your passport and your ship. What now?"

"To see Reba, and then I'll go to Harrisburg. Thc rest is best kept between me and my crew."

"Whatever you do, I'll listen out for news of it."

"You won't have to wait long."

Soon they came by the junction, turning south from Newport to Lakeside, and their destination, where Cassabian had the driver wait. Rambling outworks had been attached to Ramakrishnan's ashram, extending it to accommodate all the paraphernalia of its owner's practices and his dozens of chanting shaven-headed devotees. Outside, the gardens were unkept, a mass of undergrowth, overrun by thorn bushes. On the far side was a walled garden, full of the scents of decaying leaves; inside, the incense that wafted through a maze of cluttered rooms complemented the Hindu religious artifacts and psi-inscriptions that hung everywhere. It was like the private museum of a madman.

Ellis ventured inside uneasily, but his interest was soon absorbed by what he found. The dusty room was split by beams of intense projector light that pierced the heavy air. The glare fell upon a vast early visualiser. Ramakrishnan was a scholar of exploration, enough to have suggested theoretical means by which nexus astrogation into the Beyond might one day be possible, and to have laid the principles of design of ships that could accomplish it. Ramakrishnan's better ideas were hallmarked as simple and strange and magnificent. Until now unmanned and self-replicating ramjets had blasted out across space automatically, accelerating at three or four hundred gee towards their target systems, sometimes reaching 0.99 cee. They took years to reach their destination systems and then detonated the devices that would create the nexi through which an instantaneous transit might be made. It had been Ramakrishnan's idea to use natural black holes to vastly speed up this process. Practically it was fraught with difficulties, but the theory was all his.

Shiva, an Irishman, and Ramakrishnan's foremost devotee, a quiet man of solemn expression and few words, regarded Ellis and Cassabian suspiciously from a corner stuffed with books, candle stubs, and grotesque statuary. He leapt up to admit Farren and his master at the massively barred door.

"We must be careful here," he explained, the Vishnu stripes on his forehead rutting with disquiet as he spoke. "Some folk don't understand our ways. There are those who would like to murder the doctor."

"Have you succeeded?" Cassabian asked Ramakrishnan impatiently.

"Yes."

"And you got in without difficulty?"

"I, my good sir, could get past the three-headed dog who guards Hades' gate."

And out again, more's the pity, Cassabian thought petulantly, then he warned himself: C'mon, Pharis, he's an ally. No need for that kind of peevish thinking.

"They're taking bets in the White House," Farren said gleefully. "Marriage bets on Alia."

"I would advise against making any wager," Ramakrishnan told him solemnly.

"Yeah? Why do you say that?"

"Mr. Cassabian, what will be will be."

"*Que sera*, right?"

"Quite so."

Cassabian had considered the situation very fully. Even when he had first traveled in China, the Court of Heaven had been ruled by Shan Wen-lan, the scheming daughter of a family of Shanghai bankers. When eight years old, she had been caught in a revolution and narrowly escaped a traditional punishment for losers—being chained naked to the ramparts of the city to be raped to death by Republican soldiers. When fourteen, she had been married off to Tso-peng, then chief minister of Sian. By this means Earth Central had sought to bring Sian, Shenyang, and Tsingtao into Yamato's hands, but Tso-peng had married low blood to no advantage: the territorial dowry had turned out to be mere promises. So Wen-lan had suffered a marriage of great ignominy. Insults were heaped upon her by a husband whose love bed was filled instead by the voluptuous courtesans of Taiyuan. The taking of Wuhan and Nanking and the defeat of the Republicans had made Tso-peng Warlord-Emperor, and on his death she had grabbed power with both hands.

Cassabian recalled the Wen-lan he had seen. A narrow-shouldered, broad-buttocked woman with bulging eyes, shrew nose, and thick lips. Even so, Wen-lan had birthed seven children, five of them male. Three of those still lived.

For ten years, so the saying went, China had been the anvil of Known Space surrounded by hammers that beat upon it. For almost as long there had been talk of a marriage of alliance between President Kane and one of Wen-lan's sons. The suit of Prince Fa Hsien had foundered on the President's revulsion at the idea. She had told Lubbock that, since he was a Chinese, the marriage would bring political turmoil to Amerika once more, and after the example of the disastrous marriages of Korean princesses, the project had been dismantled. But now, with Yamato and China and Earth Central poised to form an unholy alliance, marriage was a weapon that could not be ignored. Four weeks ago on Wuhan a peace had been declared that had made it imperative that negotiations be reopened.

The Dowager's patience was exhausted and there could be no revival, but if a marriage was agreed with at least one of the three living brothers, that might be enough. A marriage in principle.

Cassabian watched Ramakrishnan, nauseated by his spookery, but unnerved by the man's eccentric brilliance. Wen-lan might have the Tao weirds of the Confucian seminary at Tai Hu to advise her, he thought with satisfaction, but

Ganesh Ramakrishnan's suggestions have a core of hard practicality. So much hinges on our assurances that President Kane is fertile! So much rests on the possibility of an offspring to cement the alliance. Damn the Chinese and their weird way of thinking.

When Farren had told Ramakrishnan of a Chinese-paid spy in the White House, his strange genius had supplied the perfect solution. If the Chinese wanted proof that Alia had not yet passed through the menopause, proof they must have!

The Chinese idea of using the chemically active chrysalis of the White Emperor moth to detect Alia's monthly pheromonal changes had been totally brilliant and virtually impossible to fathom. But Ramakrishnan had solved the riddle and supplied an answer. Already they had spawned fifty reports to the Chinese ambassador. All doubts regarding the President's capacity were eradicated and the way had been opened again.

"What do you mean, advise against it?" Cassabian echoed.

Ramakrishnan shook his head sadly. "The future is not as we would have it."

Ellis got up and walked across the room to where the visualiser beams converged. He inspected it closely. The quadrant displaying in twenty-one-centimeter detail was the buffer between Kalifornia and the Neutral Zone.

Cassabian spoke. "Well, now, Doctor. I see you've had some thoughts about the Neutral Zone. What do you think of the future in that respect? Dr. Farren tells me you've been reaching conclusions about . . . about an Amerikan *empire*."

Ramakrishnan stirred. "An unfortunate term. I mean to foster interest in exploration of the Beyond. There are many in Amerika that are eager to push our boundaries out faster than the relativistic limit allows, and you cannot deny Amerika's need to grow. In the fullness of time we shall find the means whereby that rate of expansion may quickly be multiplied a hundred- or a thousandfold."

Ellis turned, heady thoughts consuming him. This time tomorrow he'd be back at Harrisburg apron and counting. Two months from now and he would either have Duval standing at his side or a cargo bay full of expensive compensation. "Dr. Farren told me you'd made some breakthroughs in singularity theory. Maybe you've found some way of penetrating the dense dust clouds that have been wrecking the robot explorers in the Sagittarius branch."

"The President's request was that I think about the problem. She said that if territorial competition within Known Space was to be as vicious as it has lately become, perhaps we should look to extend our Sector into the Beyond. I have petitioned her for a patent to search, find out, and view such remote systems as we know exist beyond the dust clouds of this galactic arm. Should a method become possible, we shall try to settle colonists under laws agreeable to the form of the laws and policies of Amerika without reference to Earth Central."

Cassabian grunted, disappointed that Ramakrishnan's thoughts were as yet apparently only hypothetical. He got down to the heart of the matter. "That's all for the future. For the moment we have no choice but to dispute territory with our neighbors. It's my policy to move against Yamato, and that may be done in three ways. First, we must destroy their capacity to invade us. Second, we must lever them out of the Korean system. And third, we must carry the fight into the very center of the Zone. All those ambitions call for nexus ships. Better ships than we now possess, better than Yamato possesses also. And we need people of similar strength of mind, people like my friend Captain Straker, who is preparing to light out into the Zone tomorrow. Bend your thoughts to all of that, Doctor, and you'll do us your greatest service."

"What do you want, Captain?"

"Give me detailed information on nexus instability and high-resolution visualisers that will help me get through where others can't follow. In return I'll bring you back the best empirical information I can gather from the Zone."

"Done!"

Cassabian said, "And the other thing, Doctor? The thing we discussed?"

"I have it here. Shiva! Bring me the article."

The Irishman brought out a stainless-steel box four inches square and he laid it portentously on the table.

Ellis eyed it with interest. "What is it?"

"Something very valuable. A wonderful thing!"

"A new instrument?"

"Ha! An amplifier. It's unique. It was created by a psientist whom Conroy Lubbock invited to Amerika from Varanasi. His work on the crystals of power had brought him in contact with Hans van Hoorbecke, a Europan known to Dr. Farren. Unfortunately both men are dead now."

Farren opened the box and revealed a huge pendant diamond on a chain. "See! You wear it."

Ellis examined the egg-sized jewel carefully and saw that there was a light shining inside it. It was secured by a thick chain because it was heavy. So heavy that it must contain a good amount of aurium, argentium, or platinium. Instinctively Ellis put it round his neck, seeing nothing but a hazy patch of light in its center changing color slowly.

As he did so, Ramakrishnan swept aside the curtains and flung wide the window. He held the jewel up, carefully pressing it to the nodal point of Ellis's forehead.

"The man over there. The devotee sitting cross-legged. Concentrate *through* it, not *at* it, man! And shut your eyes if you can't achieve focus."

Ellis's inner eye blurred and adjusted as he did as he was told. He saw the halo of the robed man moving swiftly and shaking as if he was on fire. All seemed strangely darkened and set with fringes of red and blue—and then he heard the man's thoughts. They were loud!

Ommmmm . . .

"Aghh!"

He let out a gasp and dropped the jewel as if it was red-hot, jumping back from it. Then he stared out of the window again, his mouth agape. "Jeezus! That was painful!"

"Have a care!" Ramakrishnan picked up the jewel and examined it testily. "The devotee is in meditation. But even so you might shock yourself. You are very sensitive."

"Where is it?" Ellis demanded, peering across the contemplative garden in agitation.

"Where's what?"

"The giant bird! I saw it clearly!"

Ramakrishnan pointed. "There it is."

Ellis looked again and saw the sparrow in the swaying branch, as it had been. "It's not possible," he said, turning to Cassabian who watched him eagerly. "I read a *bird*'s mind? I saw its own view of itself?"

"Little birds are very confident creatures. Try again."

He took the instrument once more, but with great reverence this time, and held it to his forehead. He concentrated through it, astonished, hardly hearing Ramakrishnan's explanation.

"It is an amplifier. It allows you to read forebrain intentions."

Ellis felt the hairs rise on the back of his neck. He panned his attention speechlessly to left and right, seeing foxgloves and the bricks of a wall and the high-rise living spires a mile or two away. He became aware of a low-level background hum, like rain hissing or white noise, but there was also organisation in it, incredibly so! Like . . . almost like the interlaced conversations of a crowded party, listened to from above by a man drowsing into sleep, a hum with peaks and toughs. He concentrated through and then suddenly into a peak, hoping with determination to catch the drift before it escaped. A matrimonial argument. Heavy sense of injustice. A dead love. I'm going to leave you, bitch! That was it. Clear as clear.

"*How can it be?* A man's thoughts and yet I've overheard them."

A sudden hammering assaulted the door of the house. Instantly Ramakrishnan snatched the jewel from Ellis's hands and spirited it away. The Irishman took a blaster from his robe and went to the door, shouting out for identification.

"Open up! Squad!"

"What do you want?" Ramakrishnan bawled.

The hammering started again. Stun-rifle stocks. "Open! Or we'll break down the door. I've got a heavy duty meson plexcutter and fifty men surrounding the building out here."

Ramakrishnan slid back the heavy ion bolts and the door was slammed back, flooding the dark, incense-filled entrance with sunlight. An army of men were outside. A Squaddie, helmeted and clad in studded red and black leather, strode in, his Squad gear glinting. He was one of the District's elite corps, granite faced, unyeilding. He held up a warrant smart card with Straker's image in it. "Your rights are deemed read!"

It was an arrest.

Cassabian demanded of the officer. "By what authority?"

"The Secretary of State's orders."

"On what grounds?"

"Captain Ellis Straker is alleged to have brought one Yi To Man into Amerika against nexus restrictions and carrying Earth Central lies about the President."

Ellis surged forward. "You can't arrest me! I've got work to do! I've got a passport to leave Harrisburg tomorrow!"

"It's revoked," the Squaddie replied, motioning his men to seize Ellis's arms. "You're going on vacation—to Camp Worth until a trial can be arranged."

SADO

The toothless smile of Wataru Hoshino greeted him broadly.

"Hey, Senmu-san."

"Hoshino-san, my friend! *Konnichi wa!*"

They embraced, slapping backs, and the old man held him off, looking at him with faded eyes. "You're looking so good! Like a rich man."

Duval's clothes were simple but of good quality, white cotton undershirt and a pair of baggy pantaloons that had once belonged to Katsumi.

"Where are you going?"

"To Niigata, so sorry. The *kin kaigun* is due soon and I must be there to meet it. I have to supervise arrangements for Admiral Kurita's ships."

"You'll take tea?"

"You're too kind, Senmu-san."

Wataru Hoshino had passed through Chiba three times, each time arriving in his beat-up air-car. Each time he had sought out Duval, sure of a welcome. The first time he had seen the hospitality of the bare little room at the back of the lab. Later, he had visited a back room of the main house itself. Then he had slept on a blanket outside, on the broad veranda. After many years of itinerant living, he had told his host, it was difficult to sleep under a roof. If a man woke up in the middle of the night, it was a comfort to see how far the stars of Sado's pretty constellations had moved and to know how late or how long before the dawn.

"I have traveled many years, Senmu-san," he would say, unwilling to attempt Duval's unpronounceable name, fingering the coin he wore on a leather thong round his neck. The coin was of brass and worthless, a square hole in the middle and stained green by the acids of Wataru's skin. "You know this was once Lord Takeda Shingen's? You want to trade it for your ring?"

"A good gold ring for a worthless trinket made by slave Chinese antique fakers yesterday?"

"You see, Senmu-san, old habits die hard! I've been bargaining at too many *ya*."

"Tell me. I want to know everything about this planet."

"Everything? There would not be enough time if we sat here until the Judges of Hell came for us."

"I envy you, Hoshino-san. You're free to range across it all while I'm trapped here."

"But look! You have a place of your own." He had banged the main roof support cantilever of the research lab. "A place you've seen built to your own personal specifications. There's satisfaction in that. It's almost finished, yes?"

"Yes."

"And soon you will need aurium?" Wataru had said, looking out from under his eybrows shrewdly. "And argentium for making the power device? I know a mountain that is built entirely of yellow argentium sulfide—the purest in existence!"

"Which you, doubtless, can bring here?"

"Oh, no. The mountain is very holy, so holy that it is named after the greatest mountain of Old Japan. There is a curse on it: the dragon will come out to punish anyone who interferes with the mountain's riches. But aurium, maybe some old weapon mountings and parts. I can bring you these things from the salvage yards at Niigata. I've seen how the weapons on the Amerikan ships were melted out with disrupter bolts, but some bits and pieces survived."

"Better to have a wholly new gun and mount," he had said. "And not have to worry about compatibility with old parts. You see, the secret of range is in the design of the gun barrel. Partly shape, partly purity of material, and partly the frequency at which the magnetic fields fluctuate in the—"

He had stopped himself then. How easy it was to forget. How easy to slip into old enthusiasms. He had thrust the *sake* flask at Wataru, saying, "Here, you drink it. Then tell me about some other wonder of this world that I will never see."

At first, during the building of the facility, he had assumed a detached and remote attitude, cynically allowing the test range shed structures to be erected inadequately and letting the laboratory equipment manifests go fantastically over budget for no reason. But as the facility took shape he had remembered his long studentship at RISC and recalled the envious feeling that had flushed through him as a youngster. It was a dream of those days to have a research facility of his own. A dream that one day he could experiment with all the small ideas that had come to him. All the tiny improvements, the suggestions he had wanted the senior men to listen to, and which they had never once listened to. They had scorned him, keeping to tradition and form and their own status. And he had grown up and learned to be the same, knowing that he would never have his own research or manufacturing facility, never have total control, or satisfaction from those unanswered questions: What would be the effect of increasing the proportion of barium in the helical coolant? And could a barrel be more efficiently shaped if his obsession with catenary curve surfaces was put aside?

And what was the white substance that sometimes appeared on the iron 56 plumstones *and that glowed in the dark?*

And now he had been given it all! Freely! His own grotto of delights!

He had started to find pride in what was his own personal project. Kenji-san had marked the change in him and given him encouragement. Eventually he had ordered the mistakes torn down and shown them how to really make a research lab, and at nights he had told himself that none of it mattered because he would never, never, never give away the most important secrets.

Later, he'd moved into the Hasegawa house. "I envy you the new family you have, Senmu-san," old Wataru had once said. Duval thought of the third and latest time he had come by way of Chiba. "What a shame you're not a Japanese, Senmu-san. I do believe you would make a Sado girl a fine husband. Of course, you'd have to take a proper family name first. You can't give her 'Saturaka.' I cannot even say it! That's why I have named you Senmu-san. You are the chief director. You have a big responsibility! So now you are Senmu-san."

"I could never marry here," he had said, and he had felt that curious tension in his stomach, the same he always felt when he tried to repress a difficult thought. "Anyway, what Japanese mother would call her son 'Mr. Chief Director'? And what mother would want a *gaijin* for a son-in-law? It's an impossible thought."

"Then why don't you come with me to see the Zen teachers in Chiba? They're good men. If they teach you to understand the concepts of their discipline, you'll feel more at home here. And if they ask you if you are seeking after truth, answer them yes." He had winked. "We're both men of the world, Senmu-san. Neither of us would deny there are more important things in life than the *cha-no-yu*. But the tea ceremony is important to many people. You and I both know also that comprehending proper form is essential for true acceptance. Acceptance can bring a man much comfort."

Duval had neither nodded nor smiled, but feeling something stifling closing in around him had pressed the old man to speak instead about his wanderings.

With dreaming eyes, curving his hands in a lewd way, Wataru had spoken: "This world is like a disobedient woman, Senmu-san, with a wicked tongue and full of deceits—but also delights. And it has a woman's temper! I have been south into the mountain lands and the jungles of the Great River. I have journeyed north also. Beyond the Tropic of the Dog. I know it is a worthless land, more inhospitable than Gobi, a land of desert scrub and lizards that can never amount to anything." He had poured more tea. "I lost a good friend there. In Sekigahara, while exploring in the caves of the volcanoes. It is rumored that aurium exists there in huge quantities, but I do not know."

They went into the laboratory together, and he showed Wataru the machinery that had been constructed to manufacture projectors. The furnace was almost fully tested and there was a waldo-rigged hot room.

"Where's this argentium sulfide mountain of yours, Hoshino-san?"

"That is easy. You have been looking at it every day. There!"

"What? Fujiyama?"

"The holy mountain. The local people call it 'Fuji-san.' In Yamato there are many mountains holy to the Shinto religion. Every inhabited planet has them—Mount Osore, Mount Hiko, Mount Ishizuchi. They're Shugendo—where a man may commune with the *kami*."

"Come on, Hoshino-san. You're a realist. You can't believe in all that geomancy stuff."

Wataru looked shocked, then his gold teeth flashed. "Maybe it's *because* I am a realist that I believe in it. Did you never talk to Yao Wen-yuan about *feng shui* and *di li?* Did you never ask your brother about psi-forces and the nexus patterns and how they relate to ley lines and the ancient sites on Earth like Stonehenge and the places of the Inca? If you didn't, then you should have."

"Tell me about Mount Fuji."

"Its crater is a boiling mass of argentium sulfide, a thousand *ken* across. It stinks like a devil's armpit! And two *ri* away there are places in the ground that are so hot that you can bury a chicken's egg, come back in five minutes, and it is hard-boiled!"

"What? Even with snow capping the volcano?"

"Oh, yes! But that's nothing. There was a great eruption twenty-one years ago. I saw that. A great dragon power. A great dragon power in the earth." He grew suddenly weary. "It makes an old man think of life, and of death and how foolish we are to worry over small things."

After sundown, they ate a meal of pickled fish, soy sauce, runner beans, *kaikon* radish, and rice, and after it, a glass of Duval's amateur beer. It had a pleasant taste and soothed the old man, making him mellow for storytelling. He brought a scratched card from his pocket and passed it to Duval, whose interest surged as he put it into the reader. It was from Helene di Barrio on the Komatsu *han*.

As Hoshino relaxed into his chair, Duval watched the translucent face appear above the reader. It was poor quality, ghostly and unreal, reminding him of the images of kidnap victims in the unending hostage mess on Levant IV. The voice was oddly poised as if carrying a subtextual message, but not as if Helene was speaking under duress.

"Duval? How is it with you, old buddy? Long time no see. As I hope you can see, I'm quite well. The people of Kanazawa have been kind to me, and the family I serve have allowed me to pass on a Christmas message of peace and goodwill to all—if you see what I mean. Did you know that Juli Dexter has found a rich family in Joetsu to live with. David Alexander and Torven Jones are both married to Chinese women in Komatsu and Paula Heeney to a *sangokujin* man from Taiwan. Who else? Oh, yeah, Davey Marks got sent to the Home Worlds, but as for the others I can't say."

Duval watched the face carefully, knowing there was something hidden in what Helene di Barrio was saying, but unable to grasp it.

"As for myself, well, you know me, Duval, I can't settle down—never could, eh? I went to Kanazawa a few days ago, and—do you remember John

Oujuku, who knows your brother?—well, he's running a *ryokan*—you know, one of those little guesthouse things—it's called the Ryokan Lombok. John's married to a terrific Chinese lady named Cao and I hear they're both doing well on the convention trade. He wants to make himself rich and would just love for you to drop in. Listen, if you can, drop me a card. Wataru Hoshino is a friend, though he plays a mean hand of poker. Hi, Hoshino-san, if you're watching. But make it soon, Duval. Next year I may be gone from here. Take care now, y'hear?"

Duval guarded his feelings as the image dissolved, but inside he was jumping. He had already had to readjust his thoughts to take account of new circumstances. Can I readjust again, he asked himself despairingly, on the slim strength of a carefully coded letter-card?

A year ago, the question of escape had never been far beneath the surface of his thoughts. Hopes of somehow leading his crewmates down to the apron at Niigata Terminal and stealing a ship home. The vision had always been piecemeal, lacking in details, and with no plan at all, but there was always the glorious vision of the thirty of them pulling off the runway at Niigata in a captured nexus ship. Always it was a moonlit night, always Governor Ugaki was in the tower, shaking with fear and sweating, and the impotent daimyo in a rage on the vidicom. And then there had been another detail: Michie, sitting on the bridge, wrapped up in his dress uniform cloak.

But the dream had slowly faded into noise like a letter-card image. How stupid it was to think of escape when those same shipmates were scattered all over Sado and making new lives—some married, some with children even! And if there was to be no escape, what was he doing hanging on to his silly delusions and his defiance? Everything had had time to mellow into something deeply personal on the *han* of Hasegawa. The worst of it was they liked him: the *genin* laboring men, the *kokata* undermen, and the *oyakata* overmen. Yao Wen-yuan, the comprador; Kenji-san, the lord of the *han*—everyone. He had been here so long now, and he knew the people here so well, that defiance would just be bad manners and resistance would seem like nothing more than a lack of gratitude. And as for Nishima Jun, he couldn't even remember what the daimyo looked like.

Perhaps it was as Hoshino-san said. Bend like a rice stalk in the wind. Accept the strange destiny the gods gave you. You were born in Amerika, you have to die somewhere—you may as well live in Chiba.

So—now John Oujuku was loose in the space lanes again and raiding, God damn him! Perhaps I should send a reply to di Barrio, he thought guiltily. Suddenly everything had been raked up and was laid open.

As Wataru took himself away to sleep, Duval walked out under a sky bright with stars, his head throbbing with tumbling memories and the chirrups of the *semi* insects, and found Michie.

"Do you like pearls, Michie-san?"

"Oh, yes. What woman does not appreciate the beauty of a real pearl?"

"Then, does it have to be a real pearl?"

"Yes again. As with the tea ceremony. As with so many things, we take enjoyment from the old ways and genuine things. In Amerika you can have a giant pearl the size of a baseball from a genetically altered oyster. In Yamato we would prize higher a perfect pearl the size of a pea so long as it was taken from a natural oyster that had lived in open sea."

"I'm beginning to understand that, I think."

"These are truths that cannot be explained. You have to feel them. If Wataru-san tells you his coin is eight hundred years old and belonged to Takeda Shingen, then he is playing an old rogue's game with untruths. But what if the coin *was* real? Then its value would be very great."

"There was a place we used to trade," he told her in a lost voice. "A planet called Masae."

"Oh! That is my mother's name."

He savored the moment. The delightful way she expressed girlish surprise at some of the things he said made him love her. "Yes, like your mother, but it was not a planet worthy of the name."

As she sat down on the swing seat that had been hung from a bough of the shade tree, the *semi* chirruping stopped. "Was Masae a pretty planet?"

"It was a very poor planet. It was just after the annexation, and the daimyo was very tough. There was only one business he was interested in: pearl fishing. He didn't have many troops and ships at his disposal. They couldn't keep us away from the local people who lived on the far side of the planet, Chinese and Taiwanese who had emigrated from their own Sector and then been enslaved —*sangokujin* you call them. We sold them all kinds of products even though our traders knew what was happening."

Michie held the ropes of the swing lightly. "What was happening?"

"The daimyo had a plan for the newly annexed planet. He was systematically enslaving the population. The fittest he took off to his pearl fisheries. He found that a system of replacing his workers was cheaper than feeding them, so he worked them until they died, sending them deeper and deeper after oysters until they drowned or until their lungs burst."

He plucked at the swing rope absently. She broke the silence softly. "Masae is my mother's name. I don't know why, but this seems to magnify the shame I feel."

"You don't have to feel shame." He looked in her eyes. "How can you be responsible for the crimes of a daimyo fifty light-years away, a man you've never met?"

"We are all of us responsible for one another. Isn't that so, Duval-san?" She kicked up her feet, letting the swing move. "Do you miss your home planet?"

"Sometimes." He said it wistfully. "When the sun is at its highest and the ground is parched, I think of cool, gentle rain falling on green meadows. I'm sure there's no green like it anywhere else in Known Space, a patchwork of fields that have been the same for a hundred years, automatically tilled, seeded, fertilized, harvested, and fallowed for a hundred orbital periods. Machine-groomed land has a particular quality about it. And great forests of mature oak and elm reaching up like the buttresses of a cathedral, full of peace and cool darkness and carpeted with delicate wildflowers."

"Do you yearn for that?"

He looked away from her suddenly and put his face in his hands. "No."

And she laid her hand on his shoulder then, and felt him cry silently, like the cool, gentle rain falling on green meadows.

36

On Friday, in the almost completed weapons facility, he told them precisely how he would make them a singularity gun.

"You have to understand what I'm going to need. First comes the confinement chamber. Integrity must be built up from topologically involute fields—or the singularity will devour the gun."

"There's a good Moebius field technician working at the Komatsu *han* near Kanazawa," Yao Wen-yuan said, jutting his chin towards the capital. He was a tall and spare Chinese with long wispy moustaches and a permanent sporadic stubble except where a complicated scar meandered over his jawline. He had a bald patch on the crown of his head which he took immense pains to hide from the women of the *han*. From time to time as they spoke he cast a judicious eye over the men that he had appointed to make up Duval's team. They listened and considered and nodded at one another, absorbed in the challenge.

"We'll have to test the integrity of the confinement fields first. It's a pity that we're not still in Niigata. A grav generator and a stabiliser from a hulk would be an admirable start—that is, a test rig on which to distort the prototype, and the field must be intense. More intense than the gun's own, to leave a margin for oscillation. Like so." He drew his marker through the trivee, representing the chamber resting in grooves on two breech blocks. He added the four levers, projections from the thick end of the chamber, like capstan spokes, to permit the chamber to be turned. Streams of super-heavy antimatter ions with energies in excess of ten-to-the-twenty MeV coming from the accelerators would collide in the center of the chamber and fuse until a certain critical mass of two-point-one times ten-to-the-minus-five grams had been accreted. Sixth-force generators then created a compression field intense enough to form a localised quasi-singularity. A stabiliser from a ship had to be able to cope smoothly with two- or three-hundred-gee accelerations. Suitably adapted, it would be able to hold the singularity in the center of the confinement chamber until it had been fed up to the requisite mass by tapping a universe of antiparticles on the other side of the continuum hole. A standard particle-pair creation process.

"The next stage is to release it. And then we must accelerate it tightly along the barrel. In Amerika we used to make barrels from black-metal alloy, but any super-rigid will suffice. The singularity must be fed into the slowly rotated spindle and compressed tight. A difficult job when the gun itself is moving with respect to the ship's own fields and the ship with respect to planetary and stellar bodies and the galactic node. Don't forget that by vastly increasing the local value of big-G we have created a singularity with an effective mass of two tons, but an event horizon as much as a foot across—instead of the ten-to-the-minus-twenty-four of a meter we would ordinarily obtain."

"The computation is applied to that manifold surface?" Kenji asked, raising his voice above the whispering of Duval's pupils.

"Yes. Of course, even and odd particles annihilate into a blaze of gamma photons unless they are channeled separately. To balance the mass equations, there's a requirement to leave this universe mass heavy. With this weapon we thought it would be environmentally more acceptable to have a single discrete event-object, or 'plumstone' as we call it, of real iron 56 rather than antimatter iron 56. You can imagine how unpleasant it would make a system that had just been exposed to a battle if several hundred two-ton bolides of antimatter were moving around afterwards. We can calculate how much unintentional destruction would be caused in a battle such as that fought at Niigata. A single thirty-*tan* antimatter annihilation would be productive of four thousand kilograms times cee squared—that's three-point-six times ten-to-the-twenty joules—and we can't have that."

"But thirty *tan*—four thousand kilograms—so much antimatter will take a very long time to accrete using particle accelerators," Yao Wen-yuan objected.

"No. The pulsing rate is the important factor and the accretion does not come from the particle accelerators. Those argentium nuclei are there only to initiate the formation of the quasi-singularity—to create the initial collapsible mass. The two tons appears from the corresponding quasi-universe by energy-mass conversion. We tap it as ultra-hard radiation from the ten-million-degree hearts of antimatter stars."

They breathed as one, touched by the magnificence of the idea, and began to nod at one another with smiles of intellectual delight. So! No need to carry vast masses around. No need to divert the vast power to operate the gun from the engines.

Duval went on. "While the mean temperature of collisions is maintained at a high energy level, the quasi-singularity must be rotated constantly to prevent it from breaking up. At RISC we used an ion injection system to charge the initial particles and a rotating magnetic field to drive it round. But it's better if the particles themselves have a spin excess, hence the use of the specific isotope mix we have chosen."

"Ingenious. But what about the program itself?" Katsumi said with an aloofness that irritated Duval. He ignored him and turned to Kenji instead. "When will we have a prototype operating?"

"We haven't even considered the propagator mechanisms or the grav compensator yet," Duval said.

"Yes, of course." Yao Wen-yuan's face was screwed up in concentration. "That's true. How do you make them move?"

Duval rocked his forearm up and down in explanation. "There must be mechanisms on each side of the barrel that allow the movements of the barrel to be compensated for, and an accelerator to compensate for the maneuvers the ship may make while the singularity is accreting."

"It is to be hoped that these guns will have a more aesthetically pleasing aspect than their forerunners."

Duval nodded, silently deploring Katsumi's pride in understanding nothing of the design problem. "All external fittings are attached at the stage. In Amerika it's usual to apply the seal of state, the Aquila eagle and stars of our Sector, and the gun's identification plate. They're made of plex and contain a unique trace pattern."

"You're not in Amerika now. Submit your designs to me," Katsumi said coldly. "I'll ask Nishima-sama to be good enough to look at them."

"Perhaps you could obtain drawings of what the daimyo desires by way of ornament and bring them to me. But I suggest that the patterns are kept simple and the decorations to a minimum."

"Your skill is wanting in this respect?"

"Nishima-sama can have his triple *ginkyo*-leaf *mon*—he can have cherubim and seraphim and vine leaves encrusting the barrel if he so desires. But tell him that each vanity will prolong the manufacturing time greatly."

"What do you do after that?" Kenji asked impatiently, staring up at the machine that rose above his head.

Duval made more explanations, each building on information he had previously offered. Kenji nodded and the technicians listened attentively.

"This is a far more complex process than I had imagined," Yao Wen-yuan asked, rubbing his chin. Duval had noticed that whenever Yao Wen-yuan was in the presence of Katsumi he reflected the other's concerns in his behavior, acting like a weather vane to Katsumi's moods.

"A two-ton weapon—that is, thirty *tan*—is a highly advanced piece of equipment."

"How long will it all take?"

Duval bowed to Kenji. "That depends on many factors, Lord. But it could be a matter of weeks. Each barrel is an individual shape dependent on the particular fields generated by the constrictors, and suited to the particular ship and the place on that ship where it is to be mounted. As with your samurai swords, singularity guns cannot be made in large batches. The production methods suited to beam weapons cannot be applied."

"That is very unfortunate," Katsumi said, clearly unhappy that so much costly preparation and material must go to make each and every gun.

"Remember that the gun, when completed, is the best weapon ever invented for use against nexus ships."

"So the next step is to create a working prototype?" Kenji asked hopefully.

"Not yet. The magneto-hydrodynamic model must be produced."

He put down his tri-vee marker and pointed overhead at the heavy waldos that would hoist the half-built chambers into the test rig, explaining how first a scan would be made inside the chamber to examine it and an irradiation to destroy all traces of gaseous impurities.

"It's essential that no instabilities are allowed to form in the chamber. There would be uncontrolled expansion that would lead to a gun disintegrating when fired," he told them. "I've seen it happen, and it's terrible. Inside the blister of a ship it would be completely devastating."

Katsumi nodded knowingly. "The power of these weapons is not easy to appreciate until you have seen them used yourself at close quarters. If the singularity did not propagate, the gun would be torn apart and a thirty-*tan* event-object brought into being in its place. Anyone standing within ten *ken* would surely risk death."

Kenji motioned Duval to go on. He picked up his marker and sketched the catenary surface, saying, "Gentlemen, I expect you've realised that to create a barrel from the surface as we have it would be to create a barrel of which the most important part is missing."

"Missing?" Katsumi's eyes studied the model; Yao Wen-yuan scratched at his bald place.

"Gentlemen—the barrel must be completely solid. There is no bore." They nodded and tutted and leaned in closer towards the representation. "We need a core: an iron bar, longer than the barrel by a small amount, and about half the diameter, inserted into the barrel to gorge the singularity on its passage along the barrel.

"It's suspended inside the barrel with an iron crown ring and chaplets that must hold the core in the very center. The positioning is critical because the accuracy of the gun depends on that, and also the range—if the core is only fractionally off center, the singularity will expand prematurely, and it will ream the barrel, or even annihilate it completely."

"But when you propagate, won't the core and these chaplets disappear?" Kenji asked.

"The core does disappear. That's the idea. And you're right about the chaplets, all but the studs. You must have seen this, Katsumi, having seen the guns fired. The studs are ejected mechanically, and a fresh core is loaded into the barrel before each firing."

"Yes, of course."

Duval grinned. "You see, Kenji-san, these guns are tricky devices. Our engineering must be made reliable to a very high degree."

Kenji walked a few paces away across the floor. He folded his arms and looked around at the machinery appreciatively. "You have done well. This is very impressive. When may I expect to see the first of your prototypes functioning?"

"A matter of months."

"Good. Good. And you guarantee that they will be as effective and as powerful as Amerikan guns?"

Duval hesitated momentarily, thinking of the many factors that combined to give the weapon its phenomenal power. He knew that given time and the necessary materials, he could equal the performance of Amerikan guns, but should he try? His professional pride wrestled with his loyalty to Amerika. He knew that without any objective comparison, he could claim what he liked. Finally he said, "Yes, Kenji-san. I can assert as much with confidence."

Kenji's eyes narrowed. "Then you'll have no objection to my arranging a test."

Duval shook his head blankly. "Test? Of course, all the guns must be fully proofed . . ."

"I mean a trial. Between an Amerikan weapon and the first prototype of your own manufacture."

"If only you could do that," he said, with Japanese regret in his voice.

"But we *can* do that," Katsumi said.

Kenji nodded. "When Wataru Hoshino next comes through Chiba, he will bring with him an Amerikan weapon." Duval looked back blankly, and Kenji continued. "Nishima-sama has seen fit to comb the hulks at Niigata apron very carefully. The remains of the *Thomas Jefferson* have yielded up one intact gun. That may be fired."

Katsumi's forehead went back and he looked down his cheeks at Duval. "So in two months' time we shall have the gun and we shall see if you are as good as you claim, *gaijin*."

He laughed uproariously and the circle of technicians laughed dutifully around him.

Damn you! he told Katsumi silently, trying desperately to straighten his thoughts. What can I tell Kenji-san now? Think!

"There may perhaps be a problem."

Kenji looked at him. The guffawing had died.

"A problem?"

"A singularity gun is one thing. But there is not one built, nor will there ever be, that can operate without argentium tubes."

"We have argentium!" Katsumi said.

Duval shook his head very deliberately, seeing his chance. "No good."

"What? These Amerikan guns must have Amerikan argentium?"

"They may be charged with local argentium but it is poor stuff. How can you compare guns on an inferior power source? That's like racing two stallions to see which is the better when neither is allowed to leave a trot. To see the full power of the guns you must bring an experienced isotopist here and we must make a blend of argentium isotopes that will have the correct atomic weight." He held up the tri-vee marker.

Kenji considered. He consulted with Katsumi and Yao Wen-yuan quietly but rapidly, breaking off to ask, "You have adequate chemical facilities, have you not?" Duval assented and there was more talking and shrugging. "Where is argentium to be found?"

"Fuji-san, Lord!"

"We must go there." Duval pressed his advantage, knowing he needed to learn more than Helene di Barrio's letter had told him. "I need my own isotopist. His name is Horse. He was one of the Amerikans captured on the Blood Moon."

Kenji nodded briefly and the three samurai left, unsure whether Duval had all along been laughing at them.

37

The volcano dominated all.

For two days they had striven to conquer its lower slopes, striking temporary bivouacs and marching hour after hour up the steep stony tracks. Only now was the summit in sight, and they left a dozen of the heavier, slower men at the final encampment and pressed on with half their donkeys.

At this height, twenty thousand feet above mean sea level, their long ascent reached its final stage. Duval could see small white clouds peppering the air above the valley, moving *below him*. To the northwest was the vista of Sado's central valley—a hot plain with its salt lakes and roads and *han*. It's a strange illusion, he thought. These commanding views were immensely more impressive than he had imagined they would be when, three days ago, he had looked up at the volcano from the plain.

An incredible, God-like panorama was laid out before him. Duval felt it was a privilege to experience this protest the planet had thrust up against the terraformers' handiwork, to survey in one long sweep the vast continental territory that had been broken with ferocious diligence by the settlers of Yamato. It was a landmass that stretched beyond the dusty horizon, outward and outward, for thousands of miles, sprawling across the equatorial belt, and it had all fallen to the fathers of the men who stood around him. Such a feat! And such a generation of men! What heroic resolve they must have had, he thought wonderingly, to believe that they could turn all this into a complete neo-feudal society within one generation. It seemed an impossible exploit. But they had achieved it, and in doing so had reaped glory for themselves, far greater than the lesser men who had come after.

He put aside his thoughts and reviewed their own progress with smaller respect. The fertile land they had traveled through on the lower slopes was forested, but here the trees were becoming smaller and gnarled and were petering out, and above them the volcano rose in sheer walls of banded rock, fabulously colored in red and gold and purple. Despite the burning sun, there were patches of fossil snow in the shadows, and, he saw, a convenient rocky crest along which they could climb to the crater.

Horse turned and wiped the sweat from his thin face, looking back down the valley. He was glad to be speaking his own language once more. "This is a cruel bastard, ain't it, Gunner? How far do you think we come now?"

"Fifteen, maybe sixteen thousand feet above the valley."

"And how far to go?"

"As much again is my guess."

Horse's glance was skeptical. He was sinew and bone, with gaunt cheeks; his dark-dyed face lined, clawed by life. "It don't look that far."

"Deceptive. They say that about mountains," Duval said, detesting the man. Horse had changed. His stay in Sado had transformed him from a quiet, even-tempered man into something moody, suspicious, and nervy. For the first time on the ascent they moved out of earshot of the samurai, and Duval faced him. "God help me, Horse. Tell me what's your bitch with me or I'll swing for you."

Horse's words were flinty. "I wish you'd never brought me here, Gunner. I do, and that's a fact."

"What's the matter?"

Horse stabbed a thumb over his shoulder, towards the valley. "I was digging a fortune down there. Meaning to make a break when I could. Until you interfered, damn you. It's the luck of a lousy steer that's lived all winter and dies before the summer."

"Quietly!"

Ahead, three samurai led by Katsumi were lifting themselves wearily up the slope, digging their toes into the friable rock. Dust rose up around them, acrid and sulfurous. Occasionally they stopped, panting for breath, before they turned and resumed their upward toil. No Shinto priests had been willing to pathfind, he recalled. To a man they had been terrified rigid when Katsumi had tried to compel them, clucking and tutting their fears.

"Why the fuck couldn't we use an air-car?" Horse asked.

"I told you. It's a holy mountain to them. No access. The religious authorities only agreed when Kenji-san told them it was a pilgrimage. Strictly no technology."

"That's just fucking typical of these no-hope sonsabitches."

He looked back to where Kenji and Michie plodded with the rest of their men. Fifty of them followed, leading donkeys loaded with empty sacks. Kenji had chosen to come, drawn to visit just once the fire mountain that watched over his *han*. Once he had told Katsumi of his intentions, Michie insisted on coming too. And her brother had shrugged. He watched her now, Duval saw, sullenly waiting for her to falter, but she showed no sign of weakening.

He turned back to Horse. "Now, tell me what you've heard."

"Not now."

Yao Wen-yuan caught up with them. "It's hard to breathe. And getting worse. There's no oxygen."

"Yes. My head's aching," he replied, switching smoothly into Japanese, his interest absorbed in this fantastic landscape higher than clouds where the air was running thin.

"What if the oxygen runs out altogether? Kenji's beginning to tire."

"Wataru-san told me that we're not the first to come this way. It's hard but not impossible. Why don't you cut Kenji a staff before the trees run out?"

"That doesn't make it any less steep."

Duval slapped his companion's shoulder wordlessly.

Yao Wen-yuan's mind was on the laboratory. He insisted on going over details endlessly. How long must the test range be? How many *tan* of aurium would they need as moderator? Was he sure that the chemical reduction plant would be big enough?

Duval made reassurances, wondering how much of it Horse understood, and feeling shamed as the depth of his collusion was revealed. Deeper down inside, he was trying frantically to piece together the details of what he had learned about Oujuku.

Oujuku's ship was prowling the Zone. He had taken a dozen small ore ships, routinely ordering them to cut power, depriving them of all they carried, and exploding them with great pyrotechnic displays. Always he put the crews down, making his name known as if his aim was to advertise it as widely as he could. Then, each time, he had disappeared into a nexus as swiftly as he had come.

As Yao Wen-yuan dropped back, the quiet exchange with Horse began again.

"He tried to ransom us, Gunner. Oujuku tried at Niigata. What do you think of that? When the others thought we was forgotten. I knew he'd come for us. I kept faith."

"Is that the truth?" Duval felt a pang of excitement.

"That's the very word. From Guam to Lombok, the watchword's being whispered, 'Beware the Black Dragon!' That's what they call him—our Captain John. What do you think of that?"

"You can't get to him."

"I can try."

"It's madness to think you can make a rendezvous with him. If you run away they're sure to catch you."

"No! I want home. And I've got a plan."

"Make Sado your home."

Horse's whispers grew strained. "I tell you, I want home, Gunner! And I'm fucking going home. I hate it here. I hate everything. Everything! I want to take my profit where I can spend it. Only, you've jiggered up my plan real good!"

Duval stayed tight-lipped for a moment, then he pulled a small black instrument from a fold of his kimono and said, "I've got a job for you."

Horse spat and took the device. "Fuck you, Gunner. Getting me out here when I had a plan. I've got four children back home. What about them?"

"You get home and they could freeze your ass for piracy! What about that?" he warned.

"I'll take my chances!"

When they called a halt, Duval joined Kenji. He sat on a boulder next to Michie, the cool wind ruffling him, but something colder and more penetrating battered at his conscience. He picked up a handful of stiff, smutted snow and crunched it in his hands, washing the dust from them. The sounds of the men drinking water and shrugging off their gear were all around him. There was tension in them, an uneasiness emanating from the land and from the awesome mass of rock above. But he was lost in his thoughts and he did not listen to their talk, nor participate in Kenji's conversation. There was a bleakness in the air. He knew with utter certainty that trouble was coming.

A rolling, deep-throated rumbling began.

Above them the hillside shook. Tiny stones trickled into crevices. No one uttered a sound.

Duval felt his chest tighten. The silence was overwhelming. Even the wind had dropped, the birdsong stilled. It was unnatural and deafening, until somebody shouted an obscenity into it and destroyed it.

All eyes were cast up at the mountain, and suddenly Kenji pointed at the ragged lip of the crater. A thin, almost elegant wisp of smoke coiled from the summit and dispersed in the air.

He stood up, and the soldiers stood also. They began coaxing the donkeys forward hurriedly.

"Jeezus, Gunner—what was that?" Horse asked, wide-eyed. Life on Sado had made him brittle to shocks. Now he had the look of a horse that might bolt on an instant.

"A little indigestion," Duval pacified him, thinking to himself that it was the mountain *kami*'s judgement on Horse's malice, or on his own guilt. Perhaps the isotopist was right. Perhaps he should be trying to find some way to escape. But why should he? Wasn't it just a maniac's dream? How could he possibly know where to find Oujuku? And why should he want to? It would be fine to see Ellis again, but what else was there to go back for? "Yep, just a bellyache for Fuji-san."

Horse showed his teeth. "Just so long as he don't spew his filth over us, eh, Gunner? That'd be a reward for all this climbing you've caused me."

As the sun-star climbed towards the zenith, they pressed on, ever upward, onto the shoulder of the volcano. There the ground was flatter and easier, and the walk to the top was across beds of refrozen snow that hurt the eyes with their glare. Duval traversed it, marveling at the way it crunched underfoot, aware that heavier snows were common here and that he was fortunate in the season because now the rock strata were revealed and it would be easy to find the sulfur beds.

As they crested the final rise he was breathing heavily, his lungs bursting. Then he saw the pit. The crater was huge, elliptical, half a mile across and five hundred feet deep, and its floor was ruptured and fissured with steaming vents that poured a choking, fuming stink into the air. Fortunately the wind was carrying the plume of gas eastward, over the opposite lip.

Then the thought struck him. Perhaps the snow's thin because the volcano's hotter than usual. Perhaps Horse's right. Perhaps it's getting ready to erupt.

The wounded ground held his eyes. He shivered, reliving the walls of singeing heat that he had felt blast across the burning apron. Suddenly the horrifying image of his brother's face filled his mind. The nightmare was always the same. A face which he loved puckered in agony. In the kamikaze fireball, he had held so tightly on to the drain floor he had been unable to breathe, and still the shock wave had blown the air from his lungs.

He shook himself, looked back at Michie, and was able to contain the rising panic in his mind.

Horse stared into the pit openmouthed. "What do you think of that?"

Yao Wen-yuan gasped. "It's *kuei-men-kuan*, the doorway to all hells," he said, fascinated by the molten mass that surged and spat far below. Hot rocks belched up into the air, higher than the rim, and rained down back into the crater, leaving trails of smoke in the air.

The isotopist twitched. "It looks primed to blow to me."

"I hope you're wrong about that, Horse."

"I don't like it. Don't like it at all. I wish you hadn't brought me here."

The samurai lined the rim, their clothes rippling as they watched the spectacle of raw power bubbling in the guts of the planet.

"You see that?" Yao Wen-yuan said to Horse. "That's your hell. When you die you'll be chained in there forever."

"Maybe you been there, Chinaman, with your incense sticks and your Confucian temples."

"I worship my ancestors. But you—" Yao Wen-yuan shook his head grimly. "You're going down there, my friend."

Duval intervened, pointing a little way back from the crater to a place where a vast wall of yellow, crystalline sulfur had formed. He led Horse to it, saying, "I didn't like the shock we felt earlier. Best get our chore done and get down."

When they reached the deposits, Horse gasped. The sulfur was feathery and pale. The whole wall was crumbly, like sand and hot, seeping, gummy red resin that was another form of raw plastic sulfur. There were veins of deeper yellow, cheesy and aromatic. The isotopist scraped at it, taking a mill in his hands to crush and assay the grains. He sniffed and tasted it, grimacing.

"It's damn near a tenth of a percent pure!" he said, astonished at the find. He looked at the reading. "Jeezus, Gunner! Argentium sulfide. There's tons of it! Perfect natural refined sulfide straight out of the guts of the planet! I ain't never seen it so pure."

"Good enough for you?"

"Good enough?" Horse looked around suddenly, then grabbed Duval's kimono, pulling him close, his breathless voice urgent and fierce. "I told you. I ain't doing your filthy job. Did you see the black? There's quadrazine below here. You're not wanting me to show them that, are you, Gunner? Show them how to line their tubes with quadrazine and refrigerate their charges so's they don't crust their terminals?" Argentium power tubes were "refrigerated" not because they had to be kept cold, but because they had to be kept at a constant temperature. Their stability was dependent on maintaining a critical 282.3 degrees Absolute within a 3-degree margin, and Horse knew that recent Amerikan advances had used quadrazine, itself an argentium compound, to achieve improved stability.

"And what about deuterium doping?" he went on, anger welling up within him. "You don't want me to tell them about that, do you? They don't know how to make their tubes deliver an even charge. They don't know how to make it work. And you want me to tell them. That's why you brought me here!"

Duval stiffened. "Shut it! I know how to engineer tubes better than you ever could. I brought you up here because I wanted news. News of Oujuku. And you're one man who could bring it to me."

"You're lying. What about the weapons you're making for them? I seen the way you kiss their asses." Hate flared up in Horse's eyes. "How did they buy you, Gunner? What did they promise you?"

Duval shoved him back, but Horse clung on and he slipped awkwardly so that they rolled to the ground together.

"You've sold us out, haven't you? *Haven't you?*" Horse's eyes were red, stinging from the acid fumes, and the wind blew jaundiced dust over them as Horse straddled him.

"I got you out of the hog sty! I kept you alive! All of you."

"Yeah! And yourself! You want news? I'll give you news. We're at war with Yamato now, Gunner, and you're a goddamned traitor!"

Horse raised his fist. Then the ground under them heaved. A terrifying quaking began, malevolent in its intensity.

Duval heard a woman's scream.

With sudden strength he threw Horse off and pulled free from his grasp, running towards the rim of the crater fifty yards away. Michie and Kenji struggled on the brink, while the samurai stood like statues, transfixed by the inhuman power of the fissure as it blasted hellish gouts of molten rock higher and higher. Then he watched in horror as the outcrop on which Michie fought to save her father began to collapse. A black cleft snaked across it, cutting them off. He saw Kenji, furthest from him, slide towards the edge, scrabbling in the dust helplessly. The opening yawned and the nearer face of the outcrop disintegrated, taking Kenji down.

"Michie!"

He came out of his trance and leapt forward, grabbing Kenji by the legs as he dangled head-down over the chasm.

Avalanches deep in the crater echoed thunderously from the walls. The ragged break was two paces wide now, threatening to cut off the entire outcrop on which they would ride to their deaths. Each thrust of his body promised to plunge them into the crater, each desperate wrench only kicked away more of the ground from under him. Duval strove to reach Kenji's sash.

He looked up and saw Katsumi and the others confounded by the heaving ground. He reached across the split imploringly, knowing that his weight might easily carry away the rock against which he was braced. Then he dived flat across Michie's body and grappled her, trying to link them in a human chain.

Another shock assailed them. Pinnacles of red and black rock that lined the crater wall collapsed, spinning dizzyingly into the void. Yao Wen-yuan ran forward, reaching the outcrop. Two of the donkeys had broken free and they pirouetted in terror around him, caught up in each other's guide ropes. Duval watched him break free just as they toppled sickeningly over the edge and plummeted down the sheer cliff.

Michie screamed again as her grip on Duval's hand slipped. He shouted for her to save herself. Then Yao Wen-yuan's hands were on her, wrestling her away. Rope lines surged across to them. Duval grabbed, wrapped the rope over his hand three times, and heaved, the samurai retainers hauling himself and Kenji back from the abyss as the ledge crumbled.

"God help me!" Duval gasped as his forearms took the strain. The loops of rope tightened on his hand, squeezing it, cutting into his skin. He felt something crack in the center of his chest. A jagged pain exploded across his rib cage and he felt himself passing out. In the thin air all exertion was a death struggle, but holding on to Kenji's leaden weight was ripping him apart. Still, he couldn't let go. A man's life was hanging from his fingertips.

After what seemed like an age, the strain across his chest stopped. The intense pain in his hand stopped. Blood began to pump again in his arms. He was lying on firm ground again, and Kenji lay with him.

He raised his arms weakly towards Michie.

"Duval-san," she cried. "Can you hear me?"

Her face and hair were thick with dust. He was unable to answer her.

Kenji was lying on the ground also. Duval saw him hazily; then Michie bent over him, careless of her own hurts. There was a backdrop of sparks, fireworks exploding. His vision began swimming nauseatingly, then someone remarked on the white of Kenji's face and his blue-tinged lips.

"Stand back! Give him air!"

"We must get him down to where the air is good."

"Yes. Right away. We must all try to get down off the mountain before sundown."

"It's too far," Katsumi said.

"We have to try."

He saw Kenji hoisted between two of his men, unconscious. They dragged him away from the crater, stumbling as they went, wanting only to escape the nightmare violence of this airless hell. The dragon was now hurling up red-hot boulders as if from a giant mortar. A rain of debris and small stones began to spatter down around them. Yao Wen-yuan caught him up and half carried him after the others.

"Quickly! I cannot hold you. Find your feet, I beg you!"

They ran for the pathway, following the remaining donkeys and most of the retainers who had, at no one's bidding, already begun to look for a way to the security of the lower slopes. Duval stumbled after them, feeling Michie guiding him and Yao Wen-yuan's strength support him.

The next four hours were a waking dream of horrors. The huge dragon of the mountain, risen and angry, pursued them and tore their hands and knees and the clothes off their backs as they descended in a desperate effort to escape his fury. It was only after they had scrambled down to the tree-line encampment once more that they paused and saw that the volcano's anger was abating. Behind them a vast plume of dense, ash-laden smoke reared up, filling the sky as the wind changed. Shocks still traversed the land, sending avalanches of rock and cinder and ice down after them, but their frequency and intensity were diminishing.

Duval drank greedily. Michie washed his face.

Katsumi's men were counting the cost of the enterprise.

"Why don't you stop?" Yao Wen-yuan yelled, shaking his fist at the peak.

"Who can say? This mountain is an evil dragon."

"A dragon who does not want to yield up his treasures."

"That's so. Just as the priests warned!"

"We're not wanted here."

Duval sat down, and when Michie turned her dirt-streaked face to him, he saw that her eyes were full of fear. He comforted her, knowing that she wanted to cry but would not. She whispered, "Thank you. For the life of my father. And for my own. Surely we would both have been consumed if not for you."

She bowed to him. Despite his exhaustion, Duval felt a pure shaft of joy spear him. He was still alive. Michie was still alive. For the moment they were beyond the reach of the smoking dragon, and that was all that mattered.

The retainers, bruised and ragged and with the remaining beasts, were packed up and ready to move out now.

The journey down was arduous. With Kenji strapped up in a bier of sacking slung from a hastily cut pine pole, and Duval walking unaided, they forced their aching legs to go on until they could no longer see the way ahead. Duval saw that the entire company helped inflate the tents and light the fires. Food was shared and bottles passed around unselfishly. The mountain dragon's driven us away, he thought, but it's also brought us closer together. It's the same camaraderie that bonds a nexus ship's crew after action or disaster. Everything is suddenly so lucid. Why? Maybe it's like warfare. I've been brought close to death and I can suddenly see with all the clarity of a man who should be dead but isn't. All the small weights that oppressed me have turned to thistledown. My conscience is reborn, fresh and unblemished.

The fear of fire was gone.

It was only then, under a vast cloud whose underside pulsed yellow, then orange, then vermilion in the darkness, that Duval realised their company was incomplete. Horse was no longer among their number.

38

LIBERTY

"Time for lunch, Captain!"

An ion key jangled and then turned the lock. Ellis looked up at the familiar sound. A fat synthetic brought in a covered tray and set it down on the table among the cads.

The room was the best Hawken's persuasion could get: plex-walled, set high in the block above the camp, and light. There was a bed, a chair, and a table on which he had an engineering design encyclo, a terminal, and tri-vee designed cads—tiny plex replicas of various parts of a nexus ship. Outside, the corridor was always scanned. Beyond that, the rest of the maximum security jail, then the rest of Camp Worth: a military base garrisoned by elite Army personnel. Escape by sinew was going to be impossible; escape by wit remained.

"Dover steak medium rare and salad today, and a black coffee."

"Cut up by you again, I see."

"It's my function to see that you get no more than meat in your steaks, Captain!"

"You have to be so damned cheerful?"

The synth chuckled contentedly. "If my manner offends you, just say so. You're the guest. And one enjoying greater comforts than any I've seen in this place, except when the vice-president, Mr. Henry, lived with us. You're a lucky man, Captain."

"Well, I guess it beats eating space-whale blubber."

"Space whales?" The incorruptibly naïve synth was perplexed.

Ellis explained patiently. "If you must know, I was on a ship and the Dovers were busted flat and there was nothing on the menu and we came across a school of space whales, okeh?"

"And you wanted to eat *them?*" His expression flipped from perplexity to bright disregard. "Yes, of course! What a good idea!"

Ellis sighed. "Get outta here!"

"Yes, sir. Anything to oblige a guest."

I'll be as fat as you are soon, he thought sourly, watching the even-humored synth leave and lock him in once more. Helluva thing, talking to synths. And how long before I'm tried and locked in here permanently? Lubbock's men must have a heap of evidence against me by now. What's holding him up?

He reviewed the letter-card that had come by Butler four days ago. The sight of it daggered him. In it, Hawken spoke optimistically about the trial, but warned that Pharis Cassabian had gone on an extraordinary embassy to China. Conveniently out of the way, or so it seemed. What justice could an innocent man expect when he can't trust to the telling of the truth to get him off the hook? he thought wryly. The joke is that I didn't know what Yi To Man was carrying or what he planned. Neither did Hawken, who got pretty angry when the news came out, and who's been trying to make amends since. But Cassabian knew. It was his idea. What if I threaten to tell the true story and implicate him? My word against that of the extraordinary ambassador to China? No, Ellis, they'd say you were a man clutching at any lie that would give him hope. Can I trust Hawken to side with me against Cassabian? Doubtful. How true that shit falls downward. And there's nobody below to pass on my troubles to. No one that's not been gotten to already. In any case, I may end up standing accused of more charges than even the wicked Mr. Yi. What happens when they figure out the truth about Kim Gwon Chung, as they surely will do?

He took a sip of coffee and paced the floor. Then he sat down and loaded the data that Ramakrishnan had sent, scrolling the flat pages with a dejection he had seldom felt so deeply.

For months, he thought, I've rotted here, with just one thought in my head—the harrowing of the Neutral Zone. Now it seems that I'll never get there. Why am I continually searching through these records and reports? It's foolish to fill my days with foreign designs—how best to equip and power a marauding nexus ship, which location on which continent on which planet in which system of the Zone will best serve as a secure raiding base, what is the least number of men that might hope to take Sakhalin, and how many times has the Index got above fifty percent in that nexus? He looked at the cads, unhappy with the form of the lateral transom and the thrust plate that sprang up and out and aft from it. All his hopes seemed suddenly remote, and he felt a pang of hopelessness, but he recognised it and cut it down instantly, shouting defiantly at the wall, "By God, if I don't get out of here and use these studies, others will!"

The echo died away to silence. His mind drifted, helmless, entangling him in frustration. He stood up again, trying to think, but whenever a plan of escape became clear to him, it dissolved into a hindrance. Always a hitch, a block, a problem!

He beat his hand on the wall. Then an inner discipline seized him and he heard his own crisp voice say, "When I brought the *Richard M.* home, I thought I was a lucky survivor. When Hawken and I came to Lincoln, I thought that we'd both end up here—waiting for the freezee. And when I lay naked with Reba, I told her how I was walking the razor's edge. I should have lifted off then. But I missed that tide of fortune and so my psi ebbed away to that place far across the Zone where I should have been."

He sat down on his bed, put his feet up high, and drank his coffee almost down to the bitter grounds. This time his voice was consoling to him. "Like the fat synth's always telling me, this is better than regular treatment. It must mean something. While I breathe there must be no despair. Now! *What to do?*"

No answer came.

The sight of Hawken's earnest face plagued him in the visualiser. He threw his cup at it, slashing coffee through the image.

"And damn you to the deepest hell of all, Kurt Reiner!"

That was better said. Some acid bile coughed up at last. The sharpest barb in Hawken's well-meant letter was not any false sympathy on his confinement, nor any false hope regarding the possibility of getting out, but the news of a date set on Reba's wedding.

He had told Butler, who he knew was programmed to accomplish such things, to return an urgent letter-card, and warned him on his synthetic life to do it straight. It had been a real threat, backed by Bowen, who was to shadow Hawken's synth and cut out his plastic heart if he deviated.

The letter-card had contained two messages, one sealed with Reba's terminal code that had passed through the kitchens in the Lubbock mansion and, so Butler promised, would go from synth maid to synth maid, and come at last into Reba's hands.

"Reply to me, or I think I'll go insane," he had told her, among many other private things that he could never have quite said to her face.

Now it was the fourth day, and still no news. He phased the wall to full transparency. A quiet Sunday. No compound sentries barking challenges at visitors. No messengers. A gospel choir from somewhere, and the noonday bugle. Not a sign of anything.

He closed his eyes; the pale light of a still overcast fell across his face. Then as he dozed, his arms over his eyes to block out the glare, he fancied he heard a noise in the approach drive. He imagined the jailor's flat footfall and another, lighter.

Again the jangling sound of the lock.

Then the door swinging on its huge hinges.

"One hour," the synth's strangely altered voice said. "No more."

Ellis lowered his arm as the door banged shut and saw that it had not been a dream. There was someone else in his room. Reba had come.

39

As Cassabian entered the secretary's room, he focused his mind on the several reasons he had come in secret from China.

Lubbock admitted him but chose to keep Jiro Ito by his side, perhaps imagining that a witness might inhibit discussion. It's a pity Jiro Ito's no babbler, Cassabian thought. The more witnesses to this, the better. Since the matter can no longer be buried.

"Congratulations on your promotion, Conroy," he said immediately. He knew the reward Alia Kane had conferred on her secretary was for his competence in steering the ship of state through the nexi of the last three years. In that, Cassabian thought wryly, Otis le Grande has also succeeded: he's buried the name of Halton Henry forever, though I doubt whether he likes the alternative that's risen up in his place.

This was the first time Lubbock and Cassabian had met face-to-face since the vice-presidency had been conferred last February; Cassabian's embassy in Peking and the delicate negotiations with the Court of Heaven had kept him busy. Much too busy for trips back to Liberty on purely ceremonial matters, he thought, prickled now by jealousy.

"Thank you, Mr. Cassabian."

"Yes. It's a reward you deserve," Cassabian said, "and one that I see you intend to enjoy."

"You can rely on that."

"Oh, I will. I will."

He left more unsaid and smoldering: You can't deny that you have your eye on the presidency; they say that when Nikolai Belkov moves to the Navy Commission you'll take control of the Treasury too. I wish you good luck. But what about me? Where's the recognition for my part in the continuing defense of Amerika? What position shall I have?

Preferably none!

It's not position but power that I want: a position of influence, and call me what you like. Titles are meaningless unless they give a man control over events. I want to hold the linchpin. And you'll give it to me. And if I have to scheme a little more, then so be it, Conroy Lubbock. And since you've stepped out of a secretary of state's robes to don those of the VP, those old robes can be mine.

"How was Peking?"

"Hank Morris sends you his regards. We're both optimistic about the outcome there. A lot is agreed already, which is no surprise. In their words: 'If the brother of the future Emperor of China shall marry the President of Amerika, the Dowager will consider herself and her son well favored by fortune.' "

Would Lubbock have backed this match off his own initiative? Cassabian asked himself. Will he back it now, when it's me who's the main architect of it? How deep is he in with Yamato? Worry and more worry is coming from Otis le Grande on these points. Worries I maybe can't afford to ignore.

"I want to know what you think of the President's marriage," he said directly. "Are you for it or against?"

"You have my word as VP that I support the marriage implicitly."

"And your word as Conroy Lubbock?"

"That is my own affair."

"Then there's a problem. One that concerns another marriage. I must have this out in the open. Now. I think you know what I'm about to say."

Lubbock faced him, sitting motionless under his huge allegorical painting of "Power and Glory," giving nothing away, nor making any sign of dismissal to Jiro Ito.

"You're insisting that your daughter, Reba, marries Kurt Reiner."

"It's been known for years that they'll eventually marry."

"Yes, so what's the sudden urgency?"

"Young love is impatient, Pharis."

"Oh, how true." Cassabian screwed at his wedding ring. "But at what price?"

"What do you mean? The dowry? A few token Halide stocks."

"I've heard that the dowry is to be the traitor's reprieve. Halton Henry's life. That price is too high for Amerika, and too high for me, Conroy."

Lubbock sat up, unsettled by the directness of Cassabian's charge. "Of course, you have evidence of this—agreement?"

"It's no secret that you're seeking to make important marriages for each of your children. That's understandable. What isn't, is how you can propose to give Halton Henry his freedom after what he's done. That he's cousin to a man who will soon be your own son-in-law is perhaps reason enough."

"That's a hell of an allegation."

Cassabian blew out his breath explosively. "You signed Henry's release from Camp Worth. Why? On the pretext of placing him under house arrest. You've installed him in his own property, virtually bailed the man. Why? To demonstrate his innocence and the lack of seriousness with which his crime is considered. You've tried to rehabilitate him as much as you can. Why? To show the United Worlds that he is forgiven."

"Halton Henry is a repaired man, Pharis. He's apologised. He's cleansed by confession."

"This was Kurt Reiner's idea. I think that the deal was this: in return for Henry's pardon, Reiner has agreed to marry your daughter—*even though your daughter is pregnant!*"

Lubbock stared. Then, swiftly, he recovered and waved his hand dismissively. "Is that what you think, Pharis? Let me tell you, Halton Henry's part in the rising is old news. The issue's been dead a long time. He told us all about the plans of Waters and Westmoreland, in detail. And it was the President who said she preferred him alive, not me. You spoke of evidence, Pharis. Present it. Or stop these allegations."

Cassabian pulled out a sheaf and laid the flexiplex surveillance records on the table one at a time. His voice was smooth and uncolored. "Item: Halton Henry has reaffirmed his oath of loyalty to Alia Kane, but denied his intent in a private letter to the Korean minister—the original card is in my possession. Item: Henry has been contacted by Yi To Man. And here's evidence that since Henry's release he's been in constant touch with the financier. Evidence that Yi, in turn, has talked to Okubo, to Baron Harumi, and even to the chamberlains of the Emperor's Court. Evidence that ultimately he plans to talk to Earth Central also. Evidence, in short, that since his release Henry has spent every waking hour trying to secure Yamato's help so that his sister may once more attempt to take the presidency."

Lubbock gathered up the sheets and scanned them, thunderstruck. He had already been shaken by the quality of Cassabian's accurate intelligence. How could he possibly have known of Reba's pregnancy? Whom did he have in the Henry household? Was Cassabian now in league with Otis le Grande?

He summoned Jiro Ito from the shadows and talked privately to him. Cassabian's eyes followed him as he left.

"You must believe that this is a surprise to me." Lubbock watched Cassabian shrug amiably. "It's true that I wanted to give Reiner what he asked. My grandchild must have a father. It's true also that the President wants to pardon Halton Henry. But the fact is I saw him as a counterpoise to Otis le Grande. He hates him totally for the betrayal he planned, and I also judged that if Otis le Grande is continually watching and riding Henry, then he's in a political straitjacket."

Cassabian rose and went to the window. "This is too important for either of us to misunderstand one other. You're VP now because you preserved the peace with Yamato. But you've got other ambitions. You want that peace to continue, but you also want Otis le Grande controlled and curbed. You want your daughter to marry Reiner. And you want the father of her bastard killed."

Lubbock stamped the heel of his hand into the desk. "And you, Mr. Cassabian? What are *your* ambitions?"

Cassabian turned, carefully hiding his smile. "I want my President to marry the Chinese prince—because then the Korean rebels will be protected and because it holds promise of a Sino-Amerikan pact against Yamato, making a buffer out of Korea. I want Henry executed and Okubo expelled—for justice's sake. And I want Captain Straker released—for my own reasons. And I believe that with luck we may each of us have everything we desire."

Lubbock's eyes hardened. "Ah, no! You want the President to marry so that Korea may be crushed by Chinese forces. You want Henry's head to be carried on a plate to Otis le Grande. And you want Okubo thrown out to sever relations with Yamato. Lastly you want Ellis Straker released so that he'll clash with Reiner and bring down a man you despise and whom Otis le Grande despises."

Cassabian smiled and cocked an eye at the novelty of the idea. "Neither of us is a fool, Conroy. So let's be open about it. Take the Chinese marriage: You've already consented to that in principle. You've said you'll not obstruct it. But neither will you facilitate it." He turned back to the window. "However, despite the fact that we're opposed, you and I are nevertheless in some accord. We both see value in the *prospect* of the President's marriage. Even the rumor of it is sufficient to deter Yamato arms, and while they're deterred there can be no war between Yamato and Amerika. That's how your peace will be preserved."

"And Otis le Grande?"

Cassabian's smile became knowing. "At the moment, you can blackmail him with the contract that he rashly made with Halton Henry. You ask yourself—what if Henry is executed? How can Otis le Grande be kept from my throat then? I'll tell you the answer to that: the death of Halton Henry, your tacit opposition to the President's marriage, and the release of Captain Straker will be enough to convince him to drop his efforts to depose you."

"Straker must be tried! Because he helped publish a malicious Earth Central proclamation on Alia. And for my daughter's sake."

"No! Without his release, Otis le Grande will have no guarantee of your continuing good faith. Your daughter's social standing as the wife of Kurt Reiner is his hostage. If Henry is arrested the day after the wedding, I promise you there will be ample evidence to implicate Reiner also. That evidence can become yours, and with it you'll be able to control him. The price is cheap: Ellis Straker's freedom."

A fleck of spittle showed at the corner of Lubbock's mouth as his frustration exploded. "*Why?*"

"I have uses for him."

"What uses?"

Jiro Ito reappeared, followed by an armed party. They brought with them a man whom Jiro Ito threw down in the middle of the room. "Here's the man, sir."

The prisoner scratched and shivered. Cassabian saw that he had been a big man once, muscular and erect, but now he was shrunk by the rigors of the Probe, cowering and hunched. His pitiful state made Cassabian turn his head away.

"Who is he?" he asked disgustedly.

Jiro Ito's voice rasped. "Speak! Tell the congressman your name!"

"Three-two-oh-four-five-oh, Ingram."

Lubbock looked at him dispassionately and his eyes locked on Cassabian. "This man will testify to a whole stack of underhand plots dreamed up by Ellis Straker. He's informed me that Straker made an unauthorised deal with the nexus pirates led by Kim Gwon Chung to molest Yamato ships in the Korean chain."

Cassabian's voice became wearily disdainful. "It's a great pity, Conroy, that the full force of Ellis's dealings with Kim Gwon Chung was never felt. The idea was to land a force to seize the Korean port of Pusan as soon as Harumi's army had started its invasion of Amerika."

Lubbock's anger overflowed. "He had ideas to develop the foreign policy of Amerika just as it pleased him! I could not allow that!"

Ingram began to cough and hawk.

"Why don't you let him go?" Cassabian asked disgustedly.

"He's detained here for his own protection. But his allegations range far and wide, and they implicate others. He says that he witnessed Straker bring Yi to Man into Amerika with the Earth Central proclamation. That alone is sufficient to freezee him as an evil traitor."

"Only a fool fails to arm himself against the future," Cassabian said with sudden anger. "Evil men are found all over Known Space. Some are ordinary people. Some, more evil still, become politically powerful, and the most evil of all sometimes win the glittering prizes. Ellis Straker brought Yi To Man into Amerika on my orders. There was no malice against the President in it. Consider: it was not *he* who drew up the proclamation against Alia Kane, but the judges and cloistermen of Earth Central. No purpose is served in keeping the news secret in Amerika. I wanted security tightened around the President. I wanted the pro-Yamato elements that still exist in Amerika *warned* of their true position. I also wanted the real intent of Yamato drawn out for everyone to see. Yi, with his plotting and scheming, has proved to be the best possible agent for all three aims. Ellis Straker therefore is no traitor. He must have his freedom."

Lubbock watched Cassabian's face carefully. As extraordinary ambassador, Cassabian's efforts in Peking had continued unabated for almost a year. Hadn't he returned to Amerika periodically since Straker's arrest? Once on so-called vacation, and later, in January, to attend the opening of the Amerikan Trade Center, at Lombard Hill. That was a tangible result of Korea's partition and ruin; approved by the President and renamed the Amerikan Center of Trade and Commerce. Its grasshopper crest flew over the District like a weather vane of mercantile ambitions. How closely was Cassabian connected with the growing Trader powers in Lincoln? Hadn't he dined with the Hawken brothers many times? Perhaps he's persuaded others of the immediate benefits of antagonism towards Yamato. It was a sound argument for ten years' time, but surely the time is not yet ripe. Amerika must play the quiet hand still. Growing and prospering in trade and in military capacity, building a head of force to overcome the Emperor and his dictates. To go off now, half cocked and unprepared, would be a disaster.

The wind was changing. Ever so slowly and by degrees, the Sector of Amerika was gaining confidence and people in all walks were seeing new opportunities. Prudent folk were building up their affairs. But others looked outward. Otis le Grande was fond of meddling in foreign wars, Cassabian wanted to champion the Korean cause, the damnable Ramakrishnan filled the President's head with fanciful notions of pushing the boundaries of Amerika into the Beyond. Then there was Jos Hawken and his private argument with Yamato. And now this amateur tinkerer, Straker.

Lubbock bristled as he thought of how he had been abused. He rued the day he had allowed Straker into his house. The man's audacity had shocked him. Crime upon crime, he had come to blows with Reiner. Then he had had the face to lie with Reba and get her with child. A grandchild conceived in a Camp Worth prison cell. The shame of it!

Straker's crimes were numerous: He had shamelessly purloined a million credits from Okubo and spent it on equipping a nexus ship in which his fellow conspirator John Oujuku had lifted off from Harrisburg, without passport or clearance, to maraud in the Zone. He had brought in Yi To Man and plotted an invasion of one of the systems where Korean resistance was ready to surface. What else could be expected if such a man was let loose on Known Space?

He said, "No. I can't release him. He's too dangerous."

Cassabian pressed forward. "You want to get rid of him, don't you?"

"I'm rid of him already."

"And if he'll swear that he'll not see your daughter ever again, or Kurt Reiner, or try to harm him, or breathe a word about the child?"

Lubbock wavered. He pinched the bridge of his nose and then looked up. "Could he be persuaded to promise that?"

"Certainly."

"And he can be trusted to keep his promises?"

"Yes."

"I guess there's always the chance he'll die in some nexus accident or a ship malfunction, goddamn him!"

"That I can't promise."

"Ha!" Lubbock sat a long moment, watching Ingram, who shivered and stared wide-eyed. There was no doubt what Cassabian was really saying: that he, Lubbock, could no longer hold Straker. He would have to bring him to trial or let him go. If Straker was let out, he would fall in with Cassabian's designs. In Amerika he would be a lurking presence around Reba, promise or no promise, of that he was certain. Out of Amerika he was a menace. Only a saint chooses good over evil every time, he told himself. Where there are only evils, a wise man chooses the lesser. Do I trust Cassabian enough? What does he really want with Straker? Wasn't it obvious to him that as soon as Straker was released he would cruise to Sado with some half-chewed notion of ransoming his brother?

Ingram broke into another bout of coughing. He motioned to him, telling Jiro Ito, "Give him some credit and let him go."

Jiro Ito goaded the pitifully grateful prisoner from the room with barked orders. As the door irised shut, Lubbock offered Cassabian a glass of Utah red wine to seal the business.

He accepted pleasantly.

"Tell me why you're protecting Straker. I don't believe he knows anything about you that you want kept quiet," Lubbock said, gathering his sleeves onto the table. "And I don't believe he's a New Year's present to Otis le Grande."

Cassabian sipped, looked up. He said, dueling mildly, "At least your line will be vigorous through your first grandchild. He'll have psi-talent coming out of his ears. He might even be President one day."

"It's dangerous to look too far ahead, Pharis. But you? What are you after? Are you thinking of a pact with China, with yourself as power broker? Or will another rising suit you better?"

"I'm loyal to the President."

"And tomorrow?"

"The long future is a hard place to make plans. But there is one thing." Cassabian said the word distantly, like a guru's revelation. "Hainan."

The battle at Hainan had been fought three months ago and Cassabian had heard of it some days later. According to the detailed intelligence reports he had received, a huge fleet of two hundred and seventy Chinese assault vessels under Admiral Lui Te-shan had been met in the Zhanjiang system by a force belonging to Yamato, the Slavic Federation, and Earth Central. The Emperor's bastard half brother, Prince Sekigahara, had commanded the league's navy: two hundred turtle ships, backed by a hundred transports packed with hundreds of thousands of samurai, and spearheaded by six vast globe ships that mounted fifty beam weapons each.

Prince Sekigahara had carried the Emperor's *sashimono* banner into battle, falling on the fleet of the Heavenly Admiral with incredible ferocity. He knew that failure would give the entire quadrant of Hainan to the Chinese and lay open a defenseless flank to them. It would also destroy Yamato fleet power and encourage the Dowager to send her hordes against Shikoku.

In the titanic struggle the Chinese admiral had become an especial target. The samurai boarders had surged from the locks like motes, flickering across the spaces between the ships as they maneuvered, penetrating the shields in a way energy weapons could not. They had massed on the hull of Lui Te-shan's ship with meson cutters, thousands falling to the antipersonnel devices, but still they had carved their way in and fought through the interior of the ship yard by yard, bulkhead by bulkhead, until they reached the bridge. Admiral Lui had fallen in single combat, and when Prince Sekigahara ordered his severed head raised in the scanner beams, the sight of it on all the Chinese monitors had turned the battle.

Fifteen thousand slaves were taken. Only fifty Chinese ships had got away. The rest were destroyed or captured, and Prince Sekigahara's gamble had succeeded.

"Hainan," Cassabian repeated. "With the Emperor's victory his Sector is secured. How long can it be before the full might of Yamato is directed against us?"

40

The sound of a big Bristol air-limo echoed back from the high, lit-up windows of Richmond Gate at the rear of the White House.

Ellis jumped to the ground, and Otis le Grande's officials led him briskly on and through a security check under a night sky filled with glittering diamonds. Even at this time of night, they passed clerks with inquisitive eyes and secretaries who started talking about him. He was met there and taken inside by Otis le Grande himself.

"C'mon, Captain. We can't afford to waste time right now."

"What about my blaster?"

Otis le Grande shook his head. "You're joking, aren't you? You couldn't get a butter knife into this place."

At their swift passing Marine guards stamped rigid, their smart officers saluting. Each double door was flung open. The long brilliantly lit corridors rang to their shoes; the suite of rooms where a ceremonial guard was posted was sumptuously decorated by carvings and ancient paintings and hung with a giant chandelier. Ellis saw, glancing to right and left, that the opulent hangings and allegorical paintings seemed to extend forever in every direction. After his confinement it seemed to him a huge and inviting open space. Finally they came to a door that was not open, nor could it be opened by Otis le Grande's arrival alone. The guard demanded ID, and what business he might have, and when Otis le Grande gave his summons card, it was taken by a machine and ingested.

"What now?" Ellis asked, swaying his weight from one foot to another and back anxiously.

"We wait."

"And when we're inside? What then?"

"I'm not coming with you."

Ellis was struck with a sudden pang that stiffened him. "But . . . hell—I can't go in alone."

"Why not?"

"I . . . er, I don't know what to say to a President."

"You're *summoned*. And therefore you will do as you're told. Don't worry."

"I heard you have to talk in allegorical form to the President." Ellis scowled. "At the least, tell me what I'm supposed to do."

"Relax yourself a little, and be polite. Call her 'Miz President' and don't venture your opinions unless you're asked for them. That's all that's required. Now, can that be too much for a person to bear?"

Ellis's stomach gurgled. It was almost ten P.M. and he hadn't eaten since three. He stamped one foot forward and thrust out his hand. "So right off, I'll shake hands."

"No, no. No!" Otis le Grande said, appalled. "You're meeting the President of Amerika, man, not thrusting at some plexing tutor. You don't touch the President at all!"

The face of the Marine guard captain had turned the color of a beetroot. Ellis shot him a venomous glance.

"Hell! I don't know anything about protocol and stuff."

"You don't say," Otis le Grande said. "You should come forward like this. Like the goddamned supplicant you are. And wait."

He stood with his feet together, rocking back with his hands clasped behind him. Ellis thought it looked like an effeminate way to stand.

"I know it's hard, but just—you know—be deferential!"

Ellis shook his head and shrugged. Then, before he could ask another question, the doors were flung open and he was urged forward.

He saw the President, seated at a huge desk and surrounded by her aides, to her left Lubbock and to her right Cassabian. Ellis approached, thirty pairs of eyes following him, and nodded with the deepest humility he could muster.

He heard her voice, icy and hard and utterly terrifying.

"So! This is the man with the reckless plans? Never mind that he's spent the last few months at Camp Worth, eh, Mr. Cassabian?"

Cassabian's face assumed a smile of massive insincerity and Ellis cringed inside. "He's a good man who's been trapped by circumstance, Miz President."

Alia Kane gazed up at him and snorted. "Caught up in your machinations, I shouldn't wonder. And you want me to let him go?"

"I . . ."

She continued to stare at Ellis, her eyes penetrating him. This is the moment, he thought, the tension inside him building unbearably. What should I say? I don't know anything about political allegory or allusion. What can I ask? Give me permission to waylay the ships and subjects of a neighboring power? Grant me the right to maraud a foreign empire at will? Let me go beyond the limits of your jurisdiction, and though I've just come out of prison, I'll be worthy of full trust?

"What do you want, Captain?"

His mouth was as dry as dust. "Three things, Miz President."

"Only three?"

"I wouldn't like to have to choose between them," he mumbled.

"Out with them, then."

"First, I'd like my ship back."

Lubbock bent to whisper an explanation in her ear. "*Your* ship?"

"She was promised to me by Jos Hawken, whose name you may know."

"This is the ship *Constitution?*"

Ellis swallowed hard, his nerves jangling. "Commodore Hawken has been minding her for me, as you might say, Miz President, while I reflected on my—reckless plans—inside Camp Worth."

The strike of light in Alia Kane's eye was deadly. "And the second thing?"

"The second thing is just a no-account square of plex. I imagine it's a pretty big square, because it seems that without it my ship can't lift off."

The President pursed her lips testily. Her cutting voice split the air. "The ship of your friend, Captain Oujuku, didn't have any such difficulty. He didn't wait for a passport at all."

Ellis produced his nod again. This time it was semi-apologetic. "Yeah. Well, John's kinda like me, a man who knows what's right, but sometimes doesn't know what's the right way."

"He's a criminal!"

The President's fingers grasped her armrests. She got up from her seat and touched Lubbock's arm with an almost reassuring gesture. The material of her sleeves crackled and soughed as she went to the middle of the room. The decoration sewn on her handmade bodice sparked brilliantly. She turned on him suddenly, much too close. "And if I accede to these two requests, what's your third?"

"Only this, Miz President—"

"Come here, over by the window. I want to look at the sky."

He followed, awkwardly. Until they were almost alone, separated from the aides, separated from Lubbock and from Cassabian also. He held his tongue, remembering Otis le Grande's advice that he should wait for her to speak first after any pause, and seeing that she was deep in thought.

Then she said, "When I was a baby, the very first thing I saw was the sky, and the way the stars gazed back at me. I've never been out of Amerika. Tell me about the Neutral Zone."

Ellis searched his memory frantically to recall the many wonders he had seen, but he could not. There was nothing in his mind connected with the Zone. Nothing at all. He looked inside himself and found only the thought of the lunch he had eaten and he felt the hunger gnawing at him. He tried desperately to focus his brain on something—anything—but it was blotted out by an overpowering desire to blurt out the third request he would ask. How can I ask the President's personal protection for Reba against Kurt Reiner? he asked himself, stricken with a dread he had never known. She can't prohibit the marriage, or annul it and make it void. He began to sweat and his heart hammered. Jeezus! This is agony.

His voice faltered. "Well, I guess . . . I guess I could try to describe a psi-storm . . ."

She tutted at him. "I've no wish to know about them, Captain. I want to know something essential about the Neutral Zone. Quickly now."

From the far side of the room Cassabian watched Ellis anxiously. The man's awkward embarrassment lit him up like a torch. I represented him to her as a brave and capable man, he thought. A man to command and inspire other men. A chief. He's barely in command of himself, goddamn him! Don't say he's going to attempt an allegory. Ah, these received notions! I wish I could hear what he was saying. This is a disaster!

Then he saw that Ellis had stopped his stuttering. His hands began to move like ocean waves as he spoke.

"Miz President, the Neutral Zone is more than a buffer between the two most different cultures in Known Space; it is a great sea in which no oar is dipped. And upon that sea all men must be free to go where they please and trade where they please. Without that capability there can be no freedom, and without that guarantee Amerika is prey to an oppression as monstrous as any that has threatened the great liberties we have always proclaimed . . ."

Incredibly Alia Kane's prickly temper softened. She began to listen closely. She took off her pin and gave it to him. Then she laughed.

Ellis talked to her for more than ten minutes, the President interrupting at intervals. When he was dismissed, it was fondly.

Cassabian followed him, catching him as he turned the corner.

"What the hell did she say?"

Ellis rubbed at the back of his neck. He regarded Cassabian suspiciously. "She asked me to tell her about the Neutral Zone."

"What did you say to her?"

"I told her about it."

"And the third request?"

He darted another dark glance. "I asked permission to carry her pin aboard my ship to remind me of my duty."

"And she agreed?"

He held up the silver pin.

Cassabian blew out a great breath of relief. He slowed as they came to the great hall. It was hung with huge Taylorian oils depicting classical scenes, and the long tables were being laid for a banquet under them. Ellis was heading towards the courtyard under full power. Cassabian called out impatiently after him, his voice ringing off the silverware. "How did you charm her? What the hell did you say to her that made her laugh?"

"That's none of your business, Mr. Cassabian."

Ellis strode from the palace and into the courtyard. The gull-wing doors of a flashy air-car were opened for him by Otis le Grande's chauffeur. It was the Bristol he had been loaned by le Grande to ride to Harrisburg apron before the President changed her mind. He breathed deeply. A spring night! And the air was full of promise, and he saw that at last his road was straight and unencumbered, and open all the way to the Zone.

"You know, sir, there's nothing as good for a busy man as a really fast and comfortable English car," the chauffeur said fatuously.

Cassabian caught up with him once more. He reached in to clasp hands. "Godspeed to you, Ellis Straker."

"Thanks for that, Mr. Cassabian. And for everything."

"But—what did you say to the President?"

Ellis felt a burn of embarrassment and he settled himself into the upholstery to cover it. "I told her about space whales."

Cassabian stared at him blankly. "Space whales?"

"Yeah—I told her all about them."

Ellis thumbed the door shut; Cassabian watched him as the vehicle drove smoothly past the Richmond Gate, and once past the White House checkpoint it gathered speed and spurred swiftly up into the air lanes.

Now, at last, the enterprise he had planned for was under way.

BOOK 3

23RD YEAR OF KANEI/A.D. 2425

Sending my dear,
Back to Yamato,
I stood in the dark of night,
Until wet with dawn's dew.

Even when two go together,
The autumn mountains
Are hard to cross.
How will my lord pass over
them alone?

Princess Oku
A.D. 661–701

Material excerpted from "A Manuscript Found in Space,"
by A. Hacker:

Material excerpted from the Ozma Vault
Transmission Package KVFG #0131,
Copyright Synthetic Educator Corp, Orenburg, VIR.,
By Permission of the Central Authority,
Old Earth. A.D. 2401

[Ref. Module MCXXIV-024.240354 /Engl.]

[Cross-references to other SEC modules in CAPS.]

AURIUM

Begins: rticular chemical elements make possible advanced industries: aurium and ARGENTIUM. Both are transuranic elements found in the island of isotope stability in an extension of the periodic table beyond the Actinide series. Argentium has atomic number 125, and aurium 126, the principal isotope being Aur-310. Both are super-heavy, super-dense stable metals with very complex chemistry. A third super-heavy metal, PLATINIUM, makes up the tri#

. . . HACK INTERRUPTED . . .

#Vela supernova of 13,000 B.C. exploded giving rise to the Gum Nebula. (The next nearest remnant is the CRAB, at 4,500 lys.) Cold ejecta has entered Known Space, and several planets exist that were terraformed from debris originating in the Vela exp#

. . . HACK INTERRUPTED . . .

#la Pulsar (0833-45). The Vela pulsar (2CG-263-02) is an SNR (supernova remnant), like the Crab Nebula pulsar, only somewhat older. The associated nebula now covers 30–40 degrees of the sky seen from Old Earth. The pulsar emits high-energy gamma rays. It has an approximately 90 mS period, a rate of slowing of 1.5 × 10(−5) sec/yr. The pulsar itself was originally identified with a 24th magnitude star appro#

. . . HACK INTERRUPTED . . .

#ospecting in the NEUTRAL ZONE in search of "blue gold." The systems of SADO and OKINAWA both have rich super-heavy element deposits which are being rapidly and exclusively stripped whilst the demand for aurium and argentium continues to increase. Unfortunately both elements exist only in tiny amounts and are formed under physical conditions so vastly energetic that they are only found in matt#

. . . HACK INTERRUPTED . . .

#he key to several crucial processes. Both are used in the manufacture of PLEX, the light material that is universally used for its strength, durability, and versatility in building. Ship hulls and city domes are made almost exclusively from plex. Both are used in the basic DOVER process that allows terraforming and the transmutation of water, carbon dioxide, and energy plus trace elements into synthetic foodstuffs (fats, sugars, carbohydrates, and proteins). Both are also used in the transport technology that allows NEXI to be created and permits GRAVOMETRIC machines, like ships' gravity/acceleration force compensators, to operate. A radioactive isotope of argentium is used to power a new class of sh#

. . . HACK INTERRUPTED . . .

#generate defense fields. These remarkable strategic materials are found in very limited quantit#

. . . HACK INTERRUPTED . . .

#the only place where atomic nuclei so heavy could have been forged: Class Sp. XIa supernova remnants. Being stable, they do not decay radioactively like other transuranic isotop#

. . . HACK TERMINATED.

41

THE PALAWAN SYSTEM, N.Z.

"Unidentified ship bearing green two-oh-nine azimuth ten on the forward scanner!"

The shout from the helm galvanized Captain Kondo Izumi. His stomach began to clench in anticipation, and his eyes moved eagerly across the forward screens. Seeing nothing, he quickly punched up the scene to starboard, promising to have the monitor operator disciplined if he had made another false call.

The other ships of the outward-bound *kin kaigun* aurium fleet powered in on a steep orbital approach path. The Palawan system had a bright AO primary star, diamond blue, a fast-burner fifty times as luminous as the Sun. Vega, that's what the *gaijin* call it, he thought, and it possesses a big gravitational field that moderates the nexus exactly as expected, making the passage easy.

He saw that the ships were steady, staying tightly formed-up in their convoy to starboard during deceleration, Admiral Kurita in his flagship, *Musashi,* and twenty-six other ships, big and small, burning the giant retro-engines that would brake them into the system, shedding velocity at between a hundred and two hundred gees to bring them down from the 0.9 cee they needed to transit this nexus. It was sobering to reflect at such times, Kondo thought, that if the gravitational compensators failed, everything within the plex hull would instantly be pressed into mush by the braking forces. If.

The bridge of the *Kogyo-Maru* was in operational lighting, a sullen red lit only by the screens and the spangle of stars that glared through the overhead blister. Kondo Izumi strode across the bridge and leaned against the rail, until his line of vision to the forward scanners cleared the obstruction of the helm console. Balanced there, he waited, watching for the appearance of the *gaijin* pirates.

Still nothing.

May the gods castrate the monitor operator if he's wrong this time, he thought, angered by the shout.

Kondo was unsettled. The alarm six hours ago as they came out of the nexus had skinned his nerves, and this new disappointment was sharp in his throat. He realised he would have to endure longer in purgatory before a real chance to show his samurai spirit arose. But when that chance did occur, it would be glorious. Of that there was no doubt.

The *Kogyo-Maru* was a remarkable vessel, a unique ship, with extraordinary qualities, new to Kondo and untried by all aboard. The thought of her powerful concealed armament filled him with impatience. He looked up through the plex blister at the primary star and damned the lookout once more; to the helmsman he muttered, "If he's wrong again, I'll have the knife to his topknot, Noma-san."

"It's a clean system, Captain-san. It's hard to make a mistake now the nexus's properly cleared."

Noma Shimei made his reply deliberately soothing, sensitive to Kondo's brittle temper. A bluff man, craggy-faced but with heavy brows, he was also a capable first officer, highly experienced at handling a nexus ship and its esoteric apparatus, which was why Kurita had insisted that Kondo enlist his services.

"No. He's tired," Kondo said. "And not properly mindful of his duties as a samurai."

"Takano is keen. I know his family. He has good blood." Noma turned suddenly to a loitering fifteen-year-old cadet. He bellowed, "You there! Boy! Go to the main scanner bay. Find out what Takano is shouting about."

"*Hai!*"

Cadet Takano's record was not without blemish. Naturally awkward, he had been the last of his watch to get to stations when the *Kogyo-Maru* had come bursting out of the Celebes nexus. After the initial deceleration was complete the master at arms had handed him the punishment pill and nodded at him phlegmatically to swallow it. Takano had then gone to the airlock, suited up, and shot himself into space, and there, seventy feet above the ship and directly visible to the whole bridge, secured himself to the communications gantry, knowing that he must remain there without sleep for twenty-four hours, straining his voice on the comms channel, singing "I Did It My Way" endlessly over and fighting the steady loosening of his bowels brought on by the laxative pill. It was immensely humiliating for Takano but caused great hilarity among his all-male crewmates.

Of course, he had fouled himself audibly within the first hour, after which they had switched him off, but he had had to remain singing on the gantry for the full punishment period, then clean out the suit to the master at arms' satisfaction. Perhaps it had been more than Takano's aristocratic dignity could take, as the captain said. As they had come blasting into the Palawan system, his alert had brought all hands to stations and inconvenienced everyone at a critical moment. But somehow it did not seem like Takano's way.

"Yes, Captain-san, Takano is a good man."

"That good man made fools of the entire crew last night," Kondo said stiffly. He underlined his point, placing the flat of his hand deliberately on the rail before him. "I *must* have my ship perform to the utmost limit, Noma-san.

That means a disciplined crew. And a lesson for those who are slow to commands. You know this is no ordinary ship. We cannot afford slackness."

Noma scratched his head. "Yes, Captain-san. Of course you're perfectly correct. I've never sailed any ship like this before."

"No one has, Noma-san."

The *Kogyo-Maru* was a vessel of five thousand tons, a four-engined nexus freighter deliberately rigged to look much older than she was. Her dorsal hull strake had been extended with sliding plex blisters that made her high-charged, and her thrust plates were emphasised with bulky strapping that ran from stem to stern and gave her a ponderous appearance.

But she was not ponderous. Her balance was superb. Her center of gravity was set more forward than the placing of her hull indicated. Beneath the mid-line she was smooth and handsomely swept back, so that she cut through orbital maneuvers like a fast battle cruiser.

The seven beam weapon ports that ran along her side were flush, disguised by integral ray reflection shields and internally opaque at all scanner distances. And behind the ports were powerful pieces of offensive weaponry. She was Admiral Kurita's brainchild, laid down to his specific design, his answer to the Amerikan and Chinese and Korean pirates who were coming increasingly into the systems of the Neutral Zone.

Kondo's thoughts turned to the extraordinary man who was his admiral. Ever since the debacle at Niigata, Kurita had worked hard to erase the stain on his honor, but the indictment of his subordinate had required more than just carefully chosen words. So while Kondo had languished in confinement, Kurita had used his connections in Kyoto to petition Prince Sekigahara, the Emperor's brother.

Unhesitatingly the prince had secured a command for Kurita, whom he respected both as an admiral and as a man. Kurita had been placed under Baron Harumi, to lead a squadron of ships against the Chinese, and at Hainan Kurita had repaid the imperial trust that had been vested in him. He had triumphed and had returned covered in glory, yet even in the midst of his victory, when another might have basked in the praise of his Emperor and set his sights on higher things, he had not forgotten the disgraced Kondo.

During the long months awaiting his appearance before the tribunal on Edo, Kondo had been a broken man, his career shattered into a million shards, his status as a samurai hanging by a silk thread, but Kurita's evidence had been irrefutable, his support magnificent. Kondo recalled the day he had swept into the court wearing the sash of the Order of the Chrysanthemum to speak on his behalf. His bearing and humility before the *bakufu* daimyos had dazzled the judges. They had acquitted him, and Kondo remembered how he had burst euphorically from the courtroom, blemishless once more, uttering a catechism of thanks to the gods who protect star travelers, and slamming his forehead into the dust at the feet of the admiral.

But the day after, Kondo had discovered that he was no longer vicc-admiral of the Yamato Guard. Despite the verdict there was to be no reinstatement, no pension, and not a single word of explanation. He had been discharged from the Emperor's service, without honor and without a future.

He had wandered the Home Worlds like a Buddhist soul in purgatory until the admiral's agents had come upon him one night in a pleasure house in Yakiyama, insisting that he follow them to the apron at Kure. He had been astoundingly drunk, spent out on despairing carousals and cheap *sake*, vulgarly rude and sword-happy. He had rejected them, *ronin* style, but they had ducked him in the mama-san's ornamental carp pond until he became reasonable, and had taken him red-eyed to a secret meeting.

He had been incredulous when Kurita had shown him the *Kogyo-Maru* in her secret hangar. He had been utterly astonished when Kurita had assigned command of her to him. "You'll master her, Izumi-san," he had said with dark humor as they stood under the gilded chrysanthemum figured into the ship's nose. "I want a man who's hungry for the task and you're the hungriest man in Yamato. You'll take her with the next aurium fleet to the Neutral Zone and you'll seek out the Amerikan pirates. To those *gaijin* curs the *Kogyo-Maru* will seem the perfect victim. To their eyes she'll be an old and fat freighter, holds stuffed with a dense aurium cargo, massy, wallowing helplessly, hogbacked, without speed and lightly armed. And the scum will be drawn to her like rats to a *shoben* sluice. But look at this!"

Yes, Kondo thought now, remembering how Kurita had kept faith. The daimyo's condemnation on Sado might easily have cut my topknot, not to say my belly, had it not been for the admiral. I owe him my life. He's given me a chance to redeem my honor, to prove that I'm neither incompetent nor a coward. May the gods help me do my utmost to repay the trust of a great admiral.

His thoughts were brought swiftly back to the present by the urgent beating to quarters over the comms channel. Crewmen were swarming to their stations, but below he saw the cadet whom Noma had sent after Takano. He was cupping his mouth and shouting back at them excitedly.

Kondo felt his hopes surge. Then he too saw it on the screen.

At first he could not be sure, then his eye latched onto the gray speck. "Make a signal to the *Musashi,*" he told the ensign at his side. "Unknown ship bearing: azimuth red one-four-one; range: two-one-oh-five-decimal-four *ri*."

The ensign spoke into his pickup, transmitting the signal, and drew a fast response from the *Musashi*. Kondo exulted at the message: *plan cherry blossom*.

Here, in the outskirts of the Vega system, interplanetary space was a clean, fathomless black. Low gas and dust levels made it easier to maneuver without abrading the ship with millions of submicroscopic particles and vestigial gas pockets that taxed the shields and dissipated energy. Here was the chance to sully its transparent beauty with Amerikan wreckage. This place where the ether was infinitely clear and frigid was surely a most fitting place to settle the blasted hulk of a General Dynamics ship. He would send its arrogant remains into an endless hyperbolic orbit, plummeting forever into the cold blackness that lay between the stars. May the gods grant that she's Amerikan, he prayed. Kondo unsheathed his ancestral sword and closed his right hand upon the corded fish-skin grip.

"By the gods, the Emperor, and Yamato!" he said solemnly as he raised it above his head, once for each article of his faith. All over the ship, his officers did likewise.

Look at her, sniffing at us like a prowling shark. Come on, *same*, let's see your teeth!

Think like Miyamoto Musashi, the Sword Saint. Think as the warrior you are, Izumi-san . . .

She can't be a Yamato ship. If she was a smuggler, she'd be shy of us because of the fines Edo would impose as soon as she was identified. Nor can she be a regular freighter—nobody jumps nexus points in the Neutral Zone without being part of a convoy these days. She can't be Chinese, not here. So . . .

What else?

Only an Amerikan would be working up towards home this far out, ignorant of the newly made nexus points at Matsui and Taiseiyo Tokai, unaware of the great chain that could carry a ship towards the Boundary. So . . .

Hai!

My prayers are answered! She is an Amerikan ship! Probably loaded with thieves' booty, and no doubt red-handed with the blood of Yamato settlers. Is she from one of the Kalifornias? Too far to tell yet. Either way they're pirates. Either way they'll pay for their crimes now with their lives!

"Ready starboard shields," he ordered tersely.

As the ship on the scanner steadily resolved itself into a three-engined trader-warship looking like a hammerhead shark, a long aerial was extended along the *Kogyo-Maru*'s lateral line, generating confusing signals, the images of a near-critical engine failure.

It was a deception the crew had practiced often, and at which they were smoothly skilled.

Hidden from the enemy by the ship's ailing signals and sunk in the drone of false noise, the real power of the ship was waiting to spring upon the pirates. Already, Kondo felt the *Kogyo-Maru*'s acceleration falling off. The compensators groaned and creaked, complaining at the extra resistance. The shields flamed at the bows and he felt the slight pebbling as they passed through Trojan-point debris. Moments later he looked to see how much the remainder of the *kin kaigun* had pulled away. The *Kogyo-Maru* was gradually falling back. A wounded animal limping after its herd.

"Let the engine failure commence!" he shouted to the men on the consoles.

The compensators suddenly juddered as their pent-up energy was released. The effect was spectacular. It was as if the upper port engine had blown out. It was as if it had overheated furiously, then failed, and drones were sent edging along the maintenance wells as if to begin stripping it down.

Kondo watched the prowler carefully for a reaction. She seemed to edge a point or two closer. Yes, you barbarous pigs, come closer. You see our one balanced engine straining to give us one gee and you imagine we're bursting our hearts to get away from the shark!

"Run out emergency booster motors and rig for close order maneuver."

Noma passed on the order urgently to the officers of the watch, knowing that the frantic activity inside the ship as the drones tried desperately to repair the defective engine would be scanned by the stranger and interpreted as a bid to outrun them. He ordered more men aft to increase the illusion of panic. The other ships of the *kin kaigun,* now strung out half a million miles ahead and to starboard, were also accelerating. Steadily they began to pull away. Escaping. Abandoning their weakest to the predator.

Still the lone nexus ship approached, on an interception course, with no sign of her slackening. Her hull was stealthed out in a blanket of radio black so that the ship was hardly visible. No call sign or corporate device could be made out in her muted emanations. Nor was there any identification jack on her hull. That *proved* she was a pirate.

Kondo watched the ship grow larger. As she came closer, her aspect changed, she showed her hull in UV and visible wavelengths, and he realized that the pirate planned to cross her bows and capture her with grapple fields. Then he'll come round abaft and run with us, stealing up on us with his better maneuverability. That's when the ultimatum'll come, he told himself savagely. And that's when they'll see they've cornered not a lamb, but a lion!

As the marauder came to within two thousand kilometers, Kondo's high-penetration scanners began to resolve the men aboard. They were heavily armed, he saw, and five boarding parties were crammed into the central deck airlocks. He expected the forward-firing beam weapons to loose a ray across their bows soon, and to hear the hated order to surrender on all hailing frequencies. Only then would he respond.

He turned to the ensign. "Are the drones clear of the wells?"

"Yes, Captain."

"Are you ready to cut free?"

"There's a man at the bulkhead, Captain."

"Let go the instant I command."

Below the bridge, on the orlop, fourteen beam weapons were being manned behind the reflective screen-proof layer. Harmless holos of cowering passengers were being broadcast in their place. All the guns were small antipersonnel lasers. Their blisters were masked by two long holos of deck activity, wonderfully real like a ship's interior and indistinguishable. Kondo knew that the numbers of men he had sent up and down the ship would have been enough to give the impression that the *Kogyo-Maru* was commanded by an inexpert captain. The apparent chaos of her decks was carefully rehearsed.

Two shots from the pirate's forward beam weapons crackled out, pluming the airwaves with pink noise as they seared into the weakened shields. The accuracy of the beams impressed Kondo and he saw Noma look away from him wordlessly. He knew that the man thought him reckless, and his tactics overly flamboyant, but for all his skill in ship-handling Noma was at heart a shrinker from action. He could scent caution about the man like a bad smell. He thought of the Sword Saint's words: "In the Way of Strategy, those who study as warriors think that whatever they understand in their craft is the Void. This is not the true Void."

As the two enemy beams fed energy into the shield, it tested the hardness of the fields. Instead of remaining rigid, it began to deform, bending inward at the bows. The shield was soft and flaccid. Within a few minutes it could be penetrated and the shriveling energy of the beam brought to bear on the plex hull itself. The plex would stand up to it, but the silvery liquid crystal motes suspended in the plex, the motes that allowed the hull to change color and reflectivity, would begin to burn and the plex would either "fail black" and heat up in a huge white-hot patch, or worse, "fail clear" and permit the beam to go straight through.

The hands in the *Kogyo-Maru*'s nose began to panic as the other vessel bore down on them. It looked certain that the beam would intensify as the ship closed, the shield would continue to buckle, and a hull contact would be made. Some men scattered, others shook their fists defiantly. Then, at the last moment, Noma ordered the single engine cut to bring their acceleration to a dead zero.

The beams stopped.

"Close down shields!"

The *Kogyo-Maru* broached. Waited, shield naked and apparently helpless. The pirate flashed across their bows, beam-sighting laser after beam-sighting laser drawing patterns on their hull, frighteningly close. Every detail of her threatened under bright arcs as she circled. The gleaming muzzles of her armaments were twitching and she could easily have loosed off a staggering blast that would have fried the inside of the *Kogyo-Maru* instantly.

The sweat stood out on Noma's hairless head. He stared at Kondo, disbelief in his eyes.

"Cut compensators!"

"Captain-san! What are you thinking? Can't you see they have us at their mercy?"

"Cut compensators, damn you! And prepare to open all channels."

"Captain-san, please!"

But Kondo's attention was riveted on the pirate. Slowly she came around so that the ships were abeam, separated by no more than a quarter of a mile.

"Closer, you bastard! Closer!"

Noma's complaint was doubled. "Captain-san! Order the firing, I beg you! Before they come astern!"

Kondo's eyes were unseeing. His ears unhearing. The pirate was so close, undoubtedly coming astern—just as he had gambled.

"Captain-san!" Noma's voice was hoarse. He grabbed Kondo's arm, but he threw him off.

"Order our weapons to fire before it's too late! Please, Captain-san!"

"*Enough!*"

Then the critical moment ended as their target passed out of the arc of fire.

In the monitors he could see the arcs glinting on their helmets and gloved fingers, see their ears, the enemy's faces burned dark but originally fair. No Mongoloids these, but Caucasian peoples. Of the three figures on the bridge none was dressed in clothes fit for a captain, but the foremost wore a dark blue cross-belted coat trimmed with white piping and a broad white collar that stood open under his golden beard. The man's lieutenant hailed from the other ship as she came about; the guttural order was sharp and uncompromising, delivered in bad Japanese.

"What ship is that? What ship is that? What ship is that? Identify yourself."

Kondo replied immediately, his voice strong despite the tension in his belly. "*The Princess Nukuda,*" he lied, "rare earth trader, out of Shikoku. I am Captain Murano Shiro, carrying the daimyo of Bizen to Osaka under the protection of His Imperial Majesty, the Emperor of Yamato. Whom have I the honor to address?"

Two small beam weapons down among the engines and a pair of *yubi*—swivel guns—mounted high on the tail were all that the *Kogyo-Maru* could train on the pirate now. In the terrifying silence the surge of low-level static in the comms channel filled the bridge. The rest of the *kin kaigun* had passed beyond full-resolution scanner range, and there was suddenly the immense oppression of being alone and friendless in the wilderness of space.

Inch by inch, it seemed, the other nexus ship moved across their stern and came round so that her beakhead lay a few hundred yards off their starboard quarter.

"Captain-san, stand off from them. They'll see the holos for what they are and realise we're fooling them," Noma warned. "The animation will begin to loop and they'll see it repeat!"

"They're not close enough." Kondo gripped his courage in both fists.

"Look! They suspect something!"

Kondo wheeled on him, hissing, "That's no naval ship. They're pirates! Greedy bandits who live on what they can catch. They want to take us, not destroy us."

"What if they open fire and fry us?"

"They want to take us as prize!" Kondo's voice raged at his subordinate. "Damn you to the nine hells! Where's your spirit, *hinin?*"

Noma was suddenly sobered by the insult. He seemed to realise that his cautiousness had been seen as cowardice, and his jaw jutted. "I'm only thinking of the ship, Captain-san."

"Don't think. Just do as I tell you."

Kondo's mind tried to bury the distraction. His heart hammered and his *bushi* spirit soared as he tried to bury the knowledge that the moment he had dreamed about had come upon him. Soon he would know whether he could afford the reckless luxury of sitting shieldless at point-blank range. And soon he would discover how the *Kogyo-Maru* and her crew would behave in their first real action.

"Come to me," he whispered through gritted teeth.

Simulated beam weapons stood visibly unattended in their transparent blisters, but under the holos, out of sight of the enemy, real gunners were poised at real beam weapons. Kondo watched the pirate ship drift inexorably into position with the smooth motion of an automatic tea house shoji. Her captain would want to put her in the most threatening place he could—abeam as close as possible, so that all his larboard guns were trained on the victim's waist. A pirate would trust to no code of honor. To him, the Covenant of Shipping would mean nothing; he would want to come alongside and secure umbilicus tubes and send boarding parties thundering into the *Kogyo-Maru* to disarm all opposition before he came himself. To do so he would have to get into bed beside the *Kogyo-Maru*—naked.

Kondo heard indistinct orders being shouted aboard the pirate as the sound detectors listened in. What language was that? He saw that the chief of the rabble, the great gold-bearded brute, was so sure of himself he had scorned helmet and fighting gear. When the man put his hands to his mouth, the same arrogant gruff hail rang out across the comms channel, again in pidgin Japanese. "Order your people to put down their weapons and assemble in the aft mess, lying on the floor with their hands raised, Captain Murano. We're coming aboard. If you resist we'll fry you all."

Yes! The swagger! The temerity! The unmistakable insouciance of the man. They were English scum, the same that had almost closed up the spaceway into Europa through the Baltic chain.

Kondo raised his hand. He closed one eye, and with his thumb he mentally obliterated the mocking figure as he would a dung fly on a windowpane. Down below, at the head of the gun deck, the gunnery captain raised his hand also, and when Kondo brought his arm sharply down, the other did the same.

There was just enough time for the pirate to realise that it was not a sign of acknowledgement but an order to fire. Seven head-bursting explosions of light tore across the vacuum between the ships. The *Kogyo-Maru* shook under his footing and heeled as the energy hammered from her cells. Momentarily the hull of the pirate was obscured by an intense aura of brilliance over which her bridge and tail fin thrust like the head and tail of some monstrous dragon, then the plex snapped into transparency—a fail-clear!

As the light play began to die, Kondo steeled himself against the reply, but none came. Furious shouts on the talkback told him that his gun crews were ready. Then his heart leapt as he saw the devastation they had wrought. The pirate's gun deck had been burned away. Instead of five airlocks along the side of the ship, packed with boarders, the whole of her side between channel wale and lateral line had been turned into a smoldering mass. The load-bearing members of her frame were like the rib cage of a blasted corpse, arclight spilling across the debris from above where human fragments and the wrecks of gun mounts and umbilical tubes lay hideously mingled. Atmosphere swirled from the airlock doors, and a shout from his own deck told him that the pirate's power cells were cracking and splintering, their protective coverings burned away.

Before the light echoes of the blast died in their eyes, his own boarding crews had begun screaming like berserkers. Transformed, they jetted from the airlocks, armed and lusting for the fight. A fourfold grapnel field was flung towards the enemy, binding the stricken ship in a powerful tractor lobe. Teams of men on fore hull and tail were cutting into their victim with meson projectors, others trying to blitz their way inside the burned-out airlocks as the charred corpses drifted out.

Kondo was suddenly filled with the sweet knowledge that whatever happened now he had carried the day. He turned to his men and raised his naked blade, shouting, "*Banzai!* For the Emperor and Yamato!"

A tremendous wail of answering war cries went up across the talkback, and the assault began.

Umbilicus tubes with special adhesive termini and meson ring cutters were slammed across from lateral line to lateral line, and men poured across them, seething out like ancient warriors, *katana* clamped in their fists. The cracks of blasters could be heard, and the pirate rabble were smashed back before they had time to regain their senses. Then the *Kogyo-Maru*'s samurai were bursting across the interior, hacking and slashing, until the transparent belly was awash with blood and strewn with convulsing bodies.

Some of the pirates bolted through unsealed bulkheads, others found themselves cornered and leapt from intact airlocks into space, and still others swarmed into the nose, prepared to make a stand or crying pitifully for mercy. Kondo himself crossed with the second wave, cutting his way into the enemy's bridge, towards a looked-for duel with her captain.

But he was too late. The man was dead, a lifeless mass of gray entrail looped out beside him, his lower jaw blasted off bloodily, and his shaggy blond beard with it, now raised aloft as trophy by a delighted samurai.

Kondo saw that battle had become rout; it was, he knew, the point when, if left unchecked, desperate courage soured to fanatical savagery. He cut it short, watching which of his men came down latest to his order. Such men, he knew, were always the cowards, the least obedient, those with the brittlest minds, men who needed most watching, and whom he would be rid of as soon as he could. He sent them off the smoldering ruin, back aboard *Kogyo-Maru,* and the rest speedily into the cargo bays, to search out captives and whatever booty should be discovered before the gutted vessel lost its atmosphere.

42

In his magnificent cabin aboard the *Musashi,* Admiral Kurita laid aside his log feeling hugely gratified. Kondo had carried out his orders to the letter and demonstrated the power of the *Kogyo-Maru* to lure sea thieves to their deaths. The single-minded courage of her captain had been quite superb. Kurita felt certain that had he given the task to any other subordinate, the execution would have lacked that particular edge of daring that was Kondo Izumi's gift of rebirth. It's true, he thought, congratulating himself. The plucking of Kondo from disgrace had been a masterstroke, and of course he had performed his duties with that special eagerness encouraged by his difficult position. In another's hands the *Kogyo-Maru* might have proved less than worthy, but the unfortunate pirate had met a man for whom there could be no release from torment, except through death or glory. Certainly the value of a man so fortified by the spirit of *bushido* was impossible to overestimate.

Kurita was about to open his cabin door when he saw the silken robe woven with the subdued steel-gray barred-spiral device of the *kempei,* and immediately his pleasurable thoughts abated.

"Admiral-san," the *kannushi* priest said, his voice rising questioningly. "If I might please beg a moment of your time."

He was *metsuke* Fukuda Ikku, a man of bird-like frailty whose skull-like face was pinched and unsmiling. About the ship and on the bridge and in the sight of the men, he habitually wore the hood of his office and carried the *o-gohei,* but in private quarters there was only the pious shaven head shining like a jaundiced moon. The *o-gohei,* a stick carried like a short inverted spade but with four flagged plates cascading down from either side of the blade, was once simply the *gohei,* the Shinto symbol of divinity, but when dignified with the honorific "*o*"—"great"—it became much more. It was the rod of power and authority presented to *metsuke,* the inspectors general of the cultural police, the *kempei.* These powerful men were appointed by the *toshiyori,* the five elders who did the Emperor's bidding, but acted independently of the general staff. Their function was "to conduct surveillance of vassals, great and small, to report to government on infractions, deviation, and subversion, and to maintain cultural integrity within Yamato and all the territories of the Empire."

Fukuda had come aboard with an Imperial rock melon, the symbol of the Emperor's personal gratitude, and he had brought with him a terminal full of imperatives. He had been appointed to carry his mission into the Co-prosperity Sphere, for the glory of Yamato, to safeguard men's spirits and the Way, in the Emperor's newly gained systems across the Zero Degree Boundary. Kurita knew his reputation and hated the cleric with such detestation it was hard for him to reply civilly, but he managed to make his voice coolly formal. "*Ohayo gozaimasu.* All is well with you, I trust? Please, come in."

"*Ohayo.*"

The admiral's cabin was luxuriously appointed. All the stern accommodation aboard the twelve-thousand-ton flagship was fit for the highest-ranking officers of the Empire, for their families and their extensive staffs. Every effort had been expended to see that the greatest convenience was provided for. In a voyage that would last two months, and which might be intolerably crude or confining to an aristocratic state official, a premium had been placed upon comfort. They dined using the best real porcelain and pairs of real bamboo *hashi*. *Sake* was liberal and of the best quality. Real wood embellished the quarter galleries and private *cha-no-yu* chambers. Real first-grade handmade tatamis and actual cedar and rice paper wall fittings gave the illusion of a Kyoto villa, their shoji sliding open to reveal mural holos of breathtaking seascapes or contemplative gardens. And because the officials who ventured across the nexi on the Emperor's errands and the *kannushi* of the Imperial Court were notoriously unused to the sensations of transit, the futons were triple thickness and expensively appointed with silken quilts stuffed with down plucked from the breasts of year-old geese. Even so, Fukuda Ikku and his coterie of zealots had strayed from their quarters repeatedly, to accost the crew and interfere with the working of the ship.

Kurita went down on one knee and bowed, his twin scabbarded swords jutting back from the left side of his sash, cutting edge upward, as tradition demanded.

Uninvited, Fukuda Ikku folded his legs under him, kneeling in the admiral's place, raising his fingers to decline a shallow receptacle of *sake*. "The barbarians: how many are there?"

"Twenty-one."

"Why have you had them brought on board your ship?"

Kurita politely put his knuckle to his lips and coughed, trying to conceal his resentment at being examined. Fukuda was exceptionally skilled at asking questions. He obviously relished the sense of power it gave him. It's the same with all physically weak men, Kurita thought with sudden penetration. Don't they always try to compensate for their lack of stature or girth in other ways? And isn't it the sexually constrained who are the worst? Have you ever in your sixty years had a woman? he asked the old man silently, watching his soulless eyes search everywhere but his own. Never! And if you had, how would you have performed? I can see you as the novice you were forty years ago, white-faced and straining to shoot your seed into the belly of some seminary whore. It was overzealous offal like you who drove the Emperor's son mad with your excesses and started the trouble on Kyoto. Filthy-minded priests twisted tight with lust and perversion. Wasn't that the truth of it, for all their piety? Down on the raw floorboards, or in the dust, copulating under the Emperor's all-seeing eye. Peevishly surrendering to your animal lust and taking a peasant woman by force. Ah, I'd give plenty to know how you performed when your spirit craved the flesh! Was it the head priest's slavering mouth? Or the anuses of prostitute boys from the local pleasure house? Or perhaps you were the victim—the buggered runt of the seminary? That would explain the serpent of hate which writhes in your hollow chest. There are many ways a man dies inside—what was it that snuffed out your spirit?

"These prisoners are my responsibility," he said, keeping his voice neutral. "They are Europan pirates, and the laws of Earth Central and the Code both require that I execute them for entering what is now Yamato."

"Ah! Thank you, Admiral, but I asked you why they're on board the *Musashi*. Why were they brought from the *Kogyo-Maru?*"

"Since it is by my authority that they will be executed, it is only proper that they be brought before me. I shall explain to them their crimes so they may understand them before they die."

Kurita made a final gesture that should have stopped further inquiry, but Fukuda Ikku seemed suddenly alerted. He tried another attack.

"Of course, they are worthless individuals who have surrendered, but they have a purpose. Is it not your duty to make their deaths shout an example to your men? Are you not familiar with the precepts of *bushido?*"

"I know my duty, Fukuda-san. And my understanding of *bushido* is my own affair." He regretted that as soon as the words had left his lips.

The *metsuke*'s eyes traveled slowly to his. "No, Admiral-san. Your understanding of *bushido* is my concern also."

Kurita felt the muscles of his stomach knotting. He tried to deny it to himself, but realised that he was experiencing something he had not felt since he was a young man—a spasm of cold-blooded fear.

"The beheadings will be witnessed by the men, Fukuda-san," he said guardedly.

"It has, quite naturally, occurred to you to execute them as a warning to others, but—please correct me—you will kill them for *piracy?* That's an example to no one. Unless you suspect that there are those among your crew who are liable to turn pirate themselves."

Anger rose in Kurita. "The crew of the *Musashi*—all my crews—are loyal to the last man!"

The other smiled insipidly. "Ah! Your obligation to them is such a marvelous example. It is good that a samurai has faith in his subordinates. But you miss my point, for there is a much more glorious example to be made, a greater loyalty to be tested—to a principle much higher than obedience to the Emperor's statutes."

Kurita's fists had bunched and he carefully relaxed them. He had divined the direction in which the priest's octopus words were leading, but he knew he had to oppose Fukuda Ikku, to show him that here, in space, the admiral must be absolute master. Still, the strangling tentacles of the Shinto *kempei* were many. He must contain his impulses. It was madness, he knew, to gratuitously make an enemy of one of the *kempei*'s most exalted and ruthless instruments.

"Do you not agree?" Fukuda Ikku was asking. "Do you not hope, as I do, to inculcate some understanding of the Way in all men, however worthless, before they die?"

Kurita bowed his head humbly, feeling nothing but disgust and revulsion inside. "Within *bushido* alone have I lived my life. The Way is sacred to me."

Fukuda Ikku's words sharpened as he felt the resistance in Kurita. "I ask you: shall we behead pirates as common criminals?"

"That is the law."

"The law. And what of the Emperor's edict? That law says that barbarians shall die by crucifixion."

Kurita felt the grip of the octopus tighten about his throat. With an effort he raised his head. "It is a matter of practicality. We cannot properly crucify men aboard a nexus ship, but we can behead them. Unless you would have me carry them all the way to Sado?"

"You are a warrior commander, Kurita-san. You think like a man of action." The priest's smile lingered, then suddenly his aspect changed and his tone grew subtle. "I've heard reports of your gallantry in the great battle against the Chinese. Did you not command a squadron bearing the *mon* of Prince Sekigahara? And was it not your own vessel that carried the banners of the Heavenly Throne from Lui Te-shan's vessel? They say it was ripped and urinated on by their officers when they were ordered to do so by the prince. Defiled until its vile symbol was made invisible. What men will allow defeat and then do that? Only non-men. Because we secured victory, the chrysanthemum standard, emblazoned with the symbol of our Emperor, suffered no blemish, not a sword in the whole fleet was broken, not a single *sangokujin* entered any Yamato vessel. When men act honorably and according to the will of the gods, they are protected and favored. Are they not?"

Kurita stared into the bloody dregs of his wine, despising the priest even more as he remembered the horrifying truth of Hainan. The Chinese had been a fearsome enemy: when they took the planet of Hainan, they had skinned the Yamato garrison commander alive, stuffed his skin with excrement, and sent it as a trophy to Peking, and when news of the outrage had reached Kyoto, the Emperor had been persuaded to act. The Yamato fleet had surprised the Chinese in orbit, surprised them utterly.

With the enemy unprepared and in confusion, the battle had been over in half a day. The Chinese Blue Dragon and Red Lion squadrons were smashed and routed. The remains of the Golden Palace squadron, under Admiral Cao Yung, had struggled away—a mere thirty ships, badly mauled, seeking the chains of Zhanjiang, or falling crippled into the huge green oceans of the reconquered planet. On Hainan's main island fortress, dusk had decayed that day over a scene of absolute devastation; the sick sea for miles around had been stained with blood and strewn with the broken bodies of crashed ships, and of men. And through it all the shuttles and air-cars of fanatical Shinto priests had plied with sword and blaster, personally chopping down the surviving enemy. When night settled, the ghastly flare of the citadel's burning had continued to illuminate the carnage, sending tongues of flame towards the sky so that the work of the gods could go on.

Kurita felt the tensions within him polarise. Maybe the priest's right, he thought with dread. Maybe my belief is failing. He knew suddenly why men clung to the Way, for without the Way the world was too terrible to contemplate, a chaos of evil, a catalog of inexplicable atrocities. He remembered how his own victorious ships had made for the Weizhou Dao system, where he, along with the other admirals, had received the grateful thanks of Prince Sekigahara. The ceremony of victory had been celebrated there by the officers of the *kempei*, under a magnificent pavilion bedecked by the purple blooms of almond trees and accompanied by the thundering of giant battle drums and the chanting of Confucian monks, and at the word of the prince each ship of the fleet had fired a salute that lit up the sky brighter than daylight. They had lost seventy thousand men and more than twice that number sullied by wounds; the Chinese had lost two hundred fifty thousand.

Fukuda Ikku's voice came to him, insistent and cold. "The purpose of the execution of barbarians is not to dignify the condemned, but to put fear into those who are witnesses."

"Excuse me, Fukuda-san, but I will have no crucifixions on board my ship," Kurita said, rising to his feet. His words were hard and final. He had made his decision. The next move was the priest's.

The *metsuke* regarded him silently for a moment, then gathering his robes he rocked back on his heels and stood up.

"I shall pray that you see fit to alter your resolve."

He went to the cabin door and without turning back left the admiral alone with his choice.

The next day a compromise was agreed.

And the priest was allowed to address them, holding out before him a great scroll with golden stoppers and great tassels, and it seemed to the admiral that Fukuda Ikku's eyes never once strayed to the parchment, but roamed thirstily over the faces of those upon whom he broadcast his words.

"Hear me, now, men of the Way, samurai and priests, officers of state and of His Imperial Majesty's ships, technicians and soldiers, men of every condition, quality, and degree, whose attention to this will result in the purification of your minds."

The *Musashi*'s assembly area was formally hung with silken banners, and all the secular splendor of state was displayed for the occasion. The entire complement of the *Musashi* was paraded below. Five hundred men knelt in rank and file in their color-coded coveralls, the samurai of the first class, and behind, those of the second. Above them were fifty more in ascending rank, seated on collapsible stools along the quarterdeck, and above them all Kurita, the admiral. Five captains from the fleet's other ships flanked him, including Kondo and the *Musashi*'s captain, Takashi. Then came the commander of assault troops, with his lieutenants at his side and a line of fully armored soldiers. The ship's lesser officers dressed the rostrum, the astrogators, the engineers, and, ranked behind, the gunners and surgeon. Even the merchants and other passengers and the Emperor's revenue officers with whom they dealt were assembled. Last came the scientists, the Dover chefs, and the cadets.

Fukuda Ikku's voice grew incisive. "You are hereby warned to declare and manifest the things you have seen and heard of any person or persons, alive or dead, who have defamed or acted against the Way; or who have cultivated or observed the filthy laws of the barbarians or of the *sengokujin;* or who have perpetrated any crime of cultural impurity. Do you know any who say that the Emperor is not the true descendant of Amaterasu? Or the true Son of Heaven? Have you heard any man or woman deny that? Deny the purity of *bushido?* Say that the Way of the Warrior is not virtuous? Or that the shrines of Shinto, wherever they may be, are not holy and inviolate? Or who say or affirm scandalous libels against the sacred office of the *kempei* or its officers? Or who assert that the Three Imperial Treasures—the Jewel of the Moon, the Mirror of the Sun, or the Sword of Lightning—that the Emperor possesses are not the true relics of Nihon? If you do, then I command you to speak now!"

Twenty *gaijin* prisoners were shackled in a miserable line below the rostrum. One had died of his wounds overnight and had been dispatched through the toxic-waste chutes before news of the death could be communicated to the *metsuke*. Facing the English-speaking barbarians now were the Emperor's own officers. There could be no denying the visible authority of these men: Fukuda Ikku, their chief with his purple robes; Hishikari Noburo, his studious companion who carried the *o-gohei*. It was he who had spent years examining and censoring the library of the Imperial Court itself, excising unwholesome histories that did not accord with the New Truth. Kurita knew that Hishikari's obsession with *sangokujin* heredity was total; he prayed that neither Kondo nor any man would be foolish enough to admit that their ancestry was tainted with Korean blood. Beside Hishikari sat Suzuki Tokuji, and to his left Wada Zengo, the recorders. Both were cowled and sinister.

Kurita boiled with indignation. He had made a compromise, but he had not given permission for this. Fukuda Ikku had agreed to the beheading, and in return for that concession he had asked to deliver his sermon, to address the men on the evils of impurity. Surely the admiral could not deny the sacred office that small thing? Even an admiral who regarded the common laws above the wishes of the Emperor? Kurita had let the insult pass. Fukuda Ikku might be beneath contempt, but he was also above the law.

Kurita watched the proceedings with an immobile face, unwilling still to focus the malign spite of Fukuda Ikku's fanaticism on himself or his officers. That much he knew was expedient. But doubt raged in the private quarters of his mind. One part of him wanted to put an end to the priest, the other part was sure he was giving in to weakness. Men must be punished for what they do, not for what they are, he told himself, and he replied, equally angrily, that surely what men did *made* them what they were.

No one moved, and Fukuda Ikku lowered his scroll a little, growing more intimate with them, his gaze dwelling in turn on the officers and merchants.

"And if anyone here knows of any person being children or grandchildren of a barbarian already condemned by this office, let him come forward. For those vile offspring are disqualified and may not make use of any office, or bear arms, or wear silk or fine cloth, or ornament themselves with silver or gold, stones or pearls.

"And is there a man here who knows of any once-condemned person who now possesses confiscated or forbidden goods? Furniture or apparel, jewels or credit? If so, come forward!"

This is outrageous! Kurita thought, suddenly awake to what was happening. The *metsuke* was delivering no sermon, he was conducting an exercise in terror. But still Kurita dared not move to intervene.

Now Fukuda Ikku leaned back, angry with them. His shrill voice blasted them with threats now, rushing like a torrent.

"If you have knowledge and, after the period of amnesty, will not speak and still hold your spirit obdurately, know that it is greatly to the burden and prejudice of your family. You shall have incurred the sentence of exile and exposure, and you shall be proceeded against as an abettor of impurity. You shall be denounced, denied *seppuku,* separated from the Empire and its colonies, cursed by all, and spat upon by *hinin*. And upon your heads, and upon the honor of your families, and the memory of your ancestors, shall be loosed the corrections that befall all who deny the Way.

"Loathsome is the man who abjures the Way! May he be afflicted in living and dying, in eating and drinking, in working and sleeping, and may his body suffer pain without respite. May his days be evil and few. May his children be orphaned and his wife and swords be used by *hinin* overseers to dig dung. May his family remain in disgrace and may none help them. May they be turned out into the streets and trampled down to die in want."

Fukuda Ikku stared at them, filled with a terrifying power. He saw the light emanating from his hands and feet, felt the fear in the *kami* that appeared before him. Incense sticks burned, perfuming the air. The *gaijin* were goaded back and forth at his command, dressed only in *fundoshi* loincloths, men and women alike. They were made to kneel down, bound, so that their heads might be shaved. Water was cast over them as the sentence was read. Hishikari's voice rose shrill above the bowed heads before him, terrifying the captives who suffered it uncomprehendingly. Then his hand was thrust out and the *o-gohei* pushed into each face so that each was turned away.

"See how they flinch from the symbol of divinity?" Hishikari demanded.

The *gaijin* stared at one another unable to understand.

"They are without value!"

The incense sticks fumed, the long robes swirled, as the officers of the *kempei* passed now among the crew. Fukuda Ikku raised the *o-gohei* above the crew now, reciting a list of impurities.

"Your admiral will bring his ships into the system of Sado in thirty days. Half that time shall be your period of amnesty. If you know, or have heard of, any Koreans who eat the flesh of dogs or who continue to speak the Banned Language—come forward! Which among you falls short of his duty? Come out! Yes! Which of you has unsatisfactory thoughts? Yes! I promise you will not suffer serious penalty if you admit it now. Step forward! Come out, obediently!"

Kurita remained fixed to his camp stool, mesmerised by the mounting wrath of Fukuda Ikku's oration. He wanted to act but he could not. He knew he must order the *metsuke* to stop, but something powerful smothered his will, making him listen to the insistent words. Below him, the men's mouths dropped open as they contemplated the rapturous questions. Fear warred within their minds but their spirits were captured. Kurita raged inwardly as he watched his crewmen wrestling with the terrible urge to make an admission. Then he felt his hatred rise up and burst the invisible bonds that held his own mind fast.

"Enough!"

"Admit your imperfections! Do not wait for others to denounce your crimes! Confess! And it will be the better for you!"

"Halt! I command you!"

"Confess! I am waiting!"

Fukuda Ikku was deaf to Kurita's words. Blind to his presence. As he swept down the central aisle the *Musashi*'s crewmen ground their foreheads harder into the flooring. He walked, sure of his power now, erect and bigger than he had been, hands opened before him menacingly until he was beside the airlock. The ecstasy flowed in him unstoppably as he approached the climax of his work.

That morning he had ordered twenty-one steel crosses made. He had suggested the craftsman could hang the crosses in the main egress airlock and cover the airlock port with a silk banner as part of the formal dressing to conceal what he had done.

Ah, yes! Look how they revere the Spirit of the Way, the familiar voice said inside Fukuda Ikku's mind. Their respect does them credit, but who can deny that they are all lost to the Way? Tell them they are to witness the deaths of impure creatures.

He told them.

Tell them they have the chance to show the Emperor how they glory in the destruction of impurity!

He told them.

They are simple men, and simple men are weak, prey to all manner of deviant thoughts. They must be helped to confine themselves to the Way.

He cast boiling water over the English.

"See how they shrink from the Way! See how it eats their flesh!"

He stalked along the line of kneeling prisoners. They began to wail, imploring him for mercy in the vile English tongue, caught up in the horrifying power of the ritual, and as they showed their fear so the samurai who held them increased their grip.

Ah! How their animal spirits cry out to me. But how they fail to understand their shortcomings. It is impossible for a *gaijin* to have worth except by the purifying elements of pain and fear. Though their bodies are tainted clay, we shall purify them with death and return them to the state of dust from which they came!

He threw back the silk covers, revealing the shining crosses within, and the stink of stale airlock air swirled out, making men groan with understanding.

"Only suffering can destroy the stain within men," he shouted.

"Bring the captives! Attend the gas valves!"

The order rang out from the chief maintenance engineer who had been induced to prepare the punishment. Three hands ran to obey.

"*No!*" Kurita grabbed the arm of the first man and threw him back, his face contorted. To allow the captives to be attached to the steel crosses in the airlock and the oxygen partial pressure progressively altered to enhance the agony as the *metsuke* wanted was not something he had agreed to. He had to stand up. Whatever the cost. Whatever the risk. He had to.

"I will not allow it!"

Fukuda Ikku turned on him. "You cannot prevent due punishment."

"This is not what we agreed!" Kurita shouted.

"Stay where you are!" Fukuda Ikku's fingers clawed out. "No man may interfere with the Emperor's will. No man here will allow that!"

Kurita halted, a thousand eyes locked on him. His way was barred by his infantry captain. "Araki! Step aside! I order you! Honjo, you will prepare for a beheading! You there, Sergeant! You will decapitate the prisoners now! Move!"

No one flinched. The men's eyes were riveted on the hem of the *metsuke*'s robe.

"Move, I say! This is mutiny!"

"They will obey only the word of the Emperor! Take him!"

"No!"

For an interminable moment all were frozen in a terrible stalemate. Kurita saw that he had lost. He went for his sword, then the universe crashed sideways and he was carried off his feet.

The ship's deck had canted hard over, sending men toppling down or scrambling for a handhold. Over the talkback, klaxons wailed a priority failure warning as the *Musashi*'s frame quivered. The huge ship jolted, then jolted again, her decks convulsing like an earthquake before she quieted. The symptoms were of an imminent and incapacitating stabiliser fault. Immediately Kurita realised what had happened and he thanked the gods.

In the confusion, Kondo came from the shadows under the main deck arch. He drew his sword and advanced on Araki. "Obey the admiral—or I shall execute you! The rest of you, get to your stations! Now!"

Instantly the confusion of men in the assembly area threw off their doubts and dispersed, driven by the familiarity of orders and suddenly awakened from the terrifying spell that had been cast over them.

Kurita tried to order his thoughts, but his mind raced feverishly. He damned his own foolishness. Incredible how Fukuda Ikku had spellbound everyone with his sorcery! And thank the gods that Kondo had had the strength of mind to get to his terminal on the bridge and call up a training simulation of main stabiliser failure condition one. What a mistake I made! I was disobeyed by my own men. It was mutiny until Kondo slapped them back to their senses. The way the *metsuke* bent them all to his will was truly amazing. I felt it myself. Kurita's spine chilled at the thought. Even the psi-talents were hypnotised by him. But how can I oppose him now? I can't placate him—the affront was too much for him to ignore. How can I stop him?

He seized his panicking thoughts and savagely bent them to the present. At all cost, the initiative Kondo had gained must not be lost.

"We must carry out the beheadings immediately," he told Kondo. "The quicker the better."

He knew his authority depended on it. Fear spurred him, crept into his voice as he fired his orders to Takashi, the *Musashi*'s captain.

Hands were rushing to action stations, unaware as yet that the emergency was only a simulation.

Kurita ordered that the twenty captives be brought to the airlock. The English were hauled to their feet and marshaled quickly into line. Some began to pray, some to struggle, others to defecate.

Kurita searched out Fukuda Ikku. The *metsuke* leaned drunkenly against the bulkhead, his whole body racked with a strange seizure. His eyes were rolled up white and his lips curled back, flecked with foamy spittle. Kurita struggled to understand. It must be the sickness of the Void, he thought, horrified. The same that sometimes afflicts Zen astrogators awakened from their trances after a difficult passage. Then Kurita saw what he must do.

He sent a man to begin the beheadings. Then he steeled himself, seized Fukuda Ikku, and shook him until the pupils of his eyes looked once more on the living world.

"Come to the airlock!" They must die, he thought. "Here! Execute them with your own hand!"

He closed his grip over the priest's fingers and clamped them to the handle that fired the explosive bolts on the egress hatch, holding it there, unmoving, until the executioners were clear.

The inner door sheared shut. Warning lights flashed orange above them. Kurita heard the interlocks impact with a deep, smothered thud, then the gas valves were squealing, super-pressurising the lock, the indicators climbing to maximum.

A computer-generated androgyne voice repeated auditory warnings with enthusiastic urgency. *"Please be careful! Airlock pressure is very high! Please check with your superior now! Please be careful . . ."*

He jammed the priest's palm against the handle, and the outer hatch blew off, and the headless corpses, empty egress suits, helmets, and steel crosses were jerked altogether off the floor and wall pegs and out into the stream of exploding air. They soared up for a sickening moment until their tangled limbs hit the hatch rim and were snapped through.

Kondo watched the twisting bodies tumbling in space, the severed heads like sport balls, then he stared at the vacant eyes of the *metsuke* and knew that the admiral had done his duty excellently. Fukuda Ikku was shaking, the hollow husk of the man who had addressed them minutes before. The admiral had been magnificent: what courage it had taken to stand up to the *metsuke* at that moment!

"Have Captain Takashi see to the airlock personally," Kurita told him, his voice infinitely weary now.

"Yes, Admiral-sama."

"And—thank you, Izumi-kun."

"Honjo, take Fukuda Ikku below and confine him to his cabin. Have the surgeon sedate him."

"Hai!"

Kondo felt his burn of satisfaction fade. He saw that Kurita had pitted himself against an implacable enemy.

"What have we done?" he asked.

Kurita shook his head hopelessly. "We have a *kami* by the tail, Izumi-kun." The suffix "kun," more informal than "san," was customary aboard nexus ships after an emergency; the looseness of it emphasised their differences of rank and celebrated the triumph of the team over whatever had caused the problem.

"Yes."

"I don't know what can be done with him."

"You've locked him in his quarters and had him sedated, sir?"

"Yes. But I can't keep him confined there forever."

"You'll have to, Kurita-sama, at least until we reach Sado."

Kurita wiped his mouth, then he took his hand away and nodded. "Yes, I can do no other. But then what? When we reach Niigata I'll have to release him."

Kondo swallowed hard. He knew well that the *metsuke* would demand revenge for his humiliation. The thought of the impeachment that must greet them when they returned to the Home Worlds turned his bowels to ice. He looked around him at the few men who remained in the assembly area; all were intensely occupied, working furiously at whatever tasks they could find. They had been deeply scared by what they had witnessed.

"Did you see his eyes, Izumi-san?"

"Yes. They were—without life."

"He's mad. You know that?"

"Yes."

The admiral's voice dropped. "Do you know what we must do?"

The terrible thought broke over Kondo like an ocean wave, followed by another, more sinister consideration. He blanched. "You can't mean that. Unless—"

"What are you thinking?"

"I dare not say."

"I order you to tell me what you're thinking."

Kondo clasped his hands together as if in prayer. "I asked myself what we would do if—if we discovered that Fukuda Ikku was *possessed*."

Kurita stared at him, unable to believe his ears. *"What?"*

"What if it could be proved that his mind had been taken over by an evil *kami?*"

"Those are dangerous thoughts, Kondo-kun."

Kondo seized his arm. "Yes. But thoughts that might explain a lot—and perhaps solve much more."

Kurita's eyes widened as he began to understand the implications of Kondo Izumi's words.

"Think of it, Admiral. If an inspector general of the *kempei* was possessed by a demon."

"Ai-eee! That's meddling with unspeakable things. Can you imagine the upheaval that would follow if it were to become known that so exalted a functionary of the Emperor had been possessed by a demon?"

"Precisely."

"You're suggesting I make that *known?*"

"No! That would certainly destroy you." Kondo's face was taut with anxious hope as he pressed his plan. "But as a threat, what better lever can there be to control Fukuda Ikku after he's made planetfall? Tell him that if he wants revenge, the price will be his own exposure. I'll back you. And I'll see to it that other witnesses do likewise. We can easily—manipulate—the ship's log. It's the only way to contain him."

Kurita closed his eyes. When he opened them again, he said, "I agree. I'll put it to him just as you propose. Such a threat might deflect him—it might conceivably save our skins—but it won't contain him. He'll find some other way to slake his thirst for blood. And may the gods help them all on Sado."

SADO

Michie saw the ceremonial water gate and squeezed her father's hand. Her precarious side-saddle seat on the white horse was made even more unstable by the sleekness of her silk kimono, and she almost lost her parasol. The *torii* of Nikko, she knew, had stood here for fifty years, its two huge timber legs as red as crab flesh and rooted in the tidal mud, its crossbar curved up like a sword blade and roofed in grass-green tiles. The ebbing tide of the Great Lake had left an inch of water, making the mud of the inlet a mirror, and the reflection of the *torii* rippled as she watched, delighting her.

Dedicated to the ancient goddess Ama no Uzume, it had been erected shortly after the terraforming of Sado had stabilised, marking the planet as one destined to become part of Yamato. It had stood unchanged since the days of Bashi, the Shinto *kannushi* priest, who had come with the first settlers more than half a century ago. He had dedicated his life to building the Nikko shrine.

The shrine was built from massive timbers, polished cedar walkways jutting above algal green mud that flooded with warm, clear lake water twice a day, and twice a day was a mass of worm casts and lungfish and tiny freshwater crabs with eyes on stalks. Above the shrine complex, tiled roofs glittered like new steel, and within, incense smoke curled up ceaselessly, blackening the rafters. At night, a thousand lanterns would bob and dance in the breeze, and the shattered image of Sado's huge red moon would lie over the water, but now the primary star that acted the role of Sado's sun was almost directly overhead and the shrine was a cool refuge from the brilliance outside. On the land beyond, trellised blooms hung about the cliffs, brilliant climbers garlanded the leathery trees, and aromatic shrubs loaded the air with their perfumes. Nikko, her father had told her, had been built to mirror the ancient flower gardens of Old Japan where for hundreds of years the Japanese people had gathered decorations for their ceremonies.

"Are you nervous, my daughter?" he asked her.

Michie nodded and searched out her father's hand. He was leading her horse, watching for the priests amid the rioting flowers. She looked out also and sighed at the beauty of it. Bright sun had baked the mud to a crust away from the walkway, sending the crabs and lungfish into their burrows, but its rays were kept from her by the bamboo and paper parasol which he held delicately over her shoulder.

On the far side of the neighboring *han,* square rice fields of new green stretched to the foothills of the Kanto-sanchi range; behind them the rocky outcrops were planted now with pines, and small streams cascaded between mossy hummocks. She thought it a fitting landscape and knew that her father had been right to insist on this place, and on a small gathering in the shrine, despite the wishes of her mother.

How her father had shown strength! A quiet resolve, persuasive and encouraging. He had swayed her mother and brought her round to see that this must be the only solution.

Kenji caught her looking at him. His kindly eye strayed to her face and he grunted amiably.

"You have been completely dutiful, Michie-san," he told her proudly.

"Thank you, Father."

"You seem to have no regrets."

"I have none, Father. It is my duty."

She thought of her brother's opposition, but banished it from her mind instantly.

"I hope your mother reminded you about constancy? I'm sure she did. They are her most precious words, treasured up in her head for thirty years. She received them from her own mother's mouth—after it was found that a handsome but foolish young samurai called Hasegawa had begun to find her beauty irresistible. She has been a faithful adherent to those high principles of duty ever since, even though the man she married never deserved such devotion."

Michie protested at her father's modesty, dwelling on the sentiments her mother had passed to her in the quiet of her bedroom the night before.

"My dear little dove," she had said, tears glinting in the corners of her eyes. "The gods know that you are our own flesh and blood, but it is my duty to instruct you as my mother earnestly charged me. Who else will tell you what it is becoming for you to do and what to avoid? Neither must you forget the things your father has told you, since they are all wise and most precious, but there are things no man can tell you. First, take care that your garments are decent and proper, and do not adorn yourself with finery, for that is a mark of folly; remember that a courtesan may be taken for a lady, but never must a lady be taken for a courtesan. When you speak to servants, do not hurry your words from uneasiness, but remain calm and deliberate. And when you walk abroad, do not carry your head overly erect, for that is a sign of ill breeding and shows your people that you do not care for them as you should. Always show a modest countenance; have no shame, nor arrogance; do not paint your face like a *maiko* girl, but that your husband may not dislike you, adorn yourself, bathe and take exercise twice daily." She had drawn closer then, enfolding Michie's hands with her own. "Listen, my daughter: in this life, it is necessary to live with prudence and circumspection. You must treat your husband with respect at all times, then he will respect you. Do not cross him in manly matters, or he will secretly despise you, and when the day comes to ask of him that which you desire, he will spurn you. Beware that in no way should you commit the treason against him called adultery. See that you give no favor to another, for this is to fall into a pit from which there is no escape. According to our law, you shall be thrown into the street and despised by peasants, and the stain will spread to all your family and your nobility and your honor of birth. And remember that even though no man sees you, nor your husband learns, still *the* kami, *who are in every place, see you.* You shall be maimed or struck blind or your body will wither or you will come to extreme poverty for daring to injure your husband.

"My dear daughter, whom I brought into this world, see that you live in peace and tranquillity and contentment all the days of your life. See that you do not disgrace yourself, that you do not stain your honor, nor pollute the luster and fame of your ancestors. And though I remember the day when your husband-to-be first came here and I would not have him enter our house, I now bless you both, so that the gods may prosper you and your marriage."

The grove of trees parted as the horse came round the last bend of the road. She felt a fluttering within her as she heard the chanting of the monks, growing louder as she neared the shrine. What will the daimyo say when he finds that his permission has not been sought? she asked herself. The daimyo's permission was not requested, even though strictly it might be expected in so complicated a case. Katsumi had not taken the announcement well, nor after that the oath his father had demanded of him. Kenji had announced his final decision after careful thought and expected his son to render him the filial duty he owed by swearing to treat Duval as a racial Japanese.

"But this will not reflect well on the family, Father."

"Nevertheless, that is my choice. Swear."

"I cannot swear to acknowledge him as I would a samurai husband. The shame is too great for me!"

"I am your father, and you will do as you are told!"

"I also have a duty to Nishima-sama. A higher duty."

"You will do as I say! Swear to me that you will acknowledge him as 'adopted husband.' "

"I cannot!"

So it had gone round and round. Everybody knew that it was the custom for samurai families to arrange the marriages of their children, and it was the children's duty to accept their parents' choice. In almost all cases, marriages were samurai-samurai, the first rank usually marrying the first rank, and so on. And it was expected that the wife would go to live in the family house of the husband. But not in this marriage. This marriage was very different. Michie was aware that her father's decision was unique.

But then not everyone married normally. Occasionally a rich member of the commercial classes would attempt to marry their sons into samurai families, because the offspring of such a marriage would be samurai, and the samurai family would sometimes agree for money. Although the social status of samurai was paramount and highly prized, their incomes were a fixed proportion of the income of the *han* where they belonged. Often the lower classes, those of technicians, slave-farm owners, and traders, commanded high incomes. Only samurai family heads who dwelled in the impoverished fourth and fifth ranks would consider this option; it was unheard-of for a prosperous *han*-holding family of the upper second rank, such as the house of Hasegawa!

But even so, this was not the basis of the objection Katsumi was making. Even rarer than transclass marriages were the cases of "adopted husbands," when a family took in a man for their daughter. In such a case, the man's surname was erased from his family records as if he had never existed, all his filial duties, or *giri*, were transferred to his wife's family, including his surname, and he was accepted on the same terms that a wife would normally be accepted into her in-laws' home. What had enraged Katsumi was that this practice was carried out by families who had succeeded in raising only daughters and were therefore without heir. The choice of Duval as adopted husband, Michie knew, had been a severe slight to Katsumi.

"The marriage will change his surname," her father had said in conciliation. "He will be one of our clan. And because his personal name is impossible, I have decided that from the marriage day he will be called Zinan—second son."

"Does that make him one of us?" Katsumi had said bitterly. "It's as if you believe that we can all be who we want to be. That we can alter our state at will. That is contrary to all that's sacred in our society, Father."

"What is most sacred is that sons obey their fathers!"

"And everyone the law!"

And that was another consideration. The legality of the marriage was uncertain. There was no specific statute against marriage to a *gaijin*—since Yamato had been effectively closed to outsiders for generations and since nobody would dream of marrying a *gaijin* even if it were possible. There had been no need for such a law. Michie understood that her father had chosen this course because an adopted husband was bound to his wife's father and his business by bounds of *giri* closer than any other tie. Her father was quietly doing his duty to Lord Nishima by advancing the weapon project and at the same time clearing his debt of honor with the man who had saved his life—and hers. He was breaking no specific law, but perhaps there were those who would not approve—Nishima-sama included. Like all daimyos, Nishima-sama was accountable to the *bakufu* in Kyoto, of course, for whatever went on in his domain. He could be replaced at any time, and because of that he had to be careful. But what Nishima-sama did not know about, he could not very well object to. By not informing him, Kenji was doing his duty by protecting him; by swearing Katsumi to accept that plan, he was swearing him to secrecy. But Katsumi had not sworn, nor would he.

A small knot of women were gathered at the door, maids and servants and others wearing kimonos in pastel shades. Beyond them was a group of laborers, who knelt and bowed their heads as she slid carefully from the saddle, staring at the fine silk wedding kimono she wore.

Her head felt hot inside the heavy marriage wig, an object made of real human hair woven into a traditional style, lacquered stiff and stuck with long, decorative pins.

Her father led her on his arm inside the shrine, where light filtered sparingly onto the polished floor with wisps of incense rising. It was cool and clean, austere after the flowers. She looked to her kneeling mother and searched her face, saw that Katsumi was not beside her. Then she was filled with sobriety as she gazed upon the great golden *gohei*. She walked to the front and stood beside the official go-between and before the priests and smelled the incense and tasted the salty sea air in her mouth, and the minutes were strung out like pearls, hardly passing.

The recorder came forward. "On this penultimate day, in the second month of the twenty-third year of the Era of Kanei, in the shrine of Nikko, we receive Hasegawa Michie, daughter of Urawa no Hasegawa Kenji; and Zinan, this son of unknown parents, to be married in accordance with the imperial wedding statute . . ."

Michie repeated the words of the oath with solemnity beside the man who had come into her life and won her and who had taken the Way for her, so he could be her husband. I know that Zinan can truly become like us now, she prayed. May the gods destroy me if I lie, if he lies. And I know he loves me as much as a man ever loved a woman. When my father came to him with thanks for his life after the struggle on the fiery mountain, he offered him his pledge. "What shall I grant you?" he asked. "You have only to name it." I watched him playfully appraise Kenji's favorite horse, and then his long sword; I saw the smile on his lips as he stole a glance at me. He must have seen the look in my face. And then he boldly said, "I ask only permission to marry, for there is a woman I want." And my father, who is a good man, nodded and drew himself up. "One life for another? That is fair and just. But will this one that you desire be an appropriate choice?" Zinan looked to me then, and he said, "Yes, Kenji-san. I can say that." He was right. Whatever he may have done in the past, he is not a *gaijin* now. He truly may become one of us. And I will do my duty by him.

The shrine was completely silent as the vows were asked of them. He promised to protect her and she to serve him, come what may in life and unto death. Zinan, her husband. Michie, his wife. The witnesses were hushed, but into the silence the sounds of air-cars circling closer rose, drowning the official recorder's words as he began to speak again.

"*Kokoni osuwari kudesai* . . ."

He beckoned them forward and they knelt. He placed a band of gold on each successive finger of her heart-side hand, removing it each time, then he slid it finally onto her third finger.

"I, Zinan, give my body to you, Michie, as your loyal husband."

"I receive it. I, Michie, give my body to you, Zinan."

"I receive it."

The recorder placed his hand over theirs, which were entwined, making the moment solemn. "I join you in marriage in the name of the Emperor and his sacred laws."

She looked to him as if for the first time and saw that his face was filled with adoration. Unhooded, she had taken his ring, the universal token of a man and a woman joined, and the recorder said, "You are now made one."

He kissed her, his eyes full of colors, so that she caught her breath with shock.

The tumult outside the shrine grew louder. The clangor of war gear and shouted orders and the whining engines. She turned, and saw her husband turn also. Then the screens of the shrine parted, and in the glare the cool interior flooded with unmuted sunlight. Outside, her brother, proud and armored—Katsumi at the head of two ranks of armed men. All heads turned; the recorder raised his hand and man and wife walked hand in hand toward the light, uncertain, for what had been witnessed and made Nishima-sama could now unmake.

Kenji shaded his eyes, rising from his contemplation, and in the brightness fifty swords were pulled from fifty sashes and were laid before their owners, who knelt in two lines. Then Katsumi knelt also, and they went in procession, followed by their pages, by Kenji and his wife, walking the gauntlet of samurai which Katsumi had brought from the daimyo to salute them to their marriage bed.

He warned Yao to treat the test with respect, remembering that terrible day in his first year at the RISC lab at Lakeside when the compression chamber had lost stability and a half-ton singularity had bubbled out towards Nate Smith, the mathematician, and killed him.

With so many people gathered here now, Duval had plexed off a space ten feet around the testing pit, but there were few who could bear to stand closer. The field reactor was working now, the static field surrounding them spiking their hair like iron filings on a magnet and making their skin prickle. The field was intense, rushing from the open maw of the test chamber as its heavy door was irised open periodically. And above it the great black power skeins looped evilly.

"Everything is almost ready," Duval announced with satisfaction, walking back towards the assembled dignitaries. It was the same everywhere when weaponry was developed. As the climatic moment arrived, the pace of work heightened, illustrious visitors were invited, and the testing was done with great ceremony. Necessary witnesses were those connected with the factory, the purchasing authority, and the state. It was a tradition that Kenji insisted must be observed.

Duval paused appreciatively, enjoying one of the few moments when his attention was not demanded by some practicality. The industrial councilors of the *han* were here in full uniform. Visitors from Niigata and Kanazawa had honored him in their regalia, and the *hatamoto* and other officials representing the military, resplendent in their martial uniforms. Even the local judge and the secretaries of his legal bench had come to enjoy the occasion and the lavish entertainment that was to follow. To be seen in the company of the daimyo was an opportunity too good to miss.

Nishima himself stood on the raised plexed-in gallery that had been built for the most important visitors; Kenji and Katsumi were both at his side. They gazed up at the heavy machinery that stood idle now above the buried chamber, and down at the field reactor. Michie waited proudly with the ladies, the wives and mothers, and the young children, close to the big factory office doorway, away from the noise and the field and the danger of explosion. He saw Masae-san there, engaging the formidable Fumiko-san in conversation and gesturing towards the daimyo.

Duval was being questioned closely by the samurai. He explained how the pit had been made, how the six biggest chambers—those of the prototypes—had been lowered in one by one using the massive waldo that hung from the frame. They were placed vertically, he said, not too close to one another, muzzle end uppermost, and their lower ends bedded in plex "sand." Then they had lowered in refrigerated argentium tubes, this time further from the accelerator point, then filled the pit with more plex granules, and finally they had made up the rest of the space with a variety of equipment, mostly monitors and transducers, so that the behavior of the chambers now buried up to their filter heads could be thoroughly investigated. Six technicians had spent the morning tamping the plex sand down with stamps, not too tightly, and Duval had supervised, dampening the mixture with ordinary water at intervals, but sparingly, so that not too much moisture was allowed to seep in around the carefully positioned chambers.

"Of course, the top of the pit slopes this way," he told them, sweeping his hand across it and speaking up at the daimyo's party. "At its highest it must be lower than the injection hole so that the initiator particles can be fired in from the accelerator, and lower still as the distance from the accelerator increases. Relativistic effects alter the spacing of the pulsers as the particles approach light speed. The initiation will come via this vacuum chamber here and flow along these field line channels. You can see the way they branch. Each branch leads to its own individual chamber."

"What's that man doing?" the daimyo asked, indicating the technician who stood on top of the pit. He was delicately adjusting valves on the channels with a torque reader and a small pair of ion keys.

"Two hours ago the channels were heated to drive off gases and harden the vacuum, Excellency. His responsibility is to do this evenly by means of small heater elements in each section along which the stream will flow. He's simply testing the integrity of his work. Remember that the particle stream is of such high energy that any collision with stray gas molecules in its path will produce cascades of gamma radiation. If this is above a critical figure, it will affect the fields."

"Ah! And these small gratings you've placed in each channel?"

Katsumi answered. "If you will permit me, Excellency. As the particle stream begins to focus, the grating will be phased open so that the stream can be collimated."

"Of course. Yes. I see that."

"Excuse me, Excellency," Duval shouted up. "It's ready. With your permission I'll begin the test now."

He climbed the ladder swung up onto the top of the reactor and crossed it, heading for the control room. He was tired. For the past day and night he had been on his feet unceasingly, checking the field figures with which to charge the test. And his obsession with secrecy in this had driven him to hide his procedures, especially from Yao.

At first, the mixing of units had been a problem, so ingrained had the Amerikan system become in his mind during his own training. He had laboriously learned from his men the Yamato equivalents—the *shaku,* or Japanese foot, which was slightly less than an Amerikan foot: 11.930542 inches. Ten *sun* made a *shaku,* and ten *bu* made one *sun.* A *rin* was a tenth of a *bu.*

"The dimensions of the chamber are fundamentally important," he had patiently explained to Yao, who had struggled to calculate the form equations of the chambers using the Japanese system, which differed from the Chinese system he was used to. "Above all there is the interfocal distance of the concentration chamber. That's essential. We must get it right."

And Yao's openness had betrayed him again. His eyes had gleamed and his lips pursed. Someone—Katsumi, Duval guessed—had charged him with learning the key secrets. But Yao was a poor spy because he had become a good friend; he had helped him build the facility, he had been the man who had stood and given a speech on his behalf at his shoulder at his marriage feast, and Duval had asked himself, How can I lie to him now?

So far he had given Yao all details freely and without deceit. But these were techniques already well known to Yamato's military engineers, and to Koreans and even to certain Chinese. The compression chamber secret was different. It was what lay at the heart of the gun's practicality, what permitted it to be used with reasonable safety, what permitted greater accuracy when the gun was fired, and, ultimately, what lengthened the effective range of it.

The problem had kept him turning in his sleep knowing that soon he would have to divulge his secret to the enemy. But then he had realised his error. Where was this enemy? No man who worked for him at Hasegawa Industries was his enemy. The household of the *han* were, none of them, his enemy. His new family? How could they be his enemy? Even cold Katsumi and the haughty daimyo were simply acting as functionaries of the state. All their moves had been sanctioned and prescribed by circumstance. It had been their duty to imprison him and the others. And afterwards, had they not shown incredible clemency to mere *gaijin?*

The daimyo had been right: Jos Hawken had been guilty of breaking the laws of space. He had deliberately provoked Yamato, which, in truth, was the conqueror of this Zone and had the right to use it as it pleased. Who did the Amerikans think they were to interfere?

"What's the matter, Zinan-san?" Michie had asked him tenderly that night as they lay on their futons. "Is the heat keeping you awake?"

He had sighed. "That and an unquiet mind."

"Perhaps I can help."

"Perhaps."

And he had told her and she had listened, and all the while he had remembered Horse's stubborn and suspicious mind and his accusations, and he had asked himself what kind of man could keep himself so stiffly apart from others and reject the hand of friendship as consistently as Horse had done. Only a barbarous Amerikan, a stupid, self-gratifying egotist, blind to the way of purity and discipline. Without refinement, without subtlety in his language, or place, or tradition, how could he know? He could never learn.

In Amerika there lay a deep and insane spirit which held on to its people and never, never let go. Left to itself it slept, but once stirred up it awoke and roared out with ferocity as it had over Hiroshima and Nagasaki on Old Earth so long ago. It was a crazy spirit. And manic. And it seized people and caught them up blindly. He could only see it now because he had been separated from Amerika and all things Amerikan, and by chance had come to see as an outsider sees. No wonder the rest of Known Space saw Amerikans as they did, as men possessed by a desire to free mankind, convinced of the rightness of their crusade, single-minded in their unbalanced beliefs. Always they spoke of rights, but never of duties.

The insight had chilled his heart. There was something awesome about that knowledge, and he wondered how much of the crusading freedom spirit was dormant within him. He watched Michie: the night's blue-blackness fired her hair, the silken surface of her body was dark and magnificently arousing against the white futon on which she lay. He felt himself harden as he told her, "Do you know that if Amerikans see a racial Japanese in Amerika, they assume he's a spy?"

She had laughed at that.

"And are there many Japanese in Amerika? Fumiko told me that the Amerikans are all ugly—hairy with huge noses and bad smells. But you are Amerikan, and you are quite the most beautiful man I have ever seen."

"I was Amerikan. And your eyes are a wife's eyes." He kissed her forehead. "In Amerika there are many strange people. A great variety. In Amerika they think variety is a good thing."

"Do you think variety is a good thing?"

He placed his hand flat on her stomach, his fingers splayed, his touch infinitely soft. "Since we married, I've wondered many times how it might have been for a Yamato scientist stranded on an Amerikan planet. I don't doubt that, had I been a racial Japanese and arrested on Texas or Maine, I would now be doing much the same thing." She placed her hand over his, and he lightened his words. "The difference is that I would have found it much harder to adapt to Amerika."

Michie's teeth showed white in a smile.

"Then maybe variety is a good thing."

"Yes. Maybe."

He held her for a long moment then, watching the *hotaru* fireflies dance in the garland of jasmine flowers that surrounded their window. The air was heavy with fragrance and filled with the high-pitched sound of *semi* singing in the trees. Then they made love, unhurriedly, until the futons were damp with their sweat, and the huge limb of Sado's bloody red daughter world rose up over the mountains.

Afterwards, they had lain together until their hearts stopped hammering, and he had told her what really troubled him.

"Surely you can still make working guns without the dimensions that are so special?" she had asked at last.

"Yes."

"Then do so. Give the daimyo adequate guns, but deny him magnificent guns."

He had sighed. "I can't do that. Because I love my profession. I have my pride. Don't you see? I have a duty to science and I owe my best to my work."

"You feel you must live up to that?"

"Yes, I do. But those who entrusted this knowledge to me—and who therefore saved my life—are Amerikans. It would not be right to betray them. To give their secrets away would break the oath I swore when first admitted to RISC. I can't do it."

She thought for a moment, then said, "I know a way."

He lay back, smiling at her words; it was as if she thought there could be a simple solution. "If you do, then tell me."

"Your science was learned in another life, an old life. And in that life you were true to it. But now you have a new life, on a new world. You must be true to that also. Tell no one how to make the special chamber, *but make it all the same*. Order many ingredients that you do not need as a blind, use sleight of hand. Cover your actions, and design your equipment so that it falls to pieces if anyone tries to get inside it. That way you will make your fine guns, but the secret you will have kept to yourself."

He had made up his mind then, giving in to his vanity. They would be *superb* guns! The best he could make. Long projectors and a way of imparting spin to the singularity to improve its endurance. Ten miles must be possible. Must be. A more powerful field, more concentrated, and with a flash-over of longer duration. Yes, and a more tightly wound propagator so that the singularity would go further and faster and straighter. It could be made smaller and more compact, the initiator rods condensed and turned back on themselves. Lastly there *would* be self-destruct catches, just as Michie said there should be, a globe shield of thin plex containing every important part, arranged to consume itself in a confined and stationary singularity if its integrity should be violated. The guns would bear his name—the Hasegawa Zinan gun—and no one would know but him how it was done, and when asked how, he would lie . . .

Yes, he was tired, he decided as he stood by the test control bench. Tired, but only through lack of sleep and the gyrations of this crazy double planet, and this was the great moment he had been waiting for, the one he had anticipated in his dreams for five strange, difficult, rewarding years. A buzz of delighted expectation tingled in him.

The equipment was ready, its power humming, its temperature exactly stabilised. The watchers waited as the compensators came on, bending the light paths across the test range, twisting the scene like something seen in a distorting mirror. Duval began the initiation sequence by driving the main console. When he withdrew control, a gush of golden light and heat, like liquid metal, radiant like the sun itself, glowed inside the transparent channel and flowed, splitting at each branch into three, four, then five incandescent streams. He stepped forward as it sprang to life, raising the field strength to 5.52 *yukawa* at the filter heads, and he saw how the smooth flow of light reached the testing pit and disappeared down into the five chambers.

It had been a long time since he had done this, and never had he supervised a test solo, let alone with equipment he had virtually designed and built himself, but his intuition had not deserted him. The equations that steered his actions were solid. They defined the precise moment to close off the particle flow and concentrate it by pulsing the field. More automatic choices were made, this time differential alternations to the internal field in the prototype chambers, then again to reverse the effects, and finally one piece of destructive testing, one containment being deliberately ruptured so that the probes could pick up data on the behavior of the distorting singularity.

As the power was cut, the equipment died, its vitality spent. He went down to the lab floor, looked up, and saw a hundred faces looking on, silent and engrossed, so he held his hands out to them, like a showman might, to tell them that the show was over, and there were nods of appreciation and a discreet round of applause.

The pit was opened and decontaminated. At the sight of the men in orange flexiplex removing the packing from the pit, people emptied from the facility and went out into the yard, where tables had been set up for the dedication ceremony.

Katsumi walked with him. "His Excellency is anxious to see the weapons perform. When may I tell him they will be ready?"

"It's difficult to say until more work has been done, Katsumi-san."

"You know that he's losing patience. The fortifications at Niigata and Hitachi are nearing completion. Of course, we have possession of one whole gun and certain parts from three of the guns salvaged from the Amerikan wrecks, but a large battery is planned."

"I hope our new weapons will soon be ready."

Katsumi nodded shortly. "Good. It is the daimyo's hope that he may have the weapons in place at Niigata in time to protect the next aurium fleet."

"Protect it from whom?"

Katsumi seemed surprised at the question. "From pirates, of course. Amerikan pirates."

46

A week later, Duval prepared to meet Kenji and the daimyo at the proving ground. A dozen weapon mounts were lined up along the wall. Before them was the newly mounted barrel of the *Thomas J.*'s singularity gun recovered from the apron at Niigata, still a malevolent matt black and still with the marks where he had destroyed the end stops to use it to smash into the ship's strongroom. The sight of it turned his thoughts again towards his brother. He touched the boss of the gun with his fingertips, felt the black smoothness that after five years of development work now looked so obsolete.

He drew his hand back suddenly. It was as if an electric charge from the gun had tingled his hand. Suddenly he knew, he had sensed, that Ellis was alive.

Where was he now? Could he be one of the pirates prowling the space lanes of which Katsumi had spoken?

He tried to put the painful thought away, but he knew that if Ellis had survived he would surely come back to Sado. Strange that he should feel this anxious excitement. There had been a great sense of loss at their parting; perhaps this was its counterpart at Ellis's return. He considered Katsumi's words for the fiftieth time, then he examined his feelings and saw a greater deception.

"It's because I am changed now," he said aloud, feeling afraid at the traces of regret that came with the declaration. Anger stiffened him. Go home, *a-ni*, he said silently. Go home, elder brother. For the brother you once had is long since dead and buried. This is my home now. I am Zinan, a new man. A married man. Reborn on a new world, in a new life, with a new name. And of the other there is no trace remaining.

Beside him, his technicians worked amid the machines and tools and laboratory benches making more parts for the prototypes. They whispered anxiously, wondering at the illustrious party that had arrived and laying bets on the performance of the weapons. The guns had almost reached the stage where they could be mounted and powered up.

"Wen-yuan, Dae-woo, Watanabe-san—you must take off the rim and break the seals before you take out the cores," he had told his men the day after the machining. "Then, if everything is satisfactory at my inspection, your teams will go ahead on the actuator insertion. For the largest gun that will take a day and a half. You'll work in teams of two until the job is done."

"Then we'll be ready to assemble the barrels?" Yao Wen-yuan had asked.

"Yes! And be careful to collect the spent casings you remove. They'll be useful in future."

He had checked each gun carefully to see that the cores had remained straight during machining, and he had supervised the mounting of each one in the great compression lathe. Then he had set the plex tools that would cut out the bore, each barrel descending fraction by fraction, under precise control onto the cutting tool. The tool, geared to a mill, was forced round at hundreds of thousands of revolutions per minute until, twelve hours later, the bore was completely reamed.

"We must remove precisely the right amount of metal to accommodate the windage," he had explained, moving an ancient laser micrometer across the cut-away diameter of the demonstration hologram. "A bore precisely one plus pi-to-the-minus-four times the diameter of the event horizon of the singularity being projected is the ideal."

"So sorry, but what is this for? And how do you arrive at that expression?"

"Excuse me for not explaining myself more lucidly, Watanabe-san," he had said, and launched into a long mathematical derivation at the chalkboard. "See? Quite simple."

They had smiled and nodded, not really following his leaps of logic, so he had checked the sums over again slowly before pushing on. Peering minutely at the *hiragana* symbols used in chaos math, searching for the mistake he knew did not exist, but which he had to search for to save his colleagues' face.

He had worked meticulously over the weapons, his teams duplicating his work on the components, and he had seen them grow jealous of their parts of the project and the importance of the segment they were given to work on. He had smiled inwardly at that, for this was how it should be. They had learned that the esteem of the master and his trust in them were expressed in this way, and to them all his praise was of the highest importance.

Next he had shown Mori-san how to install the vent—a hole narrower than his little finger that would connect with the implosion chamber. It was the means by which the singularity was propelled into the projector on firing. He specified that each be tilted back towards the cascabel at pi-by-three radians, the most convenient angle for the injection.

Yao Wen-yuan had come to him full of woes. "We'll never be ready in time!"

"Don't worry."

"I'm not worrying!"

"We'll soon be finished."

"But we have yet to prove the weapons, Zinan-san!" Wen-yuan shook his head.

"Leave that to me. We can't prove an unfinished weapon," he had replied with satisfaction, polishing the best of his prototype barrels on its elegant black snout.

"She's perfect now! Perfect! What more can there be? Hasegawa-sama demands that we are ready before the daimyo comes here again on *kin-yo*, the agreed day. He says Nishima-sama's patience is at an end."

"One thing remains."

"Not a big thing?" Wen-yuan had said, resigned to the fact that the weapon-making would never end.

"The most important thing of all."

And that afternoon he had done it, proudly incising the maker's mark, the fallow deer, and his name, on every base ring.

Now four of the five big guns were set up on the benches of the covered test range, a two-mile-long plex shed with high transparent roof echoing to the sounds of men and machines. Each barrel was a masterpiece of polished chrome, weighing five hundred pounds without its mounting and a waldo hung overhead to move them. The fourth weapon, the best of them, was in its mount, feather light to the touch because it had been so accurately counterbalanced, but still with massive momentum. Charged and ready, it stood beside the weapon that had been salvaged from the *Thomas J.* and restored to action. Both weapons were hooked up to massive black power cables.

Kenji met the daimyo in the administration block, and they walked towards the range together with a dozen stern-faced *rikugun* officers of the Yamato Guard who followed Katsumi. When Duval asked them to inspect the unmounted guns, the daimyo's irritation overflowed.

"How long before the weapons may be fired?" he asked rudely.

"In due course, Excellency. Please excuse me."

"Answer my question precisely."

Duval felt an unexpected shaft of anger at the daimyo's curt impatience. Yes, he thought darkly. There's much more to making a singularity gun than you first imagined when you brought me here. Much more. But you'll not hurry me, and I'll give you what I promised you and more. "I beg your pardon, Excellency. I can discharge the weapons immediately if you wish."

Kenji intervened. "Please, Nishima-sama, if I may explain—" He raised a placating hand, outlining the targets that had been erected down the vast shed exactly one mile away. The biggest was in the form of a huge cast ingot of plex a yard square and two hundred yards in length.

"You intend to fire at those targets?" the daimyo asked, screwing up his eyes. It seemed to Duval that Nishima was unable to believe that the weapons could project that far, much less work on the target.

"When I first started the project, I was asked to demonstrate the performance of my best gun and to compare it with the gun from the *Thomas J.* in a straight contest. In those days there were those who believed I could not be trusted to render my best skills to the Emperor's service."

The daimyo's sidelong glance was condescending. "Let us hope his doubts were groundless."

Katsumi regarded the mounted weapon appraisingly. "The first gun seems impressive, Excellency."

"It is," Duval agreed.

"Perhaps we should proceed." Kenji moved to the daimyo's side.

He grunted. "Yes, demonstrate the weapons. Show us that your skill is all that you claim, Amerikan."

"*Hai!*" Duval nodded briskly, unsettled by the daimyo's manner. The way he had called him "Amerikan" had been deliberate, and he was clearly preoccupied with some weighty matter. That made him dangerous.

"Before I demonstrate the guns may I ask you all to retire to safety."

The daimyo looked about him. "Safety?"

"It is usually unwise to stand too close to unproven weapons, Excellency."

"Unproven weapons? I told you they were to be ready. Today. Now."

"So they are, Excellency. Ready to prove. As you can see the weapons have not yet been fired. I thought it would be best to—"

"You thought to wait until I arrived?" The daimyo's manner froze still harder.

"It is customary in Amerika to give the customer guarantees that what he is buying will work."

"Guarantees are implicit."

Duval indicated the plex-screened viewing gallery that had been erected fifty yards away. "May I request that your distinguished party retires to the gallery?"

Katsumi began to lead his officers to the rear, but stopped when he saw the daimyo was not moving.

"You will come too."

"I cannot." Duval made a gesture of apology. "I made the weapons. It is I who must test-fire them."

The daimyo laced his arms together. His suspicions were aroused and he watched Duval steadily. "Then we shall stand with you."

"That will not be practical—"

"I said, we shall stand with you."

Duval blew out a breath. "As you wish, Excellency."

Katsumi and the others began to gather again uncertainly, their cap insignias glinting as they looked to their lord with sidelong glances, detecting the mistrust in him. Finally the daimyo said, "You seem ill at ease, Amerikan. Explain to me the real reason why we should not stand here. Why are you insisting on firing the weapons yourself?"

Duval's pride overcame him, but he trod warily, facing the daimyo with coolness. "I have faith enough in my own skill. I can assure you that in service these guns will perform properly."

"Then why do you suggest that we retire? Do you think I am afraid?" The daimyo looked to his officers imperiously.

Duval stared at the floor. "Of course not, Excellency."

"Tell me: have you made unsound weapons? Are they unsafe?"

"It is merely that a singularity weapon, any weapon, no matter how well made, may be dangerous. That's what a weapon is for. This is the first firing." Duval met the daimyo's eye insolently. "And, were it not for one small fact, I would welcome your standing beside me as I fire the first round."

"One small fact?"

"I've made a powerful prototype, many new components, many innovations. The weapons are powered to their limit and will be operated to the limits of their components, perhaps beyond. Consequently, if there is anything I've overlooked, I want it to show on this first test firing. With me standing here. I don't want any one of my team to pay for my mistakes. In Amerika it's a traditional saying that the inventor of the airplane pilots the first flight."

The daimyo looked flintily back and Duval saw that his certainty had deserted him. He enjoyed the moment. He allowed a slight smile to play over his face as he explained quietly, "If we stood here, and the gun malfunctioned on proof, it would turn us all nicely into butcher's offal, Excellency."

The daimyo's response was sharp. He barked an order to Katsumi, who ran up and came to attention before him, then he turned back to Duval. "I have made it plain to you that your function is to manufacture singularity weapons for my batteries. How dare you jeopardise your life unnecessarily? This man will prove the weapon."

"But, Your Excellency, it is my duty—"

"Silence! Your duty is to do as I order!"

Duval made a gesture of concession. The blood had drained from Katsumi's face. He turned and saw the development team regarding him with little respect.

"Katsumi-san is not technically compet—"

Nishima rounded on him furiously. "Weapons are weapons! Tell him what to do."

Duval's eyes were fixed on the daimyo's own. Then he shook his head slowly. "I must apologise humbly, Excellency, but I cannot allow Katsumi-san to prove my weapon."

Nishima's anger grew and his fist closed over the grip of his *katana*. "You will do as I say!"

"With respect, Excellency, I will not. I must be sure that the gods intend Yamato to have my skills."

Nishima halted, bottled his threat, seeing suddenly that nothing he said could counter Duval's twisted Amerikan logic. "Very well. Retire!"

Duval watched them go, feeling the sweetness of his victory as they trooped towards the viewing gallery. His team buzzed with anxiety but he calmed them, saying nothing about the modification that only he knew had been strapped to the new gun. He motioned his crew away to safety, spitting the dryness from his mouth. Everything he had told Nishima Jun was true, everything except one detail. There could be faults. His life was hostage to that, to his skill and his conviction, as was only right. Then why had he lied about the modification? Why had he set a fifty percent power margin, over and above his safe firing limit?

It was a reckless, foolhardy action. Had some part of him secretly wanted to goad the daimyo to stand here beside him and blow them both into Shinto hell?

No. It would have been very easy to have manipulated the man's dignity to that end.

Then what was it? And why, when Nishima had retired, had he felt himself sweating? He knew suddenly that the modification was enough to carry the prototype's performance beyond that of the Amerikan weapon. If successful it would open up a whole new area for advancement. It also made the outcome a true gamble: a disaster*—or the reward of making known what was previously unknown*. He had told the daimyo the whole truth when he had spoken of the gods. That single massive discharge would in one firing prove the weapon, the theory, and also the weapon-designer's destiny.

The end of the range house was being opened. Grav compensators clicked on, distorting the interior of the test range in a fish-eye manner, like an image reflected in a mercury droplet. The all-clear sounded. He sent his team away to the gallery, then, alone, he stood behind the weapon he had built and put out his hand to the firing levers and took a deep breath. Like a man looking down from a high building, he felt an irrational impulse. It would be so easy to turn it on the viewing gallery and end everything now. He mastered himself and pulled the firing triggers.

The concussion was terrifying. The cold argentium tubes delivered their charge, and the explosion flung the gun and its mount back against its recoil springs and ripped him to the ground. As the gun crashed back, smoke blew around him. For a few seconds he was enveloped in it, then he saw his development team running towards him. He stood up ecstatically, deafened by the roar, finding his notes and throwing them up through the air like a madman.

The gun was intact!

In the distance, vermin pigeons that had leapt from their roosts as the sound thundered down to them fluttered out, flying crazily through the compensator fields. Far away in the fields beyond, slave rice planters straightened and looked up. He looked to where the daimyo stood, saw Kenji raise his hand and wave it in congratulation. He ordered the weapon repowered immediately, this time with the modification bypassed. They brought fresh argentium tubes out from their floor recesses, their interiors maintained at a steady low temperature to fight the chemical instability of the special isotope mix. Then the team were dismissed to safety.

Why the hell was it smoking?

Again the gun bellowed and bucked. Another great plume of smoke filled the air and drifted thin above him. All was well. They repeated the repower, faster this time. And a third angry blast roared out.

Duval began to feel the ringing in his head, the peculiar gun-drunkenness that stretched time and made everything euphoric and unreal. He felt as though he had been clouted hard on the ear, slightly concussed, but paradoxically able to aim the weapon the better for it. He handled the argentium tubes with infinite care, set the power catches until the range was correct, sighted the target, and laid the gun's azimuth.

The shot threw the gun back violently with another ear-shattering roar. Further gouts of lightning and acrid smoke spewed out from the muzzle, and Duval watched the pads of burning liner arc to the ground leaving smoky trails. He moved to the side so he could follow the propagating singularity. The cameras downrange showed that the singularity had carried just over the target.

He ordered a repower and fresh barrel core and moved ten yards away to the *Thomas J.*'s gun, checking the sighting once more. It was intact except for the mechanism that recored the barrel for rapid firing. It was already charged up and ready to fire, but he altered the gun fractionally to the left with a twist of the mount adjusters before firing it off. This time the cameras showed that the singularity had blipped out short of its target. A plumstone appeared and continued towards the target like a giant bowling ball. It struck with tremendous force, but the plex target was as unmoved from its anchorings as if the iron object had been made of ultra-light helithene.

He felt the urge to destroy overwhelm him, just as it had that day on the apron at Niigata. The plex targets became real, his memories vivid. He urged his technicians to double their efforts each time they repowered and replaced the core, shouted at the crews ferociously, exhorting them in savage language, willing them to work faster against one another, to compete.

They had never seen him like this, but they did his bidding, restoring each of the weapons to firing condition within half a minute. With the next two shots the target was penetrated, the range found. Then they scored hit after hit. It was too easy: a sitting target, no movement to compensate for, no variables. His hungry singularities began to lance the plex into pieces, and he saw exultantly that his own was the deadlier. He had created one of the most precisely destructive weapons ever made.

First the target was eaten away, then the anchoring ramp, then the steel backing screens punctured neatly, but Duval continued to fire, now with his own gun, now with the gun from the *Thomas J.* After two dozen shots, the barrels were almost too hot to touch. The air tasted of burned liner. His technicians were slicked with sweat. A dozen shots more, delivered as fast as they could fire them. Still he shouted them onward, and they saw how he was touched by a *kami*. Angry, yet not angry. Time passed, but its passing did not reach him. Nothing diminished the passion and intensity of the attack. The target that had once been the epitome of durability was reduced by the test to a splintered block of gray shards, but still he urged another repower and another and another, until all fear and all grief and all anger and all hatred were pouring from him, on and on and on and on, until there was no more will and no more breath and no more strength in the technicians' arms and legs with which to feed the guns and the terrible flame within their master.

As they fell to their knees, he took up the tools and the argentium tubes himself, threw off the hands of those that tried to stop him.

"Enough!"

Then the officers of the Guard were hurrying towards them. They saw the glaze in his eyes, the stark rawness that lingered there, and they knew they had witnessed a man who was prepared to push himself to the utmost limit to demonstrate his skill.

The daimyo looked at the new gun with awe and fascination. From the very first shot he had been profoundly impressed by the demonstration, by the range, the consistent accuracy of the shooting, the power of the singularity to destroy. The anxieties of the morning rose up in him again as he faced the Amerikan. He had been half expecting, half hoping that the demonstration would prove nothing. After so many delays it was not unreasonable to suppose that the results would not justify the expense, that the experiment would prove a costly and inconclusive failure, but the Amerikan had done all that he had promised and more. Such a pity that the prize must soon be lost, he thought. Duval is now a real asset and not simply a potential one. How unfortunate it has taken so long to manifest itself. How cruel the turn of events back in Kanazawa.

"That was magnificent shooting, Amerikan. I congratulate you."

Duval's eyes were staring through him blearily. Kenji took his arm, wiped the sweat and grime from his face, his own breathing fast and excited. "Do you hear that, Zinan? Such guns! Who now would be our enemy?"

The daimyo watched his host's delight grimly. If we had a hundred of these guns, fully finished, with loading and charging and coring functions completely automated, we might subdue the entirety of Known Space, he thought. But this is hardly a start. Is there still time? *Is there still time?*

"Hasegawa-san, you will immediately put your facility into full production. By this time next year, I want a hundred of these weapons in my possession. No delay is to be tolerated. No expense is to be spared. Do you understand?"

"Yes, Excellency. Thank you. It's a great honor, but perhaps a *hundred* singularity guns in a single year is too many for our small facility to produce."

"Then you must build another. I will pay whatever is necessary. You will start tomorrow. Today. Now."

"You do us too much honor, Excellency."

The daimyo motioned the *han*-holder aside. "Can it be done without the Amerikan?"

Kenji seemed not to understand the question.

"I ask you: can the facility operate without the Amerikan? Have your men learned enough?"

"I—I don't know, Excellency."

"Then find out. You have a year to make those guns, Hasegawa-san."

But the daimyo knew that he did not have a year. That very morning he had learned from his council that Fukuda Ikku, imperial *metsuke* and inspector general of the *kempei,* was preparing to put out his hand in search of impurity. To begin its quest the office wanted first to examine the captured Amerikans, and the name "Duval Straker" was at the head of their list.

47

"KABUL BASE"—A SECRET LOCATION IN THE NEUTRAL ZONE

The Yamato Guard had come here and found their base and all was destroyed.

Oujuku stood on the blasted crete and stared at the fire-blackened ruins two hundred yards away, feeling the pain in his leg and tasting the bitterness of yet another disappointment. Behind him, the landing party stirred uneasily, watching the purple undergrowth and straining to listen for dangers despite the wind.

"So. The sonsabitches've found us out," he said.

"We've been betrayed!" Pelgar Rosen, his second-in-command, came to his side. "They must have learned from those who we left for dead at Okinawa. From Ramirez or Esterhazee."

"Yeah, and maybe it was just bad luck!" Frane said. The belligerent Ohion third officer threw down his cap. He and Esterhazee had been close. "We've got bad psi, I tell ya!"

"Shut your mouth, Frane. The captain don't allow that kind of talk."

The shuttle crew fanned out across the mountain shelf. A cold wind howled in the peaks, driving small clouds westward, giving movement to everything in land and sky.

Oujuku shaded his eyes and looked from the base to the *Lexington,* to the *Valley Forge,* then back to the base again. This had been his secret stronghold, the place he had code-named "Kabul Base" because of the drabness and the deep valleys and the towering white peaks that stood over them. Behind, the land was clothed in dust, rising steeply—god-awful with the sun sinking low, casting the shadow of the mountain across it. A rock stood at the entrance to what had been the underground complex, and not far from this place a frozen waterfall of pure crystal that he had first washed in almost two years ago. This place was hard to find unless you knew what you were looking for.

They followed him warily toward the ruin, pushing through twisted metal, their sensors fluttering. Kabul Base was to have been their base of operations: a secure port where he could replenish his ships and stockpile the booty they had meant to take from Yamato ships. But now their stores were stolen, their provisions spoiled or carried off; there was only snow and charred metal and the threat of ambush. Kabul Base was known to the enemy, and so it was useless.

"Are you a'right, Captain?" his thick-spoken shuttle coxswain asked once more.

Godblind yah, Frane! he thought uncharitably, wanting to savor what the enemy had done, the better to decide on a fit way to get them back for it. The deep wound in his calf muscle raged, echoing the disaster that had befallen them at Okinawa. Three months had passed since then and still the leg had not properly healed. He hated it because his men thought him a cripple and because it reminded them of the bloody failure. *His* bloody failure.

"Get the landing party back aboard. Let's piss off out of here."

"Aye, sir!"

They sat meekly at their controls, the huge windshield buffeted by snow flurries, waiting for him, watching him limping up into the shuttle. The leg burned as he stepped up the ramp.

Frane hesitated. "Captain—"

"Get about your tasks," he shouted, his voice rasping hoarsely.

The new loss infuriated him. The shame of it. *This piss-burning poisoned leg!* He'd have to have the bastard off if it didn't improve in three days. He strode inside and heaved himself into a seat smartly, knocking away Cao's helping hand, unwilling to fill their eyes with any more of this goddamned crippled-captain sideshow.

He looked at their faces and saw they were all troubled and lined. None would meet his eye. He knew they could not lightly put aside this new setback. He read their thoughts: Betrayal. Fuming anger. Above all, disappointment. Ramirez and Esterhazee again. Stupidity! Ramirez. Wanted to be a hero. Ramirez, the comms expert, was certainly dead, his brains splashed out by a sniper, but Esterhazee might have been alive.

Oujuku folded his arms to stop his hands going to his knee. An analgesic might stop that blood-pounding ache. Oh, no! Suffer and smile, you sonofawhore! Put your mind to something else.

There was another explanation. What if Ellis Straker had been taken and had talked? No, surely not. Not Ellis. His men, then? But Ellis alone knew the full extent of the plans; he alone knew the location of Kabul Base. Ellis would have died before telling anybody. And he wasn't indiscreet in marking up his visualiser log.

So it was Esterhazee. Fucking Esterhazee. The rat-faced little scum-bucket. Maybe not . . . maybe they cut his balls off first. Yeah, think about that, John, and save your recriminations up for them that can defend themselves to your face.

When they reached the *Lexington,* the shuttle swung inside the hangar deck. He climbed out with gritted teeth, looked for and found the furtive way the rest of the crew regarded him. None of them would hold his gaze and that angered him more, and the anger showed and made them more evasive still.

He cast about him with his jaw tight as a fist and his lips protruding, and went below to his quarters. Immediately he broke out a bottle of mash, but there was no comfort in it and no spirit to light up inside him. He could not put out of his mind what he had seen in the faces of his crew.

At the outset he had promised them riches beyond imagination.

"You all heard of Mitsu? That's the chief *zaibatsu*—a kind of Yamato mega-corporation. It means 'secret.' And this is it's symbol—" He had held up a *kanji* that looked like a bunch of fishhooks. "Mitsu is the outfit that contracts and ships most of the aurium out of the Zone. Now, how many of you guys wants to become a corporate raider?"

They had grinned at that, but so far there had been struggle and toil and death. Twenty-five of them had fallen in fighting, five more to ship accidents, and two taken by local fauna. And the remainder had seen neither credit nor a single flask of Mitsu's heavy compounds with which to redeem their promises.

That had been the original plan: take enough to buy the men who had been grounded on Sado, finally discharge the debt that Jos Hawken had run up in the marooning. But what to do now? The Amerikan they had picked off that Yamato ship had changed everything. The isotopist had given him plenty to think on.

Still, a promise was a promise, but Okinawa aurium was better spent on Liberty than at Niigata, whatever Ellis Straker thought about it. They would have to talk it over.

He remembered how they had seen it in the raw, tons of it, stacked in spherical ingots, in the metal vaults of Aurium Terminal on Okinawa. After Sado, Okinawa was the biggest super-heavy-element shipping point in Known Space, and like Sado, pretty poorly defended. Nobody had dreamed of interfering with the place before. But it was rich: aurium and argentium *and* platinium, plus a few exotic decay nuclides—long-lived radioactive fusion products that were associated with the supernova wreck of the Gum Nebula. All in all, it added up to something worth hanging around a pulsar for. But the mission had misfired and they had got away with none of it. *As a leader, he had failed them.*

It had been a sorry debacle. He had bluffed his way into orbital stack around that unlivable hole of a world using captured ID interrogation equipment and intended to land at break of Okinawa's short seven-hour day, and storm the metal vaults, but the party under Jerry Dyson's command had made their landing prematurely at 0300 UT, in pitch-blackness, using full suits, and they had been forced to follow up. Then their four shuttles had been rumbled by a patrol ship; and the high-security compounds had been alerted before they had even scrambled out of their vehicles.

It had been chaos! Caution and order had flown away. Totally disoriented, they had assaulted the dome complex in a screaming panic, searing down the defenses, running and shouting like madmen, careless of life and limb, into the guard fire that had peppered them randomly from the blackness. Crashing about because of the shitty gravity. Utter indiscipline. Utter, uncoordinated, piss-boiling chaos!

Incredible, but the shooting had died away.

It turned out to be Taito, a town the size of Harrisburg, maybe twenty, twenty-five thousand inhabitants, almost all of them Mitsu Aurium Terminal workers and their dependents, because this place was nobody's idea of paradise. Under plex-dome cover, dust like gray talcum everywhere, filthy mineral flats and blue-green algae scum and poisoned, acrid air. Like Biak a real terraforming gone wrong. It had been emptied by the alarm. The townsfolk fled before them, panic-stricken, crying in their terror of the Mongol horde that had come out of the night, but the three shivering prisoners they grabbed had told them of the vaults and the fabulous treasure they contained and so they had swarmed through the narrow streets, their mission coursing with undeserved good fortune, riding unhindered on the back of surprise.

"You know how to breathe ammonia, fellah?"

The question had taught one of the captives to speak a little English.

"Okay. You know what this is? It's a meson cutter! We'll blow your fucking dome wide open, y'hear me? Now move!"

Oujuku smiled bitterly at the memory of it. What a nonsensical miracle. They had taken him there, and there had been ion interlocks on the vault. By psi alone, by his own eerie inner certainties, he had guided them to the very place where the wealth of Known Space was concentrated. Tons of argentium! Great big, assay chop stamped pure 99.9999% refined bars. One for each day of the year—and there were five hundred fifty-two and one-third days in Okinawa's year. Three fortunes for each Amerikan raider. Bars stacked six feet high in the main vault, filling the space completely. It had gleamed like moonbeams under their torches, astounding everyone who gazed on it, because it was without doubt the greatest single repository of argentium in all creation.

But in the queer tension before a psi-storm, when the claustrophobia inside a suit is thick enough to curdle milk, a man's mind can easily slip away from reality, and then argentium seems like some other, baser substance, fresh-poured lead or bright iron.

He had forbidden them to touch any of it. Trusting his own mind, he had been sure that another place was nearby that contained the same immense hoard—*but of aurium.*

And so it had been! In the Mitsu warehousing by the apron they found the unattended strongroom bursting with it. Their glee had been unutterable—Rosen and Frane and Zaratini and Cao and his own brother, Frank—all his lieutenants had run their hands over it, capered and gawped, seeing the stuff and the super-heavy cast spheres—metallic blue in tint. They had stared with the eyes of wonder at those pawnbroker balls, those golden goose eggs that could buy the future of Known Space. Next they had turned their gorged eyes on him and he had exulted in the knowledge that he had delivered them here and that his promises to them were thereby fulfilled.

"Didn't I tell ya? Didn't I? *Didn't I?* Eh?"

Then the Mitsu guard had come to their senses, and the sounds of personnel carriers grinding into the complex was raw. The craven garrison had composed itself and returned, seeing their four shuttles and understanding how pitifully few they were, and as the guard came on to repossess their treasury, the astonishing vision had vanished. Their surprise was exhausted. They would have to go.

But it was the whole point that they take this stuff away!

He had felt strong and charged with confidence, unbreakable and unstoppable, but how his followers had read the omen differently. Huddled in that queer light, amid an immeasurable wealth flashed blue by damaged lighting panes, those deep superstitions had flared up in them.

The many awed voices had spoken out in their paralysis, the repairman turned pirate and the stevie looking for excitement, and the nexus hand who'd become a corporate raider because it sounded real smooth.

"I don't like it!"

"They're coming after us, John!"

"We've gotta get outta here!"

And that awed voice still: "But look at it! It's a dying man's dream!"

"Captain, we'll never get away with it. It's too much. They'll hunt us down wherever we go!"

"Remember, it's Yamato we're stealing from."

"Oh, Jeezus! We're going to die!"

"We can't take it!"

"Come on, let's get gone, Captain!"

And he had risen up in a mighty fury at them. His voice had filled with power and flame. "Listen to me! I have brought you to the treasure house of the *universe!* Follow me, until the job is done! Because if you leave without anything, you can blame no one but yourselves!"

His rage had shaken them. The spell of fear had abated. They had activated the waldos then and begun to shift Mitsu's monstrous eggs down onto floating pallets, running them out to the waiting shuttles, knowing, because he told them so, that if they were to leave them here, then that sonofabitch Emperor would use it to trouble the last outposts of freedom.

"Do you want them to come into Amerika to pillage your own people? Rape your wives? Smother your babes?" An egg of vast weight had swung in the waldo fist. "*This* is the pay they give their samurai."

Then the firing had intensified. There had been an almighty explosion, and he had let out a groan and staggered in a sudden faint. And they had seen the air jetting from the hole in his leg and the flame within him guttering.

Those foolish stevies and adventurers and repairmen had abandoned the treasure to pick him up. They had slapped a pressure pad on him and carried him to the shuttle and took him away, still their captain, and still much more precious than any Emperor's load of scrap.

"Take the aurium and leave the man. Surely I taught them that much?"

he said, sick at their misplaced loyalty. "And tan their hides for it, because our mission is to rob and to plunder, and not to care a damn for anyone, least of all a fool who gets his leg slit open.

"Godblind me! *Why do I feel so weak?*"

Oujuku stared dispiritedly into the mirror. The man he saw before him was a sorry piece of loot, black skin peeling. A mane of dready hair, elfed up in a headband that was stiff and caked with dust. There was a line of jigger lumps on his neck; where he had scratched at them to get at the burrowing ticks they were skinned raw. He stripped his shirt off and examined his chest, then the muscles of his upper arms and the smooth forearms also knotted with muscle where he had worked alongside his men in building Kabul Base. When his heart moved in his chest, each beat sent a pulse of pain down his thigh and into his calf muscle. It was hard not to give in to the urge to have treatment, but he had his Naturalist principles to stand by. No medication. The natural way, for good or ill. But the microfauna of Known Space was so diverse now, there were always evil strains of something appearing, something the medics couldn't handle. It would be a hell of a thing to die of a cut on the leg!

Sullenly he looked inside himself, finding a pervasive fatigue there, like the sour dregs of a water tank swilling in his belly. I did fail them, he said silently. They look to me alone for their future. Mine is the driving force. But there's not a lot remaining within, and nothing I can do to stop the soreness growing in my eyes. And I don't look like I ought to—not like a captain. That I must do, at the very least.

He took another belt of mash and wondered suddenly on which planet his heart would beat its last, how many beats it still contained; then he was ashamed of the thought. It was the first time in all his life he had asked himself such a question. He stoppered the flask and vowed never to ask it again.

But listen, he thought, slamming the flask back in its place in his cabinet, it's only me, John Oujuku, that's carried the burden of hopes and fears for a hundred volunteers these past few months. Only me that's filled them with dreams and hassled them on, never asking anything in return except a bit of faith. And they've followed me gladly and without complaint, suffering trustingly, some even dying, because I'm their leader. Their captain. And it wasn't fear or compulsion that made them do it, but free will and trust. Be worthy of them, John, you sorry bastard! You hear me?

When a knock came at the door, he was ready for it. Pelgar Rosen, his tall, unsmiling second-in-command, came in, surprised that her captain was stark naked. Oujuku was wet shaving his cheeks and chin. His hair was combed and had been trimmed back short.

"Well?"

"I'm sorry, I thought—"

"What did you think, Pel?"

"I—the helmsman wants to know if you're ready to light out, sir."

Oujuku's reply was distorted by his shaving. "We must find ourselves a new place to lay up, but I'm undecided as yet. What would you do, Pel?"

"Set up another stronghold down the chain, maybe Tuamotu."

"Not further down? To Tahiti or Raiatea?"

"Seems to me, sir, preying on nexus traffic's our only hope of profit now. Unless we make some hits, we'll start to run out of vital stores. Lube, for example. We'll have to find plexoline somewheres—we really have need of a new base where we can refit properly when necessary."

"Where do you think it ought to be?"

"A new place remote from Yamato. So's we're not displaced again."

Oujuku looked up and shook his wet hair so that droplets flew from it. "I want none of that, Pel. We're here to do a job of work. We'll keep close by our quarry."

"If you say so."

"I say so. In any case, the fall is coming on in Liberty and I mean to hit a rendezvous that's been agreed for November of this year."

"Oh?"

"Yep. There's a man who, if he can, will meet us at a pleasant little dustball between Upolu and Savaii. A man we owe plenty."

Rosen's face lit up as she realised whom Oujuku meant. "We're to meet Captain Straker at Apolima?"

"Yep."

"Will you tell him about the isotopist?"

"I'll have to, though it'll break his heart."

Oujuku shrugged on a fresh shirt. His kit was newly broken out, laid out on his strap hammock. He would change into the kit he had sworn not to wear until they had something to celebrate.

"Help me with my boots, Pel."

Rosen took hold like someone shoeing a horse and eased the boot on. The right was easy, the left impossible even when Oujuku sat down on the lip of his strap. They gave up.

"Shall I fetch the surgeon?" Rosen asked, too circumspect to make direct comment over the gash. Oujuku flexed his ankle so that the calf was laid open from top to bottom, and the flesh all around was swollen. It had slashed badly when a jagged lump of steel had spun off in the firefight. Now it was full of yellow pus and smelled nasty.

"Surgeon? No! The bastard's too happy to put a man in a unit. I've got an aversion to synthetic parts being attached to me. And, well, they say it leaves you woozy for a week."

"It's the easy way to get fit. You're a Naturalist, aren't you?"

"Bodies were meant to heal naturally. Don't you know never to trust a ship's doctor? When he took the poison out of my leg, the sonofabitch nearly killed me. He'll have my leg off quick as a wink and then what'll I say to Ellis, hopping around with one half of a white leg?"

Rosen was unamused. "C'mon, sir, they got black below the knees in the freezee."

"I'll not waste good limbs on a little-biddy flesh wound, and that's flat."

"I booked you in. It'll kill the pain."

Oujuku straightened instantly. "Hey, do I seem to you to be in pain?"

Rosen shook her head. "No, Captain, but the impairment—at least take a course of sepsin."

"I told you, I don't hold with medication. I need a clear head, and there's a better way. One I learned from Ayrton Rodrigo. Open the cabinet. You'll find a tub of yoghurt there. Bring it to me."

The yoghurt had been thrown away, and in its place was a mass of maggots. They had been rotting inside the tub in the cabinet for a week. Oujuku took out half a dozen pale-colored grubs with the tip of his knife and grinned. "A blow for a blow, that's what Ayrton used to say, eh, Pel? Come out of there, you little beauties!"

He placed a dozen maggots into his palm and then one by one onto the place where the suppuration was worst. They wriggled and quickly dived into the wound.

Rosen watched with absorbed horror at Oujuku's side.

"Pick the smallest for their appetites. See? When they come out of the air, they have a mighty taste for pus and dead flesh. It's their meat and drink and what makes 'em grow fat. They'll clean me up for sure. I can feel them doing me good already."

He clapped a wad of cotton torn from his old shirt over the wound, tied it round, and forced on his boot again, feeling hugely pleased with himself. He danced a reggae jig for Rosen's benefit, ending on a clap and a stamping flourish.

"You see?"

Rosen's face was green and Oujuku clapped her on the back with a full-bodied clout. "Well? Shall we get on up to the bridge?"

"Yes, Captain," she said. "Anything you say."

THE APOLIMA SYSTEM, N.Z.

It had been an uneventful planetfall, and it was good to be back on a low-grav planet in a G-type star system, good to see the primary westering red at the ending of each day. But each night there was a rage in heaven the like of which he had never seen, and it made Ellis think of his brother and the real reason he had come to this rendezvous.

Apolima was cataloged as uninhabited—surprising, since it was hard against the Yamato Boundary, but perhaps less surprising when it was realised that

Apolima was utterly without all exploitable resources except one: physical beauty.

This part of it was delightful. The night was calm. *Constitution* was in standing orbit with *Lexington,* directly above the place they had code-named "Providence," and the shuttles were drawn up on a sand beach. A score of wood fires burned there among inflatable tents as Ellis stepped down. There were no clams here, but they were going to have a clambake anyhow.

"Ellis."

"John." The clasped forearms. "Any news?"

"Not good. C'mon, have a bite with us."

Ellis sat down with a roast kale fowl to learn of Oujuku's doings. It had been May by the Amerikan Central Calendar when Oujuku had left Liberty with seventy-three men and women in the *Lexington* and the *Valley Forge.* Provisioned for a year, they had got offplanet before anyone could stop them with a countermanding order from the Security Council. By June they had reached this world, and after refitting had headed for the systems Oujuku had surveyed on his reconnaissance the previous year.

Oujuku grinned as he recounted how they had sighted the Okinawa system. "We attacked Taito in July. That's where I got this."

He pointed to the leg. The bulbous muscle of his calf was knotted with scar tissue, but seemed not to impede him now.

"You were almost killed, they tell me."

"That's aright, Captain," Cao growled protectively. The man's shipboard slang seemed strange, and Ellis remembered the terrible day Cao had first seen Harrisburg, how he had sat with him in the bar after the news of Janka's death. Then the man had shown outstanding qualities.

"I hadda carry him out the Mitsu strongroom myself, he was so heart-set over them eggs."

"I fucked it all up," Oujuku confessed disgustedly. "Suit puncture. But I swear it'll take more than a chunk of tin to put me down for good."

Ellis poured more beer into his mouth and ripped the white flesh from a kale-fowl breast. "You got away with their aurium, then?"

Oujuku shook his head ruefully and told the tale, the bright firelight flickering across his face. Despite the failures, Ellis thought he seemed utterly at peace with creation, except for one thing.

"Bewitched, it was! In my palm and my fingers closing over it, when *pssht!* Hell, there was probably too much to shift. And we weren't exactly the best-disciplined hit squad there ever was. It won't be the same next time."

"Next time?"

"Sure! I'm resolved on it. Broke but game. Give me credit for that at least."

"Pity about Okinawa. Some of it might have made the ransom—for the maroons."

"Might have." Oujuku stirred uneasily. "I was meaning to tell you . . . about something."

"What?"

"Oh . . ."

After a pause Oujuku stood up and walked barefoot towards the tide line. Ellis picked up his order satchel and went after him, knowing that what was to be said was for them alone.

Waves lapped gently there. Out of range of the beach fires the sky was brilliantly dark and spangled with stars, and the tremendous vivid veil of the Milky Way spanned the heavens. One star in particular, an intense blue-white point, riding at forty degrees elevation in the north, was vastly brighter than all the rest, magnitude minus six or seven, its light reflecting on the water. Ellis looked at it unhappily.

"The supernova terrified my people at first," he told Oujuku. "Half of them just knew it was their home primary, though that's impossible."

"I confess it weighed heavy on my own mind for a while. Wondering what system it was. *What* it was."

"And when you located it as Nagoya?"

"I worried again."

"A bad sign, you think?"

"Ain't nice to see any star go suddenly nova, and if the system's cataloged as inhabited . . . it's unthinkable. But listen, I don't believe it was a supernova."

"Well, it wasn't a nova, Ellis. Too big for a nova, and I don't have Nagoya's primary down in my catalog as a cool Main Sequence-plus-white-dwarf binary, which is what they always are. Mass transfer's the mechanism—"

"John, I didn't say it was a nova."

"Then what? Check it out. The classic type-one supernova was 1054 Taurus, eighteen hundred and forty parsecs away. The 'Crab' reached magnitude minus four as seen from Earth. That's equivalent to, let's see, five plus *m*, plus five-log-ten of . . . there you go: minus fifteen-point-three. That's about a hundred and fifty million times as bright as the sun. The event at Nagoya was smaller. It'd show as minus fourteen or so otherwise."

"So it's a small supernova."

"No."

"No? Why not?"

"Because they don't happen that frequently. Forty or fifty novae per year per galaxy, sure, but very few supernovae."

"And it's in Yamato. So it's suspicious."

"Correct. Look, this is the furthest any Amerikan has penetrated towards Yamato, and what do we find?"

"Yeah."

"The light from that whatever-it-was took forty-nine years to get to here, John. It's still lit up at peak. That peak is five times ten-to-the-thirty-four watts of radiation. Nothing, not even a supernova, can keep supplying that kind of energy for more than a year. Ergo, the thing blew less than fifty years ago."

"You think they kept us out of Yamato, with that sonofabitch edict and all, to stop us finding out about Nagoya?"

"I wouldn't put it past the Emperor's government."

"But why? I mean, so what?"

Ellis continued to stare at the sky. Like Oujuku, his astrogator's instincts had been greatly disturbed by the apparition and what it might portend. It blazed like a diamond, a jewel bright enough to cast a shadow, and because it shone in the black of a moonless night, it was even more impressively luminous.

What was Nagoya?

Before the last jump it had been invisible, then, after the transit, he had seen it blasting out as bright as an uncharted white dwarf in the Apolima system. He had immediately embargoed the computer records on that location hoping to hold off speculation until he had figured out what to do. He had said nothing to Angelo, his co-astrogator, or to Bowen, but the following day they had come to him to demand he level with them.

Novae did not suddenly appear in space; they were unstable binaries—all crews knew that. And Ellis had had no better answer for them. The stellar sciences, as Ganesh Ramakrishnan had acknowledged, were by no means exhausted. Long hours of study had taught Ellis that the stars were as variable and sophisticated as the members of the plant or animal kingdoms. Even the Main Sequence stars in their pedestrian courses of evolution sometimes behaved according to a far from predictable plan. The Earth ancients believed that in times of earthly crisis odd things happened in the sky, for it was a mirror and in it all things were reflected. How right they were.

The thought reminded Ellis of crucifixions and the forgotten roots of his religion. There had been a report of a new fixed star coming into the sky unannounced two and a half thousand years ago, the one the three wise men had seen.

"Doesn't it send a shiver through you?" Oujuku asked, troubled. "My crew have asked me how we'll report it. What we'll tell them back in Amerika. What do you think I should say to them?"

Ellis studied the unwavering spark, deeply shocked by the message he knew it carried. He quoted Rorenzo: "*Ask rather what earthly matter can be of such importance that a new star must herald it.*"

"Huh?"

"Never mind."

"You're not going all bookish on me, are you, Ellis?"

"What, me? No, to answer your original question, I think we ought to swear both crews to secrecy, bind everyone to it."

Oujuku stared at him, hard. "Why?"

"I don't know yet."

As they walked, Ellis told him the startling news he had received at Harrisburg whilst he had gone through final preflights aboard *Constitution*. In that communiqué Hawken had told him that Halton Henry had been executed for his crimes and that Okubo had been ignominiously sent out of Amerika after an attempt to have the new VP shot down in the street, but there had been another report enclosed, recounted in harrowing and despairing terms. It had come from Cassabian in Peking, and told of an infamously bloody massacre.

The Dowager had, on the Feast of the Wall, ordered the assassination of the Korean leader and the entire pro-Yamato Cabinet. The mob in the capital had had their own ideas about how to react.

Oujuku was stunned. "So the running dogs of Peking have fallen on their neighbors."

"All Koreans, of whatever rank, indiscriminately butchered on Peking alone. Tens of thousands until the Yangtse itself ran red. Cassabian admits he was completely unprepared for it. Up until the very day he was continuing political marriage negotiations with the Dowager. They even had to fortify the embassy against the murder gangs that roamed the streets when it turned into a general riot against foreigners. It's said he barely escaped with his life."

The killings had plunged Amerika's position into doubt once more, changing everything. As Oujuku's oaths against the atrocity subsided, Ellis took from his satchel the hard copy he had been waiting to give him. Sweeter news, but needing explanation.

They walked along the lapping water, hearing the boisterous carousing of the crews at their barbecue fires, shouts and laughter and the strains of vambo and E&L music on the sound systems. Oujuku concentrated on the documents in the flickering glow, finally grunting scornfully.

"This is all bullshit!"

"Better than we might have hoped for." The hard copy was passport confirmations, letters of marque, and a permit signed by the chairman of the Security Council; accompanying them were copies of the financial arrangement Ellis had bargained out.

"Better, you say? Then you're a poor judge of a stinking deal!"

"You're wrong, John." Ellis kept his face stern and lowered his voice. "We're backed by powerful factions now, you and I. Otis le Grande's put credit into our voyage—without him I couldn't've raised a crew. Capital's come from Cassabian too, and there's the money I took from Okubo. Our mission may not be official, but we're watched for, and our dealings will be closely followed at home."

Oujuku thrust the hard copy back at him. "You're fucking crazy! Jeezus God, the President's seal comes at a helluva price! With so many ways to cut the apple pie, we'll be lucky to come out with a bite."

Ellis felt his anger rise unstoppably. "Look further than your nose, John. There's more to this than the credit involved!"

"Is that a fact?"

"Sure. Don't you see? There's no alternative."

"No?" Oujuku squared with him. "We could choose piracy! Then what we do is totally to our own advantage!"

"Come on! This is a better way. We're Alia Kane's instrument of policy. If I've read her intentions correctly, we have permission to punish Yamato just as we see fit, so long as when we come home we turn a profit, and so long as we turn half of it over to her."

"Sheeee-it!"

Oujuku's face set in a mask of grim mistrust, and Ellis went on. "Because we're financed by private subscription we're unaccountable to the Security Council. That means we bypass Lubbock's—the VP's—authority. We're free to conduct a private war, with profit at its center, and free to take from Yamato anything we can shift."

"And if we fall into Yamato's hands?"

"The President'll deny all knowledge of us."

Oujuku spat. His voice dropped scornfully. "That's a real balanced deal you've got us there, Ellis. You begin to sound like Hawken. The government risks nothing and gets half. What do we get by alliance with Alia Kane?"

"We keep our asses when we get home. Total amnesty. Protection. And leave to walk about in Lincoln as rich men."

"Ha! I can nexus-hop to a pretty fine planet up beyond the Europa chain—Suisse—and live there just as happily!"

"Never more to see Amerika or your wife?"

Oujuku's defiance stood firm. "She can easily be sent for, or brought out by a contract man at a price. Yeah, and anyone else who wants to visit me."

"And how will you spend your credit in Suisse? What will you spend it on? Get a big ranch? Get a Bristol air-car or two? Buy yourself some friends? Hell, John, you don't ski and you don't even speak French!"

Oujuku grunted, and Ellis saw that his tantrum had blown itself out. They sat down and he came again with his plan, more coolly now. "Our duty is to Amerika. We're all moths flying round the President's flame, and the Security Council is the window through which we can fly in. Those fifteen people watch after Amerika as if it was a lover, jealous of everything—mostly one another. Think! We want credit and revenge, and, after that, status among our own kind and the knowledge that we kept the Emperor's greedy hands off Amerikan liberties. That's what the new star foretells for us. We'll carry home enough of Yamato's ill-gotten glory to bankrupt her economy."

"But a clear half of all we take, Ellis! It's fucking usury!"

Ellis picked up several small white cockleshells from the sand. "Don't imagine the government's motive is avarice."

"Oh, yeah?"

"From each pound of aurium we bring home, they'll take a sixth for the maintenance of the Navy fleet at Harrisburg." He threw a shell away. "And another for the shafting of Yamato's plots in Korea; and a twelfth to loan to the independent Korean leadership; and another twelfth to help the insurgents in Hainan." The last shell he held up significantly. "D'you see now?"

"Alia Kane confided all this personally to you, did she? You who's spent the last God-knows-how-long being a guest in Camp Worth, and almost had your ass freezeed by her?"

"Yep. I spoke with her directly."

Oujuku levered himself to his feet, shook his head. "Oh, yeah! They use the Probe on you, or something?"

"Jos Hawken is very well connected."

"Yeah! Jos Hawken is!" Oujuku's voice was edged with steel. "But you said you spoke *with the President herself!*"

"You better believe it."

"I don't believe Hawken. And I've got my own schemes that won't cost me a bloodsucking." Oujuku stabbed a savage finger toward the zenith. "There's *Constitution*—Hawken's ship. Built to his specifications. I think he's using you, Ellis."

"He has talent in that line. Also the services of the finest ship designers in Amerika—which means the finest, period. But *Constitution* is mine."

Oujuku took a deep breath. "Can you satisfy me that Jos Hawken isn't still working you like a puppet?"

Ellis's chest swelled up. "Is this a puppet you see standing here?"

"I don't know. But I don't believe you. Or you've not told me the whole story yet. Hey, Ellis! Aren't we confidential with each other anymore?"

The pause between them dragged out, tormenting Ellis until he felt he must break it.

"I was sworn to silence."

"I knew it! And we're sworn to be straight with one another."

"Okeh, Jos Hawken never had a part in any of this. If you want to know the reason, then I'll tell you: I was in love!"

"In love? You?"

Ellis caught Oujuku's surprise, and the angry part of him got hot. He gestured at Oujuku dangerously. "Yes! Me! In love! And I married—in spirit—just as you did in body and soul."

In the light of the fires, Ellis's face was as hard as iron. The words spilled from him, telling how he had come to love the secretary of state's daughter, how he had pursued her and played a dangerous game under Conroy Lubbock's nose. He finished, stilting his words, and sat down again on the powdery ground, his head in his hands.

Oujuku was shaking his head in wonder. "You *crafty* sonofabitch!"

"She was married to Kurt Reiner, the Halide heir, in St. Anthony's before I left Liberty. With Alia Kane in attendance, and a guest list like Who Knows Who. And my son was in that bride's belly." He lifted his head, staring at the painfully bright point in the nameless constellation. "You see that star? It shines for my boy. It's his star. But when he's born there'll be a better bed for him to sleep in than the one this nexus rat could give him. There'll be wise men enough around him. And the President herself will be his godmother."

The waves lapped slowly on the gently curving, shallowly sloping beach. Some of the fires had burned down to embers, some of the people were stretched out, ankles crossed, elbows out from their ears. Others had crept away into the darkness. Some told likely tales, still others laughed at them. Happy crews with an adventure ahead of them and no cares about tomorrow.

"I want my brother, John."

"I know you do."

"Are you gonna help me or hinder me? I must know which, because with you or without you I mean to get him back."

Oujuku sighed. "You can't now."

"I can. There's not a man alive that can't be ransomed out of Yamato if the price is right."

"No."

"Listen, if—"

"No, Ellis. No!" Oujuku laid hands on him.

"Why no? Explain."

"Just this: I've had a little news of my own. News you won't find a whole lot to your liking."

Oujuku shouted for Frane, who went on his errand, reporting back with another of Oujuku's crewmen. Despite the way the man's cheeks had caved in with the loss of his teeth, Ellis recognised him immediately.

"Good God, aren't you—"

Oujuku cut in. "I hoped to be able to spare you this, Ellis, but you won't be put off," he said, then he turned to Horse. "Tell Captain Straker the same tale that you told to me."

"Okeh."

Ellis listened silently but with mounting dread as Horse recounted his story. He spoke about Chi no Tsuki and Sado, and how he had been imprisoned by Nishima Jun. Then he spoke of his working in the argentium refineries, but this was only preamble to a more shocking tale. When he told of his visit to the *han* of Hasegawa, his march to the great volcano Fuji-san, and his subsequent escape offplanet, Ellis felt hollow inside. He was unable to speak.

Oujuku questioned the isotopist some more, then dismissed him. When they were alone again, Oujuku said, "We picked him up when we took a trader bound for the Marquesas chain. He was working his passage, calling himself a German isotopist, looking to get to Europa, and eventually, so he says, to ship for home. I heard his story some two months back just as you've heard it now."

"He's lying!"

"No, Ellis."

"He's lying, I tell you!"

"Why would he lie? For what reason? Eh?"

Ellis's mind boiled with impossible explanations. The shame of it! It couldn't be true. Not Duval. Not his own brother—making secret weapons for Yamato? A big thing going with a Japanese woman? No, it was Oujuku's lies! All Oujuku. He'd put the man up to it! Yes.

"You've set me up—"

Oujuku leaned back, his face showing his compassion. "It's no setup. You know the isotopist. You know he went to Sado four years ago. He's got no reason to lie."

"No. I don't believe him."

"All right, maybe you'll believe this." Oujuku pulled out the ring. Its gold glittered in Oujuku's palm. It was the same ring Ellis had once passed to Chambers. "It went from Jon Chambers's hand to your brother, and from him it was taken by Horse in their struggle on the volcano, and from him to me. You'll have to face it, Ellis: your brother's made a fool out of you."

Ellis twisted the ring over and over in his fingers, burning with humiliation. By God, how could Duval have done it? According to Horse, they had not tortured him or put him to the Probe. He had given up his priceless design skills freely.

"I can't believe it," he whispered, knowing it was a lie.

"He's made fools of us all"—Ellis tried to shut out Oujuku's words but they came at him like relentless daggers—"and he'll do so again." Oujuku spoke flatly, but he could not keep the reproach out of his voice. "Once Sado and Okinawa and Dozen and all the other ports along the Boundary are fortified with singularity guns, we can kiss goodbye to any more raids. We'll be reduced to scavenging orbit ships and thieving nickel-'n'-dime traders and running like shit from the Yamato Guard—"

"Jeezus, that's enough!"

"I'm sorry, Ellis. But you had to know."

Oujuku walked away, went back to his bonfire, and Ellis let him go. His plans were in ruins.

And his soul was in hell.

SADO

The daimyo's apartments were in darkness. Nishima Jun lay on his cushions, his satisfactions over the work of fortifying Sado temporarily driven from his mind by a maddening sexual itch. It took all his willpower to turn his mind away from the deliciously illicit liaison he had entered into six days ago.

The supple young body of the Taiwanese girl. Her full lips and black eyes. The wispy hair of her pubis. The fire of her *sangokujin* blood. Her resistance. How he had delighted to break that down, to smother her protests, to threaten her and then promise her, to take her and enter her and sate himself, and then to order her not to run away, not to tell anyone. Or her family would all suffer.

He wanted her again—such a delight—once, twice, three times a week. Oh, the smell of her. He could take her daily. Twice daily. "Wei," he whispered, pronouncing the syllable of her name slowly, repeatedly, enjoying the way it sighed across his tongue.

What if she tells? What if she has my bastard? he asked himself, suddenly disturbed that he could be proud at the idea. That would show Fumiko. If ever she found out. If ever. But that's why I spilled my seed outside the maid's love tunnel. I must be careful. It's too dangerous these days. A man must be oh-so-careful! Because fornication with a *sangokujin* is not the way a daimyo should conduct himself. It is contrary to the Confucian ideal, and only death and disgrace can come of it. No one is immune from the *kempei* now.

His thoughts went brooding out over the night's darkness, across the sculpted roofs of the city to the place where the *kempei* had installed itself, and he knew he had made a serious tactical mistake. He could not afford to have them know of his weakness. No, that would upset everything.

He heard footsteps through the wall behind him, but no challenge from the guard. The shoji slid open, Fumiko came in, and the attendant closed it after her. She approached him, put her hands together, standing so close that the folds of her long robe touched his oiled swept-back hair.

"This heat!"

"Does it keep you awake, Fumiko-san?" His reply was ice cold.

"Don't you want to go to bed?"

"I'm not tired."

She faced the spray of willow fronds that arched from a fine porcelain vase. "A marriage bed is not only for sleeping, Jun-chan."

He drew in a loud breath and moved away from her, but continued to stare out of the open window. Oh, how the sound of her voice drained his desire. *Wei.*

"The law commands men and women to—"

"I know what the law commanded."

"Then why don't you obey?" Her voice was hope-lorn.

He tried to smile. "What would be the point? You are barren, Fumiko-san. We both know that."

"But I've completed another application. I've received permission for an operation. Three nights in the medical center on Kyoto, if you will only agree. A new womb and ovaries. The gods have favored me, the donor is samurai. It's certain to be a success. Please, Jun-chan, can we make love tonight. For my sake?"

"Not tonight."

Her words hardened, cut at him as she turned away. "You're the one who's afflicted. You have no love of duty in your heart. You're not a real man."

Always the same. Blaming him. If only she knew. If only she had seen the copious seed that had gushed over the belly of the maid. Potent seed. He had been stiff enough this afternoon. Poor, clever, studious, barren Fumiko. Couldn't she understand that no transplant could make her desirable. To use another woman's ovaries was merely to be a bearer of counterfeit genetic currency. He would never desire her. He would never give her a child.

"Go to bed, Fumiko-san."

But she had already begun to leave the room.

He lay back, rubbed at his eyes. He was tired, but he had to unknot the problem before he surrendered to sleep. Go over it again, he told himself. Once more to get it clear. From the beginning.

The first ominous sign of trouble had come when the *kin kaigun* had landed. News of Fukuda's arrival had preceded his appearance in Kanazawa by two weeks, wild rumors carried across the continent from Niigata that had inflamed the whole planet like a disease. Immediately a committee of samurai worthies had formed and he had agreed to meet with it, ostensibly to prepare a welcome for the distinguished *metsuke,* but the true function of the meetings had been otherwise.

The coming of the *kempei* had long been dreaded by the *han*-holders who were already established in the Co-prosperity Sphere, and would be greeted frostily by many of the samurai who had pioneered it. In all the years since the conquest never had they been subject to the control of the *kempei*. In all those years Kyoto had respected the status of the worlds beyond the official limits of Yamato. As a matter of practicality the men who were the source of the Emperor's wealth were spared the spiritual policing so necessary inside Yamato itself where mixed bloods and secret *sangokujin* had to be rigorously controlled. But over the years the inspectors general had been able to build up an irresistible pressure on the Emperor's government. They had used their unearthly influence on the shogun, who in turn had approached the Emperor, and so the hand of the *kempei* had reached out across the nexi and come at last to Sado.

Nishima recalled with sour regret the way he had recognised the threat the *kempei* posed to his own temporal powers. He had seen a way to accommodate the office, and to deflect for the moment the fears of his *hatamoto,* but the committee of worthies had been right about giving the office a single grain of rice and expecting them to be content with it.

Fukuda had virtually requisitioned the grand house across the main square, next to the shrine, and decided that it was best to call to question first the famous Amerikan interlopers—especially those that had become integrated into the fabric of life on Sado.

The orders had been read out and notice given that the Amerikans were suspected of impurities and must come to account for themselves. They were sent for and searched out in all parts of Sado, and proclamations made, upon pain of confiscation and exile, that no person should keep secret any *gaijin*.

At first, Nishima had done nothing. He had taken no steps to protect his investment, deciding that discretion might be a more effective policy. He had sent Hasegawa Katsumi to speak with his father about the weapon-designer, and to reassure the family, but nothing more. After all, wasn't he now an adopted husband? Hadn't he taken marriage vows and been doubly confirmed in his spiritual purity by absorption into the highly respectable Hasegawa clan? The man had a new name. He applied himself assiduously to his work. He was confined on the *han*. With luck, Nishima had thought, it could be years before the *kempei* came to Chiba.

But Duval had been betrayed. By whom, it did not matter. A servant, a priest, one of his own men, another of the Amerikans who knew where he was, had learned of his work and chosen to point the finger at him . . . Whatever the means, the *kempei* had found out about him and he had been taken.

At this point Nishima had pressed his daimyo's privileges. As proconsul to the *bakufu* he had certain rights, could make certain small demands. He had indulgently explained about the new guns. "A matter of the utmost strategic importance, Fukuda-san. I'm sure you understand?"

But the *metsuke* had stared back unmoved. At their second formal meeting, Fukuda had been at pains to clarify his position. "Your Exalted Excellency may be the tool of government, but please remember that our office is the instrument of the Emperor himself."

"Of course, and we agreed that all *gaijin* should be exposed. But this man is not a *gaijin*."

"Agreed?" Fukuda had echoed, leaning back without any hint of his former amity. "I was not aware of any agreement between us. The term '*gaijin*' includes so-called adopted husbands and all those who cannot trace their ancestry to Old Nihon through the paternal line."

"Please excuse me!" he had cajoled, pricked by Fukuda's inflexibility. He had swallowed his pride again. "How can that be? This man is an adopted husband. He's given up his identity completely. His old life is over, his former self is dead. He's as good a Yamato citizen as I am."

"Indeed?" Fukuda had paused significantly until the debating point was both scored and acknowledged. "I salute Your Excellency's noble efforts on our behalf, but I must point out that accurate measures of depth of belief and sincerity of conviction are quite impossible. However, that small and worthless skill in inquiry that a *metsuke* such as myself possesses must now be applied. If the gods allow it, an interesting outcome may result."

He had sighed, humbling himself further. "But surely this one man, who may do His Imperial Majesty great service? Surely he could be overlooked?"

Then the *metsuke* had laid the closely written scroll open to his inspection, passing a hand over the names. "It is the Emperor's will that all—*all*—herein proscribed shall be brought captive to the city of Kanazawa and committed separately to prison cells to undergo examination."

"And if you should find him pure, Fukuda-san?"

"Ah." Fukuda's smile had shocked him with its ugliness. "If he was found to be pure, then we should release him. But who amongst the living is really pure?"

"I'm gratified, Fukuda-san," he had said, readying himself to leave. "Gratified, and so pleased we understand one another."

Nishima's eyes continued to dwell on the house whose plex annex had become a prison, one cell of which held the man who remained the key to military victory. It's too bad, he thought, scratching at his scrotum vigorously. I tried. But the Amerikan's survival is probably no longer an issue. He's served his purpose now; his gun secrets have almost certainly been learned by his team. I pray to the gods that that's so, because I'll wager a ball of aurium to a bamboo cup that he'll never get out of that house alive.

He examined his fingernails in the muted light and a frown clouded his face. "Wei! You filthy young whore," he muttered, suddenly realising about the prickling at his groin. "She's lousy. And the disgusting little *sangokujin* has made me lousy too!"

50

"Do you believe in the divinity of the Emperor, Duval Straker?"

The inspector general, a small, gray man in purple robes, knelt on a slightly raised rostrum. To his right sat another, Hishikari, a severe, heavy-browed man in his late forties, in a black kimono decorated with gray barred-spiral galaxies as a repeated motif, crossed tightly at the neck and stiffly winged at the shoulder. He was silent, staring down at his papers. To the left, Wada, a younger man in plain brown, taking notes with practiced ease into a five-finger keypad as they spoke, and in the shadows at the side, seated against the wall, a big man in a loose black *haori* robe. Another, whose name was Suzuki, was concealed behind a black lacquer and mother-of-pearl screen.

On the low table, which was spread neatly with a cloth of white silk, stood a small replica of the *gohei*, an ink block and brushes, some hardcopy sheets, and a half-unsheathed disemboweling sword. Alone in the center of the table was a scroll containing the *metsuke*'s imperial mandate.

"I ask you again: do you believe in the divinity of the Emperor?"

"Yes."

"Witnesses say that you do not."

"What witnesses?"

The man seated to the inspector general's right spoke. "Many good people offer themselves to our service. A person needs only a clean heredity to help our office discover error."

"Who informed on me?"

"It is our rule never to say."

"Tell me who alleges I am impure now."

"We do not break rules. We adhere to our methods."

"What is the specific charge?"

"It is our practice not to divulge that."

"Then how may I defend myself?"

"It is not for you to prepare defenses, only to answer our inquiries with the whole truth."

"Do you believe in the divinity of the Emperor?"

Duval's thirst raged, blood pounded in his head, and the light from the translucent walls pierced him. He had been confined in absolute blackness for a long time. How long? Three months? Six? Nine? It was impossible to say. The trailing of the inked brush over the sheets fascinated him, the sound plucking his nerves raw. He watched the soft light sharpen on the semi-revealed edge of the *seppuku* sword, glinting at him as the questions were repeated endlessly, the same questions put to him time after time until he longed to answer them with other words.

On the striking of a large, distant gong, a new question.

"Tell us about yourself."

"There is nothing to tell."

"Every man has one story to tell."

"Some have more than one," Hishikari Noburo said.

"Can you read Japanese?"

"Yes."

"And write?"

"Yes."

"How many *kanji* do you know?"

"I don't know—four, maybe five thousand."

"You know what this is?"

"Of course. It's a writing brush."

"Take it."

"Why?"

"Take it with you to your cell. A lamp will be allowed. You will record for us a full confession of your life. Every detail, exactly as you recall it. Not until that is done and we have examined it will you be brought before us again."

"And if I refuse?"

"You will not refuse."

He ached all over.

He could not tell if it was night or day. He might have been here a month or six months or a year, but there was no way to tell, no regularity about the appearance of rice and water or the times when that intense, blinding blue lamp was lit for him. No natural light penetrated to the hot, humid cell, but still the flies found their way in through the ventilators, attracted by the stench in the corner.

His ears were sharp to the sounds that came from beyond the seamless door, muffled sounds, as if the feet of the guards were bare to deaden their noise. They had ordered him to make no sound, and they had beat the soles of his feet to insensation when he had disobeyed. No one spoke outside, though often he could hear them faintly, passing by. No human sounds, except a distant coughing, a wretching, or the screams that trailed away beyond another muffled door.

How long before they came to beat him again? The dread kept him awake interminably until his mind grew as heavy as aurium and his thoughts melted into chaos. Am I ill? he asked himself, unable to understand the incredible lassitude that filled him. Am I dying? Have they drugged the water? Have they given me a disease?

He lay back, imagining the room upside down, that he was falling. He dreamed that he was dreaming fractured dreams on the frayed and fetid tatami that served as his bed. He felt the need to relieve himself, but he could not get up, could not will his legs to lift him. He had written the confession after the third beating, filling the sheets with every item of his past that he could recall, and after that they had come and collected the sheets but left him in his corner. He felt the pressure in his bladder, but he could not move and he could not raise the effort to halt the unmistakable series of relaxations in his belly. He tried to hold his muscles shut, but it was too late, and he felt the hot urine flood his groin and the smell was rich and dark and uric, but he could do nothing except lie there and tell himself that it did not matter because it was not real and that the nightmare was only a nightmare.

When he was called again into that intense light before the *metsuke,* they told him quietly that they had read all the sheets he had written. They were seated as before, and they told him their names as before, and examined him and commanded him to explain for them certain Zen *koans,* or riddles, which he could have responded to at one time with ease, but somehow as he addressed the words he found his mind wandering, and they gave him some water so that he could continue like a man and not caw like a crow. He thought of Helene di Barrio and the rest. A great many, he knew, would be able to make nothing of a Zen *koan,* other than to call it a half-assed piece of mystical bullshit.

Then they demanded in thin, flat voices, "What is the sound of one hand clapping?"

"The sound of the wind from nowhere."

"Where is this nowhere?"

Duval said nothing.

"Answer."

"If I must answer, then nowhere is the place the darkness goes when the light is turned on."

"Do you believe in the divinity of the Emperor?"

"I do." It was true. In one way, Mutsuhito was a god.

"Ai-ee!" The one called Suzuki exploded with anger. "You're lying, trying to save your life. You know that if you answered as you truly believed, you would die."

"I want to die."

"What were you taught as a child?"

"To believe in logic."

"Nothing else?"

"To believe there are many ways, all valid. To believe in the fundamental rights of mankind."

"*So desu ka?* Truly? You were forced to believe these lies?"

"In Amerika there is no compulsion to believe."

"Then where did you find such chaotic ideas?"

Duval swallowed, awarc that he was being maneuvered into a trap of self-condemnation. He said, "My childhood was poor. Deficient in all kinds of learning. Which was no fault of mine."

"But as an adult you did not correct your errors? Why was that?"

"In all my days in Amerika, no one questioned me as you have."

"There are many errors in Amerika."

"The minds there are never silent."

"*So desu ne.* I agree. Who commands that?"

"It is the Way of Amerika."

"An impure way!"

"A different way."

"In Amerika there is no understanding!"

"There is no *bushido.*"

"Therefore, there can be no honor."

Silence.

"You and the other Amerikans allowed yourself to be captured in battle. This is the real reason why you are now so obedient to the Way. You are dead."

"This is not so."

He began to shiver, his teeth chattering together like ivory dice.

"Explain?"

"The people first imprisoned by the authorities were freely exchanged hostages. The people who were brought down from Chi no Tsuki were marooned. I was not captured in battle. I was arrested several days after the battle whilst trying to obtain food."

"Then your status is that of a thief."

"Attempted thief."

"There is no such status as attempted thief. Yamato law does not concern itself with motives, only behavior."

"Then I am not a thief."

Fukuda stirred, his purple robe crackling as he adjusted a fold in the sleeve. "It is not our purpose to inquire into your status in law, only your state of purity. You may know that it is not possible for a man to become a *go* grand master unless he begins to play the game regularly before the age of five. So it is with the Way."

"I had no control over where I was born."

"The fact remains: you spent a quarter century in total ignorance of the Way."

"Not in total ignorance. There were some writings on *bushido* available. The *Go Rin No Sho* is a book found in many libraries in Amerika in English translation."

"Do you know how much you have revealed your ignorance by that remark? Japanese is much more complex and subtle than any barbarian language. Japanese cannot be successfully translated into any barbarian language. It is impossible to render an ancient classic like the *Go Rin No Sho* into English."

"Some people in Amerika learn to speak Japanese, just as I learned."

"You learned this as an intellectual exercise?"

"Partly."

"Yes or no?"

"Yes."

"Was it not to distinguish yourself from those who willingly remained ignorant?"

"We did not consider ourselves ignorant. Amerikans think there are many ways, and that all ways are valid."

"You behaved and believed according to that philosophy?"

"I behaved and believed as everyone around me did."

"*Wakarimashita!* Ah, as a sheep does?"

"As people do."

"Yet you say there was no compulsion of belief in Amerika?"

"It is the law in Amerika to guarantee all men and women certain fundamental rights and freedoms."

"Such an idea is dangerous and repellent. Law and order of this kind is an attempt to pervert the natural order!"

"There is a saying in English: no man is an island. It means that we are none of us isolated. We are all affected by the context in which we live."

"Then you admit that you did not behave and believe of your own free will."

"How could I?"

"So you were acting contrary to your culture's imperatives."

Another asked him, "Were there never days when you had doubts? Never days when you preferred not to endure the foolish ideas of rights without duties?"

"There were no days like that."

"Were you taught about the Way?"

"Not formally."

"You had a word for racial Japanese?"

"We called them Yambos."

"Do you believe in the divinity of the Emperor?"

"Yes."

"Open your eyes."

Hishikari consulted the sheet, adjusting it to the light. "I read your history and I ask myself this: what can account for the recent change in your convictions?"

Wada Zengo, the recorder, explained. "We find as the honorable ancients found before us that the mind of man is as a clay vessel, malleable at the first throwing upon the potter's wheel, but as a man ages so the vessel is fired. The form is imprinted indelibly and may no longer change."

"And when pressure is applied," Hishikari added unsmilingly, "the vessel shatters."

"And yet you say you changed, Duval Straker," Fukuda said. "And you did not shatter."

"My beliefs are as changed as my name, which is Hasegawa Zinan."

"*Masaka!* It is no matter to change a man's name."

Wada said, "All criminals maintain aliases."

"I am not a criminal."

"And alibis."

"I am not a criminal!"

Hishikari slapped the signed sheet before him. "Is this your alibi, Duval Straker?"

"It is the truth, as you asked it of me."

"Strange, then, that it does not accord with the confessions of certain other Amerikans."

"What?"

"They condemn you."

"That is their fear talking."

"Do you have no fear?"

This time he did not answer.

Then Fukuda asked, "Did you agree to become an adopted husband of Hasegawa Michie only that you might be allowed to live?"

He stared at them, his anger suddenly stronger than his fear or his exhaustion, but the mention of his wife's name sent shivers of panic through him.

"If you will only tell us the truth, you will be set at liberty."

"I have told you the truth."

"Are you sorry for the infractions and offenses you committed in Niigata against the imperial government of Yamato?"

"By the gods it was nothing to do with me!"

"Why did you make no mention in your confessions of your Japanese heritage?"

"What are your saying?"

"We have carried out a genetic test and found you to be half Japanese."

"Impossible. There's been some mistake."

"I warn you again to tell the truth."

"Probe him!" Hishikari demanded.

"Must we Probe you?"

He knuckled his eyes, his mouth was dry again.

Fukuda renewed his question, his voice cooing now, redolent with regret that such action was necessary and unavoidable. "Must we?"

"Yes!" Hishikari shouted.

"If only you would be frank with me and make a sincere confession."

"I have told you everything."

"Oh, wicked half man. Show him what is coming."

They had recruited *hinin* and Koreans for their stainless-steel shop of terrors, and some who enjoyed watching the pain brought up in others.

An electric branding rod glowed red in its stand, and liquid crystal tattoo inserters and other implant instruments. This place was where the *han* administration office had once IDed slaves, but now its function had been taken over by the *kempei*. Through the window, he recognised the horrible twisted figure of Jeff Smith hanging unconscious from a punishment frame, his marked body suspended upside down. He had been there some time: the blood had pooled in his head, making his face purple, and rivers of dried blood patterned his body. It was not possible to tell if he was still alive.

They took him past a side room, where Kentwell Harper's naked body was bound to a bench, his head confined in a hood, his nostrils plugged with cotton, his throat packed, and water was being dripped into his mouth through a funnel. Next door Kai Boscovitch's feet had been smashed with hammers. Her face was a hideous yellow. As they dragged Duval into the room, a pail of water was thrown over her, rousing her to groans. The steel frame below was bloodied, and she screamed at the sight of her broken legs, unable to stop.

A Shinto priest stood at Boscovitch's side, with the *gohei* held up before him.

"Help me! Oh God, help me!"

"*Doshi mashita?!*"

"Help me!"

"*Yorokonde.*"

"I'll do anything." The victim screamed again, her eyes popping, her breath pumping. "Anything!"

"But the truth is what we require."

"The truth . . ."

"She's fainted again, Hishikari-san."

"Here's another. He is special. You will Probe him."

"Yes, Hishikari-san."

They made him look at the Probe, secured his ankles and his wrists, gagged his mouth, levering his teeth open so that the packing filled his mouth like a horse's bit, and twisted it tight, then the cage was put over his head, the mechanism clicking as they turned the machine on.

Where are you, Michie? he thought, his brain beginning to blind with terror. Are you thinking of me?

And then the true agony started.

51

Michie had not hesitated to steal either the heirlooms or the air-car. She had finally broken free from the confinement her family had imposed on her at Chiba and come to the city of Kanazawa to do what she could. Night and day she had lingered outside the daimyo's residence with her petition, but the guards would not admit her without authority and she had not dared to reveal her identity for fear that her father's searchers would find her.

She had fixed her hopes on Katsumi. Surely her brother must help her. Surely he would fix her an interview with Lord Nishima. But when she asked after him, they told her the honorable officer was far away in Niigata.

Friendless, the city was a changed place. A dark pall of fear had fallen over it. Well-to-do samurai doors were barred against her. Few dared listen to her pleas, and those who did professed themselves as helpless as she was, or took the opportunity to remind her of her father's foolishness in ever thinking to marry her to a barbarian. Some even tried to trap her, to send her back to Chiba. So she had fled.

She had sold the conspicuous air-car for a robber's price and got herself lodging at an inn in a bad part of town. Here technology was either banned or shunned. The town was a mass of semitraditional-style shanties all tumbled one upon another. She had dressed in the white false silk of a low-class widow, but her bearing and mannerisms constantly gave her away. The fawning servility of the lower orders had evaporated here. In their own territory and with no samurai to watch them they were tough-bodied and flint-eyed and their language stung like salt in a wound. She endured the whispers of the street. The *ikki* women thought her mad. They gossiped acidly at her misfortune and speculated at what had given her delusions of samurai status. She could not really be samurai—could she? She bore unflinchingly the stones of *hinin* children who made faces at her and danced out their parents' superstitious hatred insolently in front of her. And the stinking drunks that encountered her at night pressed themselves on her when they saw her fine looks, making foul suggestions and pawing her until she showed them the razor-edged short sword she kept concealed in her robe.

There had been talk. Her father's people had heard the rumor. Yukiko, her maid, and two of her mother's servants had laid hands on her to bring her away, but she would not surrender herself, telling them that they should help her rather than hinder her, but they only repeated what her father had said. So she had pulled out her *aikuchi* dagger and threatened to spill her own blood if they did not let her run from them.

So she had come at last in utter desperation to the domicile of Wataru Hoshino.

"Please, Wataru-san! You must help me!"

"Come in, Lady. Come in."

He had made a place on his floor for her and offered her green tea and noodle soup, which she would not eat, and apologised for his humble home, smiling toothlessly but compassionately, until her tears dried.

"What can be done for you now?" he asked, facing her across his low table, stroking the long, graying head of his old dog. The heady stink of dog permeated the room, and dog hairs were stuck into the weave of the tatami. Through the slightly parted door, on the other side of the street, she could see a tattooed *yakuza* delicately stripping the insulation from a humming 550-volt power cable with a knife, prior to making an illegal tap.

"You know that Zinan-san is imprisoned," she said.

"I heard the proclamation, Lady."

"I must try to save him."

He patted the dog's head and clasped his hands together. "In your heart you believe that to save him now is too much to hope for."

"No!" Her face was white, drawn with anguish and lack of sleep. "I can't believe that. I must not believe that. They are going to crucify him, Wataru-san. Do you understand? *They are going to crucify my husband.*"

"Hush, hush."

"Wataru Hoshino, you are an honorable man. You have been a soldier. You must help me or I shall die by my own hand!"

"Quiet, now, Lady. Listen to yourself! Are you not a daughter of the Hasegawa clan? I will help you. Take courage. And plan, as your father would plan, to think how you might make the *metsuke* change his decision. But take care also for your own life. Those black priests will see your devotion only as the taint of the *gaijin*."

She nodded rapidly, recognising the wise counsel of an old man. "I must find a way to see Fukuda, explain to him that Zinan is a true subject of the Emperor, that our marriage was real. But the guards he has posted on his door will not admit me."

Wataru put up his hands. "No, Lady! You must not go to Fukuda Ikku."

"But if any man can reverse the decision of the tribunal, surely it is he."

Wataru's eyes clouded. "There is nothing you can offer him that will change his mind."

Michie reached inside her robe and took from it a leather bag. She opened it and spilled a glittering assortment of super-heavy nuggets across the scarred wood: aurium, argentium, and small, green-tinted nodules of native platinium. "Look! These can be his ransom."

"I don't think so, Lady."

She went on breathlessly in fervent hope. "But I have been told that Fukuda's rapacity is boundless. Doesn't the *kempei* finance itself through confiscation? These are not conterfeit, they are completely genuine and worth exceptional credit!"

"Then, for your own sake, Lady, do not show any of them to Fukuda Ikku."

"But—"

Wataru was shaking his head. "I have seen the *metsuke*'s like before. And in Niigata the men who came on the last *kin kaigun* told me about the time his zeal was unleashed on board Admiral Kurita's flagship. No, Lady, he is a complete fanatic. You cannot bargain with him. If once you show him your pretty nuggets, he will take them. Then he will be forced to commit you to his prison to cover his theft."

"But how, then?"

"We have few allies in this battle, Lady."

"Even Katsumi is in Niigata." Her mouth twisted with bitterness. "All of those who I thought were my friends have deserted me. I could hardly believe their cowardice."

"Don't fault them. They are scared. You must see that when the Amerikans are used up, the *kempei* will begin looking for others to indict."

A canyon of silence opened.

"So Zinan-san must die?"

Wataru's head lifted on his shoulders. "Do not lose hope."

"Do you think he will escape?"

"He's imprisoned alone and well guarded in a prison with plex walls. He cannot escape. But—"

"Yes?"

Her eyes were luminous with tears; her whole being hung on what the old man was about to say.

"I know one thing, Lady. Your brother, Katsumi, is certainly not in Niigata."

Then he told her what she must do.

The city square was in darkness as she ran through it. The sculptured roof of the daimyo's residence stood out starkly against the star-peppered sky, and the wooden edifice of the *kempei*'s punishment stage was eerie and empty. At the gates she was stopped by the guard, who looked at her *ikki* garments and denied her entry.

"Go away, woman! You cannot come here."

The guard was armored, a soldier but not a samurai, with pocked face and tattered beard.

"How dare you speak to me in that manner?"

"Go, woman, before we set the dogs on you." The other, a man of slighter build and shorter ways, thrust his torch into her face. "Go!"

She stood her ground. "I am the sister of Hasegawa Katsumi. I must speak with him."

The first guard shifted his weight and peered at her, apparently unconvinced, but when he spoke, his mode of address had altered. "The man you name is not here, Lady."

"Don't lie to me, soldier."

"He is not here, I tell you."

She produced a nugget of bluish metal and held it up so that it reflected the torchlight brilliantly. "This says that Hasegawa Katsumi is dining with the daimyo tonight."

The slighter guard took the nugget and examined it, spitting on it and polishing it on his cotton sleeve. He looked about him and weighed the stone in his palm—there was no doubt it was aurium.

"I'll inform Hasegawa-san, Lady."

"Quickly."

He vanished and reappeared moments later with Katsumi, who was furious at the disturbance. He seized her roughly and brought her inside, out of earshot.

"Michie-san," he whispered fiercely, towering close over her. "Are you mad? What are you doing? Don't you know that our father is here in Kanazawa, combing the city for you? Where have you been?"

"I want to see the daimyo."

"Don't be stupid. That's impossible!"

"Katsumi-san, I must see him!"

He shook with anger, plucking out a hair and holding it at her. "Don't you *understand?* By the gods you are that far—*that far*—from getting us all impeached by the *kempei*. Thank the gods I've found you. Now your father can put you in hand."

"You didn't find me! I found you!" Her voice rang out in the timbered interior, then grew intense, pleading. "You must help me, Katsumi-san. If ever there was a time a sister needed her brother's help, it's now. Do not deny me, please!"

"Help you? What for? So you may find a way to get the Amerikan out of prison. You'll get us all killed and dishonored."

"He is your brother-in-law. Where is your duty?"

"I warned you at the very first not to look at him, Michie-san. But you disobeyed me."

"Hypocrite! Don't give me your lies. You brought him to me in the first place. And now, for fear of the *kempei* you deny all. Bring me to the daimyo, or I'll denounce you to the *metsuke* as a secret worshiper of the Christian God!"

"Sister, control yourself!"

She inclined her head and set her words in a deadly threat. "Take me to Nishima-sama, or I will do exactly as I have said."

All around faces appeared at corners. Doors cracked open. He hurried her deeper down the candlelit corridors, to the heart of the residence, a quiet flagged quadrangle with moss rockery and stream, then he stopped again and implored her, his hands curling in the empty air at his breast. "Think carefully, I beg you. I have been to the daimyo once already, and I have heard his answer. He'll never back down. And if he did, what could he do? He has no authority over the *kempei* prison. Even he is powerless to save your—"

"Take me!" she shricked, and the sound echoed like a *katsu* shout in a Zen temple.

He clapped his hand over her mouth and led her away to a great, carved wooden door, guarded by two sentries, who snapped to attention as they saw Katsumi's uniform. Neither looked at Michie, but gazed ahead, allowing the daimyo's principal lieutenant to pass. Inside, Saionji Hidemasa, the daimyo's chief *hatamoto,* was at his station.

"Excuse me. Is Nishima-sama within?" Katsumi asked without ceremony.

Saionji, a man in his forties with eyeglasses and a shock of sleek black hair, looked up slowly from his reading, appraising the grime-streaked woman who stood beside Katsumi. "He is, Hasegawa-san. So sorry, but you can't go in. The *metsuke*'s with him. Excuse me, but who's this?"

"Thank you." He looked dangerously at his sister, but when he turned for the exit back into the courtyard, she refused to follow.

"Michie-san—"

"So sorry. We'll wait," she blurted out.

"As you wish, woman." Saionji shrugged and sucked a tooth. "So sorry, but His Excellency may be quite some time. May I inquire the nature of your business?"

"So sorry. It's confidential."

"Very well."

Michie stood with her eyes downcast; Katsumi stood with his back to the secretary. His intense embarrassment that Saionji should see him thus exposed showed in the color of his face, which was reddening. He seemed to be waiting for Saionji to offer some slight, but the secretary merely unfolded the wires of his spectacles and looped them over his ears, allowing disdain to be suggested by his indifference.

Was Wataru-san right? she wondered. Was the inspector general so terrible? Should she throw herself on Fukuda Ikku's mercy when he appeared? What sort of man was he? Surely a man personally entrusted by the Emperor would have compassion. For the sake of her husband she would throw herself at his feet, beg him to reconsider, and the daimyo would add his voice to hers and Zinan would be saved.

The daimyo's door opened and everyone bowed low, holding their bows. Michie was surprised to have seen Fumiko standing at his side. Nishima-sama was subdued, almost reverential before the tiny man in purple.

She steeled herself, not daring to look up. This was the moment. If she was going to fall at the *metsuke*'s feet, it must be now.

As she raised her head, the daimyo looked up suddenly, seeing them for the first time, but his expression was so full of displeasure that she froze.

"What's she doing here?" he muttered furiously, touching Katsumi's sleeve, then he swept past with the *metsuke,* his wife conversing banally with him.

As the echoes of Fumiko's nasal tones died away, Saionji said to Katsumi, "So sorry, but I warned you that the lord was extremely busy tonight. Would you like to stay a little longer? I'm sure he'll be back presently."

"Thank you, but we'll leave now."

He grabbed her arm but she fought him off. "No! I won't go!"

When Nishima returned, he ordered Katsumi and his sister immediately into his sanctum. "Explain yourself, Hasegawa!"

"Excellency, I'm sorry. My sister—"

The daimyo turned his anger on her. "What are you doing here? Don't you know that your family's worried about you? That it's dangerous for you here?"

"I—I *had* to see you, Excellency," she stammered, terrified to be confronting him this way. "It's about my husband."

"What of it? He's under arrest. I can do nothing for him."

Fumiko came in, eyeing her coldly.

"Please, you must save him. For your own sake, Lord."

"What does she mean, Jun-san? Speak up, child."

"The weapons. It's the weapons. Zinan told me that he has kept the secret of how the gun is made in his head. Without knowledge of the general equation of state for the form of the compression chamber the facility cannot make others. If he dies you will not impress His Imperial Majesty with your work, and he will not order you back to Yamato."

The daimyo's eyes flashed to Katsumi. "Is this true?"

He made a helpless gesture. "I don't know, Excellency. It might be."

Fumiko watched her husband sit down on the tatami heavily and begin to stroke his moustache. Though they knelt to lower their heads below the daimyo's, Fumiko seethed with anger inside. You're a fool, Jun-san, she thought. Why didn't you stand up to Fukuda Ikku like a samurai of the first rank? Now we're both trapped here on this vile colony planet forever. I'll never see Kyoto again. Never. I hate you, Jun-san. I hate your weakness and your pride and the way you treat me. You think I don't know? I have eyes to see and ears to hear, and I am not a fool. God knows how many days and nights I've endured your humiliating me with your filthy *sangokujin* whores. Must I endure it forever? The Emperor will never have you back in Yamato until Prince Sekigahara, who aided you in your murder of Prince Kono, is dead. But Prince Sekigahara is not yet thirty years old, and his life is charmed in war. You will die, Jun-san, and I will die long before he does. You knew the new weapons were our only hope, and yet you let Fukuda Ikku take the Amerikan away. And tonight, instead of working for his release, you humbled yourself before that stinking little jumped-up priest. Don't you care that we're marooned here beyond the outermost edge of civilisation?

"Do you know why the inspector general was here tonight, Michie-san?" Nishima was saying. He was calmer now; regret edged his voice. "Tonight I asked him for your husband's release, but he refused me. There is no legal way I can countermand him."

"Then please try to find some other way. I beg you!"

"Hasegawa-san, take her to her father. She must understand that she can do no good here."

"Yes, Excellency. Come here, Michie-san!"

Fumiko stepped forward. "It would be better if you left her to me," she said. "I know how to calm her. It's a woman's comfort she needs, not harsh words."

The girl was shaking as she allowed herself to be led from the daimyo's rooms. When they were alone, Fumiko said, "Tell me, child, how do you know that the Emperor would be reluctant to recall his daimyo from Sado should my husband desire that?"

Michie looked up at her, suddenly speared by the realisation that she had revealed her knowledge about the daimyo's past, but she seemed no longer to care. She said, "I saw long ago that Nishima-sama's appointment here was in effect an exile and that he wanted the singularity gun as a means to recover the Emperor's favor."

"That's very perceptive of you, Michie-san."

"I know also that the Emperor sent him here because he committed a great crime but at the same time a great service to His Imperial Majesty."

"And do you know what that crime-and-service was?"

"No, Fumiko-san."

The young woman's perfect oval face stared up at her unsettlingly, paining her unbearably. She might have had a daughter like Michie-san if she had not wed a man unwilling to give her permission for a transplant in twenty years of fruitless marriage. Jun-san has ruined my life, she thought as she watched those grief-reddened eyes. It is time he was made to pay.

"I will tell you the daimyo's crime," she said imperiously. "Then, if you so desire, you may use that information to persuade him to help free your husband."

THE OKINAWA SYSTEM, N.Z.

Ellis stood on *Constitution*'s tall tail fin at peace with the world, arms laced together, deep in contemplation. The morning on this idyllic world was cool and pleasant: the K-type star of this system low on the eastern horizon, lost in a great tangerine haze. Mists clung to the edges of the forest clearing in which they had set down. The plex underfoot was still wet with dew, undried as yet by the sun and smooth under his boots. Here and there on the broad wing, huge patterned moths shivered for warmth—green triangle wings, powdery mantles, feather antlers, thorn legs, and amethyst eyes. So beautiful. Each one the intricate handiwork of evolution. They had been blown out of the forest on the fetid breath that the jungle exhaled nightly, and Ellis wondered fleetingly how many countless millions of them were scattered as bird bait over the endless tracts of broadleaf in Okinawa's southern polar continent. Beautiful but wasted, unseen by any human eye. Wasted like the rain that fell over an ocean. Wasn't it strange that it rained at sea? A glitch in the efficiency of nature. An unknowably idiotic phenomenon but one that no terraformer had thought about bettering.

He took another turn about the tail plane, and his thoughts focused down on practicalities once more. His eyes followed the experimental stealth aerials. A new radio black dipole, four-stranded, twisted right to left, attached to a strange horn-like transmitter device, quite unlike anything he had seen before. The Yamato trader they had taken it out of had been rigged with it. "Ninja," the comms officer had called it, said it was brand-new and he didn't know how to switch it on. He ran his fingers over one of the dipoles where it was half-wave loaded. It had been his intention to renew the stealth equipment as necessary with a totally new rig, but he decided against it. After so long away, a man grew to know his own stealth gear, how it performed in space and under different magnetic conditions, how much it would take, where it would fail, and where it would go beyond spec. He had learned from Ayrton Rodrigo how to get the best from it, but this new Yamato stuff was reengineered and highly refined. Using it, a ship could be virtually invisible. And what had been built for shipping that wanted to avoid pirates could also be used by the pirates themselves.

Thoughts of Ayrton turned to thoughts of his brother. Horse's words haunted him now, shamed him with images of Duval sitting comfortably on some Sado *han* with a wife and his own research lab, making weapons for the enemy, *being* one of the enemy. After all the moments he had imagined Duval's peril, all the nights spent in Camp Worth worrying over the problem of his release like a dog at a bone; the defiance, the risks he had taken—and for what? It had soured him more deeply than anyone among Oujuku's crew, or his own, could know. The samurai had taken Duval bodily: that he could understand—for that he could almost forgive them man to man, could conceive bargaining Duval's release in civil terms. But they had cast a spell on his mind, the foul priests had suborned his spirit, and, by God, for that they must now pay.

But slowly, and by degrees, with planning and plenty of forethought he would descend on the Emperor and take from him due compensation. A brother's ransom it would never be, but he would take a million credits from Yamato for each ounce of Duval's body weight.

Since the time he had assembled his crew around him, Ellis had worked on them like a hammer on white-hot metal, forming them to his principles. He had quietly told Tom Brophy and Leah Glass, his second-in-command, that leadership was an art he'd like them to learn.

Both were like Bowen, capable of being brought on. It was born in a person, but leadership could also be encouraged by good policy, and in combat it was essential that the team hauled together: "Make yourself respected by your sections. If they don't like you, then you have to use fear, and fear is a poor substitute. But either way, respect they *must* have for you. In punishments, an officer's anger has no place. In all cases, first have the problem put right by the wrongdoer as far as it can be done. Allow no disrespect against your subofficers and take a crack against one of them as you would against yourself. Trust your people but demand as much of them as you think they're capable of delivering. Beware of those with too much mouth. Give them small secrets and follow those secrets to see who betrays you, because when a big secret is to be trusted, you need to know where it will end up. Always remember that in a fight situation five fearless volunteers will always outperform ten fearless volunteers and one coward."

In the days and nights of their passage, his principles had seeped into the flesh of all the people on board, armoring them more securely than any plex hull. And although they knew that they were just one hundred seventeen in number, they had faith that the captain's plan must succeed—whatever it was.

The Okinawa *kin kaigun* was expected to form up in convoy in several months real-time. Meanwhile the *Constitution*'s crew had made excellent progress on Okinawa. They had taken five small ships on the planet, stripping them out: equipment, cargo, personal effects—everything they could want. They had arrested the grounded ships with little opposition, each time releasing their crews and demolishing the pillaged vessels. No blood, but inordinate fear, and fear was a contagious disease.

The trackless idyllic southern continent of Okinawa had been their base. It was the place where the ore was mined and refined, vast open-cast pits where Mitsu's immense machines had penetrated the planet's skin. The refineries were heavily guarded.

The filthy, dusty heat of the equatorial belt with its ammoniac fumes and its one-hundred-Celsius-plus temperatures was where the Mitsu terminal was that Oujuku's crew had attacked. The dome town of Taito sat on the stinking gray wastes of the equator itself. Ships leaving the high-gravity planet loaded with super-heavy cargoes needed as much grav assist as they could get, and Okinawa's fast-rotating equator provided a slingshot to ships needing to get into orbit. It also gave rise to vast Coriolis forces that wound up deep atmospheric depressions and flung typhoonicanes across both temperate zones a thousand times a year.

A spur of land connected Okinawa's two landmasses, and a monorail link ran down the middle of it. That too seemed invulnerable to attack.

"Best of luck, Cao."

"O-keh, Captain."

Cao's tight smile had flashed in the blackness of that awesome night, the whites of his eyes yellow in the sodium glare: he was embarking on the most dangerous course of all, and alone. And all those who watched him depart wondered at the mission he was to try, knowing that if the Okinawa authorities should catch a *sangokujin* saboteur near their railroad, he would be skinned alive.

After that, Pel Rosen had landed a shuttle full of goods in the southern continent: survival commodities and gifts to offer the escaped slaves who were known to inhabit the less easily policed areas. Near a steep cliff they had found a sizable cave and hidden equipment containers in it: tools and a stock of plex, a readied shuttle, stores, suits, spares, listening gear, and new and expensive weaponry—enough to blow Yamato out of the Neutral Zone.

Then they had taken their task force northward. The Yamato astrogator from Rakahanga had told him much, that the *kin kaigun* was expected on the Taito apron in a short time, that her commander was Admiral Kihei, and that the metal would not be waiting in Taito for fear of another raid, but would be transported at the last minute by rail.

"Attack Amerikan ship make alter habit of Yamato," the astrogator had said. "They know two Amerikan ship here. Maybe come down, but no danger in Taito. Maybe hold metal until admiral bring ship planetside."

"How can we attack Taito after Captain Oujuku's attempt?" Brophy had asked after they had put the astrogator down. "It'll be like a hive of wasps."

"We're not going to attack Taito," Ellis had said.

"Then where, Captain?"

"All in good time, Tom."

At length, they made camp within sight of the coast exactly at the mouth of the Kin River, at the very narrowest part of the isthmus, and waited for Oujuku's ship. There, in a clearing near the coast, they materialised from the forest, the chameleon-skinned ship blipped a sudden bright yellow on her underside surfaces to acknowledge contact. Ellis discovered that Oujuku's party had come close to disaster.

"Twenty-eight've died so far," Oujuku reported. "A virus."

Ellis feared the deliberate microbes which had been introduced onto some worlds. Sometimes they were too sophisticated or just too simple for the atmosampling filters to catch, and without blood conditioning they were often fatal and provided a practical barrier to unwanted visitors. He saw concern lay heavy on Oujuku's mind and probed him. "A planetary welcome bug, you think?"

Oujuku shook his head, shrugging off the suggestion. "The epidemic's past now, but the fight's gone out of the rest of my crew. Most of them want home. They figure a promise that failed their dead shipmates might just as soon fail them."

"And you?"

"I'm human too, Ellis."

"Be careful your people don't catch onto that."

Oujuku did not smile; he scratched at his arm. "We're few, and growing fewer. Another blast of fever and we're broken as a raiding force." Then, seeing Ellis's eyes upon him, he admitted, "Two of my brothers died—Zeh and Joseph.

Zeh in a half-assed attack I would never have mounted had I been there with him. Joseph of that piss-boiling fever. And the surgeon that freezeed him didn't outlive him by more than four days."

"I'm sorry, John."

"Yeah."

"And a real good officer was Joh."

"Yep."

Ellis studied him again, seeing him bottle his grief, remembering Oujuku's bluntness when Horse's report had been made. "Then we'll have to punish Yamato for three lost brothers, eh? And put heart in the crew for the job."

"Yep."

53

Three days later, Ellis received the message he had been hoping for. The comms channels were insecure, and so a prearranged signal had been arranged and watched for. Smoke smudged the top of a hill nearby, and he went secretly a short way along the coast, alone in one of the surface skimmers they had brought to take the news. Then he had consulted with Oujuku urgently.

"You came by skimmer? Are you crazy? What about the wake? The surveillance satellites Mitsu operates can resolve a pinhead on the surface. Why've we been keeping under the trees?"

"Relax. It's overcast, isn't it?"

"Optically, yes."

"Their infrared resolution's poor. And besides, we're not the only living things on the continent. They have settlements and there's the escapees. That's why they're troubling themselves to mount surveillance in the first place."

"Yeah, to target strikes on anything suspicious. Keep the vermin down, eh. Us, like."

"Fact is I laser-blinded the one that passes over here midmornings. By the time they check it out and send a vehicle for a look-see, we'll be gone. And we're looking out too."

Oujuku's temper rose. "Ellis, you and I agreed no unilateral action. You don't get final cut on this mission without consultation."

"O-keh, o-key. Calm it. What's the reason you brought me out anyway?"

"Well, I'll tell you. I had rumblings. Prickly back. It's time we did something about the morale around here. Some of them're scared, I think."

"You want to give the people the old one-two?"

"Tricky, Ellis."

"We'll do it after you brief them on the mission."

". . . a'right."

That night, in the *Constitution*'s open cargo bay, the captains laid their carefully rehearsed plan before both crews. They gathered late and the atmosphere was broody, cut by the sultry heat of the night. Oujuku smoothed the big visualiser clear in front of him. He punched up a map of the isthmus and began to poke at it with the tip of a pointer.

"The land bridge runs north-south. This is us here—the north part of the south landmass, latitude minus seventy-one degrees or thereabouts; along this track we've reconnoitered. Here"—he stabbed at a spot on the middle of the equator—"is Taito. A place some of you people might just recall. And this is the rail link. At the other end is their number one refinery at Kin. Both terminals are now strong and well defended. But you can see that to bring their stuff up from the south and send it into orbit, they must first load it at Kin and rush it overland to Taito. This they do on monotrucks, following the *kinto*, along thisaway." He touched a button on the pointer and scored a red line between the two ports.

Leah Glass raised a hand. "Excuse me, Captain, but I can't figure why they use a monorail to take refined aurium north. I mean, if it was massive trucks of ore, yeah, but refined stuff? There's escaped slaves kicking around in the southern jungles, so why not just put it on an air-freighter, and zip, straight off to Taito?"

"Their own security regulations," Oujuku answered patiently, pleased by the question. "They built the rail link after an air crew mutinied and tried to heist a squillion credits' worth of the stuff offplanet. They don't want to tempt anyone else into that kind of thinking."

They looked at one another, some making low whistles.

"What about the slaves? Don't they want to give their ex-masters a hard time?"

"They don't have weapons. And not much they can do with aurium in a jungle in any case."

Ellis listened to Oujuku explain further and watched him finally stab the middle of the line and leave the pointer hanging there, suspended by the field. It was time to intervene. He scanned the faces of the mingled crews, saw them lit variously with greed and the promise of a fight, willing and unwilling, seeing with pleasure the eagerness in some as they crowded in on him. He noted most those that seemed least hungry for action, then, just as he and Oujuku had prearranged, he stepped back.

"C'mon, Captain Oujuku," he said, acting his part with relish. "It's a tough request for your people. Are we gonna pick twenty candidates and hope to overcome a thousand guards? I know which of my people are up to it."

"So your people are capable, and mine're not, that it?" Oujuku replied with mock rebuke. "You think your crew's hot, and mine's a pack of shipneys?"

Ellis leaned in on him. "I'll tell you this, John. Any of my crew would cut your throat on an order from me, despite the fact they like you and respect you." The eyes of the hundred who clustered around them stood out in disbelief at what thcy were hearing. The attention of the last of them was nailed to Ellis as he continued, "It's to fight Yamato that we've come here. Yamato aurium is our aim. Tons of it, yep, and argentium too! And things like this!" He drew a nugget of native metal from his waist pocket and rolled it in his palm. "Big and blue and heavy as hell. And there's more where that came from. Spherical ingots the size of a grapefruit that burn with an electric fire, each sphere worth a million credits. Enough to make everyone here rich as the Mitsu daimyo's bastard.

"What title does Mitsu have to it? That's a philosophical question I want you to think about. Who does the aurium really belong to?"

No answer came.

"Fact is the Zone was made an independent territory by unanimous treaty over four hundred years ago—*in perpetuity*—and that means forever. They talk of a Co-prosperity Sphere, but the truth is they annexed the Zone by force, and they did it to provide their industry with the means to mount a massive invasion of Amerika."

They stirred uncomfortably.

"Until now, they've been forced to use subversion within Amerika, to stimulate rebellion and to threaten us with troop-massing operations. We've always been able to halt their plans because we've prevented them from completely destabilising us at home, and because they have to come through the nexus points of the Boundary worlds where we can concentrate our firepower. But they won't give up. The culture they have made their religious ideal was forged during five hundred years of civil war. They treat the *hinin,* the lowest class of their own people, like filth—the word means 'subhuman.' They honor samurai like minor gods, and they have an unshakable belief that they're superior to the rest of mankind. You've seen the way they herd their slaves like pigs. You've seen the way their soldiers scorn death. You've seen the way they're obsessed with rank and with duty. But they *can* be beaten."

Nate Allen, Oujuku's expeditor, shouted an oath and some of the crew smiled, then Ellis's face clouded and Allen remembered himself again.

"We're not slaves. We're a free people who know about duties *and* rights. We don't believe the universe is fixed and that our fate is immutable; we believe we can affect the outcome of events! And that is our strength!"

"Yes, sir!"

"Yeah! We can handle it."

"Hey, you're making sense, Captain!"

"We're with you!"

"Remember, he who attacks carries the day, and he who thrusts at the enemy's softest place will be the victor. How can we fail when right and justice are on our side?"

He saw them fill with belief, some shouted out, others whooped and made agreement, and all the while he and Oujuku were looking them over, sorting out the ardent from the fainthearted, knowing by their attitudes which of them were only carried by words and which were at heart fit to take on the most dangerous part of the mission, and which again were fit to put in charge of the ships and shuttles they would depend on for escape.

Ellis grew serious now, seeing it was time to draw them back from an excess of encourgement, and he began to put to them the opposite view.

"There's not many of us. Twenty of us can be spared to go on the strike. Twenty only. Ten from the *Constitution,* ten from the *Lex*. I have to make that choice: this is a wilder planet than it seems down here at the pole and fraught with dangers. Thank God, then, that we're not alone in our mission."

"You bet! God's got to be on our side!" Patrick Navajo shouted.

"Yeah!" someone else assented.

"Amen to that," he said. "But I have somebody else in mind, as you'll find out."

Then Ellis pushed through them, clearing a way before him until he had reached the open cargo bay doors. He jumped down from the ramp, cupped his hands to his mouth, and brought in the armed, silent crew members who had been planted in the fringes of the forest as sentries in lieu of the guard fields that would have given their position away. He brought them in and made them sit all together and called again into the darkness three times in a loud voice and they waited and watched until their eyes deceived them with expectation.

After a space they heard movement in the undergrowth. Oujuku hissed at one of his men who reached for his Wesson, and stilled him. In the gloom the palmito leaves parted and a squat figure in black garb ran crouching out from the darkness.

As he approached, the arclight picked him out and the crew began to shout his name and yell out because few had thought they would see him again.

"Cao!"

At his back was a host of Mongoloid warriors who came out one by one and waited, some crouching down, some standing with spears and with bows. Only one came forward and Cao presented him to Ellis and to Oujuku with great ceremony.

His code name was "Kuwa"—"Mulberry"—headman among the Okinawa *gurentai* of *hinin* and escaped *sangokujin* slaves, whom he had turned into a small bandit force. There was nobody in the Neutral Zone who hated the samurai more, nor knew their habits on this planet better.

54

The next day, the mission was finally prepared, weapons issued, battle suits passed out to those that were chosen and to their newfound allies. Use of the shuttles was ruled out by the possibility of emission surveillance, and the difficult ground made land vehicles impossible: it was going to be a long march. Cao interpreted tirelessly to discover from the *gurentai* what was best to take and how precisely the land would be against them. The first day's trek inland was arduous, the second and third more so, and at certain places *gurentai* scouts were dispatched ahead, pathfinding and leaving a trail of subtle signals by ripping leaves and snapping jungle stems. Silence was imposed on the rest as they walked. Stealth was their watchword.

All morning they climbed higher into a land filled with the chattering of monkeys and exotic birds, scaling the mountains that stretched east-west like a spine down the isthmus, Ellis swearing that they would find no rest until they had broken the back of the land. Some time before noon local time on the fourth day, Oujuku called a halt. The *gurentai* chief pointed to a thickly forested hill lying a mile or two off the track. Its peak rose above the general lie perhaps a hundred feet, and Ellis agreed that now they should take the weight off their backs for an hour. Although it was approaching the hottest part of the day and the sun had burned away the morning mists long ago, leaving the day clear and bright, the trees hereabouts were lofty and full of shade and the red earth beneath was moist and cool.

Oujuku came over, his ebullient face gleaming with sweat.

"I've spoken with Kuwa. He says there's something he wants to show us. Will you come?"

Ellis felt the ache in his thighs. The climb had been steep and growing steeper as the morning wore on and as the climax to the pass neared. He slumped against the bole of a tree and charged his mouth with water from the recirculator tube, swilling it round his teeth before swallowing. The distraction unsettled him.

"Hadn't we better rest now? And keep our minds on the business in hand?"

Oujuku put his chin back, balked. "It's worth it, Ellis."

"I've eaten enough of the local game, and I have no great taste for more of Kuwa's forest lore."

"It's no hunt, Ellis. I've got something to say to you."

Ellis sighed and found his feet.

"All right."

"That's right."

"I'll swear you were born with the energy of the devil."

"Energy conquers all. And that's a fact."

"Okeh," Ellis admitted, realising it was probably important. Reinvigorated by the thought, he picked up his Wesson, gave instructions to Nate Allen, and followed. "What is it? Sighted a settlement?"

"Better."

"I can think of nothing better at this particular moment. Except maybe a strap hammock."

Ellis followed the two *gurentai* who took them along the spur and to the ridge that led to the hill. After a deal of walking Oujuku thrust out his hand.

"Look! There!"

"What?"

"Don't you see? Near that tree?"

"John—*this is a fucking jungle!*"

"C'mon! There. There! Look!"

"What is it?" Ellis followed the line. A glint of light, a straight line abhorred by nature even more than a vacuum. It was clearly artificial. He took the glasses. A massive span stood across a clearing, a plex structure, slender, die straight, supported by gossamer uprights. "Yes, a plex span. What is it, a road?"

"A bridge."

"I swear I'll—"

He stopped, looking at the line that stretched tantalisingly between walls of living rock.

Oujuku clapped a hand on Kuwa's shoulder. "Looks like our hosts are right, eh, Kuwa?"

"*Hai,*" the *gurentai* leader agreed gravely.

Ellis raised an eyebrow. "Great. A bridge."

"Yep. Coming up the rock?"

They threw off their suits and climbed to the best vantage point fifty feet above, seeking handholds and footholds where they could pull themselves up the rest of the way, until they came to the highest part.

Oujuku was first into the rough slit trench at the summit where the view burst upon them spectacularly.

"Jeezus, Ellis! Would you look at that!"

Despite himself, Ellis absorbed the panorama with an inrush of breath. The quiet moment that followed was heightened by his bodily tiredness, a moment of soft peace and silence, filled with the green smell of the forest tops and the echoing cackles of rude-faced monkeys and other strange creatures. In the distance the cordillera stretched away magnificently. To the west they could see the faintly shimmering White Jewel Ocean, to the east another ocean, blue and infinite. It rent their eyes with its color and shimmered vastly.

"That's not just any bridge," Oujuku said. "That's *the* bridge. The one that carries the rail link. The one they use to carry the aurium up to Taito. Not many miles from here is Yomitan, the midpoint of the link. Kuwa says that's where we'll get our information."

55

They turned north and marched another short day until the forests subsided, to be replaced by tall knot grass, tracts of open land which had been cleared by burning. Kuwa insisted on greater care and secrecy, knowing that they approached Yomitan, and after consulting with him, Oujuku suggested that they go to a more secluded place along the link. Up close, the scale was apparent. The rail link was much smaller than he had expected. Small tunnels only eight feet in diameter bored through the rock outcrops.

"It's like a mine train."

Oujuku nodded. "Makes sense, if you think about it, I guess."

They doubled back and looked for the protection of a dry riverbed, following it some distance until the luxuriant forest came up around them again. Then, as they were passing along a gravel bank on an eastward bend of the river, they heard the noise.

Ellis ordered silence. What was it? The link causeway was narrow here and overhung with big trees that followed the watercourse. Instantly the whole raiding force fell unseen into the shadows under the rail embankment.

The rhythmic noise came again out of the gray plex rail: diffuse, light-pitched, murmuring like children's voices, then the sound grew plainer and Ellis picked up his glasses and saw the vehicle sliding smoothly round a distant bend. He estimated its speed as cautiously slow, maybe forty or fifty mph, probably to give the track-check scanners time and reduce the risk of a mishap on this difficult section.

"It's now or never," he muttered, almost despairing that their timing had been so misinformed as to jeopardise the whole mission.

The horn sounded like a lure in the distance. On maximum magnification he made out five sleek trucks, coupled one behind another, each burdened with two one-ton flasks. The guards rode in special open carriages, seated back-to-back, staring outward. At the head a gun with its crew of three mounted on a special truck followed by a carriage of twenty armed soldiers, then the traction car. At the tail another gun truck. Each guard carried a quartered rifle blaster and a bandolier of power tubes around him, staring out at the land under tight discipline.

When Ellis looked towards the southern horizon, he saw with amazement that another train followed on some miles behind with a further seven trucks, separated by more soldiers, and a third of six trucks. He silently calculated that together they must contain more than *thirty-six tons* of refined aurium bullion.

A soft blasphemy escaped Nate Allen, who hugged the ground beside him.

"Radio black those suits," Oujuku told them grittily.

The first train came on unaware of the men that crouched under the riverbank ahead of them. He prayed that surprise would be advantage enough to overcome the guard, but there was little time to deploy.

The trains continued to approach. Oujuku sent a dozen men scampering over a bend in the road with Cao, a further dozen working back one train length, and the rest up ahead with him. Ellis took the remainder, six *gurentai,* Kuwa, Jenkins, Allen, and Brophy, with him forward another train length. He pulled Kuwa down behind the stem of a plantain tree.

"Tell your people I want no shooting until the train stops," he whispered, his voice a rasp, his hands making explanation. "Do you understand?"

Kuwa nodded, his suit camouflage blending perfectly from moment to moment with the dappled light. He turned and passed on the command, dispatching his people to hidden locations on each side of the track, then he drew out his blaster. This time it was no practice, it was for real; the rifle was set to cut and to kill, a big punching Esandubya, a full six pounds and a half in weight. He knocked off the safety and crept out of sight.

Ellis's heart thumped and he breathed deeply to calm himself. Somewhere in the distance he heard the sound of rushing water. It mingled with the rail sounds, filling his head with music. He picked up a branch as thick as his leg and dragged it across the track as if it had fallen there from one of the trees. Then, methodically, he primed his blaster pistols, charging them with power tubes from his belt and adjusting the set to maximum. The clicks as he rotated the lever seemed to echo through the forest.

Twenty yards away, Allen grimly loaded his meson cutter with a tube and began to carve out a slice of the plex track.

The horn sounded, the vehicle began to brake, slowing as it detected a fault on the track. The train came on at a walk, the guards blithely unaware of the true danger ranged about them, and their officer stood up. When the lead gun truck had come to within five yards of Ellis, it stopped and the officer jumped down. Ellis leapt out in front of him, Wessons in hand.

The officer pulled up sharply.

"*Konnichi wa!*" Ellis greeted him, his eyes deadly on the man's own.

"Aggh?"

The officer's face contorted. The incredible challenge had stunned him. He recovered himself immediately, but before an order could escape his mouth a beam slashed out of the forest and across his throat and he crashed to the road at Ellis's feet.

Then all hell broke loose. Once, twice, Ellis squeezed his triggers, blasting the nearest two samurai back into the arms of their comrades. Instantly the answering reports of other blasters came out of the forest. More heavy weapons, impaling the infantry and showering the track with severed foliage. The samurai guards, panicked by the sudden ferocity of the fire that assailed them, tried to scatter, but the raiders surged across the track and cut them off, preventing them from falling back.

Another volley of burning rays sliced into them. Two samurai fell. A third fought on, smoldering, until shafts cut into his shoulders and back. When the guards got off their replies into the shadows, it was at random. Then Ellis felt himself wheeled round as if by a giant hand slapping his pelvis.

Jeezus, he thought, that was too close! He looked down and saw the burn holes plucked in his suit. The reflections zinging off the track had blown one of his belt tubes. The guards' blasters could fire a tight beam with enough energy to penetrate a battle suit at four hundred yards, and their burning power was instant death at this range, except that at the moment of the ambush they had been set up to deliver spray fire. At close quarters the virtue of this was that they could blind and incapacitate as well as kill when fired into an ill-defined group of men.

Blood began to trickle from somewhere on his head and cascade into his beard, but he ignored it. Three samurai guards were advancing on him, the desperation on their faces grotesque. He cut them down with the last of his tube, making his blasters useless.

All around now the road was a struggling mass as raiders came crashing from the undergrowth and into the guards, slashing and stabbing beams with their new weaponry. There was no time to reload with fresh tubes, and the raid was degenerating into a terrifying hand-to-hand fight. Through a blur of red, Ellis saw men stumbling closer to the edge of the track. Their feet clawed for purchase on the crumbling earth that overhung the riverbed by ten or fifteen feet. Jenkins darted from his cover with his side arm and plunged into the blinded men, rending them. Those closest to the drop began to topple, crashing over and rolling helplessly into the green pools below. Others were forced down until a dozen were kicking and flailing in the shallow water.

Ellis flung a hand over his face and brought it away sopped with blood. It trickled from him so that it seemed there must be a big gash on his head. He groped out for a rifle blaster instinctively. Then more guards were on him again.

Ellis's anger hammered in his head. He pulled the trigger, knowing that if the gun had been abandoned because it was empty he was a dead man. It jerked and chopped a huge swathing beam into the first man's rib cage, notching him so that he went down immediately. The next trooper flung himself on Ellis and struggled to use his sword. A *katana* lunged at him but he deflected the blade down so that it passed between his thighs. Then he drove his fist into his assailant's face, knocking off the man's unlaced helmet. But he was now unbalanced himself and falling to his knees. He staggered back, fingers reaching wildly, and the third, a man with no breastplate, came at him wielding the butt of his firearm like a club. He rolled away from the initial blow as the man tried to dash his head open. His fingers found the chin strap of the plex helmet that had rolled within reach. He swung it up, launching it with desperate strength into his attacker's way. The sharp brim bit into the man's fingers where he gripped his weapon and it fell from his hand. It was enough to buy Ellis the split second he needed. He tore his knife from his belt, gripped it ready for the upthrust, remembering what his combat instructor had taught him about killing:

that a man's ribs are shaped like a louver, that a down-stab jags off the bone, but an upthrust slides in.

The man was defenseless before him now. All he needed to do was hug him close and dispatch him, but he saw the stark fear in the man's face. He was not a guard at all, young, hardly able to grow a beard—probably the operator. In that moment there was a change in the sounds around him: the solid rage of battle resolved itself into a hundred separate noises and fell away from his ears.

Through the blood, the man Ellis gripped seemed suddenly to be so like his brother, Duval, that at the last instant, instead of the kill, he doubled his fist and knocked the wind from his opponent, then he kicked him down, furious at his own weakness.

When he looked up, he found that the remaining guards were fleeing back along the track. The *gurentai* were expending their last tubes, crouching in their strange way, their rifles held flat and horizontal, their middle fingers hooked awkwardly under the trigger guards. He called them back.

Two hundred yards away Oujuku's force had already triumphed, and the rest of the guards were in rout.

Ellis felt exultant. A wave of intense triumph beat through him as he realised that they had actually won. He felt the blood course down his cheek and drip onto his shoulder, the burning points on his thigh and hip where the tube had blown dug into his flesh, a distant discomfort, but he felt no pain. Only numbness and elation.

It had all been so *easy!*

A vast treasure. A staggeringly vast treasure. *They had just taken an aurium train.* Just like that. Here, on a gray plex track in the middle of a polar rain forest, was more wealth than had been raised in taxes in the whole of Amerika since Alia Kane's inauguration. It was awesome. Immense. Impossible to comprehend.

"They'll be here soon."

It was Oujuku, slinging his gun.

"In God's name, John, we've *done* it!"

Oujuku grinned evilly. "It's not ours yet."

Yomitan was close by, and the garrison there would turn out immediately the first survivors reached it. At worst, there might be an airborne patrol riding down on them within the hour and a thousand troops combing the forest before nightfall. While Nate Allen's work had cut the track, the two following trains would not be coming through. They had already slammed into reverse and were gone, guards and all.

Ellis and Oujuku took stock of the situation.

"How many dead?" Ellis asked.

"A few. Theisen and Kennedy for sure. Pollack's burned pretty bad."

"Kuwa's boys?"

"Ten maybe. And a dozen hurt bad. You can't say they lacked enthusiasm."

"We have to get off the track."

"Which means unloading this lot now."

"Thirty-six tons?"

"Jeezus' sake! There's more than we can carry."

"Half the job's to take it, half to keep it."

"We can keep some of it, by God!"

"Each of those flasks weighs around a ton. There should be—uh—twenty spheres in each one. That's seven hundred and twenty in all. Aurium's around three and a half times the density of lead, more than twice that of uranium. Each ball weighs about a hundred pounds apiece."

"We'll bury what we can't move. The main part we'll take into the forest. Fifty pounds per man. Absolute max. Tell your people only aurium. Cut the spheres in half. Leave anything else."

"Is there time to sort it and bury it? They'll surely find fresh-dug earth."

"We'll have to get on with the job of cutting the spheres and burying the rest. There's the ideal place!"

"Where?"

"Down there." Ellis pointed to the stagnant pools. "Bury it under the riverbed."

"Yeah! And we'll shatter the rest and dump the pieces into land-crab burrows for them to discover. Maybe disperse a few spheres into dust along false trails. That should hold their detectors up a while."

Ellis's fingers searched through the blood-matted hair at his temple.

"Let me see that." He submitted as Oujuku satisfied his curiosity. "Not much: a cut no more'n an inch long. And no depth to it. It's pretty well cauterised."

They got to work with the meson cutter, spilling out the contents of the flasks across the track, rolling the grapefuit-sized spheres down the banks, digging out trenches, and sinking the spheres into the green water pools. They blasted a few spheres to dust, which scattered and settled all around. The *gurentai* looked on, at first with cool amazement, preferring to collect their own trophies from the dead guards. To them, neither aurium nor argentium was of the least account, weapons being their prized booty. They menaced the wounded and the captives, declaring that they would take their victory payment in the traditional way—in ears and noses and genitalia—until Ellis told Kuwa this was no way to hurt his ex-masters, who loved aurium better than life itself, and that if the *gurentai* would help in the rest of the job, they could have all the small arms the *Constitution* contained.

It took them five arduous days to recross the mountains and come back again, through rain and wild weather at the tail of a typhoonicane, to Akarie Ue, the place where they had arranged to meet with their shuttles. But there was no sign of them.

Instead, a Yamato Guard frigate cruised overhead, and Ellis looked up at it, heartsick.

Nate Allen voiced the great fear of them all. "If the shuttles are taken, then we're blipped, Captain. They'll torture them and learn where our ships are hidden, and the *kin kaigun* will be in strength on the Taito apron by now!"

"C'mon, Nate. This is no time to lose heart. We've got to keep trying."

Oujuku railed against the disappointment, then his temper cooled. "At worst, if our shuttles are taken, the Yamato commanders must have time to search them, time to probe the crews, time to mount their counterstroke. The *Lex* and the *Constitution* have both got pretty good stealth measures operating. And that big bird has got a whole goddamned continent to comb. If we're lucky, we can still get to our ships."

"The enemy haven't found us yet," Bowen stated. "Guard frigate or not."

"Yeah, but as soon as we break comms silence they'll be down on us like a ton of aurium. We going to walk to the ships?"

Ellis added more hopefully, "Look, if the shuttles were late coming here and arrived to see that vulture buzzing the area, they might just be lying low. Have you all got so little faith in your shipmates?"

They wasted no more time in idle speculation. Oujuku led three scouts west to check out the number two zone, leaving Ellis to comfort the remainder with encouragements. He told them they were sitting on a treasure that amounted to only one tenth of the haul they had taken, but that was still an immense prize. And that as soon as they made the ships they were as good as offplanet and through the nexus.

Two hours into the dusk Oujuku returned in the shuttles, and by nightfall of the next day they had regained their ships. As they slotted the craft aboard, everyone wanted to know exactly how the enterprise had gone. Powerfully Ellis lifted the five-inch aurium sphere from his pack and bowled it heavily across the decking.

"Oh, pretty well."

They erupted with cheers. Against his own orders the boss had carried twice the limit—one hundred pounds—across rough terrain, and he had got it back successfully.

That night they divided the spoils, paying off Kuwa in the way he wanted—blasters and as many spare tubes as they could give him. They ate a festive meal. The local meats imparted flavors the Dovers never made, and they started to drink and to sing in the way all hunting parties had done since the dawn of time.

Doones started it off. Bosco joined in, then a third, Jenkins, the top gun with a voice like a bassoon. Together they raised a dozen verses, and while the crews caroused, Oujuku and Ellis consulted together to unburden their minds.

"You know that I want to take my ship home," Oujuku told him. "I've half a mind to overfly Taito with our guns blazing, to show them we don't give a good goddamn about them."

"And you know that I want to stay in the Zone—to prove as much."

"Then our partnership must dissolve."

"I wish you good psi, John. Will you carry our share home with you?"

"I sure will. And I'll save it against your return."
"It's a deal. Now let's get the hell out of here."

56

SADO

They came out into the Sado daylight to the beating of gigantic war drums and the ghostly blowing of the *shakuhachi*, and the mass of people confined beyond the high bamboo lattice fence wondered what could be the reason that these terrible *gaijin* were feted in so important a fashion when they were only here to die.

Duval walked on in procession, sweating under the weight of the heavy punishment collar and the iron chains they had attached to his wrists and ankles. He felt a sudden faintness; fear daggered him. Where was Michie now? Was she here among the crowd? Was she imprisoned? Was she about to go through the same terror that he had suffered? He had not dared to ask after her, even via the arcane *komuso* monks who appeared to offer him only support. He allowed himself to trust no one, fearing that any questions might precipitate her arrest. The residual paranoia left by the Probe had paralysed his mind, but the monk had unknotted his terror, and the dread and loathing had passed slowly away.

Pray for my rebirth, Michie-san, he asked silently. Pray for mine as I pray for yours. If only I could see your face. Once. Just once more. But no, an answering voice said. Don't wish her here to see your degradation. You must wish her far from this hell. Imagine her far away and happy and free. You're together in spirit. The thought of her safe deliverance will give you strength to acquit yourself like an adopted son of the Hasegawa clan should.

He stared ahead towards the market square. The open graveled square had been transformed. A scaffold that was a hundred feet long and thirty high had been erected in the punishment grounds off the Square of Perfect Harmony, surmounted by dozens of crosses, one for each of the accused. Some of them were inverted, others made in spread-eagle form. The monstrous punishment ground was fronted on one side by the towers of Kanazawa's castle-like ramparts, and on the other by the daimyo's residence, the veranda of which now formed a part of the upper tier. Forty steps led up to the stage on which the *metsuke*'s rostrum was placed. Opposite was a rectangular space towards which they were being led, and all around were the huge timber tiers of the theater that had filled with the ranking samurai hierarchy of Sado. Down below, a crowd vast enough to have emptied the city waited, all the low classes without official entitlement to a surname: merchants, technicians, clerks, industrial workers, and land workers—everyone except *sangokujin* and the *hinin.*

The special cedarwood stage for their "trial" had taken many weeks to craft. The sounds of hammering and hewing and sawing of timber had penetrated even to the dark quarters in which he had been imprisoned in these last few days since their bodily sufferings had abated. It was like a deliberate taunt, magnifying their terror.

Duval was revolted by the eerie pomp of the rite and the way it consumed reason and displaced all that was good in men's minds, how it had been designed to make a vile spectacle of the intimacies of death.

When the sessions of interrogation and torture had stopped, and the severity of their confinement relaxed, he had called it mercy. But his flood of relief had been stemmed by the realisation that this was not mercy, merely a time set aside for reflection, a span in which a man might be tempted to surrender himself utterly to the Void.

The words of the sacred *Kensei,* the Sword Saint, Musashi, had been repeated to him: *The spirit of the Void is nothingness. The Void is unknowable to man. But by knowing that which exists we come to know that which does not exist. Men of this world do not comprehend. They imagine that which they do not comprehend must be the Void. It is not. That is only bewilderment.*

Through all that time *komuso* monks had visited him daily, soothing him at first, then urging him, as one friend might urge another, to meditate. They had been patiently deaf to his protests that he was a son of the Hasegawa clan and should not be treated like this. Even so, the *komuso* had interceded on his behalf. They were not like the priests of the Black Brotherhood, but Zen monks of the order of *Fuke-shu.* They wore dark blue kimonos tied with a red sash, and high-blocked *geta* sandals, and were never without their hardwood *shakuhachi* flutes, which they could wield with the defensive skill of a sword master when attacked; but their strangest piece of apparel was the *tengai,* the woven reed basket that covered the head and protected the monk from worldly identification. Their efforts had brought him light and food and then a short period each day in the high-walled yard to exercise alone. Lastly the rule of silence had been withdrawn and he had been permitted to associate together with the others.

"A woman can't trust her eyes and ears," Helene di Barrio had said wonderingly on that first day of greeting.

Duval had embraced him, but Jeb Womak had searched the blank walls, full of suspicions. "Yeah, they'll give us this and then take it all away again."

"I guess they're making their judgements now," Juli Dexter had said ominously.

"It's their rule." Duval had understood the procedure. The *kempei* ensured that their victims were watered and well fed, that the injuries captives had suffered in the torture chambers or under the Probe were sufficiently healed prior to their coming out for judgement.

"We're soon to go for trial."

"Wouldn't do to crucify a cripple, would it?" Torven Jones had grinned sourly. They had taken out each of his gravestone teeth to teach him humility.

"Yeah. These bastards have taken care to keep us alive—or else how could they murder us?"

"The *kempei* are not allowed to kill us, according to their law," Duval had said, his voice laden with irony.

"Oh, sure!" Davey Marks had snorted. "Except maybe in a great big public ceremony, to show the poor bastards who're watching how high their power stands. That's their way."

"Still, we're safe until then."

Duval had been assured by the *komuso* that the *kempei*'s own rules forbade killing within their prisons, that the office was merciful and just. He had debated the matter from his nightmare bed, asking how they could justify the weeks of terrible torment they had inflicted, the physical and mental pain, the repeated tortures. The *komuso* had explained earnestly that what they had suffered had not been *repeated* tortures. Unlike other less enlightened authorities, the *kempei*'s rules allowed torture only once, and therefore he had suffered only one torture. One torture *continued* over many sessions. That was the Way and the measure of their duty. There could be no repeated amputations and reculturing of limbs, no conscious dissection under medical control, no sadistic Chinese practices; in fact, most modern techniques were disallowed, except the Probe, and that was a purely mental agony.

He had told the monk about it. "Mind rape, they call it in Amerika. I feel as though my brain has been turned inside out and picked over by strangers. When I first came out, I felt completely worthless. As if my most personal intimacies had been tampered with. I couldn't face myself. It's a disgusting device."

"I will help you to heal yourself."

"You cannot."

"I will try."

There had been sessions of deep meditation during which the monk had relaxed him and rebuilt his confidence. Duval had told his shipmates what he had gleaned from the *komuso* about the *kempei*. "Since they can't kill us themselves, they'll have to hand us over to the civil authorities for execution."

"That's a real fine distinction, Straker!" Matt Kaiser, Horse's closest friend, had been set to work as a slave overseer in the aurium mines. Prosperous and married to a Taiwanese slave, he had been making the best he could of his life until the *kempei* arrived. Now his thin red hair was all gone, but the wounds on his face were as livid as the hatred his captors had stored up in him. He had spat. "Does it matter to somebody like you?"

Duval had bridled at that. "What do you mean by that, Matt?"

Kaiser had looked away. "To a collaborator."

"I'll tell you: to me the *kempei*'re guilty of crimes against humanity. They're trying to wash the blood from their hands with legal niceties. I'm saying that I'm beginning to understand how they think."

"You think maybe their Shinto consciences plague them? Like yours maybe?"

"You got something against me, Kaiser?"

"They say you married into a samurai family, yeah, and even took their religion!"

"And you took their credit!"

"Credit? You got a nerve. I *earned* it honestly, Straker. In the mines. Every day. Toiling and sweating. What was *your* pay for?"

Di Barrio had got between them and calmed them. "Hey! You're both married men, anxious for your wives. Beating up on one another won't help."

"Yeah. Don't give 'em the satisfaction. They're spying on us." Dexter's single eye roamed the walls. She thrust a finger up insolently at the sightless socket of a surveillance lens.

"See there, they're always watching us," Jeb Womak whispered, pointing.

Then Horner spoke softly to Duval. "Haven't you heard the rumor? It was your brother's interference that brought us all to this place, Gunner."

His mouth fell open. "My brother?"

"You mean you don't know?"

"No. Tell me."

"The word is that Ellis joined up with John Oujuku to bring off an incredible heist. They landed on Okinawa and busted out a whole heap of refined bullion. They've stirred up Yamato like a nest of Mexikan hornets, smashed Mitsu's finances, and spread panic throughout the Zone. It's even said that the Empire's economic stability had been shocked, that the loan rate is twice what it was last year. Believe me, Gunner, they're angry as hell."

Duval had let out a whistle, stunned by the news. "Which is why we're going to be scapegoats?"

"Some of us believe so."

"And you?"

Horner had shrugged. "As for me, I think they'd do it anyway. Seems to me that the supreme and untouchable *kempei* does what it wants. The Emperor thinks an O-type supergiant shines out of the *metsuke*'s asshole. He takes no notice of the *bakufu*, or any other level of Yamato's government, much less your brother's doings."

Then Duval had sunk back against the wall and there had been silence until Dale Seeback's feather-light singing voice had floated up, sweet as an Irish flute. "The Emperor's got us in his grip—"

Answering voices had given the refrain. "*Fly, men, fly!*"

"The Emperor's got us in his grip—"

"*Who's a fool now?*"

"The Emperor's got us in his grip, but through his fingers we shall slip."

"*With heart and head and hand and hip, Who's a fool now?*"

Duval had watched the old song cheer them, whilst above, shuttered windows had opened and shaven-headed acolytes had goggled out at the crazy *gaijin*, mystified that there could be laughter in such a place. The song had made them think of the old days, made an Amerikan crew of them again, but despite the first smiles to light their pale faces in a year, they had all known, deep in their hearts, that none of them would slip from the Emperor's fist; each had understood that those that were deemed pure would be flayed through the streets and then sent into Yamato to be chained in slavery; those that were deemed impure would be nailed to crosses to die. Duval had known then with great certainty what his own sentence would be.

A month later, the *komuso* had brought him news that a proclamation had gone out, warning the citizens and people of Sado that the judgement was to be served in the Square of Perfect Harmony, and that all must lay aside their toils or their leisures and attend to hear the sentences solemnly announced. Those of the populace who attended would be granted intercession at the shrine of their workplace, the monk had said in his fervent way, adding at Duval's asking that those who failed to attend would be chastised.

Last night they had all gone without sleep, *ashigaru* soldiers incessantly marshaling and drilling them in the prison yard so that they were set in order and given instructions where they must walk and who must follow whom. Then, in the waning hours of night, Wada Zengo had arrived with a squad of men. They brought out the punishment collars, the white *hachimaki* headbands, and rough pajamas like judo suits but striped in broad red, the color of the criminal. All was meticulously cleaned and made straight. Hishikari had passed the headbands out to the prisoners personally and with great reverence, telling each one that the *hachimaki* would hang one day in the rafters of the great warrior Zen temple on Kamakura, as immortal reminders of their correction. All bore the red sun of Yamato in front and ancient black ideograms intended to be read in the Chinese reading: Earth, Water, Fire, Wind, and the Void. The punishment collars were painted red and intended to demean and to humble the wearers.

At dawn they had been breakfasted on rice, raw fish, and a cup of rice wine. A shower of rain had quenched the dry earth and gone away again, and, two hours later, the great procession was begun, marching a crooked mile through streets packed with people, headed by a column of soldiers in full armor, carrying long ceremonial bamboo pikes and the long flags of the various *han* of Sado strapped to their backs. Next came a cadre of the Black Brotherhood, attired in black kimonos, with white obis round their middles. Following them a dozen pages carried the barred-galaxy standard of the *kempei* and, after it, the Standard of a Thousand Gourds, to represent the *rikugun*, the military power of Yamato, all flanked by guards in charcoal gray and moss green.

Duval moved forward at the solemn pace the cruel ceremony dictated. Now he saw the *hatamoto* take their places in the procession, headed by Nishima Jun, a distant, upright figure, clad in his formal kimono of midnight blue, and deviced with the three-leaf *mon* of his clan. Along the far side of the Square of Perfect Harmony Duval saw the ladies of the nobility ranged at balconies and windows overlooking the scaffold, peach pastel in their finest kimonos, and fanning themselves under multicolored parasols. Today had been proclaimed a great public holiday, but the buzz of gaiety and expectation was fueled by a dark and seething fear that he saw keenly in their faces. Every spectator, no matter what his rank or station, knew that though this day they watched the procession from afar, tomorrow they might be walking in a similar one themselves.

Duval walked as if in a dream, flanked by the basket-headed monk and another, younger monk, who watched and prayed continuously in droning rote verse. Around him were raised the horrific effigies, as big as life, of those of his shipmates who had perished when they had first come ashore, or who had died since, and whose names the diligent inquiries of the *metsuke* had brought to light. Horse's rice-straw image was there as were those of the men who had been killed on Chi no Tsuki. They were raised up on poles, dressed in the same fashion. Also, there were coffins of red lacquer containing the remains of Kier Rider and Jim Collier and Denzil McFadden, whose obstinacy had killed them in the *kempei*'s cellars, though publicly it was said that they had died of fever.

Each Amerikan was accompanied by two *komuso*—monks who, like his own, had prepared them for death as they walked. Each prisoner's collar was linked to the others before and behind by an iron chain as they walked. The uncontrollable Juli Dexter had been manacled and gagged to stop up her shouts. Behind her, Matt Kaiser mouthed the Lord's Prayer, his eyes burning red as coals. Those that had wives and children that they cared for went quietly, knowing that their families were hostage to fortune, hoping with good behavior to save them.

The tri-vee cameras followed them as they went, capturing the moment, beaming it to every receiver on the planet, and soon to every planet in the Emperor's domain. Duval suddenly saw the fallacy of his last hopes. My skills will save me again, he had thought. Surely Michie-san has told her father that I retained the secret of the singularity gun. Surely Kenji-san must have passed that on to the daimyo. Surely the daimyo has struck a bargain with Fukuda Ikku. He must have. Yes, he must have. He's not the sort of man to give in so easily. But what if he hasn't? And what if the *kempei* wants to demonstrate revenge for Okinawa more than they want singularity guns? I'm trapped, he thought, looking around. Trapped. It's insane. I'm letting them lead me to my death. Without complaint. Without a fight. Is that what a sane man does?

Panic rose in him. His eyes searched to left and right for a way to escape, but there was none. To the rear the procession snaked on with the representatives of each samurai family walking two-by-two in their distinctive gear, followed up by a column of brightly armored horsemen. On each side double ranks of pikemen stood shoulder-to-shoulder along the way, holding back a pressing mass of people. Every window was full, every gallery also. People fringed the rooftops and clung to any high vantage point they could find in every building except the daimyo's residence itself.

The rumor swept before him that this was the brother of the pirate who had raided Okinawa, and heads turned as he came into the square. At the first sight of them a huge shout went up. He saw the shiny black crests of warbonnets, like stag-beetle horns, the signs and symbols of mounted officers riding ahead, making a way through the massive crowd, the sun glinting on a drawn sword as it was waved.

As he breasted an alley he smelled thc tang of woodsmoke from a chestnut vendor's fire. Dread boiled up in his belly. He remembered the kamikaze ship that had smashed into the *Thomas J*. The terror of impending death he had felt. The face of Iwakura imploring him. Then the deep memories of the fanatical crucifixions that had happened on the park-world came upon him. They had played in his mind in that dark cell, haunting his unguarded moments. And he had confessed it. They had written it down.

The death of his mother and the way he had been helped by his brother to buy the education his intellect deserved . . . His mother had been a strange woman, loving but very secretive. His father had never treated her well and had disappeared soon after her death. The park-world crucifixions had been around that time, but he had been too young to understand. And in those days of mild warmth between Amerika and Yamato, when Lucia Henry had been President and the government had played Yamato's tune, there had been a huge cover-up. Only later, when Alia Kane had exposed the iniquities of her predecessor, had he seen the tapes and seen his mother's body hanging there.

The *kempei*'s command to confess all had made him dig deep inside himself, deeper than ever before. He had confessed too to believing their genetic report on him. Half racial Japanese, they had said. Father's side. There was no doubt. He had not known anything about it. Hadn't there been an official visit to Liberty by the Emperor and a huge entourage? And the touble between his father—Ellis's father—and his mother . . . it might easily have been. Easily.

He had signed that declaration, but they had smiled, delighting in the special terror he had for the sudden rootlessness it gave him. Once a man's past was taken from him, he was nothing, a confused wanderer, a man with no certain rock on which to build his identity.

He stumbled then, but his *komuso* took his elbows and helped him up. He stiffened, but they pulled him on until they reached the timber stage. There the prisoners were urged forward to climb the steps and take their places for the solemnisation of the proceedings, and he suddenly saw himself as others must have seen him, cringing and being carried forward as a coward. Something unbearable squeezed his heart. Will you stand up, or will you be led like a beast, Duval Straker? Choose! But look how Juli Dexter battles them every step of the way; she gets nothing but bruises and only rouses the crowd further with her resistance. So is that courage, or cow stupidity? Isn't courage nine parts stupidity? Isn't that what Ellis used to say? And the last part was what? *Defiance!* He heard Ellis say it clearly. Show the world you defy it and it runs like a kicked dog. Dare to do as you please. Lift your head up! Go boldly, and be proud!

He felt the tight fist in his breast loosen. He shrugged off the hands that held him, climbed unaided. His shoulders went back. His head lifted. And courage did fill him, driving back the terror as he mounted with the others into the prisoners' dock.

A huge gong clashed and reverberated. Silence was called. The great banner of the *kempei,* as big as a nexus ship's tail fin, was broken out on a tall mast, rippling across the most impressive square on Sado. A huge silken rectangle on which the golden image of the *o-gohei* was represented, fluttering for the cameras. Then a tiny form in flowing purple garb mounted his high podium under that immense banner, and soon the goggling crowd was silent, bowing, down on their knees in a full kowtow, hushing children and straining all to make sense of the piercing words ringing out of the speakers.

"By the authority of the Emperor, the Imperial Office of the *kempei*, and of the Council of the Supreme and General Bakufu of Kyoto, according to the precepts contained in the Instructions of Nikko, I do hereby declare this judgement made."

Fukuda began to read out the sentences. He came first to those that were dead or escaped, dealing with them at length, discussing the baseness of their crimes. As the man spoke Duval watched the mood of the people change; a great stirring in the crowd began, swirls of ill temper rising up like a wind passing across a rice field, ruffling the sea of heads as their feet shifted and shuffled. He could feel their indignation grow into hatred; their voices raised in ritualistic answer responded louder each time. One by one, the vile effigies were taken up and imprisoned in cages, each to be absurdly lectured at and shown in ridicule to the baying crowd.

Then a gate in the dock opened and Dean Jarvis, the *Thomas J.*'s chief armorer, was hauled up.

"Gunner, can you understand it?" di Barrio whispered suspiciously. "What's the *metsuke* saying about him?"

"It's a very old form of Japanese. But he said that Jarvis secretly urinates on the graves of samurai and that the *o-gohei* weeps and sheds blood for shame at it."

"The devils," di Barrio said. Her thick brows set close over her eyes. "What the hell was all that truth shit about, if they were going to condemn us on lies anyway?"

Jacob whispered. "I was on Panay in 'twenty-two when the *kempei* took a buddy of mine on the evidence of whores and thieves, and the year after Captain Lennon was taken for straying into Yamato itself."

Di Barrio nodded grimly. "I heard they took him to the Castle of Himeiji, the *kempei*'s fortress in Kyoto. They Probed him like they Probed us and stripped his mind bare like a maple tree in winter."

"They're insane," young Cadet Philips mumbled.

"No, Cadet. They took him for his ship, and all her cargo and above two million in credit. That was how Fukuda Ikku got his first fortune—by plain robbery!"

"And they call us pirates!" Chambers said.

Horner scratched at his chin. "The money I had stashed up! Jeezus, it makes me sore as hell."

Mario Agasi grinned tightly, full of false bravery. "That brother of yours'll punish 'em now, eh, Gunner? They got no answer to men that's aboard nexus ships. Free men curdle their blood!"

"No man'll save us now," Jeb Womak told him balefully. "We'll be locked up till we die."

"You think that's what'll happen to us, Gunner?" Jacobs asked hopefully, not daring to face the other possibility. "That we'll have to wear these stinking necklaces forever, and all?"

"We'll know that soon enough."

Horner pointed to the crosses waiting at the execution ground. The road to it passed under an arch on which was built an old guard tower at the northernmost corner of the daimyo's residence. It was next to the kitchens and now served as a loading hatch for rice. The deliberate withholding of technology from areas of life where it was not strictly necessary was a major part of the Yamato ideal. The *han* system of agriculture and industry tied the population closely to a patch of ground where they could be controlled absolutely. Despite the spread of Dover technology, rice was grown manually, harvested manually, and transported by road to the cities to be cooked in the old way. Only food handled in this way was considered properly edible outside the ruling classes or the military. The cities themselves were built almost exclusively from traditional materials; only samurai of the first and second ranks and a few technicians and *han* retainers were permitted to deviate from these rules, and then it was a scrupulous matter of necessity. It had never seemed odd to Duval that Buddhist nuns rode donkeys in the square or that ox carts were often to be seen standing under the arch and rice sacks being hoisted up by simple pulley into the house of a planetary ruler of the twenty-fifth century.

Now the same arch was dressed with soldiers of the daimyo's personal guard.

"Look at those ugly bastards in brown. Trust the daimyo's men to get the best view of the killing."

"They'll be severe on us," Jeb Womak said. "Don't doubt it. They all fear what Ellis Straker can do, and they want us for examples!"

Philips's voice quavered. "What became of them, Captain di Barrio?"

"Who, Cadet?"

"Captain Lennon and the other one?"

"They got away, don't you fret now. And they both got home and went on the broadcasts. Saw one of them on a gossip show when I was at Harrisburg one time. Just like you'll be doing in a year or two."

"You think so?"

"Sure."

"Yeah, and if Lennon hadn't escaped, we might not be getting nailed up now," Kaiser whispered fiercely. "He was my hero as a boy. He was the only reason I signed up."

Young Philips swallowed hard, staring at the crowds.

Di Barrio leaned across. "They'll not crucify you, son. You're too young. Plenty of work in you yet. It's the old gals like me they want to get rid of. Folks set in their ways. They know there's no hope of keeping this Amerikan down. Now, get your chin up, Cadet."

"Yes, Captain."

A hush swept across the Square of Perfect Harmony as sentence was made on the armorer: to receive three hundred lashes and condemned to serve on the Imai *han* as slave if he survived. He was led out of sight by another way. Juli Dexter was next to be dragged out. She fought like a wild thing, mouth still gagged, nostrils flaring, her single eye vicious. Her headband came off again and she knocked down a guard, but her hands were bound to the yoke around her neck and her struggles soon subsided.

"What's he saying now, Gunner?"

"Crucifixion."

"God help her."

Agasi's "Amen" was echoed a dozen times among the remaining prisoners.

Next, Cadet Philips was brought out and told he would be taken to serve in a Zen monastery for the rest of his life. He also was led away. Duval strained to watch the way he went, disappearing behind the staging and reappearing briefly before being clapped astride a donkey and conducted under the arch towards the *kempei* prison. It was at this place at the corner of the daimyo's residence that he had lost sight of Juli Dexter a second time. He had passed under the guard tower arch and had been taken right instead of left, towards the execution ground instead of the prison. Already part of the crowd was breaking away from the main body and trying to get through the bottleneck to congregate in the spots that gave the best view of the crosses, but the soldiers forced them back. On the far side, partly obscured by the residence, the crosses were visible, too many of them to give any hope to those that awaited sentence.

Another was led up before the *metsuke,* then another and another in strict order. One by one the rows of kneeling prisoners were emptied. Nausea rose in him at the sight of those vacant places. Then the next man was called, the first of his own row. Spaczynska and Mathias and then Roberts went up, then Shamir and soon van Heever. Beside him Helene di Barrio was pulled to her feet. She turned and offered her hand in a final gesture and Duval took it. For the first time he saw fear sparkle in di Barrio's eyes.

"God love you, Helene."

"And you, Gunner."

Then the gate was opened and di Barrio went out to receive her sentence of death.

57

Wataru Hoshino climbed into the ox cart and stood up to get a better view, but what he saw dismayed him. Things had come to a pretty pass. It wouldn't have happened like this in the days of the last Emperor, he thought. Not in those days, when this planet was a truly new world and the only samurai in it were heroes—real men, soldiers and pioneers that blazed the path and knew the Way, not like those that followed them, jumped-up bureaucrats, half-witted administrators, power-hungry monsters like Fukuda who twisted Japan's ancient and honorable culture to suit their own cravings.

"Get down, old man!"

The shout made him turn in anger and brandish his fists at a lumpish, flat-faced *ikki*. "Mind your manners, peasant!"

"Hoh, what's this, old man? I don't see your topknot!"

The face of the man's wife screwed up tight. "Oh, leave him alone, he's not samurai, he's just crazy."

"I can't see through him or his damned ox cart."

"Get on! Yah!" Wataru turned away furiously, pushed two children off the high, latticed sides of the cart, and lashed the oxen. One groaned languorously, both moved forward. People parted before the pair as they stumped towards the cleared roadway. The big spoked wheels creaked and turned, plowed a furrow through the crowd. Necks craned forward to hear the latest sentence. Those he displaced looked on him with annoyance and offered insults, others tried to hush them.

"Where are you going?" the rock-faced sergeant demanded, flourishing his stick.

Anxiety swept through Wataru's belly. What if they stopped him? Or held him up? Had he moved too soon or too late? His head bobbed and his manner became fawning. "I am ordered to the execution ground, Sergeant-sama. Ritual *sake* for the celebration."

"You can't go that way."

"How else can I get there?" He put a horrified expression on his face. "I have very big orders."

"I said, you can't go that way!"

"But I cannot disobey the orders of the lord!"

"What orders? By who's command?"

"A mighty captain," Wataru said.

"Which captain?"

He looked around and pointed across the square. "The one in the fine *kunari-kabuto* helmet, with the *yoroi* armor. Him. There, you see? His clan is Hasegawa, and he said that if I had any trouble with—"

"All right, old snake. Come with me."

The sergeant laid hold of the ring in the nearest animal's nose and tugged. Once again the beasts lumbered forward, into the lane down which fifty condemned *gaijin* had already been led to their reward.

Another orchestrated roar swelled out from the crowd, but this time it was louder. It echoed under the high arch of the disused guard tower at the corner of the Square of Perfect Harmony, and round the dark chamber within which Michie had hidden herself. The room was dark, but shafts of dusty sunlight speared the gaps in the tiled roof, piercing the gloom. The sounds of the vast show trial filled the space around her.

Oh, the gods must help me. Please, family gods of the Hasegawa clan, help me. Oh, the Seven Gods of Chance, the *shichi fukujin,* I beg you all, invisible *kami,* intervene and save him. Her heart hammered under her sweat-soaked peasant shirt. She tried to still the shaking in her fingers as she knotted the frayed end of a rope that ran up over the roof beam and down in a coil; she had tied it to the beam and knotted it at two-foot intervals, but it would be useless unless she could shift the heavy rice sacks and open the hatch which they covered. She sank down, braced her back against the wall, and kicked out at them, but she could not shift them.

"May the gods give me strength!"

The hatred of the people had blazed up each time sentence was passed, then each *gaijin* had been put ignominiously on a donkey and led beneath her to be pelted and abused by the crowd. Each time she saw it she had gone over the plan in her mind, growing more and more certain that it could never work, but knowing she had to try.

The sacks were of polished rice and milled rice flour. Each alone was too heavy for her to move, and the terrified kitchen servant who had let her into the store had fled, taking one of her nuggets in payment for aiding her so far. He had refused to help her further, no matter what else she offered him. The block and tackle hung above her head on its steel eye as if mocking her stupidity. She had unthreaded the rope from the pulleys and knotted it and there was no time to repair her mistake. She kicked out again at the sacks in frustration as the roar of the crowd rose to a new menace.

This time the *metsuke*'s denunciation attained a terrible pitch. His acid speech dwelled upon the treacherous robbery on Okinawa and the murdering pirates that swarmed in the Co-prosperity Sphere.

"*How shall you deal with these* gaijin *devils?*" he demanded of the crowd. "*Tell me!*"

The answering cry was poisonous with hatred: "*Crucify him! Crucify him!*"

Were they leading him down so soon? The thought filled her with panic. She stumbled in her haste to get to the window. Fell. Lifted herself up.

Pressed her eye closer to the broken slat of the louver and stared out into the brightness.

There, standing upright and alone in the center of the great stage in his heavy collar, was her husband. She had no time to think. He would be under the arch in a matter of minutes.

"This evil criminal was treated with all courtesy by the Emperor and his daimyo, and by the people of Sado, but how has he repaid you? Even now his evil brothers lie in wait to destroy all who venture into the void! How shall we deal with him?"

"Crucify him!"

Michie cast around in desperation, then fed her trembling fingers through the shutter and broke away the dry, jagged wood, turning it over in her hand like a dagger. One of the *gaijin* was clattering below on a donkey. She could see his huge craggy face set in a frightful mask. Then she saw Wataru's oxen appear to the right, led by a sergeant of the guard.

It's too soon, she thought desperately. Go back. Go back! By all the gods, we're lost! Lost!

She watched Wataru's eyes stray up to the small shuttered window and then dart away. He nodded very slowly. As the cart rumbled twenty feet below her, she saw that its steep woven sides were bedded with hay and that it carried two great earthenware wine flasks, each big enough to contain a man. Between them was a long-handled weeding blade. She saw the old man reach for it, sun flashed on the newly honed curve of steel, and then the cart passed out of sight under the arch.

She looked at the sliver of wood in her hand and then at the sacks, cursed herself for a worthless idiot for not thinking of it sooner, uttered a silent prayer to Inari, the rice goddess, who had surely put the idea in her mind, and set to work ripping into the sacking.

Duval watched the storm of malevolence surge around him and abate. Silence suddenly filled the yawning space. Ten yards away Fukuda Ikku's head was a shining skull. His sunken face was turned skyward, his hands stretched out in a piteous gesture of appeal.

"Receive sentence now, you polluted and impure interloper whose sins are so grievous and whose crimes are too evil to be heard! The Emperor's most humble servants demand that you show humility."

Hishikari put his mouth to Duval's ear, whispering hideously. "Bow down and humble yourself in front of the cameras and you will receive clemency, even now!"

"Do as he says. Please!" his *komuso* begged him. "For your own sake!"

Terror swarmed in him again, but he shook his head. He would never kowtow before the *metsuke*, bowing down before the whole of Yamato in obsequious respect! Never!

"You may be spared the suffering," Hishikari told him, his features twisted imploringly. "Consider the punishment, Duval Straker! Think of the nails biting through your flesh, the pain inescapable as you hang there slowly to die! Show the people your obedience, your acceptance of the *metsuke*'s ruling, and the executioner will strangle you quickly! Bow down like a samurai! Or you'll be reborn a dung fly!"

"The *metsuke*'s been correct all along." He heard himself say it, coolly, defiantly. "I am not a samurai. I'm an Amerikan. A *gaijin*. And Amerikans do not bow down to anyone."

Then they were leading him from the stage and down the steps, his hands bound numbingly tight, and they put him on a small donkey so that his toes almost touched the ground. The animal trotted stiff-legged under his weight, stepping through the dung of the others that had come this way. His deadening fingers felt the roughness of its neck hair, bunched the bristled mane in his bound hands; his thighs felt the bulbous abdomen of the beast; the ridge of its spine knuckled his testicles as it walked, parading him before the shouting peasants. He looked straight ahead, unseeing, and as the street closed in he felt the dream falling from him. The killing ground beckoned.

Feculence rained down on him, strewed his way, spattered the street with stinking swill, spattered the dark blue kimono of the *komuso* that led him. The pungent smell of filth and corruption filled his nostrils. Suddenly he saw with great clarity. This was the circumstance of his own death march. It was real. Sharp. Actual.

I must ready myself for death, he thought, confronting the inevitability of it for the first time. He looked about him. The details of faces impressed themselves upon him. They were no longer a crowd. The sound of every throat was distinct. He saw each watcher—young and old; man and woman; samurai and *ikki*—as an individual vessel, each the receptacle of an individual human spirit. He saw that some wanted to see him nailed up, others to excuse him. He saw hate raw in the eyes of some, and in some there was horror. Souls dull, souls radiant, hysterical souls, souls pleasured by the prospect, others ashamed, how some were twisted with guilt, how some had pity and some mere curiosity and others yet a wonderful human compassion.

The crowd thinned as the lane narrowed. In the square the ranks of soldiers on each side had stood shoulder-to-shoulder with overlapped pikes held horizontally across their breastplates like a human fence against the press of the multitude; here they stood singly at attention, backs to the wall of the daimyo's residence. Several had left their stations, and as the shadow of the guard tower passed over him as cold as death, he saw why.

An ox cart blocked the street in the bright pool of light beyond. Soldiers struggled to unhitch the team and clear the way, but one of the oxen lay heavily in the middle of the road, lowing fearsomely. He saw oozing red on its hocks and hindquarters where it had been untidily hamstrung.

"Clear a way, there!"

Orders rang out. Troopers tugged helplessly at the deadweight, dragged on the horns, holding their wide-brimmed helmets back out of their eyes as they tried to unfasten the yoke. The cart shaft lifted, bucked suddenly upward, the cart tipped back throwing out its bed of straw, and a big *sake* jar was dashed to shards on the ground, splashing gallons of heady rice wine across the ground. Another rolled and tumbled, guttering its contents out also.

A sergeant jabbed the air with his sword. "Watch him!"

"You there! Get back to your prisoner! And you! Get that old idiot away from the cart!"

The cart driver scrabbled in the ruts bathing his hands in his lost wine and the straw that was scattered all around, bemoaning pitifully. Then Duval suddenly saw the man's face. It was Wataru Hoshino.

This can't be happening, he thought, his mind knocked sideways by the confusion. It can't be!

He almost shouted the name of his friend, but saw the intent in the old man's face. Wataru's eyes met his disbelieving gaze as a brawny, rock-faced soldier grabbed his waist.

"Get out of here!" he shouted directly at Duval, then he twisted away and began to wriggle out of the soldier's grip, raising as much noise as he could.

"Hold him!"

Duval heard a scraping sound above his head, then movement drew his eye upward, but he looked away again instantly, certain that the tilt of his head would make others lift their eyes. White grains began to rain down from a hatch that was hinging open in the planking high above his head. It's a miracle, he thought. Either that, or I'm already dead. What's that falling? God's eyes, it's rice! Then a heavy coil of rope dropped on him from above and he grabbed for its knotted end instinctively, at the same time kicking out at the man who held his donkey, sending him sprawling and the beast skittering away.

"Zinan-san!"

The shout mortified him. "Michie-san!"

"Quickly!"

The square above his head filled with her hair and face and great gouts of rice. All around the arch, the hard grains showered down, spattering off the guards' armor like hail. He locked the rope under his wrist bindings. The rope jerked tight, wrenching his elbows half out of their sockets, and he was suddenly above everyone's head and climbing for his life, his bloodless hands as weak as a baby's. He lifted himself up to the next knot, clenched his thighs on the rope, got purchase with his feet, and thrust. Below, the soldiers came to their senses. A hand closed over his ankle but he stabbed furiously with his heel and shook it off. He pulled himself up another knot.

"Look out!"

A ripped sack toppled, pushed over the edge of the hatch, and fell past him to burst on the ground in a cloud of rice flour. Another knot. Then the sergeant was under him, thrusting up with his sword. The evil blade jabbed, lanced through the bindings of his leggings. He felt the back of the blade strake his shin as it ripped away. He was nearly halfway up but the strength was dying in his arms.

"Climb, Zinan-san! Climb!" Michie was screaming at him, showering the torn sacking and its load of rice flour into the eyes of those below. Her hand groped for his wildly and then his foot slipped off the knot and he almost fell back. He was blinded. Blinking. Rubbing his eyes on his shoulder. Coughing. Choking on the flour—each breath caught in his throat. The world was spinning sickeningly. And his hands! They were insensible to his commands, all feeling gone from them.

"Help me!"

"Get up after him! *Dekiru dake hayaku!*"

"*Ita-i!* He's falling!"

He felt the rope tighten under his instep. One of the troopers was climbing, but the man's weight only served to hold the rope straighter and stop its wild twisting. Then he felt Michie's fingernails graze his arm. Her grip closed over his elbow with manic strength. His head butted the lip of the hatch as he burst through, panting, rolling on the floor as she dragged him inside.

"The rope! Cut the rope!" His voice was hoarse.

She stared about her, looking for the slat of broken wood she had used to rip open the sacks in order to move them. It was buried under the flour or gone through the hole. There was no time to find it. And it would never cut through rope. The rope was creaking, twisting. A trooper's crested helmet appeared in the space.

Duval got to his feet as she swung the heavy trapdoor over on its hinges and slammed it down. It failed to close flush because of the rope, but the falling cry of the soldier told them he had dropped. Michie untied the slack rope and let it fall also, then they were out and running, through the maze-like corridors of the daimyo's residence.

59

THE DAITO SYSTEM, N.Z.

Ellis Straker's ship followed the nexus chain towards Yamato, her galactic longitude discretely decreasing as she receded from the Twenty Degree Worlds; her galactic latitude remained almost fixed, as near as possible in the equatorial plane.

This system was a complete and utter bastard. They were lying a dozen AU off the largest planet of the white A2-type subgiant Daito—a system primary known to the Earth ancients as Gamma Scuti. Unfortunately the inner planetary system had never accreted into respectable planets, and a vast Saturnian ring girdled the star in a rare and beautiful stellar debris belt. The time they would waste getting out of its way was irritating. They had to cross it, opting for a catenary trajectory arcing up and over the ring towards the Yod-Four-Six nexus. An easy transit to galactic south lay the aprons of Banaba where the *Constitution*'s sudden appearance a week ago had thrown the system into confusion, but she had cruised on, ignoring the bristling hubris of the enemy. Her engines creaked and her stabilisers squeaked drily now, making Ellis think of the many schemes of running maintenance he had been obliged to put in hand of late.

On the bridge, meson cutters fulminated violet, throwing up the characteristic full-bodied aroma of marzipan as the drones applied plex solution to the seams. The methodical chunking of a wheezee sounded as a bulkhead was reshaped. The drones bleated. Above, the bridge dome was leaden and opaque, the shields troubled by an unrelenting meteoritic peppering that was beginning to annoy everyone, a day of restless peace and short comfort for a captain and his crew who hated to cruise blind. It was a ship-day that seemed to presage violence and unlooked-for trouble.

He sat in his command seat on the bridge in the waning UT forenoon, riffle-edged hard copy spread across his knees. The quality of tabulated information was clearer on hard copy. He had noticed that. The same data was on sheet, screen, and visualiser, but somehow the mind latched into one easier than another, and it was important that his mind latch correctly. He was planning the last piece of daring of this campaign and needed to think over the matter, but the stuffy air would not clear his head. For a while he allowed his mind to steer where it wanted, but too frequently his thoughts returned to that fine Sado *han* constructed in his imagination where his brother enjoyed gains more ill gotten than his own. It was a picture on which his mind's eye often brooded, and one which distressed him greatly.

The chime of the talkback as it turned noon reminded him that they had precious little left out of the tons of logistic stores that had left Harrisburg with them. He stretched, called for a juice, downed it, and sent the steward down for one of the small, sweet real *mikan* oranges that ripened in his cabin. When he closed his eyes, there was a bright Liberty landscape, fresh with snow, glorious cold on his cheeks and frost numbing his toes. Oh, for a Lincoln winter, he thought. A wind that bites and blows through a man, skeleton trees, iced ponds, and those subtle grays that hold more hidden colors than any garish outworld scene. How I long to see the familiar constellations high in the night, and the Wild Goose overhead, ah, so much Duval has lost . . .

The talkback sounded and Ellis opened his eyes. The black ring-stone of reproof glinted at him from his finger, the eagle motif a reminder that according to the original boundaries fixed by Earth Central, Amerika stretched from pole to pole between galactic longitudes thirty degrees and sixty degrees, in the general direction of the Old Earth constellation Aquila—the Eagle.

The steward reappeared with the orange. He took it, thanked the steward, and began to peel the fruit. It was how Ayrton Rodrigo had first showed him the astrography of Known Space: an orange two hundred parsecs across, with the Sun and Old Earth at its center, and the Beyond out there, outside the peel.

He broke out an orange segment and looked at it. The Sectors of Known Space were ever expanding at close to the speed of light, the outer limits being pushed relentlessly outward by relativisitic robot exploration. Their longitudinal faces were theoretically separated from one another rigidly by Earth Central treaty along galactic longitude lines, though the treaty had many times been violated and the boundaries redrawn: zero degrees to thirty, the Neutral Zone; thirty to sixty, Amerika with its associated semi-autonomous quadrants of Kanada and Kebeque and Izrael, occupying the orange segment between the Neutral Zone and Europa; then Latina, Slavia, Brasilia, and Afrika, each thirty degrees of galactic longitude. Between two-ten and two-forty degrees Izlam; neighboring them, Hindostan; then the two Sectors of China: the Indo-Chinese Confederation with its amalgam of small quadrants, and Han Central, called by them "Chung Kuo"—the Middle Realm—ruled by the Dowager. Last, and pointing toward the galactic center, the power-hungry Empire of Yamato.

There it was in his hand: Known Space, a giant *mikan* orange with twelve Sectors, six hundred fifty light-years cusp to cusp.

Ellis ate Yamato and chewed it to juicy pulp, spitting out a pip into his hand. Though Duval was long since disowned, he was not forgotten. The shame of him could never be completely stamped out, nor could a man stop himself from wanting to see his brother again—if only to put unanswered questions to him directly. He flicked the pip at a drone, bouncing it off the curved casing with a *ting*.

This was the fourth day since they had come zipping from the nexus, and his meticulous collection of astrographical data in the last three systems they had visited were by now fully notated with readings and braking instructions and reminders of debris hot-spots and landing markers cunningly downloaded from the pilot computers of captured vessels. These were the real treasures he would bring back to Amerika because they would enable others to follow in his star-wake and significantly improve their chances of success. He looked on them with great pleasure, but there was a worm in his satisfactions, because there were just lately a whole stack of new problems to overcome, problems born not of failure, but of success.

Each month, the *Constitution* had plowed virgin systems, cruising eastward as far as the Solitaires, grazing the riches of Pandora and of Rotuma, before disappearing for a time to recuperate. In June, without warning, they had surfaced at Pine near the Ten Degree Worlds, taking some useful small game —two transiters and a bigger ship—among the Tonga planets. Then again at Bismarck, lighting up the *Constitution*'s hull with anti-Yamato slogans to terrorise and infuriate the new army of occupation just as Oujuku had done to give the slaves hope and ideas of rebellion. In October they had taken a great bucket of a ship in one of the Korean chains, a trunker full of tributary presents meant for the Emperor and sent by the Dowager of China, in which he found a casket of superb emerald jewelry belonging to the captain. He had leveled a Nambu blaster at Ellis's breast to protect them, but its power had been flat, or its mechanism faulty, and without doubt good psi had prevented the discharge.

Ellis had had the samurai ignominiously stripped naked and poked round the ship with his own electric slave prod to roars of laughter. Then he had "bought" the emeralds for a bottle of water and a *komuso*'s straw hat when the villain was about to be sent off in his shuttle fifty AU from the nearest inhabited planet—close enough to save himself, far enough away to give him a raging thirst and shivers from the radiation belts and to make him think again about his laughing persecutors.

"Tell your compatriots these little green gewgaws are presents for my President," he had told the man as he was put aboard his own shuttle. "Who, if you're still in any doubt, is Alia Kane of Amerika, and is real pissed with Yamato right now. So *domo arigato* and fare-you-well, you unpleasant little sonofabitch."

In the year that had followed, Ellis had cruised the *Constitution* into all the main systems that the enemy held in the Zone and found that no big ship could catch her. Those speedier craft that could overhaul his eighteenth-power-rated engines were too light to hit him, and he knew that while he kept his crew in good spirits he could afford not to worry about pursuit or ambush, because, thanks to Ganesh Ramakrishnan, in the matter of locating ships before they located him, he could certainly have no equal.

In December of last year they had harried the Ontong Java and Nukumanu systems from a temporary base in Choiseul, and in spring they had come upon the Honjara apron and took a guard frigate there, relieving it of four hundred pounds of argentium. Ellis's confidence had grown with each success, and he found his fame had spread among the nexus men on which he preyed so that now few dared to resist when he closed with them. In all the systems of the Zone no Yamato commander could explain Ellis's ability to find and assess enemy ships or how he was able to distinguish which were ripe and which to be avoided. He had not told Oujuku of his clever trick, and he never divulged his method to any other man, no matter how trusted.

Bowen was the worst for curiosity, and after him, Brophy. Feldman Sark, the gray-bearded software techie, thought it a hell of a thing but knew better than to ask silly questions. From the corner of his eye, Ellis had many times seen Bowen and Brophy standing together, trying too hard to be surreptitious during each spell he had taken himself into the astrogation chamber to use the Ramakrishnan jewel. They had even gone so far as to rig a microcamera in the chamber to spy on him. And after that he had mercilessly wound them up to breaking point.

"There's no big deal," he had told Bowen blankly when his best officer had brought the subject up for the fifth time. "Good ship-handling and a great crew. That's all. Competence. No more to it than that."

"Yeah," Bowen had replied, unhappily scrubbing at his head. "But how do you *know* when a ship's worth the taking when she's no bigger than a pixel on the highest scanner range?"

"Oh, I just play a hunch."

"But why do you go into the astrogation chamber by yourself? There's not another captain I know does that unless he's planning a transit."

"It's quiet there and I like to think before we engage the enemy. C'mon, gimme a break, will ya?"

"Ellis, won't you tell us what's that little box you pull out, and that necklace thingumee you kiss and put on your forehead each time we sight a ship?" Brophy had asked. "What are those *incantations* you whisper?"

He had stood up then, shocked at their intrusion on his privacy. Then he had been grave-faced. "You've been *spying* on me?"

They looked like kids caught with *choko* round their mouths.

"All right, Mr. Bowen, Mr. Brophy, you got me cornered. I'll tell you."

"Yeah?"

"Okay, Captain!"

"Well . . . it's black magic."

"Black magic?"

"Yep."

"Jeezus, Captain!"

After a while Bowen had said, as mournful as a bloodhound, "I guess you're not gonna tell us, are you?"

"Nope."

Bowen and Brophy had gone away unsatisfied, and Ellis had known that one or both of them would be back, a week later, two weeks, two months—whenever the next ship was found and his inexplicable feat repeated.

Smiling to himself, Ellis settled deeper in his command seat now and watched Bowen. The problem was worried ragged now, but still unsolved. He had told no lies. The secret of taking nexus ships was indeed mostly discipline and the correct keeping of his ship and crew. And there were other factors: his policy was always to promise his intended victims that they would be accorded clemency if they surrendered, but that on the first shedding of Amerikan blood no quarter would follow. And he had abided by that, landing prisoners within sight of habitation and playing host to their captains, generally with good grace, and by this means he was able to plant the seeds of rumor in his guests and in return learn news of the Zone and draw off intelligence and therefore come to some understanding of how intensely his operations pained the Emperor's officers and how those operations might be made more troublesome still.

Ellis eyed the leaden dome again with disapproval. It was more depressing than radio black, but necessary. Debris against the shields became incredibly annoying as it flashed the bridge intensely with random light. There would be no letup to the blindness today. Another day lost in the quest to correct his sectional charts for field variation, and in arriving at a better estimate for the differential time elapse rates—general relativistic time lag—in deep-grav-well worlds. Luckily big primary star mass meant a fierce burning star and therefore temperate settled worlds were a long way out, and since energy flux and gravitational field strength both fell away as the square of distance, there was never much correction to worry about. The man who has the most accurate pilot computer model is the man who lives longest out here, he thought.

So far, their blend of good information and good psi had held them above trouble. There were enough uncharted dim M-subdwarf primary systems in the Zone to plant a thousand bases, and enough slaves to free on Yamato-annexed worlds to provide each with a permanent garrison. They had discovered side chains for use in time of low Index or to elude enemies. Onplanet, the men made good use of their time and relieved themselves of the wants that starfield trash must endure. Bowen had gotten three women with child at least, and in three separate systems. He had sworn to each that she was his only wife, though none were that in any Christian sense, as Nowell, the Southern Methodist lay preacher, had scolded him. Despite Nowell's frowning disapproval many of the men had done likewise, and he himself had eventually yielded to the carnal temptations that psi delivered his way. As for the female part of the crew, they had been more responsible over pregnancy—just as was expected of them—but even more enthusiastic sexually. It was a well-known fact that a man reached his physical sexual peak during his late teens; for a woman, it was her late twenties. Most of his crew were in their late twenties . . .

A happy crew, then, he mused, and a contented captain. But there were times when he was alone and quiet when he was reminded that there was more to his life's quest than bandit enjoyment and the arresting of Emperor Mutsuhito's lesser traffic. The strange pseudo-nova star which had wiped out Nagoya had remained in his mind. Here it would be a another fifty more years before its radiation wavefronts lit up the blackness of the sky. It would be even longer before any other Amerikans discovered it, and he thought again how right he and Oujuku had been to put a moratorium on the information. Policy had changed at home before, and one day he might need to use it.

And like the waning of a nova, he had progressively forgotten the shape of Reba's face, the timbre of her voice. How was she faring? As a mother? As a woman? How was she faring as another man's wife? And there was that bottomless question he had had to ask himself in solitary and soulless moments: is she even alive?

Lately he had begun to think about the real aim of his labors—to return home with the means to take what was rightfully his. But that remained a ransom greater than any he had yet won. As season passed into season, and year into year, Ellis had seen the boldness of his crew increase in step with their competence. It gave him cause to consider, because he found that to keep his people sharp he had had to give them greater and greater challenges. They had begun to spurn the small trunkers that had once been their staple diet, looking instead solely to the bigger ships. Each arrested vessel had outstripped the last in bounty and the richness of its pillage, and he understood that soon they would meet their match when their power to intimidate by reputation alone would fail. It was the fate of many a privateer who had grown too greedy. Eventually a pitched battle would be joined on adverse terms, good people would be lost, they would not prevail. It was something Ellis knew they must avoid at all costs, because the people of his crew were no longer poor nexus rats with nothing much to lose. They were all of them wealthy with immense credit fortunes stacked up, and there were many who wanted to go home to spend it.

At first he had put them off easily, a joke here, a petty threat there, but their unrest had become cancerous. He had told Bob Butcher, the drone specialist who never could keep his mouth closed, that the aurium that had gone back to Liberty with Oujuku was in trust, and that Oujuku had agreed to deliver shares only if Ellis returned. The rumor had persuaded some to give up their agitation, but eventually a formal deputation had asked him straight: "When can we go home, Captain?"

He had roughly reminded them of their oath to him on Oujuku's departure when the choice had been put before them which captain they wanted to follow.

"You'd be traitors to our mission and to me! You gave your word to it, all of you! Gave your promises to me!"

Stubbs, their ringleader, had spoken up. "Captain, a person can live in only one house at a time and marry only one partner at a time. What more have we got to get to satisfy you? How many years and months more? We want to go home."

"We sail home when I decide. Not before. That was the agreement."

"Captain, our fortunes're made. We've lost our appetite."

He had shouted at them, brought to the boil by that. "I'll piss crystals before I'll have it said of me that I was defeated by my own crew! That my own people copped out as soon as their bellies were full! Goddamn you all if you don't feel you've got a duty to Amerika to live up to!"

So their opposition had subsided into muttering, and to teach them to count their blessings he had taken them up into Kiribati, to a frigid, Plutonic lump of space-rock, and planted the choicest of their booty in deep-dug pits and gone quite secretly about it in case some among his people entertained other ideas. Then he had ordered Xavier Dunstan to modify the *Constitution*'s strongroom so that the walls phased clear and everybody could see the empty space inside.

"How hungry are you now?" he had asked when they were ranked up before him on the following Sunday. "The President herself ordered me to take an Amerikan ship into this Yamato-controlled territory and do what I could to harass them. And so I have. *And we will not go home until I say so*. Got it? Good! And now, if it's excitement you want, I've got just the thing, boys and girls."

After that, there had been more digging, this time back on Okinawa, but the gun-loving *gurentai* whom they met with again told them that most of their stolen aurium had been got out by the authorities, but that a typhoonicane had hit shortly after, and the rains had washed away the spheres which they had sunk under the riverbed, so they had contented themselves with what little they could find and fled to the Cabezas, leaving three aurium mines in ruins and more than half of Yomitan stripped of its domes. He had seen that both Taito and Kin were bristling with new beam weapons and Ellis knew then that there was no alternative: he would have to find a big ship and take it, or go home unfulfilled.

The first likely ship they came upon got away under cover of radio black. The second scudded for a secure nexus and so also escaped. The third was no easier prey. They followed her for forty AU across two nexi and into the Hog Sty, and she was fast, almost taking them for fools in the maze of small worldlets, but when she saw she was cornered she made to fight, struck her Yamato ensign off her hull, and scintillated a black field set with a white skull, which enraged them because that was *Constitution*'s own private ID and it looked like mockery. Ellis had cursed aloud, though his profanity was shot through with disappointment because the joke was that the ID now made the other ship impossible to attack—she was a friendly vessel, and her captain a man know to Ellis.

"She's a captured hull," he told Bowen angrily. "That's Kim Gwon Chung's trick. He's a totally crazy man, and he's only got one thought in his head, and a whole lot of the independent Korean way about him. He'll steal anything, even a man's reputation!"

"Shall we put the frighteners on him, then?"

"Put the frighteners on Mad Kim? Hell, no! I want to know where he's been and where he's going and what he's doing here without my goddamned permission."

Bowen had grinned. "You speak like he's a trespasser across your own backyard."

"He is. Though a welcome one now he's declared himself."

Kim had come roaringly aboard and Ellis had received him with a fancy dinner, but that night the Korean had said much to unsettle them all.

He had taken out his knife and cut a paring from his thumbnail in the pause. Black hair stuck up from his head like iron filings on a magnet, a great tuft of it bound up at the crown into a stiff fountain. His black eyes were half lidded as he scraped the filth from under each of his fingers in turn. His English was heavily accented. "You ask why I come out here. Answer I give not please you. We Korean pee-po throw out from your Sector. You President she turn against us. Appease the Emperor of Yamato."

Alarm had run through Ellis, and he had stared hard at his officers to quell them. Another turnabout in Amerikan policy was precisely what he had most feared and he wanted to open Kim Gwon Chung out. Doubts for Oujuku's safety and the safety of their profits seized him. "Go slowly, Kim, I've been away a long time."

"We Korean pee-po sent out of Amerikan system to do for ourselves, ey? Order was: no goods can be brought to Amerikan aprons for fleet serving Keun Whan Pai. That no way to treat allies, ey? And then what can we do? Just go back to Korean worlds? You remember idea we had long time ago about we take Pusan back from Yamato?"

Ellis had nodded. That plan had been to land a force on the planet and to resupply it from Amerika. "Yes. I remember."

"I make plan real, ey? Without ally we throw back on own resource. Still, we hold Pusan and one week more we take Taegu also."

"Desperation makes good fighters," Ellis said, seeing Kim Gwon Chung's resentment and fearing his news more than ever now. How far can I trust the Korean's account, he had asked himself, knowing that there was little chance he could now predict the reception he would find on his return to Amerika, or learn of the reception Oujuku had received? If Conroy Lubbock's counsel had held sway, the President would have been persuaded to open negotiations with Mutsuhito, perhaps even to offer to mediate between Yamato and the Korean independent leader, Keun Whan Pai, power-broking in order to get Amerikan rebels repatriated out of Yamato territory, and to set the seal on a partitioned Korea. A mantle of pleasantries would have descended over Amerikan-Yamato relations, and Oujuku's head, or his own, might have been an appropriate token for Lubbock to lay at Mutsuhito's feet. That, and the expulsion of the Korean privateering force from Amerikan space, might just have bought the conditions Alia Kane so wanted to secure.

"So the rifle of Korea has backfired on Mutsuhito?"

"Oh, shu. That very true," Kim Gwon Chung went on. "We find many way to stop them. When Baron Harumi came with big army to squash us, we blow nexus at Pyongyang. When Yamato attack Kangnung, they lose two hundred thousand troops, and at Samchok we send many skimmer across flood to relieve city." Kim's thick lips swallowed up another chicken leg, but his eyes were tempered by hard memories. His hand waved and banged extravagantly as he explained. "Because Harumi can't crush us, Emperor recall him like dog. Baron Makino go instead because Emperor think he better to talk, but we keep our base and shut the chain tight and starve him of everything until he terrify to death. No credit and no order, ey? When he die his scum go crazy, my friend, they riot through whole place. Burn and loot everything. Wonsan completely ruin and hundred thousand citizen dead. They delare Cho Sen of half quadrant. Very very double minus bad. But in independent Korea very different, ey? Keun president now. He take other half of quadrant and now too late talk because Yamato fury has unite everybody!"

"You say Baron Makino is dead?"

Kim bolted his mouthful and swilled beer after it with a gasp of satisfaction. "Last year. Of assassin."

"Who is his successor?"

"Who you think, ey? He's name as Prince Sekigahara, but I come here before he come there. My work in Korea finish, ey? I no have political fight now." Kim Gwon Chung nodded shortly. "But I still try get rich. I kill Yamato, which I can't do now in Korca—or Amerika."

Ellis had sucked in his cheeks. Prince Sekigahara, Yamato's new commander-general in Korea? Could it be true? They're calling their annexed part of the Korean quadrant "Cho Sen," their old name for Japanese-dominated Korea. What could that mean? But if the terms of peace really included a free, partitioned Korean quadrant with Keun Whan Pai as president, just as Kim said, then Lubbock's policy had triumphed. The many factions in half of Korea united against Yamato tyranny? The army of occupation in that half to be disbanded? Mutsuhito still nominal Emperor in Cho Sen, but all liberties secured? No, he thought. It's more likely that Kim Gwon Chung's adventuring in the Zone has been prompted by another, more personal cause. I'll bet that you've been run off by the traders for some reason, Kim. You must have many enemies among the Korean merchant community after the way you gorged yourself indiscriminately on their cargoes during the blockade, and you're no diplomat. But what if you're telling me the truth? If Prince Sekigahara's really about to take over in Cho Sen, it can only mean that Mutsuhito wants to bring the quadrant totally under his control once more. Under the bastard prince's personal command, forces can be raised and gathered for a strike, and hadn't Cassabian always said that Prince Sekigahara's hawkish ambitions were the main danger to Amerika? The prince believes that Yamato can never consolidate power in Korea until Amerika is brought down to the status of the Emperor's vassal.

"I see by your ship that you've had success," he had said to Kim, switching the subject sharply.

"Some. You not first Amerikan we meet, ey? Many Amerikan beyond Ten Degree World. They say they suffered great loss. More ship destroy this three year than all time before."

"The Emperor's daimyos are under orders to reinforce their planets."

"That not reason."

"Then what?"

Kim's scowl had revealed an engrossing fear. "Don't know. But you be careful, something very bad cruising around, take men and ship wherever strike at Yamato. Maybe new gun Yamato have. Europan say too many their ship disappear off Palawan. They say monster loose in this space. I believe. That's why I take *Tenno* and destroy my own better hull, to go under Yamato ID."

"And then mine?"

"Oh, shu. That a joke, ey? Between two friend."

"You showed my hull patterning, Gwon. You stole it."

Kim Gwon Chung dropped the knuckle of meat into his plate, splattering himself with gravy. Slowly he said, "I hear Yamato hate your gut, Straker. They say you dog—can smell fear in victim. That good enough for me."

Ellis had grinned at that, knowing that his own ID channels seldom carried any recognition device until he judged good reason to allow interrogation. Only then did he show his death's head. He said, "I've never heard of a sheep in wolf's clothing. No more skulls, Gwon. Understand?"

"If you want, Ellis."

"I want."

He had bidden Kim good luck then, and given him a download of his data on Solomon and the fascinating system called Ball's Pyramid to help him in his prowling, then they had parted umbilici to trust to psi in their separate ways, knowing that once out of sight the Korean would continue to ID with the skull just as it pleased him.

That had been a month ago, and Ellis roused himself from his thoughts; the Index was rising and the noon chime had sounded, bringing up the starboard watch, so he went below to eat. He spooned down a fast meal, then he kicked off his boots and read a while, drowsing in his strap hammock until his mind was triggered by a commotion on the talkback. By the time Dannyl Peeters, his steward, had brought his boots back he was looking around, barefoot.

"Scanners pick up engine spectrum, Captain."

"Yep. Give me my belt."

Peeters's hands were red. He hovered anxiously. "You'll be wanting your flexi too?"

"I'll call for you if there's any likelihood of fighting."

"Thank you, sir."

Peeters took himself away sharply. His concern for his captain's safety was commendable, but Ellis wished he would restrain the urge to make him wear his flexiplex vest whenever thc prospect of a little brawling came up.

As soon as Peeters was gone, he took the ion key from his neck, opened the safe, flung out his most precious belongings onto the floor, and unlocked the secret compartment in the back, sliding out the small box from inside. Then he took himself forward, clamped his secret cargo under his arm, and began to climb up to the astrogator's chamber. When he reached the vault door, he glanced down at Brophy, who was shouting something silently back down the corridor. He hooked Brophy towards him with an angry finger and sent him on a time-wasting errand to check out the port stabilisers before locking the vault and putting the jewel to his forehead. What he dreamed made his heart beat faster.

"Yes, by God! Look at that!"

Through Ganesh Ramakrishnan's wonderful device the alien ship became a babble of thoughts against a background of absolute three-degree black-body silence. The captain stood out among a rainbow of spurious colors that boiled like a summer's heat haze with that odd echoic feel the instrument gave to distant thoughts. She was a big ship: four-quad engines and a sense of security. Five thousand tons, if she's fifty, he told himself with unholy joy. His blood began to flame at the prospect. She's doing fifty gee, or I'm a Mexikan. What a beauty.

"Steer for her, Mr. Bowen!" he shouted. "Alert condition one!"

The answering cries barked up at him from the talkback.

This was what he had been hoping for. With luck, she would be as mass-laden as she looked. In his third eye he watched her hull turn slowly above the stellar pattern, then, some minutes later, she began to shear off from the nexus.

He met Brophy on the bridge with his astounding conclusion. "She's a Yamato nexus ship, and she's seen us," he told him, unnerving the man hugely. "She's out of Seram, heading, I trust, for Dolak and the way home to Yamato, but it's my belief she'll try to hide in Tanimbar or Aru if she can. She's worth taking."

"If you say so, sir."

"Do you doubt it, Tom?" Ellis turned to Ridgeway, who was sitting at the helm console. "Follow her, keep alt green one-ten and to starboard and close as soon as you can."

As the seconds ticked away, the nexus ship grew, fulfilling the predictions Ellis had made. The asteroids and dust and unaccreted debris of the planetary system were strung out all around, slipping by as the UT afternoon wore on. The victim was making for the dense co-orbital plane of the belt like a rat bolting for its hole. It's her only chance of shaking us off, Ellis thought, as he watched the maneuver. In a straight chase she would be relentlessly overhauled by *Constitution*'s better speed, but the high mass of the transport was a powerful reason not to stray too far into the dangerous dust belt. The extra momentum made her vulnerable to collision with a lump of rock the shields could not deal with. Material objects could pass through a shield with an ease inversely proportional to their impact speed. Up to around a relative velocity of fifty miles per hour they would move as cleanly as a shark through water; after that the fields really started to bite, and even massive objects were slowed like a Ping-Pong ball trying to rise through a column of molasses. The energy shedding led to internal heating and usually burned the object up in a fierce flash of energy. If the object encountered was really massive, several times bigger than the ship itself, the burning would be explosive and would blast the ship with X-ray and gamma radiation. The only strategy then was FRM jinking—fast reflex maneuver. But in an environment like this, with thousands of potential collision objects, FRM would tax any ship to its limit.

I felt she had a desperate astrogator aboard, he thought. One who knows this system well. And a good pilot computer to take control as the ship threads her way. It's what I'd do, if I were in her captain's position. This one's got spirit and is willing to make a fight of it. The ship's a water buffalo, heavy, and crossing to Yamato. She has more than a hold full of freezees, but I couldn't tell what. Maybe she's rich. Maybe she'll be our last prize and our passport home. We dive through the ring plane in five hours. With good psi we'll catch her before then, and we'll find out.

60

Captain Arima Yoshisabura sweated as he waited for the pirate to close on him. He was a fleshy man, broad like Chiyonofuji, his sumo hero, and rolls of fat wreathed his neck. His good ship, the *Kawabata Yasunari,* belonged to Senpaku, a rich merchant corporation headquartered in Shikoku. Her holds were full of aurium, and her stern quarters carried twenty-five passengers, from the exalted brother of the daimyo of Oshima, who had embarked on the first day of the second month of this 29th year of the Kanei era, down to the *ronin* and his pregnant wife, who had come aboard three days ago at Chichi-jima and whose waters had broken the moment they had sighted the pirate.

"Why do the gods trouble me so?" he asked the screens. A shout of *mutsu*—six minutes—came from the helmsman. The ring was approaching as the ship bore along the steep trajectory. "I knew I should have denied that woman."

The cries of labor came from the passenger quarters, upsetting the crew and making them mutter about bad psi as they worked. I knew there was something suspicious about them, Arima decided, watching the *ronin* standing anxiously at the bridge rail. And yet I allowed them to come aboard. The woman is beautiful, far too beautiful to be a wandering, lordless, half-witted, minor samurai's wife. And she has the bearing of nobility about her—I'd say a top samurai family, at least second rank. It was she who had done all the talking, and the *ronin* has said little. He wore the two swords, but once he had thrust them into his sash cutting edge down, so they curved up like a monkey tail. That was something no real samurai would do. His accent's strangely unplaceable, that alone should have warned me. The men are right: nothing has gone right since they came aboard.

But there had been the aurium nugget which she had paid for passage. It had been too much for a man to resist. In Chichi-jima he had thought the nugget was stolen and she the thief wanting to escape to Yamato, but there had been no evidence of that, and since the ship was to sail on the next launch window with one corner of her accommodation yet to be filled, he had decided not to deny her. Even though the woman was perilously close to her confinement, and he had explained to her that the voyage would last at least five weeks, she had implored him.

"You understand that there are no special facilities aboard my ship for a woman who must give birth?" he had told her kindly on the Chichi-jima apron, turning the heavy nugget over so that it caught the light. "No freezee facility. No surgeon. Only paramedic."

"So sorry, Captain-san. Do not trouble yourself. I have been on board a ship before, and so long as I may have privacy and clean linen I shall be content."

"Your need to leave Chichi-jima must be urgent to put yourself in this position."

She had taken the nugget back angrily then. "With the *kempei* killing hundreds in Chichi-jima, Captain-san? My husband is *ronin,* and the *kempei* blame us for everything, as if having no lord were our fault. When the Old Man died without issue, his *han* was broken up and his less useful retainers scattered to the winds. My husband is not very quick in the head. Which course would you try? I must think of what is best for my baby."

So he had shrugged and allowed her to come aboard, even after she had produced her idiot husband—it was truly a very valuable lump of aurium—but he had begun to watch the man closely, and he had seen the way his apparent imbecility fell away from him when he thought himself unobserved.

Look at the way he regards my beam weapons to distract himself, Arima thought. Is that not an *examination*? He says nothing, but sits alone watching my men come to quarters, but is he not itching to tell them their errors when they run in and run out? And errors are not difficult to find, for this crew has been gleaned from every low terminal hole in Chichi-jima and Sado and is the scum of the entire Sphere. They are without even the basest elements of gun control. But, by the gods, there's no doubt—that's a look of appraisal if ever there was one! This man propped against the control console so innocently is no idiot *ronin*.

Arima looked out at the screen once more, eyeing the pirate solemnly. Because control of the ship was with his system software, he felt redundant and extraneous. This pirate was fast and would be upon them within the hour. He had gambled that they might shake her off among the dangers of the belt where no navigation system with special knowledge could help them. Without sufficient occupation, Arima's brain fretted for the safety of the Oshima daimyo's brother who was samurai of the first rank, samurai to the core, who would rather die than allow himself to be ignominiously ransomed. If the pirate was of a certain kind, he would think nothing of destroying them all for having dared to attempt escape. Pirate gun crews knew the business they lived by, but *Kawabata Yasunari* was a big ship and her guns were adequate and pirates feared the loss of their means of escape. A volley of well-placed beams might penetrate her shields and send her off after other carrion. And there was still a slim chance that she would vaporise on the treacherous asteroids of the debris belt.

He descended the bridge companionway, passed hurriedly by the nearest starboard side gun blister and by the *ronin,* who leaned against it, then he turned as if in sudden absence and commanded him to hand him the arming key.

The *ronin* bent to it immediately and his fingers closed over the handle of the ion mechanism used to actuate the arming of the gun. Then he froze, realising his mistake, and bowed his shaved head.

"So, *ronin,* you know something of beam weaponry and the firing of ship's guns."

"*Iiye,* Captain-san. No. *Gomen nasai.* So sorry—I don't know, sir."

"Don't lie to me! I'll order you frozen down."

Duval Straker stood under the captain's eye, thinking furiously and damning himself for his foolishness. The privateer, which was almost certainly Amerikan from the shape of her hull and the cut of her tail fin, would be upon them before the Hour of the Horse was up. That meant a running battle or surrender, and judging by Arima's actions so far and the stories he had heard of what lay in the vessel's cargo bay, there would be no surrender. He heard Michie cry out in pain from the baby in her belly, and icy sweat broke out over his face. The fear of battle or a stray beam that forced its way through the shield could easily affect the birth if they made a stand of it, but if he refused to aid Arima and the privateer overcame them, what then? How might a pregnant woman be used aboard a pirate, Amerikan or not? He itched to punch Arima's mouth for his rudeness, or to show him what he could do with a gun, but he maintained his humble stance.

A shout rang out from the bridge. "*Itsu-tsu!*"—five minutes!

"Please let me go to my wife. The birth is starting. Please, Captain-san, I only heard the technical words your crewmen speak."

"Liar! You are not samurai."

"Please, sir. I'm *ronin,* dispossessed of the *han* of Yamaguchi on Chichi-jima these past two years."

"I don't believe you."

"It's the truth, sir. I swear by my ancestors."

It was no lie. The escape from Sado had been miraculous. Almost the entire guard had been in attendance on the *kempei* show trial, and Michie had led him to the courtyard where a fast air-car waited. They went unchallenged as they fled, following totally deserted air lanes until they had run out onto the eastern flightway and the open country. There, Michie had proposed that they turn north and head away from Chiba to the place Katsumi had designated as a rendezvous, but he had overruled her on a powerful certainty that the escape had been too easy and that the daimyo's hand was deeply in the matter.

"Did you tell Nishima-sama that I alone possessed the formula that defined the shape of the compression chamber?" he had demanded of her.

"I had to, Zinan-san. To secure his help."

"Then we have to go east!"

"But Katsumi-san is waiting for us."

"Yes! He's waiting, all right! With a troop of soldiers and a Probe. Don't you see? It's not me they want to preserve from the *kempei*'s crosses, but my secret. Katsumi would take it from me and send me back to Fukuda Ikku like a dog!"

"You must shave the top of your head."

"What?"

"Shave your head. And get a change of clothes. It's the only way. If they think you are samurai, we may be able to bluff and bribe our way out."

They had torn the engine out of the air-car, winging towards Niigata, where the *ya* would be packed with strangers, and then they had gone down to the apron and taken ship for Chichi-jima, where the *kempei* had not yet spread. They had transited to Chichi-jima and hidden themselves in a small town there. He had lived like a *ronin* so that their identities could remain hidden, and for two years he had drudged at bits of work, until Chichi-jima too began to come under the basilisk stare of the *kempei*. He was recognised by a soldier in the marketplace in the town where he had gone to sell hens, and immediately he had known they would have to leave, despite Michie's condition.

Arima's impatience flared up. "I warn you, foolish man, don't try my patience. I give you a choice: If you are a gunner and agree to help us fight, then you may stay here. But if you insist you are *ronin*, you'll be a *ronin* below, in the brig. Now, answer me."

"Captain-san, am I not a paying passenger?" he wailed, feeling himself tighten inside. "You cannot do this. Let me go to my wife!"

"*Yotsu!*" Four minutes!

Arima let out a gasp of frustration. Four minutes! The belt was growing dangerously dense, but no matter how dense it became, the raider would always have the option to follow. "Take him away!"

Two men seized him and pulled him below. Then the muffled boom of a contact sounded and a plume of orange light fountained off the shields overhead. It was the pirate's longest range beam—a range testing shot rather than a power shot. Arima wheeled and went to his command chair, forgetting about the *ronin*.

The pirate had come within range and it was time to make a decision.

Ahead the belt was beginning to widen menacingly. The probability computation gave him a result.

"*Chiku-sho!*" Damnation!

They would have a less than even chance of coming out the other side. Arima saw that now there would be no chance of shaking off the pursuit, and he determined to make his stand if the gods gave him the hint of a chance. He asked the helm to take a parabolic trajectory over the upper surface of the ring and then head for the open space where he might at least have unhindered time to bring his own weapons to bear. The pirate followed, understanding his decision and waiting for the moment menacingly. It began to dawn on Arima that there could be little hope of outthinking this predator. He ordered beams fired off from his forward blisters, for the purpose of exaggerating his report, then he gave orders for his ship to come to match velocity for tractoring. The words were as bitter as gall in his mouth.

The ID was full of interference across the intervening stretch of space—too much debris, and the words were indistinct and in strangely constructed and enunciated Japanese.

"Please to speak with us, for we are Amerikanmen and therefore well disposed to all if there be no cause to the contrary. Those who will not, or those that run from us, then his be the blame! Know also that if there be cause for warfare, we will be demons rather than men!"

Arima's fleshy frame quivered with frustration. Then he shot a glance at his first officer and said, "Tell them we'll comply."

61

As he was guided below through the fusty darkness, Duval could hear the soft moans of his wife's efforts. He was banned from attendance at the birth by custom. But a real samurai would have belonged to a *han* and that *han* would have had maternity facilities and equipment and midwives to assist instead of one terrified maid who knew nothing.

"Please do not imprison me, I beg you," he implored the hand. "My wife is helpless."

"Captain's orders," the man said woodenly, then he relented. "I have children of my own. Go to her and help her if you can."

"I promise I will not leave my wife's side," he said gratefully.

"See you keep your promise, or I will lose face, and the captain will punish me."

A makeshift delivery bed filled the narrow test-room chamber that was their accommodation. The narrow hole was crammed between the hot starboard stabilisers, just under the mid-hull airlocks, and was ablaze with small screens showing the output of every conceivable monitor or scanner aboard the ship. The plex spacers that supported the deck above thrust out across the cabin only a couple of feet above Michie's head, and she had braced her hands against them to fight the contractions. At her side a horrified young girl, the servant of a Senpaku corporate *bucho*'s wife, who were the only other women on board, dabbed sweat from her face with a rag.

"You can't come in," she cried when he appeared. "The baby's coming."

"Calm yourself," Duval said, wishing he could do the same. "I'll help."

The stifling heat was almost unendurable, the bed was soaked. Michie looked up at him and her exhausted eyes broke his heart. I wish I could help you, he thought, but how can I? He held her hand then, squeezing, willing his strength into her. Her pains ebbed and she breathed pantingly, so tired and waiting for the next surge. When the forward beam weapons fired, the maid jumped, but Michie merely rolled her big eyes up, oblivious to anything beyond the confines of the room, then the sweat began to stand out on her face again and she gathered herself to fight a fresh wave of agony.

Duval looked up at the dozens of monitor and scanner screens and glanced at those that showed the privateer. Through the light-haze of dust particles that glowed as the shields were peppered, he saw the two ship fields coalesce. A shuttle was approaching, probably packed with armed men. He could see from the markings that they were Amerikan. That's something at least, he thought. At least if they come here I can bargain with them. Or maybe not. Was it just propaganda that Amerikan pirates killed everyone. Was it? And what would they make of his samurai hairdo? With luck they'll loot us and leave and there'll be no firing, he thought. God forbid that there's any firing.

Michie's hand tightened and he held her as she grunted. The young maid knelt between her splayed legs. She looked up over the great swollen belly with a look of awe on her face. "I can see the baby's head. Push. Push harder!"

The wonder of the moment possessed him as he looked on. He heard the sounds of a boarding party entering the mid-hull airlock, of heavy feet on the deck above, then the oaths and gruff shouts in Amerikan of a body of raiders systematically combing through the ship for loot. But Duval Straker had only ears for his wife's grunts, and eyes only for the wrinkled head that was emerging from her. He stared, mesmerised by it. Wisps of dark hair and, incredibly, a small bloodstained face screwed tight against the shock of the living world, then a narrow shoulder, slick inside its mucous coat, and a perfect tiny hand. He reached out to deliver the arm and the torso and the purple trail of cord which he cut with his sword as soon as the legs came free.

Michie lifted her head to see.

"It's a boy, Michie. A son!"

He wiped the face and saw the toothless gums as the mouth opened, and some instinct told him to clear the slime from it with the tip of his finger to allow the first intake of breath. And there was a shuddering angry wail, like that of a small animal. Michie received the baby in her arms immediately and cradled him, and Duval saw the joy and adoration shining from her and he knew that he had witnessed the mystery of a profound miracle.

Slowly he became aware of a deathly silence pervading the ship. The Amerikans had gutted the *Kawabata Yasunari*'s cargo bays and gone, and he pictured Arima's men dourly watching the shuttle struggle away with their wealth. Then a torrent of cries rang out from somewhere, and he turned and looked up at the miniature monitor screens again.

There, sliding out into scanner range from the concealment of the ring plane, was a big warship. And her ID was Yamato.

62

On his bridge Ellis Straker watched the boarding party returning, and he took a reported assessment of the value of the haul they had brought off. It looked good. Very good. Bowen was on the screen, elatedly waving his arms from the copilot's seat of a shuttle that was loaded to its non-tare limit by the mass of four aurium flasks. He had told Bowen particularly: "No greedy diversions, no time-wasting. You'll take only what's in the cargo bay and the strongroom and we'll be away again. Don't even bother to disable her guns, she'll never catch us."

The *Constitution*'s own fearsome singularity weaponry was conspicuous in its obvious blisters, trained on the enemy's bridge dome, guaranteeing there would be no rash change of heart by her captain, but as Ellis watched he saw that there was activity on the other's decks, more than there should have been. When on previous occasions under similar circumstances they had lifted spoils from their victims and let them proceed, Ellis had almost been able to taste the burning humiliation of the ships' samurai masters. It had manifested itself as a sullen paralysis. No shouted insults, no bravado, just the shame of defeat and a skulking resentment. But this was different.

"Look, Captain! She's moving!" Brophy warned.

She can't be, Ellis told himself incredulously as he too saw the victim pulling away very slowly. The shields decoalesced, snapping into discrete ovoids, still ringing with a faint pink light of dust impacts. Because of the Hakon Effect, nexus ship shields repelled one another, but would coalesce like soap bubbles if a sufficient force carried the ships together. The fact that the repulsion force remained between the two ships when both were enveloped in the joint shield meant that pirates usually preferred to order their victim's shields shut down —unless they were very good at close-quarters steering. Unlike soap bubbles, however, the shields did not add algebraically: two coalesced shields were actually stronger than the sum of two individual ones—a classic case of the parts summing to a greater whole. A certain force had to be overcome in making the shields separate, and it was that kick that had alerted Brophy.

Ellis saw the *Kawabata Yasunari*'s gun blisters springing to life as the shields separated. Can't her captain see this is no bluff? he thought. We've position and enough firepower to tear her to pieces. And she's already lost her cargo. Jeezus, what's he doing? Okeh, at this range she'd cripple us if she could hit our shields for long enough, but we'd blow her to hell before she processed a byte.

"Keep us matched on her quarter, Feldman!" he shouted forward.

"Okeh, sir!"

A vision of horror came into Ellis's brain. They're unpredictable, these samurai, hotheaded, yeah, and as proud as cats. What if he's weighed his losses and decided he can't take responsibility for it? What if we've brought so much off him that he can't show his face again? Ever? He'd risk plenty to counter that, but he must be aware there's nothing he can do. He's raging! That's it. The mad sonofabitch's slicing his own belly open!

Ellis swept up the device that hung inside his shirt, licked it, and pressed the jewel to the node of his forehead and searched the other ship. He registered two men at the beam weapon on her dorsal blister, lining up on the shuttle as it drifted through the enemy shield towards *Constitution*. But there was something else, something undefined that rippled his psi-sense with instinctive alarm. Then he saw the scene dissolve in bright light, and the sound of the discharge reached him a split second later and the beam slammed into the shields. It was closely aimed, virtually stripping the tiny halo shield off Bowen's shuttle and throwing the craft into a violent spin. Had it been a destructor, it would have blipped the shuttle to atoms, but it was not.

"Get our own tractor on her! Now!"

Then pandemonium broke free on the talkback.

"Unknown vessel approaching! Azimuth red three-zero-decimal-two!"

"Captain!"

Ellis turned, taken totally by surprise. The screens showed the hull of a trader ship cutting into scanner range. The ship was thundering up from the mass of objects that made up the ring. He saw at a glance that she was a big, old trading vessel, with few guns and what there were probably old and weak, but she was accelerating towards them very fast, and her radio black must have been very good to deceive the discriminators so long. He located a commanding personality, a samurai who knew himself as Arima. Despite his thoughts being in Japanese, Ellis saw that he felt the fierce emotions that were associated with shame and the desire to avenge himself, and now unexpected hope directed towards the second vessel. Ellis realised immediately that the *Kawabata Yasunari*'s captain had registered her approach and it had fired his courage—and stimulated his fear.

"We can take them both without trouble," he told Brophy, holding the jewel to his forehead. "Starboard beam blisters, train on ship."

"Guns locked on," Nowell, the gun captain, shouted back.

"Teach them a lesson they won't forget, Jake!"

"Sir."

A second beam tautened from the *Kawabata Yasunari*, locking dangerously onto the shuttle. It was a powerful tractor, and the two beams wrestled for the craft, jerking it under huge stress forces in the space between the ships. *Constitution*'s tractors responded massively. Ellis reflected on the acuteness of their situation. Bowen's shouts of "Puuull! Puuull!" were anxious. They had a mile or so to drag the shuttle, but it was a tug-of-war they could not win.

"She's out of singularity range and taking the shuttle with her, by God!"

"Fire!" Nowell's brassy voice bellowed. *Constitution*'s full complement of beam weapons seared out, flinging lines of luminous energy at the *Kawabata Yasunari*. Tongues of raging fire were spattered up from her shields, shuddering her. Ellis turned to the new ship, something eating at him about the speed she was making. She'd be in range in seconds. He lifted his jewel once more and studied her echoing mind images. At once the unease grew within him. Nothing squared. She was closing with all speed, maneuvering as if to come deliberately alongside his guns. But there was total silence on her bridge.

Not even deep-sleeping minds were that silent. Not even freshly dead corpses. Something was wrong. Was it possible that some quirk of the ship's design was acting as a shield to the amplification powers of the jewel? Ellis studied the ship's trajectory carefully.

Either her captain's a fool or he's the bravest man alive, he thought. She can't fence beams with *Constitution*. Surely he can see that? Surely he can see what we're doing to the other ship! He can't be trying to bracket us. Then his third eye ran along the smoothness of her sheer. She was handsome in profile, and under the beakhead the lateral lines were neatly tapered into the stern engine pods. He followed their line back across the bridge and dorsal line, searching for an echo image. He found nothing except a curious rippling, and as she rolled into a banking turn he clearly felt it: *the entire length of her main deck and bridge were empty*.

"It can't be!" he roared. There were certainly minds aboard, but where? He just couldn't locate them.

He squeezed the jewel in his fist in exasperation, polished its big flat facet on his shirt, looking to Bowen's shuttle and willing the tractors to somewhow prise the craft from the other's grip. He lifted the jewel, fitting the clean facet once again to his node. The strange rippling image was still there, and there were defocused voices coming from behind it too! Almost as if the decks were . . . *hidden behind holo animations?*

It was crazy. Tri-vee holos, got up to look like deck activity! But why? To conceal what? *My God!* Look behind! Jeezus H. . . . Look at the firepower she's mounting!

The *Kawabata Yasunari's* reply roared out. One after another, three energy beams stabbed toward the *Constitution*. One crashed into the shields and was deflected in a monstrous red plume, another moaned through the space between them and began to force their shield inward with intense pressure, but the third was tightly aimed at the place where the tractor beam emerged, and a snaking bolt of energy discharged inside the shield above the bridge, blasting the dome with intense radiation. The ultra-optical shutters sheared closed over the dome, but the ship was jolted. The deck bucked, a partially stowed meson cutter overturned and was flukishly activated by the static field. By the time the drone had caught it, it had sliced a hole two feet long by ten inches wide in the millimeter-thick plex base of the dome. The one atmosphere of standard air in the bridge began to blast out of the slit like a steam jet. A gale ripped through the bridge. The A-section near Ellis was carried away and he was thrown sprawling. When he regained his feet, he was momentarily dazed.

Brophy ran to him. "Captain, you're hurt!"

"Get back to your station, goddamn you!" His ears were popping and he was swallowing like fury to ease the pain.

He searched the deck for his jewel. It was gone. When he reached the slit, he saw that it had been plugged by a raft of loose objects torn away in the sudden hurricane, including Sherl Martini, and that a drone had already creted over her lower half with some pink tacky gloop to seal the depressurisation. A sickly marzipan smell filled the air. Through the dome he saw the mask of her face, surrounded by a halo of long, straight blond hair, each strand standing out stiff as if with fear, but actually because of the intense static charge on her body. Her eyes were open and her mouth flapped horrifically. She would be dead in moments. There was no way to do anything for her, and everyone who saw her hammering soundlessly on the dome knew that it could easily have been them.

The *Constitution*'s second broadside charged the air with ozone, punishing the enemy's shield.

"Give fire to the other ship!" Ellis shouted, marshaling his people to get the *Constitution* under way. "The fight we came here for has sure as hell started. Whatever happens, we've come to our last battle. Show them Old Glory!"

Colors broke out along the entire hull. Down in the blisters and across the lateral line his gun crews struggled to line up on their new quarry. A running fight the newcomer wanted, and a running fight he would have. He looked at the efficiency and commitment of his crew and knew there was no force in God's universe that could match them when their spirit was in full flow. Suddenly his oppressive fears left his shoulders. His lungs filled with hi-ox air and his soul flamed. All the injustices of Niigata were ranged before him, and he felt the omnipotent power of the Great Satan of the Court of Kyoto falter and fade. Nobody could face down the sons and daughters of Amerika's ideal when they were free and fighting. Nobody. This was the beginning of the end for Mutsuhito's foul, slaver Empire, and the warriors of freedom would not be denied.

Bowen watched with slitted eyes as the mother ship's maneuver engines fired. The space between his shuttle and the *Constitution*'s bay that his own engines had valiantly fought to narrow began to widen—a quarter mile, a half mile, three quarters, as the engines glowed brighter. No matter how hard their own engines labored, they could not catch the *Constitution* now, but that would not stop him trying to the limit of his ability. His crew were terrified. They looked over their shoulders at the Yamato ship and he saw their agony. A couple more newtons per square meter from the *Kawabata Yasunari*'s tractors and they would be taken.

"We're losing," Zpinskoye cried.

"Yhare! Puuuull, you sonofabitch!"

He saw Stubb's face on the screen. "We're gonna have to let them have the shuttle, Bowen."

Bowen's fist crashed into the console. "I'll rig the destruct. Die clean and take a few of those bastards with me!"

"No, man! Bale out! We'll take you by tightening the tractor!"

"Can you make three one-ton flasks?"

"Let's experiment!"

They suited up and slammed up the overrides. The big doors sheared open and, one by one, three aurium flasks ejected, to be accelerated away by the tractor. Zpinskoye's red-suited body tripped out and dived away under the tight-beam force, followed by the rest of the boarding party. Meanwhile Bowen worked fast on the destruct panel, twisting in the two big ion arming keys and estimating the time.

The Yamato ship's tractor dragged at the shuttle inexorably, and it was accelerating faster as the balance of forces was upset. Bowen threw himself out, coiling in space and lashing out with his arms and legs. The *Constitution*'s beam picked him up and began to spin him back towards the shuttle bay. A dozen suited hands fell on him, hauling greedily, and as the *Constitution*'s bay doors sealed and the area pressurised, a dozen helmets came off.

Meanwhile, a new beam volley had blasted out from Nowell's weapon banks, shattering against the shields of the false trader that had stolen up on them. Ellis knew that the seven high-energy guns that were jammed along her lateral line would be lethal, that her captain knew she only had to close until they were virtually shield-to-shield and then a prolonged power blast with the big guns would cave the smaller Amerikan vessel's shields in. All pretenses had been dropped, and he thanked psi that he should have had the ability to see the threat soon enough to escape it.

"That's the bastard Kim Gwon Chung spoke about," he told Brophy.

"Yeah! I'll bet she's worked that trick on many a ship. She nearly worked it on us—and she might have a few other tricks."

"Not as good as the trick we've got for her!"

"Closing to singularity range, sir!"

"Fire at will!"

Nowell's guns blasted through the decoy ship's shields. His singularities cut through her raked-back hull just below the bridge dome. The devastating mass-eating saucers propagated through her, ripping her systems to ribbons.

"We'll see her bleed her atmos before we leave!"

Without her engines balanced, the enemy ship's tail juddered, spilling energy from her shields, and her captain was forced to crash off all power. The compensators failed. The hull bled gas at her stern, a cloud of evaporating solvents breaking from the neat holes in her. Amerikan fists punched the air. Cheers rang out. Lockjaw Smith flung Nowell's hat on the decking and stomped on it.

As the strange particle ring of Daito sped by beneath them, the *Constitution*'s singularity guns slowly reduced the Yamato vessel to a hulk. Unstoppable shots set her bridge alight, and searing explosions inside the now crazily transparent hull blew out of the pierced holes like volcanic vents. Ellis watched the *Kawabata Yasunari* flee away at a hundred gees, to save herself, away from the maze of asteroids, and he allowed her to go, seeing her shuttle bay smashed to a ragged pulp by the exploding shuttle. In that condition she would not make the Yamato Sector, and he was not surprised to see her captain take advantage of a shift in the Index to make a run for the inner system nexus, towards Chichi-jima once more, back the way she had come.

The rejoicing that night was prodigious. Bowen had succeeded in bringing aboard three flasks of aurium, and after the accounting, Ellis told them all on his life that he was satisfied, that they were done with roving the Zone, and that they would return home by way of their buried hoard for lack of any more space to fill in *Constitution*'s cargo hold.

There was a gawping silence, followed by a trickle of cheers.

"Have we really got to go back right away?" one woman somewhat crestfallen at the news asked him.

He left them, shaking his head, and found his own quarters then, to muse on the mighty awkward nature of crews and what they professed to want.

63

LIBERTY

Marsh mists hung low over the Potomac. The tide was flowing, but the skimmer sliced over the gray waters like a knife cutting silk, bringing the President's guest to the White House. The orange disc of Liberty's primary was scarcely above the eastern horizon at his back. It was half past seven by local reckoning, a week short of Liberty's northern winter solstice: he had been away for exactly two thousand days UT.

The velvet waters glittered with embroidered silver like the dew that gathers on autumn spider webs as the red-bladed propellors pushed them steadily upriver, forcing the sharp-prowed vehicle forward and shattering the peace. At the stem the gilded eagle of Amerika stood erect, the flag of the President fluttered at the sternpost. Amidships the engines and abaft them the canopied seat in which Ellis Straker sat like the President himself. His muscular calves were knotted inside his trousers, an old dress uniform jacket hung tight around his shoulders, making them massive; in his lap lay a casket of huge Yamato emeralds, the report of which he had sent on ahead to security.

At the pier the engines sputtered; Squaddies used their batons to keep back the curious and the idle who were gathering at the yellow barriers. Despite the earliness of the hour, an honor guard had been got out. A blaze of guns announced him as he stepped on Lincoln's shore.

"Well met, Ellis."

"Mr. Cassabian, it's good to see you."

"You will remember Otis le Grande?"

"How are you, sir?" Ellis nodded abruptly and crushed le Grande's hand. The strains of political life had marked his sallow face, but his wit was intact.

"I see you've forgotten your lessons on Lincoln etiquette."

"Captain Straker has had little occasion to show respect for anyone these past five years," Cassabian said pointedly, and Ellis felt the turn of his words like a razor slash. He had forgotten the keen edge that politics and the daily pursuit of power put on a man's tongue in Lincoln, and felt momentarily disadvantaged. Perhaps there was some battle going on between them at present. He decided to tread with care until he had learned more, thinking fondly of the judicious preparations he had made against things falling out badly on his return. He said jocularly, "Too few I've met with just lately have been Amerikans, and those that weren't generally had a hard time of it."

"Indeed!"

"And you, Mr. Cassabian? I hear that you've become secretary of state, the office Conroy Lubbock once occupied."

Le Grande jumped into the explanation: "He's our whip in an unruly administration."

"Aren't you Congressman Cassabian or Senator Cassabian?"

The spymaster avoided a direct answer. "I don't care for titles. You know that, Ellis."

"Jeezus!" Le Grande grunted and gestured undiplomatically. "The President's policy has always been hinged on recognition. You understand that Alia Kane makes a man work for his honors. The rarer she makes them, the more prized they become. But don't worry, Pharis's star is in the ascendant."

"He deserves it."

"Thank you, Captain, but it's not a good idea to praise a bridge until you're over it. We've got work to do."

"Events aren't going to your liking?"

"Could be better."

Ellis glanced around and stopped. He had expected Hawken to be here, and his absence had put him further on his guard. "Tell me: how was John Oujuku's return taken?"

There was silence, then Cassabian pulled on the tab of hair under his lip and walked on. He said evasively, "Well, you've got to realise that his return was somewhat—inopportune."

"Oh, yeah?"

"We were obliged to act on his behalf."

A shock of concern speared Ellis's belly. "Where is he now?"

"You expected him to be here to greet you?"

"Yes."

"John's not around. But don't worry about your unfinished business. I have your credit safe and I'll give you the details presently."

Ellis's frown deepened to anger. "Stuff the credit, Pharis! What about John? He's okeh, isn't he?"

"He's alive," le Grande said gently. "But we don't speak about him out loud these days."

"Will you pcople stop talking in circles!"

"Calm yourself, Captain. Otis only means that Oujuku is not with us here on Liberty. Ask in Norfolk and Harrisburg and you'll hear that he's trading to Europa. Ask the Free Korean merchants in the Exchange and you'll find talk of an expedition to Chung Kuo."

"But you know better," Ellis said, his fears multiplying.

"What if I tell you that his most important voyages recently have been to the other side of Lincoln?"

"I swear, Pharis, if you don't explain yourself, I'll—"

Cassabian whispered genially, "To the ashram of delights up the river."

"Okeh! I understand." Ellis grinned and punched Cassabian's shoulder with unseemly enthusiasm. If Oujuku had been to Ramakrishnan's ashram, it must mean there was some expedition approved by government under way. Doubtless some grandiose undertaking. "Where? The Zone? Slavia? Izlam? Afrika? They say there's a fortune in rare earths comes out of there each year. This is your doing, Mr. Cassabian!"

"Partly."

"Cassabian's credit backs the voyage," le Grande said. "Secretary Belkov is the principal investor."

"Nikolai Belkov, eh? He's rich and getting richer. Must be about the biggest fortune in Amerika by now."

Le Grande ignored the remark. "I'm also part of the venture. My nephew too. None of us have any particular quarrel with the Free Koreans."

Ellis racked his brains thinking of the charts he had seen in Ramakrishnan's ashram and visualising the parties that must have assembled there during the long, light evenings of the Lincoln summer: men of daring and men of imagination. What destination would they have chosen? What would they attempt?

The Beyond! Ramakrishnan's dreams lay out there. To find a way of pushing the boundaries of Known Space out faster than 0.99 cee. But Cassabian and le Grande would certainly have been more interested in a project in which Oujuku spent his time actively damaging Yamato . . .

"Yamato!"

That was it! Whether Cassabian had said it or not. Oujuku had gone across the Zero Degree Plane, into Yamato itself!

The extravagance of the plan captivated him.

Once inside the boundary nexi of the Zero Degree galactic longitude plane, Yamato's nexus lanes would be wide open to attack. All of Yamato was an exclusive preserve. Only Yamato ships were permitted through the heavily defended guard nexi, only they were allowed in the five-thousand-transit network of the Sector. A whole slice of ten million cubic light-years was lying there for the taking. Yamato transports plied those routes, filled to their bridges with all kinds of valuables, utterly fearless of attack because no foreigner had ever dared to come inside Yamato. Unarmed ships carrying the Emperor's wealth would be at Oujuku's mercy—if he could find a way there.

Reluctantly he laid aside his speculations. There was immediate business to put in hand. It was important to learn where he stood and what changes had overtaken Amerika in his long absence. He probed le Grande on the main elements, saying nothing of his chance meeting with Kim Gwon Chung.

So, Ellis thought as he listened, Cassabian has got his promotion. He's been principal secretary since Christmas of '26, and Lubbock has so far resisted the pressures of le Grande and Cassabian to intervene in force in the freeing of Cho Sen. The President has kept her hand on the controls of Free Korea by spending vast credit there and sending "military advisors." So—Kim Gwon Chung had broadly spoken the truth about affairs across the Boundary.

As le Grande's fountain of information ran dry, Cassabian briefed him with further details, warning him that he had to understand a good deal before he met with Lubbock. It was no easy task to appreciate the intricate web that had been spun by the President's ministers, but in essence it was simple: the disquiet in Korea remained Amerika's great guarantee. The expulsion of Free Koreans from Amerika had been a masterstroke conceived by Cassabian's fertile mind; the notion had been transplanted whole into the mind of Lubbock, where it had taken root and begun to flourish.

Cassabian watched Ellis's easy muscular movements as he walked beside him through the sprawling White House grounds. The years had changed the big man, coarsened his manner and filled him with a confidence fit to break empires. He had thrived on his crusade and put behind him the consuming distraction that had once driven him, that of his captive brother. It was just as well. For in coming time Amerika would have need of all her heroes.

Cassabian recalled the day he had advanced the idea.

"Convince the President to throw out the Free Koreans?" Timo Farren had asked from his deathbed, mystified by the suggestion. And at supper that night Ursula had looked at him questioningly. "You bend credulity to its limit, Pharis. Beware. One day soon your policies will snap in two and you'll slide back down the way you came. If that happens I won't complain. It'll be a blessing."

But he had comforted her, understanding that his continual business with spies and extra-Sectoral correspondents had tried their marriage. Most of the finance behind his initial rise to prominence had come from Ursula's father's will, and she had aided her husband's ambitions. But now she was sorry that the same fire still drove him so fiercely.

"You'll see that there are great rewards hidden at the rainbow's end," he had told her.

"You talk of rainbows, Pharis, but it no longer holds any luster for me. You've been saying it for too many years."

When they lay in bed that night, he had offered her a lucid observation. "I'll be principal secretary within the year, and you'll have the fine house on the river. The one I've been promising you."

"By throwing honest Free Koreans to their doom?"

"I think so."

"You'll be the Emperor of Yamato before Alia will do that. I hope I'm pricking your conceit, Pharis. And your conscience."

"C'mon, Ursula!"

"I will not c'mon."

"See, Lubbock wants a settlement with Yamato over the Zone. He's talking to Baron Harumi through the Trade Commission. He'll see the idea as an appropriate overture."

And so the President had ordered the Korean raiders out of the Kalifornias and Hawaii, just as Mutsuhito had wanted. But the Koreans that departed Amerika's aprons were not the pathetic refugees that had landed ten years before. They, like Kim Gwon Chung, had grown strong and dangerous, nourished as they were by the killings they had made in the Neutral Zone.

"Yes, Ellis, they were well-armed and equipped, desperate people. I thought that if Mutsuhito wanted these privateers expelled from Amerika, he might as well be obliged, eh?"

"You think Conroy Lubbock saw your design for what it was?"

Cassabian smiled. "Well . . . he certainly thought that Harumi—and the Emperor himself—would be very pleased by the President's new accommodating attitude."

They came to a courtyard containing a modern junk-revival sculpture, a fountain filled by rainwater channeled from the roofs and raised up on stilts in the form of angels. Under it, four naked-man holos faced in the cardinal directions, attending a bizarre machine of rods and levers and toothed wheels. An urn filled patiently from a slow dripfeed and tripped the mechanism as they watched. The holos' muscles glittered like real bronze as they pirouetted in a graceful dance and came to rest again, showing the time.

Cassabian told Ellis elaborately of how a presidential decision had expelled Keun Whan Pai's ships from their safe Amerikan havens, sending him into the Zone. "Lubbock sent Jos Hawken to do the dirty work. They went straightaway—all of them, Kim Gwon Chung's maniacs too." Cassabian examined the back of his hand. "As sweet as you like and without complaint. Then they took Pusan a week later."

Ellis gave a broad smile that recognised the genesis of the plan. "To take up old business."

"Keun and I thought that Pusan might be a good idea: a fair system, not much of a garrison, a serviceable apron. The inhabitants welcomed the privateers like liberators. We sent supplies of weapons and equipment and so on. And I seem to recall that there were a few Korean Amerikans who responded to the call for volunteers. A call that was somehow posted in every military base in Amerika."

"Korean Amerikans or Amerikan Koreans?"

"What's the difference? But they must have been some kind of Korean because they found their way around the quadrant pretty quickly. They landed at Wonsan and Samchok—and took both."

Ellis laughed, seeing how the tactic had been to strangle the quadrant and seize the greater part of it.

"There was a happy coincidence," Cassabian went on innocently. "Keun's brother, secretly in Cheju Do with twenty-five ships, and General Kwang with more marshaling in Taiwan."

"A three-pronged attack."

"Mutsuhito called it 'an unfortunate coincidence.' "

Cassabian had known that it was more than enough to keep any thoughts of offense out of Harumi's mind. Attack was just a superior form of defense, but the impecunious Kwang had been held up on the Boundary and Lubbock had gotten wind of the extent of the plan, and his meddling had turned the plan into a standoff between Free Korea and Yamato, with Amerikan aid to the privateers regulated tightly to keep the pot simmering.

"Lubbock was convinced that once Harumi was destroyed, the Free Koreans would pour into Cho Sen and seize it, with all the consequences which that must bring for Yamato policy against Amerika."

"There can never be victory without a decisive blow," Ellis said, watching the water clock's artful operation with interest.

"If only I'd succeeded in marrying Alia to the Dowager's son." Cassabian shrugged his shoulders in regret. "Then we might have joined forces in obliterating Harumi. But the President was turned. She became opposed to a policy that would completely evict Harumi from Free Korea. We were commanded to engineer the most level balance we could achieve in that quadrant, Yamato counterpoise to the Chinese—that was her ideal. But I didn't believe that our promise to aid Harumi against the Chinese would guarantee the ancient freedoms of the Korean people, or free them from Harumi's tyranny, or expel the *kempei* from the Zone. But—" Cassabian threw up his hands in a gesture of loss. "The Peking massacre changed everything. With the Cho Sen puppet leader dead, Kwang's brave gamble failed. He retreated to his stronghold systems."

"Which must have affected the shogunate," Ellis said.

Cassabian remembered the way that the President's looked-for balance had almost been achieved through Lubbock's patient diplomacy. Cassabian told Ellis, "As a gesture of amity, Baron Harumi was taken out of his post and replaced by the less martial Baron Makino. But in March last year he was poisoned, and Mutsuhito's *bakufu* council chose to send Prince Sekigahara instead. It was a costly decision."

Ellis nodded as if the information was news to him. "The victor of Hainan? But his repuation is that of an extreme hawk."

Le Grande said, "He's had a setback. Before he could reimpose control on his army, they mutinied and sacked Wonsan, which did not please the Free Koreans at all. The demands made of Prince Sekigahara were uncompromising: they wanted the samurai soldiery sent out of their quadrant altogether."

Ellis listened unmoved as le Grande explained, then said skeptically, "Do you suppose Free Korea can remain free from Yamato domination? A self-governing quadrant, with guaranteed liberties?"

"No. Even if Cho Sen continues to recognise nominal sovereignty, Yamato will not allow that."

Cassabian redoubled his efforts, seeing from the gestures of the water clock sculpture that there was little time. "Listen! I know much better than Lubbock does that all balances are unstable; without constant care they're easily disturbed. Lubbock is an intelligent man, but he's a bureaucrat to the bone marrow. He thinks Sektorpolitik can be managed by quiet tinkerings and fine tunings and in his scheme there's no place for men of fire and imagination. What he doesn't comprehend is that without them any power must slowly slide into complacent decline. The worst of it is that because Lubbock himself lacks imagination, he supposes that that applies to everyone else. I tell you, Ellis, that is a big mistake. Prince Sekigahara is no weakling; he'll never concede to Free Korea their demands. The Korean president knows that and will never accept the prince's demands. Deadlock, so far. But I cannot believe Prince Sekigahara will crawl away with his tail between his legs."

Cassabian knew that although the prince's outward design was to pacify both Koreas, he held another, less ostensible ambition. Now he had his proof: Prince Sekigahara had fostered strong links with pro-Yamato Amerikans exiled abroad, with the renegades' seminary on Juno, and with the arch-traitor General Waters. Through his spies there, he found that Prince Sekigahara planned to embark his troops for Yamato, *but land them in Amerika*. He had boasted that he would marry Alia Kane himself and then order her to commit *seppuku*, as would be his right.

"That's where the President's credit will go, Ellis. Of the vast riches that lie in your ship in Harrisburg, one hundred billion credits is already earmarked as a loan to Keun; fifty ships and three divisions of first-line infantry and a thousand assault vehicles are to go out under Colonel Northridge's command. We'll make Free Korea accept Keun's brother as their leader, and insist that Sekigahara's troops are sent off to the Zero Degree nexi, by a ten-transit backwater chain that keeps them off our Boundary. If the President will only listen to reason."

"Do we go to the President now?"

"No, to Lubbock. He has news you'll not want to hear. In your absence you've been outmaneuvered by a consummate businessman, as he'll no doubt tell you himself."

64

"That's our contract, Captain. You understand the terms as well as I do. One half of the total belongs to Amerika."

"As it has done since it was taken from Yamato's ships."

"A further quarter of the—cargo—is to be divided among the following investors." Lubbock read out their names—twenty-five of the richest and most powerful men in the Sector—along with the percentages they would receive. Lubbock's own name was not among them. "That leaves you the remainder."

Ellis tried to appear outwardly gracious, but saw that the VP was feeling for his true opinions. "The remainder for myself *and* my crew. My own personal share is a little less than a half of what you're showing there. Also, you can exclude the most exquisite item. I intend to make that a personal gift to Alia—let's say a Christmas gift—a quantity of emeralds, a debt of thanks to her faith in me. So that's twelve and a half percent for the crew, who bought the stuff with their blood and their sweat, or for their bereaved kin, and ten percent for their captain, who figured it out in the first place."

"Do you wish it was more?"

Ellis shrugged. "If I'd thought that, I'd have gotten more."

"A pity you didn't, then." Lubbock's eyes narrowed in a shrewd look. He rose from his seat and touched his hand to the real fireplace. "Because the investors I just named all sold their shares to me. Two years ago, when news came back that you were dead."

"Remind me to thank you for your faith in me," Ellis said sourly, concealing his shock and anger as best he could. "I hope the shares didn't cost you too much?"

"On the contrary. The price was cheap. They cost me half what I would have paid on your departure, plus the going rate for a believable rumor. I wish to build a house in Northrop, and my mansion here in Lincoln is a costly enough place to run as it stands. However—I can afford to make some of my gains over to you and your crew. Enough to make them all blissfully wealthy men, and yourself a Liberty magnate, with enough credit to buy half a dozen ships."

Ellis's voice betrayed him. "Oh, yeah? I can be a Liberty magnate, can I? With what's mine already? I must be witnessing a goddamned miracle!"

"I can make you a man of means."

"Is that a fact?"

"Yes. It's a fact."

Ellis's voice sank low, but his eyes never faltered as he stared at Lubbock's own. "Strange to think that you believe I can be transformed into a man of means. I kind of thought that you were of a different set of mind: that a man's quality lies in his possession of Halide corporate stock."

Lubbock's confidence was undented. He said mildly, "Men have been given position for serving their Sector's interests before."

"Government sinecures are not yours to give."

"Nevertheless, I can confidently promise you one."

"Your promises are other men's burdens, Conroy."

Lubbock delighted in the danger into which the exchange was plunging. "Let's turn our minds instead to—"

"No, Conroy! Let's think of what gives a man self-respect and what does not. It seems to me a matter of achievement and reward, as in your own case."

"What do you want?"

Ellis's gaze remained steady. "You know fine well what I want."

Lubbock sighed and put up his hands. "My daughter is a married woman."

"In name."

"In *fact*, sir!"

"Not according to my understanding."

"Damn your understanding. And damn your eyes! You forget yourself!"

"I forget nothing, Mr. Vice-president. I've refreshed my mind daily with the thought of my Reba and of a son I've never seen yet. I will see her, and you will not interfere with that!"

Lubbock felt anger prickle him, whipped by the coarse tongue of a man who had no proper humility, who had issued only commands to others for five long years. He turned, tight-lipped and furious, and began to stalk away, then he halted, and he knew precisely why he had done so.

Lie to whomever you want, Conroy, his conscience told him. But never lie to yourself. It had to be admitted. The last five years had been years of continual torment to his daughter. No sooner had Ellis gone to the Zone than Kurt had begged the President for permission to give him a passport also, so that he could go into the Zone in a big nexus yacht he was fitting out. She had, of course, refused him, liking his presence at her White House soirees for the sake of his dancing and his manners and perhaps for his quarreling spirit, which she admired in young men and enjoyed watching.

Reiner had thought the prohibition was Lubbock's doing, and there had been some truth in that, because he had given the President honest opinions on the matter. "The spoiled brat'll kill himself," Lubbock had predicted balefully, part of him wishing as much could be arranged. "A yacht allowed into the Zone with Kurt as its captain will be loaded with three kinds of bad psi."

Oh, yes, he had thought, a triple helping of the worst psi: one, in that Kurt would surely have caught pinkeye, or got atomised in a psi-storm, or had himself blown to fragments in an engagement with a *rikugun* patrol ship; two, in that he would bring the President to grief over this—and she hardly to be in a position to need bad press; and three, in that he would probably provoke Yamato sooner or later, if he didn't die, and in so inexpert a way as to result in his capture and expensive ransom, or, conceivably, the rupturing of that delicate membrane that kept Amerika and Yamato out of war with one another.

Reiner had sworn to revenge himself on Reba.

"I'll see her cry her eyes out," he had warned poisonously. "I'll damage her. See if I don't!"

Lubbock had humbled himself to plead: "You know the President herself says that you can't take your yacht beyond the Boundary, Kurt. You want to disobey Alia?"

"*Disobey?* I don't take orders from anyone! If she doesn't let me go, I'll go fight in Korea as a mercenary, and find honor there!"

And he had gone, without the President's consent, relieving Reba, who had grown to detest the tread of his foot across the threshold. "May he be shot through the head," he heard her pray one night. "Swift and clean, but final. Sweet Jeezus, I want him away from me and my child."

It was then that Lubbock had known the depth of his daughter's anger and despair and the enormity of the error he had made, and how right Vara had been in the matter of her daughter's wedding. But he had set his face and, like everyone else, part of him had assumed Ellis Straker dead. A year and a half without word had been a long time, but still he had traded those shares in Straker's adventuring mission, just in case, swapping them one-for-one for shares in Oujuku. Then Oujuku had come back with his booty and his wild tales, and many had sniggered in private because he had sold out on a winner and bought in on a dead man.

But they were not laughing now. Not now. And Lubbock felt no pleasure, nor even gratification, only a cold dread at Ellis Straker's return that outweighed the credit. *Why?* And in any case, what was done was done. And though Reba might wilt as a flower wilts in a climate that does not suit it, she had married and her vows had been made at the altar, before God—and more important, before the President. But that was not accounting for her willfulness.

After the Korean episode, in '27, Lubbock had had Reiner smuggled home by the mercenaries who were glad to be rid of him. He had induced him to apologise to the President, which he did genuinely. Having seen a little of war—in the flesh, so to speak—Reiner had renounced it as disgusting and unworthy. His pretentions to an adventurer's life had already been reduced, diverted from this to that by the news of Okinawa and Oujuku's fabulous reception. A marvel how the publicity over that had turned every other young man in Liberty into one ardent mass ready to cruise into the Boundary, but Reiner had shunned the celebrations, calling the whole privateering thing an adolescent fad of which he had wearied. And so he had returned instead to his youthful posture as a poet of genius, because in that pursuit there was no hard standard to be set against him, only opinions and critiques which might be easily twisted to his self-satisfaction.

Lubbock cringed inwardly as he thought of the burbling hexameters that Reiner had offered up for praise, and—God save us all—the tight band of dissolute hangers-on whose whole game was to wait upon Reiner as if he was a new Messiah. The following year Lubbock had disbursed him a sum sufficient to take him off on a tour of Europa, to Milan and to London, but he had returned home within a year, crammed with new poses, totally conceited, overspent, and sporting a new Bristol air-car and perfumed clothes and canvas after canvas of fine art. He had presented a Freud painting to the President, but there had been nothing for his wife, and thereafter he had been a stranger to her, and she almost banished to the mansion of Xanadu.

Cassabian had been disgusted, and le Grande delighted, until he was brought to the brink of choking. "What does Kurt imagine he looks like?" he had said, laughing scornfully, but out of Reiner's earshot. "Jeezus H.! A Goochie hat, like an oyster. And all those French cambric shirts! Ha! I've seen better-dressed men on Dakota II!"

It was Simon Belkov who had caught the bile that should have been vomited over le Grande, for poet or not, fashion-maker or not, Reiner's violent temper was intact, and he had made war on le Grande's nephew with offers to duel and even an extravagant contract on his life.

Lubbock looked at the iron-hard man who stood in front of him. Tempered in real war and toughened by genuine adversity. Here was a man who knew exactly what he was, exactly what he wanted, and would brook no opposition to that. Small wonder Reba contrasted him so readily against the man to whom she had been matched in wedlock.

Lubbock faced Ellis stubbornly, sure in the state power at his disposal. The time had come to employ it. "You swore never to speak of my daughter again."

"That oath was made under duress. It is *revoked.*" Ellis's fingers snapped, recalling the day the soldiers had taken him blood-drained and amazed from Ramakrishnan's ashram.

"You're a shameless sonofabitch!"

"No, Conroy! It's *you* who's shameless. Didn't you force your firstborn daughter into a bad marriage against her wishes for your own ambition? Didn't you deny your grandchild his birthright? *Didn't you do that?* Eh, Mr. Vee-Pee?"

"I warn you, Straker—"

"And I warn you! Not a Cho Sen *jeon* of the aurium I've brought out of the Zone will reach you, or the Treasury, until you oblige me."

Lubbock straightened, weasel sly. "It is unwise to threaten me, Ellis. I have your ship on the Harrisburg apron—under armed escort. This time, you can't get away. Guards!"

Six servicemen sprang into the room, their blasters leveled on him. Ellis fell quiet, stared at his feet, inwardly delighting that his foresight had put him in this position. Even so, he remained carefully self-possessed.

"I had no intention of trying to get away, Conroy. I guess the whole planet'll be wanting to talk to me tomorrow."

"Your arrival is still secret."

"It can't remain secret for long."

Lubbock, recollected now to his cool and reasonable self, called his private secretary, who brought the papers. "The people want to see you on tri-vee, and I don't want to interfere with that, because the people's wants are my wants and my responsibility. But hear me well, Captain, if you want to cause me trouble, I'll just as soon take the people's hero away from them and put him in Camp Worth."

"You did that once before, I remember," Ellis said.

"You dare to smile at me?"

"I'm not smiling at you, Conroy. Simply at your bribery. I think that you're about to make a new offer."

Lubbock's anger showed but he locked it away. "All right: keep your word and you'll be a world-state governor. You'll have the federal warrant for Utah. What do you say to that?"

Ellis thoughts leapt again to John Oujuku, to how Amerika had gratefully received his billions of credit from the Okinawa adventure, and paid him off with little thanks and a sinecure as deputy assistant gewgaw of Nebraska.

As the conflict with Yamato had cooled, Oujuku's embarrassing presence in Amerika had had to be dealt with; he was sent to Nebraska to make laws on moonshine mash and grizzly bears.

Oujuku had hated it. "A fair fight at best, something to get my teeth into, that's what I like," Ellis had heard him roar after Okinawa, though to tell the truth, Captain John Winston Oujuku preferred huge odds against, believing like an ardent Amerikan must do that he was a free man and could only prove as much to the satisfaction of all by overthrowing a burden of oppression somewhere. That he had gone off on his extravagant expedition now was a mark that he had lost none of that firmness of belief. A man *complete*, sure, full of his own self. A *man*.

An image of John single-handedly attacking a grizzly with a rolled-up hard copy of a bear-control statute leapt to mind and made him smile. Ellis felt suddenly careless of the circle of servicemen who surrounded him. He brushed one blaster aside, ignoring the way the remainder made at him threateningly. Seeing the intimidation fail, Lubbock signaled them impatiently to put up their arms.

So Lubbock thought it convenient to let Oujuku leave, Ellis told himself. He could have vetoed Cassabian and le Grande and all the rest of them had he wanted to. Yet Cassabian said that Yamato's irritation with Amerika was boiling up once more. Ellis felt the change in the Index and steered accordingly. For what reason did Lubbock want a valuable privateer commander to kick the butts of klansmen in barbarous Utah? It's a diversion—shelve me, keep me from the Zone, keep me from Reba also. Stick me in a backwater, neither at home nor away.

"What do you say?"

"I say no."

"The offer's good."

"Utah? To be governor of a piss-pit like that? No chance."

"You *will* oblige me in this."

"No."

Lubbock shook his head and looked down at the contract, striping a line through it matter-of-factly. "In that case your ship is confiscated, and all it contains. And you, you sonofabitch, are under arrest."

"A real shame."

"You'll soon think so, you respectless devil!"

As the guards closed in around him once more, Ellis thrust up his hands as if addressing the heavens. "Lord God, take me from this stupid old bastard before I split my sides!"

And the peals of his laughter rang out as Jiro Ito escorted him away.

65

Ellis got down from his air-car, thoughts of Christmas turkey and Kansas klaret far from his mind now as he parked. The ground was white with snow and deeply covered; the east wind had blown everything dry and hoary and crisp. He was alone and strung so tight inside that he felt he was about to snap.

The house of Xanadu seemed to him dreary and quiet under its steep roofs. There were flakes in the air, and no echoes because of the white blanket. The white walls were made creamy against the virgin burden of the roof. A snowman stood on the lawn; pebble eyes, twig nose, and a huge grin to welcome him. It wore a cloak and wide-brimmed hat and held a broom, but it might have been a *katana* for all that it struck him with shivers.

His mouth was dry. At his back the air-car engines ticked and cooled.

The day Lubbock had imprisoned him he had marked the afternoon with a nap and the tuneless whistling that often accompanied his most strategic thoughts. He had counted the hours until enough had passed for a Revenue car to get to Harrisburg and back, then he had listened out for returning footsteps. Ito appeared within the hour to fetch him before Lubbock, who was white-faced with rage. He had shaken his fist in Ellis's face and demanded, "*Where is it?*"

"Where you can't get it."

"I swear I'll give you the Probe, Straker."

Ellis said nothing.

"I'll Probe your crew!"

"A-a. They don't know anything."

"That won't stop me."

"How will the President take it when she hears that you're victimising her privateers?" He had sucked in a breath and shook his head like an air-car mechanic looking at a lemon. "Her mood'll deepen if she can no longer execute her policies in Korea for lack of finance."

Lubbock spat at him, enraged. "Amerika has enough credit for that."

"Oh, yeah? Does Congress know about that? And what about the credit she needs to rebuild the Navy?"

He pushed open the gate, sweeping a sector of snow up behind it, trying to savor the moment he had imagined so differently so often.

As he did so, he grinned, thanking psi that he had remembered the rumors that had surrounded his and Hawken's return so long ago, rumors of how they had buried their profits to avoid the Revenue.

All that had happened since planetfall proved the wisdom of his prudence: he had told Lubbock that the aurium was buried in Kalifornia.

"*Kalifornia?*"

"On a desolate little asteroid. Five hundred feet down a bore hole where nobody can spend it until I'm real satisfied."

In actuality, he had had it committed to a Yamato store hulk taken in one of the Aleutian systems and brought right into Norfolk. The whole treasure lay there now, a few miles away, packed into containers and guarded by Bowen with a singularity gun rigged ready to swallow the lot and all the jealousy of a dragon on top of a hoard.

Ellis took off his driving gloves and walked slowly up the path, his boots crushing the snow with a sound like grinding teeth. He was suddenly hot and he loosened his collar and threw open his jacket. A small brown bird fled from him, shaking down fine snow from a twig and putting a nursery rhyme about robins into his head.

Then he caught a flash of fair hair and a twitch of curtain at the window. The light, high voice pierced him and he steeled himself to lift the heavy knock-ring, but as he reached for it the barking of big dogs began within, and the sound of them rushing to the door made him step back.

When the chained door cracked open, it revealed their dripping muzzles and their anxiety to be at him, but a female "servant" shouted for aid to restrain them, and Ellis was roughly asked his name and his business.

"I am Captain Ellis Straker, and I'd like Mrs. . . . I'd like Reba to know I'm here."

"The mistress does not receive callers."

A small voice squealed. The blond-haired boy he had glimpsed at the window galloped into the hallway. He wore a tidy little one-piece and straddled a hovering plex toy made like a shuttle. He stopped when he saw Ellis looking at him and twisted about with incredible coyness. Then he slapped the nearest dog's eye and told it to hush, which it did resentfully.

"Is this Mrs. Reiner's only child?"

The servant nodded. "He is, sir. But you can't—"

"How old is he?"

"Five years UT, but I must ask—"

Ellis knelt to the boy, "What's your name, son?"

"Hayden."

"Hayden," he echoed back tenderly, taking his hand. Then he drew a large, brown love bear from his jacket and gave it to him. "Hold him tight and he'll hear your heart beating and go to sleep."

And as he turned he saw the woman in somber green standing at the head of the stair. It was his Reba.

BOOK 4

29TH YEAR OF KANEI/A.D. 2431

Summer grasses,
All that remains,
Of warrior dreams.

Matsuo Basho
1644–94

Material excerpted from "A Manuscript Found in Space,"
by A. Hacker:

Material excerpted from the Ozma Vault
Transmission Package KVFG #2975,

[Ref. Module MMVII-124.288762]

[Cross-references to other SEC modules in CAPS.]

KNOWN SPACE

Definition: at any one time that sphere of interstellar space centered on the SUN and lying within the exploration boundary surface. Presently approximately three hundred LIGHT-YEARS in diameter.

Following the first statements of the GRAND UNIFICATION THEORY and the FUNDAMENTAL HYPOTHESIS OF PHYSICS [Ref. Module MDCDXVII-507.873523], the way had been opened for interstellar exploration. By the twenty-second century A.D. technical control of the GRAVITATIONAL INTERACTION [Ref. Module LCXI-000.976432] had become relatively sophisticated, by A.D. 2100 comparable with command of electromagnetic forces achieved two centuries before. GRAVOMETRICS [Ref. Module LCXXI-002-495271], useful techniques connected with gravitation and the manipulation of space-time geometry, were employed in the creation of the NEXUS [Ref. Module MDCXVIII-115.2936] network of KNOWN SPACE [Ref. Mod. *ibidem*].#

. . . *HACK INTERRUPTED* . . .

#two key technological developments allowed colonisation of space: the discovery of a means of faster-than-light travel, utilising nexus [Ref. Mod. *ibidem*] points, small space-time singularities which could be detonated anywhere in EUCLIDEAN SPACE [Ref. Module MCXXIV-024.240354]; and the technology of TERRAFORMING [Ref. Module DCCIX-929.220922]—the fast transforming of suitable seed-planets from chemically hostile environments into quasi-Earth-like environments with atmospheres, oceans, imported ecologie#

. . . *HACK INTERRUPTED* . . .

#tomatic ramjet spacecraft, a VON NEUMANN MACHINE, traveling at near-CEE has arrived at a nearby star system, it "detonates" the nexus, a semi-stable torus quasi-singularity, rotating in the imaginary time-domain. The PIONEER DRONE then replicates and the daughter craft move on to the next closest systems. It is then possible for near-instantaneous communication to be effected from other systems which also contain a nexus point. (At a constant acceleration of one hundred GEE, it takes the pioneer drones approximately three to four days, UT, to reach 0.9 cee, and about the same time to decelerate at their destination. Typically a four-to-five-year journey lies in between, during which its computers are closed down, hibernat#

. . . *HACK INTERRUPTED* . . .

#sts giant TF ships can be sent to each new system to start the work of terraforming. Any system based on a single (nonbinary) Main Sequence star with a spectral type in the range A to K can be searched for planets, and if suitable bodies exist in TEMPERATE ORBITS, then virtually any orbiting body from a mass as small as Mars to one as great as Uranus can be modified using gravometric techniques to create a planet close to a one-gee gravity. Chemical reconfiguration and planetary architec#

. . . *HACK INTERRUPTED* . . .

#ultant exploration and terraforming has happened. At present a geocentric globe of space has expanded until it is some six hundred light-years in diameter. This volume is referred to as Known Space; it is 113 million cubic light-years. The star density in our vicinity of the SPIRAL ARM is approximately twenty-five stars for every ten thousand cubic light-years. So Known Space contains some quarter million stars, of which half are uninhabitable multiples, whilst three quarters of the remainder are dim M-type primaries. Only half of those that still remain contain easily terraformable planets. Nevertheless, that still amounts to more than 15,600 systems, all linked together by the nexus netw#

. . . *HACK INTERRUPTED* . . .

#is why nexi have been described as "smoke rings in space." They are rotating quasi-singularities with a toroidal event horizon through which ships are able to navigate, so long as they have a PSI-ASTROGATOR aboard. The semi-stable nature of these nexi means that they are prone to almost unpredictable PSI-STORMS. They must be approached at speeds ranging from a half cee to 0.9 cee, at the correct injection angle and ship attitude. The choice of these parameters is an intuitive rather than a mechanical process. The psi-astrogator is a talent, a rare individual who has PSI-abilities to "feel" his or her way through these holes in the fabric of space-time.#

. . . *HACK INTERRUPTED* . . .

#esponse to the crushing overpopulation of EARTH and the oppressive forces of uniformity that developed, the EDICT made provisions such that each SECTOR could develop its own ways of living, and live according to its own laws, unmolested. The intention was to re-create the cultural diversity that was an enriching feature of Classical Eart#

. . . *HACK INTERRUPTED* . . .

#e Edict allowed Izlamic, Han Chinese, Hindu, Anglo-Saxon-Skandinavian, Afrikan, Brasilian, Slavic, Latin, an#

. . . *HACK INTERRUPTED* . . .

#Izrael occupying part of the Amerikan-Europan boundary along the sixty-degree plane. The twelfth Sector, pointing in the direction of the galactic center, is the NEUTRAL ZONE.

Over the centuries the boundaries have shifted and distorted, and discoveries at the expanding outer shell of each Sector have been a source of territorial dispute as new nexi were detonated in the BEYOND. What was not foreseen was that the most zea#

. . . *HACK INTERRUPTED* . . .

#in Euclidean space, the distances between planetary systems is vast. Even with nexus technology a trip from a given star system to its neighbor takes several days. Ships have to "run at" the nexus, approaching the gravitational SINGULARITY with a certain minimum kinetic energy that necessitates accelerating to a significant percentage of light speed. Transit-capable ships must also approach at precisely the correct injection angle to prevent tidal forces ripping the ships to pieces. Only psi-astrogators are able to accomplish this relia#

. . . *HACK INTERRUPTED* . . .

#. To travel from one side of Known Space to the other is difficult and expensive. It requires more than a hundred nexus transits and approximately two years' journeying. Since only matter may penetrate a nexus (light, radio waves, etc., are stopped by the QUANTUM SKEW EFFECT), there is no way to create a practical network of intersystem broadcasting that would link the Sectors tog#

. . . *HACK ABORTED.*

66

SEOUL

To Choi Ki Won the knowledge of the president's death was like a knife constantly twisting in a wound.

He dismounted heavily, swabbed the sweat from his face, and riffled the mare's hogged mane affectionately with a broad hand. "We're in a big hurry now. Still, a horse must drink, eh? You see how I take care of you?"

The low morning sun played on his horse's dusty quarters as she lowered her head delicately to the trough. Then, as she finished, he remounted and scanned the road that he had traveled a hundred times before with his pigeons, knowing that never in his life had he felt such urgency and damned the technology ban that existed beyond the Seoul City limits.

He had ridden hard for almost an hour and was midway on the journey, coming from his house in Seoul City, going to Pangojin, the village near Kunyang where the rumor had originated. He had known that, given the faintest hope that the story was true, he must go himself, and quickly. As the mare pulled around he brushed his heels across its sides, sending it cantering down the rocky decline towards the village, and towards the "ghost ship" of which the fisherman had spoken.

A crashed ship, blackened and deserted, that's what they'd said, so he had left, immediately and as unobtrusively as possible. Like so much valuable news to come out of the low-tech preserve, it had reached him first. Starting with the sardine fisherman, he'd always taken pains to maintain a cordial relationship with the people who lived between Kunyang and the Cape of Pangojin on the coast. It was important—after all, they were his eyes and ears, and had he not grown rich keeping his eyes open and his ear to the ground in what was, in effect, a telecommunications and transport shadow zone? The low-tech zone included almost half the single Borneo-sized continent of Seoul; the rest of the world was a shallow ocean, except for the uninhabited polar landmass.

What business was better than selling information? he thought. You've got a commodity. You sell it. You've still got it. What could be better than that? Unlike Amerikan wine, however, information rarely improved in value in the keeping, and the information Choi Ki Won dealt in was volatile and, now that President Keun was dead, immensely dangerous.

Choi Ki Won geed his horse again and slapped its withers. He was well liked by the people of the merchants and farmer classes with whom he dealt, famed for his garrulous good nature and as the father of five grown sons. His family made a good living from all the settlements on the main continent of Seoul, buying from foreign traders, sending bonded technology inland as far as the mountains, and handling luxury foodstuffs for what remained of the Amerikan trade. He could afford to be a generous man, a man who kept a big open household, mostly out of choice, but also to show everyone that he had nothing at all to hide and that no one need fear anything from him.

But difficult times were coming, and in difficult times a man needed a staff on which to lean.

"Yes," he told the horse, "that's the Choi Ki Won everyone knows: a man who spends his time listening to local gossips and quietly building his prosperity. The townspeople, my fellow traders, Captain Yim at the garrison—even the filthy pro-Yamato politicians—they all know that I'm a good and generous man who'll help anyone and harm nobody."

And yet I'm sure there are those who wonder at my luck, and there are certainly some who draw their livings from the seaports of the Seoul City hinterland who're jealous of the inexplicable way I've grown richer than they have. They're the dangerous ones.

He saw the ship the moment he arrived at the quiet line of gray and white fishermen's houses that made up the village of Pangojin. She was lying in ocean a quarter of a mile down the inlet. Many times he had seen damaged nexus ships limping into Seoul's massive apron after being caught in psi-storms, but this ship was exceptional; she was almost a hulk. She was seriously damaged: her plex hull was blackened in parts and both her cargo bay doors had been taken off by what must have been a huge explosion. What remained of her radio black had been upset by the seawater, and her hull patterning tried feebly to keep pace with the sparkling sea. A gantry of sensor aerials had been jury-rigged at her bows and left to melt away to stumps on atmospheric reentry. But she was right way up and seemed to have soft-landed.

She might have been in the sea for days—or months—blown in like flotsam from the deep ocean by fresh east winds; she sat low in the water as if she was sinking, but he saw that her bottom was grounded on rocks as the waves lapped about her; water swilled into the cargo bay, but there were no signs of life aboard.

By her lines she might easily be a Yamato ship, he thought, but what made Choi Ki Won view the battered hull with greater interest was that she had been in a firefight—and she had been severely beaten.

Choi Ki Won's spirits rose. So! Old Tian had been right! There *was* a "ghost ship"—and she had come into his arms. There was good credit to be made in salvage. This was not an opportunity to pass up lightly. Already there were too many villagers on the beach, scratching their chins and wondering how the ship had come to be in the middle of the estuary. But the women were chiding their children and sending them indoors and the men had pulled their fishing boats high up on the beach. No other outsiders had yet come to the village, and Choi Ki Won realised that time was critical.

Tian Meng, his young local agent, hitched his bridle and helped him down. Tian's grandfather, Old Tian, a man twenty years Choi Ki Won's senior, white-haired and leathery, was by his side.

"I don't like it," Old Tian said, mistrust flashing from under his rambling eyebrows. "I don't remember anything like this ever happening before. It's because the president died—"

The young man shifted uncomfortably. "You must excuse my grandfather, Mr. Choi, he is a very poor businessman."

The elder drew himself up. "What of it? Our family have been here on Seoul for more than a hundred years. I am a fisherman, from a long line of fishermen, and proud of that."

"A noble calling, Mr. Tian, if I may say so," Choi Ki Won said, knowing Tian's great-grandfather had been one of the ten Chinese refugees to have come here after the Shenyang disaster. The whole community still clung dutifully to the Chinese tradition, unabsorbed, unintegrated, despite their long history on Seoul. Only Tian Meng was a black sheep.

"Is not the August Personage of Jade's wife herself, goddess of the sea?" Choi added indulgently.

"Of course. And the Empress of Heaven, T'ien Hou, also."

"Then I am in good company."

Young Tian put his hands on his hips and jutted his chin towards the ship. "That could mean a lot of credit. For *us*, Grandfather, don't you see?"

"She's a ghost ship, I tell you. You won't persuade anyone from here to row near her—no matter what you offer. She's bewitched."

"But she's not a ship, she's a spacecraft!"

"It doesn't matter, you young good-for-nothing! We're simple people here. It would be better for you if you had fewer of your big ideas."

"These superstitions!"

"When did she come in?" Choi Ki Won asked.

Tian Meng began to answer but the older man raised his voice stubbornly. "In the dead of night, Mr. Choi. She came in on the early morning tide all lit up by the moonlight. I saw it myself. I was out in the bay in my boat, with my lamps, casting for shrimps, when she rose up out of the ocean like a—"

"Like a gossamer ship blown here on a moonbeam! Ha! Therefore she must be a ghost ship. Isn't that right?" Young Tian's sarcasm was incisive and very disrespectful. Choi Ki Won hushed him and gestured for the old man to go on.

"Well, I rowed home as fast as I could. I am not as young as I used to be, Mr. Choi"—Choi Ki Won nodded indulgently—"so I said to myself, 'Tian,' I said, 'this is the very work of the Supreme Lord of the Dark Heaven, who is also the Regent of Water.' And what does a man do with news of supernatural events? Of course, if he is a pious and dutiful man, he takes his report to the proper authorities."

"You informed the authorities?" Choi Ki Won asked with ill-concealed dismay.

The old man cackled, regarding his grandson's expensive silk shirt. "No, no, Mr. Choi. I thought immediately of my son's son. Where the gods are concerned he is the one to consult! Fine feathers make a fine bird, but fine clothes do not make a fine man!"

Young Tian stifled his irritation, muttering under his breath.

"Time is short," Choi Ki Won told him quietly. "By now news must have reached the Hill. Plenty of army people will be here soon. They take every opportunity to inquire into 'celestial events' and this ship will be no exception."

"Yes, sir."

"Venerable Mr. Tian, may I beg a favor of you?" he asked, extending his hand to touch the old man's arm. "May I borrow your shrimp boat for just a little while?"

"I'll not go out there, Mr. Choi. Not for any credit you might offer me."

"Grandfather!"

"That's not necessary. I'm sure that Meng is willing to row me to the ghost ship."

The old man shuffled uncertainly. "You say there may be credit out there? *Gold* credit?" he asked. A flicker of interest lit his dim eyes.

With a show of conspiratorial secrecy Choi Ki Won unhooked the purse from his belt and loosened the drawstrings. "Here, one golden *won* slottee. For you to hold."

"Eh?"

"It's a new Amerikan idea. Anonymous credit in discs of silver and gold."

"They're not plex," Tian said suspiciously. "Are they really credit?"

"Of course, of course!" He bent the fisherman's horny fingers over the heavy coin with its square central hole. "And a promise that if we do not return with your boat, you may go to my son, Il, and ask him for a quarter the coin's value. That's twenty-five *jeon!*"

"I don't know about this. It's not the same as a plex smart card. You always know where you are with plex!"

"Try it, Mr. Tian. The old-time Chinese had great respect for gold metal."

Old Tian chewed on the gold and spat. He said something in the old language followed by a shrug of acceptance, then he dug a finger at his grandson. "Be careful with my property, you young viper. Master Choi is a worthy man. I can trust him—but it's more than anyone can say for you."

Choi Ki Won took the old man's arm and nodded towards the other fishermen. "I want you to persuade them to keep back. Tell them I have a best-lacquer idol blessed by the great god Ts'ai Chen against sea misfortunes. Ask them if they have any such protection."

Old Tian cackled, screwing his face into a grin. "Oh, master, you are a wise man."

Tian Meng watched his kinsman wander away with an exasperated stare. "That was too much, Mr. Choi. Twenty-five *jeon* for the ransom of his water-logged shrimp boat. He is a villain to take your coin."

Choi Ki Won laughed. "Don't worry, I intend to return with it intact. Which is his boat?"

"There, the blue and green one. Please."

They crunched down a gravel beach that smelled of crusted salt and sun-bleached fish heads. Tian laid his hands on the stem and slid the boat out clear of the pebbles so that it rocked in the water, then Choi Ki Won waded knee-deep and heaved himself in, steadying the oars.

It was a pull of five minutes. Choi Ki Won put his back against the sternpost and studied the ship carefully as they approached. When they came to within thirty yards, he told Tian to row them no closer. He cupped his hands and shouted. The greeting echoed back eerily, but there was no answer.

At a word from the merchant, Tian sculled slowly in, meeting the ship on the beam. The plex hull rose up thirty feet above them and Choi Ki Won could see beards of deep green weed pulsing on the rocks below the waterline. Could she have been abandoned? he wondered, his fingers tingling with hope. He had heard tales of nexus ships being caught in psi-storms or orbital emergencies, of them being grounded and then left by their crews. Perhaps a privateer attacked them. Perhaps the crew are all dead and it homed down on autopilot. But why would it be using chameleon-skin stealth if not to deliberately avoid detection? It's a mystery!

"Ai-ee!"

He shouted again. Still no reply. The young man was searching the empty gun blisters, fear contending visibly with avarice on his face. "Ai-ee! Anyone there?"

"Maybe there really is no one on board."

"If that's true, then she's ours. We found her, didn't we?"

Choi Ki Won swallowed, wishing despite himself that he had the fictional best-lacquer idol to brandish. "Free Korea is not a signatory of the Inter-Sector Salvage Treaty. According to the law we have only to board her to claim her."

Tian licked his lips. "Maybe we should go back for weapons—for the others?"

Choi Ki Won turned towards the beach. Three upright figures in red robes and black three-tongued hats had arrived there in a six-wheeled rough-terrain vehicle; they sent a shiver through him—Harmonious Apron Police.

"Go back? And share the prize with the Revenue? Are you mad as well as frightened?"

They sculled inside the echoing cavern of the flooded cargo bay. Impulsively the younger man stood up and leapt for the rail. He heaved himself up onto the platform and froze there, listening and looking into the airlock.

The emergency release mechanism cycled faultlessly. Inside, the gun deck was empty, there was no sign of life. Choi Ki Won watched the youth's caution as he surveyed the empty corridors. Truly it was as if the crew had been lured away by T'ien Hou herself.

According to the legendary Chinese story, the Empress of Heaven had once been a girl on the planet of Mei-chou, which was a celebrated place of piety. She had four *tao* astrogator brothers who plied the space lanes in the same convoy. One day she fell in a swoon and was only brought back to life by powerful drugs, but as soon as she regained consciousness she complained that she had been brought back prematurely. Later, three of her brothers returned and told of the psi-storm that had assailed them, of how she had appeared to them and saved them. The fourth brother's ship was lost.

The girl of Mei-chou died soon afterwards, but it was said that her spirit frequently intervened, helping astrogators in peril or ships attacked by pirates. After that she became Princess of Supernatural Favor, then a Celestial Queen, and finally she was rewarded by the title of Empress of Heaven.

Tian looked back over his shoulder momentarily, and Choi felt the hairs lifting on his own spine. A Yamato ship, he thought. This was a big craft, no warship but a trading vessel, lightly armed to allow bigger mass cargoes, like most of the ships that plied the Neutral Zone routes. Tian went as far as the assembly area and looked down the companionway into the darkness.

"There's no one here at all," he shouted, and returned to help Choi Ki Won up into the vacant lock.

With fervent hopes that the derelict was filled with valuable cargo, the merchant went first to the container lift and found it inoperative. Then he went aft. It smelled foul and dense, like fermenting brewers' soy mash. The captain's cabin would be the place to start if he wanted to unravel the mystery. Oh, most certainly she's Yamato, he decided, glancing up at the squiggly *hiragana* and *katakana* script that was embossed here and there on the plex walls. He knew the script and the hateful language very well from the days of his youth when it had been his mother tongue. Yes, Yamato-built, and Yamato-worked, he thought, feeling the old panic rise in his guts. He had seen many different ship hulls in his time and had learned to distinguish the external signs that showed origin, but with Yamato ships it was often difficult—they were rarely distinctive, but owed their lines to Amerikan or Europan or Chinese designs. This dogfish was certainly made in Yamato, and the shipyard's maker plate in the bridge confirmed that the frame of the ship had been constructed in 2416, at the Nissan Yards on Kure, specifically to be operated in the *kin kaigun* fleet. Could it be? Had she really once been one of the Yamato *aurium* transports? Choi Ki Won's hope soared, but he steadied himself. But she was now owned by Senpaku, and crews did not simply abandon fortunes in aurium, even at the cost of their own lives. What horror had evacuated the ship?

He went further aft, passing out of the harsh bluish light. The smell of fermentation gave way to a cloying stuffiness. Thc hum of power looms and microscopic switching as fans and pumps deep within the ship ducted and recycled the air and conditioned the shipboard environment. The ship's nose lifted and settled on each gentle motion of the tide, sending unearthly groaning noises through her. How much simpler if she had been Korean or Amerikan, or even Cho Sen, he thought. But the August Personage has seen fit to send a Yamato ship, and that could only mean officials and bureaucratic investigations and endless delay. Ultimately it must mean confiscation, for this was Korea, and Korea's independence was still a poor and threadbare thing.

If only our President Keun had seen sense, he thought. Why in God's name did he go in that car-cade? What stupidity! What madness to jeopardise the free Republic! Aiee! An official visit to the Front Line Worlds was an expensive and ludicrous exercise, no doubt an idea put there by an advisor whose pockets were a-jangle with Yamato aurium. That Keun should be killed without any credible minister to succeed him! There's only Vice-president Park now, Keun's aged uncle, and beyond him Mutsuhito the Accursed, who waits like a crocodile to devour our quadrant. It's their design to destroy our cherished independence. They know the vice-president cannot hold this fledgling state together for long. There is no one except Park, with whom Mutsuhito must contest ownership of Free Korea. Oh, how the work of a single vile assassin, the death of a single peerless leader, casts all of future history onto an unhappy track!

A more uneven contest was difficult to imagine. The vision of Free Korea subdued like Cho Sen and the so-called Neutral Zone by Yamato's military-industrial machine burgeoned garishly in Choi Ki Won's imagination. Already Mutsuhito had armies stationed along the Boundary. He could now lean so heavily on Free Korea that her state policies, both internal and external, would be distorted out of recognition, whoever ruled. Mutsuhito itched to absorb his independent neighbor and snuff out the ancient identity of the Korean people. The strategic and material benefits of a bloodless conquest of all Korea would be overpowering when set beside Mutsuhito's greed. And Keun has given him the perfect excuse! Two years, maybe three, as the senile Park loses his grip on the coalition—then what? Butchery and terror—or the meek acceptance of Yamato domination. And then it will be the death of all good things.

Choi Ki Won damned the watching fishermen on the beach. They had brought him the news, but they had also propagated the rumors that had brought the officials. He damned Mutsuhito to hell. To the deepest, hottest, and cruelest of hells. Then he damned all things out of Yamato.

Yamato embargoes on Amerikan ships and Amerikan goods, the *kempei*'s terror in Cho Sen, Yamato's meddling in Free Korea—these things have slashed my profits by half, Choi Ki Won thought, staring into the gloomy depths of the ship. But, by all the gods, they'll repay me!

Is it not an invariable rule that the horse of a warlord tramples the poor merchant underfoot? There's no justice in the cosmos, only the eight Great Immortals who enjoy irony. Still, they comfort the suffering people in times of great loss, and I know they stand by those who seek to stand up for themselves.

Choi Ki Won gritted his teeth at his secret thoughts. He detested Yamato fulsomely, hated the idea that it could seize Free Korea. Yes, a Yamato ship!

Maybe she became detached from the annual *kin kaigun* in a psi-storm. It often happens that ships get lost. Perhaps pirates have not attacked and stripped her. Or maybe she's a lone private milk-cow that attempted the crossing in secret so that Senpaku could avoid Mutsuhito's shit-eating taxes! Now, that would be justice!

The way the mill wheel has come full circle! Aiee! If I lose credit this year I'll have only myself to blame. My monthly accounts will certainly show small returns on hardware, but the sale of information is much more lucrative. The facts concerning the scheduling of ships into the vast and complex Korean nexi must be worth more than all the hardware in Seoul City, though the payment I receive is comparatively meager. Think positive, Choi!—as those Amerikans always say. Yes, I will think positive. Perhaps this ghost ship is sent by the gods as a reward!

He pushed open the door that led to the captain's cabin and entered it, filled with a growing confidence. Then the confidence left him as he felt the touch of a muzzle between his shoulders and whirled to see a ghastly face and two Nambu blasters set to "burn" and pointing at his belly.

The apparition was fierce: yellow eyes with pinpoint pupils, a clenched jaw, menace in every fiber of him. The man was shaking as if from a terrible fury, raving as if in fever, and his voice was like a demon's.

"Put your hands up, dog!"

The order was sudden and savage, but Choi Ki Won understood the Japanese. Involuntarily he took a step back and raised his palms above his ears. Then he watched with incredulity as the man's unearthly eyes rolled up, one of his blasters almost trembled from his grip, and his knees gave way under him so that he crashed to the deck.

Then Choi Ki Won's shock was penetrated by a familiar noise. It took him a moment to identify it because it was the last sound he could possibly have expected to hear in this place. It was the wailing of a baby.

Duval Straker staggered, overcome by another wave of agony. Desperately his mind clung to the sounds he was hearing, and he fought back to consciousness and tried to muster his faculties once more. He got to his knees, and his blaster wavered in an opaque blur. Stand up! Find your feet, or you're a dead man. This is Yamato! Yamato, don't you see? Lord God, how could you betray me like this? We've landed while Arima Yoshisabura's still alive. Didn't I promise you I'd believe in you again, if only you'd smother that worthless bag of rotting shit before we reached Yamato? Wasn't that the bargain? How many times did I tell you that the captain's going to betray us to the *kempei?* Michie and the baby, who I've fought so hard for—*they're going to die!* Don't you understand? The bad guys will have won. Who's more important: Arima, who lies stewing in his own black vomit, or your innocent little baby? Shall I murder Arima now we're safely down? Shall I cut his throat with his own sword as he lies there writhing? Come on, God answer me! Wouldn't that just be a mercy to him as he suffers now?

Duval's eyes popped. The sound of screams in the dim distance, the music of rage ringing peals of bells in his head. It was as if a giant hand had slapped him. Listen to your son cry, Duval! Listen to him cry! You must stop gawping and seize the initiative now! Do what's right!

He saw, penetrating through veils of mist, as the frightened man raised his hands. The man was well dressed, an expensive robe and boots, his girth supported by a wide, sagging belt, a strange pinch collar, and above it a forty-year-old's face, nut brown, high forehead, badger-streaked beard, and eyes full of surprise. He did not have the shaved pate and topknot of a samurai. Why don't you rush me? Why don't you try to burn me with my own gun? Can't you see I'm next to helpless?

"Please don't—"

"Get back!" Duval growled, fighting back the dizziness that threatened to engulf him. "Try me and I'll burn your throat out!"

"Don't shoot, sir. I mean you no harm. I am not armed." The intruder's Japanese was oddly accented.

"I told you to put your hands up! Up! Higher!"

"Are you the captain? What ship is this? I only want to help you."

"Back, now! Move yourself! In there!"

The man fell back before him into the cabin, Duval keeping him on the end of his Nambu; he did not take his eyes off him until they were safely inside.

Arima groaned from his bed. Suddenly Duval's mind became lucid as the wave of nausea passed from him. He forced himself to remember how he had come to be locked into this dangerous strategy. However he looked at it, there had seemed no other way. Didn't Arima try to have me locked up? Didn't he swear to me he'd tell the *kempei* at the apron terminal as soon as we came in sight of the Home Worlds? But in the attack he lost so much equipment and so many crew sealed in blast-proof compartments he could hardly run his ship. The Dovers were smashed, many of the systems disrupted including the freezees and the med units, but luckily the maintenance nerve center of the ship where Michie and the baby and I were stuck had gone into an emergency lock-out spasm that could not be overridden from outside. The software was convinced that the ship was still under attack. Without food the situation grew desperate, and when I finally got out, I was turned on as a competitor. I was forced to systematically stalk those of the crew who remained, just as they stalked me. They used meson cutters to try to get into Michie. I evacuated the atmosphere from the compartments they were working in. Those who survived suited up and continued. I found a way to remotely shut off the power to their cutters. They used egress cell packs. I dummied round behind and sniped at them. They gave up, and I burned their cutters, hoping there were no more, and resealed the bulkheads with a noninterruptible mask to keep them bottled up.

Finally I got to Arima, knowing that I needed the astrogator alive, and I hit him and burned him badly. I brought him an emergency medikit and it was then he swore he would keep our true identities to himself after we landed. He saw us through three nexi, but I still don't trust him. He's a pragmatic man, who cuts his promises to suit his situation. And he's in need of credit and dignity now, and the awe of the *kempei* has too powerful a grip on his mind. He must hate me for what I did to him and his ship. He'll recant his promise for a few *yen* and he'll blame us for everything, and they'll arrest us and deliver us to torture and the Probe and the hideous crosses all over again. I should have burned Arima's brains out last night. But I couldn't then, and I can't now. Not a pitiful starving wretch with the stink of death coming off him. Not in cold blood. Even when Michie's life and my son's life and my own life all depend on it. Maybe he'll die yet. Maybe. Maybe . . .

The shaking was starting again inside him.

"You'll be my hostage," he told the man through chattering teeth, grimly hanging on to his blaster butt. "That's a fair bargain. A rich merchant like you, in exchange for passage to Amerika. I want nothing more than that. The means to get my wife and son off of this planet. A bargain. Just like the one at Niigata. Only this time there'll be no payment, no trusting to treaty, and no mistakes."

"How many are you?" the intruder asked. Despite the order to keep his hands up, he bunched the broad sleeve in his hand and clamped it over his nose and mouth, then he leaned over Arima. "This man is close to death."

"Yesterday there were ten alive. All dying just like him. All bottled up in the nose section. Today I don't know. The thirst . . ."

"Please, sir, put up your gun. I want only to help you."

"Get back from me!"

Duval felt the crest of the feverish tremor pass over him. Each day the lassitude of starvation had made it more and more difficult to concentrate his mind, to climb from deck to deck, to roll from his strap hammock, but he had hunted down meat, and Michie kept producing milk for the baby, and he was still well enough now to pull a trigger. He looked at the hostage, then down at the unconscious Arima. Die, you sonofawhore! he told the man silently. Die and let my secret die with you!

"You must let me help these men, sir. If they are dying. Where are they?"

Arima opened his eyes. He would not give up his life easily. He was a fighter, and though his struggles had brought himself and his crew to the gates of hell, he had done as he had sworn to do. He had brought his ship home. After the pirate had disabled the *Kawabata Yasunari* he had tried to make Chichi-jima, but the Index had been low and the nexus had tossed them towards the side chain where contrary psi had seized them. For two days and two nights they had fought on, but the power of the nexus had left Arima unconscious and they had drifted helplessly until they had identified the destination system as a branchless dead end, and they had had to go back the way they had come.

Arima had sent out all but one of the ship's distress beacons, hoping to get a message to Chichi-jima, or the Twenty Degree systems, but not one had returned, and for weeks they had languished in the miserable system of Delta Scuti, 6.6 parsecs away from Daito, running short of everything, stuck like flies in amber, until in desperation he had realised that they must attempt another transit or they would all perish.

"Can you hear me? My name is Choi Ki Won. Where are the others?"

"I hear you," Arima said weakly but coherently. "My crew are dead, or dying like me. I am the captain of this ship—"

"Hold your mouth, samurai!"

Choi Ki Won's eyes narrowed at Duval. "You are not samurai yourself? Then what are you?"

As Duval's feral alertness returned, he jabbed the blaster forward. "I'm Amerikan. I want food and water and passage aboard an Amerikan nexus ship," he told the man, his voice rasping now. "I demand—"

Choi Ki Won stroked his chin warily. "You're in no position to make demands, sir."

"I'll shoot you before I'll rot in any Yamato prison. Do you hear?"

Then, incredibly, the tenor of the man's voice came back at him in puzzled amusement.

"But, sir, you are not in *Yamato*."

"Not Yamato? Then where?"

"This is Seoul. *You are in Free Korea*."

Duval felt the resolve drain from him. If this was Free Korea, there was no need to hide. If this was truly Seoul, they were safe . . .

Then a young man's arms came around him from behind, seizing him in a plex-like grip, and the blaster was wrested from him.

67

Michie was sitting in the adjoining room with Choi Ki Won's wife, and the sound of their laughing came to him. The tuna fish dinner had been exquisite, and after the fine red wines, as rich and heady as Kansas klaret, he felt relaxed and receptive.

The ocean was dappled with starlight in the narrows that sheltered Seoul City's harbor. From the window Duval could see the water chopping up as it became the open sea, the Western Ocean that stretched around the planet, twenty thousand miles along an unobstructed parallel of latitude to the far side of this same continent.

"Look at the fishing junks, Kenichi. See that one with the red lights?"

He stroked his two-year-old's hair gently, but failed to capture his attention. Kenichi began to cry. Choi Ki Won swept the infant up and stood him on the sill, careless of the precipitous drop below.

"Be obedient to your father, Kenichi," he said, pointing up at the night sky. "That's where you were born. Out there in space. Someday you'll cruise the space lanes as your father did and win glory for Free Korea."

The sight of the sea and the velvet sky soothed the child. Duval too felt the restless draw of it. Memories of past rigors no longer had the power to hurt him. He was healed. How different was this pleasant house and the soft comforts it afforded to the horrors of the *Kawabata Yasunari;* how delightful the hospitality of his good and generous friend, Choi Ki Won.

"You know," he told him wistfully, "when I first set out to cross space, my shipmates used to call me a Yambo, owing to my looks—as a joke, you see. And I would laugh with them. Then when the *kempei* came, they told me I was half racial Japanese. Now I'm in Korea it's hard for me to know where I belong."

Choi Ki Won smiled. "You are at home here! You are a Seoul dweller. Seoul Immigration says so!"

He remembered the official confirmation that had arrived two days ago; it was nominally the reason for the celebratory dinner they had just eaten. "I thank you for that. And it is true, you have made us very welcome."

"But something tells me you yearn for your own world still."

"I have no home world now." Duval drew a lingering breath. "At one time I was Amerikan but was called a Yambo, next I was a stateless slave, and then an honorary samurai. After that I was told that my genotype was not derived from the people I had thought were my parents. Now I am in Korea—but only as an officially accepted foreigner. In truth, I don't know what I am."

"You might go into Amerika when the next convoy comes in. Many ships that come here are out of Liberty, as you know, and I have the friendship of many an Amerikan shipowner."

Duval shook his head soberly at his friend's probings. "I can't have a Japanese wife in Amerika, Ki Won. Race as such is disregarded there, but she would be obliged to adapt her behavior. It would hurt her to think she was losing her cultural heritage. And if there was ever open war—I would fear for the safety of my family."

"Is there more tolerance for you here?"

"Thanks to you." He smiled. "I have a living. And I have friends, and harmony at last."

"But for how much longer? Go to Amerika, my friend."

"Why should you say that?"

Choi Ki Won lowered his voice, and as he spoke his words grew bitter. "The peace is crumbling. Though Park is Korea's choice, Mutsuhito has a dynastic marriage link with the old Korean Emperor's line of Yi. According to the old ways, his blood claim is undeniable, and he has massed his legions on our Boundary so he can impose his will. Each week, more and more Yamato traders are flooding into Cho Sen and all the Open Ports. They are the shock troops, sent in advance with their bribery and casuistry." He checked himself, remembering that he must keep his loathing for Yamato partially concealed. For all that he hated them, he had to admire their efficiency. The way they had persuaded the Seoul authorities to send Harmonious Apron Police to impound the *Kawabata Yasunari* within hours of its discovery, and afterwards, how their tireless diplomacy had arranged her repair and speedy dispatch to Yamato, robbing him of his windfall.

But he had robbed them of a far greater thing. He had struck a blow that had been waiting to be thrown for twenty-five years.

The Harmonious Apron Police had seen Tian Meng waving at intervals from the bridge, beckoning them, and so it was that half an hour later they had come out in a second fisherman's boat, three of them, with three constables and Captain Yim in the bows. Poor Yim, with the imperiousness of the minor nobility, impractical and hot-tempered, and utterly under the sway of his own ego.

Yim was a tall, thin man in his early forties wearing the immaculate scarlet robe that was part of his superintendent's uniform, with that look of complete, single-minded self-possession that only those schooled in Seoul's Academy of Harmonious Corrections could attain. Choi Ki Won had winced at the sight of him.

Old Tian's empty shrimp boat had been drifting aimlessly fifty yards away and so he had waved his arms and shouted out of the airlock to them. "Thank the gods you've come at last, Captain Yim! And you too, brave policemen!"

Yim had ignored him, cupping a microphone to his mouth and hailing the ship with a distorted blast. But one of the constables had peered into the flooded cargo bay inquiringly. "What are you doing here?"

"Our boat drifted. That good-for-nothing Tian Meng can't even tie his father's boat up properly. We were stranded here, Captain. If you hadn't come I can't imagine what would have happened to us."

Then he had clamped his sleeve tightly over his nose and mouth again while Tian Meng had stood beside him, mutely under orders.

When the frightened fisherman in the police boat had shipped his paddle and brought his fishing boat alongside, Yim had asked, "Is there no one else aboard? We thought you must have been attacked."

Then Yim had tasted the air suspiciously. "Why do you hold your sleeve to your face, Mr. Choi?"

He had given a hacking cough. "Can't you smell the stink? This ship is full of corpses, Captain. And others alive still, but covered in red sores."

"Red sores? How many?"

"Yes, ten, I think. Maybe a dozen. It's so hard to tell. I've seen nothing like it in all my life. It's horrible. Here, help me down into your boat."

"Get back!"

The captain had seized the oar and pushed the boat back from the lock. His face graven now with fear and anger.

"Please, Captain Yim! What are you doing?"

"It's a disease!"

The Apron Police had looked from one to another in panic.

"No, no—please. Don't think that. Come now. You must let me off this stinking wreck."

"Row for the shore!" Yim had ordered. "It's one of those terrible plague diseases!"

Instantly the stern oar had been unshipped and the wobbly little boat set in motion.

"But Captain Yim!" His helpless plea had rung out and he had begun to run from side to side in the airlock, secretly delighted at the success of his ploy.

"You must stay there, Choi Ki Won. With the hatch shut. I command it! This ship and all its disgusting microbes is quarantined. For forty days, do you hear me?"

"*Forty days?* But there's no food aboard. I shall starve! And these poor men—"

"Food will be sent."

"But they need a medical unit!"

"Do what you can for them."

"No! Captain Yim, I beg you! Come back!"

The boat had stroked rapidly away, and under cover of night Tian Meng had swum to his father's boat and recovered it and they had crept to shore with the Amerikan and his wife and the baby.

But there had been a good deal of substance to the ruse. Choi Ki Won recalled the scene that he had witnessed in the nose section, men wasted with starvation, ragged and feverish, dead or dying. None except Arima able to stand and he a yellow skeleton. He had had a samurai's tenacity that drove him on when other men gave up. Perhaps he had survived, for the Yamato ambassador's people had found the courage to board the ship the following day. In any case, they had found him gone, and because of the delicacy of the negotiations surrounding the *Kawabata Yasunari*'s release, and because the imposition of a quarantine order would have hampered them, his name had appeared in no official reports, and within a week the entire ship had been sealed in a vast flexiplex bag and the lot air-lifted back into orbit, doubtless to be taken off to Kyoto for examination.

"Do you think there will be much resistance?" Duval asked him, bringing him back to the present. "If Yamato invades, I mean?"

Choi Ki Won put his hands together thoughtfully. "It's said that Mutsuhito's appointed Baron Harumi to head his invasion. If he's opposed, Yamato troops will destroy our pitiful army and then they will trample Seoul City. They could raze all of Korea as they choose. We are already in their power. That is why my advice to you is to get out now, while you can."

Duval glanced at his friend, reminding himself that Choi Ki Won knew only that he had escaped the *kempei*'s cross. He had never told him his true profession, nor the reason Arima had valued his discovery. So far as Choi Ki Won was concerned he was nothing more than an academic who had been victimized by the *kempei*, and in that, somewhere, had been the bond between them.

"You're a wise man, Mr. Choi."

"If you permit me to write a letter to my son, he will arrange passage on an Amerikan nexus ship."

"No."

"But you don't know if Captain Arima survived. If he did, and spoke of you to the *kempei,* you will already be marked. Once the invasion is complete—"

"I ran once, I cannot run again. I'll trust that Arima died, or that he chose to forget me."

"Reconsider, please."

"Thank you, but no."

Choi Ki Won put out his hands in appeal. "I beg you. For Kenichi's sake. For Michie's. Listen to me."

His son began to cry again, wanting to get down from the sill, and Duval lifted him to the floor. Ki Won's words are wise, he thought, beginning to feel the weight of his friend's persuasion. In a Korea ruled by Yamato a single indiscretion could uncover us and unleash the terror again. But there's no place in the cosmos that's any safer for us than here. At least in Seoul City we're among friends. Living here in the low-tech zone suits us. It's almost like home to Michie. In Amerika we know no one, we have nothing. Twelve years is a long time to be away, and they say that in an Amerika at war there would be no peace for any racial Japanese.

"We'll stay here."

Choi Ki Won sighed, his tact failing. "President Park has support in New Wonsan. Perhaps that will remain truly Korean. Perhaps if you—"

"No. I said I'm tired of running, Ki Won. We'll take our chances in Seoul City. For good or ill we'll make our stand here."

"Is that to be your final decision?"

Below, a delivery car rumbled by loaded with crates of chickens and fresh vegetables, gutted fish, great stoppered jugs of wine, water, pails of shellfish, and big hocks of meat for tomorrow's markets. He remembered the first day of his deliverance in Korea in this same house. He had wanted to eat ravenously but had known that the shock of food on a starving body was like swallowing red-hot coals. He had drunk a little and he had fed Michie very sparingly and tried to make sure she did not gorge herself. Then doubts had speared him. His mind had tried to unknot the problem. Choi Ki Won was a rich merchant. Surely he only wanted to ransom them to the authorities—yet he had insisted that he did not. All along, Choi Ki Won had been at pains to comfort him and to provide for his family. He had jeopardised himself to become the willing helper of an Amerikan. That doesn't make sense, he had reasoned. No one in Choi Ki Won's position would want to clash with the authorities. I can't understand why he's working so hard to preserve us. Would either of the Hawken brothers have reacted that way if they'd come aboard a Yamato ship downed and half wrecked in the Rappahannock Estuary on Liberty? No! Then what was it that had made a serene man like Choi Ki Won hate Yamato with such a personal animosity? And what was it that made him hate samurai most particularly?

"Why are you doing this for us?" he had asked him directly.

Choi Ki Won had given his patient smile and pointed to Amerikan ads on the terminal building of the Seoul apron. "I told you. The owners of some Amerikan ships are my friends. Before the troubles Amerika and Korea traded for years as allies and our friendship has prospered both Sectors."

Duval had been unconvinced by Choi Ki Won's superficial reply. "You're asking me to believe that you'd risk your life to save us. Why?"

"In Korea as in Yamato, Mr. Straker, the merchant has little status. Big men make promises and the small man keeps them. We must protect our own interests. For the merchant, taking risks is our way of life."

Duval had felt deep guilt at the way he had doubted Choi. Then he had looked into the man's dark eyes and he had thought he recognised the mark of an honest man.

"I ask you again: is that your final decision?"

"Yes. I will not leave here of my own free will."

The broad, kindly face of Choi Ki Won clouded then. He became grave and stern. "Well, then, come with me to the cool of the garden. We must talk, you and I. For all is not what it seems here in my house, and if you will stay in Seoul City, you must know the truth."

They went down past banks of tamarisk and gorse under which night lizards darted. Among the green blades and purple dragon-headed blooms of flowers-de-Luce they walked side by side, Choi Ki Won speaking and Duval Straker listening, until the Korean had told of the other trade in which he dealt, the trade in secrets and sealed reports, and the place where he sent them.

The Amerikan felt himself sober up, despite the twice-fermented rice wine that ran in his veins. He judged himself fully admitted to his friend's confidence now, and so he likewise unburdened himself, telling of the skills he possessed, to which Choi Ki Won nodded sagely as a man does who receives a great responsibility.

In trust he listened to Choi Ki Won then, and heard him speak with difficulty of the first family he had had, the one of his youth, a quarter century ago, when he had been a samurai and the *kempei* had discovered him wanting. And as he listened he discovered the answer to a question that no one else knew enough even to ask—what a man born a Yamato samurai was really doing living in so grand a house in Seoul City.

68

LIBERTY

"Mr. Straker, there's a gentleman to see you!"

Ellis Straker looked up impatiently. Reba, sitting quietly in the boat's prow, scrolled the page of her book. The servant was breathless; his shoes, thick with mud, thumped the dirt bank, sending rings rippling over the glassy surface. Vibration at the lakeside always disturbed the fish, and this would ruin them for the rest of the afternoon.

"You can see I'm fishing, Matthew," he called back gruffly as he picked another roach out of his pail. It was four inches long, and its gills heaved as he threaded the barbed hook into its back. When it touched the lake it fled, red fins blurring as it towed the float on a line of micron-thin plex.

"He says it's urgent, sir."

"Damn you, you foolish object. Can anything be more urgent than a twenty-five-pound pike?"

"I didn't think to ask him that, sir."

"Did you think to ask his name?"

"Oh, yes, sir, but he won't tell it. He's a fine gentleman, though."

Ellis roused himself from his study of the reeds, exasperated by the synth servant that Reba could not be persuaded to get rid of. "Then, tell the fine gentleman for me to take his ass off of my property."

He had been brooding over the neo-Puritans of the town who had recently somehow conceived the idea that the owner of Xanadu was living in sin with another man's wife. If one of them had had the balls to come here—

The boat swayed as Reba laid aside her book and sat up. Ellis spread his legs to steady the boat.

"Perhaps you ought to attend to it, Ellis."

"If he hasn't got the manners to give his name, he can't expect civility."

"I'd like to think that any visitor to our home might expect that. And I wish you'd treat Matthew as a creature entitled to a little dignity."

Ellis looked at her calm determination and knew he had been justly corrected. Of course she was right. It was unnecessary to be so sharp towards the synth, who was always so amiable and polite. But for all her composure Reba must have had some small suspicion, as he did. Was this nameless visitor the one that they both knew must eventually come to disturb their quiet life together?

In the time they had lived here, Reba had borne him a second child, a daughter, Kat, and another, Deb. And there had been inevitable unvoiced questions among all kinds of people, seeing as how the Halide heir *never* came to his wife's house, and it was odd how the nexus ship captain appeared to have taken his placc. But Ellis was no longer a nexus ship captain. For the sake of his family he had forsworn space travel and all it had once meant to him. Except for business visits to Lincoln and frequent trips to the various aprons of Liberty, he had renounced nexus ships forever, telling himself that he had fulfilled all promises and realised all potentialities. This little lake was his cruising ground now, and the twenty-five-pound pike his only adversary.

It seemed only yesterday that he had pushed open the garden gate and come inside to reclaim his Reba, but it had been almost seven years. That first Liberty spring he had secretly acquired Xanadu through an intermediary, relishing the power of his outright ownership. He had demolished the Yamato-style tea house in the garden to make way for stone brought from a local quarry, and then he had built two new wings so the house had the form of an "E," to literally stamp himself on the place, but perhaps more to erase all trace of the previous owner.

The house now contained no plex and no curves, a strange choice for a man who had lived so long in a nexus ship. It was built from the bones of the planet; his home, rooted in the stuff of Liberty, this quake-free planet, whose architecture was characteristically solid and strong and aspiring, and therefore, he thought, inspiring. So he had chosen it: a foundation of stone, walls of Liberty redwood, a roof of Algonquin slate covering all, solid and stately. And though there was an antique stone fireplace, that had once graced a big house on Earth, that was his one concession. He had had no doubts that the swell of Liberty's green hills was his proper surroundings, or that the best occupation of a wealthy man was philanthropy and the management of credit and materials through signature. For seven years he had played the mercantile game and consigned his privateering past to a locked chest somewhere in the back of his memory. But it was undeniable that the spirit of the times was altering, and that Yamato's martial spirit had been undimmed by the distractions of Korea. Events were moving swiftly towards the day when he must open that dusty chest and look in upon its treasure once more.

He regarded Reba with love and with respect. Her power to surprise him had never waned, and her intellect was an awesome thing that made her advice indispensable, especially when he retreated into the smoldering angers that once might have been doused by a little action. They would ride their Palominos together when he needed space, racing across the green hills to the fringes of the forest. Or he would hew timber with an ax until his muscles were sweat-oiled, and the fresh summer light of Liberty's primary turned him to bronze.

"The weather's changing," he said stiffly.

"Yes."

"I don't suppose we'll see any more of the pike."

"If you say so."

"Yep."

Cloud blighted the sky above the slate planes of the house. A rain of golden leaves shimmered from the aspen trees beside it. He closed his eyes. Yep, there was more than just the weather changing. More than the season too. He could feel it in the air, just as he had felt it back in '25. Throughout the uneasy peace,

Amerika had steadily built up her defenses and her economy, finding new trade in Germani and the United Baltic States for her manufactures, sending raw materials and know-how to Muscovi, and pushing boldly into the markets of Brasilia and Afrika to do trade with the new republics. Ellis had made astute investments, growing richer still, putting his credit into the Eastlands Corporation and helping to set up a new venture to trade into Hindostan/Pyxis/Puppis. But the weeping sore of Korea had continued to fester, and Mutsuhito's annexation of Free Korea had added to Yamato a much greater power to strangle and control any who dared oppose the Empire. The worlds just beyond the Boundary had grown as perilous for the Amerikan shipping as the Twenty Degree Worlds had once been to Yamato shipping, and the immense riches of the Zone, Outer as well as Inner, were as much a Yamato preserve as ever. In Lincoln, too, many things were in need of setting to rights. Too many conversations there had verged on treason and brought him to overturn tables that he no longer gained any pleasure from the city. The President's party itself seethed with factions that wanted to see a détente with Yamato bought on any terms, and too many of those that remained were cowards who could not see the inevitable.

He grunted. "Who would come here and refuse to give his name?"

She sighed. "Go and see!"

"Yes. Okeh. I will."

He wound the line back and stowed his pole, giving the last captive roach in his pail its freedom. As he propelled the punt deftly forward, a cloud passed over the sun, there was a sudden chill, and the water's surface lost its silver. The Liberty summer, a maid of fickle mood, had grown capricious, and before they had reached the house a heavy, dousing rain had begun to fall.

Ellis's muddied Texas boots crunched across the path, skittering gravel. He strode around the corner of the house trailing the pink-faced androgyne, Matthew, in his wake. Anger lay like a coiled diamondback in his chest and he wished he had his firewood ax in his hand. Then he saw the Bristol air-car.

I'm gonna beat on Kurt Reiner's man until he's black and blue, and send him away to think again, he told himself. It was not a course open to a respectable businessman. Okeh, then, what if I treat his boy real polite and get a meeting with that drunken sonofabitch, and then break his head?

He turned the buttressed corner of his entranceway and sensed a figure step out through the rain behind him.

"Git yo' hands up, ya lazy bear!"

He whirled.

"John!"

"*Senator* Oujuku—let's have some respect, now, brother."

He advanced on Oujuku and they gripped forearms, hugely pleased to meet each other again. Rain dripped from the brim of Oujuku's hat, spangled his black beard with diamonds. The scar that had been put between nose and eye by a misadventure during his voyage into Yamato wrinkled as he smiled broadly.

"Ah, let me look at you, now!"

"Man, you look like Lord Shit!"

"And you his butler."

"Is that any way to address a senator?"

"On my patch of ground, yes. But this senator is very welcome. What brings you here?"

Oujuku's voice went dark brown. "Y'know . . . just passing through."

"Come inside. Will you smoke a stogie with me?"

"Gladly. And you can tell me all about your retirement."

"Retirement? I don't think of it as such."

They passed under the arch side by side. It was good to see Oujuku buoyant again, buoyant enough to rib his friend over his quiet style of life.

Their last meeting had been unhappy; the one before that, glorious. That had been the triumph of Oujuku's return, when he had landed the *Arizona* back on Harrisburg apron after three years laden with fifty billion credits of Yamato aurium. Then Oujuku had received the highest accolade the Sector could bestow. The President had thrown off all objections and come herself to Harrisburg, to the very cargo bay of his ship, to meet him. And how Ellis had basked in the glory of it, knowing, as his President gave her best profile to the foreign cameras recording it, that by her act the diplomatic snub to Yamato had been made immense. Drinking with Ellis afterwards, Oujuku had said delightedly that the simulcast was bound to reach Mutsuhito's own tri-vee screen and would cause the sonofabitch to spit bile, and both had pledged themselves to firing up their wild pasts at some future time when the Sector's need arose.

They had been great days. This Amerikan had fought his way into the newly constructed nexi amid the Blue Beacon supergiants of Ara and Scorpius. He had thrown himself against the might of Yamato and had put such heart into Amerika for his pains. But last year Oujuku's wife, Marie, had died and he had grieved her deeply. They had spoken together again then, and Ellis had aided his friend as he had once himself been aided, and both had been uplifted. Still, as if by mutual consent, neither had renewed their ideas of going out again into the Zone.

This year the Index had risen again for Oujuku. According to his occasional calls, he had found employment working on the Navy Commission. He had been elevated from governor to senator and he had found the love of an heiress in Justice Secretary George Packer's daughter. It seemed to Ellis that the prospects of making a good marriage had brought Oujuku to fine condition.

They sat down in armchairs, surrounded by mounted ship models—*Constitution* and *Lexington* and *Valley Forge*—and indulgently reminisced, Ellis speaking of his investments and Oujuku telling tales of Court, both sucking on tobako stogies until the room filled with a noncarcinogenic blue haze.

Oujuku regarded the polished wood and tall windows with approval. "So you're enjoying your leisure?"

"Certainly am." Ellis nodded. "And you? How're you doing with the Navy Commission?"

He watched for Oujuku's reaction. In the time since Hawken had been appointed Navy treasurer, Oujuku had mentioned his Navy work only once, and that dismissively.

"You know, I been doing a lot of thinking about our little secret. I don't know how much longer we can rely on the people who saw that nova—or whatever it was—keeping quiet. There were nine of them who knew something was amiss, the amnesia drugs only worked on five, two're dead now, the other two're on a helluva pension each. Kort, she's okeh, but Keever—I think he wants to split it. And he drinks more than he ought."

"And?"

"Well, I don't know. I wonder if we shouldn't split it first?"

Oujuku said it so lightly that Ellis tuned immediately to the bass chords of his guest's manner, to his gestures. Yes, he thought, there's definitely something amiss with him, and it's not connected with the quasi-nova. He fenced in his curiosity and, equally lightly, said, "I might think it over."

"Okeh. But I tell you, I feel kind of spooked."

"You think Yamato's discovered the ultimate weapon, don't you?"

Oujuku's eyes searched his face. "Yeah, Ellis. I do."

"You think they figured out how to destabilise a stellar interior and wipe out a whole system."

"Ellis, what if they have?"

True, it wasn't any ordinary nova. But it had been in an inhabited system. An experiment gone wrong? Maybe. But the shock and panic that would escape across Amerika was unthinkable if it was suspected that Yamato had a weapon capable of destroying a whole system in one go.

"The way I see it, there's two alternatives," Ellis said. "If we sit tight, we got plenty of time. I don't see anybody else getting near the Zero Degree Boundary, not the way Yamato's fortified since your little holiday. If nobody's going in or out of Yamato, that's it—in regular space it's axiomatic that light only travels at one light-year per annum, John."

"It's been more than ten years."

"Okeh, but at the Earth radial distance we're talking, it'll take decades before the waveshell breaks past the Twenty Degree Worlds. Listen, if what we saw could be demonstrated to be a natural phenomenon, then we got nothing to worry about. We could talk about it, tell the defense chiefs, et cetera, et cetera. If we could show that it couldn't possibly be a usable weapon, we'd be okey."

"But we can't show that."

"Right! Mention it and we have an instant panic that no crisis management team could damp down. That leaves us with two critical courses. Either the thing is a weapon or it's not. If it's not, we won't have served any purpose in talking about it, nor protected much in keeping it secret. That's a low-payoff strategy eitherhow."

"But if it *is* a weapon, what then?"

"Then we'd be in deep shit. And so would the rest of Known Space. But then that would be true whether anybody knew about it or not, so it may as well stay our little secret."

"But if we talk now, we can develop a similar weapon! Threaten them when they threaten us!"

"It's not the weapon—*if* it exists—that's the problem. It's delivering it to its target. While we've got a strong Navy we're safe. We go where we please inside Amerika, and no one comes here from Yamato unless we give them the say-so."

"That's what's bugging me, Ellis. The Navy—"

"Oh, I'm content to leave Navy matters to Navy men." Ellis deflected him, probing subtly with his maddening disregard for what Oujuku was trying to tell him. He knew that if he got involved, it would be up to the neck, and he had made his promises to Reba.

Oujuku reacted, changing the subject abruptly. "Did you know that when President Park came to Amerika for aid, I spoke to him?"

Ellis cocked his head. "Oh?"

"It was at a White House dinner. Everybody in their parrot suits. 'Give me that knife,' Conroy Lubbock says. 'Would you look at that! If that hybrid vegetable don't remind me of Ping-Pong,' you know—the Dowager's youngest son. And Alia says from right down the table, 'Conroy, wasn't that the Chinese prince Pharis wanted me to marry?' "

Ellis grinned at Oujuku's gesticulations.

"Yeah, and there's the Chinese ambassador sitting not ten feet away, and he don't know where to look. And, later, that sonofabitch Belkov, who's richer than hell just lately, he comes up beside Otis le Grande and tells him about the latest terraformed system up against the edge of the Beyond. You know, the one that's just coming up to completion. 'Of course, Otis, I'll call it "Virginia," in honor of Alia.' But Otis is full of booze, and running off at the mouth, and he tells him back: 'Hey, now—"Virginia"? That's a misnomer and I know what I'm talking about, boh.' "

Ellis laughed, then he shook his head and sucked in a sharp breath. "Le Grande and Belkov both get pretty crazy when they've been drinking."

"They'll go far."

"Or *too* far."

"Yeah."

"Yeah. Though sometimes Amerika needs men with a bit of spirit. Like now."

There was a space pregnant with silence, then Ellis said, "So, John, you been enjoying yourself up in Town. You've a taste for gossip you never had."

"I've a taste for getting what I want. And I came to see that my old straight-talking way was too blunt for Lincoln. Your advice in that regard was better than any I got from you about cruising space."

"Well, a senator's got to be amusing, and an ambitious senator something of an intriguer. Now suppose you tell me, what really brings you here?"

Oujuku's face shed its smile, growing suddenly serious and intense. "Dirty stuff."

"Yeah? Well, I guess it's too dirty for a man of leisure like me. One who's—*retired*."

"I need your help, Ellis."

A curl of smoke spiraled up from the tip of Oujuku's stogie. The other end of it was clamped in his teeth, and his eye was steady on Ellis's face.

"Do you, now?"

"Yeah—call it ambition and intriguing if you want, but do you remember in 'thirty-four how I planned to get up a fleet and take it into Korea? How the President agreed and then changed her mind?"

"Uh-huh."

"I'd like to put it to her again—if you'd come."

"Oh, my cruising days're over, John. There's no call for the likes of me while the peace holds."

"You're wrong." Oujuku leaned forward, fired now with his old passion. His eyes smoldered; his hands gripped the arms of his chair. "Since Yamato took Free Korea everything's up in the air. Amerika has got to prepare for war. Now. Quickly. Before it's too late."

Reba stood in the doorway, a posy of garden flowers in her hand. Her face had lost its warmth.

"It's always been the policy of Yamato to extend their power across their boundaries," she told Oujuku coldly. "But they annex by marriage now, rather than war. When Yamato arms overran Free Korea, the Presidium on Seoul recognised Mutsuhito as Emperor through his wife's bloodline."

"That's true, Reba, but they also exiled President Park, who has the democratic claim. He's the man the Korean people want."

"Then we should be glad he found little help here. When he and his loyalists went after Cheju Do with a Chinese fleet, he was smashed to atoms by Baron Harumi. Had it not been for the President's change of heart, they might have been Amerikan ships, Senator."

"I beg your pardon, Reba, but Baron Harumi's victory was a beam weapon action. In that game Yamato has no peer. But would I, would Ellis, have allowed the baron's ships to come to grips with ours like the Chinese did?"

Ellis's dismay mounted as he heard Oujuku out, fearing his infectious words and the way they wounded Reba. "C'mon, we're not gonna talk politics all—"

But Reba was insistent. "Please, let Senator Oujuku have his say."

Oujuku's fist balled. "We must fight. Because I've been. And I've seen. And I tell you, the whole Zone beyond the Kalifornia Boundary is a Yamato preserve. To their Empire they've added a thousand low-population worlds: the Remnant, a great aurium extraction plant on Sado and another on Okinawa, fabulous wealth. Yeah, and now Korea, with the most strategic of nexus chains in Known Space. But the biggest prize of all is Seoul. You're blind if you fail to see the purpose of that. They're set on overwhelming us, Ellis. They want to sweep us away in one massive blow. Don't lie to yourself that it's peace. It's just a temporary halt."

Reba dropped her flowers down onto a table and left the room. Ellis checked himself from following or calling to her. She was only thinking of him, of the children. But Oujuku was right, and right to speak. After the battle of Hainan, Yamato fears over the Chinese threat had been obliterated. The Three-Thirty Degree Boundary was secured, and when Free Korea fell under Mutsuhito's claim, two space-spanning nexus chains were put under his sole direction. The moment Imperial troops had landed on Seoul, Yamato had become a power with an easy chain stretching unbroken for two hundred light-years, and in the center of it, the greatest multiplex nexus junction in Known Space: Seoul's Yod-Seven-Seven. Overnight, Yamato had taken possession of Korea's nexus fleet—a dozen huge transports and their armaments, their naval fabrication yards, their arsenals and stockpiles. Then there were the extensive private trading fleets that plied the Twenty Degree routes, that Mutsuhito, as Emperor of Korea, could commandeer at any time. The title had given him mastery over the Zone in the same way that his destruction of the Chinese fleet had given him mastery over the Three-Thirty Boundary. The focus of his attention was shifting and his fascinated stare was now falling on the *gaijin* of Amerika without distraction.

As if from a great distance Oujuku's voice urged him. "We've got to speak with Secretary Cassabian, Ellis. Will you come now to back me?"

Ellis said nothing, only turned away.

"Not even to hear me speak to him of the crimes of Jos Hawken?"

"Hawken?" he heard himself say.

As Oujuku spoke Ellis looked beyond the great windows of the house, watching the rain slash down across his lawns, watching the ragged line of hills and the dark dappled forest. This was his peace. His home. His haven. Two of his children were next door in the library with their tutor, the third lay upstairs sleeping. At the back of the house Reba would be pacing in a fury, knowing what was happening here. Must he go to her and ask her to take it calmly and tell Matthew to ready his air-car?

He bowed his head, put his face in his hand, plowing the fingers through his hair. Oujuku, his closest friend, had brought him a bigger impediment to his life's tranquillity than any sniveling Halide creature sent by Kurt Reiner. There *was* change in the air, and he knew that what Oujuku had told him was true.

Goddamn this man, he thought, this brother who's filled the gap in my heart left by the brother I lost so long ago. Must I leave everything? Must I give up my peace?

Then he thought of the proverb that said that blood was thicker than water, and he had his answer.

69

Ramakrishnan's ashram on the river had lain deserted for a long time, sealed by the President's personal order. The contemplative garden that was walled and locked was full of dead things, its meditation niches poisoned, its grass bleached or burned. At the fringes all was overgrown with brambles, its high wall a multicolored masterpiece of graffiti, but, in the center, the garden was only brown: desiccated wood, fungi and molds, and the filthy suppurations of decay. Rain beat against the broken statuary beside a pool of green and slimy water. Once Zen carp had swum here, and the devotees of the astrogation school had learned to concentrate and cultivate their psi-talents under a strange and moody genius, but no longer. It was a sobering place to talk of treason.

Cassabian pulled the chain from the gates and pushed against complaining hinges. Ellis shut one eye against the shafting rain, following Cassabian and Oujuku out of the air-car. The secretary's men, he noted, made no move to follow from their vehicle but looked to one another superstitiously, which pleased Ellis because he wanted secrecy.

He regarded Cassabian closely. Trust your first impression of him as you stepped off the skimmer, he told himself. Sharp-tongued? Yes. A man full of political ambition and subterfuges? Again yes. An underhand dealer? It couldn't be denied. Oh, but you're a less righteous man than I once thought. And you're not a friend, because I know you keep me only as an ally. You have weak faith, because you once sold your stake in me to Conroy Lubbock. And you're hard in the soul, because your business is knowing secrets and weaknesses through the buying and twisting of other men's greed. All these things damn you, Mr. Secretary, but, by God, there's one side of you that saves you. You're not a traitor and so I can trust you.

"Tell me what you hope to find here, Ellis."

"In good time, Mr. Secretary."

Ellis looked about him at the devastation, eerily appalled. "This is a terrible place. Did it die when Ramakrishnan departed on his Europan wanderings?"

"Before. It was ruined by psi experiments. Even the life of the soil has been destroyed."

"It's clear to me why Ramakrishnan has been called a Satanist and a black magician by most of the Adventer churches, and why he's gone."

"You can't hold a man like that," Oujuku said. "So, Mr. Secretary, where's he gone?"

"It seems the great man knew enough to prophesy the arrival of his enemies on Prague three weeks ago. I can report that he escaped beyond the grasp of the Europan authorities, who would surely have expelled him had they caught him. But he's not infallible. He made a grave miscalculation going to Paris and the Rosenberg seminary."

"Miscalculation, you say?" Ellis said.

Cassabian rattled the ion keys. "Yes. So completely did Ramakrishnan convince the French of his greatness that their hospitality was extended to him indefinitely. He's to stay on Paris until he's turned all Rosenberg's psi-talents into astrogators."

Oujuku grunted and took the ion key from Cassabian. "If the Rosenberg seminary wants astrogators, they'd be better off doing it themselves."

"An altogether more difficult prospect," Cassabian disagreed drily, adding, "Ramakrishnan can't be coerced."

Oujuku unlocked the door and went inside. Ellis, following, pulled out his torch and struck a beam of light into the interior. All was musty and dank: rain had got in, birds had found their way through the eaves, liming the furniture; insects had wintered and summered in the rooms and vermin had made nests in the laps of the Buddhas. As they moved throughout the sprawling warren, Ellis realised how little prospect there was of finding what he had come for.

"Genius, I've heard it said," Cassabian said portentously, examining a carved idol face-to-face, "is in inverse proportion to orderliness."

Oujuku eyed him coolly. "This place stinks like cat piss."

"You were wrong to let Ramakrishnan leave Amerika, Mr. Cassabian," Ellis said. "Why did you?"

Cassabian took the accusation smoothly. "He was growing meddlesome in government and getting too close to the President. I was happy to have him travel elsewhere."

"A mistake. Men like Ramakrishnan are rare. A resource more precious than aurium. I thought you, better than anyone, understood that." He pulled a plex box from under a stack of moldering hardcopy, opened it, and looked inside, then he discarded it carelessly into a gloomy corner.

"What're you looking for, Ellis?"

"A copy, or a plan."

"Of what?"

"The jewel. It was an incredible device, and it might save our astrogators a great deal of trouble if we find its secret—and then someone who can make another one."

"You've brought me here so that you could look around?" Cassabian's impatience erupted. He stiffened angrily. "Our people have been through it with a fine-toothed comb."

Ellis ceased his ransacking and leveled a finger at Cassabian's eye. "I brought you here to talk. There's no better place in all Amerika, and no more important matter to disturb the silence with. This is one place you can be certain nobody is going to overhear us."

Cassabian's shoulders sagged and he acquiesced. Oujuku planted three chairs around the table and they sat down in the gloom as Ellis began.

"Mr. Secretary, the Sector's heading for war. And when war comes we have to be ready. Say what you will, our Navy is still all that stands between us and the snuffing out of our liberties, but there's a traitor in it." He thrust a document onto the table. "I have it here."

Cassabian examined it, listening simultaneously to Oujuku's catalog of teachery. Ellis already knew about it: Hawken had profited greatly from the dealings they had had with Okubo. The success of that had brought Hawken position and power. He had first succeeded to the post of treasurer of the Navy, inherited with Conroy Lubbock's connivance, from his own father-in-law, Ben de Zharian. Later, he had been promoted once more, this time to a post that gave him ultimate say over the hull-building facilities. Since then, his avarice had been unbounded.

Ellis boiled with anger as he listened to the corruption that Oujuku was reporting. Hawken had gone into partnership with the plex-manufacturing corporations of his friends, with suppliers and engine designers, and now with the procurement people. Between them they had defrauded the Navy, building their own hulls in private hangars and getting lucrative contracts.

"It makes me burn to think that this man can send Amerikans offworld in ships less well equipped than they should be because of his greed. And in such a time of crisis."

Cassabian stared back at Oujuku. The two men were so utterly different. They had never liked one another, which was why Oujuku had asked for Ellis's intercession. He said softly, "Leave the matter with me."

"Act!" Oujuku's fist slammed the table, knocking over the torch. "Make it known! Tomorrow! Unseat Hawken! And unseat Conroy Lubbock!"

"No! There's a better way!" Rain drummed in the silence, then Cassabian smiled for the first time. "On the nexus lanes, it may be your method to fight fire with fire. Here on dry land we have another way. We fight fire with a pail of water."

Oujuku's anger stalled, his forehead furrowed, and then he too smiled.

In the secretary's house the three men met again. Cassabian paced anxiously, seeing no way out. Amerika's peril ran far deeper than either of his guests could know. The spies of the Empire were secretly pouring into the Sector. Ninja, infiltrating Liberty under cover. Refugees, the vast majority bona fide Koreans, were arriving, and Amerika's liberal laws did not allow them to be detained. But there were those among them intent on paving the way for invasion, striking at the heart, sapping strength by their subversion, and reporting everything faithfully to Yamato.

It required a huge investment in time and credit to track such people, and Cassabian's resolve faltered as he considered his task. Admittedly there had been successes. Hadn't he infiltrated a swarming nest of traitors in Philadelphia? Hadn't he penetrated the Yamato network through Jiro Ito? Hadn't he arrested the seditious pro-Yamato radical leader Ali Akhbar and disposed of him? As he had lain bleeding from the ears under the Probe, Akhbar had talked, but too late to get hold of the Black Orchid Cell or Akhbar's controller. Even now, that monster was running back and forth between Kyoto and Seoul, Guam and the Ten Degree Worlds, designing revolution and the President's assassination. Hadn't that been specifically ordered by the *kempei*? And hadn't Earth Central received a deputation of rebel Amerikans, an unparalleled intervention? Why, if not as precursor to an invasion? To rally waverers and deep-run cowards and those who chose to stay quiet? But what else?

Cassabian saw it clearly now, shuddering at the force of the idea. After news of Keun's assassination and the overrunning of Free Korea had reached him, his spies had said that Baron Harumi, Yamato's foremost warlord, had wanted to assemble a two-million-strong force in Wonsan and Guam and then ferry them into Kalifornia II in two hundred hulls. With Amerika's Navy on the Boundary that idea was as doomed as it had ever been, but then Harumi had returned from his victories against the Chinese bursting with confidence and laid before his Emperor another, more ambitious enterprise.

Yes, he thought despairingly, it was the only answer! Mutsuhito must have sanctioned the massive invasion that his shogun wanted launched from Seoul: five hundred ships, fully one hundred fifty of which were gigantic purpose-built warships. Thirty thousand crew. Three million troops. The greatest single battle fleet ever assembled. An unopposable, invincible force.

This time, there would be no expensive-but-limited irritations like the rebellions of Dakota, which had been shut down almost before it had started, no abortive attempt like the one Prince Sekigahara had almost mounted before he was replaced as Mutsuhito's commander in Cho Sen by Harumi. No, this time, the entire might of Yamato would be focused on Amerika. Directly. Like a magnifying lens on dry straw. And *still* Conroy Lubbock imagined that war could be avoided!

A tremendous weight of responsibility pressed down on Cassabian as he thought of the terrifying news he had received from Yamato. Months ago, plans for an attack via Florida II had been thwarted. Under the Probe, the double-dealing Milton Klingsor had confessed to his complicity. He had run a conspiracy between the Yamato ambassador, Kamakura, and the still-imprisoned Lucia Henry. He had succeeded in sending Kamakura the same way as Okubo had gone, but what of the arch-conspirator herself? What of Lucia? To have the least hope of warding off the threat, Lucia must die. And the President must be persuaded to sign her execution.

Cassabian closed his eyes, feeling the stares of the two men at his back and the sweat beading the peak of his hairline. He wiped it away and examined his hand, imagining blood.

His spies had picked up a thousand terrifying clues, all pointing in the same direction. The darkest days of '24 were a pale shadow compared to the evil gloom that presently mounted against Amerika. She was besieged on every side. Now, Yamato was twice as rich, her navy twice as powerful. All over the Zone, in Cho Sen, in the other Korea, in the Solomon League and the systems over which Yamato arms held sway, a ground swell was beginning. And the hub of it all was the family shrine in the fortress-monastery-palace of Chiyoda-Ku. Yamato's foremost daimyos were being recalled to Kyoto, assembling in ranks to the beat of war drums, bringing with them arms and levies and the implacable martial spirit that had conquered the only unassigned part of Known Space, all gathering for a decisive blow.

Now Oujuku's and Straker's revelations about Hawken had shaken to the foundations the one pillar on which Amerika's survival depended. And Hawken was Conroy Lubbock's man.

He tried to drag his thoughts back to the present. Straker was right, Amerika needed her able men now, more than ever before. The old Amerikan worlds close to the Earth Exclusion Zone were drawing together, divisions were being mobilised, but it was being done with painful sloth. Under Conroy Lubbock and his chiefs of staff, the newly organised planetary defenses were inadequate, and certainly no match for Harumi's war-hardened veterans. The Navy was Amerika's only defense, her only hope of survival.

Ellis told him: "We must have nexus-going ships to guard the Boundary, fast vessels capable of outrunning any ship sent against us, to free our war wagons for work other than system defense. And those big ships must be of the new kind, like the *Iowa*, well armed with singularity guns that outshoot the Yamato ships at close range. This must be our strategy."

Oujuku nodded his assent. "Yeah, and we have to cut out the parasites in charge of the Navy, the ones who're sucking the lifeblood out of our defenses."

Cassabian protested. "But the size of our fleet—"

"If numbers were the crux," Ellis told him, "we'd already be dead men. Numbers are not critical. Quality is the key. Two dozen ships—that's all I ask. But two dozen like the *Iowa*!"

The meticulous designs that Ellis had worked on spilled across the table. They dated back to his confinement in Camp Worth and had been augmented by a thousand incredible ideas patiently collected by Ramakrishnan and the self-destructive mathematician, Timo Farren. Years of careful thought, refinements drawn from experience, details teased from Oujuku and from the other privateering astrogators. It was the essence of change, designs that would make an unparalleled fighting force of the Amerikan Navy.

"Though Amerika depends on it, I can't get these measures being accepted while Hawken is at Navy and while Conroy Lubbock keeps him there."

Every nerve in Cassabian's body itched to tell them that the improvements would be put in hand, but he knew that he could never present the President with such an expense. Free Korea had been a bottomless pit. The government had given Park thirty billion in inter-Sector credit units to finance the retaking of Wonsan, and sent him away with a further ten billion, and then sent a division to him with the promise of fifty billion more, all to convince Mutsuhito of Amerikan-Chinese solidarity. And still Harumi had triumphed. On the day before Keun's death, the President had sent a message to him that in war and peace three things alone mattered: credit, credit, and once again credit.

He explained haltingly, all the while searching for a way out of the problem, but as he finished, Ellis gave Oujuku a significant look. Incredibly both men seemed oddly satisfied to hear the objections wrung painfully from him.

"What I offer you, sir," Ellis said slowly, "is no expense. But a saving."

The airless room closed in around them.

"A saving?" Cassabian said with incredulity, sure only that if any argument could sway the President, the one least likely to drain her budget must win the day. "You say a *saving*?"

Ellis planted his elbow on the table. "Implement these plans and the cost of the Navy will be cut from ten billion in credit annually to half that. See, there's not a captain offplanet who wouldn't prefer two hundred and fifty good crew to three hundred incompetents—if the ships can be crewed that way."

Oujuku backed him, leaning in on Cassabian fiercely. "It's not skill we lack, but the *will* to organise."

Ellis nodded tautly. "Credit makes the galaxy revolve, as they say. If we're wise we'll plow back the seedcorn. Reinvest the saving. And pitch our prices at the right level. If we don't we're dead."

"Take our people," Oujuku insisted. "Ships are hulks without good crews to staff them. To make them good we must pay them well. Look at this: the *Missouri*. The charge of wages and supplementary sums for three hundred crew at twenty-three personal credit units per crew member is point-six-nine fiscal. The same ship with a complement of two hundred fifty but costed at twenty-seven-point-two units per hand is point-six-nine fiscal. Make no mistake, you can't expect the best people unless you pay for them. Show them their Sector values them and they'll know who they're fighting for."

Cassabian wiped at his brow once more, utterly weary, but feeling the grim capability of the men beside him. "Yes," he said. "Yes! We'll try Conroy Lubbock. He may be persuaded. If he's not, I'll go to the President herself!"

71

Conroy Lubbock received them in his office in the river precinct on Pennsylvania. He was courteous and listened to Cassabian with thoughtful silence. At last he raised his head and said pleasantly, "Let me take your spreadsheet, gentlemen. I promise I'll give it my attention. And I thank you for your concern."

"I want your signature on a warrant of arrest for Jos Hawken," Cassabian demanded less than respectfully.

"Oh?" Lubbock nodded slowly and looked Cassabian up and down. "I'll have to consider that at length."

"If you don't reach a decision by noon tomorrow, we'll be forced to approach the President directly."

"The President is still involved in fiscal matters. By her own request she cannot be disturbed."

"I *will* see her. That is my right."

"As you wish."

"And when I do, Jos Hawken *will* answer these charges."

Conroy Lubbock sighed inwardly and thought again of the tremendous economies his patient work had brought. A tight rein had been held for twenty-five years, despite the credit spent in Korea. Though rebellions had swallowed up all the extra taxes imposed in that time, still Amerika's foreign debts were paid, and the obligations left by Lucia Henry also, making Amerika's interest rate half of that Yamato was forced to pay. For twenty-five years Amerika had prospered, a quarter century nurtured by his careful guidance, which had brought with it a payoff that other, more impulsive men might have squandered on needless war.

In those years, Conroy Lubbock calculated, there had been a tripling of wealth in the Sector, but it had come only by hard work and diligent effort. The aurium that Ellis and Oujuku and the rest of the privateers had waylaid were as nothing beside that.

He smiled inwardly. It had been a wise policy. Wise to keep at arm's length high taxation that would raise credit, but at the same time buy the privilege of tinkering in affairs of state for sticky-fingered congressmen. Although he had first conceived the policy as a way of avoiding political control, it had paid immense and unlooked-for dividends in another way. Low rates of interest and low taxes had fostered commerce and the manufacturers. Successful trade and successful commerce were the key. For the first time all the wants of civilised life could be supplied by Amerikan hands at Amerikan factories, in Amerikan yards and from Amerikan fabricators. No longer did the Sector depend on expensive imports. Nor did it need Seoul. Exports went out through Europa, trade flourished with Muscovi and the Slavians. Brasilia was taking raw material and terraforming equipment. Even distant Izlam had been among the new customers.

Oh, Pharis, can't you understand that subtlety? Little by little. In military matters half the battle's concerned with hiding true weaknesses from the enemy. The other half's concerned with hiding true strengths.

"Hawken will answer these charges before the President. Confirm that to me, Conroy."

Conroy Lubbock turned on them admonishingly. "I warn you, Pharis. I warn you all. These matters are best left to me."

"In all sincerity I doubt that, Conroy. Our Sector's plunging into a war *and you will not see it,*" Cassabian insisted.

"Seems to me that some people would have us plunge in all the faster."

"Hawken is a traitor!" Oujuku burst out. "And you, Lubbock, are his protector!"

"C'mon," Conroy Lubbock told him mildly, shaking his head. Cassabian's bellicose table thumping is still dangerous, he thought. He's never learned flexibility. I was right to clip his wings in '31. That's the reason I sent him on a diplomatic mission of pacification to Peking, a mission contrary to his own stance and doomed to failure, and in the Wilderness, politically speaking. I wasted three months, but I prised him away from the management of the Sector at a vital time. That's also why I let him waste his energies on attempting to arrange the Chinese marriage. I let him embroil himself in a hell of a mess. And now he's realised the backwater he inhabits, and he understands his own impotence, his temper's got worse. He's going to have to bear the brunt of the President's vacillations, but that frustration has done nothing to break him of his readiness to meddle in affairs best left to me. If it wasn't for the growing menace on the Boundary and his sources of information there, I would have side-footed Pharis Cassabian into the gutter long ago. But I have my own sources, sources he knows nothing about, and I'm not as ill informed as he believes.

He approached Ellis, who had remained silent throughout the interview. The man's magnificent, but he's a continual embarrassment to me, a real thorn in my side. Why do I tolerate him? Because Reba loves him? Because while he's with her Reiner dare not go near her? Because while he's at Xanadu he's not offplanet? Perhaps. But perhaps because he's the devil's own trident. It's not yet time to use him, but the moment's arrived when he must be handled. He's precipitated it before I thought he would, but what does it matter now? He'll strike the blow that breaks the fleet that Mutsuhito is building . . .

He stood in front of Ellis smilingly. "Can you really believe that I'm a traitor, Captain?"

Ellis drew himself up straight. "Sir, I believe you're mistaken in your attitude towards Yamato. I believe you're reluctant to admit that war with Yamato is inevitable, though the evidence for it is clear enough."

"You astonish me. Do you really imagine you know more about the Emperor of Yamato's intentions than I do?"

"Pharis Cassabian knows more than either of us, and his opinion is the same as mine. As far as these complaints we've laid out before you today are concerned, I can't think other than that you've been deceived."

"By whom?"

"By Jos Hawken, amongst others."

"So you believe Jos Hawken is a traitor?"

"What else can I call it? There are two edges to his sword, he cuts two ways. Here's hard evidence that he's been dealing with Yamato agents. That's more than stupidity, more than plain greed. It threatens the security of Amerika."

Conroy Lubbock sighed, went to his desk, and pulled out a closely printed sheet of hardcopy. "This came into my possession some time ago. You may be interested to read it, Captain. It was dictated by a man, one Cadet Philips, who knew your brother in Sado, and who subsequently found his way back into Amerika."

Ellis was thrown for a moment, then he took the sheet and read it. As he scanned the lines his eyes clouded but the rest of his face betrayed nothing. The paper was an affidavit describing the fate of Duval, how he had been imprisoned, sentenced, and then crucified by the *kempei*.

"Your brother was making singularity guns for the Sado daimyo. Guns whose only purpose was to smash Amerikan ships. Guns that might even have been used against you yourself!"

"Yes."

"In that case you already know he's a traitor. To you, and to his Sector."

Ellis's jaw clenched. The blood had drained from his face and he found difficulty in speaking. "Yes."

"And you still accuse *me* of harboring traitors? Of shielding traitors? Of *using* traitors?"

The silence that enveloped them was punctuated by the sounds of the city that drifted up through the open window. Vigorous sounds of air traffic and crowds and daily business. To judge from the way Ellis's stiffness left him, they must have seemed deafening to him.

"I disowned my brother long ago, Conroy. It's a relief that he's dead. I would have killed him myself if I could have done so."

Conroy Lubbock's demand was suddenly as sharp as a samurai sword. "You swear that's the truth?"

"Yes."

"You swear?"

"Yes, I swear, damn you!"

"Good. Good. There may come a time when I'll ask you to remember that." Lubbock recovered the sheet and put it back into the drawer. Yes, he thought. A devil's trident. Handled, but not yet thrown.

He took up his pen. "Captain Oujuku, here's a warrant ordering your presence at the meeting of the Security Council in three weeks' time. There we'll discuss your plans to embark preemptively and in force against Yamato forces in the Neutral Zone." He turned to Cassabian. "Give me thirty days. In return I'll immediately put Captain Straker's suggestions before the Navy Commission and I'll personally insist they're discussed. I'll even require that some of them are adopted."

Cassabian considered. "And when the thirty days are up? What about Hawken?"

"When the thirty days are up, you can come to Camp Worth and put Jos Hawken against the wall and shoot him if you still want to."

72

SEOUL

Michie met her husband near the Seoul terminal as she did every seventh day at this time. It was early evening, before dusk, and the sky was full of golden streamers behind a black haze of military transport fumes. The Emperor's enterprise was gathering for the final blow.

Huge nexus ships lined the herringbone service structures, sometimes hooked up six deep. More sat out on the apron and on the auxiliary stacks: vessels of all sizes, from the small supply ships and orbital shuttles to the lumbering, round-bodied transports and the high-built sleekness of Korea's warships.

Along the terminal a great quantity of ships' stores had been stockpiled and all kinds of technicians and subcontractors had erected temporary workshops among the chaos. Thoughout the day, a vast array of human endeavor had come together, but this was the peaceful hour when the toils of the day paused and the builders of the battle fleet looked to their rice bowls instead of their work.

Michie took her husband's hand and sensed again the unbearable tension in him. He had put his own work away after a busy week; with Choi Ki Won away across continent and extra statistical analysis work coming in every day from the Seoul Port Authorities, he was ready to rest, but it was not simple tiredness she felt in him. There was something else, something worrying him and destroying his inner harmony. She squeezed his hand and asked, "Do you know why Ki Won-san left Seoul City?"

He did not look at her. "Why does Choi Ki Won do anything?"

"To trade or to talk—sometimes to see and remember what he sees."

"Then you know already what Ki Won is doing. Why ask me?"

"Zinan-san, why does he take with him his sons?"

"His sons?"

"Oh, yes. And those cages of pigeons."

"I don't know. And I don't care."

He volunteered no more, and she chose not to pursue it, seeing his nerves were raw. Perhaps he was regretting his decision to stay on Seoul, realising that the tide of events could no longer be turned, that the Yamato invasion juggernaut was now unstoppable. It seemed capable of tearing down anything that stood in its way.

I know you understand that truth, my husband, she told him silently, feeling nothing but devotion towards him. You watch the soldiers coming and the ships arriving and the invasion fleet growing stronger every week, and you feel helpless and Choi Ki Won feels helpless and, though you yearn to act, there's nothing you can do.

They walked together in silence along the broad service roads that edged the terminal, threading their way past many-colored, varishaped containers and flasks and hi-tech cabins that were being unloaded from vast multi-wheeled ground transporters and air-lifters, and transferred by great waldos into the ships that were attached to the numbered quays by looms of umbilicals so that they resembled the severely ill inside their medivacs. And all the time as they strolled they secretly noted and memorised as many details of the preparations as they could, to be recalled later verbatim to Choi Ki Won.

It had been like this for at least a year now. From the shipbuilding yards and hangars of the vast Seoul apron and from all the aprons in Yamato great ship after great ship had come here to be rigged and outfitted. Hundreds of technicians and freezee installation engineers labored at their work, putting down an average of one soldier every ten seconds, day and night, round the clock, for over a year. Ships' quartermasters and provosts supervised round the clock, overseeing the lading of supplies and the payrolling of crews. Each ship had been designated its own assembly point, transports to their main terminal stations, big globe ships to their special anchorages. Between them, a thousand craft of all sizes plied the twenty-five-mile by fifteen-mile extent of the Seoul apron, weaving back and forth endlessly with men and materials under the glare of B-type-blue arclights.

Michie saw the helplessness in his face as he watched the preparations and asked him gently, "What is it, Zinan-san? Please tell me what it is that especially troubles you."

He stirred. "What?"

"You seem so full of cares tonight."

"No more than usual. I'm just thinking."

"If you want to, you can tell me what it is that weighs on your mind."

He squeezed her hand briefly, stifled a sigh, and looked out again across the vast plain of crete and plex. "The fleet seems much bigger than it did only a week ago."

"Do you think the time approaches? That it will take off for the Flying Horse nexus soon?"

"No," he said. "I think this is only the start. It's much more awesome than I imagined. The Emperor is bending every resource to this single end. It's staggering."

To Duval, the Emperor's minions seemed prepared to spend all, apply all, risk all, on their government's fanatical desire. For months Seoul had been drinking in men: samurai soldiers brought across the Zone, *ashigaru* from every world of every prefecture of every quadrant of the entire Sector: from the biggest of the four quadrants, the main Honshu prefectures of Mino, Hida, Echizen and Ise, Shinano and Harima, and all of the forty-three others; from the six Shikoku prefectures of Tosa, Iyo, Awa, Sanuki, Awaii, and Izumi; from the twelve Kyushu prefectures and the eighteen of Hokkaido; from every Mutsu world not required to stand in defense against the Chinese; and from all *han* of the Empire samurai of every rank. Oh, yes, the fleet was far from completed. Choi Ki Won had said that it was so far only a quarter, a third, of what it must eventually become. Yet already it was an awesome sight, the greatest assembly of nexus ships ever undertaken.

Not all the contributions had been willingly given. Duval's eyes flickered over the place where the huge *Toyotomi Hideyoshi* squatted, her vast and powerful black bulk frowning down over the ships and tiny human figures that surrounded her. The massive warship had arrived in Seoul weeks ago. The idea was that she was to be sold and sent on to the Chinese. She had been called the *San Francisco* then and had belonged to the España quadrant of Latina, but Baron Harumi had taken a liking to her. He had commandeered her to be refitted as flagship of his Yamashiro Squadron, and put his soldiery aboard to make sure his plans were not overthrown.

As they continued to stroll, the outer walls of the main ultra-security terminal loomed nearby, opaque plex without color of any kind, "point four nines" absorbent black, like velvet, huge-domed and impregnable. The gates were guarded by a dozen men, and only Yamato soldiers and specially summoned persons able to show the correct ID were permitted inside. Duval thought again of the great ammunition store and beam weapons arsenal that lay within and his palms began to itch. Since Choi Ki Won told him of the armory he had been unable to put it out of his mind. Inside these walls were the high-intensity weapons that would be used to subdue Amerika's Navy. But to gain entry was like trying to get inside Camp Worth. It was impossible.

They began to return the way they had come when a voice called to them fiercely in Japanese.

"You!"

They stopped and Duval noticed for the first time a soldier ten paces away leaning heavily against a huge ship anchoring flange among the shadows. He pointed an evil-looking ID gun at them, but he seemed like a man who hadn't slept for seventy-two hours.

"Yes, you! Come here!"

Duval complied, Michie following a pace behind, with tiny steps, as was required of her. Duval's blood was rushing to his stomach, flooding his belly with fear. Their ID was not good, but they had always risked it before, knowing that security could not possibly cope with the hundreds of thousands of individuals that had every right to be here.

"I saw you looking at the gates." The soldier's voice dropped to a growl. "What business do you have here?"

Duval considered, almost denied it, then decided to gamble. "I must fill an order for statistical analysis work," he lied.

"Let me see your ID smart."

Wordlessly Duval took the card from his pouch and handed it over. It was a Korean credit smart, from the days of Free Korea; it was unmarked.

The soldier appeared to check it in his type-two reader, then he hit the device with the heel of his hand. He broke wind noisily. He stank, was stubbled, and his eyes were shot pink, rolling up as he blinked, as if he was coping with an impossible strain. He was just going through the motions. "So—you're a Korean mathematician?"

"A chaos theorist. As the ID says." He leaned forward, but the soldier pulled the reader back broodily.

"So what's your business here, chaos theorist?"

"I have a contract to do analysis work," Duval repeated. "As it says on the smart. Is there a problem? Do I have to get confirmation? I'd be happy to. My hardcopy work's a bit involved because of my specialisation, but if you want to read it, I can bring it along now."

The soldier held the reader up once more, inclining it to the light. It was obviously faulty.

"The smart's all in order. But you can't come this way. A restricted area." He handed the smart back grudgingly and gestured over his shoulder at sixty or seventy refrigerated flasks stacked inside a garish lime-green-and-black-striped container that drones were in the process of unloading. "You speak good Japanese, so you should know what those signs say: 'Danger, Argentium' and 'No Unauthorised Access.' It's my responsibility to check everyone who comes around here. You had no visual on your ID when I scanned you, see? I thought you were a spy."

Duval nodded at the man, mirroring his grim humor. "Supervisors! They always want you to do things but they don't give you the right hardcopy work, eh? I haven't known one of my corporation IDs to interrogate properly on Seoul. Maybe it's the gravity here. I'm still not used to it. Everything feels so heavy, not like Wonsan. Where's the argentium going to?"

The soldier vaguely indicated the apron; he leered crookedly at Michie, wiping the reader on his sleeve. "Who's she?"

"My—assistant."

"Korean as well?"

"Er, yes."

"It's a shame you're in a reserved occupation. I could've spent a lot of credit on you, eh, Rose Petal?"

"Is your regiment short of men?" she asked, forcing herself to smile back at him. "You seem like a man who has worked very hard."

"Short of *real* men." He reached out and grasped her arm. "You want to make a date?"

Duval broke in. "Maybe I could find you some Seoul City bad boys who'd like to come up here. Maybe we could split the credit. How many do you need? What's your name?"

The soldier's grin died slowly, then a sickly anger overcame him and he brushed at Duval, letting go of Michie. "Get on your way, Korean shit-eater! You ask too many questions!"

They retreated, the soldier still calling after them. Duval carefully stored away his thoughts on the drunken guard as he and Michie merged with the crowd. Here, along the South Boundary Road, a temporary shopping mall had been set up under transparent flexiplex, selling z-suits, tools, power packs, and a hundred thousand assorted luxuries. A knot of well-dressed samurai stood back as their representatives haggled on their behalf over the price of a tri-vee, another loitered as his twin white-faced whores looked over a garish display of Europan commodities. Next to them blue smoke drifted up where barbecued meats basted and spat on a makeshift hibachi, filling the air with a mouth-watering aroma. Lights began to come on in the gathering dusk. A hundred little stalls had been set up to do brisk business: Korean sausage and cured chicken and piglet, mummified duck heads clustered hanging on a hook, their bills pierced, their eyes black pits, the bones of their long necks visible under the taut, crispy yellow skin. Noodle sellers and sushi bars, giant melon sellers, and tubs of big, live, spidery crabs, bubbling, all locked together and struggling weakly.

Duval steered Michie through the press of customers, amazed at the increase in trade that had occurred in only a single week. It was as if every samurai in the Empire had suddenly descended on Seoul in a vast deluge to seek honor in arms on the great crusade. Every day religious orders and private corporations of troops arrived, landing in great phalanxes of shuttles and marching across the city in processions, sometimes in forced marches lasting all day and all night. Every last guesting house and spare room had been turned over to accommodate samurai officers, and acres on the outskirts of the city were now under flexiplex tentage, as hundreds of thousands more *ashigaru* made their bivouac under Seoul's bright stars.

Nunki shone down on them now, the brightest star in the Seoul summer firmament. It was a blue giant, five light-years away in what was once the Old Earth constellation of Sagittarius, blazing clear in the twilight at a magnitude of minus two, its system huge and populous with three terraformed planets and a smallish gas giant about which there had once been a sensational xeno-life rumor. Of course, it had all come to nothing—it seemed almost certain now that no life existed in the galaxy, except that which had originated on Earth and had been dispersed across Known Space by man's titanic terraforming machines. Why? When there were so many star systems with planets? So many planets within the temperate zones around their primaries? And so many planets with atmospheres and oceans and all the chemical wherewithal to allow the complex process of evolution to get started? It was now the biggest, most mysterious question facing science: are we alone? And if so, *why?* So far, the answer was a resounding yes to the first question. Not so much as a single provably xenobiological RNA analog had been detected in a virgin system. The answer to the second question—why?—was far from being answered.

The stray thought made him shiver. What a bleak aseptic universe it will be, he thought, if we don't find anything out in the Beyond. It'll take us a thousand years more to extend Known Space across the Carina-Cygnus arm of this big type-Sb spiral galaxy we live in; thirty thousand years to colonise half the Milky Way; another fifty thousand to consume the rest. Maybe "infect" is the word. When all we do is fight among ourselves . . .

He glanced at Michie and felt the warmth of her concern for him. Fighting isn't the whole story, but sometimes it's hard to see the good for the forests of evil that seem to hem us in. What an incredible, futile, insane expense, he thought, looking around the immense enterprise on the apron, trying to calculate the scale of it. How can the Emperor continue to bear it all? There's almost too many men here for the Seoul City area to support, and even with the troops freezeed down inside their vessels, each passing month is a month's fouling of the ships, a month's refrigerant and catalyst consumed, and a month's wages owing to the crews and technical support people. The Emperor's exchequer is not bottomless; he must be mortgaged to every bank in Yamato. God alone knows what rate of interest he must be forced to pay.

As they reached the far side of the terminal the last rays of sunset deserted the sky across the darkening west. These were the drilling grounds, and all around them, exercising troops dressed off in columns to be marched to camp behind z-suited officers, their places quickly filled by more lines of men. Others burdened with full assault kit formed queues to receive bowls of Dover noodles, then wandered away to sit in groups and drink down the steaming stock water noisily.

But the lethargy of the hour was stirring, pierced by shouted orders and sergeants striding among their platoons. Duval saw the multitude of men begin to rise to their feet. Rumors passed through them like a breeze rippling a cornfield, and they were alert and craning to see, suddenly expectant, as if a saint had appeared above the Mordor towers of Seoul City downtown.

Michie gripped his arm and pointed to the sky. "Look, Zinan-san!"

He saw it in magnificent silhouette: a great ornate air-car, low and slender, triple-tailed with tilted-back wings tight to a sweeping, open gondola, the engines stroking her swiftly in a banking turn. She was an *ika,* one of the special ceremonial shuttles built for VIPs who had the rank to bridge the gap between hi-tech and traditional forms. She knifed through the still, calm air above the apron, her sharp snout seeming certain to punch into the ground as she swooped. Then the drumbeats sounded from her gondola and the rhythmic shouts of her Imperial guard rang out as she maneuvered like a scorpion to confront the landing space.

Black *kempei* uniforms glittered inside. Duval remembered the sentences served on his shipmates many years ago when Fukuda had ordered them onto the crosses. He had to stop himself from searching the rows of *kempei* faces for

Fukuda and his fellow interrogators. What if he recognises you? he asked himself with sudden alarm. Then he realised that recognition was impossible: these were not *kempei* at all, but black-toothed bodyguards of the Imperial household.

The drumming beat changed and changed again, and the long shallow craft began to turn with impressive smoothness in her own length and to back, stern-first, into the landing slot.

Her stern was stepped high and pavilioned in red and yellow stripes, and a great brass arc threw its beams onto the embroidered threads of a snow-white ensign emblazoned with a centipede *mon*. It was the family device of Baron Harumi, supreme commander of the Imperial Navy.

Duval caught his breath, his heart pounding now. This was the man in whom the Emperor had vested his total trust. The invasion was his responsibility alone, all matters were in his charge, everything was under his personal control. Duval felt the anguish rise in him unstoppably. Soon he would glimpse the man who had begged to be permitted to destroy Liberty.

An undercarriage was flung down, the craft's weight settled on the runners pneumatically, and a banistered gangway was run out to one side of the scrolled sternpost. To left and right of it an honor guard in five-piece *go-mai* armor and grotesque black helmets assembled, arms clashing, flaming *sashimono* back flags raised high.

Duval was awed by the cold anger that welled up inside him. If I had a knife, I'd kill him, he thought. I'd kill him! *No! That's madness! Think of Michie, of little Kenichi.* But look, an opportunity to do something at last! To burst forward and kill Yamato's greatest warlord! *They would inflict terrible torment on you before you died!* But their shogun would be dead, and all the strategies in his head would be gone forever.

His hatred possessed him as he and Michie were swept up in the rush of men. It was made starker by the waves of respect and awe emanating from the thousand men who now rallied to the baron's arrival. Baron Harumi's standard-bearers came down, upholding his banner, and a line of robed and hatted dignitaries followed them. Then a knot of men appeared in the shuttle's gondola, tall, long-faced, and solemn. A short, solid figure suddenly emerged from among them in a hard black *eboshi* cap. He was sixty years of age, with a white handlebar moustache, and wearing magnificently corded black and red *yoroi* armor. Duval saw that below his fine silk *hitatare* his legs were armored in *suneate* to the knee. From beneath his neck guard a pair of thick cord protectors hung, his *mon* incised on each in crimson. As he advanced, they clattered against the laminae of the baron's breast with a noise like mah-jong tiles being played, emphasising the bulk of the man. His nose was very flat and his face mask-like, deeply lined as if he was in constant pain—not at all the figure Duval had imagined.

As he mounted the head of the gangway, ranked troops punched the air shouting their terse regimental huzzahs in unison and knelt on one knee with bowed heads. He walked down, then paused, nodding his approval of the martial reception, standing no more than five paces from Duval. *Five paces.* He held Michie tightly. A knife, a *sepukku* dagger, any blade at all—a sudden thrust at the jugular and it could have been over in a moment. But he had nothing. Only his bare hands. And then the baron's officers came close about him again, and the moment had passed.

Michie's hand closed tightly on Duval's arm and pulled him down.

She turned, jostling, and turned him also, forcing him to creep slowly away through the press of awe-struck soldiers, and as they broke free of the crowding men, she guided him across the crete roadway and away from the glare of the landing lights. For a moment Duval resisted. He turned her, then he saw the fear in her eyes as she tried to hide her face.

"What is it?" he asked, dumbfounded, after fifty paces. "As your husband I order you to tell me, Michie-san, what's the matter with you?"

"Didn't you see him?" she whispered with astonishing urgency. "Didn't you see who that was?"

"The shogun?"

She shook her head wildly. "No! The one following!"

"Who? Tell me who?"

"*I swear it was Katsumi-san.*"

"*What?*" He stared at her in disbelief, a spasm of panic clutching at his bowels. "Are you certain?"

"It was his armor, and the Hasegawa *mon* was on his breast. I swear by the family gods it was my brother—he looked straight at me."

He glanced involuntarily back towards the baron's party, but was unable to distinguish anyone in the pool of brilliant light. Then he held Michie tight to him and pushed her out at arm's length once more. "Did he see you?"

"I don't know."

"Michie-san! Did he recognise you? Did he? Think!"

"I don't know!"

73

Hasegawa Katsumi looked towards the citadel, following a single pace behind Nishima Jun. His mind was in turmoil, and anger gripped him. The pride of all Yamato had been wounded, and an answer had to be found.

The news from Ise was incredible. The Amerikan corsair, Oujuku, had actually dared to land a pirate rabble on the sacred soil of one of Yamato's outlying Home Worlds. His filth had looted the city of Tsu and desecrated the Jingu shrines. Now he had taken off again and was cruising back towards the Korean Boundary. If only he could know what a force of nexus ships lies waiting for him here, Katsumi thought savagely. The baron will soon turn you into dog meat!

Katsumi followed Nishima Jun dutifully. They had built a traditional battlement on a ridge half a mile high and overlooking the apron, so that the baron could stroll here and look down, God-like, across the entire mass of preparations. It was a practice he was known to enjoy. The climb to the great citadel was long and twisting, as tortuous as the strange path that had brought him here to the brink of this most ambitious of enterprises.

It had begun years ago, in the middle of an airless and sultry night in the daimyo's residence in Kanazawa. Nishima Jun had summoned him late to his private apartment and there he had spoken strangely, with an odd light in his eye, as if testing him, as if about to single him out for some immensely dangerous task. At last, sweating and dressed in nothing but a thin cotton *yukata*, Nishima Jun had delivered the stunning news: "The Emperor's brother is dead."

Prince Sekigahara? Dead? The governor of the two Koreas, dead? Calamity!

Katsumi had pitched onto his knees and bowed respectfully, but he had felt immediately foolish under the daimyo's harsh laugh. "Get up, Katsumi-san, unless you would mourn the death of a syphilitic blackmailer."

He had stared back at his superior, utterly stunned, certain that his ears had deceived him in the thick air.

"I beg your pardon, Excellency?"

"I have placed Prince Sekigahara's death at the head of my prayers every day and every night for ten years, and now at last the gods have seen fit to answer me."

"Excellency?—but I don't understand."

Nishima had turned to his window then, regarding the visible token of his domain with total abhorrence. "Momentous changes are emanating from the Imperial Palace of Chiyoda-Ku, and this wretched, insect-ridden planet is to have a new daimyo."

That had stunned him, but he had thought quickly. "May I conclude that His Imperial Majesty has recognised your magnificent work here in the Co-prosperity Sphere, Excellency?"

He had said it with trembling voice, hoping and praying that this was some kind of reward the Emperor had offered in recognition of the fortification of the main aurium source planet. By all the mansions of heaven, please promise me this is not a mark of the Emperor's displeasure, he had begged the gods silently in the streaming humidity of that Sado night. Grant me that this doesn't mean a posting to Eniwetok. Anything but Eniwetok! I couldn't stand being sent there!

Nishima Jun's deep-set eyes had locked on him, as black and expressionless as pitted olives. The dark stubble of his chin had underlined his weariness, but his voice had cut suddenly formal. "Captain Hasegawa, I ask you now: wherever I am sent, will you follow me as my principal staff officer?"

His hesitation had betrayed him. "Follow you? But *where*, Lord?"

And Nishima Jun's heartless olive eyes had fallen, and his voice had become a whisper. "What a terrible thing it is for a man to be truly alone in this life. My dear Katsumi-san . . . I see that not even you can bring yourself to trust me. If I tell you it's not Kwajalein or Eniwetok, then will you pledge your service to me?"

He had showed eagerness then. "Where? Nishima-sama, please tell me. I would be honored to serve you wherever you were, ah, appointed daimyo."

The strangeness in the daimyo's face had been made clear to him then. It was the face of rapture. *Could it be that the Emperor was to entrust Nishima Jun with Korea?*

"Where?"

"Oh, how I've waited for this, Katsumi-san. I thank the gods of good fortune the assassins took Prince Sekigahara before it was too late."

"Where, Excellency?"

"Ah, I feel magnificent. Magnificent!"

"*Where?*"

Nishima Jun had smiled then, as if answering from within a state of *satori*. "Oh, unless I'm quite mistaken, Katsumi, we're going to Chiyoda-Ku."

"Chiyoda-Ku?"

Of all the *go* stones Nishima Jun might have played, this was the killing play, the most incisive, the most devastating. Chiyoda-Ku was the location of the Imperial Palace on Kyoto, the fulcrum of power. Kyoto was a dream come true.

It had taken a year for the Imperial summons to appear, and the best part of another to hand Sado over to the Emperor's new nominee, but Nishima Jun had reached Kyoto in time to see Free Korea fall and in time to be appointed to the military council specially convened to assist the Emperor in an examination of the ways and means of subjugating that lazy and immoral monolith, Amerika.

Katsumi swelled his plex-plated breast and checked that he was in step with his superior as they mounted higher towards the tower. Apart from the apron, the power of this foreign city to impress him was slight. Proudly he could say that the tatamis of the Imperial Palace itself—the Emperor's own pavilions—had been warmed by his shins. He had worked there for five magnificent years, helping Nishima Jun to advise the Emperor. Five years inside the very heart of the Chrysanthemum.

In truth, the vast palace complex had been no decorative flower. It was like a temple raised up on a massive recurved plinth of shaped stone. A vast, perfect precinct of magnificent traditional buildings, with square white and steel-gray castle keeps at each corner, rising to pagoda roofs. Each wall was pierced by hundreds of tiny, slitted windows that watched all who approached. Within were miles of passages, thousands of rooms stuffed with Imperial treasures, a Confucian monastery, the Imperial mausoleum, and in the inner sanctum, the hermit-like water pavilion where the Emperor lived and worked in earshot of the multicolored human-faced carp that rose up and snapped at flies or lurked in the shadows around the pavilion's pilings. It was said that His Imperial Majesty had sworn to build the immense red-beamed Heian shrine to the memory of

Emperor Hirohito—whose memory he revered and glorified—and that the ancient Emperor's bones were contained in Mutsuhito's personal reliquary. It was said also that he possessed in his most private and sequestered retreat the head of another saint, a skull crowned by an iron tiara, which he consulted over the most important matters of state—the *gaijin* shogun Dugurasu Mukata.

Whatever the truth of it, the counsel the Emperor had taken had led him, in these latter years, to the greatest triumphs mankind had ever known. Year by year His Imperial Majesty had increased his prestige. The two Cho Sen prefectures and all their retinue were taken. Baron Harumi, president of the Council of Government, and Yamato's most able general, had almost completed his reconquest of the rest of the Korean quadrant; his patient diplomacy had set Korean and Korean to tearing at one another's throats once more. Harumi had dissolved the unity of the rebels, and his military skills had begun to push back the last fastnesses of the quadrant. Keun was dead, Seoul recaptured. Yes, the Emperor had chosen Prince Sekigahara's successor well. The laurels had mounted higher and higher. Even Chung Kuo had been humbled. Baron Harumi, the greatest warlord alive, had destroyed their fleet of sixty ships, and Prince Pi Wu had finally been isolated and brought to sign a secret accord with Yamato. One objective remained. One alone. How could they fail now to bring the woman President to her knees? Soon it would be time to mount the assault on the ultimate bastion of impurity, Amerika.

"What are we going to do about Oujuku?" Baron Harumi asked suddenly. He stopped, and his officers stopped also.

"The latest reports are that he's coming this way, Harumi-sama," Nishima Jun said.

"Yes, I know. I asked what we should do about him."

"When did he depart, Captain Hasegawa?"

"Two days ago, Excellency," Katsumi supplied respectfully. "He's heading along the chain of Hoganji, towards the nexus the Amerikans call Yod-Two-Two."

Baron Harumi grunted. "Of course he's heading along Hoganji."

"Oh, but that's bad psi. Very bad!" Nishima Jun said. "We must take steps."

"Steps!" Baron Harumi snorted, and resumed his climb towards the donjon.

The news had been consistently bad for weeks, Katsumi reflected, disliking Baron Harumi's manners greatly. Pirate Oujuku's fleet had appeared in force, swooping in at minus eighty gee from one of the most vicious nexi known, in the Ryukyu Worlds along the Yamato-Korea Boundary at Zero Degrees. He had such incredible good fortune: the terrifying nexus in the Nansei system that normally spat ships out with vast kinetic energy had given no ship of his fleet more than a half cee. He had injected into Nansei orbit in what must have been record time. There, with diabolical perfidy, he had demanded all the aurium on the planet from the local daimyo while setting his nexus ships to prey on defenseless interplanetary craft. Then, when he had got what he wanted, he had dropped all pretenses and allowed his pirate bands to ransack the entire capital city, doing three hundred million credits' worth of damage, stripping and desecrating the Kinkaku Temple and breaking venal slaves out of their *han* all over the continent.

"How does this despicable pirate imagine he can get away with it?" Kinoshita Heisuke, one of Baron Harumi's most experienced warriors, asked.

"Because he's got a fast fleet and exceptional psi and two thousand crew aboard, and because he knows we can't move our own troops fast enough to catch him," Baron Harumi said, adding drily, "He's not brave or foolish enough to attempt a pitched battle against a samurai army, and quite right."

"Perhaps we should put some effort into catching him and punishing his insolence," Nishima Jun suggested.

"I can't agree!" Aoki Zengo, tall and thin, Baron Harumi's elderly second-in-command, waved him to silence. "That's just what the Black Dragon wants. To draw us out of the Seoul chain, unprepared and with our swords only half drawn, so he can eat us up! The Black Dragon is—"

"Ei! I'm tired of hearing that nickname!" Baron Harumi growled, stopping and turning. He was short of breath from the climb, and equally short of temper. Here the stepped way opened out into a punishment area where several gibbets had been erected. An assortment of chained samurai prisoners awaited flogging for insubordination or execution for dereliction of duty. Their jailor barked an order and they got down on their knees and pushed their faces hard into the dust as the party approached.

"Get up off the ground!" Baron Harumi shouted. They struggled to obey. "Until your topknots are cut off you're still samurai, not animals! Remember that!" he said, and marched on.

"I agree with Nishima-sama," another general said, hardly noticing the line of wretches. "We should confront the Amerikan. Show him he can't insult us. I long for the day when I shall see his head set on one of our spikes."

Aoki shrugged his bony shoulders. "But why interrupt our preparations just to oblige him? Why else is he heading for the Seoul system if not to tempt us out?"

Baron Harumi's low growl cut across the argument. "He's not heading here."

"*Gomen nasai, wakarimasen, Harumi-sama!* I don't understand, Lord! Not heading here?"

"Seoul's impregnable. With our new heavy beam weapon batteries and orbital defenses he'll never get in, and he knows it. He's cruising this way because he wants the *kin kaigun.*"

No one but Baron Harumi had dared voice that possibility.

"Obviously he'll try for the *kin kaigun*. Oujuku's no fool—and it's what I'd do in his place. He certainly has strength enough for an interception. That's why I've already taken steps, Nishima-san." Baron Harumi braced his back, his eyes flickering now over his subordinates, clearly enjoying this demonstration of his strategic prowess. "Think about this: imagine what would happen to our preparations here if Oujuku were to succeed. His Imperial Majesty's tied down with loans that all hang on the arrival of the aurium in Kyoto. Without it we'd all be as bankrupt as *sangokujin* beggars."

"Then he could halt our endeavor whether we leave Scoul or not?" Minami Yoriyasu said, appalled.

Baron Harumi resumed his climb. Behind the party the flogging was taken up again.

"Cheer yourself, Minami-san. We cannot ignore any possibility, but Admiral Kurita and Admiral Kofuji are both experienced men. Both know what they're doing, and they have explicit orders to keep to as difficult a course as the Index will allow. I have faith they'll make the Home Worlds unmolested, but I'll say this: it's a mistake to underestimate Oujuku and his like."

As they came to the doors of the pavilion, Katsumi tried to digest what he had heard. He was greatly disturbed at the way Yamato's foremost generalissimo was prepared to accord a filthy corsair such respect. Though his blood was indisputably linked to the Imperial line, Baron Harumi sometimes exhibited the bluntness of a peasant and the manners of the gutter. Such a pity that Nishima Jun was not appointed commander in chief, he thought. But perhaps I have only myself to blame? Myself and Michie-san. Nishima Jun still blames me for allowing my sister to spirit the Amerikan out of his grasp. And I was a fool to think she could be trusted. Yes, such a pity. Katsumi rued it for the thousandth time. Especially now, when the Emperor is preoccupied with the success of his invasion fleet. The Amerikan weapons are a lost secret that might have made Nishima Jun shogun.

"Go indoors and play, Kenichi."

"But, Father, I only wanted you to mend my kite—"

"I said, go indoors!"

Duval felt the warmth of Seoul's primary star on his back, but inside he was as cold as ice. He watched his son leave him, and his stomach tightened. Above him a dozen or so plump pigeons, puffed up and strutting, displayed on the conical green-tiled roof of the dovecote. Overhead, the sky was a deep and featureless purple. He watched Choi search it once more, unable to rid himself of the bottomless fear that had opened up inside him.

An hour ago, he had told Choi of his suspicions regarding Katsumi. He knew the merchant well enough to understand that they had come out to the yard for a definite purpose. As yet, however, Choi had made no explanation, and his unhurried manner was grating on Duval's nerves.

Choi held the bird expertly in his hand, its red claws clamped between his fingers, the light fully iridescent on its neck feathers as he stroked it.

"There, my little chick. Isn't she beautiful, Duval?"

Duval was distracted with worry, his voice barely controlled. "How can you remain so calm when they're closing in on us?"

Choi's face creased with a secret satisfaction. "Maybe they are, and maybe they're not. But I'm prepared to bet that they're not as clever as these pretty little birds, my friend."

Duval looked up at the familiar high walls of Choi's house. The walls of a fort or a prison, they seemed to him now. He had brought Michie and Kenichi here, seeking refuge, and for a week they had lain low, praying for Choi's speedy return. All that time he had slept hardly two hours together, worry stretching his nerves tauter and tauter until his head ached and his hands shook.

He had sent a message to the office that he would be away on business, and for his assistants to take over. They were capable men. Trustworthy Korean academics. They could easily be left to work on the contracts, but what if they had been visited? What if there was already a search being conducted throughout Seoul City for them?

A maid slipped quietly from the kitchen door and cut across the yard, carrying a big woven basket of laundry. Duval felt the old anxious dread eat at him, dread in case Kenichi stole away to fly his kite, dread that their clothes were recognised by a passerby, dread that there would be a knock at Choi's door.

None of the servants in the Choi household were party to their master's secrets, none knew of his past identity, and none were aware that the master's friend was in hiding. Choi's wife had said it was the only way. The nature of his business life was very open and the house was frequently visited, so they could not hope to stay here in secret very long. Duval thought of Michie and the boy and felt a punishment collar tighten around his throat.

"Do people keep birds as pets in Amerika?"

He tried to rouse himself to Choi's words. "I'm sorry, what did you say?"

Choi repeated his question. "Pigeons. In Amerika. Do you know if they're kept?"

Choi's calm inconsequentialities maddened him and he shrugged. "I—think so; people like pet birds. But they prefer small, singing birds like canaries."

"For no other reason than decoration and singing?"

Duval sought Choi's eye. "I suppose not. Some people race pigeons for a hobby—and there's pigeon pie." He broke off suddenly. Today, finally, Choi had returned to Seoul City with the incredible news of John Oujuku's attack on Tsu and Nansei, and yet here they were talking about *pigeons!* "Listen, Ki Won, do you think there'll be an attack here too? A landing?"

"On Seoul?"

Duval nodded.

"I fear for my adopted home world," Choi said. He set the bird down on a plex ledge mortared into the wall of the dovecote and shielded his eyes, scanning the skies once more. "The whole of Yamato has been sunk in mortal dread of John Oujuku. He's teaching them a lesson they don't like. But no, I don't fear for Seoul because of any attack John Oujuku might launch. The place is being ruined without him. I don't know how much longer it can go on."

"Until the baron is ready to leave."

"May the gods grant that that's soon." Choi reached into a sack and broadcast a handful of corn over the yard, bringing a dozen more pigeons down. "Oh, my poor Seoul! In all quarters trade is booming but it's sick trade. Unreal commerce. The influx of so many offworlders is draining the whole place dry. Food, technical equipment—everything. Demand for commodities of all kinds has outstripped our capacity to supply it. Prices are rising every day, doubling and trebling. The poor are going hungry. It's no trouble to Yamato. More meat for their slaving gangs."

Duval shook his head. "No, they already have more men standing idle than they can use or occupy. It's an impossible job keeping their army all fed and processed into the freezees. Trouble is setting in. Desertions have begun. They've started confining whole crews and entire companies of nonsamurai troops aboard their ships. The whole fleet's like a time bomb. *They'll have to lift off soon.*"

Choi knelt among the birds that had fluttered down around them and picked one up. "The invasion fleet is too big. It will never be ready to lift off."

"Is that what you're telling them in Amerika?"

"That's just my opinion. In my reports I confine myself to the facts."

Duval watched Choi's face closely; he saw anxiety there, buried and suppressed, but it was massive. And there was surely an inconsistency too in what Choi had said.

"Ki Won, where did you go to last week?" he asked.

"I told you. To see my brother on Wonsan."

"That can't be."

Choi flashed a glance at him. "It's the truth. I have a contact there."

"Then how can you know so much about Yamato when it's in the other direction?"

Choi gestured towards the birds. "They're the reason I went to Wonsan. And also the reason I can know so much about what happens in Seoul. The authorities try to keep people under control by designating low-tech zones. Sometimes it backfires. Like this."

Duval was mystified. "Pigeons?"

"Yes, pigeons."

"But—I don't understand."

"They have a wonderful instinct to return to their home. It doesn't matter where you want them to go, so long as the apron's not more than a couple of hundred miles from their home. It's something discovered by the ancients and long forgotten."

"But how—"

Choi turned the pigeon over and began to unscrew its leg. He carefully removed the false claw. "Pigeons are by far the best messengers on an occupied world, better than one of Yamato's comms ships. Very, very secret. I ship them to other worlds, labeled as breeding stock, and my contacts there ship them straight back again. If you release them from the cargo bay of a newly landed nexus ship, they will circle once, twice, then away they go to the place where they first broke from the egg. No entry controls on them. No searches. No communication signals, however weak or scrambled or coded, to be intercepted. They would never be guessed at!"

"That's incredible!"

Choi nodded smugly. "Oh, yes, incredible. But true. And very useful. Of course they don't fly at night and they're brought down by rain, and sometimes by hawks, but even so . . . There's a network of watchers across the entire quadrant. I cannot tell you their names or which worlds they live on, but I'm their paymaster, and whenever anything happens it's relayed to me by sending a consignment of my own pigeons to Seoul apron. That's how I heard about the arrival of the *Kawabata Yasunari* before the authorities did. Old Tian contacted me from the low-tech zone and I got a head start. It's also how I know about John Oujuku."

Duval was amazed. "Who will you report the success at Nansei to?"

"An Amerikan. In Japanese, they pronounce his name Josu Oken." Choi fell silent, then he said, "Perhaps it's time I told you. Almost twenty years ago, when I first came to Korea, I lived on Cheju Do. I began working at the shipping terminal. There I made the mistake of giving succor to an Amerikan ship. She was trying to find her way back from the Zone, and I didn't know she had been in battle against Yamato ships. Like the *Kawabata Yasunari* I found her insides had been heavily damaged and she was full of starvation and I offered my help as any man would."

"What ship was she?" Duval asked, a nameless unease stirring inside him again. The astonishing workings of psi and the acausal principle had meshed!

"Her name was *Richard M. Nixon*. And her owner was Jos Hawken."

"*Hawken?*" Duval cried, numbed with shock. He stared at Choi sightlessly. The years fell away, and his mind swam back almost two decades to the apron at Sado and the way he had fought to hoist his brother's blood-sodden body aboard the *Richard M*.

"I remember he was in a high fever," Choi was saying. "Most of his crew had died. They were in a terrible condition and needed help, and so I helped. I arranged for water and food to be brought, and I alerted another Amerikan ship in the port. But then the authorities discovered what I had done. They accused me of breaking apron rules, and I was arrested and routinely genotyped. When they discovered I was racial Japanese, they made me leave." He gently cast the pigeon up so that it clattered free into the air. "Afterwards I escaped to Seoul. I made contact with Hawken again through Amerikan shippers in the Days of Freedom and he sent credit to me. All this"—Choi waved a hand towards his house—"comes from him. In exchange for information."

"Jos Hawken," Duval said again, his voice breathy with shock. "But I went with his expedition to the Zone."

Choi smiled infinitely sadly. "I know. And I also know that your real name is Duval Straker and that your brother is Ellis Straker, the famous privateer. Two years after you came to me, when it became clear Yamato would destroy Free Korea, I sent a message to Hawken about you. He said I should persuade you to go aboard an Amerikan ship, but you would not go."

"You should have told me about Hawken."

Choi spread his hands. "How could I? I didn't dare expose him as my contact. He's twisted himself in many double deals with Yamato on your vice-president's behalf. Yamato is convinced he's working for them, so much so that the Emperor has awarded him a secret dispensation for after the invasion. I couldn't risk it. If you had been taken and Probed so that you revealed him, his plans would collapse and even in Amerika he would be in danger of arrest for treason."

Duval felt an intense blade of fear slash at him as Choi's words echoed over and again in his mind: "if you were to be taken by the *kempei* and Probed . . ." Suddenly he was back inside his deepest terror, vividly, seeing the snouts of the Probe ripping into his mind and the crosses of the crucifixion grounds, and he knew that he could not face that a second time. It was not the fear of death, but the fear of mental pain. Terrible agony, piously justified, repeatedly applied, deliberately inflicted, to his mind and to the minds of his wife and son. He felt the punishment collar tighten on him further, choking him, and the panic began to rise up inside him more intensely than he had ever known. The sweat on his face turned icy. *How can I get out?* his brain screamed. *What can I do?* But no answer came, and he saw that he was trapped beyond hope, and falling, and falling . . .

Then Choi was shaking him, looking in his eyes with fatherly understanding. "What is it? Tell me."

"The Probe," he babbled. "I was dying. My legs—their strength was gone. The Void opened under me and I was falling. You must help get Michie and my boy away from here . . ."

"Calm yourself. I know what it's like. I know what you're feeling exactly. Please believe that. But we *must* be strong. We must go on, no matter what."

Shame crashed over him like an ocean wave, humbling him as he realised that Choi must be seeing him as a craven coward. "It's not that, Ki Won," he said shakily. "It's not cowardice. I promise you. I saw the future clearly. I *saw* it, I tell you."

"Of course. Of course. After the Probe a man's mind sometimes plays tricks on him."

Choi helped him inside. Maids and kitchen servants gathered, concerned to see his pale face and his distress. He sank down onto a stool, swaying.

"Give him some air!"

"Fetch water!"

"Is it an offworld fever?" a young maid asked, round-eyed.

"It's nothing at all, now," Choi told them, clapping his hands sharply. "Quickly, now! About your tasks, before I send for the mistress!"

He helped Duval into his private business room, the windowless place where he kept accounts and locked away his profits. It was cool and quiet and smelled of incense and candle grease.

As soon as they were alone, Choi brought out his microscope and opened the tiny capsule he had knocked from the hollow in the pigeon's claw. He found a minute sliver of plex, placing it delicately on the stage of the machine. He read it, then touched it into a phial of solvent and shook it until its message was completely consumed.

"Where was it from?" Duval asked, feeling the warmth returning to his limbs. He wiped his forehead and looked at his fingers. They were trembling.

"The Yamato Boundary. Bad news, I'm afraid."

"What did it say?"

Choi tried to put it aside, but Duval pressed him. The blow had been a hard one. "This year's *kin kaigun* has reached the Home Worlds in safety. John Oujuku has failed to intercept it."

Later, they sat together on the balcony that overlooked the city, trying desperately to fathom a solution. Duval felt a clarity of mind he had not known for weeks. The blackout had settled him like a psi-storm settles a nexus. In its passing the black fear that had engulfed him paled and ebbed, and in its ghastly currents he had seen the way. He knew now what he must do, and the decision was all that remained.

"What did you mean about Michie earlier?" Choi asked him quietly.

Duval shifted himself, leaning his elbows on the broad sill. The night was silent and windless. "Is it possible for you to get her to Amerika?"

"To Amerika? Why?"

"Is it *possible,* Ki Won?"

Choi shrugged. "Perhaps. I don't know. But tell me why."

"I know I'm trapped," Duval said, not knowing how else to put it. "I know I'm a dead man, and I feel relieved. I've made a decision."

"Have patience, my friend." Choi's face was that of a Zen teacher. He touched the streaks of his moustache, the whites of his eyes glistening, the stars, like a halo around his high forehead, shimmering. "It's hard to bear, I know, but nothing worthwhile is ever easy. There is a reward: there's the knowledge that you're helping to oppose a great evil. Dwell upon that and—"

"No!" he hissed, his mind absolutely made up. "Listen to me. A week ago, on the apron I saw refrigerated container loads of argentium in stockpile, and a voice inside me spoke: 'Destroy it! Do it now! Destabilise it! You can strike openly! Here's your chance for real thunder and lightning!' Do you see what I'm trying to say, Choi Ki Won?"

Choi shrugged helplessly. "But that's ludicrous. They'd replace it inside a week, and you'd have achieved nothing."

"Exactly!" Duval stepped across the balcony, his fists clenching, his voice rising. "But you don't understand. Your way there's never any tangible result. I watch and I watch and the invasion fleet grows and grows. Unstoppably. Swallowing up everything on the planet like a great mouth. I'm full of rage and I must act. But I'm just one man. I'm impotent. And I know there's nothing I can do that'll have the slightest effect on the invasion. Nothing. Nothing at all—*except one thing.*"

"What's that? To make a big fireworks show?" Choi said, trying to keep his words soft despite his dismay at the eerie change that had overtaken his friend.

"No. Not fireworks. That's just how I began to see what I must do. The same night I happened to see the baron arrive. Baron Harumi himself! He stepped down onto Seoul amid a thousand troops. He was as far from me as you are now. And I knew that if I'd had a knife I would have used it. I would have plunged it into him, Choi Ki Won. Do you see now?"

Choi looked at him, aghast. "You can't be thinking that. Oh, no! That's madness!"

"I could have killed him a week ago."

"But it was just sheerest chance that his shuttle landed beside you. And you said yourself he had a thousand fanatics around him. May the gods bring you to your senses, he's inside a high-security fortress. *High security*. You can't get in there."

"I know how I can get inside."

"But even if you did, you'd never get near him. He's guarded everywhere he goes. It would be suicide!"

"I'm a dead man already."

"But you're *not* dead!"

"So sorry, Choi Ki Won, I've seen the future and I know what I must do."

75

LIBERTY

The Potomac's muscular waters were restless under an equally troubled gray sky.

"The river's up higher than I've ever seen it, Ellis," Hawken said. They stood five paces apart in a narrow sloping street that ran down to the bank, Ellis loathing him utterly. "The rain god's in a mighty rage today, wouldn't you say?"

He faced Hawken as a man might face his mortal enemy, having no stomach for small talk. Hawken had twice asked for this meeting, and he had twice turned him down, believing that nothing Hawken said could possibly assuage the despicable crimes he had committed, nothing he did would restore the respect Ellis had once had for him.

"It's just a wet month and the spring tide."

"No, it's a rage," Hawken insisted, his eyes hard on Ellis. "I can smell it in the air. Can't you?"

"The only smell hereabouts is the stink of treason."

He had agreed to meet after Hawken's third time of asking, but only after Reba had whispered that he must. But he had not gone alone. Dressed down like a stevie, wearing his thick belt and a cap set back on his head, he had a Wesson sitting on his hip, but even so, the first sight of Hawken had raked up a mix of powerful resentments that put him immediately on guard.

"Say what you have to say," he told Hawken abruptly, planting his feet. "And we'll have done."

"Not here on a street corner, Ellis. I've plenty to say to you, all of it personal."

"This is as anonymous a place as any."

"Criminals seek anonymity. I want security. I have words that can only be said in confidence. I'll only speak them aboard the *Chesapeake*."

Alarms rang in him. "Oh, no."

"It would benefit you. And I'll not speak freely except aboard my ship."

"I'd be a fool to follow you there."

"Why do you think that?" Hawken's smile showed narrowly. "What're you afraid of? That I'll murder you? Has your trust fallen that far? In any case, I can see that Wesson on your belt's no ornament."

Ellis put his fingers to his lips and blew a shrill blast. Hawken stepped back suspiciously, his hand straying inside his jacket. "What's this?" he demanded.

"Who should talk about trust now?"

Instantly two men appeared from nowhere and ran to present themselves to Ellis. He turned his back on Hawken and whispered to the taller, then dismissed them.

"Who are they? What did you say to them?"

"They're my insurance. I told them that if I'm not on the Memorial steps by seven o'clock, they're to complete the contract on you. Now, where's your air-car?"

"I have no air-car here."

Ellis knew his surprise at that must have showed. He remembered pretty well the incident years ago when Hawken had been viciously gunned down by one of his enemies whilst riding in a ground-car along Pennsylvania. The attack had been in broad daylight, in Lincoln's widest, most prestigious thoroughfare, and Hawken had almost died of his wounds. Since then he had maintained discreet precautions at every level. To trust himself alone in an air-car with an armed man who was now all but sworn against him was almost unthinkable.

"You've no transport here?"

"How can I expect your trust if I don't show that I trust you?"

"*Trust?*" Ellis's laugh was short and bitter. "Your stocks are bankrupt there, Hawken."

Hawken turned away, tight-faced. "I'll call a cab. Unless you want to."

Perhaps it is a trap, Ellis thought, but some of the tension fell from him as the skinny young driver who had won the haggle steered them away from the waterfront.

"Norfolk apron."

"Yessir!"

All the while the lad chattered at them in high spirits, spinning a tale and offering fifty services for sale, until Hawken told him roughly to hold his tongue.

No, the lad's no killer, Ellis thought, nor in anyone's pay but his own. And Hawken seems to want me aboard *Chesapeake* badly. If it's not a plan to detain me or kill me, what is it? What can he be wanting to say? He faced his old employer warily as they pushed out from the cluster of small craft waiting beside the tall, round-towered, weather-stained building known as North's Tomb. The tide of vehicles was now reaching its peak, taking the air routes out of town and blackening the sky with rush-hour shadows. Watch Jos Hawken, he's as slippery as a sumo wrestler, still massively involved in intrigues, deeply scheming on all fronts. He's slid out of the belt hold that Cassabian threatened to hoist him with well before Conroy Lubbock's thirty days expired. And it was done with such smooth grace and skill that a man just has to respect it—but not necessarily admire it.

Of course, it's Conroy Lubbock who's protecting you, he said silently as he watched Hawken's eyes scanning the shore. He's paid off Oujuku and Cassabian handsomely to maintain you. A miraculous pretext arises for privateering, one that in less crucial times would have been quietly suppressed in the corridors of the White House, but which instead you made sound important. A carrot to dangle in front of John. Yes, a chance of going into Yamato again: the only credit that could have bought John Oujuku for you, and you knew that, didn't you? And Conroy Lubbock's style of management is written all over it: the inconsequential arrest of some small Amerikan nexus ships that tried heading into the Earth Exclusion Zone and were stopped. Suddenly it's mushrooming into a patriotic cause. How? Like this: credit spent; the word put about; the broadcasters getting out lurid programming and tri-vee catalogs of Yamato atrocities; public opinion lit up and the flames of indignation fanned; then plex-hard political pundits demanding retribution—that's how Oujuku had got his mission.

Yes, Ellis reflected sourly. Oujuku had dutifully lit out to punish Yamato and then off to the Zone with a fleet of twenty ships to give the Remnant hell and havoc as he really wanted.

Cassabian also had fallen silent. Some deal had been struck there, but it had been too deep and too secret in all its convolutions for even Reba to have fathomed it out. The most obvious bribe was that Cassabian's stepson, Carlyle Balaban, had been given a Navy commission and made Oujuku's second-in-command in the Sado operation, but there were other ingredients that were as yet hardly rumors.

So Oujuku got out of the Sector and Cassabian appeased; it was obvious that Ellis too must have his price. Paid off. Bought off. Put off. But they'll never buy me like that. The moment Hawken suggests it I'll burn his guts out.

"Was this meeting Conroy Lubbock's idea?"

Hawken shook his head. "No."

"I don't believe that."

"I'd like to shake the pride out of you, Ellis," Hawken said in the tones of a man who firmly occupied the moral ground. "I'd do that for the VP willingly. I'd have done it years ago, but he would not permit me."

Ellis watched Lincoln slide by below slowly as traffic piled up in the lanes. Air-cars impatiently breaking from the designated zones suffered a mandatory tractoring. At Borobridge the quays with their barges and heavy lifting waldos were shaded by the skyway blizzard. Behind, the soaring, spireless towers of the financial district, a buttressed stump dominating an endless clutter of buildings that tumbled down to the waterfront: Squad Central. Ahead a hundred traffic tractor towers held up the sky above the mass of the city: St. Martin's, Walbrook, Burlington, the spire of the Hill. On the south bank the Palace of Pleasures and Paris Garden and the riverside walk where lovers came to stroll, and the oval arenas for open-air *tai chi*—all were congested with traffic.

"You gotta pay the toll," the cabman reminded Hawken.

Hawken nodded his assent. "Let's see you ride this thing, boy."

"Wanna get there fast, huh?"

"Correct."

"Okeh—if you want the backways."

Ellis settled himself against the seat, his hands unconsciously poised to grip his blaster as they spun down out of the lane. A sharp fetid riverine tang lay on the wind that streamed past the polycarb dome, and the sound of rushing air from the fins. Up ahead Ben Thompson Market spanned the river, plex and very modern, with buildings precariously erected on twenty narrow arches seeming about to topple into either Faneuil Park or the Potomac. It had been a very wet week and the ebb was at its height; the great boat-shaped piers on which the Market stood forced the river into a series of narrow gorges on this side, and the press of water churned and foamed in each tunnel-like gap.

Ellis felt the tractor grip the youthful cabman's vehicle as he steered the nose of his cab for the nearest span. Clearly he lacked experience and did not want to risk his livelihood shooting the narrow channels at full ebb, but he had got the fare against stiff competition only by agreeing to take them direct to Philadelphia apron and the *Chesapeake*. The only way to do it was to somehow break the inexorable grip of the tractor before it spiraled them down to a waiting traffic violation drone.

As the Market loomed up he aligned the cab as best he could in spite of his fears. The river was up too high. There was no clearance. It was insanity! Ellis felt the suction leave them abruptly and the cab spurted suddenly forward. Where the sharp piers cut into the river, swirling vortices of churning brown water were shed, roaring water breaking up and echoing under the arches. Then everything went black and it was as if the bottom of the cab had fallen out. The front end pitched down and a gout of water sluiced up over the dome and through the window and over Hawken's knees. Then the roar was behind them and they were out in the light again and only the marbling foam of water beneath the cab spoke of the danger they had faced.

The cabbie piled on the power; the tractor had been broken and the run to Norfolk took them just five minutes. He looked at the *Chesapeake* visible now up ahead on the Norfolk apron and, as he turned, his sharp-featured face was smiling.

"Wanna stop off at a rest room and clean up?"

Hawken grimaced at him, his best cut of clothes drenched. "That ain't funny, boy! But you won't be laughing soon. You've lost your fare!"

Ellis cut him. "C'mon! Leave him be. It was you told him to ride out of the traffic lane."

"Yeah, and he took the job on! Asshole."

The youngster's eyes slitted and his mouth set. "You'll pay me in full, or you'll walk from here, even if it is three hundred feet up."

"You young runt! I'll knock your teeth out!"

"You wanna try it?"

The lad coiled like wire in his seat ready to spring should Hawken try for his neck. In the lad's hand an ugly stunner had appeared. For a moment, Ellis considered pulling his blaster, but decided against it. Instead he asked mildly and with raised eyebrows, "Do you know that you're threatening a real famous nexus captain? One that's cruised into the Zone and back more times than you've eaten burgerettes?"

The youth was plainly unimpressed. He remained bunched up against the door. "It's him that's threatening *me*. And I don't give a sack of shit who he is. This is Amerika, not Yamato. I'll tell you something, my name's Jimi Derby, cab guildsman, and I'm the captain of *this* ship, so what I say goes, else I'll land and whistle up a few of my good buddies to you."

Hawken continued to look darkly at him, but Ellis grinned and held out a credit smart forward. "Here's your fare, fellah. C'mon, take it."

The young cabman made no move. "Jeezus, that's authorised for ten thousand. You real?"

"Take a credit tip—for your spirit. You shot that hole like an astrogator."

Hesitantly the cabman reached back, his stunner still gripped in his left hand and a feral light in his eye as he tried to see the trick. Then he quickly took the smart and striped it through his slot, watching both his passengers mistrustfully as he recovered his seat and steered them past Sears and the Reformed Synagogue and the half-built Murdoch Tri-Vee headquarters.

"Thank you, sir," he said grudgingly a moment later. "And anyway, how do you know I ain't a psi-talent?"

Ellis winked at him. "You might say I was in the business, once over. Next time, take the widest span and relax your mind from the stomach."

"Relax my mind from the stomach? What the hell you mean?"

"Here, see, from the diaphragm. Loosen up. And take this card to the address marked on the back, if you want to develop your psi. I'll tell you now, it's dormant there."

The lad looked at the card and his eyes lit. "Hey, thanks, Captain Straker."

The *Chesapeake* was set down on the very end of the apron, beyond Wright Terminal. Ellis went aboard her after Hawken, admiring the sleek lines of the ship despite himself. The caretaker crew seemed orderly and well disciplined. Their first officer welcomed Hawken with due dignity and answered the owner's questions promptly until he was dismissed. Then they went aft to the captain's cabin, Ellis expecting some surprise every step of the way but there was none.

"Will you share a bottle of mash with me?"

"I wouldn't crack a bottle with you if it was the last bottle in Known Space."

"Ellis, Ellis. Sometimes you're a difficult man to deal with."

"We're on your vessel. I'm ready to hear you. Say what you want to say quickly. Then I'll be away before your corruption makes me spew."

Hawken drew himself up then. "You've got me wrong, Ellis. And I hate to see a man whispering behind my back."

"You're a swindler and a thief, Jos Hawken. Yeah, and a traitor. How's it sound to your face?"

Hawken showed no anger at the insult. He dashed amber liquid into two small ceramic *choko* and set them down, pushed one towards Ellis, and lifted the other.

"Ellis, you're a stiff-necked bastard. And blind. But unless you're stupid too, you'll listen to me. There have been developments since you took your slanders to Conroy Lubbock's office." He held up his hand and ticked off the fingers. "Firstly, John Oujuku raids Yamato and the Zone. Secondly, Ramakrishnan has made a breakthrough regarding the Beyond. Thirdly, Bernardo Spitz destroys five Yamato ships on an apron in the Zone. Fourthly, your crazy pal Kim sets up a base at Marshall IV from which to harry the Remnant. Fifthly, your improvements go to the Navy Council for consideration. Sixthly, there's a plan up before the President to send ships to intercept the Yamato aurium fleet before it reaches Yamato. Now, do you think all that's coincidence?"

Ellis's stare was as heavy as lead. Everything Hawken had said was true but irrelevant. "Have you finished?" he said levelly.

Hawken's anger exploded. "No! I have not finished! It's Conroy Lubbock's work, Ellis. All of it. Everything's happening with Conroy Lubbock's knowledge and consent. Jeezus! You're not the sole prophet of Yamato's intentions, you know."

"I never said—"

Hawken cut him down. "You have embarrassed me, Ellis! You've *accused* me unjustly! And when I could make no public denial. Had it not been for Conroy Lubbock's patient handiwork, I might have been shot by a Daughter of Freedom, or arraigned for—" Hawken pressed his thin lips together, stemming the outburst. His face was pale with anger, but still he seemed able to find the resources to control himself as he stood up and paced. "I'm a broad-minded man, Ellis, and I can understand why you did what you did, but I'll never forgive you for swallowing John Oujuku's allegations whole and setting yourself so hard against me. Couldn't you see that most of this has come from Kastner and Belkov and the Lucia Henry people? I *made* you, Ellis. I grew you from a seed! And yet you turned on me. I credited you with more intelligence. Yeah, and more loyalty."

"Loyalty?" Ellis struck back angrily. He knew that the expense of keeping nexus-going warships in commission was great, and although the Navy was controlled by Hawken as joint chief, the posts of surveyor of ships, surveyor of weapons systems, officer of supply, and clerk of ships were all occupied by his main political enemy, a man whom Hawken had himself accused of obtaining a vast income from corrupt practices. Now he was trying to shift blame to Nikolai Belkov again.

"It won't work. John Oujuku brought me evidence. Written evidence. What should I have done? Ignored it because you were once my employer? No, Jos Hawken. You got the wrong man here. I won't put any one individual before Amerika."

"Oujuku is a great astrogator, greater than I ever was. He's full of courage and he's an admirably honest man, but more than that, he's a hothead. He always has been. All fire and fury. And because his honesty is so complete he has no skill whatsoever at secret maneuverings. He doesn't understand them. But you, Ellis—you should have seen through all of that chickenshit."

The scorn in Ellis's voice was bitter. "You're not fit to stand on the same planet as John Oujuku, you fucking snake!"

"*Don't you understand?*" Hawken's face was contorted as he struggled to change Ellis's mind. "My God, and after all I've taught you. It was *me* who showed you how to give a juicy rumor to a young cadet and see where it ended up *so's to test him*. Are you forgetting that? This rumor went to John and then to you. And although Conroy Lubbock warned you, you wouldn't leave it alone. Like a goddamned *T. rex* at an illegal circus, the pair of you! Jaws snapping. Slavering for blood. And Cassabian whipcracking like a meddling ringmaster . . ." Hawken's hooded eyes dropped, then fixed on him like shards of sapphire. "When I first took to running the Navy's affairs, they were in a pretty fine state of disarray. In the first deal I struck with the President I promised to clear out the corruption and end the decline that had dragged Amerika's defenses so low. And so I did! But I made enemies, Ellis, enemies of the self-same men whose bubble I'd burst, and as soon as they could they came back at me, saying that I'd framed them and defamed them and abolished their posts expressly to benefit myself. I had to have those parasites out."

Ellis shook his head slowly, mockingly. "So it was lies, then? All those accusations and suits served against you by half the administration?"

"Yes, lies! Secret, premeditated opposition. A campaign against me. Deliberate. Willful. They wanted to tear me down! Nikolai Belkov wanted to push me out. Lucia Henry wanted to see me thrown off Liberty. Do you see, Ellis? Do you see now?"

"And that's the truth?"

"I swear."

Ellis's face remained immobile. His eyes met Hawken's own, staring him down. "You're a goddamned liar. When you first got hold of the Navy's affairs as a joint chief, in 'thirty-two, Amerika's Navy had two hundred and twenty nexus cruisers. Now, after six years of your misrule, we've got two hundred and thirty. Do you call that preparation for war? I saw signed orders. Requisitions that had come from your office. Hardcopy transferring the Sector's aurium and argentium stocks and the Sector's dockyards and the Sector's credit to your corporate business cronies as 'surplus to requirements.' Government facilities hived off to become yards to build merchant ships for your own profit! Yes, you sonofabitch, ships like this one! To line your own pockets and to sell out to Baron-goddamned-Harumi the moment his samurai come pouring out of the Kalifornia nexus."

Hawken's fist pounded out his words. "What you saw was false accounting."

Ellis stood up, suddenly enraged by Hawken's barefacedness. His seat scraped back across the luxury flooring with an ugly sound. "*False accounting?* Do you think I don't know a scam when I see one? Can you really take me for so complete a fool?"

"There were hundreds of requisitions! I dreamed them up! I wrote them all! Every last one!"

"Then you *admit* it! You sonofabitch!"

"No!" Hawken stood up also. He too was angry and stabbing with his finger, Ellis's muscular bulk totally disregarded. "I admit nothing. You're so goddamned quick to accuse, ain't ya? You're so goddamned sure of yourself. Well, let me tell you this, Mister-fucking-Clean, you don't know the first thing about politics on Liberty. You're as blind as a newborn babe. And John Oujuku, who collected the evidence against me so patiently, he's blind too. Together you were the danger! Unwitting—yes! From the highest motives—surely! But you were more dangerous to Amerika's Navy than any Yamato flotilla." Hawken broke away, leaned heavily on the psi-screen console. "Of course, war is coming. I've known that since the day we dined with that rat, Iwakura, back on Sado, and you saved my skin by your action. Oh, I haven't forgotten that: I remember it when I chose to sell you *Constitution;* I remembered it again when you were locked up at Camp Worth and I walked the White House corridors, wondering how I could get you out; and I remembered it again when I argued on your behalf before the President that she ought to maneuver Kurt Reiner into selling Xanadu mansion to you."

"*You did that?*" Ellis hissed, astonished at the discovery. He could not find the words. His amazement was so complete that he sank back into his seat. "You interfered even in *that?*"

"Sure, I did. And more," Hawken said, aggrieved bitterness building in his voice. "Many things have passed between us. Most of them were unknown to you, and all of them were kept from the public. But because they were done in secret, does that make them any the less constructive? Hush-hush. That's always been my way in business. It's the foundation of my fortunes. What kind of conceit is it that would make my dealings common knowledge from the Senate to the bars on Sunset Avenue? No, sir! I don't allow it! Secrecy. Stealth. Discretion. These are my watchwords. They're what beats an enemy in the end. *And so it's got to be with the Navy.*"

"But . . ." Ellis felt his anger draining away as Hawken's words bit into him, then he sagged inside. Suddenly everything was starting to become clear and the enormity of his error was dawning.

"But *what?*" Hawken saw that he had taken the initiative and his voice turned scornful. "Are we so witless a people that we've got to tell every goddamned individual in creation our private business? Only a fool tells the opposition what weapons he's got. The stock market swarms with two-faced Chinese financiers, the Yamato embassy here on Liberty is full of sophisticated listening gear, all our ports and aprons are covered by *kempei* spies; each day they report the strength and disposition of our fleet and the readiness of our vessels to repel an invasion. So are we going to advertise the exact measure of our ships into the bargain? 'Sure, Mr. Emperor, we got four ships here, five there, over thataway a half dozen more?' That would be real clever, Ellis!"

It was as if Ellis Straker had been hit by a sumo wrestler. He shook his head slowly.

"This ship," Hawken said, jerking his thumb up at the third-deck blisters. "Is she a warship, or is she a merchantman?"

Ellis said nothing, understanding perfectly what Hawken was saying, letting him run on and spend his anger and accepting the humiliation as he knew he must.

"You don't know, do you? Because you can't tell by looking at her! If she's laden with cargo, then she's a merchantman; if she's tooled up with guns, then she's a fighter. Her purpose is not implicit in her design. You can't tell what she is. And if you can't tell, neither can Baron Harumi's spies!"

Ellis bowed his head. The lessons being read back to him were the same he himself had first set down at Camp Worth thirteen years ago for Ramakrishnan.

"You . . . you were taking the guru's counsel, even then?"

"I was taking *your* counsel. I intercepted your every letter. It made good sense. 'Versatile cruisers mounting singularity guns, not fixed-function ships equipped with beam weapons, that's what Amerika needs.' You wrote that. And you were right. Yamato's admirals are living in the past. They still believe space warfare can be a matter of emerging from a nexus and blasting their way into a system with a sledgehammer. Baron Harumi proved as much against the Koreans. Without constant thought, war strategies become obsolete faster than any other work of man. The Emperor's spies will count the two hundred thirty battleships of our fleet and he'll think they're the same outdated hulks that Lucia Henry left us with. But they're not the same. Internally they're totally rebuilt. Baron Harumi and his advisors will hear reports of small, weak engine clusters and he'll think they're freight carriers. But he sure won't have reckoned with the guns those babies'll be carrying!"

Chow time chimed throughout the ship. Ellis felt a tremor pass through him hollowly, as if his guts had been torn out by a singularity. He had made a cardinal mistake, one for which he would have pulled up any cadet: he had allowed his personal dislike of a man to interfere with his judgement. Shame for the way he had hounded and insulted Hawken rushed through him, followed by intense relief that his accusations were unfounded.

"I owe you my apologies," he said throatily. "I was wrong. Very wrong. Completely wrong."

Hawken's pale eyebrow lifted, then his expression softened almost imperceptibly. "Yes. You were. But I'll tell you this: I'd have done exactly the same in your place, which is perhaps a testament to how similar we are under the skin."

"Then you'll accept my apology?"

"I'll accept. But there are three conditions. First, should I ever ask you, you must put your seven ships freely at my disposal. Your crews too."

Ellis nodded, deeply chastened. "Agreed."

"Second, when John Oujuku returns from across the Boundary, I want you to help me build this Navy into something that can stop anything Yamato sends against us."

"Agreed. And the third condition?"

"That you drink this *choko* of Jim Beam with me now."

"Agreed!"

Ellis stood up and lifted the ceramic cup, thinking ashamedly of the time and how he had set a limit on his return. He despised himself for his motivations of two hours ago. "Sure, I'll drink with you, Jos Hawken. I'll drink a toast to the man who grew me from a seed."

"And I'll drink to a faithless sonofabitch who became an oak tree."

76

Within a week of Oujuku's return from beyond the Boundary, Ellis met him in Hawken's company on Fort Bush, the main orbiting station of Liberty's planetside defense chain. The fort occupied a stationary orbit, standing guard over the atmosphere of Liberty and the freight dockyards at Port Wilson where the silver bulk carriers appeared with their vast loads of mineral wealth from the moons of the outer system gas giants. Fort Bush was a vast spinning top, peppered by a million tiny fosfors that shone like starlight. Oujuku had been away ten months, and during that time Ellis had labored ceaselessly to put Amerika's nexus cruisers into good fighting order. An ominous pall was hanging over all of the Sector with new rumors every week increasing the nervousness of Liberty. In the White House, it was said, the President was like a mad thing, half crazed by anxiety. Her aides avoided her—servants fled, secretaries curbed their tongues and their manners, no one dared ask for either favor or reward. Conroy Lubbock himself had twice been sent out of the Oval Office, his ears on fire, cursed at and screamed out. Although Oujuku's return had muted some of the more doom-faced oracles at Long Island and Harrisburg, Alia's mood continued to feed off the unease of her presidential staff, and the mood of Amerika took its key from her.

But above the planet's surface the talking was straight.

Oujuku, on his way up to orbit, had already received Hawken's full account of the current state of naval preparation and had been told of Ellis's work. In return, he had given a report of his actions in the Zone, a report he was most reluctant to repeat.

Oujuku counted his voyage a failure; it had achieved nothing in terms of creditary return or strategic dividend and, though he had done much to lift Amerikan morale, he was accustomed to far greater achievements. Ellis quickly learned that Otis Le Grande, the Hawken brothers, and the President had been chief among the syndicate which had backed the voyage. Unfettered enterprise had grown up in the Sector and everyone was benefiting, but this deal was crucial. Other prominent shipping parties had been involved also, and Ellis began to wonder if he had been deliberately excluded from the syndicate.

He watched Hawken's dog, a big, gangling, foolish hound with a liver and velvet coat, brown nose and eyes and whip tail, zigzagging restlessly around the station, sniffing at everything and marking territory on every corner. Hawken had given it a studded collar on which was written, "My name is Tojo: 1400 Pennsylvania Avenue." Ellis wondered again what the real reason was for the truth being kept from him concerning the allegations he had made against Hawken. There had never been anything tangible, but he had sensed that Hawken was keeping a whole lot from him still. It had played on his mind for several months now, ever since the day he had stepped out from the shadow of the *Chesapeake,* chastened and humiliated and feeling like an idiot.

"The President blew hot and cold over my departure," Oujuku was explaining unhappily. "She's still swayed by the peace lobby, from meek and deluded souls who believe it's possible to avoid war with Yamato. I told her that ninety percent of wars were ultimately about trade, that that was the lesson of history, but she wouldn't have it. She was convinced that Amerika's ships should stay in the Amerikan Sector."

"What did you do, John?"

"Just looked for some alteration in her that would prohibit my going. Then there was some trouble with a pack of the President's aides who wanted to come on what they called a 'fact-finding mission'—as if it was some kind of pleasure excursion I had in mind. I eventually left, September fourteenth, in *Ticonderoga* with twenty other ships and eight shuttles, most only half prepared and half staffed, again through fear that the President's countermanding order would turn up at the last minute. We cruised about in the Zone long enough to prove to the Emperor that Amerikans don't care nothing for his ass. Even so, if we'd been quicker getting away, we might've had something less abstract to celebrate. As it is, the rest of my account's pretty dismal."

Ellis listened as Oujuku related how he had missed the '38 aurium fleet by a single day, and how he had cruised instead to Sakishima Gunto to antagonise the Emperor's subjects further. There his crews had picked up a virulent fever and it had killed some of them before the medics had been able to get a program on it. He had sighted Ishigaki Shima a week before Christmas and set about a systematic unpicking of Yamato's illegal possessions. He had stormed and taken Shika; at Iriomote Shima he had done the same, but he had missed the '39 aurium fleet, and too many astrogators had died of the fever by then to mount the intended attacks on Hateruma and Yonagumi. As he returned he had attacked the Yamato presense in Taiwan and touched down to bring away prisoners captured off the ill-fated *Potomac,* but there was little joy in Oujuku's mind about any of it.

"What do you think?" Ellis asked him directly.

"Too little. Too late. After last time, a lot was expected of me. I made some pretty rash promises, but I brought back only seventy-five ticks on the credit to my investors, which makes it hard to call what I was doing trade. I missed the fleet, Ellis. Both times. And it's my fault. It's gonna cost us."

"Shit," Hawken said stiffly, his eyes searching for his errant dog. "But you're right about the cost. Two years' aurium is enough to pay off all Yamato's outstanding loans, and their success in refining it'll make their bankers the braver when it comes to advancing more. Also, the damage is doubled because the aurium might have been ours. Without it, we're gonna be hard-pressed."

"About Lucia Henry and Nikolai Belkov—have you had any more trouble from them?" Oujuku asked, determined not to dwell on his failure. "It was a wise move to sign Belkov's son aboard my expedition. Lucia Henry is a creature

I heartily dislike." He turned to Ellis, his ebony face brightening. "By the way, your brother-in-law acquitted himself like a man in the fighting."

"Thanks."

"I've already commended your son's handling of the *Roanoke* in dispatches, Jos."

"Yeah." Hawken took the compliment condescendingly. "My son knows what he's about. He'll go beyond Known Space one day, exploring the Beyond, John. If Ramakrishnan's right, he'll make it to the Galactic Center someday. God grant that he gets the chance. As for Lucia Henry and Belkov, they've almost given up. They're beaten and they know it. But the truth is I wish I was rid of the pair of them. They're old, with old minds, and neither has it in them to adjust their views. The President did the right thing appointing me above gray old bureaucrats like Belkov. It's a good policy to make a businessman the head of any undertaking."

They walked on, Ellis feeling the tension in the men around him who manned the fort's plex corridors. It was as if each one of them saw the war approaching—a war against an enemy that would expect and give no quarter. He told Oujuku, "For every nexus ship officially on the Navy lists there's a private vessel of equal maneuverability and firepower in the hands of a commercial shipping operator. That means we maintain crews and operational ships at nil cost to the taxpayer." He pointed through the observation blister with pride. "Al Vega's *Nebraska* is a good example, a fine ship of six thousand tons mass, available for Navy charter with minimal notice. It's expensive to keep ships in commission, as the Emperor must have discovered. And with the credit we've saved and funds Congress has allotted we'll build eight nexus-going cruisers, two good warships like the *Kentucky,* and one nexus plotting ship . . ."

They debated for more than an hour, Oujuku still moodily ashamed at his half-failure, Hawken lecturingly, striding along the curving concourse of Fort Bush, throwing Doggi Choos from his pocket for his idiot animal to catch, all the while saying that time was short and that they must look to the future instead of the past.

To revive John Oujuku's spirits, Ellis showed him the real strengths that lay beneath the superficial appearance of neglect. He went through the foremost points with enthusiasm, detailing especially the proposed change of manning, and all the while, Ellis was thinking of the question he had wanted to ask Hawken. He had perhaps been waiting for Oujuku's return before putting it. He felt bound to Hawken now by promise, oath, and duty, obliged to atone in full for his past misjudgements of the man. He was working hard for him, trying to make it up.

It's an unnatural state for me, he thought, knowing that Hawken alone in Amerika had the trick of manipulating him. Christ, how I wish I was back aboard the *Constitution,* shooting through on a nexus, cruising free, making my own decisions where to go and when to fight. On Hawken's staff I'm like a dog on a lead. And I want to be off it!

Secretly he thought of the mess John Oujuku had made of his chance to upset Yamato's plans. I'd have done the job properly, he thought with some shame for his arrogance. But it's a fact! God knows it's not right to damn John for his one failure, and I don't know enough about the circumstances, but we sure needed to stop that aurium fleet. Hasn't John demonstrated his capabilities? He's a great astrogator. A great captain. He took his ship through uncharted nexi and home again with a hold full of Yamato's aurium, but still . . .

Ellis sighed. Still the uncharitable thought would not leave him. Jeezus, I'd never have set down on Sakishima Gunto, it's famous for designer diseases. And I'd have taken the aurium fleet instead of hanging about on Ishigaki Shima. Next time it'll be my chance. My chance.

Apropos of nothing, he suddenly asked Hawken, "Why weren't John and I told the truth when we first put our accusations on Conroy Lubbock's desk?"

"Maybe because a secret is best kept by fewest people," Hawken answered carefully, stepping from between them. "Conroy Lubbock wanted the scandal to break out long enough for Yamato to get wind of it so they knew pretty well the deficiencies of Amerikan defensive strength."

"We could have played our cards close to our chests well enough," Ellis said.

"There's no play realer than real life, Ellis."

Oujuku held his tongue, watching as Ellis pressed the point. "We were deliberately kept in the dark, and for an unnecessary period. Why didn't you deal straight with us? It's as if you didn't trust either of us."

Hawken laughed. "Hardly so. John was trusted with twenty ships and a mission against the Yamato aurium fleet."

"Some might see that as John being deliberately got offplanet and out of the way. I remained on Liberty, but still I wasn't taken into your confidence."

The smile fell away from Hawken's mouth. "I asked to see you twice and was turned down."

"Oh, sure. You could have gotten to me."

"I never deal against the play." Hawken grew jovial once more, his dog bounding up to him with a chewed piece of cable insulation. "Ellis, what is it you're saying to me?"

Ellis let it go, knowing that this was not the time to pursue the matter, then Oujuku asked Hawken about the thrust of current policy, leaving him to ponder on the soundness of the answer he had received.

"I know you want to put up a blockade around Yamato. But the President won't countenance any direct and unprovoked act of war. I told her, and Conroy Lubbock told her, that we must prevent Yamato from equipping their fleet at all costs."

"An expedition might be the answer," Oujuku said, warming to the idea. "Refugee Koreans might be got together under their exiled ex-President's leadership. It could be a big deal if we brought in the Chinese and—"

"I've thought of that," Hawken told him. "And I've put as much to Congress, but that too was vetoed as aggressive. What they don't realize is that Yamato ships cost three times as much as ours to get into space. Already Baron

Harumi has assembled a fleet of four hundred ships and a hundred thousand shock troops on Seoul and there's a second force almost as large concentrating in the Hokkaido quadrant. He sure as hell isn't gonna want to wait long."

Ellis rubbed at his chin as he listened to Hawken relating the precise strength of the Yamato fleet. He stared through the plex blister at the bright points of light that were the other orbiting defense forts, wondering suddenly how Hawken could have such detailed information at his fingertips. He said, "I'll allow that a blockade of the key trans-Yamato nexi is untried, but it's worth the attempt. Our biggest ships can stand off the nexi for a couple of months at a time before needing to return to Amerika to refit. If the most crucial months are chosen, we might hamper them enough to make them cancel their plans. At least we could delay them until they're forced to rethink, and every day we succeed is a day costing Yamato three times what it costs Amerika."

"Even so, the President won't allow it. Too many voices close to her doubt whether a blockade of Yamato can work," Hawken said cautiously. "The argument used against us in the Security Council meetings is that of a Yamato fleet getting through despite the blockade. If they broke out and our ships were evaded, Amerika would be dangerously exposed."

"So we're just gonna sit here and wait to be attacked?" Ellis asked, aware that his disappointment was showing.

"You heard John's view of the President's attitude. It took all Conroy Lubbock's persuasion to make her agree to the reprisals on Sakishima Gunto, and even then she was only finally swayed by an outcry of public opinion and the survey of voting intentions."

"We're gonna wait like lambs in the slaughterman's yard," Oujuku said grimly, walking away along the fort's main access corridor.

Hawken looked to him sharply, shouting after him, "Nobody wants to be at the sonsabitches more than I do. It might've been possible if you'd come back with a bit more aurium." He turned to Ellis. "The truth is, his failure's crapped it up for us all."

Ellis's fist balled with sudden fierceness and his eyes met Hawken's own. "It's by decisive action that wars are won. Give me a strike force of fifty nexus ships and I'll do the work. A massive preemptive blow. I'll blast into the Seoul system and smash Baron Harumi's invasion force to ions."

"I've told you," Hawken hissed back with unexpected violence. He looked around as if checking that they were not being overheard. "Don't even think that way."

"Sanction it, Jos! Imagine! Just as the whole goddamned hive is stirring—"

"Quietly." Hawken's voice sank to a whisper. "As I said, I don't have the power to sanction that."

A series of yelping barks rang out. Hawken's dog had found a maintenance drone and was trying to turn it over, but the drone was unimpressed and at every turn the dog flinched back, blue sparks from the drone's meson tool crackling at its nose.

"Get away from it, then, you stupid animal!" Hawken roared at the dog, striding across to slap its flanks with the lead.

Ellis followed and grabbed Hawken's arm. "Try Conroy Lubbock, then. Make him see sense!"

Hawken looked slowly down at Ellis's hand until he was released. "Not even Conroy Lubbock. The President is dead set against stripping Amerika's defenses for the sake of any damned fool adventures." He paused. "Besides, the Seoul system is sealed up tighter than a silex reactor. You'd never get in past the beam weapons, and if you did you'd never get out again."

The fire in Ellis's belly burned up higher. "What does that matter so long as I got amongst them? And I know I can. I can get into any system, and I've thought long and hard about Seoul and its so-called impregnability. See Conroy Lubbock. Persuade him."

Hawken shook his head. "Conroy Lubbock is busy with Cassabian."

"What do you mean?"

"Just that. Lubbock is involved in difficult matters. Matters of the utmost importance."

"What the hell can be more important than this?"

Hawken watched him a moment, considering. Then he said, "It's confidential. My duty to him prevents me from speaking of it. Even to you, Ellis."

"But you know what it is?"

Hawken nodded slowly.

"Tell me."

"I can't."

Ellis watched after Hawken, watched the dog bound after him as he followed Oujuku. Inside his head alarm bells were ringing loud now. From his tone Hawken was certainly hiding something, but what was it? And what was it that had made him rile up at the mention of an attack on Seoul? Whatever was being stitched together by Lubbock and Cassabian, he wanted to be a part of it.

"Please sit down, gentlemen."

Ellis placed himself in one of the wooden armchairs in the VP's study. Apart from Ellis, only Hawken, Cassabian, and Oujuku had been called in here. The meeting had been convened at Conroy Lubbock's house, in camera, and under conditions of great secrecy. Guards had been stationed at both ends of the corridor to prevent eavesdroppers, and the cold courtyard below the electroscreened window was empty except for a pair of women standing at attention by the gatehouse. A roaring real fire blazed in the grate, filling the room with radiant heat.

Conroy Lubbock had grown gray in the guardianship of the Sector. His long face was as pale and mournful as the high winter moon of Liberty, accentuated by his white beard and the velvet cap which was set askew and back from his high forehead. He put out his power in measured words. "I have called you here to tell you how it's going to be. A conspiracy of circumstances stands against us and I've chosen to undo them, with your help, by the means I'll set before you. Tomorrow we'll begin the first moves in a chain of events that will save our President's neck, yes, save it for her—*despite her own best judgements.*"

Every man in the room stiffened at that. Ellis thought of the time he had brought the *Richard M.* home, the time in the Cheju Do system when he had been obliged to put down a mutiny. Then he thought of the other time, just before burying the *Constitution*'s aurium hoard in the bore holes, when he had seen signs enough to prevent a rising. Conroy Lubbock's words sounded unwholesomely close to mutineers' talk. Only this time it was not the overthrow of a ship's captain that was at issue but the captain of the Sector—and that crime was not called mutiny, it was called high treason.

"I can see what you're thinking," Conroy Lubbock went on. "And you're right to think it. But hear Pharis Cassabian out and you'll understand the reasons. I hope we can reach accord, because if we cannot we're all of us dead men, and Amerika is lost."

Cassabian sat on Conroy Lubbock's right, strained, tired, swathed in fawn and tan except for a neat collar of white Afrikan cotton that enclosed his throat. Grave-faced, he said, "An invasion of Amerika must always be built on three columns: an army to threaten us, a navy to convey that army to us, and a rising of Amerikan sympathisers to aid and applaud it as it makes planetfall. This last pillar has as its pedestal Lucia Henry. For above a year, since the last attempt on Alia's life, Lucia Henry has been kept incommunicado by order of the Council. It was hoped by some that this measure might pinch off the diplomatic intercourse that passes between her and the Boundary, enough at least to disable any pro-Yamato faction betrayals of Amerika. However, some time since, by my own initiative, I deliberately opened up a channel by which coded hardcopy might reach her. In June, four months ago local time, this deception paid me back in full. I intercepted a message from a certain Tony Bola, a young lawyer enrolled at Armstrong College and known to me to be onetime associate of the traitors Lewis de Campion and Robert Jansen. He is the instrument of a conspiracy to bring spies into Amerika. Bola's message was looking for Lucia's approval for a rebellion, her full compliance in a Yamato invasion, and her explicit agreement to the assassination of the President. In her reply, Lucia Henry put her name to all of these plots."

Ellis sucked in his breath at that. Oujuku was half out of his seat. Both looked to Hawken, who nodded grimly as Cassabian continued. "I had Lucia's message copied and then I allowed the original to reach its destination so that others party to its intentions could be apprehended. I need not belabor the point that by these free actions the ex-President has transgressed the New Statutes of last year in that she did as an Amerikan citizen willfully involve herself with a plot against the President's life. In consequence Lucia has laid herself open to the death penalty."

"But she's an ex-President," Ellis said, astonished at Cassabian's intentions. "How can she be executed?"

"Oh, she'll be tried. Before a commission of judges, security councilors, and congressmen. And once she's found guilty she'll be speedily dispatched to Camp Worth and the bore hole. Once she's brought to trial no power in the cosmos can save her, except Alia herself, who might still refuse to sign the death warrant."

As Cassabian flashed a glance at the VP, Ellis's mind thundered with the revelation. Now he saw the reasons for the incredible storms that had swept the White House, for Alia's refusal to sanction a foray against Yamato, and why when Hawken had personally put the idea to her she had spat bile at him and allowed him only to take the fleet to its Boundary stations. With Lucia Henry dead everything would be plunged into turmoil.

"Lucia is a foremost ally of Yamato," Ellis said, putting his view direct to Conroy Lubbock. "If she's executed, surely the storm in Yamato will be so great that the Emperor will be driven to back the efforts of Harumi all the more, multiplying the danger to us."

"No!" Cassabian cut in. "Naturally, when Lucia is executed there will be howls of indignation from Yamato, but the Emperor will find himself without a recognised ally to lead any insurgency."

"But you have a point, Captain," Conroy Lubbock said, nodding towards Ellis so that his fine white beard shook among the dazzling threads of his jacket. "The President fears that the execution will so tarnish the ideals of Amerikan justice that we will lose every last stitch of credibility among the other Sectors. It's my belief that unless we're able to armor her against accusations of murdering a political opponent, and an ex-President, Alia will not permit Lucia's death."

Ellis shrugged tautly. "So how can your plan proceed?"

"That's no concern of yours at this stage," Conroy Lubbock told him sharply. "Understand that this matter is disclosed to you on pain of death, Captain. It is disclosed only that you can be properly briefed in another matter. Jos?"

Hawken leaned forward, propping one fist on his hip, the other on his knee. The gravity of the matter clearly pained him. "As soon as Lucia is dead, the last hope of the appeasers is smashed. She is the compromise solution, and without her, Alia's unseating means their accepting as a puppet president some other figure from their own diversified ranks, a leader none of them will be able to agree on, because without Lucia they're split. The alternative is to accept the direct Emperorship of Mutsuhito himself. That will not appeal to appeasers of any persuasion, so Harumi's armies will find no enthusiastic reception on any Amerikan world."

Oujuku spoke up, seeing a flaw. "But conversely, wouldn't Lucia's death remove the last obstacle between Mutsuhito and the absorption of Amerika into the Greater Yamato Co-prosperity Sphere? It'll become full absorption or nothing."

"Yes," Hawken agreed impatiently. "Which is why we'll then be forced to take direct steps against Yamato."

Ellis stirred in his seat. He had noted the oblique way Hawken was approaching the kernel of his argument, and his heart had jumped to his throat at the implications: by forcing the issue Conroy Lubbock and Cassabian were making a preemptive strike against Baron Harumi's forces not only permissible but *essential.* Suddenly the undertaking he had been perfecting and pressing on Hawken and pleading for over the months was more than a possibility, it had become a likelihood.

"The assault on Seoul!" he said as if suddenly filled with light from supernova.

"Yes," Conroy Lubbock said. "Assault, if you will. I'd prefer to call it a naval action, carefully designed and planned." He turned to Oujuku. "I'll inform the Security Council, who are apprised and firmly with us in all points, that you, Congressman Oujuku, will command the expedition. I shall further inform them that you'll appoint Nikolai Belkov as your vice-admiral—as protocol demands."

Ellis felt a cold hand seize him inside, utter disappointment descended on him, then his jealous suspicions ballooned. He saw clearly that in Conroy Lubbock's mind he was unrecognised. He had always been placed and rooted in Reba's father's consciousness as a scheming pirate, a psi-happy astrogator, a criminal system-robber to be despised and ignored. The distinctions conferred by a role in the political pyramid had never been his, had never lifted him above the rank of citizen as they had with Oujuku, who was a congressman. That he had crossed Conroy Lubbock had deepened the resentment, excluding him completely from any commanding role in the very expedition that he had studied and planned for.

Ellis's flesh crawled and his nostrils filled with the stink of Conroy Lubbock's hypocrisy. He saw starkly etched on the VP's face the admiration for false values that only a politician could believe in so totally. I'm the architect of this undertaking! he raged at Conroy Lubbock silently. And what part am I being given in my own mission? None! You know how deeply this cuts me, you bile-pissing bastard. You understand that I ought to be appointed to lead it, and though you know how much this operation means to Amerika, still you humiliate me! Still you try to keep me from my right and due! Still you try to pay me in your counterfeit credit!

Icily he said, "Am I to have *any* part in the operation, Conroy?"

Lubbock ignored him. "The precise form of the mission will be in your care, Congressman Oujuku, but if it all goes as I hope, you'll have a number of Navy ships at your disposal. It will be your last chance to intercept the invasion fleet before Baron Harumi's preparations are complete. Now, go and think it over. Amerika and the future of Known Space are in your hands."

Conroy Lubbock looked hard at Ellis before signaling that Oujuku should leave and that Cassabian should accompany him. Oujuku laid a consoling hand briefly on Ellis's shoulder as he passed. Then he fingered his compac and within seconds one of the guards was at his side. He gave quiet instructions, his fingers playing about his lips, and the guard departed.

"I ask you again, Mr. Vice-president. Am I to have any part in this mission?"

Conroy Lubbock regarded him for a long moment, then he said, "Do you remember when we met last time, how different the circumstances were then?"

"I have apologised to Jos Hawken, and he's accepted my apology," Ellis said, his spine rigid now.

"Good. It was about time. But relax, I've no wish to carry on any part of that unfortunate and *unnecessary* debate." Conroy Lubbock adjusted the sleeve of his garment fractionally. "You may also recall swearing to me an oath on that occasion? One concerning your brother?"

"Yes . . . but I don't see . . ."

Lubbock moved on, deliberately switching away from the source of Ellis's unease. "This meeting was called for your benefit, Captain. You're a cunning man and I think you must have understood that the intentions expressed in the last few minutes are a complete volte-face of the policy I've always promoted. Also, you must have guessed that I was driven to agree to it." Conroy Lubbock paused again as Ellis nodded. "I regret the solution we've proposed, but I believe that Pharis Cassabian and I have arrived at the only accommodation that'll give us any hope at all of preventing total disaster. You see, it's become apparent to us that if our Navy were to wait for the invasion to arrive in Amerika, we would be totally overwhelmed."

That's not true, Ellis wanted to say. Even in the last resort, we stand a better than even chance. We have the ships and the guns to assault them, to herd them out of their formation, then to run them down and pour fire and brimstone into them one at a time with our singularity guns, blasting at close range until they're destroyed or sent running. But something stopped him; Conroy Lubbock had closed his eyes as if shutting out a terrifying vision of the future. Hawken began to speak, his own eyes never once meeting Ellis's.

"I had hoped to avoid this, Ellis, but events have caught up with us. Your brother is alive—"

The room closed in around him.

"—Duval's on Seoul. He's making singularity guns for Baron Harumi."

"No! God, no!" Ellis was paralysed by shock. He felt his face drain, and he buried it in his hands, the throes of anguish rushing through him. Despite the cool currents drawn across the room by the aircon, the atmosphere was suddenly too cloying to breathe. His mind filled with a hundred knotted questions, but none became clear enough to ask.

"I didn't know the whole truth before." Hawken's words were hurried, as he fell over himself to get them out. "I knew that Duval was alive. That he had escaped the *kempei*. That he had somehow got to Seoul. He married, has a son. He's been working for my Seoul contact, the man who was the center of our intelligence network in Korea. You remember Choi Ki Won, Ellis? The same man who helped us when we put down on Cheju Do aboard the *Richard M*. He was fired and went to Seoul. He became my business contact in the days of Free Korea, and when Yamato began to threaten he became an admirable spy and crucial to our efforts there. He was such a key man that I didn't dare risk his life. Duval's life depended on that. You understand me, Ellis? I didn't dare risk him. Not even to you."

Ellis's mind swam in the welter of words as he struggled to comprehend. "Then Duval's no traitor . . . If he's working for you, he's no traitor. Yet . . . yet you say he's making singularity guns for Yamato? I don't understand."

"Duval was caught. Or gave himself up. Choi's dead and we have only a hazy report of events, but at least we know he's in Baron Harumi's possession and that Yamato's using him."

Ellis gasped. Then Conroy Lubbock was right! With singularity guns the invasion would be impossible to stop at the Boundary. Suddenly the sight of Hawken's dog snapping at the maintenance drone came to him. The electrostatic sparks had made it yelp . . .

He heard the sound of footsteps in the corridor. Conroy Lubbock told the Marine guard to enter; he led two oriental women in. One was of middle age and graying, shrewd-eyed but puffy-faced with crying. She was dressed in a long, dark cloak that completely enclosed her. The other who followed was taller and some fifteen years younger. A woman in her prime, beautiful with high cheeks and olive skin, and samurai pride shining in her face.

Ellis swallowed involuntarily as he rose from his seat to greet her.

"Ellis, this is your brother's wife."

78

They walked like trespassers through the banqueting hall, where the walls were covered in rich oil paintings in bright, gorgeous colors of gold and crimson and verdant green. The paintings were seven in number, each six feet tall and ten or fifteen yards long, big enough to clothe the entire room. They were from the Old Earth White House, from the days when Old Earth had been consumed by the fad for the enigmatic symbolist school. They had been hung here to show visiting ambassadors that people who performed Amerikan high politics could match any of the courtly convolutions of Yamato or Chung Kuo when it came to metaphorical double-talking.

"Wait here, Captain," Cassabian told him. Ellis thought of the complex web that had brought him back here to the White House, and the irony of his position. Since Lucia Henry's execution, Conroy Lubbock had been banished from the President's apartments. Alia's public fury had been like hell's furnaces. So totally had she dissociated herself from those who had "maneuvered" her into signing Lucia's death warrant that she would see neither Conroy Lubbock nor her principal advisors. At least Cassabian had had the presence of mind to temporarily install the eminently expandable Jolen Davison as secretary in his place, and a diplomatic ailment had meant that it was Davison and not he who had brought the death warrant from the President. Davison had become the scapegoat and had gone to Camp Worth.

"She's coming," Cassabian whispered, seizing his arm and turning his back to the Marine guards. "Remember, she's read the letter, but your meeting is not arranged; it must seem coincidental. Now I've got to leave you to it."

He hurried away, leaving Ellis bare seconds to compose himself. This is the crux, Ellis told himself, steeling his nerve. That the future could depend so completely on this carefully arranged chance meeting appalled him.

"Why me?" he had asked Cassabian.

"Why? Because it's your plan. You'll have to plead for it, and as eloquently as you can."

"But what about Hawken? Oujuku? The Navy admirals?"

Cassabian had shook his head. "The Navy is too closely tied in with Conroy Lubbock, Hawken likewise. And John's brusque charm has little appeal to her after his financial failure, even less to the ambassadors who know his reputation."

"But I'm no statesman," he had said. "She won't talk to me."

"Oh, you underestimate her, Ellis. She certainly remembers you. You never once failed her and—she likes you."

The approaching commotion in the corridor grew louder, then all at once the hairs stood up on Ellis's neck as Marine guards snapped to attention and aides began spilling into the hall.

The President appeared. Her incredible presence seemed to fill the entire place. Then she paused, and her retinue stepped back, parting so as not to crowd her.

She had seen him.

Immediately he took off his hat and nodded, sweat trickling down his back, staring fixedly at the floor until she came over to him.

"Who're you?"

He looked up but he was unable to meet her eye.

"I asked you who you are?"

"I . . ." he stammered. "I'm . . . my name's Ellis Straker."

"Ellis Straker?" She aimed a long finger at him. "I remember you. Aren't you the privateer who took a brotherly interest in Conroy's daughter?"

A ripple of laughter passed through the assembly.

"All right, then, Ellis Straker, what are you doing in here? What do you want?" Her voice was a stiletto.

His heart raced, hating the jokes she was making at his expense. He looked to the wall and back, knowing he was lost. "I was . . . I was inspecting—admiring—the fineness of your Old Earth paintings, Miz President."

"Yes?" Then she asked him sharply, "And how do you like them, Captain Straker?"

"Oh, they're real pretty, Miz President."

She turned suddenly, her eyes searching his face for embarrassment. Her aides were at her elbow, mischievously watching him. "Oh? And which one's your favorite?"

Ellis cleared his throat and looked quickly at the two that hung closest, entitled "Music" and "Dancing," subjects dear to the President's heart. He rejected them. You must have permission to embark, a voice told him. Impress her now and the presidential warrant to cruise beyond the Boundary could be in your fist by tonight. But take care! She's a difficult one to steer. A wrong move could cost you the chance you've been aching to take.

"Let me see . . ."

"Stand back! Give the captain a little room!" one of the aides said.

Alia noticed his eyes dwell briefly on the hanging of "The Deadly Sins." He seemed not to approve of it, still less of "The Triumph of Time over Fame." "The Triumph of Fame over Death" and "Hannibal" were quickly glanced over.

"Don't you think this is the finest one, Captain?"

She opened her hand at "The Triumph of Death over Chastity." The significance of it, as of them all, was clear to him. Alia Kane would never marry Prince Pi Wu, nor anyone: she would die a spinster. She watched his forehead furrow, his shaggy blond brows knit over the choice.

"To my mind, Miz President, the subject hasn't got much appeal."

"Is it the same mind that imagines the shape of our Navy? And fantasies the future of Amerika on my behalf?"

She noticed his hands flex as Conroy Lubbock's did when he was in combat with any problem. He was simmering now under the eyes of the dozen aides, men and women experienced in the ways and word games of high politics. They knew how suddenly a pleasant stroll through the White House in the company of their President could turn into a penetrating cross-examination of political motive and loyalty. Ellis was obliged to answer.

"If you mean that our fighting ships are now the envy of Known Space, I guess you're right. I've worked to improve them. As for the fine arts, well, I don't understand too much about that, but I would say that there are two paintings here that I like."

She heard an aide whisper to her; the man's piercing blue eyes glittered and she took his suggestion.

"Let me guess your choice."

Ellis watched stricken with paralysis as the President walked the length of the room, her heels echoing on the hard polished floor, filling the high ceiling with their sound. She paused and paused again, then returned, facing him with ice-green eyes that stabbed through to his soul. The russet fire of her hair blazed in tight curls around her head and her slim hand fingered a great emerald pendant that hung from her neck on a chain of worked platinium. He saw that it was the finest of those he had given to Cassabian to present to her as a Christmas gift so long ago. Then it had seemed he and his crew might be shoveled into the diplomatic fires that burned between Amerika and Yamato, and the gift had been a symbolic monument. He had made a pact with a she-devil. The cold fire in the massive jewel exactly matched the meson flame in her eyes.

"No," she said. "I can't guess."

The aides were frozen like statuary. They saw the way she looked at him and recognised the ominous tone in the President's suddenly coy perplexity.

"Captain Straker, I can't see at all what you have in mind. That worries me greatly. Tell me, do you like *this* one best?"

She stretched a bony finger at the painting entitled "Dancing."

Holding himself tall he said politely, "No, Miz President. I don't."

She drew back her hand, suddenly irritable. "Then which?"

Ellis took a pace back and turned. He strode boldly to stand before "The Triumph of Fame over Death." Deliberately he turned his back on it, then pointed across the hall to the painting depicting Hannibal bringing the spoils of Cannae to Carthage.

"With your permission, Miz President, I'll tell you straight. That's my favorite."

The aides drew breath as one, then there was silence. The canvas depicted the legendary general of far antiquity in the glory of his victory over the Roman legions. Everyone present knew that at Cannae Hannibal had destroyed the power of the greatest empire of the classical world, annihilating an army of fifty thousand men and laying bare the defenseless heart of Rome. The meaning was clear.

The President, standing back by her stony retinue, threw wide her arms and tossed her head. The stridor of her laugh tore through the hall.

"Captain Straker! That's good. Very good. You'll have my blessing for it —and your ships."

The presidential party swept on, following Alia Kane from the hall, leaving Ellis to stand alone, watched balefully by a pair of rod-straight Marine guards. They held their blasters stiffly at quarters.

As soon as the great doors banged shut he punched the air and whooped like a Texan.

79

SEOUL

As he watched the elite of Yamato's military hierarchy enter the citadel and make their way up the steep steps toward the council chamber, Katsumi thought of the singularity gun maker and felt a powerful thrill of anticipation run through him. Tonight a glorious war would be made in the blaze of a thousand torches. Here, inside the closed and heavily guarded fortress that dominated Korea's capital, a heavenly rage would be formally launched at the impure heart of Amerika. It was good to be alive now that the pact was sealed. He felt the strength that only warriors know, the intoxicating taste of best-quality White Heron *sake,* and he knew that his own future, Nishima-sama's future, all of Known Space's future, depended upon a decision as intricately complex as the placing down of a *go* stone.

Whichever way the stone was placed, he knew, the killing play would be Duval Straker, coupled with the solemn and murderous agreement he had made with Lord Nishima only twenty-four hours ago. War was opportunity and war was glory, that's what Nishima-sama had said. In war ambitious men were noticed—especially those fortunate enough to be distinguished within sight of their commanders. And those so distinguished became, in time, commanders themselves. That was the Way; the Way as it had always been. The Way of the Warrior.

That's why tonight is the real beginning, he thought. Tonight the armies of white stones and black stones will clash, and I, Urawa no Hasegawa Katsumi, will be privileged to see the confrontation. I am no longer a young man. This is my last chance for true recognition. And if the groups Nishima constructs do not turn out well, then I shall, as agreed, overturn the board and scatter the stones in the six cardinal directions!

Katsumi followed as they took their appointed places along the giant, low map visualiser table. Baron Harumi knelt cross-legged at the head, his commanders, accompanied by their *hatamoto,* ranked to right and left. On the tatami around this board was gathered the greatest concentration of samurai chivalry since Hainan: Aoki Zengo, Baron Harumi's second-in-command, was paired with Admiral Kurita Imari. The two Yamaguchi admirals, Kofuji and Matsumoto, cousins who hated each other, were discreetly placed at opposite ends of the position plan, separated by General Cho and General Sumita. Minami Yoriyasu and General Yonai faced them. Nishima Jun knelt in the middle, facing General Uehara, his electric-blue formal attire provocatively woven with the ring-dragonfly symbol of Yamato.

All were distinguished men, men of proud accomplishment and prouder bearing. All wore the badges of their rank and the honors of past victories about them, and the sign of their high station burned as much in their faces as on their armor. These were the custodians of armies and navies that had fought victoriously for the Emperor for a hundred years and who now ruled, at the command of the gods, virtually the whole of the Two Sectors.

The hall echoed into silence as they settled to business. The admiral astonished them by drawing out his sword, an incredibly fine blade made by the Old Earth smith Munechika. It was said that the gods allowed the swordsmiths to make only one sword in a thousand years as perfect as this, a sword that never lost its suppleness or its cut and never rusted. The intricate *nioi* patterning that covered the blade testified that this was Mutsuhito's priceless personal gift to his shogun.

"This meeting is long overdue," Baron Harumi told them, his voice a low growl. "His Imperial Majesty is growing tired of delay. He will bear no more excuses. And now there is another reason why we must decide finally on the battle order of the *kaigun*. It has been communicated to me tonight that His Imperial Majesty's agents in Lincoln have reported a great crime. The Amerikan usurper has executed the rightful leader, Lucia Henry."

The whole assembly knelt in stunned silence while Baron Harumi went on. "Therefore, before I close proceedings tonight you shall know my decision regarding the ordering of the fleet. First, though, hear me out on the generalities of the matter."

Despite his shock at the news of Lucia Henry's death, Nishima smiled inwardly, knowing that his appointment as generalissimo of the planetary invasion troops was virtually assured. The order was as good as signed by the Emperor himself. The Henry woman's death changes nothing, he thought. Alia Kane has merely set a useful precedent for her own execution.

"Each of you will have the opportunity to contribute your thoughts in due course." Baron Harumi looked from face to face as he spoke, his pained eyes and the way his fingers gripped his leg tightly just above the knee the only evidence of his unremitting physical discomfort. He bent over the visualiser campaign maps, touching the images with the tip of his sword.

"My intention is to assemble all nine squadrons of ships here at Seoul. As soon as conditions permit we shall venture along the Seoul chain, keeping at all times within formation, until we enter Hawaii. Then we shall strike out across the Amerikan Boundary, taking advantage of the excellent Index, on a course that will take us to the nexus of the Floating World, here, ten light-years from the Amerikan system of Kalifornia II. This means we will enter the Sector as far along the radius as possible and then track along that chain. The purpose, of course, is to terrorise the Sector. Every planet, every city, every apron, and every orbital station along the entire flank of Amerika shall see what a mass of arms is thrown against them. Every man, woman, and child will know intimately the strength of Yamato resolve, and how useless it would be to contemplate opposition."

The assembly began to nod, relishing Baron Harumi's plan. All without exception were absorbed by the baron's words and felt privileged to hear so accomplished a master strategist expound his thoughts. "It is my intention to catch the western squadron of the Amerikan fleet in its bolt hole of Carolina. If it is there, we shall enter and destroy it. Then we shall sail immediately to the nexus of the Lone Pine, here, midway along Amerika's main internal chain. There, at Massachusetts, I shall land a force of six hundred thousand troops to establish a beachhead, occupy the system, and obliterate all resistance. With the eastern aprons in our hands the main landing will be made. Our main army will be able to disembark with little opposition and begin their thrust across the Red Plains chain towards Liberty." He paused, looking around the table appraisingly. "As soon as this force is landed the fleet will light out again and continue to the Marshalls, where a second force under the command of General Yamaguchi will be embarked. There our task will be to screen his transports as they cross the Boundary, and run escort from Korea to the three Kalifornias. Thus, by the time Yamaguchi lands in the Liberty system, we will have their capital world between hammer and anvil, ready for the crushing. Then and only then will our fleet engage the remains of the Amerikan Navy."

Baron Harumi watched their enthusiasm rise. He quieted them, then added, "I call upon General Uehara to explain in detail how his army will approach Lincoln and lure the Amerikan planetary forces into direct confrontation."

Nishima stared, totally unable to believe what he had just heard. Uehara's army? Uehara, that oily-haired upstart? But *I'm* to command the landing force on Liberty. The Emperor himself has said so! Beside him Katsumi paled. The stone had been played. And the group had proved one-eyed—as dead as if they had been played by an amateur. Never mind, he told himself. We still have *sente*. We still have the initiative—Duval Straker.

General Uehara, grizzled and meticulously formal and supremely self-confident, rose to his feet and bowed. His voice was steely. "Honorable Lords, we would do well to remember that the Amerikans have suffered no real external threat since the creation of Known Space over four hundred years ago. And whereas our troops have yearly hardened themselves against the Korean rebels, there has been little action to exercise the Amerikans for better than half a century. Even now they possess no satisfactory army; just a rabble of untrained levies who hardly know one end of a blaster from the other. Our samurai infantry will easily push them aside as I approach Lincoln from the southwest of the main continent." He called a detailed map of northern Liberty in front of them. "My first objectives will be to seize and destroy the fleet aprons of Harrisburg, Philadelphia, and Baltimore, and to raze the cities in the region between. As you can see, all these targets are conveniently north of the equator and should pose no problem to a force approaching from a high polar orbit. At the same time our transports will cross the Liberty nexus here and descend directly upon the impure heart of Lincoln itself. By the time that city's buildings are burning, our main infantry force will have straddled the western continent. If it is found that the usurper has fled to Detroit, this will have driven a wedge between her and Lincoln; if not, she will be prevented from finding refuge there. Simultaneously a second force will strike east to cut off the northern paths of retreat from the city before turning south to close on it. It is said that much of Lincoln has overflowed its old defenses, and the manner in which our troops acquit themselves among the hovels and Christian temples there will continue the baron's example in Harrisburg. Alia Kane must be pinned down in the southeast, for then all resistance will collapse. At all costs, she must be prevented from getting offplanet."

Minami Yoriasu, a highly experienced commander who had served in the Hainan campaign, had been listening coolly. He now offered his objection. "What if the Amerikan fleet is blocking the Lone Pine when we come upon it?"

"What of it?" Baron Harumi asked.

"Shouldn't we bring them to battle as soon as possible, Baron-sama?"

"No. In that case we shall cruise immediately for the Red Plains."

"Surely we would have better strength to overwhelm them if we engaged them *before* disembarking our troops?"

Suddenly everyone was speaking and Baron Harumi waved his sword flat across the visualiser image to halt the discussion. "You forget that this is a joint operation with General Yamaguchi's army. If we are able to land a single force of five hundred thousand men on Liberty, Amerika will be ours. Nothing there can withstand one Yamato army of that strength, let alone two. The disembarkation *must* remain our priority."

Aoki Zengo nodded in agreement. "It makes sense. Why attack the Amerikan fleet when we can bypass it? They will not dare approach us so long as we maintain order and keep together. I say we follow Uehara-san's plan to the letter."

The young General Cho spoke up cautiously. "We must not underestimate the power of Amerikan naval weaponry, Baron. It was my father who brought His Imperial Majesty to Amerika thirty or more years ago, and he was impressed by their fleet even then."

General Sumita, in his sixties but as dashing as Uehara—it was he who had captured the Chinese flagship at Hainan—spoke next, his tone scathing, dismissive. "Their fleet has long since moldered away. And the present one has been wasted by the miserly policies of the woman they call President—it's only half the strength it was then! They're all pirates with pirate minds and no understanding of organisation. What do they know about the proper maintenance of a fleet?"

More nods of agreement were exchanged, then General Cho put in keenly, "I agree. A landing along the Red Plains is repeating history. That's the chain our Emperor traveled when he went into Amerika. Our troops will think that a good omen for success. Not that we need to depend on omens."

"May we consider what happens if the Amerikan fleet launches an all-out assault on us?" Aoki asked Baron Harumi.

Baron Harumi smiled, pleased to deal with the question. He understood the apprehension that frothed just beneath the surface in all of them. It was the unspoken horror of the Black Dragon and his fellow privateers that now permeated the whole of Yamato. Baron Harumi knew that their terrifying reputation was justly deserved. The damage they had inflicted on Yamato pride during their assaults had been out of all proportion to the actual physical destruction they had wrought. The baron saw his chance to allay his subordinates' fears; he had conceived a strategy that would cope with any attacker.

"If that happens," he said, his hands moving up and apart in a sweeping circle, "we shall adopt this formation. It's a shape we've all seen on the Imperial standards at Hainan—the radiant sun. When held tight, the Hakon Effect works to add the shield defenses of our ships. With hundreds of ships, an impregnable defensive formation will be formed! Our globe ships and transports in the middle, protected by an impenetrable wall of warships at the outside."

Nishima boiled as he watched Baron Harumi explain the tactics. The flush of pride he had felt at the prospect of being appointed Mutsuhito's generalissimo had been obliterated at a word from the baron. Over the months he had come to understand that Baron Harumi's position was absolutely central. The baron dares to overrule the Emperor himself on strategic matters and to direct the *kaigun* as his own, he thought angrily. All major decisions are being taken by him alone, and how these naval men defer to him! Uehara too—doubtless because he knows he's going to get his own way. But that's going to change. Oh, yes, that's certainly going to change.

His eyes strayed to Katsumi, suspecting his aide could almost read his mind.

"I sympathise, of course, sir," Katsumi had said the night the singularity gun maker had fallen into their hands. "But surely it's Baron Harumi's prerogative to shape the enterprise as he sees fit."

"Unfortunately, yes. But with Duval Straker in our possession once more we can arm the *kaigun* as it should be armed. Think about it. You've seen how tired and drawn Baron Harumi looks. It's clear he overexerts himself. He's starting to make bad decisions. Naturally I've mentioned it to the Emperor in my dispatches."

Katsumi's reply had lacked conviction. "But the Emperor will not tolerate any postponement. I understand he's writing to Baron Harumi daily urging him to launch the invasion."

"I have heard that the sex disease that afflicts Harumi-sama is going to kill him within the year," Fumiko had said balefully. She hated Seoul as she had hated Sado, and Baron Harumi had become for her the living reason for her forced removal from Kyoto and for all her discomfitures. "Perhaps the baron can be persuaded to exert himself even more. After all, he's not long for this life. The Emperor has never liked stubborn men, men who oppose his will. Once you remove him, you can use the Amerikan to your own benefit at last—like you always wanted to."

"He's unimportant," Nishima had lied. "And Harumi-sama is strong enough to see the invasion out. The Emperor thinks he needs him."

"Well, you can always help his decline a little," she had jibed. "That's one thing I know you can do."

He had given her a daggering look then and tried to gloss over her words, but they had obviously registered with Katsumi, so he had switched his plan, daringly laying out his most secret thoughts in a last bid.

"Suppose Baron Harumi does die before the attack can be launched," he had said slyly. "Have you considered that?"

Katsumi had pondered. "The Emperor will have to appoint someone else. Someone in favor and in full health, someone capable of becoming commander in chief, of becoming shogun."

He had smiled then. "So who do you imagine he'll promote?"

"Obviously, Aoki-sama. He's second-in-command."

"No, no. That won't happen, Katsumi. He's old, and he's too much Baron Harumi's man. With the baron dead he'd be like a geisha without a mama-san. And I know that the Emperor doesn't approve of him."

"Then the choice will be between Admiral Kurita and Admiral Kofuji—and, of course, yourself, Lord."

"Quite so. *Quite so.* Therefore we must take care to foster the Emperor's goodwill. We must demonstrate our loyalty and our capability. What do you suggest, Katsumi-san? You have an organizer's mind. What case can we make for ourselves?"

Katsumi had grimaced. "Lord, at the moment it's a case of great haste and small speed. The operation is a logistic shambles. Some ships are half manned while others have twice what they need. Some crews are incompetent, others have experienced men in superabundance. And the apportioning of weaponry is ludicrous! There's simply not enough heavy beam weapons to go around, and even at this rate we'll have no more than thirty tubes per gun. Of course, we still have the Amerikan. Perhaps it's time to use him."

"Yes. How many singularity guns can he make for us between now and our departure?"

As Katsumi made his calculations Nishima's thoughts had dwelt on Kurita. What of Kurita? What Katsumi said is true. The man's a formidable nexus fleet commander, renowned for his service to the Emperor. He's from much the same mold as Baron Harumi himself. I don't fully know how the Emperor regards him, but whatever his standing I can undermine him. Mutsuhito won't want his invasion commanded by a man whose adherence to the Way is in doubt, a man who once stooped to blackmailing a *metsuke*. He accused Fukuda Ikku of possession by demons, isn't that what his enemies always maintained and were prepared to swear to? No, Kurita should be no obstacle at all to me.

"At least fifty, Excellency. Though that will mean purchasing more argentium to energise them."

"Then I'll ask for a hundred. Prepare a budget for that. The expense of the invasion has already amounted to four years' contributions of Sado argentium. A little more won't hurt the Emperor. He's resolved on his great enterprise whatever the cost."

"Couldn't you write to him and beg him to come to Seoul himself?"

"Why should I do that?" Nishima had asked, surprised at Katsumi's naiveté. While the Emperor remained on Kyoto, writing despatches to his nephew in Korea, to his ambassadors everywhere and to Baron Harumi, all was safe. "No, Katsumi, that the Emperor never leaves the Imperial Court is our greatest strength. He's a virtual recluse, and that's good, because the last thing we want is his meddling here. This way, I describe everything that happens in Seoul and he has no choice but to believe what I say. That's power." He had sipped at his *choko* of *sake* then, pleased at the way events were leading. "You may be right about our weapon-maker. Perhaps now the time is right to use him against Baron Harumi. But one thing still puzzles me. Why did he give himself to you, Katsumi?"

He had asked himself the same question daily since Duval Straker was first taken, and the answer Katsumi had given then had stayed with him.

"I don't know, Lord. He seemed to think we were bound to find him sooner or later. Of course, I had him Probed—"

"You had him Probed?"

"I wanted to discover what he had done with my sister, Excellency."

"I hope you didn't damage him."

Katsumi had picked off his sandal, pulling at his toes one at a time in his maddening way. "Duval Straker was temporarily rendered half conscious, and it was then that he spoke of Michie-san. He seemed to be worried about her. Perhaps he thought we had taken her. I wanted to discover where she was."

"And did you?"

"Not yet, Lord."

"No more Probings. That's an order. I'm only interested in his skills. He's a very rare commodity. Don't jeopardise him because of some whim about your sister."

"Yes, Lord."

That had been months ago, and since then, Duval had been confined in secret until the right time to produce him arrived. To have produced him sooner would have given him to Baron Harumi. He was sure of that.

"I still can't explain why he came to us, Lord," Katsumi said. "Perhaps he's telling the truth, that he just wants a sum of credit. Who can say how the minds of barbarians work?"

Nishima had grinned then, pleased at the miraculous gift. "Haven't I always forgiven you your sins, Katsumi-san? I didn't punish you as some might have done after you mislaid him on Sado. You see how the gods reward the virtuous?"

Katsumi's silence had made him think of the night they had put the old man to death. There had always been a cruel streak in Katsumi. Though Wataru Hoshino had been the mainstay of his plan to allow Duval Straker to escape crucifixion, he had turned viciously on the old man when the plan went wrong. He had taken him to the rendezvous outside Kanazawa, but when the wait had turned out to be fruitless Katsumi had stroked his sword through the old man's neck, thereby satisfying, he had said later, Hoshino's wish to die as a soldier. After that, despite intense searches by both the secular authorities and the *kempei*, they had never discovered any trace of Katsumi-san's bitch of a sister, or of the

Amerikan. Of course, reports had been many: Guam, the Marshalls, Korea, even tales of a nexus wreck and one of escape to Amerika, but there had never been any hard evidence. Until his reappearance. It was amazing. Perhaps too amazing. Curious that he should offer himself like that at such a time. What can he want? Still, he's too precious a resource to have Katsumi snuff out in a rage.

"Yes, you must treat Duval Straker with care," Nishima had said, leaning back against his cushions. "Are you still loyal to me, Katsumi-san?"

Unhesitatingly, "Yes, Lord."

"And to the Emperor?"

This time Katsumi had paused, evaluating the trap. "Without reservation, Lord."

"I wonder." Nishima had stood up, recklessly abandoning himself to the idea in his mind. "Yes, I wonder. What would you do if I told you the Emperor's patience with Baron Harumi is at an end? That he wants the shogun dead? And that I had offered your name as a mark of your fealty to him?"

What indeed, he thought, relishing again the way Katsumi's jaw had fallen at that. He rubbed his palms together unobtrusively, his mind suddenly alerted to Baron Harumi and to the present by the striking of the nearby shrine's great bell.

Nishima looked around the assembled Council of War, then studied the Baron closely. Yes, I'm still not sure about you. They say your blood's poisoned by the sex disease and you'll be a dead man soon, but will you be a dead man soon enough? On the other hand I've always been able to rely on Katsumi. He won't take my word alone, but he's stupid enough to have no qualms about disposing of you once I show him the correspondence I've received from the Imperial Court.

Mutsuhito's last dispatch was the most urgent yet, complaining of Baron Harumi's sloth. In it the Emperor had asked to be advised minutely of the state of readiness of the invasion fleet, to have a detailed evaluation of the baron's intentions and a list of proposals for how Baron Harumi's difficulties might be eliminated. The tone of the letter had been characteristically ambiguous, and Mutsuhito's dispatches had always been capable of two or more quite separate readings.

Yes, he thought, stirring from his smoldering reverie, just as I was used by Prince Sekigahara to murder Mutsuhito's lunatic son, so I will use Katsumi to murder Baron Harumi.

The invasion of his thoughts was sudden and unexpected. "What have you to say, Nishima-san?"

"Lord Harumi?"

Harumi fixed him with the stare for which he was famed. "You seem to be anxious to say something."

Languidly Nishima knelt up straighter and made his bow. "I should like to underline the need for proper armament. It is my belief that we should wait until we are able to ship singularity guns. Half the research establishments of the Two Sectors have donated their best minds. It would be an insult to the Emperor to depart before we had the means to—"

Baron Harumi's eyes sheered away arrogantly. "Yes, I was forgetting. You're an expert on how ships may be properly armed to oppose the Amerikans."

General Uehara saw his opportunity and spoke. "Surely more important than that is a quick and decisive infantry campaign. Naturally that will depend on quick departure. What date can we now expect to light out from Seoul?"

"Patience, Uehara-san, you'll be at them soon enough," Baron Harumi assured him, still ruffled by Nishima's obstructive attitude. "Your men will fight soon. We shall depart in the fifth month, the sixth at the latest. Six weeks after we cross the Boundary you'll be standing on the ramparts of Lincoln's fortifications and the next day drinking green tea in the ruins of the White House. I can promise you that."

"Excuse me, but is that possible?" Kurita asked, knowing also that Mutsuhito was growing increasingly irate at the delay. "Are we really able to ready the fleet by then? That's only eight weeks away."

The baron drew himself up. "We could leave now if I chose to order it." Kurita bit his tongue, and Baron Harumi continued. "I'm only waiting for the squadron now assembling at Chongjin. As soon as that arrives we'll get under way."

"But we're still short of heavy beam weapons," General Cho said bluntly. "Nishima-san's quite right. It's something which needs to be rectified."

Baron Harumi's voice rose, something of the pent-up anger that had made him a living legend at the Imperial Court showing itself. "I can't agree. So long as we have sufficient firepower to keep the Amerikans at a distance we'll prevail."

"Excuse me, but does that mean you are prepared to gamble the whole invasion?" Nishima pressed. Immediately all eyes locked on him and he cloaked his following question in a mantle of lukewarm indifference. "Of course, I mean no disrespect, Baron-sama, but aren't you in your anxiety to light out jeopardising the entire operation? In my opinion it would be better to wait another month. We could still take Lincoln in the way you have planned, but our ships would contain armament lethal enough at shield range to destroy any ship they sent against us."

Kurita said, "Yes, most honorable Baron, what difference will another month make? Why must we light out by the sixth month?"

"Because the Emperor says we must!" Baron Harumi rapped out furiously. "And if we lose a few ships, so what? That's to be expected. We are samurai! Samurai with pride! Soldiers! Warriors! We know war means risk, but we are not cowards, we glory in it! Isn't that so?"

Some showed their approval, others bowed their heads wordlessly.

Baron Harumi looked hard at Nishima, imposing his will. "Isn't that so, Lord Nishima?"

"Of course, most honorable Baron, it's just that—"

"That's right! There *are* no objections! And who says otherwise? We are Yamato's sons! We follow the Way. We know our duty! No man may tell us our business! No man may beat us down! No man. If the Emperor says we shall invade Amerika—*then we shall invade Amerika!*"

No one moved to Nishima's defense. Baron Harumi's eyes bulged with anger and the vein in his forehead stood out. His gaze dwelled upon them all in turn, finally falling on the man to his left. "Admiral Kurita?"

Kurita hesitated, then said with cool courage, "There may be some wisdom in what Nishima-san says, Baron. Several times the Yamato Guard has experienced the effect of these unstoppable Amerikan guns. At short range they can be devastating. However, I agree there's little to be gained by waiting. We may supply the whole fleet with singularity guns in three months' time, but by then the Index will probably have turned against us and we might be forced to wait another year—"

"That's not necessarily true," Nishima interrupted, racking Baron Harumi with yet another reason to delay. "No one can predict the way the Index will move with certainty. I tell you that the weapons facility houses here on Seoul can be producing these incredible new guns, as good as Amerikan ones, in little more than a month from now."

"Impossible!" General Yonai retorted.

"*Sumi masen ga* . . . Is this true?"

"What are you talking about, Nishima-san?"

"Silence!" Baron Harumi's order stilled them. "In little more than a month from now we shall be cruising the nexus lanes, moving against Amerika. His Imperial Majesty has ordered it, and so it shall be. Now, Kurita, I want the battle order announced."

"Yes, Baron." Kurita bowed and began reading from Baron Harumi's notes. "The most honorable baron shall personally command the Yamashiro Squadron of fifteen nexus ships, ten of which shall be assault cruisers, supported by five transports. The flagship shall be the admiral's own *Ieyasu Tokugawa,* of twelve thousand tons, presently at Chongjin.

"The Kuzuke flotilla shall be commanded by General Cho: ten transports and four assault battlecraft, including the *Ieshige.*

"The Squadron of Shinano: General Sumita. Fourteen transports, two battle cruisers.

"The Bizen Squadron, ten transports and one globe ship, to be commanded by Lord Kinoshita.

"The Settsu Squadron of eleven transports, two battle cruisers: General Cho.

"And finally in the first battle line, the Shimofusa attack column, the ten globe ships of Admiral Matsumoto, who shall be aboard *Iemitsu.* Nishima-sama will travel aboard the *Takeda Shingen* with Aoki-sama."

There was a stirring and Baron Harumi examined each man for his reaction. Some had yet to be named, others would not be named at all. But the compromise had been the best he could work out, and though no one seemed to be fully satisfied, still none were resentful to the point of a public demonstration, not even that loathsome practitioner of dumb insolence, Nishima Jun.

"Are there any questions?"

"Do I have your permission to go ahead with my efforts to equip your ships with the new guns in case there should be any delay?" Nishima asked humbly, inwardly delighting at the way he was tearing Baron Harumi away from his best instincts and forcing him to publicly announce his intention to light out within the Emperor's ludicrously tight schedule.

"Nishima-san, as fifth in command, you must try to restrain yourself from tinkering with matters that do not concern you. Your task is to make certain General Uehara's troops are properly equipped and embarked on the appropriate transports at the right time. Nothing more." Baron Harumi regarded him briefly, as if drinking in his stony response, then he turned to Kurita. "Read out the rest."

"*Hai!* The second battle line is to be as follows . . ."

As Kurita spoke again, Nishima's eyes glowed like coals. He watched Baron Harumi's imperious gaze ripple across his subordinates.

"Does anyone have anything more to say? No? Good. I have one thing and one only." Baron Harumi paused for breath. "I have commanded many expeditions and fought in numberless campaigns, and each battle has taught me that success in warfare is absolutely dependent on the correct functioning of the chain of command. Those beneath must take orders from those above. Immediately. Willingly. Without question. I have chosen you all after careful consideration. Some of you may not be happy with the gifts of duty I have bestowed, but whether you are or whether you are not, I solemnly ask each one of you to put your personal feelings aside and to pledge loyalty to me and to your Emperor."

Admiral Matsumoto offered himself first. Then each in turn showed his humility and Baron Harumi went from man to man, to bow formally and receive his promise, face-to-face. Finally Nishima gave his word, seeing that the moving little ceremony was giving the admiral considerable satisfaction. "You'll have all the support I can give you," he promised as they locked eyes, "so long as you shall live."

Baron Harumi took in Nishima's bow and nodded back to him stiffly. "That is well. Now I call upon the priests to bless our enterprise."

They knelt before the Shinto priest to dedicate their mission to the glory of the Emperor, the Son of Heaven, each man wearing a string of beads on his hands as he pressed them together in supplication. The priest's voice began to intone a droning chant, but he had been mouthing only moments when he was drowned out by shouting beyond the door. The remonstrations with the guard grew louder. Heads turned from the priest. Then the baron leapt to his feet.

"What's this?" he raged, appalled at the intolerable intrusion. "Who dares to disturb our prayers?"

The door burst in and a messenger, quaking with fear and white-faced from his tussle with the guards, ran to the baron. He crashed down before him, offering up his communiqué in both hands.

"What is it?" Baron Harumi demanded.

"A terrible calamity, Lord!"

"Calamity?"

"It's the Black Dragon! His flagship and a great fleet of other ships! He's been sighted in the Chain of Heavenly Peace! He's tracking here, to Seoul, to destroy us!"

A SECRET RENDEZVOUS POINT IN THE NEUTRAL ZONE

In his old cabin aboard the *Constitution,* Ellis turned his ears to the familiar sounds of his ship. She was just like she had always been, kept trim by Johnson Curtis, her quartermaster, and Gedi Bolton, her captain. It would be magnificent to feel the command chair under his butt again, the ship's engines putting out two hundred gee, and her nose diving towards nexus Resh-Four-Nine. The promise he had sworn to Reba was suspended. Never more will I ride the nexi, he'd told her, but this was no recantation. She had released him from his vow. This once. As she'd known she must for the sake of his self-respect and his sanity.

He lay back, drifting as he tried to unravel the reasons why Hawken had kept Duval's existence in Seoul secret from him for so long, only to reveal it once the mission to shatter the Emperor's shipping in the Korean aprons looked certain.

With foreboding he called up the file of sealed orders from his chart organiser and peered into the screen at the locked pages as if trying to divine their significance. Today was the day that the files would lose their classified seal. The day they came into the Chain of Heavenly Peace, the main nexus route to Seoul. He saw the seals blip off the documents, but he did not open them. Opening sealed orders was an admiral's duty. And John was the admiral.

He looked down at the data the Yamato woman had given to Lubbock. She had said it was computed by Duval's own efforts, that he had made this detailed survey of the Seoul astromechanical approaches and defenses himself. Could this really have been compiled by Duval?

There were two injects, the main transport orbits that ran over the poles, and the high equatorial zone stacking-lane, crammed with standing satellites and way stations, which was treacherous and monstrously protected. The Seoul City apron itself was patrolled by a squadron of fast, armed air-cars, and across the whole stretch there were fortresses and beam weapon batteries that made entry impossible to any enemy. But what was the plan? And what about the promise he had made to Lubbock? The news that Duval was thought to be arming the Yamato fleet troubled him. He knew that with singularity technology an invasion of Amerika must surely succeed.

It was five seconds to one UT. He counted them down and—*thunk!*—the engines cut out and whined down and the compensators switched into free-fall mode, maintaining one gee smoothly. With his peace unsettled he scrolled the data and went up to the bridge, where his ensign waited. They went to the shuttle deck. The new craft was fast, his pilots happy to show him what they could do, and within the hour he was walking along the umbilicus of Oujuku's *Kalifornia*.

Oujuku had been appointed admiral with Nikolai Belkov his vice-admiral, just as Lubbock had wanted. Hawken had explained that Belkov was there to conveniently remove him from Liberty and so part him from the mischief he was planning. He had said that the sealed orders would explain the rest.

"So you persuaded the President that Rome was there for the taking?" Oujuku had roared gleefully on Ellis's arrival at Harrisburg after gaining the presidential warrant to mount the preemptive strike. "I hope you didn't tell her we'd do it with elephants!"

Ellis had grinned back. "I promised her we'd stomp on his shipping."

"Okeh!"

The Harrisburg terminal was heaving with crew who had waited for this day. Since getting down from his air-car Ellis had met countless ghosts from his past: Cornelius the Irishman had come down with Captain Bowen and Tom Brophy the Texan, whose own ship was renamed the *Kiss My Ass*. Nowell the gunner was there, and he saw an oriental face grinning from the mass, Cao, a silex merchant and shipowner for the last ten years; he'd come from Phildelphia in his trader-warship to see what he could offer. There had been other men who had suffered with him on the Niigata apron, and many more who had shared the riches of the happy homecoming ten years on from it. Oujuku too had attracted his old adherents. There had been no shortage of experienced nexus rats to set against Yamato.

Then Oujuku had taken the warrant and read from it to the assembled crowd: "Whereas it has pleased the President of Amerika to grant to John Oujuku her commission as admiral, dated March fifteen, A.D. 2441, for an action to be carried out with a privateering force and four assault ships and two attack frigates of the Amerikan Navy . . ." And they had cheered.

The promise of the Navy's four ships had triggered the cautious stock market. Alia's presidential seal on the commission had been enough to demonstrate her approval. He had pointed out where it had been signed by a crew of financiers, investors, fund managers, bulls, and wolves—Cordell, Watts, Banning, the Boreman Corporation, Hugh Lee, Robert Flick Inc—all Ellis's mercantile acquaintances willing to venture a fiscal credit or two in hope of a profit. They had fitted up a fleet at the Newport News Hull Corporation hangars: on hardcopy, ten "armed merchantmen." In reality they were battle cruisers.

There was no point in keeping their intentions secret any longer. To loud acclaim he had offered a flourish to the broadcast cameras: "We're ordered to 'impeach the territories illegally claimed by Yamato, to distress His Imperial Majesty's nexus ships wherever we find them.' Now, what do you think of that, people?"

And during the cheers, privately, Oujuku had listened as Ellis had told him, "It's a free hand, John. A free hand at last. Much more than Lubbock would have gotten us."

"It's precisely what we needed."

"Cassabian warns that there's a snag to it."

"What?"

"Within the week Alia will tell Lubbock that she has changed her mind, and he'll send Jiro Ito here with a message to stop us."

Oujuku had turned at that. "*What?*"

"If we provoke a war, Amerika will get the blame. She must try to prevent us—*officially*. You see?"

The fullness of the plan dawned on Oujuku and he cackled, then he thundered. "We need two days more to light out, then two under acceleration before the comms are lagged a day late and the security frequencies are redshifted into twenty-one cm hydrogen background. We can always have a malfunction at ground base. I'll send Abee Harris and Joni Fenner's cousin up to Fort Bush. They're incompetent enough to detain anyone."

Ellis had nodded approvingly. "And there's this: the comms vessel that delivers presidential dispatches, the one that'll be sent with the orders to recall us if a message fails, is the *Birmingham*."

"Yeah? So?"

"So her pilot is Jos Hawken's son."

"Oh, you're a clever man, Ellis! A real clever man!"

So they had left Harrisburg on April Fool's Day, streaming exhaust and blue fire across the waters, bristling with arms and crew, sixteen assault ships and seven frigates, all raring to show Yamato who they were.

Oujuku met them as they came aboard the *Kalifornia*. Though all of them thought Seoul was their target, none except Ellis knew their actual destination.

Nikolai Belkov, corpulent, unhappy at the indignity of having a privateer seven years his junior to command him, coming from the *Arizona;* Kent Fenner, Oujuku's man, a good astrogator and one who had been there during the last attack on the Home Worlds; Hal Bel, discreet, honest, and efficient; and Ellis Straker himself.

As usual, Oujuku let them have their way, listening quietly, then Belkov gave his reasons why Seoul was an impossible objective.

At length Oujuku broke his silence. "I agree," he said simply. "Which is why we're not going to try it."

"Not try it?" Hamilton said, shocked to his boots. "But I thought you said . . ."

"You heard me well enough. I said we'd hunt down Baron Harumi's flagship, the *Ieyasu Tokugawa*. It's equipping right now with the second force at Chongjin."

81

THE CHONGJIN SYSTEM

At three hours, relativistically corrected UT, just after local noon, on Wednesday, the nineteenth day of Universal April, they came upon the apron that basked in the fierce light of a blue giant midway between the Twenty Degree Worlds and the Korean border. The metropolis of Chongjin itself stood on a rocky island connected by a bridge to a long spit sweeping out from the mainland into a lime desert. The city overlooked the northern Outer Apron, but there was a second, Inner Apron, almost completely surrounded by terminal outworks, containing the military pads and the more secure zones within. It was from here that a vessel of Colonel Koizumi's ground defense squadron advanced to meet the leading ship of this unknown and unexpected flotilla.

That ship was the *Constitution* and Ellis sat in her command seat, exultant that he had had psi good enough to give them so high an Index on the last transit. As he watched the intercept aircraft come on, he tried to put out of his mind the terrifying instructions that had been contained in the sealed orders. At the breaking up of the captains' conference aboard the *Kalifornia*, Oujuku had punched up hardcopy and let him read it for himself. There were no orders, just a personal letter from Hawken, reminding him of his oath aboard the *Chesapeake* and of his promise to Lubbock. It had explained that Duval's work on the singularity guns at Seoul was now confirmed and that he must be stopped. Hawken had had the communication sealed for two reasons: firstly its secret nature, and secondly because he had wanted Ellis to consider it only when he was standing off the Seoul system. The request was that he bring Duval out, or if he could not, to honor his promise in full.

"What will you do?" Oujuku had asked him when they were alone.

"What can I do?"

"Hawken's right. Duval must be stopped."

He had groped for the answers. "But why me? Why his brother?"

"Because Hawken would rather you brought him away. And if any man can do that, you can."

"And if I can't?"

"You will."

But he had chosen to disregard the request. He had sensed some adroitness in Hawken's style, but he had known that he could not decide in a matter like this without deep meditation. So, for the first time in his life, he had thrown the burden up to psi, uncolored by his own desire. This time, the pure currents of chance would choose for him, and Ellis knew he would receive his answer as they passed into the system of Chongjin.

"Fire a warning over her," he told his gunner as the aircraft's spike drew dangerously close on the ranger. Two beams plumed the air on either side of her and he watched the sleek atmospheric craft sheer off. It looked like she had been expecting challenge to some harmless Korean merchantman; he imagined the panic that would ensue when ground control recovered from their surprise. As in the past, panic and John's fearsome reputation would be their best allies.

Behind, the Amerikan ships cruised on, passing through the dangerous high-meson flux levels of the lower atmosphere and closing on the planetary surface, and Ellis knew that the tactic of surprise must now give way to boldness. Almost as one the red-on-white stripes of the Navy ships broke out across the hulls, and as Ellis turned his eye once more on the apron he saw with disbelief that the squadron of ten defense craft was scrambling to meet them.

Their commander's mad to force an attack here, he thought, unable to understand what was going through Colonel Koizumi's mind. Doesn't he realize that his only advantage is speed? He can't prevent us from landing and we've beaten him once we set down. Ellis knew that had he been in charge of the interceptors, he would have sent them back to base and imposed heavy shielding to keep the Inner Apron secure, but the colonel seemed determined to prove his worth.

As Ellis watched through the panoramic bridge blisters, the interceptors appeared on visual and began to maneuver into attack formation, the classic low-level wedge that protected the flanks of the aircraft and made as small a target as possible for the beam weapon armament of the intruders as they swept into the attack. At near-ground level they could be lethal to ponderous merchantmen; their swift skimming made them a match for any nexus trade ship when it was below five thousand feet altitude, but here their show of strength was about to be wasted.

"Signal from the *Kalifornia,* sir!"

It was terse. The four Navy ships, having greatest armament, were to engage the interceptors, and Ellis was to penetrate the apron and lead the other ships in among the grounded Yamato fleet.

Ellis silently thanked the interceptor commander for his chance to lead the charge and thundered down onto the Outer Apron, under the batteries of the Chongjin terminal, steering his followers between two air-car lanes. Then his eyes lit at the sight that greeted them. Standing on the crete stackways were thirty-two ships of over ten thousand tons mass. These were the ones intended to be sent against Amerika, but there were thirty other ships, either tied down among a Medusa's head of umbilicus tubes or in various states of strip-down. Some were without engine cowls, others were in the middle of embarking ordnance or having alterations carried out on their internal structure.

"They're cutting their cables, trying to get them into the hangars," Hal Bel, his co-astrogator, shouted. "What'll we do?"

"What do you want to do?"

"*Hit them,*" twenty voices told him.

"So who's stopping you?"

"*Aye, aye, sir!*"

At their backs Oujuku had engaged the interceptors, downing one and chasing the others away. Then the warships bent their noses south, overflying the panicking technicians who scattered like a nest of ants below. There, naked to their assault, stood rank upon rank of new ships, hooked up and helpless, without power or crews to work them, without shields to protect them or guns to return fire.

For the next three hours the entire Outer Apron was ransacked. Shuttles loaded with implacable prize-hungry Amerikans scoured the entire area, going from vessel to vessel in search of booty. Deserted by their crews, the Yamato ships were systematically looted and detonated until two hundred thousand tons mass of nexus shipping had been ruined. Only one ship defied them, a huge eighteen-thousand-ton merchantman, and they closed in on her like wolves, their singularities tearing her to pieces while the gunners who hacked her into Swiss cheese bemoaned the loss of her as a prize.

When night fell they congregated in the middle of the Outer Apron, out of danger from the heavy batteries who dared not fire on the circle of intact invasion ships that had been carefully left all around.

For some hours yet they would be safe from the massed land forces that were being defreezed, pouring to the defense of Chongjin. The apron was lit by the burning hulks that now littered the taxiways, and sporadic beamfire crackled from the batteries and towers that dotted the terminal. Oujuku called his captains to conference to consult them and get their opinions. Many of them had just doubled their personal fortunes and were willing to follow Oujuku into hell itself. But there was one dissenter.

"We've done enough here, and I say we get out while we still can," Belkov insisted.

Ellis, who disliked Belkov's manner, said nothing.

Oujuku's eyes narrowed, smelling fear and mutiny in Belkov's words. He said, "Our job here's only half finished."

"If the Index drops, we'll be trapped. Then the interceptors can come back and we'll be standing targets," Belkov said, speaking now in worried tones.

Oujuku's considered words cut at him. "There's a beginning to every enterprise, but it's the continuing of it to the end, until it's thoroughly finished, that really matters."

"You don't understand my objection."

Quietly: "Oh? Don't I?"

Belkov stirred himself. "Captain Oujuku, so far we've had good psi. We've bloodied Yamato's nose. We can't ask for more."

Ellis saw the dangerous light in Oujuku's eye, knowing very well his unwavering rule never to brook opposition from people he did not respect. Harvis Dowty had mutinied during the harassing of Yamato, and Oujuku had had Harvis Dowty put down.

"Let's forget about today. It's over, isn't it?" Oujuku asked with deceptive calm. "Let's think out our plans for tomorrow instead. Psi has no memory, as any dicer will tell you."

Belkov blustered, deceived by Oujuku's calm. "Do you intend to dice with all of us, then? I'd rather get offplanet. Quickly. Now. To retire victorious while we can. It's the only sane—"

"Shut your mouth!" Oujuku shouted. No one dared say a word. "You'll keep your mouth shut until I say you can speak. Okeh?"

"I protest!"

"Protest? *Protest?*"

Belkov's mouth tightened. "You're flouting my right to voice an opinion, and I'll report your disregard for naval procedures—"

"This is not a Navy operation, Mr. Belkov. This is a private quarrel between myself and the Emperor of Yamato, and you'd better tread carefully if you want to come away from it alive."

Belkov puffed and blew at that. The exchange had enraged him, but he backed away.

As they left the vicinity of the *Kalifornia*, Ellis warned Belkov against his course coldly.

"That was foolish, Mr. Belkov."

"But we've got to get out of here. All the treatises of naval warfare say—"

"Hang the treatises. You shouldn't upset John Oujuku, or he'll hang your ass on a meat hook—for a coward and a mutineer. He's the boss here, and you ought to remember that."

The rumors of the summary way Oujuku had dealt with the quarrelsome Harvis Dowty must have run through Belkov's mind.

"Captain Straker, I'm only here as an official observer. The VP sent me as a representative from the Navy. Some of those are our ships. I'm thinking of the good of the mission. If the Index drops—"

"Just do as you're told."

"You forget that I'm not just a mission investor. I hold a Navy rank of admiral and I'm second-in-command here!"

"Just do as you're told," Ellis repeated, his words hard as iron now. "You're scum, Belkov. John'll have no opposition from a man who misled us, *and who turned us against Jos Hawken as you did with your lies*. It was you and your cronies who were bleeding the Commission dry, putting crews at risk. We believe the punishment should fit the crime, is all."

"What do you mean?"

"Just that you can bet your life that wherever the fighting's thickest on this trip *you're* gonna be in the middle of it. Maybe that'll teach your fat ass some respect for the dirty end of policy."

At that, Belkov settled into silence until they regained his ship. Ellis saw the fear dance on his face. Sure, and piss blood, you fat-assed sonofabitch, he cursed silently. It's justice that you've been brought to book. You deserve the freezeeing John would give you if he could. Your government career is over.

But it's a shame that you're completely right about what we should do. I agree that the Inner Apron is a dangerous trap and no place for us to hang around. In his desire to punish you, John has lost touch with his inner feelings, yep, and with his reason.

Ellis knew that the lure had been irresistible. Baron Harumi's own flagship, the *Ieyasu Tokugawa*, a great twelve-thousand-tonner, was parked at the end of the taxiway. He knew how the reports must have inflamed Oujuku's imagination, and now the argument with Belkov had driven him to a poor decision. As he climbed once more aboard the *Constitution* Ellis wondered if that was the answer he had been waiting for.

When the next day dawned, they went in against Baron Harumi's ship. A swarm of shuttles approached her, blasting their way aboard, storming the hapless vessel until she was taken. They overran her, stripped her, and burned her out, then they did the same to six other ships carrying holds packed with thousands of tons of refrigerant. His own eager crews lifted a quantity of plantinium from the last of their victims, and as they landed four big strange-looking security containers on the crete beside the *Constitution,* they asked him if they could use a singularity gun to shoot off the top of them.

He agreed and they blipped out the first two locks to fragments, but as the first lid was thrown back they found nothing but neatly folded *komuso* monks' kimonos and woven baskets.

"What the . . . that's no prize!"

"It's all basket-head trappings!"

"Worth nothing! Torch it!"

"Naw! Leave it to rot!"

Their disappointment was acute. Some tried the other containers with the same result and some went off to find other booty and a few started tearing the garments for the sake of it, but Ellis stayed them. An idea had germinated, and he began to imagine its multiple possibilities. This was pure psi, he saw that. As strange an answer to his question to have received as any, but an unmistakable answer nevertheless.

The Index began to die at local noon, as they finished their work, and the raiders on Amerika's warships looked up to find themselves suddenly prey to another attack by aircraft interceptors. The terminal batteries they had scorned for a day and a night began to open up, despite the fact that their own parked ships were taking most of the hits. The vessel Belkov was aboard had sullenly swung up off the apron and had got into difficulties with the aircraft. A shuttle was sliced in two and Oujuku grudgingly ordered them to light out.

"We'll leave them something to remember us by as we go," Ellis told his crew as they struggled into orbit. The exodus was close run, the big beam weapons of the equatorial girdle targeted them, but the shields held and they made escape velocity without further loss. Behind them, the pearl of Cho Sen had been left in total ruin. Twenty-four of the thirty ships they had found were smashed beyond repair. Baron Harumi's own vessel was smashed beyond recognition.

They met together after the deceleration phase coming out of Gimel-Eight-Oh-One someway along the Seoul chain, and there Ellis announced his intention to try for Duval. Oujuku departed for the Boundary, dragging Belkov behind him to an uncertain future. He said he would see his ass freezeed down in Camp Worth for cowardice and that until then Belkov would do as he was told, as a lowly vice-admiral must.

82

SEOUL

Dawn came in bloody rags over the vast apron of Seoul City. Duval wiped the sleep from his eyes and looked down over the command citadel walls to see what the disturbance was. He had watched the comings and goings of messengers and high-ranking officers all yesterday. Something enormous, something unexpected and immensely important had happened. The reports were being beamed straight to the command citadel without interference from the apron. Tremendous activity was suddenly necessary. What had happened? It smelled like a disaster.

Duval brought his gaze back within the compass of the walls. He had been imprisoned here since his insane approach to Katsumi. Michie had screamed at him that he was killing himself, growing hysterical as she realised he could not be persuaded away from this obsession.

Choi Ki Won had finally acquiesced and had gotten Michie and Kenichi aboard a United Baltic States nexus ship that would touch Amerika enroute for her home port of Riga. He knew the captain well and could trust him. Duval felt the void inside him shift as he remembered the parting. Michie's last words to him had been that she loved him and would always love him, but that she knew in her soul she would never see him again.

That had broken his heart, and he had had enough time to dwell on it. He had been confined under Nishima's orders instead of being sent inside the command citadel as he had hoped. Choi Ki Won had sent his own wife and three youngest sons away on the same nexus ship. And within a month of Duval's surrender, he also had been arrested. It had been Katsumi's doing. After it was ordered that the Probings must stop, Katsumi had looked for another way to discover where his sister had gone. Choi Ki Won had been an easy target. Many people knew that the mathematician and the merchant were close friends. Katsumi had had him crucified on the castle walls. It had taken him three days to die.

Why doesn't Nishima use me? Duval had asked himself, unable to understand. Then, suddenly, when it was almost too late to hope, Nishima had produced him and set him to work.

During his close captivity Duval's hatred had solidified into a hard mass. He knew now he could afford to mark time and await his chance. Though the command citadel laboratories were working night and day to arm the invasion ships, their efforts would not now affect the fundamental strength of the fleet. The invasion was within three weeks of lighting out, and they had made only twenty singularity guns after the new pattern. In a fleet of two hundred battle cruisers, that was negligible—enough to arm only two big ships properly. The months wasted by Nishima had cost the Emperor dear. If the gods granted the opportunity, Duval had vowed to make him pay an even greater price.

Only one thing mattered now. To kill Baron Harumi. Without him the invasion would lose its impetus and its guiding intelligence. Without him, it would not be half as effective. *If only the opportunity would arise.*

Duval looked down across the curving plex roofs again and into the street to identify the disturbance. This time it was not a bannerman or messenger, but a religious parade. The monks approached, walking solemnly. Their heads contained in *tengai,* voluminous reed baskets, their hands thrust inside loose blue gowns that hung down to their *geta*-clad feet. At each shoulder a cloth bag swung, held by two cords representing the *yin* and *yang;* inside, he knew, would be a sword and a *shakuhachi* flute. They were *komuso,* the same order as the monk who had attended him during the darkest days of his interrogation by the *kempei,* and the sight of them awakened feelings of terror within him. The narrow road cleared respectfully before them, early morning ground traffic moving to a halt, people bowing and pressing back against the terminal walls so that the procession could continue on without breaking formation.

At the head a monk waved a fuming thurible so that perfumed smoke billowed out to left and right as he walked. Beside him another held aloft the staff and pennant of the order, a white triangle on which was set the *mon* of the Kunesoki clan. Behind came a cadre of twenty-four monks, four abreast, and behind them eight pallbearers carrying the red lacquer coffin over which was spread a white mantle. The bearers were flanked on each side by a single column of eight, and a second block of twenty-four brought up the rear.

One of the monks was chanting, a sad tremulous wail that the others took up in answer.

"Wheyeeee-ee-ee-ee . . . Whoaoh-oh-oh-oh . . ."

The sound made Duval stare. He had never heard any religious chant like it before, but the rhythmic power of it sounded strangely familiar. They must be Cho Sen Koreans, he thought. Koreans or men from the peculiar quadrant of Hokkaido. Then he saw the hands of the coffin bearers raised high in the flare of a torch, and he saw a sleeve fall away to reveal a tattooed forearm.

Suddenly he knew what the chant was: an old rhythm, often sung aboard Amerikan ships during the long deceleration periods. *Jeezus, it can't be,* he thought. *It can't be!*

He watched wildly as they came on, passing the citadel guard, who admitted the entire procession, respectfully and without question, then they passed out of sight behind the tall plex walls. He ran to follow them and found they were coming straight towards the research block.

Instinct pressed him back against a wall. Then he saw the huge coffin drop down and the monks begin to tear off their baskets and *geta*. Loaded arms were broken out: hidden blasters, cutter guns, and blocks of meson explosive appeared as if from nowhere. One of the command citadel guards stumbled round a corner, unprepared, and was hacked down, a hand over his mouth. Then several assailants lit up their weapons. Almost silently and with great discipline the force split into four separate units and dispersed.

Duval mouthed a prayer. Whoever they were they knew the plan of the citadel well enough to find what they wanted. Already the lead unit was among the research buildings, laying fire on the security systems. Someone began to yell. Weapons crackled out and three of the research workers turned and ran back inside, pursued by attackers. A violet meson flux began to lick up the outside of the annex. Then a huge explosion took off the roof and threw it into the still dark sky, throwing him to the ground. Dazed, he saw a great orange pall mushroom up over him, felt the heat sear his face.

Debris rained all around. When his vision cleared, he saw the gates of the inner command citadel slamming shut high above. Armored troops began pouring from the guardhouse below, their leaders falling as a volley of electric-blue fire ripped into them. Duval watched, shock draining him as the assailants converged on the armory. They were coming this way. *What about Baron Harumi?* his brain screamed, then something snapped inside his mind. *You can't get at him now the inner citadel's locked tight! But he must die! He must die!*

He bolted out from his cover, his obsession possessing him completely now. A hail of sniper fire was slicing down among the chaos from the citadel walls, lightning zinging off the plex walls and crete roadways. The research block had become a roaring furnace, throwing running forms into silhouette against it, and casting huge, distorted shadows across the smoke-filled yard. Then one of the destroyers saw him and charged after him, a broad-beam weapon in his hand. He saw he was trapped.

"No!" he raged at them in his native tongue. "Stop! You're ruining everything! It's Baron Harumi who must die! Baron Harumi. Don't you see?"

The attacker crashed to a halt, paces from him, his face grimed black and full of fury, his plex breastplate glittering under the tatters of the midnight-blue priest's robe. The boss on the breastplate was phased to chrome, reflecting the inferno from his chest like a burning heart.

Duval tensed for the laser slash, but there was none. Instead the blaster rang to the ground and he felt his arms seized in a demonic grip.

"Duval! Duval! Don't you know me!"

He was paralysed. This was a terrifying nightmare. "*Ellis?*"

"I've come for you, Duval!"

"No!" He shrank back from the apparition, loathsomely, struggling with every fiber of his being as he had against the *kempei*'s Probe.

"Listen to me!"

"Get away!"

"I'm taking you, Duval! Back to Amerika! To your wife and son! To your home!"

"You can't! I must stay! You're not real!"

He fought against the nightmare *kami*, fearing madness, holding to the only certainty there was. He could not leave Seoul while Baron Harumi still lived.

Again the impossible apparition raised its hand, this time to strike, but again the blow failed to come. Instead the demon with Ellis's face was blasted back from him, a sniper's beam dead in his heart.

He tore his eyes away from the body and fled to hide himself, looking back only once to see the hell wraiths descend on the body and carry it, fleeing away to where a big blunt-nosed shuttle had dropped down like magic over the walls, absorbed them into its gaping mouth, and burst away at incredible speed.

83

LIBERTY

Ellis pushed through the rain-soaked crowd and scraped the filth from his boots before following the secretary's man into the pillared splendor of the White House. He was glad that the freezing weather had abated, but the rain had blackened his mood and made his chest twinge where his ribs had been cracked last June in the Seoul assault.

The sniper's beam had caught him above the heart, but the hit had struck him square on the boss of his plex breastplate and the intense heat had spread unevenly, snap-warping the ceramic backing, breaking ribs, and knocking the wind from his lungs. His boys had carried him back to the apron where two captured orbital shuttles had fought their way up under the walls of the fortress. It had been a superbly orderly escape with only three troopers killed, and he knew he should feel grateful to be alive, but he had not taken Duval, nor had he killed him, and at that he felt only shame and huge apprehension.

The Liberty spring was upon them now and all the red-bud trees in the city had come alive. All the signs were for a hot summer, but the meteorologists had so far gotten it all wrong: Liberty had never seen rain like it, and the impending invasion had turned the once-serene avenues into slushy barricaded tangles of crete and plex and steel ready to take on the invaders in hand-to-hand fighting.

"You had a pleasant journey, Captain?" the immaculately uniformed Marine lieutenant guard inquired politely.

"Thanks, but the truth is I had a foul journey. This whole planet's awash with antipersonnel defenses and heavy transport and rain. At the gates, I came through a bunch of new draftees gawping at the building—hell, Sergeant, they're just boys."

"Ah, that'll be the Kansas volunteers. They've just hit planetside today from the Cornbowl. Organic agrics mostly. Not many of them have seen a city before, let alone the White House."

"Most of them haven't seen a goddammed house at all, to look at them. What the hell's Deke Copeland thinking of, bringing in farm boys like that?"

"Amerika must do as Amerika can." The guard shrugged. "They volunteered, Captain. And we don't turn away willing hands."

"Well, I guess not."

Ellis wiped away the last of the mud from his boots and followed the other up the steps. He had come at Cassabian's urgent request, hoping for news to equal the reports which had greeted him on his return from Seoul in July. At that time he had visited Cassabian to be told how triumphant the rest of Oujuku's mission had been, and that had gladdened him. Although the rumors of it had been rapturous, the truth had not fallen far short either. According to Cassabian, Oujuku had come back four days after Liberty's summer solstice to an ecstatic reception. It had been in celebration of his handiwork at Chongjin, because after their parting Oujuku had cruised back towards the Inchon chain where Korea's second most strategic nexi were clustered, and there he had led his forces planetside to capture the fortified stations of Andong and Wanju. These commanded the nexus chains from Chonjin to Seoul and he had waited there a month for Admiral Matsumoto's Okinawa battle cruisers, eager to take them on, until the politically motivated Del Hamilton had panicked and ordered them home. Half had gone before Oujuku could stop them, and, left with a depleted fleet, he had had no choice but to think of following.

But even as John Oujuku had swung back along the Inchon chain with home in mind, he had pulled them out of the critical path to wait up a day or so for no apparent reason. Miraculously they had happened on a great prize: the transporter *Hizen Maru* returning from Chiang Rai with her hull phased to radio black for maximum secrecy, and laden with *refined* aurium.

To anyone but a psientist it would have been called inexplicable, beyond all reason, beyond naming even, except to call it pure chance. But it had not been pure chance. John's sure psi-sense, he knew, had felt the currents of psi-energy shivering and detected the passage of the big ship into the nexus. He had *known* there was aurium and argentium on board by their sheer mass: four thousand tons of each, plus twenty thousand tons of hypon, and added to that, four hundred and ten crew captured, twenty Neutrals who had been in transit released, and even an Amerikan prisoner got out . . .

As he was conducted to the secretary's Pennsylvania Avenue–facing office, Ellis shook his head in wonder, reflecting again on the many ways their convert operations had profited their cause. Those eighty-seven days had saved the Sector—Yamato's preparations had been thrown into confusion for three months; all Amerika had taken heart at the news that a fifth of the invasion fleet had been destroyed at Chongjin; and because of the *Hizen Maru,* the spoils had been enough to repay the effort handsomely *and* to swell the Treasury's coffers by forty billion inter-Sector spot credits. Even so, the year's grace they had bought had been more precious than all the rest heaped together. Though they had obliterated twenty percent, still eighty percent of the monstrous invasion fleet remained, and, like a wounded Nebraskan tiger, it was now all the more dangerous for its injuries.

Ellis's mood deepened further as he considered again his brother's struggles against the rescue they had attempted. Duval had not *wanted* to leave. It was as though a Zen straitjacket had been put over his mind, and the shock of that moment when he and Duval had faced each other still haunted him.

He waited now outside the secretary's guarded door, noticing how security had tightened since his last visit. They took away his blaster, then he was thoroughly scanned and even patted down for concealed weapons. When the guards missed the curved knife hidden in the top fold of his right thigh boot, he surrendered it angrily to the Marine lieutenant, underscoring the lesson harshly.

"You sonofabitch! You'd have let me go in there with this! It's your job to protect the President!"

"But, sir, I know who you are . . ."

"I don't give a damn, son!"

Jeezus, I've been planetside too long, he thought. On his return to Liberty eight months ago, Reba had met him, and that night they had whispered together in the semidarkness. She had seen the black descarring tabs across his chest and touched her finger to the twisted plex breastplate where the searing heat of the beam weapon had warped it and cold-melted the backing, and he had felt the shiver run through her.

"I hated to see you leave last time," she told him, dewy-eyed in the huge bed. "I looked at the containers loading up and the flags flying on the *Constitution*'s aerials and the plex rippling with colors and your men going through preflight checks, and I was sure your ship would hit a nexus cross-ways and you'd be killed and we'd never be together again like this."

"Ah, but there's a current only an astrogator knows," he had told her, putting his hand to his chest. "A current right in here. To know what to do. When to do it. How to do it. If a man feels it like I feel it, like John Oujuku feels it, and he takes good care to pay it respect, then he'll always be okeh."

"You really are one reckless bastard! They nearly shot you through!"

"I'm here, ain't I?"

"I hate those silly space superstitions you believe!"

"I'll tell you this, Reba, it's no coincidence that all astrogators believe the same thing. On the nexus the way is clear: we have free will, and when human beings live true to their inner feelings, then they action the universe instead of being at its whim. Humans are strange animals, y'know. There's nothing like us in the Known Universe. Maybe the ancient philosopher Carl Sagan is still gonna be right, maybe there are other planets where life started independently, but we ain't found them yet. We're unique, and do you know why? We make our own fate like spiders spin silk. No other living thing does that. And that's why I hate to have synthetic life servants around. Even your Matthew. They give me the creeps. They're intelligent and all, and you can get a conversation out of them all right, but by God they don't fit into the pattern of destiny, and they don't have fates of their own. To me that's like men without faces."

She looked at him hopelessly, tears glinting at the corners of her eyes. "I know you believe all that stuff, Ellis, and I haven't loved you so long without feeling something of a current inside of you, but still you're going away, and that frightens me. I can't help it."

"There now," he said tenderly, taking the breastplate from her. This is the proof of what I believe, he thought. The belief that has sustained me. He told her: "Anything but a ninety-degree hit would have refracted and had the power to burn right through the reflecting motes, and the fact that I had the thing on at all is a miracle."

"Next you'll be saying it's a miracle the beam hit you."

He shrugged. "That the beam hit me is a mystery. Perhaps it was never meant that I should take Duval off of Seoul."

She buried her face in the pillow. "Promise me you'll never cruise away again. Remake your vow to me. *Please.*"

"I can't do that."

"I love you." Her voice was suddenly lost.

"And I love you too."

"Then promise me. You've done enough. Stay planetside."

"That's not my fate."

"Well, make it so, Ellis, you stiff-necked bastard."

He had put his head back, studying the shades of moonlight on rippling leaves outside the window, feeling also the old wound in his shoulder, the one he had taken away from the Sado apron. "There's a battle coming to make all others that have gone before seem like child's play," he said. "It's the Armageddon your father foresaw twenty years ago. I've got to cruise just one more tour, my love. One more, then I'll be yours."

But he had waited out the winter planetside while his cracked ribs healed. The season had seen tremendous mobilisation, and by spring almost the entire eligible population of the Sector had been put under arms. Huge companies of men and women drilling with small arms and whatever could be found to arm them. Combat instructors had been marshaled together, briefed in booby-trap techniques, and then sent out to every vulnerable center. Units of very green troops, uniformed and trained but only marginally equipped, had been ferried to all the strategic places where a landing was suspected. And throughout that time Ellis had had frequent cause to wonder what the result would be when the drop landings began. There would be slaughter. Massive. Bloody. Obscene.

Properly coordinated, the samurai veterans of the conquest of Cho Sen and Free Korea would smash these scratch soldiers to pulp if ever they were allowed to land.

He knew with a sinking heart that that prospect had been heightened by the dereliction he had shown at Seoul.

"I could not have killed him," he had confessed to Reba in torment at his failure. "I stood as close as we stand now, my blaster in my hand, and still I know I could not have pulled the trigger."

"You're the better man for that."

"You think so?"

"No man could kill his only brother and come away unstained."

"He wouldn't follow me. He *chose* not to come away. He deserved to die."

"Yet you didn't pull the trigger."

"Yes, but how many others are gonna die because of that?"

"That's Duval's fate, perhaps. And yours."

Now he had arrived at Cassabian's office, and as the door opened he saw the weary face of the secretary lighten.

"Great news, Ellis! Fantastic news!"

Ellis's spirits leapt. "How's that?"

Cassabian fixed him with a wonder-filled gaze. "It was no work of mine. It's just fabulous psi! Like a bolt of lightning zapping down onto Seoul, killing him just like that."

The rushing of air-cars in the lanes above and the sounds of marching men in the streets below filled the room. Ellis's voice rose. "What're you talking about, Mr. Secretary? *Who's been zapped on Seoul?*"

"The man we've most feared all along, Ellis. The cherry-blossom-assed sonofabitch himself. Oh, the shattering at Chongjin must have broken his heart like a polystyrene cup! Their admiral in chief, the great danger to us—Baron Harumi! He's dead."

84

SEOUL

"The daimyo is very pleased with what you have done, Duval Straker," Katsumi said, examining the artfully arranged *ikebana* of iris heads and willow fronds.

Duval faced him, hating him more completely than he had hated anyone in his life. To have killed him now would have given his soul the same satisfaction that the murder of Baron Harumi had given his mind. He remembered the day he had thrown Katsumi down in a Sado street, his hands around his throat, choking the life from him. How sweet that would be now, he thought. How sweet and how just. You're filth. I know why you want to find Michie, but you'll never find her now. Never.

"Yes, he's very pleased. A hundred singularity guns, and more to come before we light out. Enough to destroy the Amerikan fleet, don't you think?"

"Perhaps, Excellency."

He longed to fall upon the man. With Baron Harumi dead, what did his own life matter? Now there was no reason to live. No reason to carry on making guns for Yamato. He should have gone with his brother, but he had not known. *He had not known . . .*

He forced himself to make Katsumi the offer. "Excellency, might I ask a favor of Nishima-sama?"

"A favor?" Katsumi's surprise and amusement were rich. "I don't think he owes you any favors."

"Still, I should like to ask him."

"Ask him what?"

"I should like . . . I should like to go with you to Amerika."

Throughout the long wait, Duval had suffered the agony of knowing he had made a fatal mistake. Each day he had watched for his chance to gain entry to the citadel, but there had been no way to get close to Baron Harumi. One day he had glimpsed him coming into the shield installation, another time standing on the crete fortifications high above, but Duval was not permitted to leave the area of the laboratory and Baron Harumi never visited it, except once in formal attire to inspect the damage the Amerikans had done during their impudent raid.

The fires of that harrowing night had burned long and bright in Duval's memory. He had hidden his head, pressed into a star niche of the citadel wall, as the massive series of explosions had shaken the entire fortress to its plex roots. It had been thunderous enough to waken all of Seoul.

By noon, *sangokujin* slaves had damped the embers, and he had staggered among the smoking ruins, seeing the load-bearing members of the calibration machine, the optical alignment apparatus, the barrel-reaming lathes, everything busted out of kilter. The explosions had been the wrecking of the argentium tubes, fifteen hundred of them blown to murdering shards by a triple charge of plastic explosive and an oversized mortar bomb that had crashed through the unprotected window. The Amerikans had fled long before the inferno had touched it off.

It had been a brave jaunt, and a hero's gesture, but it had cost his brother his life, and for what? Duval knew now the loss of fifteen hundred argentium tubes was less than an incidental damage to the invasion effort. They would light out with ten thousand ship-mounted beam weapons now: the news had escaped that afternoon that Chongjin had been wrecked by John Oujuku and another year must elapse before they could mount the invasion.

A year to rebuild the research facility and the specialised manufacturing machines. A year to use his techniques in a dozen other labs. A year to make ten thousand singularity guns. With ten thousand singularity guns the invasion must succeed, and there would be no way to stop it. He could have thrown himself headfirst off the fortress wall, but it would have achieved nothing. The singularity guns would still be made. He had lived to kill Baron Harumi. Only that. And now Baron Harumi was dead.

"Amerika?" Katsumi said. "Why should Nishima-sama agree to that?"

"It is the Sector of my birth, Excellency. I would like to see it again before I die. I would like to be allowed to . . . help to liberate it. I am a trained gunner and no man knows better than I do how to use a singularity gun. Do you remember the day on your father's *han* when I demonstrated my skill?"

"Yes." Katsumi's smile disappeared. "Yes. But you're Amerikan. And I don't trust you." I hate you, he thought. Because you defiled my sister and because you keep her from me.

"Don't I deserve some trust, Katsumi-san? I offered my services to you. I did not go with the Amerikan raiders when I had the opportunity."

"We have enough gunners," Katsumi said, toying with him. Privately he was trying to hide his bitter disappointment. The news from Kyoto had been a total calamity and his temper was close to breaking point. It had been made even more fragile by Nishima Jun's rage at the Emperor's decision, and Duval's asking for favors was the last straw. Nishima-sama might want the scum preserved, he thought, but I don't. I want to see him pay for his crimes. Perhaps it's time I began to distance myself from Nishima-sama. After all the favors I've done him . . . by the gods, there's no justice! I didn't poison Baron Harumi in order to see a nobody appointed commander in chief! Nemoto Chikara? *Who is he?* Samurai, of course. A black-toothed court chamberlain and a very high nobleman, yes. But what else? A military sheep, and hardly qualified to lead the invasion! The *bakufu* and the rest of the Emperor's government have gone completely insane.

He turned to Duval, visibly angry now. "You gave yourself up in the hope of protecting your wife. The Korean, Choi, told me that before he died. And you were not taken by the Amerikans because they did not know you were here."

Duval swallowed down the hard knot of bile in his throat and bowed his head humbly. He knew from Katsumi's reactions that as soon as the last mounting plate of the last singularity gun was in place he would have him Probed again, just as he had had Choi Ki Won Probed, to find out where Michie was. Katsumi's very presence inflamed and disgusted him, but he knew he had to try once more to get himself aboard the *Takeda Shingen*.

"Katsumi-san, please excuse me but you're wrong about the raiders. They came for me particularly. They knew exactly where I was because Michie-san told them."

"*She told them?*"

"She's in Amerika. And only I know where."

85

LIBERTY

All morning the headquarters staff had struggled to keep their invasion simulations going, but the giant screens in the War Room burst with a fury of diagrams and codes that taxed Ellis Straker's mind, and he found there was no opportunity to digest any of it. From the command center the party of high-ranking brass could see the likely unfolding of the attack in sixty-four bright colors, distinct in four probability zones: to their left was the open assault simulation, dotted with ships like jewels, an emerald guard of Amerikan lookouts cruising the approach orbits and buzzing the ruby nexus points one after another; to the right the pale pearly arc of the favored approach, and, seventy degrees beyond, the sapphire interceptors stationed so as to prevent the Yamato commanders staging their invasion from the satellites of the gas giant Arcadia, currently on the far side of the primary star; straight ahead, the possibility of an appearance from the tricky hot nexus that sometimes irised open close to the star itself close by the tiny barren speck of Icarus and well within Liberty's orbit; behind them there flashed a planetside attack senario: landings on sparsely populated polar areas that were still frighteningly naked to the enemy.

All present felt that nakedness keenly. News had come today that, at last, and at full strength, the invasion force had lit out. And time and again the simulations had come up with defense failure after defense failure.

Ellis listened as Admiral Luban, saturnine, long-faced, and all in blue, thrust out his finger at the screens. "We can't afford that many ships! We'd leave the Arcadia option completely open to them."

"Amen to that." Deke Copeland, admiral and commander in chief, Amerikan Forces, bearded and in his fifty-third year, shook the fatigue from his shoulders. For almost half a year he had held supreme command for all military preparations. Now the decision was his how best to dispose the fleet. He turned to Ellis.

"I think the second plan's better. We gotta have two squadrons. Seagrave's at the main nexus to dissuade Yamaguchi, but our main force ought to lie at the Arcadian nexus to protect our most obvious weakness—the possibility of landings on those moons."

"Forget the moons!" Oujuku said, careless of the rank of the men around him. "Let's get our ships down to Yamato like we did before. In an open fight we'll massacre them."

"And if you miss them? What, then, you crazy sonofabitch? No, John, I can't risk that."

"Did we miss them last time?"

"Then they were defenseless, sitting on their aprons!"

"Jeezus! The invasion can only come one way!"

"What if they shoot the hot nexus? I can't risk it!"

"God save us," Oujuku barked bitterly towards the screen. "Because our ships won't!"

Ellis felt the worry that was eating at them all. According to Cassabian's spies, the fleet that Yamato had finally put up was vast, and with Duval's aid its armament was likely to be considerable. He repented his failure once again as he took the comander in chief's elbow. "I gotta tell you this: three squadrons. Oujuku's at Arcadia, yourself at Liberty, as you rightly say, and leave Admiral Seagrave to guard the hot spot. A compromise, eh?"

"I'll think about it."

"Better think fast, Admiral," Oujuku said from a distance, but the attack warning siren carried the words away as another defense scenario came up "Fail."

Ellis could feel his forebodings deepen. Another blast of psi-tingling ran through him.

"Will you look at it!" Copeland said bleakly.

"This is ox shit! The best we've been able to scenario all along is a zero-sum draw."

"You said it! A draw in the ball game."

Luban shook his head, his shoulders rising. "Sure, and I don't see how we're gonna get a single touchdown out of this one."

Copeland looked back stonily. "A draw's equally tough for them."

"Didn't they ever tell you in Navy school, Admiral? War ain't a ball game. In war you wanna fight on the other guy's home ground."

"All I can say is I hope God's on our side this time," Oujuku said.

"In God we trust, John. Remember that?" Copeland turned away, his responsibilities acid-etching his face. Ellis slapped his back heavily. He knew that a psi-storm big enough to scatter the Yamato fleet in hostile space as they tried to transit was the only real hope of averting disaster.

"Yep, Deke," Ellis said quietly. "You ever hear of the term 'kamikaze'? It means 'divine wind'—the wind that blew away the Mongol invasions of Old Japan over a thousand years ago. If God's an Amerikan, then we'll have the biggest psi-storm you ever saw, and for once we'll all be glad of it."

86

THE AMERIKAN BOUNDARY AT THIRTY DEGREES

The drumming to quarters began late on the afternoon of *kin-yo,* Friday, the twenty-ninth day of the month of *Shichigatsu,* by Kyoto reckoning. Aboard the *Oda Nobunaga* the commander in chief, Nemoto Chikara, had reverently unfurled the standard of the Emperor, a red and white flag of incredible age, depicting the rays of the rising sun, the same flag that the Showa Emperor, Hirohito, had saluted on the day Japanese forces had taken Singapore on Old Earth more than five hundred years ago.

The ceremony was broadcast to the entire invasion fleet. As soon as it concluded, the *Takeda Shingen*'s sailors began flying to their stations, and soldiers packed the landing modules and took positions along the hatches fore and aft. Duval Straker ran to the gun blister, his pulse beating like the drums that summoned him. Ahead he saw what could only be the final nexus. On the other side would be Liberty. At last the invasion had come upon Amerika's capital world.

The fleet had departed Seoul on the last evening in May. That was eight weeks past, and Duval had watched the Shinto priests prepare their way with offerings and *sake* each day, and he had eaten and drunk with them, feeling each time he ate that a greater burden of guilt was upon him.

On the first day of their voyage, Nishima Jun, with Katsumi at his side, both dressed from head to toe in their ceremonial armor, had delivered them the diatribe. Only the fearsome face masks were missing.

"Soldiers of the Emperor, we ride to glory. We ride to overthrow a most vile Amerikan woman. We ride to release from her bondage those in Amerika who still hold to the Way. And we ride to establish once again the rule of the Emperor. Have no fear, then, but hold in your hearts the expectation of victory. For we are the Emperor's sword and we shall not be denied. Glory to the Emperor, who has kept faith! Glory to his government, which the *gaijin* have failed to bring down! Glory to the gods of Yamato, who go with us! Take heart, for you are the exalted warriors of the Land of the Rising Sun, and your reward shall be a thousandfold. Brave soldiers, Yamato shall have the victory. The gods are with us, and therefore we cannot fail. *Banzai!*"

"*Banzai!*"

"*BANZAI!*"

"*Banzai!*"

Duval had observed the *Takeda Shingen*'s soldiers throughout the harangue. He saw the way they drank in Nishima's words. They truly believed they were invincible and ignored the Cho Sen mercenaries who stood to the rear and who had barely understood the speech. There had been not a single word to encourage these *sangokujin*, but still they were prepared to fight for Yamato.

The *Takeda Shingen* was a great ship of nine thousand six hundred tons, vice-flagship of the Shinano Squadron. Great blue- and gold-phased horns rose up from her nose; eight turrets, like those of an apron fortress, overhung her flanks; a capacious gallery occupied the three sides of her stern. On her domed bridge Nishima and his lieutenants strutted proudly in their burnished armor, and the flanks of the ships shivered with the colors of the *sashimono*, huge rippling flag-like hull patterns, bearing the *mon* of the chief officers in yellow and black and green and brown. Across the other ships, vast sunbursts, chrysanthemums, and *kanji* characters proclaimed the power of *bushido* and the nobility of the Empire; brilliant decoration crusted the stern and the long, elegant beakhead, and when the drums beat, colored flares and bursting fireworks lit up the spaces between the ships. But for all its martial pomp the fleet's outward show belied the truth.

The *Takeda Shingen*'s complement was six hundred and forty crew and thirty thousand assault troops. For most of the voyage her cargo of troops had slept between decks. They had been loaded in plex freezee tubes, smaller than coffins and in all ways similar except that they were designed to open and eject their contents alive after suspension. Of the invasion force, only the staff officers and samurai connected by blood to the foremost clans were permitted to remain sentient for the duration.

Duval, as nominally a member of the gun crew, had staked his claim to a space between the fourth and fifth starboard gun blisters in the cruiser's waist. Though open to the main corridor, the fire control bulkhead had given him some privacy and separated him from the noise of the crew's mess, and a rough, mutually protective friendship existed between the gunners. Because of the Yamato fetish for open structures, every sheet of plex on board the entire ship had been phased to maximum transparency. He knew, as did the rest of the crew, that quasi-nights under the star-filled sky would be preferable to the hell of opaque hull walls that would remind them all of the stifling overcrowding. He had sat quietly, his back against the bulkhead on those long, empty watches, playing his fingers over the calculator tattoo that still functioned on his hand, substituting different values for the constants in the equations of state of the cosmos. So many stars, so many worlds, so much of the universe beyond the blind confines of the hull, and he a prisoner of his dreaming syllabic poems.

A million-million,
Fields of star-dust, infinite,
Like stars, the galaxies.

He had explained Olbers's Paradox to one of the gunners. "It's poetic license, you see? There are not really an infinite number of stars."

"How do you know, Hasegawa-san? Have you counted them?"

"No, Makino-san. But I can show there cannot be an infinite number."

"How? Only the gods can say."

"By reasoning. See, if there were an infinity of stars beyond the hull, then wherever you looked, whatever line of sight you chose, you would have to be looking directly at a star."

"Perhaps I am."

"But then the sky would be as brilliant as a star's surface, not black. Don't you see?"

The unwilling student had cocked his head. "Not really, Hasegawa-san."

"It's because the universe is expanding. Distant light is redshifted, its energy is diminished."

"Astronomers always blame things they can't understand on the expansion of the universe. I don't believe it's expanding, Hasegawa-san. I don't believe it at all. I think the universe is the Void and that is why the spaces between the stars are black."

Six days out and Makino had snapped under the pressure of "homesickness." He had written his death poem, folded his kit issue neatly on his strap hammock, stripped off everything except a ring containing a lump of pure aurium, and thrown himself into a Dover hopper. By 0600 UT most of the crew had eaten his recycled remains. By 1015 UT the Dover generators were out of operation, their catalytic converters overpowered by the aurium nugget that scrambled the output into unmentionable offal.

By the time they reached the fourth jump the smells issuing from the ship's bowels had been stomach-turning:

"Better sitting inside your assault suit. At least you can get a whiff of fresh oxygen now and again, eh?" Saigo, chief gunner, had got up onto the power cables beside him. He picked a wad of onion fat off his dish and scooped up a mass of purple sticky rice with it before putting it into his mouth.

"You're quite right, Saigo-san."

"Want some?" Saigo had asked. He farted loudly and a rank goat smell enveloped him. "Courtesy of Makino-san and Kimura the quartermaster."

Duval showed his surprise. Since the breakdown of the Dover machines rations were strictly limited, and he had seen Saigo eat once already today.

"Here. Take it."

"Whose is it?"

"*Baka!* It's mine, of course!" He shoved another cold lump, a hybrid of Chinese duck feet, wintergreen, and dry tea leaves, into his mouth. "Why not? It's a bit mixed up, but at least it's better than yesterday. Almost palatable. And it all goes down the same hole, eh?"

"That's like saying we're all dead in the long run."

"Well, so we are! Listen, they're down on the slate as Makino-san's rations, but he won't be needing them, or anything else, where he's gone."

"Gone?"

"He's dead." Saigo shrugged. "Yesterday. He threw himself into the hopper. That's what threw the food machines into chaos. It's all his fault."

"By the gods! No one told me!"

"No one may discuss the incident. General Orders, eh?"

"It's General Orders to report a death."

"You report it if you like, but I don't recommend it. Tanaka-san was beaten just for vomiting in an officer's presence."

"Beaten for that?"

"It's true. I saw it myself. He was just clearing his throat, but Nishima-sama's man took it the wrong way."

"Which man?"

Saigo swallowed another mouthful and inclined his head towards the bridge. "That bastard Hasegawa Katsumi, of course. Come on, eat. And don't worry about Kimura—the quartermaster's in on it. Harada-san!"

The hatred Duval nursed for his wife's brother had bubbled up uncontrollably as Harada, the surly Hokkaido gun captain, came across and took a piece of octopus and blue cheese mush.

"What's the matter? You don't want any?" Harada said.

"Yes. Take a lump," Saigo told him again, thrusting out the bowl. "Those bastard officers steal what they like. Why not us, eh? Gunners need to eat—without us they'll get nowhere."

"No one knows how long it will be before we make planetfall again," Harada said darkly. "Not even our generals."

Duval recalled the look on Nishima's face after his last meeting with Nemoto Chikara. The commander in chief had invited his commanders aboard the flagship, *Oda Nobunaga,* and sent them away tight-lipped and furious. Duval had speculated about the meeting, but it had been difficult to imagine what had been said. The following day, the crewmen had been even less willing to get in Katsumi's way; clearly, whatever had been decided, Nishima had not agreed with it.

Rumors had run riot through the ship: A landing on the Arcadian moons had been intended, and it was that which had been canceled. Nemoto Chikara had ordered a surprise attack on New New York by the Hizen Squadron to pay the devil Oujuku back for what he had dared to do at Chongjin. Even that the whole invasion was a gigantic ruse and they were going to land secretly on Iowa before hitting New New York. The Hokkaido man was right, he thought: no one knew where they were going.

Since leaving Seoul nexus, psi-waves had battered them. Strong fields had forced them to rethink their approach the moment the engines had boosted them to injection velocity and taken them beyond the point of no return. One of the heavy equipment transports, the *Tsunetoki,* was damaged and returned to the Seoul apron. By the middle of the month of *Rokugatsu* the psi-storms had blown themselves out and the Index and all the other probability factors had risen again. Aoki, the astrogator, told him they were still standing at less than forty percent, scarcely better than when they had begun. Nishima's temper had flashed white at their lack of progress, while at his back the *kaigun* naval astrogators he despised began to make disrespectful remarks over the speech he had delivered to them about the Emperor's will being done.

"If it's the Emperor's will that we invade Amerika, why don't we have a painless passage?" Aoki had grumbled, but under his breath so that none of the *rikugun* military men heard him.

During acceleration the communication ports were sealed tight, and no one could egress beyond the hull. Nishima, disgusted by the crew's inability to provide hot, clean bathwater, ordered a general punishment: the entire hull was phased to black, and the interior grew even more noisome. What feeling of light and space there had been was now gone, and those quartered sentient for the duration were packed tighter than squid in their jars. At least the crew, though daily abused, were now able to make good their dignity at the expense of the haughty, usually planet-bound men that a few rough transits had turned into groaning, green-faced *hinin*.

After two weeks they had begun to run true, passing through the Hawaii system without opposition. Orders had emanated from the *Oda Nobunaga* that the commander in chief wanted all nexus ships to clear for action, and so they had, jettisoning almost everything that was not strictly necessary aboard an assault ship. The crewmen had made no open complaint, though none had been able to understand the reason why the Nemoto-sama had made this order.

" 'We shall go from here as if we were in the presence of the enemy,' " Aoki had repeated, spitting out his scorn. "What does he think this is? A screen simulation?"

And Duval had nodded in agreement. "You think he's worried about the Amerikans intercepting us when we transit?"

"If he does, he's a fool."

"Why doesn't Nishima-sama come out?"

"He's sick as a puppy dog from the transits, like all the rest of them," Aoki grunted. "I can't wait to get at the Amerikans. They're the real cause of this war. I hate them and I want to see them all crucified."

Then, as soon as the probability indices had turned noticeably more favorable, Duval had gone down to inspect the lower freezee holds with Kimura, the quartermaster.

"Those *hinin* Koreans! Sorry, Saigo-san, but this is the last straw to break the peasant's back. Look at these seals! Half of them are leaking at the anterior end umbilicus. We're losing a ton of refrigerant a day already. And if the freezees are leaking, what are the men going to be like? If air gets in, they'll rot."

"Those *hinin* technicians in Seoul have shafted us."

They smelled the stench as one of the worst-affected freezees was cracked open.

"That's tainted flesh, all right!"

"Yes! Look, I've seen that before. Rot gas bubbles out of the muscle tissue and pressure bursts the skin. The dog-eating *hinin* must have sabotaged it deliberately."

"What if it's like this aboard the other ships?" Duval had said as they frantically unearthed more and more spoiled coffins.

"Oh, *ko!* The smell! The Nemoto-sama will have to put in at Guam now, whatever the Emperor orders."

"You think he'll disobey the Emperor?" another had asked in awe.

A group of crewmen had begun to crowd at the hatch, curiosity at the reek overcoming them.

"He'll have to!"

"He'll see us die first."

"I hope they all fester in hell! Especially Hasegawa Katsumi."

"Goddamn those Koreans."

"It wasn't the Koreans who said it was the will of the gods that we must invade Amerika," a maintenance technician said.

"What do you mean by that, *inu?*" Saigo said furiously.

"Just that I pity the Amerikans when we come upon them. They'll keel over at the stink."

"Get to your stations, the lot of you! Or I'll have your guts spilled!" Saigo had slapped down the freezee lid angrily and left them, and Duval had stared stoically at the rotted corpse. Though half the losses were due to the poor quality of the seals, the rest, he liked to believe, was the just vengeance of Choi Ki Won's friends and fellow saboteurs.

So, three weeks out from Seoul, and they had had to make planetfall at the intensely cold Guam apron, losing a whole month. The daimyo of Guam, Kido Chochi, had been informed and the fleet had gathered, half in the shelter of the ice mountains, half remaining on the exposed flash-over zone. But that night a violent snowstorm had hit the town, and the ships outside had been buried in ninety-foot drifts. The *Takeda Shingen* herself had put down in a sheltered area, but still the entire fleet had to remain there a whole month until the ships that had been iced in were burned out and recovered, and while new freezees were ordered and installed. It had taken a superhuman effort, but the targets had been achieved and the fleet was once more under way.

Now Duval watched Amerikan Space coalesce outside the observation blister, recalling the panic that had flooded Guam the night before their departure. Hizen salvagemen had come down with the absurd story that John Oujuku was bearing down on them with fifty ships a mere twenty astronomical units away. Perhaps that had decided the commander in chief to order the evacuation, Duval thought; perhaps he had been encouraged by the sudden leap in the Index, perhaps he had been frightened by the Emperor's urgent communiqué that the invasion must proceed as closely as possible according to the original timetable. It was then that Aoki the astrogator had told him that the rumor about the cancellation of the Arcadian moons landing had been correct.

When the *juniji* bell sounded at noon, Duval was still gazing at the massed fleet ranged around him, watching them form into their defensive disposition. Close by stood the *Hidetada*, named after the ship that had brought the Emperor to Amerika on his sole state visit, the huge transport *Iemitsu*, and the assault cruisers *Ietsuna* and *Tsunayoshi*. To the rear stood General Sumita's *Ieyasu* and beyond her the flag of the Shinano squadron, *Ienobu*. On the far side the *Ietsugu*,

General Yonai's flagship, mightiest and newest of the Ise attack vessels, and the *Yoshimune* beside her.

Duval saw that the powerful warships were maneuvering into two groups, following what must have been Baron Harumi's original battle plan, tipping the cusps of the fleet with sword steel. Named mostly for the various supreme shogun of the Tokugawa clan, they made a tremendous sight. The *Ieshige* of General Cho's Kozuke flotilla, the ex-Korean ship *Ieharu,* and the four vast battleships of Nemoto's van: the *Ieyoshi,* the *Iesada,* the *Yoshinobu,* and his own *Oda Nobunaga*. Their combined radio black shields winked on simultaneously and the stars disappeared. The stealth technology was working. Despite all the setbacks and all the delays, all the shortcomings, the sabotage and the holocaust of Chongjin, the invasion fleet was still the most magnificent force, the greatest, that had ever assembled. Duval knew there was nothing in Amerika that could hope to stop it so long as the great ships attacked en masse and so long as they couldn't be detected until the last moment.

Above, on the bridge, Katsumi, shining in his family's ancient war gear, watched with an ecstatic expression as the ships grew luminous once more. They were passing inside the blackout, inside the vast coalesced shield of the fleet. Nishima was a distant figure, squatting austere and solitary on the highest point of the bridge with his war fan in his hand. It was black, shaped like a butterfly, and on it was a red spot with a gold *bonji* device, like the one the Japanese daimyo Takeda Shingen had carried into war a thousand years ago. Both men, in their way, were paragons of samurai virtue, haughty, proud, inflexible, completely indifferent to the suffering of their men and totally convinced of Yamato's coming victory.

Duval forced himself to look away, hating with an ice-cold anger the men who had shaped his life. I've waited to repay you for so very long, he thought grimly, turning his firing key over in his palm. I pray to my own God that the hour will come soon.

THE LIBERTY SYSTEM

At the break of the same day, in Amerikan reckoning the nineteenth day of July, Captain Tom Brophy, in a ship bought from the spoils of five years' marauding in the Neutral Zone under Ellis Straker, emerged from the Liberty nexus a quarter of an astronomical unit from the planet to discover a shoal of luminous shark hulls ranged in a loose formation, surrounding him.

Momentarily paralysed by terror, the Texan rubbed at his eyes and then told his helmsman to run swiftly out of the shield of radio black and make for Liberty. The backfire crackled their aerials to vapor, blacking them out, and they were unable to respond to orbit challenges when they injected above Liberty and were fired on. The crash landing was heavy, and Brophy broke his arm, but by four that afternoon his air-car was plunging across Philadelphia with a tale that the Yamato invasion force was no more than thirty million miles away, but pretty well invisible.

Behind him the news threw the city into uproar. Brophy found the city Defense Committee in a barbecue arranged by the mayor of Philadelphia for his Navy guests: de Soto, McKeown, Frastley, the Hawken family, all were present. Ellis Straker and John Oujuku, bearded and in dress uniform, stood out near the barbecue, a jug of beer and a heap of Dover pork ribs occupying them. They were in conversation with Admiral Copeland and the tough Rhode Islander Curtis Frastley when Brophy burst in.

"It's the bogies! The bogies are here with a thousand ships! I swear to God!"

Ellis prepared to send his empty rib plate across the lawn like a Frisbee, but the commander in chief stepped across his line anxiously.

He called after him, "Well, now, Deke, I guess you just ain't hungry."

"My God, Straker! What you got in those veins, ice water? They're on top of us! They're trying to bottle us up in orbit and they've got the singularity guns to do it!"

The aghast silence became a storm of tongues, but it was Oujuku's voice that rose above them all when the waiter tried to pick up his half-empty beer glass.

He pushed his sleeves up his forearms and hissed, "Touch that beer, son, and I'll take your head off!" Turning to Ellis, nonplussed at Copeland's agitation, he said, "We got two hours yet. Even if Brophy's right, there's still time to eat." But the admiral was already hurrying away.

Deep inside, Ellis's anxiety at the prospect of an invasion fleet as heavily armed with singularity guns as the Amerikan fleet had reached its peak. He had persuaded Copeland to concentrate his own and Oujuku's squadrons together at Philadelphia, and in the weeks following, the admiral had put everyone on top alert, his temper quietly fraying. Then news had come of the invasion force's halt at Guam. Instantly both Ellis and Oujuku had pressed their case to the Security Council. Lubbock, now readmitted to the President's confidence and freed from all pretenses, had obtained from her an order to permit the fleet to follow the attack plan, and through most of July they had been cruising about in the Guam chain, hoping desperately to catch the great fleet unprepared once again. As he watched Copeland making for his air-car, Ellis recalled ruefully how the Amerikan fleet had got to within twenty astronomical units of Guam before a contrary Index had forced them to turn back.

"Wanna settle for a draw now," Frastley said drily, mindful of the wager that rode on the manner of the Yamato fleet's appearance.

"A draw? What's that?" Oujuku said. "There ain't no such a thing."

By a quarter after four the Philadelphia apron was on fire. Hundreds of ships and shuttles were lifting off. The orbital configuration of the main defense satellites favored the attack, and most of Amerika's trim ships had to be tractored offplanet under crude jet power.

Ellis had left the apron last of all, not wanting to miss the sight. The *Constitution* was already in orbit, but this was a moment a psi-talent could not pass over.

"Not so fast," he told the shuttle's coxwain, and climbed up onto one of the stubby air wings and sat down to breathe deep and drink it in. He felt the lubed plex under his hands, micro-ridged and yielding like corduroy shark flesh and still warm from reentry. The engine cowls were smutty with unburned carbon. There was an acrid apron smell on the air and the jetting humming noises of a great fleet putting off.

The cox and his copilot watched him, kind of respectfully, kind of puzzled. Ellis Straker's psi-talent was legendary; maybe he was delaying them around some kind of foreseen disaster. They had heard tales of talents who just reached into inspection hatches and pulled near-critically failed units right out on bare intuition. It was *spooky*.

"See that," he told them, staring into the gold and peach sky. It was rent by condensation trails as the big ships lifted off.

"Sir?"

"Moment of history, boy. Moment of goddamned history. Better believe it."

"Aye, aye, sir."

The big ships rose up like primeval gars and skates, bogling and vortexing swirls of air from their backs. Copeland's *Virginia*, renamed the *Chongjin* after Congress had used some of the profits from the Chongjin mission to purchase her, cruised out in a mass of boiling air, followed by the *Arkansas*, the *Illinois*, and the *Missouri*.

Ellis felt the blasts of warm air abrade him and the heady aromatic smell of the engines. He felt the vibrations shudder through the live wing he was sitting on, dying away as the squadron trailed into specks. Then came Mac Savage's *Georgia*, covered in insignia and revolving lights. The Aquila eagle adorned the hull, glittering in gold, Altair an eagle eye—and a weapons blister. In company were the three other presidential ships, the ones that had blasted their way into and out of Chongjin: the *Pennsylvania*, the *Colorado*, and the *Massachusetts*. They phased to midnight blue as they passed overhead, leaving only their landing lights winking and rippling along their trailing edges.

He saw Hawken's *Texas*, eight thousand tons and bristling with sixteen singularity guns, coming out to meet Oujuku in his *Kalifornia*. Dain Fenwick's *Ohio* and Glory Smith's *Florida* both making to accompany the *Constitution*. The sight of those big sharks made him sigh and gave him a strange fist-hard feeling in back of the sternum. Never had such a collection of Neutral Zone traders and Navy astrogators been brought together before, and the psi-currents in his mind surged at the incredible bond he could feel.

That's the strength of Amerika, he thought. Individuals, damn right, but a tight family when there's work to be done. A man'd need to be a stone . . . He rubbed a hand over his face and slid down off the wing.

"Okeh," he growled, giving them some of the affectionate Straker abuse he knew they prized. "Take her away, you psi-damned idle pieces of hogshit."

"Sir!"

He got aboard the *Constitution* at the height of the exodus and came alongside Fort Bush before local sundown. All around the stationary orbit belt vessels were sliding slowly into eclipse towards optimum defense stations.

As the tension mounted, the fleet of Amerikan nexus ships escaped Liberty orbit, reaching open space unseen by the invader's sensors, and during the passage round darkside Ellis Straker's squadron stole silently into a hyperbolic intercept trajectory, to begin tentatively snapping at the heels of the invader. Once they were certain they had been identified, the radio black screens came down and the awesome splendor of the invader was revealed at last.

When midnight UT rang out throughout the ship, Deke Copeland's shuttle approached the Yamato flag and gave the Yamato fleet his challenge as the Code required. Then Copeland led his line into battle against General Sumita's squadron. The fighting was reserved and cautious, Copeland's line never daring to close with the Yamato fleet. At one point, by chance, they managed to isolate the ailing *Iemochi,* and like a grizzly bear surrounded by vicious pit dogs, they sent themselves against her, putting a dozen holes through her, and the success gave Ellis leave to hope.

By the end of the second day it became clear to him that they were in great jeopardy. If they maneuvered to meet the main Yamato fleet, they would be destroyed, but if they returned planetside, the invader's stately progress into Liberty orbit would continue virtually unhindered. He thought of the *Iemochi* and decided he must press his attack more forcefully, risking himself within range of the heavy but short-range singularity guns and ship-smashers. One Amerikan ship, he reasoned, sailing alone and unattached, might drive into the enemy and detach a vessel for the others to fall upon. It was desperate, and it was suicidally dangerous, but something had to be tried.

He thought darkly of his promise to Reba as the third day began to dawn. Do or die, he had said, this would be his last voyage. And today was the day they would find out which of those forebodings had been correct.

88

Duval Straker had seen the small black and white insignia stippling the Amerikan ship's tail fin and it had filled him with a tremendous urgency. As the ship closed he ordered the gunners to don their pressure suits so that they could continue to fight if a singularity hit should suddenly rob them of atmosphere. The suits were made of micro-thin flexiplex, skintight and almost transparent. They had removable gloves and a snap-up bubble helmet to dome-in the head, neck, and shoulders; four connex hoses hung limply off the torsos like used blue condoms.

He told them to arm their argentium tubes, taking care to monitor the temperature readings carefully, and looked desperately for Harada's return. He was sure at last that his chance had come.

The Hokkaido man had gone below to the *Takeda Shingen*'s aft argentium tube store. He guarded the massive arming keys, while Saigo was fully occupied supervising the forward magazine, and Saigo had ordered him below to augment the argentium on the gun deck. He knew that if the coming attack was as sharp as those of the last two days, they would certainly fire off hundreds of rounds.

The same ferocious vessel that had attacked the *Iemochi* was closing on them now, and Duval looked again at her black-fin device, confirming the flaming hope that the first sight of it had raised up in him. Yes! There was no doubt. It surely was a black field upon which stood out a pure white skull. But Ellis's ship was heading straight down the barrels of the most dangerous singularity guns in the fleet.

Harada returned with the argentium. According to a safety procedure he himself had originated many years ago on Sado, Duval looked at the temperature setting and knelt down to examine it. He turned his back to cover his actions as he did so. In his gloved hand was a small bar magnet that would make the temperature control panel read haywire.

He slipped it under the panel. Then, as he set about opening the argentium flask, he took the first sample tube in his hand and felt it. His brows knit and he tilted the flask up, at the same time hiding the magnet in his hand.

"This argentium's hot," he said, standing.

"Hot?" Harada asked, his Japanese struggling under a thick Hokkaido accent.

"Yes, hot! You can't feel it? Take your glove off." He thrust a tube of first-grade refined argentium against the man's cheek. "And look here—the temperature reading. It's way off!"

"But—it can't be!" The humorless surprise on the Hokkaido man's face showed him at a loss to explain the facts. Argentium tubes had a very narrow operating tolerance, only 3 degrees either side of the critical 282.27 Absolute.

Praying that Harada would defer to his expert knowledge, Duval waved the tube at him angrily. "Can't be? But it is! By the gods, if you've been meddling in the magazine, Saigo-san will have you flayed!"

"Keep your voice down! You think I'm a fool? I don't take liberties with argentium."

"Somebody has. And there's only you and Saigo-san been in there since we left Guam."

"I . . . Maybe it's more of that Korean sabotage."

"You'd better find out. If Saigo-san finds out—" He pursed his lips at the consequences.

Harada was aghast. He cast about him secretively, turning the stares of the others away, then examined the temperature reading again and stared at the underside of the flask. He looked up, watching the onrushing Amerikan ship, shivered by the beam weapons that lanced out, testing the *Takeda Shingen*'s defense shields. Finally he said, "Come with me."

Duval felt a spear of exhilaration, remembering in lucid detail the terror of the kamikaze ship that had blasted the *Thomas J.* to pieces on that psi-drenched day so long ago. He picked up one of the huge arming keys, that for security reasons were as big as a hunting rifle, and followed, but when they were only halfway across the deck, alarms began in the forward scanners, and the despairing yells of the crew, like witnesses to a calamity, rose to a crescendo. Harada ran back, following the line of their eyes, and saw that the Amerikan ship had sheered away, forcing General Yonai's flagship, the *Ietsugu,* to take sudden evasive action, but she had crossed the bows of another Ise Squadron ship whose shields were of identical resonance. The shields interpenetrated instead of repelling one another, and there was a collision that carried away the *Ietsugu*'s bow horns. Meanwhile, Ellis's ship was tacking round to press home his attack. Duval darted an anxious glance towards Saigo, who was striding along his guns, urging his crews to greater efficiency, then to Katsumi and Nishima Jun, who had been brought out onto the bridge by General Yonai's accident.

"Harada!"

"I'm coming."

They went below, Harada besuited, but bareheaded and now without his gloves, carrying the suspect flask close to his chest. The guard admitted them both to the after restricted zone on sight, and they rattled down the zero-gee communication shaft to the gloom of the argentium store. The Hokkaido man twisted his ID smart in the big plex door. No one was allowed here, not even a first lieutenant, and the only illumination was the baleful red glare of operational lighting. It would make looking for a nonexistent temperature problem all the more difficult.

The magazine hatch sill was built up a foot or so and the door edge sealed with huge interlocking pins to prevent unauthorised personnel getting in. Its walls were of solid plex, half an inch thick. The Hokkaido man stepped inside and bent to put the flask down. "Show me where you think—"

Duval's arming key crashed down across the back of his neck. He hit him again with dispassionate force, this time on the crown of his head as he staggered, and then he lay still, bleeding from ear and nose. Immediately Duval took up the flask and began to calculate the time he would need to accomplish his aim.

He split open the plex cover of the *seppuku* pin. Inside, the self-destruct lock gleamed back at him. Firing it would blow the *Takeda Shingen* into tiny fragments, but to succeed he must first arm it. To arm it he needed a pair of keys, and any attempt to insert them would send loud warnings over the whole ship. In addition, the procedure could be overridden from the bridge at any time. It was an immense gamble.

He licked his lips nervously. He felt no fear for himself, but something inside was shouting at him. Five minutes ago it had all seemed so simple. He had committed himself absolutely to dying if it meant the destruction of the ship and all it contained, but now he realised that his commitment had been to suicide, to an alien ideal, to a Yamato ideal. The thought repelled him.

There must be a better way . . .

To get up the comm shaft. Ten seconds to be on deck and three more to get into the airlock, say a minute to egress the hull and accelerate clear of the debris. No room for error.

Could it be done? If so, how? His mind raced as he tried to accommodate the problem.

Another powerful concussion blasted the port shields, shivering the internal fabric of the ship. Soon they would be taking singularity hits from the Amerikan ship. What can I do? Any moment now they'll miss me. They'll certainly miss Harada. It's instant death to desert battle stations, so they'll be looking out for him.

He crouched low, hugging the flask tight to his pressure suit. Put it down, went into the corridor, stared up the companionway. The guard was still standing, arms folded, back to him, his pair of swords jutting. Please God, tell me what to do. Concentrate. Think. Think! What's possible? Ten to fifteen seconds is a minimum. The only sure way's to somehow activate the *seppuku* pin, but I've only got limited resources here. The procedure's too slow and it'll risk discovery, unless . . .

Jesus, yes! If the bridge can override instructions, they must be remoted in the control circuitry! And you've got Harada's maintenance key!

He examined the panel just above his head. It was smooth and offered no means of access. The one set into the floor was more promising. He prised it open and the plex sheet sprang off. He took care: inside, dozens of colored needles of laser light jittered with gigabyte data blocks. They were powerful and would burn him. Their beams had to be wide enough to avoid data corruption by any microscopic dust that might float into the conduit, yet powerful enough to repulse anything bigger that blocked the information path.

He heard a thin squeaking coming from the conduit.

Ne . . . he thought, reacting immediately. Nothing in the cosmos has been able to stop them spreading. They go wherever men go. We have to put up with them . . . I hate rats.

His mind blanked as he read the coding on the plex grille. He searched frantically, the dagger-bladed characters knifing at his eyes and brain until he could hardly read them. Then he saw it, the *kanji* for "self" and "kill"—*seppuku!*

So! It was an interrupt system. A kind of booby trap.

How can I interrupt the optical pathways? What can I put in there that won't burn through? It must be foolproof. I've got to be certain.

The lasers were old technology, almost as old as the idea of hard wiring, invented just after the dawn of electronics, but they were used for a purpose. Old technology was tried and trusted. And no circuit on the ship had to be trusted more than the *seppuku* refresh line. It was part of the dead man's handle design: without regular heartbeat pulses sent from the central organism of the ship, the self-destruct would be set in motion, ensuring that no crippled ship could fall into the hands of the enemy. If interrupted for more than a minute, the refresh would be missed, the circuit would go into alert. Any attempt to restore the refresh without coded procedures would create an immediate detonation.

Suddenly the parameters of the problem were clear in Duval's mind: first, fix the alarm line; second, cause an interruption of the *seppuku* pathway; third, wait for one minute; fourth, restore the laser.

But how?

The microsecond the laser started up again the *Takeda Shingen* would be dust.

It was a big ship. There were three charges and three circuits, all separate. It would be sufficient to blow just one. And best to blow the aft circuit. He ripped out the alarm line transceiver.

Dead man's handle . . .

He looked at the motionless Hokkaido man and a hair-raising solution bloomed. Quickly he lifted the bloodied body upright and it fell down, with a ghastly groan as the last air escaped from its concertina rib cage. With grim curses on his tongue, Duval rolled Harada's corpse over, arranging the limbs straight, as if the body was at attention. Then he took the dead hand and plunged it into the laser.

Where the needles touched, smoldering began. The skin of the palm cooked and browned like paper under the brilliant focus of a magnifying lens on a summer's day. Greasy smoke billowed in the needle beams, and within two or three seconds the beams were emerging from the back of the hand.

Duval's neck hackled with a deep-seated fear. Everything he was doing flew in the face of the safe habits and prohibitions of a lifetime. The sweat steamed from him and his head filled with the grisly reek of charred flesh. He tried desperately to calm himself, knowing what he must do. The lasers were more powerful than he had supposed. The rat problem well catered for.

He pushed Harada lengthways into the conduit.

A sudden pang of terror overcame him and he began to tremble. My knees are going, he thought. What if my knees go? Harada's inert body smoldered horribly as he watched, then the universe blinked out. A bang had torn him away from the mesmeric sight. The vault door had been swinging as the ship yawed to escape the attentions of the attacking ship and the compensators reacted. It had slammed noisily, shutting out the corridor light. He twisted round in utter blackness. Only the smoldering needles were visible now; only those jittering multicolored lines existed in the whole universe, drilling their way inexorably through Harada's body, lighting him up from the inside with a ghastly and terrible Christmas-tree glow.

Where was the door? Where was it? As his hands groped out blindly they touched cold panes. He began to claw furiously at its edge in the jet blackness, but his nails could make no purchase. The door was stuck fast. The roasting flesh spat and crackled, the stinking smoke making him retch.

"Jeezus Christ! Help me!" he shouted, giving way to panic. He pulled the arming key from his belt and then he realised that the door opened outward. He heaved his shoulder blindly forward and burst out into hellish red light. It was flashing—blasting an interrupt warning which should have been screaming around the ship, but which he had curtailed by pulling out the alarm transceiver. He slammed the vault and locked it. Gripping the handholds, he pulled himself up the comm shaft, but it was as if his body was made of lead and his feet were held fast on the treads. He forced himself up, painfully, one step at a time, and when he got to the gun deck men were peering down at him anxiously. He tried to make a reassuring face at them, but he was shaking and he was aware of how sick his smile must be.

The guard turned. "You! Where's the other one? Two of you went down."

Another deafening concussion crashed out from the screens.

"He's there, look."

Duval looked up to where Nishima Jun and Katsumi would be standing together on the bridge, many decks above. He took a deep breath and, when the guard bent to peer below after Harada, he took two steps towards him and brought the arming key down on his head. The guard's body pitched into the gloom of the comm shaft, falling soundlessly until he hit bottom.

Three men saw him do it. They broke away from their stations instantly, yelling as they came at him. He leapt for the comm shaft, hauled himself up the weightless tube, pulling desperately on the aluminum rungs, then onto the upper gun deck, and began to make for the airlock hatch.

"Stop him!"

"Somebody take him!"

"He's gone mad!"

His own gun crew was before him, barring his way into the airlock. Saigo's face was angry and uncomprehending. Duval snapped the bubble of his pressure suit up and threw himself at the man with all the force he could manage.

89

Ellis Straker pressed home the attack furiously against the *Takeda Shingen*. She was vice-flagship of her squadron, and almost three times the mass of his own ship. Her armament was heavy and accurate and the *Constitution* had taken deep wounds from her in her attempt to close.

Ellis gritted his teeth and held his course, heartsick that Copeland's formal strategy had not worked. His impatience had burst out yesterday. Twice Ellis's orbital pilot had warned him of the folly of cruising within range of the *Takeda Shingen*'s singularity guns.

"She's a big one, sir. And though we're pretty handy ourselves, we won't live long if you bring us under those guns again."

"Hold your helm steady, Lieutenant," he had shouted back, knowing that they had no choice.

As the vast bulk of the fifteen-thousand-tonner grew ahead, he ordered the skull ensign broken out across the tail fin. Doubtless there were enough Zone veterans aboard the Yamato ship to understand and respect it. Then he had seen the Ise Squadron leader, *Ietsugu,* sixteen or seventeen thousand tons of her, thundering in, and he had tied the enemy's course in a knot and thrown her into collision with two ships so that she lost her dorsal fin and stabiliser pods.

And so they ran on, the decks jumping with the shocks of their beam weapons as they closed for hand-to-hand. The shields lit up in fantastic colors as the bright beams slammed into them.

"*Five thousand yards and closing,*" the ship's evaluator chimed.

This adversary's the equal of any in the fleet.

"*Four thousand yards and closing.*"

I'll chop her to bits and show Deke Copeland the way home.

"*Three thousand yards and closing.*"

And if we die, we'll have died with honor . . .

Suddenly, at two thousand five range and just as they were about to come under the lethal singularity fire of the *Takeda Shingen*'s biggest guns, the watching Amerikans saw the fist of God appear over the stern of the enemy and hammer her to pieces. A second later the shock of a massive explosion peppering their shields with debris could be felt, visible as a ring expanding across the clarity of space. It shook them, and the watchers saw that what had seemed to be a titanic fist was a huge blossom of twisted fragments in a blaze of meson radiation.

Ellis looked to his gunner incredulously. There had not been a beam weapon close to making hull contact for over half a minute.

"Chief gunner?" he shouted in the stunned silence, but the gunner held up his hands disclaimingly over his still-loaded weapons.

The whooping and cheering began as the fragments cleared. They watched ragged lumps of plex and metal rain into the shields all around them as they were consumed in burning white embers. Some pieces hung there spinning above the *Constitution*'s deck, where they were pointed at triumphantly. The entire stern of the *Takeda Shingen* had been blown away and everyone who had been on her bridge was dead. The rest of the crew were trying desperately to recover and seal her bulkheads so that the oxygen-fed flames spurting out from her stern could be smothered and the leaking atmosphere did not make a vacuum of the rest of their ship.

Ellis barked himself hoarse, sending the ensigns and cadets round the decks with a hundred orders. The invaders had seen the *Takeda Shingen* explode, and several of their ships were putting about to help. There were too many for the *Constitution* to fight and Ellis put her head about too, suddenly iron certain that it was the right thing to do. The warble of an alarm by the stern screens comms bank made him turn.

"What is it?"

"There's a man outside the screens, Captain," a voice shouted below him. "He's alive!"

"A man?" he called at the scanner.

"Do we blast him, sir?"

"You sonofabitch," he shouted, angered at the man's moral cowardice. "I won't have you shooting down survivors. Get a line to him. He may have something to tell us."

There was a pause. Then, "We heard they sometimes got booby traps strapped to them, sir."

"Bring him inboard, and that's an order!"

"Yes, sir."

They closed the shields down for a few seconds and tractored the lightly suited figure inboard, and moments later, with the *Constitution* accelerating planetward, the exhausted man was hauled up before the captain.

Those who watched were amazed at the way they fell into each other's arms. It was as if they had both been trying to hug the breath from the other's lungs, and for the rest of that dizzying afternoon brother had looked at brother again and again.

Ellis found himself drawn to look at his brother's face and listen to the accent of his voice that was at once dearly familiar and yet completely foreign. And often as he looked, he found Duval was looking back through the gloom of the bridge's operational lighting, as if trying to fathom the changes worked by so many years. There was so much to talk about, but a battle was being fought, and Duval lent himself to the gunners.

They shared the *Constitution*'s bridge as Amerika's defenders broke off pursuit of the massive fleet. Watching Oujuku in the *Kalifornia* and Hawken in his *Texas,* both remembered the evil that had been done to them on Sado. Duval told him that Baron Harumi had been his reason to stay in Seoul and that the Sado daimyo had been blown to ions when the *Takeda Shingen*'s bridge disintegrated. Ellis, for his part, told Duval how his son and wife were safe in Amerika, and when Duval described the circumstance of Kenichi's birth, Ellis shook his head in wonder before admitting how it had been this very ship—*this very ship*—that had attacked them.

It would have been so easy to have destroyed their ship in revenge for the deception the Yamato vessel had practiced, Ellis thought. Yet he had not. And again, at Seoul, when they had met face-to-face only to be ripped apart by a stroke of chance. How many times had he wondered about that. Why? What unimaginable reason? And when, after Seoul, he had awoken aboard the *Constitution* and had thought his brother lost to the enemy, and there had been agonies . . .

His mind heaved with a strangeness that prickled his flesh, and the psi-currents swelled up his spine. He had never believed in blind chance, and it was as if a golden aura, rooted in his life but born of mystery, enveloped them both.

"You never told me about my father," Duval said, the strangeness of his accent fascinating Ellis. "You never said we were only half brothers."

And Ellis looked at him, tears in his eyes, and told him, "A brother is a brother. You either got one—or you ain't."

That night their joy at meeting was undiminished, but Ellis took his brother aboard the *Chongjin* to join in counsel with Amerika's admirals; he had not lost sight of the menace that still towered over them.

"The Yamato commander has orders from the Emperor," Duval said, passing on what the astrogator Aoki had told him. "Orders he was intending to follow to the *kanji,* that there must be no attempt at a landing until his fleet had secured a bridgehead in orbit and the army under General Yamaguchi was made operational. Tell your army that the moons of Arcadia at least are safe."

There was a flurry of activity as the admiral ordered an immediate communiqué to Lincoln sent out, then Copeland said urgently, "You say you know all about their guns and their disposition? Our fleet mounts in total around five thousand singularity guns, but of the big long-range guns designed to hit at three miles, we have less than a thousand. How is it with them?"

"They're mounting ten thousand new pattern singularity guns, but they're not of the Amerikan kind. They have heavy, short-range ship-smashers." He turned to Ellis. "Though I respect my brother's bravery, it's my belief that his ship would have been sunk had the *Takeda Shingen* not lost her tail, and that applies to the other big ships equally. To come within three thousand yards of the fleet shield will be suicide. They're relying on the Hakon Effect, what they call the Radiant Sun Strategy—all of their ship's shields coalescing into a mega-shield stronger than the sum of its component contributions. You must stand off from it at all costs!"

"That ain't our style!" Curtis Frastley said, rising. "We must break them before they reach Fort Bush."

"Sure," Oujuku whispered to Ellis as Frastley voiced his thoughts. "We *must* close with them, or we're lost! I don't give a damn about all this tactical bullshit, but I'll fight as I've always fought, according to my best feelings—in here!" He thumped his chest. "And if Admiral Copeland don't like that, then that's his problem."

"And if you're court-martialed for your disobedience?"

"Hell, you wouldn't shoot me. I'm the best goddamned astrogator you got."

"You're pretty sure of yourself, ain't you?"

"Yep. It takes a court to shoot a man, and a court's gotta have evidence. What me and my boys get up to is something I got five hundred sworn witnesses to. That's loyalty, mister."

Copeland tried to steer them away from the issue of Oujuku's individualism. He turned to Duval. "So, because of their singularity guns, if we get closer than three thousand yards we'll be minced up, but they're shooting beam weapons at normal range. And as we've seen, our own beam armament's not energetic enough to overwhelm so many ships in so tight a formation."

Duval said, "It's their hope to keep that 'radiant sun' made up, a formation which takes a lot of power and well-skilled orbit pilots to hold because their shield repulsion tends to squeeze it apart. If they can hold it, they can't be taken."

"It ain't enough to keep wild coyote dogs out," Oujuku said fiercely.

Hawken shook his head. "It ain't enough to follow them like wild dogs follow a herd. We might be dogs and them a bunch of sheep, but we still gotta bring them to a fight in time to prevent their taking Fort Bush."

Copeland said, "He's telling us that if the guns on our ships can't bust a way through their defenses before they reach orbit—and nothing else'll disturb their composure—then we're helpless."

"Helpless?" Frastley echoed, and Oujuku told them all, "I'll burn in hell before I'll let any man of them get planetside of me. When they're well herded into Seagrave's ships, we'll go in blazing as we have today, 'cept this time we'll be at point-blank. Sure! A couple of hundred yards' range where a singularity gun'll make so much Swiss cheese outta anybody—them or us!"

"There is a way," Duval said. All present turned to look at him. His voice was soft, almost distant. He was remembering the deck of Jos Hawken's old flagship, the *Thomas Jefferson,* and the way fear had engulfed him as he saw the enemy approaching. Though it was almost twenty years ago, he was reliving the hell that had played about him on that deck: the same fires that had burned thc ship into an inferno about him had made the guns stutter into uselessness. The stability of argentium tubes was very temperature-dependent, 3 degrees Celsius either side of the critical operating temperature of 282.27 Absolute and they wouldn't work!

But how could they heat up the tubes in the whole Yamato fleet?

The Olbers's Paradox . . .

"Yes," he said. He began to scratch-pad the back of his left wrist with his forefinger, and the keys of the calculator tattoo responded by appearing on his thumb. "Yes! There is a way!"

At the seventh hour on Sunday, July 28, the day *shichiban* in the month of *Shichigatsu* in the reckoning of Yamato, the Invincible Liberation Fleet finally ended its long planetward run. It had been successful, running the fearsome gauntlet of Amerikan attacks and achieving its objective of Liberty orbit, where it injected almost completely intact.

As his ships lay tight in their defensive formation thirty thousand miles above Liberty's equator, the commander in chief and his council met again. They were invulnerable inside their Hakon Effect ovoid. Never had the prospect of landing General Uehara's and General Ida's troops been so bright; never had the success of the Emperor's glorious design been so clearly assured. Then the scanners began to erupt with warnings.

Eighty foolhardy Amerikan ships in line-abreast came stealthily out of the shadow of Liberty. Every Yamato officer knew that so suicidal an attack mounted in the confining space of low orbit could only be a measure of the Amerikans' desperation. They started to train their guns on the approaching ships, then lights flared on the shields and pyrotechnic displays began as every beam weapon in the Amerikan fleet was trained on the tight globe of invading ships.

"What are they doing?" Nemoto Chikara asked his aide with incomprehension.

"Excuse me, Lord, but I can't understand their aim. It seems to me they are committing *seppuku.*"

Nemoto's quizzical expression showed that he was mildly perturbed. "It is true that our shields can absorb beam weapon energy without fear of failure, is it not?"

"*Hai.*"

"How long can they keep it up?"

"For several hours, at least, Lord. But that's of no advantage to them."

"And you say it can't harm us?"

"They can fire every beam they have, for as long as they want, Lord, and it would not penetrate self-compensating shields. Like a knot, the harder they pull on the ends, the tighter it becomes."

"And they know this?"

"They invented the self-compensating shield, Lord."

Nemoto made a tight little gesture of surprise and his long solemn patrician face creased. Under the neat warbonnet a face so flat that it was almost concave seemed for once to be about to crack into a smile. Nemoto's teeth were lacquered a perfect Imperial black. "Then this is quite extraordinary behavior."

Soon all eighty Amerikan vessels had maneuvered into place around the Yamato fleet. Their weapons blisters had become torches of brilliant fire. Tongues of ionised particles lit up the invaders in a violet glow of Cherenkov radiation as the intense fields of the defensive shield shattered the beams harmlessly. But still raging energy continued to pour into the shield sphere until it closed around the fleet in a complete ball of radiance like a miniature A-type star.

Inside the globe, the radiation temperature began to rise inexorably. Though there was no conduction or convection of heat in the vacuum of space, the radiant surface enclosed them in four pi steradians—over forty-one thousand square degrees—each square meter pumping energy into the plex hulls like a hot, white sun.

Aboard the Yamato ships the captains received orders to phase their hulls to chrome, the most highly reflective surface available on the mote palette. Deep in the ships' interiors, refrigeration plants fought back and were then put into overload. Another round of general orders was issued. They began to de-suspend the remaining shock troops to save on refrigerant capacity. But still, hour by hour the temperature rose inside the ships, under the frightening onslaught of energy that matched the conditions of a contracting universe.

Soon the crews were sweating in their uniforms, breathing slow and deep with the lassitude of tropical heat. The temperature alarms began to pop. Computer tissue began to complain, then to stifle. Sauna conditions prevailed, turning everyone red in the face. And then the refrigeration plants began to break down. In the external engine pods, plex surfaces began to glow red, then orange, then white.

One by one, the ships experienced a slackening of power on their secondary engines, and the shield repulsion gradually began to force them outward. The perfect globe became blistered like a great fiery bunch of grapes, then the individual grapes started to break off and drift away.

Within minutes of the first separation the reluctant Nemoto's ships were scattered and in confusion. The defensive formation that had protected them was now utterly irrecoverable. The Amerikan attack was pressed home against ships whose argentium tubes were disabled by temperature instability and whose engines were failing.

Oujuku and Straker, Frastley and de Soto, Hawken and Copeland, all went in without mercy, each lesser captain following whichever admiral he pleased. And for hours the lumbering gilded giants of Yamato, hidebound monsters, their defensive globe shattered, their captains chained down with tight orders and the fear of the Emperor's wrath, were relentlessly searched out, smashed, holed, sent spinning planetside, annihilated.

An hour later, the ships' gongs chimed midnight UT. It was now the day the Emperor had appointed for glory, but the pathetic remains of the invasion force found itself driven steadily onto the lethal upper reaches of the E-layer of Liberty's atmosphere. Finally, Daimyo Nemoto Chikara, chamberlain to his Imperial Majesty the Emperor of Yamato, came out of his paralysis. The vision of future disaster that had held him in its grip was no longer a mesmeric premonition; with dawning horror he began to understand that it was now a nightmare from which there would be no waking.

As his remaining captains put away the last shreds of hope for a landing, Nemoto's fervent prayers were answered. The singularity guns and the engines began to work again, but it was not the looked-for divine deliverance.

On the assault decks of the transports, General Uehara's troops knelt in vast ritual lines, thousands upon thousands, filling the spaces from which they had intended to paravane like a rain of death onto Lincoln and Philadelphia. They composed themselves with the precision of the intersections on a *go* board. As one, following the actions of their commanders, they drew their short swords from their belts and made the first of the three lethal incisions in their abdomens that would spill their entrails agonisingly onto the decks.

Pulling out of orbit, the Emperor's proud invaders found themselves being harried away from the Liberty nexus by fierce attacks. Suddenly there was before them nothing but death and destruction on the ragged retreat to Arcadia. No Shinto shrine would now be erected on the ruins of the White House. The Emperor's dream had failed.

Low over the rain-soaked hill where the White House's east garden merged with the aspen trees, a flight of five ten-thousand-ton nexus ships roared, blotting out the sky with their immense cross formation. Their plex hulls had been phased into total transparency and their decks were dressed by Marine cadets in their white dress uniforms and chrome helmets. As one, they saluted at the moment each craft of the flight peeled off and headed for the Norfolk apron. A presidential rostrum had been erected, and below it, with great perseverance because of the downpour, a huge concourse was being readied for the crowds. Pharis Cassabian watched the erectors balefully through the acre-sized panes of the secretary's suite. He knew that this was no time for rejoicing—a war had just begun.

Across Pennsylvania Avenue, in the Treasury, Conroy Lubbock turned away from the window and received his prodigal daughter. He told her the news that the father of her children had been shot through the helmet by a samurai assault trooper during his attack on the Yamato flagship *Oda Nobunaga,* but that the beam had apparently only parted his hair, and against the orders of his admiral he was presently giving his assailant lone chase through the branch chain of nexi that terminated hopelessly in the Oregon system. The incident, Reba was told, had been reported to the President by Deke Copeland. Captain Straker's disobedience, she had said, was to be deplored. He must come and account for it in person at the White House, and she would see to it that he got his just deserts pinned onto his jacket.

Outside, Michie pulled her coat about her and stepped down from the aircar into the damp Lincoln night air. She had come at the treasurer's command and was met at the steps of the Treasury by the always poker-faced Jiro Ito. Incredibly the mood of the night had got to him and he was smiling. He informed her that her husband had been picked up from the Yamato star cruiser *Takeda Shingen* and was presently aboard the armed merchantman *Constitution,* which had been most recently reported in the uninhabited Vav-Six-Oh system—a lone star girdled by a vast cloud of gas—hunting down a fleeing Yamato ship.

Beyond the White House gates, the President's rose gardens began to fill with hundreds of thousands of half-uniformed, dancing, rain-drenched revelers. They raised jugs of liquor and torches and a bewildering assortment of street furniture and festive trophies they had been pulling up and carrying about all day. They chanted and chanted and would not shut up until their President came to give them thanks for their loyalty.

Alone on her rostrum, Alia Kane watched them with love and deep gratitude. Her people were unique in all creation, a democratic people free and unfettered under God, their rights guaranteed, their freedoms maintained, and it was she whom they had honored and chosen as leader.

Already below her were ten thousand upturned faces, drenched by the rain. This was her Sector, her Amerika. One day the histories would call her the one hundredth President, a childless woman, but they would be wrong: she was mother to all those rain-lashed and unruly children—every last one of them. The Emperor had tried to take them away from her, and certainly there was a long road to travel and miles to go before they were truly safe, but at last Amerikans were up off their knees and walking tall again, as a free people must.

Alia Kane wanted to tell them so, but in her heart she knew that the pride of Yamato's martial spirit, though dimmed, was undefeated. The cherished dream of their "Amerikan Empire" had been extinguished, but they would never give up.

Eighty days later, a terror-stricken messenger landed on Kyoto's Chiyoda-Ku apron and crossed the moat of the Imperial Palace; there he waited terrified beside the placid carp pond. Below the surface immense genetically altered goldfish slid amongst reeds and slimy water. Each had a human face.

His Imperial Majesty was at his writing stand attending to state papers. He did not look at the man who groveled at his feet, but with inhuman self-control listened to the news without pausing his writing brush.

When the messenger was gone, the Emperor rose and stood alone before the shrine where the Imperial jewels were housed. He felt utter humiliation before the spirits of his ancestors. It seemed to the Emperor that he had betrayed their trust in him.

Icily he told his most constant companion, the chamberlain, Kido, "I give thanks to the gods that I can build another fleet greater than this I have lost whenever I choose to order it." Then he turned his eyes heavenward to contemplate the serene brilliance of the Nagoya event that continued to lighten Kyoto's daylight sky.